AUNTIE CLEM'S BAKERY

BOOKS # 7-9

P.D. WORKMAN

ISBN: 9781774680810 (KDP Paperback)

ISBN: 9781774680827 (Ingram Paperback)

ISBN: 9781774680834 (Ingram Hardcover)

ISBN: 9781989415696 (Kindle)

ISBN: 9781989415702 (ePub)

SOUR CHERRY TURNOVER

AUNTIE CLEM'S BAKERY #7

For when things don't turn out quite the way you had planned.

CHAPTER 1

Erin arranged the cupcakes carefully in the display case, carefully adjusting the space between them and making sure the icing shapes would all be oriented right-side-up for her customers.

"Well, if it isn't your favorite person in the world," Vic drawled.

Erin didn't need to look at her assistant to know who was approaching. She raised her eyes to look through the glass of the display case to the young woman about to walk through the front doors of Auntie Clem's Bakery, the muscles of her stomach clenching into a hard knot. She tried to school her expression to keep a pleasant smile on her face, and smushed the cupcake in her hand against the bottom of the shelf above it.

She groaned and pulled it out. It was a good thing there were no customers in the shop at that moment.

"Sorry." Vic gave a little grimace and a shrug.

Erin grabbed a damp cloth to wipe the smear of icing from the shelf, then straightened to greet her half-sister.

"Hi, Charley."

"Oops," Charley looked at the cupcake in Erin's hand. "Looks like that one didn't make it."

"No." Erin chucked it into the garbage can. She put her hands on her hips, unconsciously retreating into a defensive stance. "What can I help you with today?"

5

Charley smiled. Having only recently met Charley, Erin still found it disconcerting to see the dark hair and delicate features she was used to seeing in the mirror on someone else's face. And she knew that particular smile was just as fake as her own.

"I came to see if I could borrow a muffin pan," Charley said. "Every time I turn around, there's some other piece of equipment I am missing. The Bake Shoppe should have been fully-stocked. I'd really like to know who has been taking stuff home with them. If I could afford it, I'd hire help from the city instead of Bald Eagle Falls, just so I could be sure I wasn't hiring back whoever has been helping themselves to everything!"

Erin wavered between sympathy and irritation. She knew that she would have been pretty angry if she'd found someone had been stealing from her, especially when the bakery was her livelihood, but she was also increasingly annoyed with Charley and dearly wished that she wouldn't reopen The Bake Shoppe. And not just because she would be in direct competition with Erin's bakery.

"You must be madder than a wet hen," Vic said, without a trace of sympathy in her voice.

Erin avoided looking at Vic.

Charley nodded. "You bet I am. Half of Angela's recipes use weights for flours instead of measuring cups, so you'd think there would be an electronic scale in the place, but do you think there's any sign of one?" She sighed. "Anyway, I need to whip up some muffins before opening and I really don't have time to go into the city to get a jumbo muffin pan, so I wondered if I could borrow one of yours just for a couple of days and then I'll bring it back to you."

Erin had already explained enough times that she shouldn't have had to tell Charley again. "I can't, Charley. They would be contaminated with gluten and I wouldn't be able to use them again."

"I'd clean them really well. And it would be cooked, so it shouldn't cause a problem for your *special* clientele. Please, Erin, this will be the last thing that I ask for."

"It doesn't matter how well you clean it, there could still be microscopic traces of gluten or other proteins on the pan, enough to trigger a reaction in someone. None of the equipment I use has ever been used for gluten-containing batters. Nothing is cross-contaminated, so people who are celiac or allergic don't have to worry about reacting to my baked goods, no matter how sensitive they are."

"But like I said, it will all have been cooked anyway. So they shouldn't be allergic."

"Baking doesn't denature gluten proteins enough for someone to stop reacting to them."

"I had a friend who was allergic to eggs. She couldn't eat them scrambled or boiled or fried up for breakfast, but she could eat cake and cookies that had egg in them, because baking changes them."

"Some people can tolerate eggs that have been baked," Erin agreed, "but it's not the same with gluten. Or they'd be able to eat regular bread and there wouldn't be any need for specialty baked goods! I can't use pans that have been used for regular muffins. Even though you scrub the pans and they look perfectly clean, there could still be microscopic amounts of gluten that would get into my baking. I'm not willing to risk it."

Charley folded her arms across her chest and pressed her lips together, clearly irritated. "Can't you help me out just this once?"

"I'll help you any way I can," Erin promised, "just not in any way that will endanger the health of my customers."

She suspected that, like a large portion of the population, Charley figured that anyone who claimed to be gluten intolerant was just trying to get attention, and that they didn't really have any health concerns at all. While some people did avoid gluten some of the time just because it was a trendy thing to do or they thought it would help them to lose weight, Erin had customers who could end up in hospital if she glutened them. She wasn't about to take chances with their health.

Erin looked over at Vic. As usual, Victoria Webster had her long blond hair put up and corralled inside a baker's cap. Her makeup was perfect in spite of the Tennessee heat and she could have just as easily walked off a runway as out of the hot kitchen. Vic arched one eyebrow at Erin. She knew how much Charley had been driving Erin crazy as the reopening of The Bake Shoppe approached. Her advice had been to stop helping Charley. Family or not, Erin wasn't under any obligation.

"So you're going to make me drive all the way into the city to pick up new muffin tins, when you could just loan me a tray for a few days," Charley accused.

"Sorry, I can't."

"Thanks loads."

"Sorry."

"You're lucky you don't have employees who steal from you." Charley looked at Vic for a moment, then back at Erin. "If I knew who was stealing from me..."

Erin imagined the former organized-crime soldier could have made some pretty good threats, but Charley didn't put them into words. "Do you think someone is stealing from you now, or is this stuff that disappeared before you got The Bake Shoppe?"

"It's still theft, whether they knew they were taking it from me, or decided to take things home after Angela Plaint died and the bakery closed. It wasn't theirs to take."

"No," Erin agreed. "You're right. I just wondered whether you were still having stuff disappear."

Charley shrugged. "I don't know. All I know is that for what should have been a turnkey business, there are an awful lot of things missing!"

Erin nodded sympathetically. "Maybe you should do an inventory before you go into the city, make sure you get everything you need in one run."

"The trouble is, I don't really know what's missing until I go to make something and it's not there."

Erin nodded. That was exactly her point.

"You should make a list," Vic suggested. Her face was smooth, no sign of the laughter bubbling under the surface. She was always teasing Erin for her endless lists. But Erin couldn't imagine trying to run a business—or her life—without them.

Charley rolled her eyes at Vic and didn't bother to comment. While she didn't bully Vic for her transgender identity like some of the Bald Eagle Falls townsfolk—knowing how Erin would react if she did—Charley clearly didn't intend to take any advice from Erin's eighteen-year-old employee, no matter how on-point it was.

"So that's it?" Charley asked Erin. "That's your final answer, you won't help me out?"

"I can't help you with your muffin tin problem."

"Fine. You have yourself a nice day." Charley shook her head and stormed out of the store, making the front door bells tinkle wildly.

Erin didn't say anything immediately. She just stared after Charley. Eventually, she spoke. "Is it just me, or..."

"Is your sister on the verge of a mental breakdown?" Vic suggested, cocking her head.

"I don't know if I'd go that far, but she does seem to be a little... stressed."

"And you weren't before you opened Auntie Clem's?"

"Well, yeah." Erin thought back to the days before she had reopened her late aunt's tea shop as a specialty bakery for those with celiac disease or allergies. "I was pretty nervous... but I had my lists."

Vic giggled. "She didn't seem to appreciate the suggestion. Really, when I think about the two of you being sisters... I don't know if I could find two people less alike."

"Charley is a little... rough around the edges. She just has some... maturing to do."

"She's older than I am."

"*Everybody* is older than you are," Erin teased. "But you're remarkably mature for your age. Charley is still in a sort of rebellious stage..."

Vic polished a few smudges off of the display case of baked goods. "I think my family would tell you I'm right in the midst of my rebellious stage too. Running away from home, coming out as a girl..."

"You being you is not a stage," Erin said firmly, looking Vic in the eye. "Don't let them get to you."

Vic hadn't said anything about having had contact with her family recently, but she normally didn't mention them in conversation unless she'd heard from them. They weren't exactly supportive of her transition.

"Thanks," Vic said softly. She looked down at the glass and polished away another invisible smudge. "And my advice to you is to make sure all of your pans and equipment have your name on them."

Erin smiled. "I'm not exactly worried about *my* employees walking off with them."

"I was thinking more about Charley," Vic said, with a nod in the direction of the door. "It would be a lot less work for her to raid your kitchen than it would be to drive into the city."

"She doesn't have a key."

"Maybe not, but having worked for the Dyson family, I suspect she probably wouldn't need a key."

Erin thought about that. "Well... you might have a point there. Do you think Willie has engraving tools?"

"Sure. I'll tell him you need him to mark everything he can?"

"Yes. It's probably a really good idea even without Charley in the equation. If we had a break-in, or even did a catering job and left something behind, it's a lot easier to recover if everything is marked!"

Vic nodded. She tapped her temple. "I'm putting it on my list."

CHAPTER 2

*E*rin was more tired than usual at the end of the day and wondered whether she was coming down with something. Or maybe it was just the additional stress of having to deal with Charley and worrying about a competing bakery opening in Bald Eagle Falls.

She had said from the start that there was enough business in Bald Eagle Falls for two bakeries, but it had been a lot easier to stay in the black when she was the only one. People who wanted to get freshly-baked treats had to either go to her bakery and get gluten-free, or to go into the city. Now anyone who didn't have special diets to deal with would have the option of a regular bakery, and Erin was a lot more worried than she let anyone know.

She didn't have much appetite for supper, opting for just a day-old roll from Auntie Clem's and a cup of ginger tea. Vic was out with Willie, so Erin didn't have anyone to nag her that she needed to eat a well-rounded meal. Or at least as well-rounded as anything that came from a box in the freezer could be. She took her tea into the living room. Orange Blossom followed her to the couch and made a place for himself on her lap, meowing and yipping chattily about how he had passed his day in her absence. Erin encouraged his story with *mm-hmms* and ear scratches until he got settled. Marshmallow, the toasted-brown and white rabbit she had rescued nibbled at the pant leg of her pajamas and snuffled her bare toes, and then eventually flopped down on top of her feet.

Erin wiggled her toes. "Do you really think I need foot warmers in this heat?"

Of course, she had air conditioning, so it wasn't like she had to put up with the outdoor temperatures. Marshmallow just stared at her out of one eye, his nose wiggling busily.

Erin tried to focus on the job at hand, which was brainstorming what areas she could specialize in; what reasons people had to choose Auntie Clem's Bakery over The Bake Shoppe. The top ones were, of course, people who required special diets. Sufferers of celiac disease, allergies, and intolerances. Vegans. And… nothing else was coming to her. There were other untapped possibilities, such as those who followed special diets with acronyms like SCD or FODMAPS, who had PKU or other digestive enzyme disorders, were trying to lose weight or gain muscle, were sugar-free, fat-free, or low carb. But she couldn't cater to them all.

She could possibly develop a low carb line; paleo recipes were popular, but they tended to revolve around almond or coconut flour and eggs, which were bad for her allergic clientele. She had been nut-free from the beginning and didn't want to leave those who had potentially fatal nut allergies in the lurch. That meant she was choosing a smaller customer base over the larger one, which was not a particularly good business decision.

There was a knock at the door. Erin glanced out the front window and saw the squad car parked at the curb. Removing the animals from their comfortable spots, she got up to open the door for Officer Terry Piper— Officer Handsome, as Vic had been known to refer to him—and his partner, K9.

"Personal safety check, ma'am," Terry said, affecting more drawl than usual, "just wanted to make sure you're safe and secure."

Erin laughed. Terry wasn't usually so playful. She liked seeing that side of him. "I could use some personal protection," she breathed, putting her arms around him and giving him a kiss. They stayed like that for a moment, just looking into each other's eyes. K9 interrupted the tableau with a high-pitched whine followed by a low grumble, as if to say, "Oh, please!"

They both laughed. Erin drew back, allowing her personal protection to enter the house. He closed and locked the door behind him.

"On that note," he said in a more serious tone, "I didn't see you check the peephole before opening the door."

"I didn't," Erin agreed. She motioned to the window. "I could see your car from the couch."

"How did you know it wasn't some *other* police officer?"

"Because my date with the sheriff isn't until Friday."

Terry chuckled. He took his place on the couch, making a motion to K9 that indicated he was allowed to lie down and no longer be on guard. K9 did so, sprawling like a teenager. He nosed Marshmallow, snuffling curiously. Marshmallow wasn't in the mood to play, and kicked K9 in the nose with a back foot. K9 sat up, affronted, and sneezed. He looked at Terry and gave a snort.

"If you're going to poke your nose where it doesn't belong, you risk getting kicked," Terry said unsympathetically. "You go doing that to a porcupine or skunk, and you'll really regret it."

"Or even Orange Blossom," Erin contributed. "He'd probably take your nose off."

K9 approached Erin. He bumped up against her leg and nosed at her hands. Erin scratched his ears and was rewarded with a lick, but that wasn't what he was after.

"Oh," Erin scratched his neck and chin. "You're looking for a treat."

Both Orange Blossom and Marshmallow perked up at this suggestion, looking at Erin to see if she were going to give them something.

"He doesn't need a treat every single time he comes over here," Terry pointed out. "You spoil him."

"It's my house, I'll spoil him if I like." Erin patted K9's head and walked toward the kitchen. "Come on, boy. You can have a cookie."

He went with her eagerly, tail waving back and forth in wide arcs. The cat and the rabbit followed close behind. Erin picked a gluten-free doggie biscuit out of the cookie jar for K9, some soft treats from a snack can for Orange Blossom, and a stick of celery for Marshmallow. She handed K9 and Marshmallow their treats directly, but for Orange Blossom, skimmed the treats along the kitchen floor, making him go careening after them in wild pursuit.

"Doggie treats," she murmured as she went back to the living room and sat down next to Terry. "That's another thing."

Terry raised his eyebrows. "What's that?"

"I was trying to think of all of the reasons people come to Auntie Clem's

Bakery, and that's another one. Grain-free doggie treats. A lot of dogs are sensitive to grains and the grocery store doesn't stock grain-free biscuits."

Terry nodded. "Right. We'd have to go all the way to the city to get them."

"And that's not something Charley is going to want to stock, is it? She just wants a regular bakery, and most bakeries don't do treats for dogs, gluten-free or otherwise." She picked up her list and wrote the thought down.

"What else have you got on there?" Terry looked down at the short list. "What about the ladies' tea?"

Erin had revived Clementine's tradition of an after-services tea Sunday mornings for the churchgoing ladies.

"There's nothing to stop Charley from doing a ladies' tea," she countered.

"Well, I suppose not, but people will go to yours because that's where Clementine's Tea Room was. Having it somewhere else wouldn't be the same."

"But you don't think they'd choose Charley over me if she did offer one? Because I'm an atheist and she's... not?"

"Charley isn't exactly religious herself. Does she even attend services?"

"I wouldn't know, since I don't go," Erin teased. "But seriously, no, I don't think she ever has. And I don't think she goes into the city or back to Moose River for services. But she's Christian in name, and that matters to people around here. Better a Christian who beats his wife and goes fishing every Sunday than an atheist."

"I don't think they're quite that bad."

Erin considered. "Maybe not quite," she admitted. She held up her fingers, pinched close together. "But it's close."

"Has someone been getting on your case?"

"No more than usual. I think they've adjusted to the idea that they're not going to convert me, but they're not happy about it and people still... make comments."

"You're never going to get people to stop talking."

"No."

They sighed in unison, then laughed.

"Does it ever bother *you* that I'm not a Christian?" Erin asked.

He raised his brows. "Me? Not a bit. Never even crossed my mind."

"It doesn't bother you that I'm not going to your heaven?"

"You might be surprised where you end up! No, it really makes no difference to me what you believe. I'm not entirely sure what it is that I believe. I'm born and bred Christian and have never considered myself anything else, but do I believe the whole thing?" He shrugged. "That the Bible and everything in it is meant to be taken literally? I don't know about that. I'll take it on faith for now... and see what happens."

"Hedging your bets? Making sure you're covered just in case it is all true?"

"Our society is built on the Ten Commandments and the Bible. That's where our most basic laws stem from. So... yes. I'll do my best to keep the top ten and uphold the law. Whether that will get me anything in the afterlife or just keep me on the right path in this life, I don't know."

Erin shook her head. "Okay..."

"What does that mean?"

"I thought one of those top ten was going to church on Sunday, and you don't do that. You go to work like usual."

Terry looked away, grimacing. "Well, it doesn't exactly say that..."

"Oh."

"It says to keep the Sabbath day holy, and I..." he trailed off.

Erin waited for him to finish. He didn't come up with anything.

"You'll take that one under advisement?" she suggested.

"Well, maybe I'll do better at that one when I'm retired."

"Sounds good to me."

They sat in silence for a few minutes while the animals gathered back around them and found comfy places to nestle. Erin added the ladies' tea to her list and read over it again. There still wasn't enough there to keep a business running. If everybody who didn't have to eat a special diet decided to go to The Bake Shoppe, Erin's business was going to be in trouble.

CHAPTER 3

"So while you're trying to figure out how to deal with your sister," Terry said, nodding to the list, "I'm still trying to figure out what to do about your former foster sister."

"Reg?"

Terry was clearly about to say something smart to her like 'how many foster sisters do you have?' and then stopped himself as it came to him that she did, in fact, have a lot more than just Reg. Reg was the only one he had met and would have brought up, but she did have others.

"Uh, yes. Regina Rawlins. We haven't been able to track her down."

Erin shrugged. "She's had plenty of experience with disappearing. She'll be living halfway across the country under a new name. You might as well not waste your time."

"You haven't heard anything from her?"

Erin considered her answer, which made Terry straighten and look at her more closely.

"You *have* heard from her?"

"Well, sort of. Just one quick phone call, and it didn't make a lot of sense."

"Where was it from? When was this? Do you still have the number in your call log?"

"I tried it again later and it didn't work. So just a burner phone, probably."

"Where?"

Erin was reluctant to give him any information. She hadn't liked having Reg around and had refused to get involved in any scams with her, but she wasn't a snitch. She'd expect her friends and old foster families to keep quiet and protect her if she were in trouble. It was the code.

"Where was she calling from?" Terry repeated. "What was the area code?"

"Florida," Erin said finally. But that was all she was going to tell him. There were lots of people in Florida, and Terry wasn't exactly going to drive there himself to go looking for Reg. He could call it in to the locals or the FBI, but no one was going to care about solving the case of a small-town cop looking for a swindler who had walked off with certain pieces of jewelry belonging to her clients. It wasn't like his investigation was going to go anywhere.

"Florida," Terry repeated, thinking about it. "I had one query from Florida. I didn't think anything of it, because the officer never returned my call when I called her back. Figured she must have sorted things out on her own. I'll have to pull it out and have another look at it."

"You're not going to find Reg if she doesn't want to be found. Why don't you just let it go?"

"She stole from your friends. You don't think they deserve some justice?"

"I just know Reg. You're not going to find her. And… I don't know… she sounded kind of strange. Wasn't making a lot of sense."

"Drunk?"

"Maybe. I never knew Reg to get like that when she was drinking before, though."

"What exactly did she sound like?"

"Kind of… hysterical. Upset or excited. Not slurring her words or anything."

"You ever know her to be like that before?"

"Well… maybe." Reg *had* behaved strangely before. Sometimes Reg's behavior could be very bizarre. "There have been a couple of times when she's… gone off the rails."

Terry leaned in closer, frowning in concentration. "Off the rails? What does that mean?"

"She's been hospitalized. For... things like depression or... hallucinations."

"Psychosis? Is she schizophrenic?"

"No. I mean, she's had a lot of different diagnoses over the years, and I wouldn't doubt that schizophrenia is one of them... but she's not. She's just... different."

"So, when you called her back, it was to check on her? To make sure she was okay?"

"Yeah. But like I said, the number wasn't in service anymore. She knows not to keep the same number for long. She probably just bought it for that phone call, or to make a bunch of one-off calls, and then she tossed it."

"But if she's trying to run a business passing herself off as a psychic or whatever she's up to now, she'll need to have a number people can reach her at."

Reg nodded. "But I doubt if it will be anything you can track. You might as well just not waste your time."

Terry studied Erin. She knew he thought she was just trying to protect her friend.

And maybe she was.

CHAPTER 4

*E*rin was happy to see Mary Lou Cox come through the door the next afternoon. Mary Lou had been keeping a pretty low profile since her husband had been arrested for the murder of Joelle Biggs. He was still in hospital or some other facility being evaluated so they could decide how to deal with him. Erin hoped that he didn't end up in prison. It seemed obvious to her that he didn't have all of his faculties.

"Hi, Mary Lou. How's it going?"

Mary Lou was neat and well-tailored as always, her gray hair in a sleek, short style. She gave Erin her usual pleasant-but-reserved smile, then glanced back over her shoulder as if she were worried someone else might have followed her in. She turned back to Erin, the smile a little less certain.

"I'm as good as ever. Things have just been so busy lately, I haven't been able to get around..."

"Busy at the General Store?"

"Well, that and home life and... just everything. I've been keeping myself busy."

"Well, good." Erin gestured to the display case. "What would you and the boys like today?"

"Campbell has gone away for a while, so it's just Josh and me. Going from four people down to two... I admit, I'm not doing much meal planning anymore. We just fend for ourselves, mostly. But I feel like I've neglected Josh a little, so I thought…" Mary Lou gazed over the day's offerings. "Everything just looks so good. Maybe some of those cranberry muffins for breakfasts. And m&m cookies for a treat."

"Sounds good," Erin agreed. She let Mary Lou finish browsing over the contents of the case and deciding how many of each item she wanted, then started to package it up. Vic walked in from the kitchen.

"Hello, Mary Lou. I hope your day is going well."

Mary Lou's smile at Vic, who she was usually uncomfortable around, was a fraction warmer than usual. Maybe she was getting more used to Vic and appreciating the fact that unlike some of her older friends who were not supporting her, Vic hadn't turned against her and started treating her like a pariah during her recent trials.

Or maybe she appreciated that Vic hadn't asked her how she was doing. She probably got tired of people being overly interested in her life and in having to come up with an acceptable answer as to how she was doing when her life was in shambles.

"Nice to see you too, Vic."

Vic went over to the cash register and started to punch in Mary Lou's order while Erin got it all packaged up.

"Where is Campbell, then?" Erin asked. "I hadn't heard that he was leaving."

"He's… pursuing other options. I'm not sure what he's going to do… he always did so well in school, but since Roger… he just seems to have lost the will to put in any effort."

"Maybe he's been having trouble with the other kids," Vic suggested, not looking up from the register.

"I expect the boys have had at least as much trouble as I have, and that has not been pretty. I always thought… I don't know. People suddenly seem very shallow. I thought we were such good friends, but suddenly other things have become much more important in their lives."

Erin shook her head. "Well forget them. We will always be there for you, Mary Lou. And anyone who isn't, they just aren't really a friend, are they?"

"I know. It's just a little sad to find out that the people you thought were real friends… well, that they aren't."

"I know," Erin agreed. She'd been through it herself. People pretending to be friends, acting like they cared, and then suddenly they were gone when they were needed the most. It was easy to say just forget about them, but Erin suspected that Vic too had lost her share of friends when she had transitioned. She glanced over at Vic. Vic flushed a little pink and nodded, as if she had read Erin's mind.

"I know it's not easy to just forget about them. But it's still good advice. You can't eat yourself up over someone who never really cared in the first place."

Mary Lou sighed. "Of course you are right. And I'm sure it will all turn out just fine. Opposing forces increase strength."

"We are refined by fire," Vic agreed.

Mary Lou paid the bill, nodded at them each, and headed out. Just as she left the shop, Charley came in. Her face was flushed pink and she looked happy for once instead of stressed and irritated.

"Hey, Charley," Erin greeted.

Charley marched up to the display case. "You are so good at this," she said. "You always have something new in there that I haven't seen before."

Erin warmed at the compliment. "Well, thank you. I'm always experimenting with something new."

"And it seems like they all turn out! Even things like this," she pointed at the pastries. "I've never seen gluten-free turnovers anywhere else. I would have said they couldn't be done. But those look just like regular turnovers. I would swear you were using wheat flour."

"They're pretty tricky. They take a lot of fiddling. I found that if I freeze the butter, and then grate it fine between each layer, and then roll the layers just as thin as I can... something like this can take twenty layers, and if it gets too warm, it won't work, so you have to keep stopping and chilling it..."

Charley shook her head. "I can't imagine the patience. I buy the pre-made filo pastry, and pre-made fillings, and put them together. They turn out pretty good. But you can't buy pre-made gluten-free pastry like that."

"Nope. Maybe someday, but until then, if people want gluten-free turnovers, they're going to have to come here."

Charley grinned. She pulled out a small spiral notebook and, looking into the display case, started jotting down notes. Erin looked at Vic, who was frowning.

"What are you doing?" Erin asked.

Charley didn't look up from her notes. "I'm just writing down what you're selling. You have such a good variety of different things. I want to be able to do the same kind of thing at The Bake Shoppe."

Erin remembered one foster mother telling her repeatedly that imitation was the sincerest form of flattery. It had driven Erin crazy when the younger kids would mimic her, and she would run to her foster mother complaining.

So what if Charley was planning to copy her lineup? There was nothing wrong with two bakeries having similar offerings. How could they not be similar?

"You have to find your own thing," Vic told Charley. "What's your specialty going to be?"

"I don't need a specialty. There's already a specialty bakery. I'm the one who is going to carry the *normal* baked goods."

"I've got to check on some cookies," Erin announced, and retreated to the kitchen. She didn't really have anything she had to check on, but she washed some dishes and stayed out of the way for a few minutes while she tried to regain her equilibrium. She knew she should go back out front when she heard the front door bells jingle. Either someone else had come in and Erin should help wait on them, or Charley was gone, and she didn't need to hide out anymore. But Erin wasn't in any hurry to get back out to the counter.

"Are you okay?" Vic asked, entering the kitchen.

"Oh, I'm fine."

"No offense, but that sister of yours shore rubs me the wrong way sometimes. The nerve of her, coming in here just to copy your lineup!"

Erin looked up from her dishes. "So I'm right, that was weird, wasn't it? Who does that? Is she really planning to offer exactly the same foods as I am, or is she just gaslighting me?"

"I don't think she's that subtle. And yeah, it is weird. She should be making her own specialty, not baking goods *just like Erin, only normal.*"

Erin shook her head. She dried off her hands and went back out to the front of the shop with Vic. "I just have visions of all of my customers going over to her bakery. Even the ones who have to eat gluten-free. That's what Carolyn was like. She just wanted to be normal and eat normal food. We didn't have all of this kind of thing. Our foster mom tried, but all we had were these loaves of rice bread that were always so dry. Or she would try to make a birthday cake, and it would be so gritty, so obviously not normal. Carolyn wanted so much to just eat normal food. So she did."

Vic grimaced. "Some people want so badly to fit in... they'll do anything. Even when they know it's foolish or dangerous."

"She knew it made her sick, but she didn't care. It was more important to be sick and normal than to stay healthy."

"And in the end, her system was too messed up to recover." Vic had heard Carolyn's story enough times to know how it had ended. Carolyn was the reason Erin had learned to do gluten-free baking in the first place. Trying to make nice things for her foster sister or for others who were in the same position.

Vic put her hand on Erin's shoulder. "You are doing exactly what you set out to do. You're making life better for people like Carolyn. Look at little Peter Foster. He adores your baking. Without Auntie Clem's, he would have to rely on packaged gluten-free goods from the city. He wouldn't get any of this nice stuff. He wouldn't have any choices. And when he went to friends' birthday parties, they wouldn't have anything for him to eat. The Fosters are not going to go to The Bake Shoppe when it opens. They're going to keep coming here."

"Mrs. Foster will come here to get things for Peter, but what about the rest of the family? It will be cheaper for them to go to The Bake Shoppe. And I don't think I can survive if only the people who have to come here do."

Vic gave her shoulder a squeeze and let go. "That's not going to happen. People don't just come here because they have to."

"They come here because it's the only bakery in town. The grocery store can't carry everything they need and doesn't have freshly-baked goods, and they don't want to drive all the way to the city for it, so they come here. But when there is a normal bakery available, they're going to go there."

"Some of them will," Vic admitted. "But a lot of them are going to keep coming here, because you've made a place for yourself here. I loved my Aunt Angela, but going to The Bake Shoppe when she ran it was not like coming to Auntie Clem's. You didn't go there and visit and get the latest gossip. You went there to get your bread or your birthday cake, and then you got out. There were no teas or children's parties or dog biscuits. People didn't linger and get something for tomorrow's dessert too, or lemonade slushes to beat the heat," Vic nodded to the new freezer case. "And you want to know why?"

Erin knew what Vic was getting at. She had met Angela only a couple of times before she had died, but she had been a hard woman. She hadn't been able to work inside The Bake Shoppe anymore because of a late-onset allergy to wheat, but she had continued to own and manage it. Erin had never been there when it was running, so she could only imagine what kind of atmosphere pervaded the place.

"But Charley isn't your Aunt Angela. She's going to do all of the things I'm doing. She's going to copy everything I do that makes me successful. And she naturally has the bigger market."

"We'll make it work, Erin," Vic insisted. "Don't let her get you down."

"But… what if we can't?"

CHAPTER 5

*E*rin wouldn't have thought that things could get any worse as she dreaded the reopening of The Bake Shoppe. There was no way of knowing whether her worst fears were going to be realized, or whether she had reason to be optimistic like Vic said and to believe that people would keep coming for the good food and gossip rather than just going to The Bake Shoppe with its normal fare. Charley had done little to endear herself to the residents of Bald Eagle Falls, but if she had cheap fresh bread, did anyone really care about her interpersonal skills?

Erin knew who Don Inglethorpe was. She had seen him around town, but he hadn't been a regular customer at Auntie Clem's. Maybe he had bought one or two emergency purchases there, but he hadn't been a frequent visitor. She knew he was a lawyer, one of the three trustees who administered the Trenton Plaint estate, which currently held The Bake Shoppe in trust for Charley and her half-brother Davis Plaint, who was in prison. Erin's own lawyer, James Burgener, was one of the others, along with a woman who wasn't often in town.

So she was surprised to see him walk in the door while she was working a Wednesday afternoon shift with Bella, but at the same time, it wasn't anything that rang alarm bells for her.

"Good morning, Mr. Inglethorpe," she greeted him as he approached the counter.

25

He was a middle-aged man, white, slightly balding and overweight. Not someone who stood out in a crowd. He was wearing a blue button-up shirt and seemed uncomfortable. Maybe that was just because he hadn't been to Auntie Clem's very much. The early-morning rush had died down, but there were still a few other customers coming and going, and maybe he'd been hoping it would be quieter. Some people couldn't make decisions when there were other people waiting on them.

"Here you go." Erin handed Melissa her purchase, a box of muffins for the police department break room. "Have a good day!"

Melissa nodded, her brown curls dancing, and smiled her wide, easy smile. "I'll say 'hi' to Terry for you."

Erin had been sure to include a couple of blueberry muffins in the selection, knowing it was Terry Piper's favorite flavor. Though he always complained that he shouldn't be eating so much sugar, he walked it off during his patrols with K9 and he hadn't put on any noticeable weight in the time she'd been running Auntie Clem's.

"What's your turnover?" Inglethorpe asked, looking into the display case.

"These ones are sour cherry, and these are blueberry," Erin told him, pointing to them even though they had clear signs in Vic's neat printing. "I have some apple turnovers in the oven, but you probably don't want to wait or come back for those…"

"Uh… that's not what I—"

"I think he means finances, Erin," Bella said, with a bubbly laugh. "What are your annual sales?"

Inglethorpe looked at the teenager in surprise. He nodded. "Yes, exactly."

"My… what business is it of yours?" Erin blurted before she could come up with a more tactful response.

"Just wondering what a bakery in this town can make."

Erin stared at him. Bella looked at Erin.

"Did Charley send you here?" Erin asked finally.

His eyes gave nothing away.

"Are you going to get something? If not, I'd appreciate it if you'd step aside so others can order."

"You've said for some time that there's enough business in Bald Eagle

Falls for two bakeries," Inglethorpe pointed out. "So I don't see why you'd have any problem sharing information."

"The only turnovers I'm going to talk to you about are these ones," Erin pointed to the pastries in the display case. "Would that be cherry or blueberry?"

He stood there for a minute looking at her. He looked back down at the turnovers. "I'll take three of each," he said finally.

Erin was surprised, but she just nodded and put six turnovers into a box for him. He paid for them without a word. Bella gave him his change.

"You have a nice day, now, Mr. Inglethorpe," Erin said politely. He gave a nod and walked out of the bakery. Erin shook her head.

"You handled that pretty well," Bella complimented. "You sure put him in his place."

"Well, I made a sale. I don't know whether he got anything out of it."

"Sure he did. He got six of those turnovers."

Erin forced a smile. "Which is six times what he was looking for, right?"

"That's right."

"He's got some nerve coming around here scoping out my business and fishing for information."

"He wasn't exactly covert."

Erin shook her head. "Well, I guess I'd rather he was obvious about what he was doing."

~

Willie was working, so Vic had joined Erin for the evening, and they were sitting in the living room with the animals, Erin making her lists for the next day and Vic paging through the weekly paper for any local news they might have missed. She stopped, staring at an advertisement.

"Holy crap."

Erin looked over at her. "What?"

Vic turned the paper around to show it to Erin. It was a full-page advertising circular for the opening of The Bake Shoppe, advertising "traditional baked goods, made the time-honored way your grandma made them, with no trendy or unorthodox ingredients." There were pictures of various kinds of baked goods, sweet cherry turnovers featuring prominently. The lineup replicated almost exactly the current offerings at Auntie Clem's Bakery.

There were a number of call-outs with notations such as "healthy foods, not health food" and "traditional family recipe."

Erin swore under her breath, making Vic giggle. Erin swatted at the newspaper.

"Take that away. I don't want to see it. In fact, it wouldn't hurt my feelings if you burned it."

"At least you know you're doing something right. She wouldn't be copying you so closely if she didn't think so."

"She mimics me and attacks me in the same ad copy! Who does that? I never did that when I opened Auntie Clem's."

"No, I know," Vic agreed, growing more serious. "You advertised your specialty and offered a free cookie or muffin for each customer. I remember."

Erin cocked her head. "You weren't even around yet."

"I was around. We just hadn't met yet. I went in, you know, and got a cookie from you."

"You did?" Erin was floored. "I don't remember that!"

"I picked a time when it was really busy, so I could hide in the crowd and you wouldn't notice me. Nobody really did; it was pretty chaotic. It was just you, working all by yourself, but you had a great big smile and were so friendly with everyone. I only went because I wanted free food. But I liked it," Vic ducked her head, turning a little pink. "I liked you. I thought you were cool."

"You never told me that! I thought the first time we'd met was that day I caught you at the bakery."

Vic shrugged and shook her head, getting still redder.

"Well, I'm just glad you decided to stay," Erin declared.

"Yeah, me too. I never would have guessed, when Aunt Angela turned me away, that things would turn out the way they did. That you'd take me in and become such a good friend to me."

There was a lump in Erin's throat. She patted Vic's knee, and sat back to look over her lists to make sure she hadn't missed anything, not wanting to get all teary.

CHAPTER 6

 here was a knock at the door and Erin got up to answer it. She didn't look out at the curb to see if Terry's squad car was there, and she didn't look out the peephole. Vic was there with her, and despite all she had been through during her time in Bald Eagle Falls, it didn't occur to her that it could be anyone but Terry, Willie, or one of their friends at the door.

She was startled to see a stranger in a long, dark coat that flapped in the wind, along with long hair that obscured his face at first. Erin's stomach clenched, and her hand tightened on the door, preparing to shut it again and shoot the bolt.

The young man pulled his hair back from his face, fighting the wind, and gave her a smile.

"Hullo, Miss Erin. I'm sorry to bother you, but I wonder if my—"

"Jeremy!" Vic was on her feet and pushing past Erin to reach her brother. "What are you doing here? Why didn't you tell me you were coming?"

Jeremy Jackson gave her a big hug. "I didn't know how you'd feel about it, so I figured it was easier to get forgiveness and you wouldn't turn me down if we were face-to-face."

"Come inside, out of the wind," Erin ordered. She shut the door once Jeremy was inside.

"I wouldn't turn you down?" Vic repeated. "Turn you down for what?"

"Well…" He scratched his head, looking sheepish. "I'm looking for a place to stay. Just for a few days, while I get on my feet…"

"Sure, of course," Vic agreed immediately. "There's a fold-out couch. I'm not sure how comfortable you'll be—I don't have a lot of space—but of course you're welcome."

"We have the whole house too," Erin put in. "He doesn't have to stay in the loft. I'm the only one here, so you could have your own room with a real bed."

It didn't even occur to Erin that she had just barely gotten rid of Reg as a houseguest. Jeremy might be even more annoying than Reg had been. Who knew what bad habits he might have? But he was Vic's brother, and the only one who had treated Vic with tolerance and love, so Erin wanted to do something for him.

Jeremy laughed. "Two offers, when I wasn't even sure if I would get one. You're both so generous! Thank you."

"Come and sit down." Vic practically pushed him into an armchair. "Tell me why you're here. What's going on?"

Jeremy got back up to take off his coat, moving slowly. He was, Erin thought as she watched his eyes, coming up with his answer on the spot. He hadn't arrived with an explanation worked out and was stalling for time.

"I decided to leave the farm," he said finally. "I had enough of the expectations, so I thought I'd take a page from the book of my little bro—sister and get out on my own. Make something of myself. I decided I'm not cut out for working the Jackson farm. It's just not for me."

Vic's eyes were wide with surprise. "You always loved the farm. I thought if anyone was a natural farmer, it was you. You loved the animals and the fields and everything about it."

"Things change. I'd like to be something… more."

"Wow!" Vic sat back, amazed. "Who would've guessed!"

Jeremy glanced over at Erin and then back at Vic. "If you could keep this all on the down-low. I didn't tell anyone where I was going, and I want some time before Pa—before Mom and Dad know where I am. Time to think and figure out what I want to do with myself."

Vic nodded vigorously. "Of course," she agreed. "They'd be out looking for you and have you back there before you knew what hit you. We'll keep it a secret, won't we, Erin?"

Erin shrugged. "I don't need to tell anyone."

"You guys are awesome, thank you so much," Jeremy said. He let out a long stream of air. "I've been all wound up, worrying about it. Thank you."

"I'm so excited to have you here!" Vic exclaimed. "It'll be just like old times."

Erin laughed. "You guys are too young to have old times!"

"You're not that much older," Vic countered, "and you and Reg had old times."

"You're babies compared with me." Erin smiled at them. "So, tell me what you did in the old days. And what changed?"

Jeremy and Vic looked at each other.

"Just guy—kid stuff," Jeremy said. "Playing games outside with the others. Climbing trees, shooting, helping Pa on the farm. Vic and me shared a room, being the two youngest. We'd stay up late talking when we were supposed to be asleep. We played cards. Tried to scare the pants off each other with ghost stories."

Erin smiled. There had been few foster siblings that she'd been close to. But sometimes things just clicked, even though they had completely different backgrounds. Those relationships had always been temporary, fleeting, and she had no idea where any of them were anymore.

Jeremy looked at Vic again, soberly. "And then... I don't know what happened. We stopped talking. Around about tenth grade. Maybe I thought I was too grown up." He raised an eyebrow at Vic. "Was I a jerk to you? Did I act like I didn't want my little brother around anymore?"

"No, I don't think so. I just... was going through a lot of stuff. I knew you wouldn't understand."

"Well... I guess you're probably right. If you'd told me you were a girl instead of a boy, I probably wouldn't have been real understanding." He scratched his ear and looked down fixedly at a spot on the carpet. "Is that when you decided? When you knew...?"

"I always knew." Vic was looking at her big brother, blinking rapidly. It had meant so much to her the previous Christmas when he had visited her, and she knew that she had one person in the family who could accept her for who she was. "But that was when I decided... that I couldn't live like that forever. I couldn't keep pretending to be something I wasn't to keep everybody else happy."

"I must have had my head in the clouds," Jeremy admitted, "because I didn't have any idea. Not for a couple more years."

"It wouldn't have been safe for me to come out. I knew that once Pa knew… I'd have to leave."

"Yeah."

Erin noticed the time and started to gather up her papers. "The two of you can talk, if you like, but I need to get ready for bed. Morning comes early for bakers!"

Jeremy looked at the clock. "I guess you've got to get to bed early too, Vic. So…"

"Where do you want to stay?" Vic asked. "In the loft on the couch, or in the house with your own bed? I know which I'd choose."

"You wouldn't be insulted if I chose the bed…?" Jeremy asked tentatively. "If you want me at your place, I'll stay with you…"

"I'm here just as much as I am over the garage. I'll see you at breakfast. Actually, who am I kidding? You're not going to be up before the rooster. You can come over to the bakery for some lunch. Or I'll see you after we close."

Jeremy nodded. "Okay. And you're sure it's okay with you, Erin? I'm practically a stranger."

"No, you're not. You're family."

"And… your boyfriend is the cop, right? He won't… maybe it's best if he doesn't know I'm here. Does he stay over…?" Jeremy looked around. "Maybe I should stay with Vic."

Erin shook her head slowly. "No, he doesn't stay overnight. And he won't be by tonight, because he knows I'll be heading to bed." Erin hesitated. She looked at Vic. "Let me just walk Vic out…"

Erin and Vic walked into the kitchen, slowed, and stopped at the back door in the growing shadows.

"Is he in trouble?" Erin asked Vic. "If he's on the run from the police…"

Vic shook her head. "Not Jeremy," she said with certainty. "I know him, and he wouldn't get into anything serious."

"They're all involved with the Jackson clan, aren't they?"

"Can't help but be. But that doesn't mean he's done anything. He would have stayed away from anything real bad…"

"So, you think it's safe to have him here?"

"Jeremy wouldn't do anything to hurt you. And nobody but you and me are going to know he's here."

"I don't like the idea of hiding it from Terry."

"It's too late to make any other arrangements tonight. If you don't want him in the house, just say the word, and he'll come to the back with me. Tomorrow we can sort everything else out."

"I'm okay with him here tonight."

"Okay." Vic gave her a hug and left by the back door to go to her own apartment over the garage.

Erin armed the burglar alarm. She turned around and just about tripped over Orange Blossom, who had decided that if Erin was in the kitchen, it must be to feed him. He yowled when she stepped on his tail, even though she knew she'd just gotten the fur at the end and hadn't stepped on the tail itself.

"Oh, hush," she told him. "Jeremy will think I'm killing you." She got him a couple of treats from the can and slid them across the floor past him. He chased after them excitedly and gobbled them up. He looked disappointed when Erin didn't give him more or stay to play with him.

"All settled?" Jeremy asked, giving Erin a charming smile. "Do you want me in here or out back?"

"You can stay in here," Erin said. "I'll show you your room." She led Jeremy down the hall to the bedroom that had first been Clementine's, then Vic's, and then Reg's.

"This isn't your room?" Jeremy asked, looking around it with quick eyes. "This is the master, isn't it?"

"Yes, but I like the smaller room. Plus, I have a sewing room and the attic hideaway, so all in, I do have more space than you do."

"Okay. If you're sure. I don't want to be taking your bed."

"Sheets are clean. It's all yours."

"That's not what I meant, but thank you. This is very generous of you, taking in a near-stranger who just shows up without any warning. I really appreciate the help. I would get a hotel room, but…"

"You'd have to go to the city for that, there are no hotels in Bald Eagle Falls."

"Yeah, so I discovered."

Jeremy went into the bedroom. Erin stood in the doorway for a minute longer, wondering if she should ask him what kind of trouble he was in. Then she shrugged. It was none of her business. He would tell her when the time was right.

CHAPTER 7

*E*rin returned to Auntie Clem's after dropping a platter of treats off to Naomi at The Book Nook for the Book Club.

"Okay, I wanted to get some more pastry sheets started for the new batch of turnovers," she told Vic. "You'll be okay out front for a bit?"

"It's quiet," Vic confirmed. "Nothing I can't handle. You'll be done before the afterschool crowd."

"Definitely."

Erin went into the kitchen and pulled the chilled dough out of the fridge. She set it on the counter, floured the rolling surface, and reached for her rolling pin.

Her hand hovered over an empty space on the counter.

Erin looked around, wondering if she had somehow misplaced it. It wasn't on any of the counter surfaces, which were gleaming and bare. It wasn't hung up on the utensils rack. She opened and closed a couple of drawers without any luck. Not in the sink. She even looked in the fridge and freezer, thinking she might have put it there absentmindedly, or in an effort to help keep the dough cold while she worked with it. There was no sign of it anywhere.

Erin went out to the front and looked at Vic. Vic raised her brows questioningly.

"You haven't seen my rolling pin, have you?"

"No. On the counter, last I saw. Isn't it there?"

"I don't think I could have missed it."

There were only a couple of customers there, and they hadn't made their choices yet, so Vic poked her head into the kitchen and looked around. She frowned. "Well, that's odd."

"I looked everywhere. A rolling pin doesn't just go walking off by itself."

"No, it would need someone with two legs to carry it."

A wave of anger washed over Erin. Vic immediately saw what she was thinking. "You don't think that…"

"Charley. Who else would it be? She decided she needed a rolling pin, and knew I wouldn't lend her one, so she just came over here and took it. I can't believe her!"

"I'm sorry," Vic looked around the kitchen. "I was out front when you went over to The Book Nook, and the back door must have been unlocked. I didn't hear anything."

"Sometimes I wish I had never found her!"

"She's your baby sister," Vic said. "You had to."

"Well, I'm not so happy about having found her, now. I'll be back as quickly as I can."

Vic nodded. Erin hung up her apron and exited through the front of the store, crossed the street, and went down to The Bake Shoppe. She tried the door, but it was locked. She banged on the glass.

"Charley! Open up! It's Erin!"

She probably didn't need to say who it was. Even if Charley didn't recognize her voice, she very well knew who was going to be looking for her. There was no answer. She was pretending not to be there, hoping that Erin would just go back to Auntie Clem's.

"I know you're in there! Let me in!"

Erin banged as loudly as she could on the glass. She didn't want to have to go all the way around the back. She knew from her previous visit to The Bake Shoppe that all of the stores were attached, and she had to go all the way down the block to get around to the back of the store. Chances are, that door would be locked too.

"Charley! Open up! You want me to call the police?"

People up and down the street were starting to pay attention to what was going on, stealing glances in her direction. Erin banged a few more times, but to no effect. She was going to have to try the back door.

35

She marched down the block, marching at an angry pace but taking care not to trip over the uneven sidewalk blocks. Around to the back of The Bake Shoppe. She stopped outside the door, her hand on it, remembering. The last time she had been there, she had spent hours administering CPR to a dead man. Not the best of memories. But she needed to confront Charley. Erin banged on the back door.

"Charley! I'm coming in."

She tried the door and found it unlocked. Swallowing her anxiety, Erin marched forward, composing her speech in her head. Charley was going to get a real talking to. Erin was done with being nice to her. She was done with being reasonable and explaining and trying to humor and help Charley. Stealing Erin's bakery equipment was going too far!

Erin stomped into the kitchen and stopped short. Her brain took separate, unconnected pictures. Flour smeared on the counter. A newly-purchased electronic scale. Erin's marble rolling pin on the floor, dirty and contaminated with who-knew-what. It appeared to be smeared with the red filling of the sweet cherry turnovers in Charley's ad. There was a sticky pool of the red filling on the floor. And there was a man, apparently drunk, sprawled across the floor.

Erin's throat closed as she looked at him, her breath whistling through the constricted pipe. A large man in a button-up shirt, spattered with the red pie filling. Balding, his face gray. She could hardly bring herself to look at his face.

Don Inglethorpe. What was he doing passed out in The Bake Shoppe? Erin supposed that he had gone there to meet with Charley. He did represent the estate that held the bakery in trust for Charley and Davis, so it would make sense for him to be there, checking up on the asset to make sure that everything was in order for the opening.

And where was Charley? Late getting to the meeting, Erin supposed. And Inglethorpe had passed out while waiting for her.

Erin had come for the rolling pin. It was on the floor. She bent down and picked it up automatically. Then the gears in her head ground and seized up, unsure what to do next. The part of her brain programmed with her schedule said that the next step was to return to Auntie Clem's to make the turnovers, like she had planned to do. That was the next thing on her list. But the problem-solving section kept her from leaving. The rolling pin was contaminated and couldn't be used in her bakery again. She would need to buy a new one.

And there was the additional problem of the man on the floor.

She couldn't just leave him there. She should wake him up, make sure that he was okay. But she couldn't bring herself to bend over and shake him. She'd dealt with drunks before. She knew that if she woke him, he might be angry and violent, and she'd have to be prepared to get out of his way.

She could just let him sleep it off there, leave him for Charley to deal with.

And then there was the little voice that told her Don Inglethorpe wasn't drunk and he wasn't going to wake up or be violent toward her.

Because, of course, he was dead.

CHAPTER 8

"Freeze! Hands up!"

Erin didn't freeze or put her hands up. She turned around and looked at Terry, not comprehending anything that was going on. He had his gun out, pointing at her in a two-handed stance. His eyes were wide, and his jaw dropped when he saw who it was.

"Erin!"

Erin looked back at Don Inglethorpe's body again. "I just… I was looking for my rolling pin."

"You need to put it down, Erin."

"What's going on here? What happened?"

"Erin."

She stared down at Inglethorpe's body, leaning closer to get a better look, feeling nauseated as her brain allowed her to absorb more of the details and to fully comprehend that it wasn't a movie, it wasn't an act or a prank, but that Don Inglethorpe lay dead in the kitchen of The Bake Shoppe, and she was standing over him with the rolling pin.

She looked at the rolling pin in her hand, not sure what to do with it. It was part of a crime scene. She wasn't going to be able to take it back to her bakery. Not that she could anyway. How could she use an implement that had been contaminated in her kitchen?

"Just put it on the floor, Erin. Away from the puddle, if you can."

She stared down at Inglethorpe, tasting acid in the back of her throat. It wasn't cherry pie filling. Of course it wasn't. Don Inglethorpe had been bludgeoned and she was holding the murder weapon in her hand. Someone had taken her rolling pin and had used it to kill the man. Charley? Would Charley intentionally implicate Erin? But why would Charley kill Inglethorpe?

Terry holstered his weapon. He ordered K9 to sit and stay so he wouldn't contaminate the crime scene. He walked over to Erin, reaching into one of the pouches on his belt to pull out a pair of blue gloves, which he tugged on over his hands.

He took the rolling pin out of Erin's hand and laid it carefully on the floor, away from the sticky red pool of what Erin now knew was not pie filling. His fingers closed around Erin's forearm in a gentle but firm grip, and he gave her a little tug.

"Come with me."

Erin's feet moved of their own accord, following his lead.

CHAPTER 9

*E*rin was sitting in a car sideways, her feet out the door, as someone helped her to sip from a cold bottle of water. It was too cold. Erin shuddered, goosebumps raised on her flesh.

"It's going to be okay."

"I…" Erin looked around her, trying to orient herself. "What happened?"

"Drink some more."

"No." Erin pushed it away. She didn't want any more water sloshing around in her stomach. She didn't know what to do. She was supposed to be making turnovers. She would have to go to the grocery store and pick up a new rolling pin. It wouldn't be a good one, like the marble one that had been stolen, but she could work with a wooden rolling pin until she could get to the city and replace it with something of quality. "I need to get back to the shop."

"You're not going anywhere. Have some more water."

"I can't drink any more." Erin wiped her forehead, dripping with sweat, with the back of her arm. How could she be sweating and shivering at the same time?

"Maybe you should put your head between your knees. You're still looking pretty pale."

"What happened?"

"You fainted."

"No, I didn't," Erin objected, though she couldn't remember what had really happened. She was sure she hadn't fainted. She didn't faint.

"Okay, maybe you didn't technically faint. I don't know if you completely lost consciousness. But you… collapsed and you couldn't talk to me."

"Where is Charley?"

"We're looking for her. You don't know where she would be?"

"She's not here. This is her bakery and she's supposed to be opening tomorrow. Is it tomorrow?"

"She might have to put her grand opening off for a few days. Why did you come over here?"

"To get my rolling pin."

"What made you think it was here?"

Erin tried to recapture her mental processes. She was feeling disoriented, out of sync with the present. "Charley took it. So I came to get it back."

"Why would Charley take your rolling pin?"

"Why?"

She realized that it was Terry talking to her, not just a disembodied voice. She looked at him, saw him there in front of her, his face concerned, but set into that serious, no-nonsense expression he took on when he was investigating a crime. She looked down at her hands, encased in plastic bags. She wiggled her fingers to make sure that she was really seeing them and that they were connected to her body.

"We need to preserve any trace," Terry said. "Anything you might have touched in there."

"I didn't touch anything."

"Okay."

"I think…"

Terry waited for her to finish her thought. When she didn't, he raised his brows and prompted her. "What do you think?"

"I think… that was Don Inglethorpe in there."

"Yes, it was."

"And he was… dead."

"Yes. Not that he's been declared yet, but there isn't anything we can do for him."

"It wasn't something he ate."

Terry's eyes searched her face. "No. Not this time."

"Did she use my rolling pin?" Erin shook her head, angered. "That was a really special tool. It's marble."

"You're sure it was yours?"

"Yes!"

"Why would anyone take your rolling pin? Charley must have her own."

"She said people had stolen things from the bakery. It was fully-stocked when Angela was running it, but people must have taken things home when it closed down. They probably didn't think it would ever open again and no one would know the difference. Charley kept discovering that things that should have been in the bakery, weren't."

Terry nodded. "Did she borrow yours? Did she ask for it?"

"She asked for other things, but I told her no. They couldn't be contaminated with gluten flours."

"And you think she went into Auntie Clem's and took it anyway?"

"Yes! Who else would have?"

"Did you see her? Did anyone see her?"

Erin shook her head. "I went over to The Book Nook. The back door was unlocked while I was gone. Vic was in the front."

"So, anyone could have walked in."

"Yes. But no one else would have wanted it. Just Charley."

"Do you have a security camera?"

"No."

"We'll see who else on the block has one. Maybe we'll get lucky." Terry offered her the water bottle again. "Have another drink."

"I don't want any more water. Unless you want me to throw up on your shoes."

"Not particularly." The corner of Terry's mouth twitched, and the dimple appeared in his cheek. Erin wanted to reach out and touch it, but it wasn't appropriate. She *couldn't* be a murder suspect again. After all that had happened, how could she be sitting in his car, her hands wrapped in plastic, the central suspect or witness in another murder investigation? It couldn't be happening.

Sheriff Wilmot approached. "Scene's secure." He looked down at Erin, a fan of fine wrinkles appearing at the corner of his eyes. "You feeling a bit better, Miss Price?"

Erin wanted to scratch an itch on her temple, but didn't think she should with the bags over her hands. She might tear a hole and compromise the evidence.

"I... I guess I'm okay."

"You're still white as a ghost. But you're talking sense and that's an improvement."

"I'm just a little... it doesn't feel real."

Terry took her by the arm and touched a couple of fingers over her radial pulse. "I would think that with the number of bodies you've come across, this would be old hat."

"It's not."

He let go of her. "Why don't you tell Sheriff Wilmot what happened while I go get a collection kit?"

"Okay." Erin watched him walk away, feeling a little insecure. She wanted him to stay by her side and reassure her. She forced herself to turn to the sheriff, and started her description of having left Auntie Clem's to find the rolling pin.

"And why did you assume that Charley Campbell had it?" Sheriff Wilmot asked.

"She kept asking to borrow other stuff. She couldn't seem to understand that I couldn't allow any of my equipment to get contaminated. So, when I reached for it and it wasn't there... and I checked the whole kitchen and couldn't find it... I figured she had popped in the back door while I was at The Book Nook and took it."

He nodded. "Okay. Go on."

Erin told him about knocking on the front door and getting no response, then going around the back way.

"Did you cross paths with anyone else going from the front to the back? Anyone who might have been coming from this direction?"

Erin thought about it. She shook her head. "I don't think so. I saw other people on the street, but no one in the alley or the side street. But I kind of had tunnel vision. I might have walked right by someone without really registering it."

"Did you knock on the back?"

"I knocked and then tried the door. It was unlocked, so I went in."

"Tell me what you saw when you walked in."

Erin described the fractured impressions she'd had on walking into the

43

scene. She shrugged, her face getting warm. "I just thought... I'd been thinking about cherry turnovers, and I just thought it was all cherry sauce."

He smiled. "Our brains do funny things sometimes, trying to come up with explanations for things that we don't want to believe. I've heard the same thing described many times. People who thought they had walked into a TV set or a prank of some sort. The victim was just pretending. Can you tell me what you did? What you might have touched?"

"Nothing. I didn't touch anything."

"Terry said you were holding the rolling pin."

"But it's my rolling pin."

"Right now, it's evidence. Where was it when you picked it up?"

"I don't know." Erin tried to replay it. "Just... on the floor. Near his head. Not in the... pool. Just to the side."

"Good. Why did you pick it up?"

"It's mine."

"But you know you can't touch evidence at a crime scene."

"I just wasn't thinking. That was what I came for, so I picked it up. It was automatic."

"What happened next? Did you see or hear anything that might have indicated someone was still here? Smell any perfume or body odor?"

The question triggered a memory, not of perfume, but the scent of blood. Even though her eyes had been trying to tell her it was just cherry pie filling, her nose had known that it was not. Erin gagged. The sheriff took a step back from her, getting his feet out of the potential splash zone.

"Sorry," he apologized. "What was it?"

"Blood." Erin swallowed, trying to settle her stomach. "Ugh. So much."

He nodded and spoke soothingly. "The door to the basement was ajar. You didn't go down there, or see or hear any sign of anyone?"

"No."

"Until Terry came in."

"Yeah."

"Tell me what he did when he came in."

Erin looked at Sheriff Wilmot, frowning. Terry had surely told him what had happened from the time of his arrival. "Um... he told me to stop. I think he told me to put the rolling pin down. But I was kind of stuck."

"Then what?"

"He told K9 to stay, he put on gloves, and he took the rolling pin away from me and put it down. After that… I'm not sure."

"I gather that's when he brought you out here and called for backup."

"I guess. I don't remember."

"Okay."

Erin saw the sheriff nod to someone outside of her field of vision, and then Terry returned. He put down what looked like a tackle box full of various swabs, packages, and plastic bags.

"You'd better take this part," he told Sheriff Wilmot.

The sheriff nodded. He put on a pair of gloves and removed the bag from one of Erin's hands. She watched as he swabbed the skin with several different swabs, putting each into a different container or bag. When they were sealed, he and Terry both scribbled their initials over the seals. Then there were sticky strips of paper that were stuck to Erin's hand, peeled off, and then preserved in evidence bags.

"How about this spa treatment?" Sheriff Wilmot joked. "A wash, a peel, and now I'm going to give you a manicure."

Erin laughed, but Sheriff Wilmot next scraped under each of her nails and clipped a couple of them back, preserving his findings in a small bag. He and Terry marked each of the bags and then repeated the same procedure on Erin's other hand. Sheriff Wilmot released her hand.

"You can have this back now."

Erin rubbed her hands together. "I'm done?"

Sheriff Wilmot looked her over carefully. "I don't see any blood or other transfer on your clothes, so I don't think we need to take those." He looked at Terry. "What do you think?"

Terry shook his head. "Don't think so. There's no spatter, nothing on her knees; I don't think she touched the body."

"I'm sure we'll have follow-up questions. We know how to reach you," Wilmot told Erin.

She smiled and nodded. The smile felt strained and unnatural.

"You don't know where Charley is, do you?" Wilmot asked casually.

"No… I'm sure she has a lot to do before her grand reopening. But…" Erin realized belatedly how everything she said had pointed a finger at Charley. "I'm sure… Charley didn't do this. She couldn't have. What reason would she have?"

"We'll look into that, I can assure you. We'll see where the evidence leads. But Charley will obviously need to be interviewed, just like anyone else connected with this business."

CHAPTER 10

*E*rin said that she was just going to go back to the bakery, but Terry wouldn't hear of it.

"Vic can manage on her own. You're not in any shape to be working right now."

"I'm okay. It wasn't that bad."

"Tell that to someone who wasn't there. Maybe they'll believe you. I'm taking you home. I'll pop into Auntie Clem's later, help Vic close up, and bring her home. You can spend the rest of the day cuddling with the animals."

Erin sighed. "Well, I guess. If you won't let me go back to the bakery."

"Nope. You need some quiet recovery time, not gossipy customers. They'll all find out what happened soon enough."

Erin closed her eyes for the few blocks back to her house. Terry parked the car. "I'll walk you in."

Erin suddenly remembered about Jeremy. "No, that's okay. I'm fine." She opened her door, jumped out, and was halfway to the house before Terry could get out to follow her. He stood beside his car, looking bewildered. Erin gave him a cheery wave and let herself into the house, swinging the door shut behind her.

She hoped that Terry would take her strange behavior as resulting from her traumatic experience and not be offended by it. She didn't want to push him away, but she didn't want to damage her friendship with Vic by betraying her brother to the police after promising to keep his presence 'on the down-low' either.

Erin moved away from the door and went to her bedroom, hoping that if Terry were watching, her movements would seem natural. She paused in the bedroom, watching his car through the slatted blinds until it pulled away from the curb. A moment later, she heard the door to the master bedroom.

"Erin?" Jeremy asked in a low voice.

"Yeah, it's me."

They both poked their heads out their bedroom doors to look at each other. Jeremy nodded and let out a breath. "What are you doing home? I know you started early, but I didn't expect you to be home before four."

"Oh…" Erin realized she was going to have to explain it to Jeremy, and wasn't sure she was up to it. "Well, something happened."

"Is everything okay? Where's Vic?"

"She's still at the bakery. Terry will drop her off later. Though now I'm not sure that's such a good idea. She should probably tell him she wants to walk, because if he brings her home, he's going to expect to come in."

"Terry is the cop?"

"Yeah."

"This is more complicated than I expected."

"A bit," Erin admitted.

He took a step toward her. "So, what happened? Are you sick?"

"No," Erin denied her queasy stomach, knowing that it wasn't the result of a virus. "I just… well this lawyer in town, Don Inglethorpe… he was in The Bake Shoppe…"

Jeremy nodded, his eyes narrowing.

"I went over there to get my rolling pin from Charley, but she wasn't there, and he was, and…"

"Who is Charley? She's the other girl who was with you when you came to the farm?"

"Yeah. My half-sister. She's opening up the other bakery, The Bake Shoppe."

"The other bakery?" he repeated blankly.

"When my rolling pin was missing, I knew she was the one who had taken it. Or I figured she was. So I went over there to confront her."

"And found Don Inglethorpe there instead."

"Yeah."

Jeremy waited for more. "And…?"

"I just… I guess it gave me a turn. I wasn't expecting that. Terry said I shouldn't go back to Auntie Clem's, but I should come home and relax…"

"This Don Inglethorpe… did you have a fight? Or you just don't like him…?"

Erin stared at Jeremy. She rewound the conversation, trying to figure out how it had gone off the rails. "No… he was dead."

At that, Jeremy looked staggered. His eyes got wide and he grasped the doorframe, knuckles turning white. "Who was dead? Don Inglethorpe?"

"Yes."

"What happened? Was he shot?"

"Shot? No. He was…" Erin suddenly couldn't frame the words. It seemed so brutal, so violent and intrusive even to say what had happened. "The rolling pin…" She made a little clubbing motion with her hand.

"With the rolling pin? He was beaten?"

Erin nodded.

"To death?" Jeremy checked, disbelief in his voice.

She nodded again.

Jeremy swore. He reached out a hand toward Erin. "Are you okay? No wonder the cop told you not to go back to work. You discovered this guy?"

"Uh-huh."

He used both hands to push his shaggy blond hair back from his face. It was strange to see him so serious, when she had usually only seen him smiling and laughing. "I should do something," Jeremy mused, talking to himself. "Should I get you a drink? Tea?"

"Actually, tea does sound good." Usually it was Adele or Vic who made Erin tea, if she wasn't the one making it. She wasn't sure what she thought of the tall young man rattling around her kitchen.

"Tea," Jeremy agreed. "That's what my mom would say." He went into the kitchen.

Erin followed him and when he started opening and closing drawers and cupboards, indicated the proper cupboard.

"Ah," Jeremy pulled down a tin of assorted teas and handed it to Erin. "Pick out what you like. There's the kettle. I'll get the water on."

He talked like he was coaching himself, giving himself the steps one at a time. Erin pictured Mrs. Jackson trying to teach her sons some civility, walking them through various little services, drilling them on what they would do in different circumstances. *What do you do if someone is ill? What do you do if they've had bad news? How do you make a cup of tea for a lady?*

Jeremy's hand hovered over the teacups in the same cupboard as the teas and service. "Do you have a favorite? Which one do you want?"

"The blue one," Erin suggested, selecting a cup with a wide, shallow bowl. It would cool more quickly than a deeper cup, so she'd be able to drink it sooner.

Jeremy took the cup carefully down from the shelf. He took down the tea tray and lifted the lid from the sugar bowl to make sure it was filled. "Do you want milk? Cream?"

"No. Just sugar is fine."

He started to take the tray over to the kitchen table, then hesitated, listening to his mother's unheard prompts in his ear. "Do you want to take it in here? Or the parlor? Or do you want to lie down?"

"Here is good, Jeremy. You're doing just fine, thank you. I appreciate it."

She selected a ginger tea from the tin and put the rest back away. Then she sat down at the table to give Jeremy a chance to finish his service without interference. They waited for the kettle to boil.

Orange Blossom came into the kitchen, sniffing the air and looking at Erin with confusion, clearly wondering what she was doing home already. He meowed loudly a couple of times, demanding an explanation and soothing words and pats from Erin.

"Silly kitty," she told him. "You should just be happy mommy is home early!"

Jeremy watched her with the vocal cat. "You have a very loud cat," he told her.

"Oh, you noticed, did you?"

"He doesn't like closed doors."

Erin laughed. "No, he doesn't. He wants to know everything that is going on in this house. Curious as a cat." She scratched the cat's ears. "Were you giving Jeremy a hard time, Blossom? You should be a nice boy. Let him sleep!"

"I was afraid the neighbors were going to be coming over to see what was wrong. He's like an alarm bell!"

"Well, at least you can be assured that it wouldn't be the first time one of the neighbors complained about him being too loud. It's a regular occurrence. Not just because you're here."

"Well, that's good," Jeremy agreed.

Erin watched him pour boiling water into the teapot, and then he placed it before her.

"There you go. Would you like anything else?" He looked around the kitchen, evaluating. "A cookie?" He moved toward the cookie jar.

"Uh, no. Those are dog biscuits, actually." Erin poured water into her cup and swirled the teabag around.

"Dog biscuits. Well, I guess it's a good thing I didn't help myself to one for breakfast. But you don't have a dog, do you?"

"No. Terry does."

"Oh, right. I remember that whole thing at Christmas. K9, right? He's recovered from his experience?"

Erin nodded. "He's just fine. No ill effects."

She grew self-conscious under Jeremy's gaze. She motioned to the tea. "Help yourself to a cup. Don't make me drink alone."

He hesitated.

"Or if you do want a cookie, there are some in the freezer."

Jeremy gave a sheepish grin and went over to the fridge. He opened the freezer door. There was always plenty of baking in Erin's freezer. He looked over the variety. "Is there something particular I should have?"

"Anything in there is fair game. In case you forgot, I run a bakery. There are always leftovers."

He looked through the zip-sealed freezer bags and settled on a couple of chocolate chip cookies.

"Put them in the microwave for thirty seconds," Erin advised. "They'll be just right."

He put them on a small plate and followed her directions. When the microwave beeped, he sat down across the table from her to eat.

CHAPTER 11

$\mathcal{E}$rin should have known that word of the murder and Erin's part in finding the body would get around town before Vic even got home. The doorbell rang shortly after she had finished her tea and Jeremy ducked back into the bedroom while Erin went to answer it.

It was Adele, Erin's friend and official groundskeeper of the woods on the property Erin had inherited from Clementine, including the summer cottage Adele resided in. Adele had needed somewhere to live, and Erin had needed someone to keep an eye on happenings in the woods, so it was a mutually beneficial relationship. Erin had grown closer to the tall, reserved woman over the previous few months.

"Hi, come on in."

Adele accepted the invitation. Her eyes went to the kitchen, then around the living room. Erin had a feeling Adele picked up on a lot more than she gave away. Adele sat down in one of the chairs, her back straight and stiff.

"Are you okay, Erin? I heard… I thought I'd come and see if there's anything you need."

"I'm okay. Everybody is treating me like a china doll, but I'm really not. I don't need to take the afternoon off, and I can do most things for myself even if I did have a shock. I barely even knew the guy, so…" Erin trailed off, not sure what that proved.

"You've already had yourself a cup of tea," Adele had either seen the dishes on the kitchen table or had smelled the ginger tea, "and probably all you want to do now is lie down for a rest. You don't need to be entertaining company right now."

"I don't mind…"

"But you don't need it," Adele said firmly. "The last thing you need is a house full of guests."

Erin was careful not to look toward the master bedroom where Jeremy was keeping himself hidden.

"If you want to talk or need anything else from me, you know how to reach me." Adele rose to her feet.

"I'll be okay, Adele," Erin assured her. "Really."

"If you need anything, call. I'll be over here in a jiffy. Okay?"

Erin nodded.

Adele leaned in and gave Erin a brief hug around the shoulders, something she did not normally do. Adele whispered in Erin's ear, lips almost touching.

"Anything, okay?"

~

Having received Erin's text, Vic told Terry that she wanted to walk home, so it was a little later than usual when she arrived. Terry had helped with clean-up as he had promised, but it didn't go as quickly as when Erin and Vic were working together, following the routines that had become habit.

"Whew, what a day!" Vic dropped her bags on the floor and gave Erin an exuberant hug. "Are you okay? Let me look at you." It was a minute before she could take a look at Erin, as she was holding onto Erin too tightly and had to release her and step back. "You look okay. Did you end up being bored all afternoon? Or did you have a nap?"

Jeremy had come out of the bedroom. He laughed and gave Vic a quick squeeze around the shoulder. "Erin had me to look after her, so she's just fine."

"Oh, what did you do? Demand that she wait on you hand and foot?"

He raised his eyebrows, putting his hand on his chest. "Me? Just because I used to order my little brother around, that doesn't mean I'd do that to Erin! I even made her tea."

Vic gave a gasp. "Tea? You?" She turned to Erin. "Should I take you to the hospital now or later?"

Erin laughed and shook her head. "He did just fine. He was very helpful. Be nice to him."

"I'm always nice to him, aren't I, Germy? So, where's my dinner?"

"You'll have to make your own. I used up all of my domestic skills boiling water."

"I have the solution," Erin interposed. "Bread and jam."

"We *do* have frozen dinners," Vic said, their other fallback when they were too tired at the end of the day to make anything else, which was most of the time.

"I can't manage a full dinner today. I'm going for bread and jam. How about you?" Erin asked Jeremy. "You can choose what you want. There are frozen dinners in the fridge, or some leftovers from the bakery today. And we still have a few jars of Jam Lady jam."

"Can I have a dinner *and* bread and jam?"

Vic laughed. "That's my brother."

Vic and Jeremy mostly discussed their family and childhood over dinner. Erin listened in, appreciating a new window into her friend's former life. Vic normally didn't talk much about her family, and when she did, it was in relation to their estrangement and how they did not accept her transition. It was nice to hear more about the good times she'd had with her brothers, the fond memories of Mom's home cooking, and helping Pa with the running of the farm.

Jeremy was cheerful, his wide grin and laughing eyes brightening Clementine's kitchen. But every now and then, the smile dropped away, and he looked troubled. Erin could see the concern in Vic's eyes for her brother, but neither of them demanded an explanation. If he was comfortable with them, then sooner or later he would tell them what was going on.

Vic leaned back in her chair, sighing with satisfaction. "Now. What's the scoop on Don Inglethorpe? What are we going to do about him?"

Erin raised her brows, surprised. "Well, since he's dead, there's not much we can do to help him."

"Except bring his killer to justice. Isn't that your other specialty?"

"No, absolutely not. I told you, I'm not a detective. Leave the investigating to Terry."

"Terry's not going to be able to investigate it. Not when *you* were discovered standing over the body with the murder weapon. He's going to have to bow out of this one too."

Jeremy looked back and forth at them, as if watching a tennis game. "Uh, exactly how many murder investigations has he had to bow out of because you were a suspect?"

"Only one!"

"He investigated the previous ones," Vic said, "since they weren't a couple yet for those ones."

"This sweet thing?" Jeremy gestured to Erin. "What is this, a Steven King novel? The baking serial killer?"

"I didn't kill anyone. I was just... suspect for reasons beyond my control."

"Why did you pick up the rolling pin?" Vic demanded. "That seems like just about the stupidest thing you could have done. You know not to touch evidence."

Erin felt her face flush. "I wasn't exactly thinking. I'd gone there to get the rolling pin, and when I got there, I was so shocked, I couldn't really understand what was going on, and I just picked it up automatically. It wasn't even conscious, really."

"You're lucky you do have friends in the police department, or you would have spent the night in a jail cell for sure."

Erin frowned, but she wasn't thinking about spending the night in jail. "Whoever did it must have gotten blood on them. There was..." she choked, "a *lot* of blood on the scene."

"I thought he was beaten," Jeremy said.

"Yes... but there was a lot of blood." Erin swallowed and tried not to think too much about the scene she had stumbled into.

"Head wounds always bleed like the dickens," Vic said. "The scalp has lots of blood vessels close to the surface. I would guess something like a rolling pin would break the skin pretty easily." She cut her eyes toward Erin. "I don't know whether he was just hit once, or more than that."

"It's a marble rolling pin," Erin told Jeremy, not answering Vic's implied question about how many times Inglethorpe had been hit. "It's heavy and hard and the ends have sharpish edges."

She could see him revising his opinion. Not just a light wooden or plastic rolling pin. An implement that could do some real damage. A deadly weapon, wielded by the right person. He nodded seriously.

"Yeah, okay, I guess I can see that."

Vic leaned forward. "But who do you think did it? You think it was Charley?"

"I… I guess that must be what everyone is thinking, but what motive would Charley have to kill him?"

"It was in her shop. Who else had access?"

"The back door was unlocked. Just like ours was. Anyone could have walked in. Someone stole my rolling pin, and someone walked into The Bake Shoppe and killed him."

"You make it sound like a frame-up," Jeremy contributed. "Do you think someone was intentionally trying to implicate you?"

Vic frowned and nodded. "Yeah, why else would they bother to take a rolling pin from our kitchen? Why not just use a frying pan or something else handy at The Bake Shoppe?"

Erin hadn't thought about that, but they did have a point. "Unless it was Charley who stole the rolling pin, like we originally thought, so it was handy at the scene."

"Where did Charley go? Why wasn't she there? I would think that with the grand reopening, she would have been busy baking and getting everything arranged."

"I don't know. No idea where she went. The police were looking for her. Maybe they'll know something else by morning."

"You don't think anything happened to her?" Jeremy asked. "That she was kidnapped, or she was hurt too?"

"Charley can take care of herself," Erin said, hoping it was true and looking at Vic to see what her thoughts were. "She had a gun and she knew how to use it."

"A gun isn't always a protection," Jeremy said.

"Why would anyone do anything to hurt Charley?"

"Why would anyone do anything to hurt Don Inglethorpe?" Vic countered.

They were all silent. Erin had to confess she didn't know too much about Inglethorpe or who would have a motive to kill him.

"Who was he?" Jeremy asked, in the dark about Bald Eagle Falls affairs.

"A lawyer, like most of the Inglethorpes," Vic told him. "Old money. Lots of history in these hills. He was one of the lawyers who made the decisions on Trenton Plaint's estate, right Erin?" Vic looked at her for confirmation.

Erin nodded. Jeremy would know who Trenton Plaint was, since the Plaints and the Jacksons were cousins.

"The Bake Shoppe was part of the estate," Vic resumed speaking to Jeremy. "The estate hadn't been settled or distributed or whatever you call it yet, so these lawyers were the ones who decided what to do with the assets until it was."

"It was to be split between two people," Erin supplemented. "When Trenton died, that just left his brother Davis, but if it can be proven that Davis conspired to kill Trenton, he won't be able to inherit it. But then we discovered Charley Campbell, a sister neither of them knew they had. Charley is the one who was living in Moose River and working for the Dysons, not knowing she was actually born into the Jackson clan."

"So there *is* a connection between Inglethorpe and Charley."

"Yes, but..." Vic looked at Erin. "Originally, the lawyers said that Charley couldn't reopen Aunt Angela's bakery. They were just going to hold it as an asset until who was going to inherit the estate was settled. But Charley wanted to open the bakery."

"She said it was losing value if it just sat there closed," Erin agreed, "and eventually, she managed to convince them."

Vic drummed her fingers on the table. "Don Inglethorpe was the swing vote."

"What does that mean?" Jeremy asked.

"He originally voted *against* opening the bakery. So, it was two-one against. But Charley was able to talk him into changing his vote. If it weren't for him, she wouldn't have been able to open the bakery again. It would have just sat there empty, waiting for some resolution of whether Davis could inherit from the estate."

"Then she wouldn't want to kill him. He did what she wanted him to."

"Yeah." Vic's eyes flashed to Erin.

Erin understood the look without Vic voicing it. "But if there was a business that might be damaged by The Bake Shoppe opening, then *that* business owner would have reason to be upset about Don Inglethorpe changing his vote," Erin said for her.

Jeremy look from one of them to the other. "You mean you. You'd have motive to kill him. And you had the weapon and were at the scene. That doesn't look good for you, Erin."

"They haven't arrested me yet," Erin said blithely. But there was a knot in her stomach. She could see how the police investigation would go. Terry and Sheriff Wilmot might not think she was involved, but when the evidence started to pile up, they'd be forced to act on it…

"Killing Inglethorpe might not change the way the trustees vote, though," Vic said. "Now it will be deadlocked, but Charley has already been given permission to open and has been getting everything in place so that she could. They won't be able to reverse their decision unless they both come down on the same side or they get a new tie-breaker who votes against reopening The Bake Shoppe at the eleventh hour. Charley is still going to be able to open the bakery, whether Don Inglethorpe is alive or dead."

Erin blew out her breath. "Yeah, you're right. Me killing him wouldn't change anything."

"Unless you just wanted revenge," Jeremy suggested. "You were mad at him for changing his vote, so you killed him, even though it wouldn't change anything."

"I wouldn't do that!" It occurred to Erin belatedly that she hadn't said earlier that she wouldn't kill Inglethorpe to keep The Bake Shoppe closed either.

"We know you didn't kill him," Vic said firmly. "We're just talking about the evidence. *Somebody* killed him. He didn't bludgeon himself to death."

"The police will sort it out," Erin said. She wasn't going to get involved. She was just going to let justice take its course and not interfere. She wasn't going to get in the way of the investigation or put herself or anyone in her circle of friends into harm's way.

Not this time.

CHAPTER 12

$\mathcal{E}$rin was back at Auntie Clem's bright and early as usual the next day. She knew she was going to have to deal with an increase in gossip and curious questions for a few days. Until some other news took over, like an engagement or elopement. In the meantime, it would bring her an increase in revenue, as people had to cover their curiosity with purchases from the bakery. No one would want to look like the only reason they had gone to Auntie Clem's in the first place was just to gawk at the murder suspect.

There was a method of increasing revenue that Erin hadn't considered when she was making her lists. Putting herself at the center of yet another murder investigation. If she kept doing that every few months...

Erin chuckled.

Vic glanced over at her with an eyebrow raised.

Erin shook her head. "You don't want to know."

They had everything freshly baked and out in the display case when it was time to turn the sign to 'open' and unlock the front door. As usual, there were a few customers already outside, ready to get their morning muffin or Danish on the way to work. Early mornings were one of the busiest times of day.

Erin was surprised to see Mrs. Foster with Peter and the young girls as part of the morning rush. Usually, Mrs. Foster dropped the older children at school first so that she only had to deal with little Traci while she was at the bakery. The Foster children were normally well-behaved while at the bakery, but were always excited and eager to get treats, and Mrs. Foster was much more relaxed if she didn't have to deal with all of them in the chaos of the morning rush.

Erin was trying to deflect questions from a couple of other regulars about the Don Inglethorpe situation. Mrs. Foster's eyes widened as she took in the questions. It was obvious she hadn't yet heard of the murder and was not one of those who had come for the sole purpose of getting the latest gossip and talking to the prime suspect. Erin saw Mrs. Foster's panicked look at her children. She couldn't clap her hands over the ears of all of them at once, and there was no way she was getting them back out of the bakery once they were in. Not without their cookies.

"Uh…" Erin fumbled to dam the flow of the conversation. "It's really not the best time."

Mrs. Urquhart looked at Erin with a frown, not understanding why Erin was trying to stop them from talking. "Whatever do you mean? I was just asking—"

"Little pitchers," Vic interrupted. She made a nod toward the children. "Li'l pitchers got big ears."

Mrs. Urquhart turned around slightly and saw Mrs. Foster's little brood. She patted at her cheeks. "Oh, dear. Of course." She gave Erin a little nod. "We will have to talk later," she said conspiratorially.

She and the other ladies quieted to whispers and the children waited impatiently for their turns at the counter without being any the wiser. As they discussed the options with each other, pointing and pressing their noses and fingers to the glass of the display case, Mrs. Foster gave a relieved nod to Erin and Vic.

"I had no idea," she whispered.

"Sorry about that!" Erin apologized.

"No, it's not your fault. I just don't want them hearing…" She looked at Peter in particular, Erin's best and most loyal fan. Erin got the feeling that not only did Mrs. Foster not want the children to hear any of the grisly details of Inglethorpe's death, but she didn't want Peter to hear that Erin was a suspect in the murder. He would find out soon enough that his heroes were not perfect.

"Mom, can I have two things?" Peter asked hopefully.

"No, Peter, you know better. Just one."

"I was just thinking that since I'm sleeping over at Bobby's tomorrow night, maybe I could have a muffin for breakfast. Bobby's dad usually makes pancakes, and they won't be safe for me."

Peter was an expert negotiator, and it wasn't long before he'd talked his mother into a cookie, a muffin, pizza shells for their dinner, and bagels that had something to do with a social studies project at school. Erin couldn't help grinning as Vic rang it up.

Mrs. Foster rolled her eyes. "That boy will be the death of me!" Then she flushed. "Oh! I shouldn't have said that, I'm sorry…"

As she herded the children out of the shop, Erin could hear Peter demanding to know what she was sorry about.

Later in the morning, Vic had whispered to Erin that Charley was back in town, but they didn't see her until it was almost closing time. After the after-school and supper rush had faded to a trickle, Charley slipped in the door, looking up in irritation at the jingle of the bells as if they had just announced her visit to the whole town.

"Charley! How are you? Is everything… okay?"

Charley's usually fresh face was drawn with fatigue. "Ugh. I just spent most of the day talking to your beloved and the rest of the police department. I wouldn't recommend it as entertainment, by the way."

Erin's face heated at the mention of Terry in such a flippant way. She was surprised that Terry would be involved in the investigation in any way with Erin as a potential suspect. She wouldn't have thought he'd be questioning Charley. Maybe that meant that they had ruled Erin out as a suspect, so Terry was not conflicted.

"Well, they didn't put you in jail," Erin said. "That's a good sign, right?"

"They didn't put you in jail either, and you were the one who was caught with the murder weapon in your hand. They tried ten ways to Sunday to stick a motive on me, but I didn't have any reason to kill Don. Having someone killed in my store doesn't mean I'm guilty." She looked at Erin. "As you well know."

"No, of course not."

Charley sat down in one of the chairs at the front of the shop. "I don't suppose you could bring me a cookie and a cup of tea, could you? I'm just so wiped out."

"Sure, of course," Erin agreed. "Chocolate chip?"

"Molasses?"

Erin nodded and got a cookie out for Charley. The teakettle was warm, so it didn't take long for it to come back to a boil. A few minutes later, Charley was sipping her tea. Erin suspected that Charley wanted her to sit down for a chat, but she didn't have time so close to closing. There were always a few last-minute customers who were trying to squeeze their errands in before closing time. Then Vic and Erin would need to clear out the display case, wipe everything down, and clear the till.

Vic was already in the kitchen preparing batters and doughs for the next day's offerings. They would turn out better if allowed to soak overnight and it would help them get the baking in the oven more quickly in the morning.

Erin served the final stragglers and turned the door sign to 'closed.' Charley was still at the table. Erin didn't rush her out. If she needed to talk about what had happened, Erin was curious enough to listen.

"You want to come to the back while we finish up? Or do you just want some quiet time to think?"

Charley got up, picking up her teacup to return it to Erin. "If *you* want to talk," she said, as if Erin were insisting upon it. She sighed loudly when she chose one of the kitchen stools and sat down.

"You're okay?" Erin asked, not sure where to start.

"Yeah, of course, I'm made of pretty stern stuff. But it was just a bit too much like being questioned after Bobby died... I kept thinking they were going to put the cuffs on and take me away. I'll tell you, I did not enjoy my time in those lovely digs."

Charley had only been jailed for a few days before bail was granted, and she had never said much to Erin about what it had been like.

"Well, you're still free, so at least I don't have to look after Iggy."

Charley's pet, Iggy, was not a cuddly kitten or puppy, but a chameleon. While Erin was impressed with how quickly he could tongue-zap a cricket, he still gave her the willies. Bugs and lizards were not her thing.

"I'll give him an extra big worm for you," Charley teased, her mouth quirking up slightly.

"Grrreat. Tell him it's from Auntie Erin."

"Why did you call your bakery Auntie Clem's instead of Auntie Erin's?"

"It was left to me by my Aunt Clementine. I just thought… it was a good way to honor her."

"Oh," Charley nodded. "Makes sense."

"You didn't want to change the name of The Bake Shoppe to something else?"

Charley grunted. "The trustees didn't think it was a good idea. Goodwill already established under the old name, people would be confused, blah, blah, blah."

"Maybe they're right. You want people to associate it with Angela and the bakery they were already used to going to, instead of thinking you're a brand-new start-up."

"If I can ever get it opened."

"You will. This might be a bit of a setback, but you'll still be able to open it."

"The other lawyers won't return my calls. I'm thinking that means I'm out of luck. They're going to change their minds and either liquidate it or just leave it sitting closed until it's not worth anything anymore."

"They wouldn't do that, would they?"

"It's a bad risk now. They're spooked. People won't want to go to a bakery where the last three owners have been killed, more or less. First Angela, then Trenton, then one of the trustees of the estate. People are superstitious around here."

"But you aren't asking them to become owners, just customers. People are curious. It will drive them there. You know how much more business we get when something bad happens? People want to talk about it, they want to see the place where something happened, they want to see and talk to the people involved. We've had a ton of extra business today because I was the one who found the body."

"Yeah?" Charley sat up a little taller. "I'll tell them that. Maybe that will help."

Erin was happy to help, but also irritated that she felt the need to. Did she *have* to keep helping her competition? Charley had just told her that she wasn't going to be able to reopen The Bake Shoppe, which would have been the best decision for Erin, and instead of simply commiserating and letting that decision stand, Erin was helping Charley to fight back.

She caught Vic's gaze on her and gave a helpless shrug. She just couldn't seem to stop herself.

Erin tidied away the washed and dried kitchen implements, putting the cheap wooden rolling pin she'd picked up at the grocery story away in a drawer.

"Did you take my rolling pin?"

Charley turned toward Erin, her expression a mask. "Why would I take your rolling pin?"

"I thought maybe you'd found that yours was missing, so you thought you'd borrow mine until you could get one. You asked about using some pans."

"I wouldn't just come in here and take it."

"Okay."

"So, who did?" Vic asked.

Neither of them had an answer for her.

"Somebody who wanted to set me up," Erin said. "They wanted to implicate me."

CHAPTER 13

*E*rin was glad to separate from Charley and go home. She tried to love her sister, but Charley was abrasive, and they had little in common. They probably wouldn't ever have become friends without a family connection. Erin was ready to go home and stop talking about Don Inglethorpe's murder. She'd had enough of it for one day.

"Hello?" Erin called out as she closed the front door behind her. There was no answer. She heard Orange Blossom jump down from her bed, but he was the only one who came to the door to greet her.

Erin picked him up and scratched his ears, listening for any other sound in the house. Marshmallow lollopped silently over. Erin couldn't hear anything else.

"Jeremy?"

There was no answering call or noise. Erin walked through the house, putting Orange Blossom down in the kitchen, and went out through the back door. Vic was just opening her door in the apartment over the garage.

Erin didn't want to say anything about Jeremy to Vic where a neighbor might overhear them.

"Vicky?"

Vic turned around to see Erin standing there. Erin pointed back at her house, then gave a dramatic shrug. Vic frowned. She opened her door and poked her head inside. She went into the apartment, leaving the door open, then came out again a minute later and shook her head. Erin waited while Vic descended the stairs and walked across the yard, apparently also wary of shouting anything that might be overheard.

"Did he tell you he was leaving?" Erin asked quietly.

"No. Not a word. I'll check my email and see if he left a message, but I did check it at noon."

"Come in for a minute. Or do you want to shower and change first?"

They both walked into the house and shut the door. Erin leaned against one of the kitchen counters. "Did you find out why he was here?"

"No. And I didn't push it. I figured he'd tell me sooner or later on his own. He just said he wants to get out on his own."

"Have you talked to any of the others? Did he have a fight with your parents? Get kicked out?"

"I haven't talked to them. Jeremy's the only one who's wanted anything to do with me."

Erin thought from her visit to the Jackson farm that the other boys just didn't know how to take the changes in Vic. They hadn't seemed antagonistic toward her, just awkward and uncertain. Only her father had been threatening.

"Is there one of them that you could ask? What if something happened to him? If we don't say anything, it might put him in more danger than reporting it."

"We don't have anything to report right now. He was out of the house when we expected him to be home. He's not missing."

"You don't think you should talk to any of them?"

"No," Vic shook her head with certainty. "He said we needed to keep it quiet that he was here. He's not just striking out on his own. He's hiding. And maybe there's a reason he's hiding from the others."

"If he doesn't show up again…"

"He will. Or he'll let us know where he is. We're not going to report him missing."

Erin breathed out in a puff, frustrated. But she knew what it was like to want to disappear. She'd pulled up stakes and left all of her troubles behind more than once. Or she had tried to leave all of her troubles behind. It had never actually worked out that way.

If Jeremy was in trouble, she had to assume he knew the best course of action to take for himself.

~

They were still talking when they were interrupted by a knock on the back door. Vic startled, then smiled. "There he is."

But it wasn't Jeremy who opened the door and poked his head in, it was Willie Andrews.

"Oh!" Vic jumped up. "Is it that late already?"

"I was expecting to pick you up from the loft. You aren't ready?"

Willie had cleaned up as much as he could, his skin always stained dark from his mining and refining activities. He was a rough-looking character, but always pleasant and happy to help.

"I just need a quick shower and change. Sorry, we got talking and I lost track."

Willie shook his head. "You've got all day to talk with each other. I don't know how you could have anything else to talk about at the end of the day!"

"My fault, Willie," Erin apologized. "I don't want to talk about all of this stuff about Don Inglethorpe in front of the customers."

Willie accepted this. "That makes sense. Murder isn't good for business."

Vic gave Erin an amused look, but neither of them argued the point as they had with Charley. Erin gathered Vic hadn't told her boyfriend that Jeremy was in town. Willie would have kept Jeremy's secret, but if he didn't know, there wasn't any way it could slip out accidentally.

"Have a good day tomorrow. I'll see you for sure on Monday," Vic advised.

They would likely see each other several times before then, but Erin was working with Bella on Saturday, and Vic was working with Bella Sunday morning, so they wouldn't both be at the bakery at the same time.

"See you then. Have a good weekend."

Vic quickly was out the door and hurrying to her apartment to get ready. Willie didn't follow her immediately.

"You okay, Erin?"

"Yeah. I'm fine, thanks, Willie. It's almost becoming routine stumbling across dead bodies."

He wasn't fooled by her bravado. "I hear you fainted."

"Don't listen to Terry. He lies."

Willie chuckled. "I am sorry you had to deal with that. Sounds like it was a pretty messy scene."

Erin tried to remain stoic. There was no need for her to visualize the scene of the crime, to think about what she had seen and the smell of the congealing blood. She put her hand over her mouth.

"Yeah, it was."

"You need anything? Is Terry coming over tonight?"

"I wouldn't be surprised if he stopped by, but no specific plans. I might just hit the sack early."

"Okay, well, take care. You know you can call on me if you need anything."

Erin nodded. "Thanks."

He backed up out of the doorway. "Lock the door and arm your burglar alarm."

"I'll arm it before I go to bed."

"There's a killer out there who is trying to send trouble your way. I think you should arm it now."

Erin gave a shudder. She hadn't thought about it that way.

"Okay. I will."

CHAPTER 14

*E*rin did arm the alarm and she did go to bed early, without Officer Terry Piper having come by for a visit. She knew he was on call and he had probably ended up having to deal with a nuisance report of some kind. She didn't hold it against him. That's just the way things worked when dating a small-town police officer.

The sound of the burglar alarm blaring woke her out of a sound sleep. Erin jumped out of bed, grabbed her phone, and crept toward her bedroom door, listening for the sounds of an intruder, trying to decide whether to go out to see what had set the burglar alarm off or to hide in her room and call Terry.

Was some crazed killer coming after her, disappointed that she hadn't been arrested at the scene of Don Inglethorpe's murder? Someone who wanted her out of the way and wasn't going to wait to see where the investigation led?

There was swearing and a male voice calling her name. "Erin? Are you home? I'm sorry..."

Erin hurried down the hall toward the alarm control panel without identifying who it was. She hit the disarm code on the panel and the alarm was silenced abruptly. Erin turned around to see Jeremy, his face bright red. She hadn't bothered to talk to him about the burglar alarm, not anticipating that he was going to take off—and then return at night without contacting her first.

She shook her head at him and went to the front door. She looked back and forth at her neighbors' houses. Mrs. Peach was looking out her doorway, phone in hand. Erin waved at her.

"Sorry! False alarm! Everything is okay."

The older woman nodded and retreated into her house, muttering to herself. Erin looked around for any other concerned citizens and didn't see any. She repeated the procedure, going to the back door and checking to make sure the siren hadn't awakened Vic. There was no sign of life in the apartment, all lights out and no movement that Erin could see. Vic and Willie appeared to be out. Erin wasn't sure what time it was or how long she had been asleep. She shut and locked the door, then turned to face Jeremy.

"The polite thing would be to let me know that you were going to be out, and when you planned on coming back. Or maybe given me or Vic a text that you were here, and would we open the door for you."

"Yes," Jeremy nodded vigorously, "I'm sorry. I should have done that. I should have let you know ahead of time. I just... I didn't want to disturb you. That was the wrong thing to do."

Orange Blossom wound around Erin's legs, staying quiet for once, but wanting to be close to her with all of the unusual activity.

"How do you even have a key?"

"Uh..." Jeremy hesitated, then opened his hand to reveal a key. It was narrow and looked as if all of the teeth had been filed down. "It's called a bump key. It's..."

"For burglarizing houses! Now I don't feel bad at all that the alarm went off! What are you doing with a bump key?"

"It's just..." he shook his head. "Sometimes you need to help a friend who has locked himself out..."

"I might be naive, Jeremy, but I'm not that naive."

His Adam's apple bobbed. "Uh..."

Orange Blossom sat back to wash.

"What are you doing sneaking in here in the dead of night?" Erin was still holding her phone, and she looked down at the screen for the time. "Well, maybe not the dead of night, but still. You don't just burglarize people's houses after they offer you their hospitality."

"I wasn't stealing anything, I was just letting myself in to go to bed. I didn't want to disturb you because I knew you'd already be in bed. I'm really sorry, Erin. Please, I won't ever use it again. I'll call you if I get locked out."

"I should turn you over to Terry."

"Yes." His voice was small, and he stared down at his shoes, looking like a little boy facing his principal. "You should. I should never have used this. If you call him, I won't run away. I'll face the music. Whatever you think is right."

Erin knew she wasn't going to turn Jeremy in to Terry, but she was not happy with him thinking that he could just break into her house instead of calling or ringing the doorbell. She studied his shamefaced attitude for signs that he was just dramatizing for her sake, and decided he was sincerely embarrassed and penitent.

"You won't ever use it again?"

"No. I'll call you or Vic, I won't use the bump key."

Erin nodded. "Fine, then. Where have you been?"

Jeremy raised his eyes from his shoes to look at her. He weighed his words, and she saw the mask come over his face. "If I'm going to be on my own, I'm going to have to find a job. A place of my own. Stuff like that. I'm not going to get anywhere just hiding out here all day."

So he wasn't going to tell her why he was really there or what he had been doing. Erin kept her eyes on him for a few extra moments, letting him know that the explanation didn't fly with her. She was not that naive. Jeremy lowered his eyes again.

"Find anything?" Erin asked.

"Uh… no, not yet."

"Did you try the General Store?"

"Well, no. That's kind of out in the open."

"The grocery store?"

"No."

"Where, exactly?"

"Just did some asking around," Jeremy said, with a hint of irritation in his voice.

"What is it you do? What kind of work are you looking for? I could help."

"I doubt you'll hear of anything as a baker. I'm not exactly looking for the same kind of job as Vic."

"What kind of job?" Erin persisted.

"I don't know. Bouncer at a bar. Courier. Something... not too high profile, but I don't have a lot of skills. Born and raised to work on the farm."

"There are farms around here. Maybe one of them would be willing to take you on as a farm worker."

"I don't want to work on a farm. If I wanted to work on a farm, I would have just stayed home."

Erin pushed a lock of hair away from her eyes. "Why didn't you?"

"You don't know what it's like to live there."

"No," Erin agreed. "I don't." She hadn't liked what she had seen of Vic's father, an angry, abusive redneck. And they were all part of the Jackson clan, which turned out to be a sort of Tennessee crime syndicate. She wouldn't have wanted to stay there. She would have wanted to get out as fast as she could. "What exactly are you running away from?"

"I'm not running away."

Erin waited.

"Vic is the one who ran away. I just... wanted to try something else."

"Vic didn't run away. Vic got kicked out. Did you?"

"No!" Jeremy flushed, as if Erin had suggested that he might also be transgender. "I'm not... I didn't..." He forced himself to stop protesting, and used a calm, firm voice. "Look. If you don't want me here, just say so. I will find something else. I mean, I'm going to anyway. If you want me out of here..."

"You can stay for now," Erin said, "as long as it's not going to get me in trouble to have you here. But I think I deserve to hear the real story at some point."

He shuffled his feet uncomfortably and didn't offer an explanation. Erin nodded to his bedroom door.

"It's bed time. Please keep me updated on your schedule."

He nodded obediently. "Yes, ma'am."

Erin scooped up Orange Blossom, and they each went to their rooms without another word.

CHAPTER 15

The bakery opened a little later on Saturdays. Bella drove in at the same time as Erin and they went in together. Bella had worked there long enough to know the routine, so she and Erin got started without the need for detailed instructions.

"I heard about Mr. Inglethorpe," Bella commented, looking sideways at Erin to see what her response would be.

"You and everybody else in a two-hundred-mile radius. Yes, I was the one who discovered his body. And yes, it was... horrible."

"It must have been," Bella agreed. "I can't imagine." She tucked her long blond curls into a net and put on her hat. "And is it true that it was done with... your rolling pin?"

"Yes. It's true. I mean, there hasn't been an autopsy completed yet, so we can only assume that was the cause of death. Either way... he was hit more than once with my good rolling pin."

"Ouch. Now you're going to have to get a new one."

"Yes," Erin agreed, smiling slightly that Bella's concern was for the rolling pin rather than the man. "I've got a wooden one for now, but I'm going to need a proper replacement. It's just not the same."

The light wooden rolling pin meant she needed a lot more muscle power to roll dough out, and it didn't stay chilled when rolling pastries like the marble did. A wooden rolling pin was fine for quick cookies.

"Who do you think killed him?"

"I don't know. I don't know who might have had motive. Do you?"

Bella pursed her lips as she considered the question. She had lived in Bald Eagle Falls all her life and might have a few more insights than Erin.

"He's not someone I knew really well. He wasn't mom's lawyer and didn't have any kids in school. Didn't go to church. Those are the people that we tend to know. I knew who he was, but I didn't really know him personally."

"You didn't hear anything about him? I gather he wasn't married?"

"No. But I never heard any gossip about why not. He just wasn't..." She shrugged. "I mean, he was kind of geeky, right? Not someone women chased after. So, if he didn't have his eye on anyone..." She shrugged. "Lots of perfectly good guys stay single."

"Was he involved in anything? 4H? Block Watch?"

"Not that I know of. He was a lawyer. They're always busy."

Erin nodded.

"I saw him with some out-of-towners last week," Bella commented. "He must take on files from outside of Bald Eagle Falls too."

"Really? Who did you see him with?"

"I didn't know them. Like I said, they had to be from out of town. A man and a woman. They didn't act like they were too happy. Maybe they got sued."

Erin nodded slowly as she flattened cookie balls onto trays. "It might be a good idea for the police to look into who he was seeing last week."

"I'm sure they're already doing that," Bella said. "They've got all of his electronics and his planner and everything. They'll be talking to everyone, won't they?"

"Yes. Of course. But they might not know that he had this fight with these out-of-towners."

"Well, it wasn't exactly a fight. Just... a heated discussion."

"It just doesn't make sense to me. I mean, Charley's right; she didn't have any motive to kill him. Unless someone can show that he had changed his mind about allowing the bakery to open. The one person who was negatively affected by the opening is me."

"But you didn't do it. So someone else must have a motive too. Maybe he screwed up on some file. Made someone lose a bunch of money."

"Yeah. That's a possibility." Erin sighed. Again, something for the police to investigate. Not something that she could find out on her own. "How does it work? Do most people get a lawyer in Bald Eagle Falls? Or go to the city?"

"Probably depends how big a thing it is," Bella said. "If it's just like a will or selling your house, why go to someone in the city for that? But if it was something big, you might want to go to a lawyer in the city to be sure. Or if it was something really specialized."

Erin nodded. Clementine had used a local lawyer. Angela Plaint had.

"What if a lawyer had two clients whose interests conflicted?" Erin mused. "That could happen a lot in a little town like this."

"I don't know. I guess they'd tell you."

"They'd have to, wouldn't they? They'd be in big trouble if they played clients off against each other or told confidential things about one to another."

Bella nodded vigorously. "That would be really bad."

"I wish I knew more. It's making me really anxious to think that there's someone out there trying to set me up. Somebody violent."

One of the first customers into the store was Melissa. Erin was surprised to see Melissa and Mary Lou together. Not because they weren't good friends, but because Melissa had been hanging out more with Charley lately, and Mary Lou had been more solitary since Roger's arrest. Erin couldn't understand why people were shunning Mary Lou. It wasn't her fault that Roger had gone off the rails. She'd been the best wife and mother she could be, but she could only spread herself so thin, and she couldn't monitor her ill husband twenty-four hours a day while trying to work to support the family and to take the boys to their various activities. She had done the best she could to get Roger the help that he needed before things had gotten so bad, but all of the professionals had said that he was fine. Erin was glad to see Mary Lou and Melissa together again.

"Morning ladies," Erin greeted. "Good to see you."

"I wanted to see how you were doing," Melissa said in a long, sympathetic drawl. "It must have been so awful for you, finding Don Inglethorpe like that. Just shocking!"

Erin nodded. Melissa did some admin work at the police department, and sometimes revealed a little more than she ought to.

"It was pretty horrible," Erin agreed. "I hope they're making good progress in figuring out who did it."

"Don't like being the prime suspect in another murder?" Melissa teased.

Mary Lou gave her a reproachful look. "Melissa! Really."

Melissa covered her mouth as if she were embarrassed, but Erin suspected she was enjoying the reaction. She loved to dramatize and be right at the heart of the action. That was, Erin was sure, the reason she liked to work for the police department. It gave her immediate access to anything exciting going on in town.

"I didn't mean to upset you," she told Erin. "I just meant, it's an awful predicament you're in, and if it was me, I'd want to solve the case and prove my innocence as soon as I could too."

"What did you want today?" Erin asked, turning her attention to the display case. She wasn't going to give Melissa's attention-getting behavior any mind until the woman started giving up some information. "Cookies for the church exchange?"

"Oh, I almost forgot all about that!" Mary Lou said, her eyes getting big. She would normally have made her own batch of cookies, but it had apparently fallen off her radar. It was less than twenty-four hours before the exchange, so time was quickly running out. "Oh, dear... yes, I think I'm going to have to go with bought cookies this year. I really don't see any way around it." She looked at Erin. "I *always* make my own. I have every year. But this year..."

"You've had a hard time," Erin said. "Give yourself a break. These were made fresh today. It isn't like they're packaged cookies from the grocery store."

"Store-bought are perfectly acceptable," Melissa agreed, though she had a bit of a smirk that told them both that she had already made or had plans to make her own.

"What would you like?" Erin asked Mary Lou. She helped her to pick out what she would like to take to the exchange.

When she looked up, Melissa was practically bursting, she wanted so badly to spill whatever news she had about the murder.

"And what would you like today, Melissa? Are you looking for something for breakfast? Dinner? You said you already have your cookies for the exchange tomorrow."

"Oh," Melissa looked impatiently over the baked goods on display in the case. "Maybe some of those cheesy pizza crusts for supper. They look awfully good. And a muffin for breakfast. Double chocolate."

Erin wasn't sure how Melissa could eat things like double chocolate muffins for breakfast and extra cheesy pizza for dinner and still maintain her figure.

"They've requested all of Don Inglethorpe's files for the investigation," Melissa confided, leaning closer but not actually lowering her voice.

"Have they? Do they think it was one of his clients, then? Something to do with one of his cases?"

"They've asked for everything, not just Trenton Plaint's trust. I don't think they know what it was about."

"At least they believe it wasn't you," Mary Lou said.

Erin nodded. "I hope Terry knows me at least that well by now. I hate it when he gets all suspicious."

"Well, I don't think you need to worry about that now," Mary Lou said in her most soothing voice. She gave Erin a smile that was just a little bit sad. Erin had her man looking out for her, but Mary Lou had lost hers. She'd lost him by degrees over the past few years, ever since he had lost an investment with Angela Plaint and tried to take his own life.

"Thanks." Erin gave a nod, but what she really wanted was to take Mary Lou by the hand and give her a squeeze and to tell her that everything was going to work out okay. And not just because that was what Mary Lou wanted to hear. She really did want things to get better for Mary Lou, but she had no idea how it would come out in the end.

"So, they haven't got the files yet?" Bella asked. "They've just asked for them?"

Melissa nodded. "Things take time. It's not all instantaneous like on TV, with warrants being granted at all hours of the night and police breaking down doors and grabbing files like it's a home invasion. They ask, and it takes time for the law office to respond, and they want to photocopy every-thing before it's out their doors, then the police have to actually go through every box and every piece of paper and decide whether it's anything that's helpful to their investigation or not. That's slow, tedious work, let me tell you." Melissa gave a little sigh, as if she had done it many a time and knew how very taxing it could be. In reality, she'd probably just transcribed a report of the police department's search of a file, not something that was very difficult at all.

"I hope they figure it out quickly," Erin said, "I don't like the idea of the killer wandering around Bald Eagle Falls free."

"It doesn't mean anyone else is in danger," Mary Lou put in. "There's no hint that anyone else was an intended target. Whatever Mr. Inglethorpe got himself into, there's no reason to think that any of the rest of us need to be concerned for our safety."

"Except for me," Erin said. "I was intentionally framed as his killer, so they must have something against me too."

"Must be someone who wants to open a third bakery," Melissa laughed. "Kill two birds—or businesses—with one stone."

Erin thought about that, but there didn't seem to be any merit to it. What was the benefit to anyone of closing down the two existing bakeries? Maybe it was someone who wanted to open a bakery for their own, but they must have kept their dream to themselves up until that point, because Erin hadn't heard any rumor of anyone else who wanted to open a bakery. Not unless Bella or Vic wanted to break out on their own. Erin looked over at Bella.

"You're not planning on starting up your own place any time soon, are you?"

Bella laughed, showing her even white teeth. "No, it's going to be a while before I've got the capital to open up my own business. And when I do, I don't know that it's going to be a bakery. And I need to get my degree first."

Erin shrugged at Melissa. "Nope, doesn't look like it. Unless you have a suspect."

"No, not me. I'll leave that job to the guys."

CHAPTER 16

*E*rin headed over to The Book Nook to pick up her trays from Naomi. It was hot, as always, but she took a deep breath of the warm, muggy air and sighed. It smelled like home. She might not like the heat, but on a clear summer day, she could almost see herself as a child, walking to the river with her father to paddle in the water and pick up rocks. It had been a long time ago, but it was a happy memory of her early childhood, and she didn't have many of those.

So Erin just stood there and breathed and pictured it and felt the warm, happy feelings she'd had then. As she stood there, she saw a couple of people down the street who must have just had a fender bender. Both had stopped in the middle of the road and were getting out to inspect the damage and to talk to each other. Erin didn't recognize the cars or either driver.

The woman was blond, maybe around Erin's age, late twenties or early thirties. She wore a camouflage hat with her hair in a ponytail out the back, an army green t-shirt, and camouflage cargo pants with lots of pockets that made her look broader than she was.

The heavyset man wore a black t-shirt and blue jeans, a black cap turned around backward, and sunglasses which he had pushed up onto his head in order to glare at the woman who had rear-ended him. Erin couldn't hear their words, but their body language said it all. They were both confrontational, both of them sure that they were in the right and ready to defend their opinions to the end. Neither one was ready to back down. Physical violence seemed a very real possibility.

Erin inched closer, wanting to hear what was being said. Normally, little dings in Bald Eagle Falls didn't require any kind of police intervention. People apologized, traded insurance information, and went on with their lives. There were occasional bumps along the way, but no one was ever so confrontational.

As Erin got closer, she could see movement from the nearby shops as well. People pushing back curtains and opening windows to hear what was being said. People coming out of the stores and standing around trying to look natural, as if they were waiting for the bus or making a phone call. But all eyes and ears were on the man and woman.

Erin wasn't sure how close she could get to them. She didn't want them to think that she was somehow involved in the accident and bring her into the argument. Then she heard barking, and saw Terry approaching them from the other direction, K9 straining against the collar Terry was holding on to.

"Let's take a step back and cool things off," Terry suggested. "Everybody just take a deep breath. Looks like we just had a little accident?" He inspected the bumper of the man's car. "It doesn't look like there's very much damage."

"You should arrest her for reckless driving," the man growled. "There are what, two stop lights in this town, and she rear-ends me? She's a menace."

The woman was chewing a wad of gum. At least, Erin hoped that it was gum and not tobacco. She couldn't understand anyone chewing tobacco, but especially a woman. The blond woman was calm, her face was like a mask. She observed everything around her, completely detached emotionally. The man could rant and scream and threaten all he liked, and the woman would just keep chewing her gum and looking at him.

"Ma'am, you're the driver of the station wagon?" Terry asked.

"Yep."

"You were following too close."

She shrugged. "Apparently."

"Have the two of you exchanged insurance information?"

"She rammed me!" the man ranted. "She did it intentionally!"

"Do the two of you know each other?"

"No." He muttered something under his breath that Erin didn't hear, but suspected was along the lines of "thank goodness."

"And you think that someone you don't know would intentionally ram your car?"

"Yes! Obviously, because she did."

"I see. And why would she do that? Was there something that happened earlier? Something that escalated?"

"No, she just came out of nowhere and rammed my car."

"Okay. If you would come over here, sir, I'm going to ask you to fill out an accident reporting form."

He skillfully separated the two potential fighters, herding the man to the sidewalk where he could start filling out paperwork. The woman stayed where she was, watching them, chewing her gum like a cow chewing its cud.

Once Terry got the man going on his paperwork, he returned to the woman. "I'll need you to fill out your report as well. Anything to say? *Did you ram him intentionally?*"

"Why would I do that?"

Terry shrugged. "People's stories can be pretty outlandish when they're upset. You also need to fill out a form. Do you have your insurance papers?"

She walked over to her car with Terry and in a couple of minutes, had handed him whatever she had in the car. He copied down the information he needed and handed the papers back. He approached the man's car.

"Insurance papers in the glove box?" he asked.

"Stay away from my car!" The man came immediately to life. "I haven't given you permission to search!"

Terry stopped. He raised his brows. "I wasn't going to search it, I was just asking you about your insurance papers. Would you like to get them out for me?"

"Just get back."

Terry took a couple of steps back from the car. The man relaxed. He sat down in the driver's seat of his car and reached for the glove box, then looked over his shoulder at Terry, hesitating.

"Maybe I overreacted about all this."

"Maybe you did."

"If there isn't really any damage, maybe we could just each go our separate directions and forget about it."

"No, at this point the police department is involved, and I would like to see the proper paperwork filed. So, if you would get your insurance papers, please."

"I just realized I left them at home."

Terry continued to gaze at the glove box. "Why don't you just check? Maybe you have an old document in there that has the policy number on it. Then we can call the agent to confirm it is still valid."

"No, no. There's nothing in there. I just got this car. All of my insurance papers are at home."

"You need to provide proof of insurance."

"I'll call my agent, okay? He'll confirm it to you. Fax or scan you a copy. Then we can get on our way. If you really think you need to go through with this. I think we can just chalk it up as lesson learned and be on our way."

"Do you have proof of valid registration?"

"I have my plate and stickers."

"But no registration papers?"

"Uh, no. Not here."

"You sure you don't want to check the glove box?"

"No. They're not in there. Give me a ticket, if the plates aren't enough."

Erin leaned against a power pole, getting tired of standing in one place. But she didn't want to make any movement to draw attention to herself. She kept waiting for Terry to insist on searching the car or at least seeing what was in the glove box, but it became apparent that he didn't have enough cause to insist on it.

"If you'll finish your statement and track down a copy of your insurance for me then, please. I'll take a look at your driver's license while you're doing that."

The man sighed and pulled his wallet out of the back pocket of his pants. He slid out his driver's license and handed it to Terry, then went back to writing out his witness statement.

The woman was writing her statement and had given no sign that she was listening to the rest of the conversation going on between Terry and the male driver. But when neither of them was talking, she looked up, scanning the area. She met Erin's eyes, then looked away again, deciding Erin wasn't anyone important. She continued to chew.

Eventually, both of the strangers had filled out their paperwork to

Terry's satisfaction, and far from wanting to have a fight with each other, they were both eager to just get back into their cars and, presumably, out of Bald Eagle Falls.

Terry watched them both drive away, and then resumed his patrol with K9. K9 had seen Erin and drifted away slightly to go to her. Terry said a sharp word to bring him back to heel, then spotted Erin.

"I didn't see you there. What's up?"

"Oh… I was just going to The Book Nook to get some serving platters when…" Erin circled her finger to encompass the street and the cars that had previously been there. "All of this happened, and I just kind of hung around to see what was going to happen."

"Happy to provide entertainment."

Erin felt her face flush, but tried to remain nonchalant. "It was all very exciting. What exactly do you think he was hiding in his glove box?"

"Either a weapon or drugs. Or both. But he was determined not to give me any opportunity to find them."

"Did he have any warrants?"

"If he had, I would have arrested him and searched the vehicle. But he didn't have anything outstanding."

"Does he have a record?"

"Yes, he does."

Erin raised her brows questioningly, not asking the next question.

"I'm afraid I can't really share any of that with you." Which Erin already knew. "But suffice to say… I'm quite sure he had something in his glove box and wasn't just embarrassed that he'd forgotten his papers or that his cubby was messy."

From Terry's previous comment, she assumed he had previous arrests for drugs and guns. Not the kind of person they wanted hanging around Bald Eagle Falls.

"Why do you think he was here?"

"Hopefully, just passing through. I don't want to see his type hanging around here. We try to keep them moving right through."

"There aren't any major problems with drugs in Bald Eagle Falls, are there?"

"No. Not really. It's mostly confined to the city, and any of our people who go to the city to party or bring back enough for personal use. Not a lot of dealing going on, other than maybe some pot and prescription meds to school kids. Not the huge problems with meth and crack and some of these other nasty drugs that you get in the city."

"And we want to keep it that way," Erin summarized.

"Exactly. Walk you to The Book Nook?"

It wasn't far. Just half a block. But Erin didn't get to spend much time with Terry during the day, so why not? They walked side by side down the street, back toward The Book Nook and Auntie Clem's Bakery.

"You need any water?" Erin asked.

"Not yet. Might stop by for some later." They reached the front of The Book Nook. "You take it easy, right Erin? I don't want you getting involved in anything…"

Erin wondered what he was thinking of in particular. The murder? Covering for Jeremy? The two strangers having a collision in the middle of Main Street? She wasn't involved in anything. He was welcome to do the investigating, she didn't want anything to do with it.

CHAPTER 17

*E*rin thought all afternoon about the strangers suddenly showing up in Bald Eagle Falls. They didn't get a lot of tourist traffic through the town. A few people who wanted to stop at the General Store to pick up some homey novelty item, someone who wanted to explore caves or do some camping, but mostly Bald Eagle Falls didn't attract outsiders. Even though Erin had been there for a year, she was still considered a newbie. In some neighborhoods, she would be considered part of the old guard after a year. But in Bald Eagle Falls, anyone who hadn't been born there was considered an outsider. And even some of those who had been, if they moved away for a significant length of time.

Bella had seen two strangers arguing with Don Inglethorpe. Erin had seen two people arguing in the middle of the street, almost coming to blows over damage that was so minor Erin hadn't even been able to see it.

It couldn't be a coincidence. And if one of those arguing strangers was a drug dealer, then how had he been connected to Don Inglethorpe? Was Inglethorpe a drug user? Was he a dealer? Someone who was just curious? And what about the woman?

~

Jeremy was there when Erin got home. In spite of her talk with him, she wasn't sure if he would be, or if he would again take off without letting her know where he was. He hadn't taken it upon himself to make supper, and Vic was likely out with Willie, so that left it up to Erin. Ordinarily, she would probably visit one of the local eateries on a Saturday night when she was by herself. Or she and Terry would go out somewhere. But with Jeremy there, she didn't feel comfortable just abandoning him to go eat on her own.

"You want to help with supper?" she suggested to Jeremy. "I'm not planning on doing anything big, but I wouldn't mind a hand."

"Sure, of course," Jeremy agreed. He went ahead of her into the kitchen and checked the supply of frozen dinners in the freezer. "I should have thought of it before. I could have had something waiting for you."

"No, you're my guest, you don't need to do that. I just thought that since you're here…"

He was competent enough in the kitchen, even if he was slow and seemed to always be consulting his mental record for how to do things. Like he'd been trained, but didn't have much experience. Erin suspected that his mother had given him instruction to make sure that he could get around the kitchen in a pinch, but that he hadn't had a lot of opportunity for building up his skills. He would have spent more time on the farm equipment than in the kitchen.

Erin was still thinking through the day's events and puzzling through what it might all mean.

"What reason would a drug dealer—or any criminal—have to be seeing a lawyer?" she asked Jeremy. "Not a lawyer representing him in court, but like a corporate lawyer."

Jeremy looked at her, frowning. "Why?"

"Just something I'm thinking of. Say a drug dealer. He's in town to see a lawyer. Why?"

"Just like anyone else, I guess," Jeremy said, still looking puzzled and slightly disapproving of the subject. "Maybe he needs a will or needs a company created."

"Would a drug dealer need a corporation? Like an LLC?"

Jeremy was chopping vegetables for a salad. He diced them small, frowning. "Not a small-time street dealer, no. But a bigger operation… they're sometimes built up to look like legitimate businesses."

"The lawyer could be helping him launder money. Taking it from his illegal business and running it through a company that does something else."

"Right."

"Like a bakery?"

"What are you getting at, Erin? Is this hypothetical?"

"Yes, of course. I wouldn't know anything about any actual criminal enterprise."

He looked at her, eyes narrow. "Where is this all coming from? You think there's something going on in Bald Eagle Falls?"

"Oh, there is definitely something going on in Bald Eagle Falls," Erin said with a laugh. "I just don't know what it is."

"What?"

Erin explained to him about the drug dealer and the collision in the middle of town.

"What makes you think this had anything to do with the lawyer who died?"

"I don't know that it did, I'm just thinking about possibilities. We don't get a lot of tourists through Bald Eagle Falls. What are the odds that a couple of strangers would be having an argument with Inglethorpe before he died and then a couple other strangers would be having an argument in the middle of town today?"

"It's possible. It could all be unrelated."

"You're right. I could be putting together two things that had nothing to do with each other. I just find it difficult to believe that they don't have something to do with each other. And if this drug dealer did have some argument with Don Inglethorpe, then maybe he had something to do with his death too."

"But why would this guy stay around? If you killed someone and you didn't have a legitimate reason to be in town, you wouldn't stay on the scene."

"Maybe..." Erin tried to puzzle it through. "Maybe Inglethorpe wouldn't agree to do what he wanted, so he had to get someone else to do it instead? Maybe he's here to see another lawyer."

"He's here now?" Jeremy looked toward the door.

"Well, not now. He looked like he left town after Terry talked to him. But that doesn't mean he's really gone. Or if he is, there's nothing to say that he can't come back or send someone else."

Jeremy nodded slowly. At a tug on his pant leg, he looked down and saw Marshmallow sitting up on his haunches expectantly. Erin laughed.

"You can give him a few veggies."

The tension in Jeremy's manner melted away, and he talked to Marshmallow and gave him the ends of the vegetables he'd been cutting up. Orange Blossom *mrrowed* and hurried over to see if he was going to get a treat as well, but when he discovered that all Jeremy had were vegetables, he hunched back and swished his tail crossly.

"Come here, Blossom," Erin called to him. He looked at her and didn't move out of his sulky pose.

"If you want a treat, you should listen," Erin told him. "If you're just going to pout, you're not going to get anything."

He looked at her for a moment, then got up and approached her. "That's a good boy. You don't think I'm going to forget to feed you, do you?" She opened the fridge and got out some leftover chicken. Orange Blossom immediately perked up, rubbing against her legs and purring loudly, letting out the occasional excited yip.

CHAPTER 18

*E*rin was happy when she heard the familiar knock at her door, but was also nervous about the fact that Jeremy was still there, shut away in Clementine's room. She had advised him that if he wanted to stay under the radar, he'd better stay quiet and behind closed doors while Terry was there. It would be pretty hard to keep his presence a secret if he decided to shower or use the commode in the middle of Terry's visit. Trained to be observant, the police officer might just notice.

"Hi, Terry." Erin accepted a kiss from Terry and gave his partner an ear scratch. "Hi, fur face."

K9 panted and sat back with a happy doggie grin.

"Long day today?" Erin asked Terry.

"Things do seem to heat up when there's a murder in town," he admitted. "Even stuff that's totally unrelated to the murder. It seems like everyone just gets a little crazy."

They sat down together, cuddling up with each other and then waiting while the animals made themselves comfortable.

"I know I saw you today," Terry said, "but I feel like it was ages ago. And I didn't find out how you are doing. I mean, if you're okay after finding the body."

Erin nodded. "I guess. I'm trying not to think about it, mostly. I didn't really know Mr. Inglethorpe and if I keep thinking about it, I'll make myself sick. So I'm just trying pretend nothing happened."

"Good." He stroked her hair. "I don't want you to be traumatized by it."

Erin tried to lighten the mood. "It isn't like it's the first body I've come across."

"No, but the violence of this one… the others were not so gory."

"But still violent. And when I think of poor Bertie…" Tears stung Erin's eyes all of a sudden. "Oh, I'm sorry. I thought I was over that…"

Terry hugged her to him. "Don't be surprised that this stirs up old feelings. That's normal. And out of everyone who has died, Bertie was the only one who was really your friend."

"Well…" Erin sniffled and reached for a tissue from the side table. "There was my father, too."

"I didn't mean *he's* not important. But it was such a long time since you had seen him, and the memories are pretty dim. With Bertie, though… that was very tragic, and right in front of you."

Erin dabbed at her eyes, trying not to cry in earnest. If he'd just stop talking about it, she'd have a much easier time staying calm.

"Have you talked to a therapist?" Terry asked. "It could be very helpful, after some of the things you've had to deal with lately."

"No. I'm fine. I don't need any therapy."

"It's not a bad thing, you know. It's not a show of weakness. It just means that you know you could use a bit of help to get through something traumatic or troubling."

Erin shook her head adamantly. "I dealt with enough therapists in the system. Now that I'm adult, you can bet that I'm never doing that again."

Terry didn't say anything, just stroking her hair. She had been expecting a fight, but not getting one, wasn't sure how to react.

"It's up to you. I'm not going to force you into anything."

Erin let her breath out. "Good."

"Just remember that everybody needs help sometimes, there's no shame in getting it when you need it. Whether it's counseling or something else. You don't have to do everything on your own."

She knew that she tended to do just that, insisting that she could handle anything that came her way all by herself. But it had been good for her to get Vic to help her at the bakery, and then Bella to help out part time. She had found that she could delegate and get others to do some of the work and not have to do it all herself.

"I know. Thanks."

They were both quiet.

"So how is the case going?" Erin asked tentatively.

"You know I can't talk much about it, especially when you are... a person of interest... but so far, we don't have a lot of leads. There are not a lot of people who had motive to kill Don Inglethorpe. Unfortunately, you are one of the few, with your livelihood possibly being threatened by him changing his vote to allow Charley to open The Bake Shoppe."

"There must have been others. Or something to do with his business. Bella saw him arguing..."

Terry raised an eyebrow. "I thought you were not investigating this one."

"I'm not... I just... people tell me things, because they know I have an interest in the outcome."

"I'll bet they do. Yes, it's possible that it was something to do with his business. An irate client or somebody he did wrong in setting up a deal or settling a lawsuit. People sometimes get riled up over the strangest things."

"Maybe he was laundering money."

Terry's eyes narrowed. Erin hated that look of suspicion and kicked herself whenever she saw it come into his eyes.

"I don't *know* anything," she told him. "It's just speculation."

"Money laundering is always a possibility. But we would need to show a connection with criminal enterprise. Organized crime. So far, we don't have anything pointing in that direction."

"And you don't think he's involved with this drug dealer?"

"What drug dealer?"

"The one today, that got into the fight. I thought that he might be one of the people that Inglethorpe was fighting with the other day. He obviously has a temper."

"It's quite a jump to the idea that he was somehow involved in something with Don Inglethorpe. You don't even know that he was a drug dealer. Because I certainly didn't tell you that."

"Well... not exactly, no."

"I didn't."

"Okay. You didn't say he was a drug dealer. But he sure looked like one."

"Things aren't always as they appear." Terry's gaze was steady. Then the dimple appeared in his cheek. "And sometimes they are," he admitted, eyes twinkling.

Erin laughed. She snuggled against him. "I just want it to be solved. I don't want to have to worry about it, and I don't want you to have to worry about it. I just want things to go back to normal."

"Normal for Bald Eagle Falls hasn't been normal since you arrived here, I'm sorry to say."

"That's just... an anomaly. I didn't have anything to do with any of the... increased crime. I'm just minding my own business."

Terry nodded. "I know you didn't do anything... except maybe ask questions when nobody wanted you poking your nose into their business. And that's not going to happen anymore, is it?"

"Do you hear me asking questions about anything?"

"Well, *I* do."

"But that's you and me, not anyone else. And you're not going to try to kill me for asking you how the case is going, are you?"

Terry nuzzled her hair. "No. You've got me bewitched."

"You'd better not say *that* too loudly. They'll burn me at the stake."

"I'm not on shift in the morning."

"That's good. You can take a Sunday off for once."

"And you're not at the bakery in the morning."

"Nope. Vic and Bella have it covered."

Terry didn't say anything. Erin turned her head to look him in the face. "What?"

"I was just thinking, neither of us has anywhere to be tonight, and neither of us has anywhere we have to be in the morning. That doesn't happen very often."

Erin started to grow warm. She searched his eyes for his intent, and then dropped her gaze. She'd been waiting for some time for him to make the next move and give her some sign he was ready to go beyond spending a few stolen minutes together or exchanging a kiss.

She wanted badly to pursue his suggestion to its natural conclusion, but all she could think about was Jeremy in Clementine's bedroom. If Terry stayed the night, Jeremy would be forced to reveal himself. Erin didn't know what Jeremy was involved in, but she had promised him and Vic to keep his presence there a secret. Especially from Terry.

"Erin?" Terry's voice was uncertain, clearly worried that he had misjudged the situation.

"Uh… yeah. You're right. We should go out for dinner."

"Haven't you already had dinner? You don't usually want to stay up much later than this."

"Well, yes. I did. I just thought you wanted to go out and do something, since we're both off tomorrow. We could… go into the city. Catch a movie."

Terry's eyebrows lifted, bewildered. Erin hated to do it to him. She wanted to be able to tell him about Jeremy being there so that he wouldn't think he had done something wrong or was on a completely different page from Erin.

"Sure, if you wanted to," he agreed slowly.

"I hear that new Marvel is really good." Guys liked action films. He'd be delighted that she wanted to watch one with him.

"Sure. Or something more… romantic, if you like." He tried once more to clue her in.

"You know what?" Erin rubbed the ticklish spot on Terry's knee. "After the movie, we could go back to *your* place."

Terry brightened a little, though he still looked thoroughly baffled. They never did anything at his place, Erin always preferred the space and comfort of Clementine's home, and since they never knew whether Terry would be able to get away to see her, she always let him come to her. She could see him trying to compute why Erin would want to go back to his house, on top of the already-mind-boggling suggestion that she wanted to go all the way into the city to watch an action movie instead of just staying in and going to bed at the usual hour. Erin was a creature of habit. He knew she didn't like unexpected changes to her schedule.

"Just stay here for a minute," she told him. "I just need to grab my purse, and a couple of things…"

If she didn't get up right away, she was just going to have to keep explaining herself, and that wasn't getting any easier. Erin hurried into her room. She pulled out her phone and texted Jeremy to fill him in on the developments. She would have to give him the code to disarm the burglar alarm, because Terry would insist she armed it before they left. If Jeremy didn't want to be stuck in the house until she returned, he'd have to disarm it.

Erin wondered if Orange Blossom would behave himself, or whether he'd start yowling when she left. He had been okay during the day, but he was used to her usual routine. If she left him alone at night with Jeremy, she didn't want to think of what might happen.

She threw a couple of overnight items in a large handbag and returned to Terry within a couple of minutes. Not long enough to be suspicious of anything.

"Uh, I guess I'd better feed the animals their bedtime treats before we go."

Terry stood up and watched her, not offering any objection or demanding an explanation, but she knew he had to be wondering what the heck she was thinking. She could give him a story about feeling funny about having him overnight at Clementine's house, but then she'd have to come up with an explanation for her change of heart when Jeremy was no longer there. It was better to just let Terry come up with his own explanation for her strange behavior.

CHAPTER 19

*E*rin stretched languidly. She knew that it was much later in the day than she would normally get up, but it had been a very late night too, and she knew she didn't have to be at the bakery, so she just let her body curl into Terry's.

There was a buzzing that seemed far away. She thought she should know what it was, but wasn't quite awake enough to connect her thoughts and be sure. Terry groaned and rolled over away from her. Erin made a disappointed sound, and in a few seconds, he rolled back into the warm pocket of blankets.

"What does your sister want?"

Erin squinted, opening her eyes just the barest crack to get more information. The room was too bright with morning sunshine and she didn't want to have to wake up the rest of the way. Terry held a phone out toward Erin.

"Reg?" Erin asked. She took her phone from him and looked down at it. "Oh, Charley. Right."

She hesitated, not really wanting to talk to Charley. She didn't want to let anything else break into their little paradise. The phone stopped buzzing and was still and silent in her hand.

"Oh, well," Terry said, cheek dimpling. "If it's important, she can leave a message, right?"

Erin nodded. Terry hugged her closer to him, his eyes suggesting that he was not quite as interested in going back to sleep as she was. Erin yawned. She knew she shouldn't be so lazy. They had the whole day together, something that almost never happened. Or it hadn't before. She might be insisting that they manage to coordinate their schedules better in the future.

Erin's phone started buzzing in her hand. She looked down at it. Charley again. She really wanted Erin. Maybe something was wrong at the bakery. But then it would be Vic or Bella who would be calling her, not Charley. Maybe the trustees had told Charley that she wouldn't be able to open The Bake Shoppe after all and she needed someone to talk to about it.

"Go ahead," Terry said, leaning back, putting a few inches between the two of them.

"I'm sorry. I'll be right back. Promise." She swiped the phone and put it to her ear. "Hi, Charley. What's up?"

There was a long blast of sound from the phone. Erin pulled it away from her ear and frowned, trying to interpret it. It didn't sound like a pocket dial. It sounded like someone's mouth was too close to the microphone and they were yelling or crying or making some other caterwauling noise.

"Charley? Is that you? What's going on?"

This time, she was pretty sure she could detect a few hitching sobs in the middle of the noise. She looked at Terry, frowning, and then back at the phone.

"Do you need help, Charley? Is someone else there? Do you need the police or a doctor?"

"No…" This time, at least, she was sure there was actually a person on the end trying to talk to her, and pretty sure that it was Charley.

Terry sat up, looking concerned about at least Erin's side of the conversation. Erin wasn't sure if he could hear or understand any of the other noises.

"Are you sick, Charley?"

"No."

"Hurt?"

"No." Charley burst into bubbling, noisy tears again. Erin was really starting to get concerned.

"Where are you? Are you at home?"

Erin thought—or imagined—she could hear a 'yes' in Charley's answer.

"Okay. I'm going to come over there. Is that okay? Is that what you want?"

More noise from the other end of the phone. Erin shook her head at Terry, unable to make any sense of it.

"I'll be right over. Hang in there," she told Charley, and hung up the call.

"What's going on?"

"I don't know. It sounds like she's crying. I think. It's really hard to tell. But I think she said she's at home, so I'm going to go over there and see if I can help her."

"I'll come with you."

"I really don't think she's going to want you there. She's got a real thing about police."

"I don't have to stay if she doesn't want me there. But I think I should at least check and make sure she's safe and hasn't been the victim of violence."

Erin nodded. "Uh... okay. That makes sense. Just don't be insulted if she acts like you're an intruder. She did call me, and I'm telling you, she doesn't like dealing with police after everything that's happened to her."

"Understood," Terry agreed. "No problem."

He got out of bed and started pulling on his uniform. Erin followed suit, grabbing her own clothes and ducking into the bathroom to change.

"You don't have to hide," Terry called to her through the door, chuckling.

Erin's face burned. "I know. It's just... faster this way..." she explained, telling herself that she could take off her nightie, get dressed, use the commode, and brush her teeth all more efficiently if she were already in the bathroom.

"I'll make some coffee. Do you want anything else? I have a few muffins in the freezer."

"Yeah, maybe you'd better thaw some out. I'm not ready to eat yet, but I don't know what kind of a state Charley is in. She might need something, or I might end up being there for a long time."

"See you in a minute, then."

Erin quickly got herself together and was in the kitchen before Terry could finish thawing the muffins. She let K9 out of his kennel, and he ran excited circles around her, his big tail making wide sweeps back and forth.

"Settle down, partner," Terry told him. "We've got work to do."

At the word *work*, K9 stopped playing and was still, waiting for a command from Terry.

"I'm going to leave you to get breakfast together," Terry said. "Throw the coffee in a thermos and find a container for the muffins. Juice or jam if you want them. I'm going to take him outside, then we'll be right back."

"You got it," Erin agreed.

Terry went outside and Erin familiarized herself with the kitchen. In ten minutes, they were both ready to go, and Terry drove over in the squad car.

"She's at her house, not at the bakery?"

"That's what she said. She wouldn't be able to get into the bakery, would she? Isn't it still a crime scene?"

"It's been processed. She can access it if she wants to. Depending on what the trustees of the estate have to say."

"She must really hate having to check with them on everything she does. She's so independent."

Terry nodded. "I suspect you're right."

"But that doesn't mean she would kill one of them just because he wouldn't do what she wanted." Erin didn't want anyone saying she was trying to throw suspicion on Charley.

"Particularly when he was letting her do what she wanted to," Terry agreed.

They pulled up to the house and Erin jumped out of the car first. She hurried up the sidewalk to Charley's door and knocked. Terry was right on her heels.

"Don't you think I should go in first?"

"No. She's just upset. It isn't a crime."

Terry acquiesced. Erin knocked on the door again, harder. "Charley, it's Erin. Open up."

It took a couple more times, then the door finally opened. Erin stepped in and gasped.

CHAPTER 20

Charley's apartment in Moose River had been neat and well-maintained. Charley had been embarrassed at having left a pair of socks and other everyday things out where they didn't belong. But her house looked like someone had turned it upside-down and shaken it. Erin looked around, gaping.

"What happened? Did someone break in?"

"No," Charley blubbered. Her face was red and sweaty, wet with tears and snot. And it was no wonder. It was obvious someone had broken into the house and ransacked the place. Erin would have been in tears too. "No, it's just me," Charley said, voice thick and choked. "I've been busy with the bakery... I haven't had time to take care of anything around here... and I just... can't... deal..."

Erin could smell the alcohol oozing from Charley's pores.

She looked back at Terry, who was trailing them into the house. If the house was in that state just because Charley was busy and hadn't been able to look after herself, then she clearly needed help. Maybe a maid and maybe a psychiatrist.

"Why don't we sit down, and you can tell me what happened?" Erin suggested.

Charley made gulping noises, attempting to stop the tears, but it appeared to be useless.

"Shh. It's going to be okay," Erin soothed. "Just tell me."

"It's all too much," Charley bawled. "Trying to open the bakery, and people stealing things, and Don Inglethorpe getting himself killed on my property, and Bobby! I miss Bobby!"

Erin was doubly shocked. Charley had barely mentioned her late boyfriend in the months since she had been falsely accused of his murder. Erin had decided that Charley hadn't really had any feelings toward him at all, but had just been attracted to someone who was powerful in the organized crime syndicate she had been working for. He might have been handsome, but she hadn't actually loved him.

"Bobby? What does any of this have to do with Bobby?"

Charley scrubbed at her eyes. "Nothing!"

"Nothing, but…?"

"I just miss him. Nothing has been the same since he died. I thought that if I came here and opened the bakery, everything would be fine. I'm not with the clan anymore, but I could start something new and it would turn out okay."

"But things haven't worked out the way you were hoping," Erin surmised.

"Why did that idiot have to get killed in my bakery? Do you know what a pain it is having someone killed in your place of business?"

Erin looked at Terry and couldn't help smiling. "Well, actually, yes. It sucks."

"Who's going to come to a bakery where someone was killed? Two people, if you want to count Trenton Plaint, but that happened before I ever came to town, so that's not my fault!"

"None of it is your fault." Erin cleared a place on the sofa for Charley to sit down and guided her into it. She sat beside Charley, giving her a sisterly hug around the shoulders. "None of this is your fault. It's just the way things go sometimes."

"I'm never going to be able to open the bakery now. So where does that leave me? I've got nothing! I was hanging on to this, thinking that if I could make it work, I could be independent of my family and the clan and just be a… a businesswoman like you. How come everything works out for you, and it just turns to crap for me?"

"Charley…" Erin rubbed Charley's shoulder and shook her head. "Everything doesn't work out for me. My mom and dad died, and I went into foster care. I had nothing. I was out on my butt at eighteen and had to find a way to survive. The only reason I've got the bakery is because my Aunt Clementine died and left it to me. And starting it out hasn't been all roses. Angela Plaint dying of an allergic reaction on opening day wasn't exactly the thing to convince everyone how well I could handle baking for people with special diets."

"But it worked out," Charley sobbed.

"Yes, eventually. But not all in a day. I had to work through the same things that you are."

"Not all of them," Charley snapped.

Erin shrugged. "Maybe not."

"You don't even know all the stuff that's going on with the clans in Bald Eagle Falls right now."

Erin broke out in goosebumps. She shivered. *All of the stuff going on with the clans?* She looked at Terry, but he gave her wide eyes and a shrug. He didn't know what Charley was talking about either.

"What?" Erin pushed a lock of Charley's hair back behind her ear. "What's been going on with the clans?"

Charley sniffled. She wiped her sweaty red face with the back of her arm. "Nobody cared about Bald Eagle Falls before. It's such a little place, no one bothered to add it to their territory."

"And that has changed…?"

"They're fighting over it. Dysons and Jacksons. Maybe some of the smaller players too, I don't know. Someone is going to get it. And there's going to be more blood shed before they do."

"But why would anyone want Bald Eagle Falls?" Erin was shocked. It was such a safe little community, despite the rash of murders, she couldn't imagine that there was any benefit to a crime family claiming ownership over the community.

"Why do gangs fight over inner-city blocks?" Charley countered. "It isn't because they've valuable. It's just to prove who is more powerful."

"How do you know all this? How do you know they're fighting over Bald Eagle Falls?"

"I might not be in the Dyson clan anymore, but I still hear things." Charley snorted, sucking back the mucousy tears. "This sleepy little town isn't as sleepy as you might think."

Erin looked at Terry. His expression was stony. This was not good news for him or anyone in town.

Erin rubbed Charley's back soothingly. "It will work out in the end," she repeated, though of course she had no way of knowing if that were true. Charley had been through some pretty rough times recently, and if the clans were stirring things up, who knew what else they all might be facing.

Images from old black and white movies about prohibition times and The Godfather series flashed through her brain. They might not be strictly factual, but she had met with a couple members of the Dyson clan in Moose River, and they weren't just paper-pushing figureheads.

Charley rubbed her eyes. "If you had any sense, you'd get out of Bald Eagle Falls," she said. "All of you."

~

Terry was quiet as they got into the squad car. They had only taken as long as was needed for Erin to get Charley calmed down, knowing that Terry needed to get in and report the rumors of a possible clan war in Bald Eagle Falls to the sheriff and to consider how to address it.

"Do you think it's true?" Erin asked.

He glanced sideways at her, not answering immediately.

"I think she spent a long, hard night drinking," he said eventually. "That's obviously going to affect her perceptions. She has been through a lot of challenges and big changes lately. That may be all it is."

"But you don't think it is."

"No," he admitted. "I've seen some signs... people hanging around town that shouldn't be. Increased chatter. I was hoping it was just people who were attracted by news of a murder. You do get people who want to be where it all happened, whenever something sensational happens. I was hoping that it would just die down naturally."

"But if it's some kind of gang war, then it's not going to, is it?"

He stared off into the distance before starting the car. "It depends how much they really want Bald Eagle Falls. It could just be a flash in the pan, and then they get bored with it. There's not that much to attract big criminals here. But if they really do decide to have a showdown..."

"I sure hope not."

"Me too. I'll talk to the sheriff, but chances are, we're going to need to get the feds in here. Our little force is just not equipped to deal with something of that scale."

They were both quiet as Terry started the car and pulled out.

"Do you mind coming by the police department with me? Or do you want me to drop you at home?"

"I don't mind coming in, if you don't mind having me around. Are you going to have to clock in?"

"No. Just because this came up today, that doesn't mean that the clans are closing in and I'll be needed for one last stand. It's highly unlikely anything will happen today. I'll just talk to Sheriff Wilmot, let him know the rumor, and we can deal with it next week."

"Sounds good. I'll hang around, then."

"He might want to talk to you anyway, get your opinion on whether Charley is telling the truth or exaggerating."

"She could be doing both."

Terry gave a small smile. "Yes, she could be doing both."

"I couldn't believe her house. Her apartment in Moose River was so neat and organized."

He nodded, but didn't have any comment about Charley's housekeeping.

"Do you think she really loved Bobby?" Erin asked, as they pulled into the reserved parking space behind the civic center.

Terry's brows went up. "Hard to say. I'm no expert on matters of the heart…"

"Just your gut feeling. As a cop."

"People get emotional when they are tired or when they're drinking. She was obviously overwrought. But does that mean she didn't love him and is just dramatizing? I don't think so. I'm sure she had feelings for him… I'm just not sure how deep they really were. You just can't tell by the way people react to a death."

"She seemed so together when it happened. Perfectly calm. She hardly gave any sign that she cared about what had happened to him. Now this…"

"The truth is probably somewhere in between. In the aftershock of a violent death, people are often less emotional than you would expect. It isn't until everything should be back to normal—after the funeral ends and everyone goes home—that it really hits them, and they begin to grieve."

"And then to be hit with Don Inglethorpe's death right in her bakery, and the possibility that she'll never be able to reopen the bakery again…"

"She could probably use a hand," Terry said, "some counseling, maybe."

He was obviously hearkening back to their earlier conversation that Erin might need some therapy in the wake of her traumatic experiences. Erin just rolled her eyes and didn't take the bait.

"I'm sure Charley will be fine. And she does have family she can go back to. They can help her get over this and figure out what to do with her life."

"You're not including yourself in that?"

"Well… no," Erin admitted. They might be blood, but they weren't much of a family. Charley was young enough that she could go home, and her parents would help her. Erin hadn't ever had a safety net like that.

She probably should have enough compassion for Charley to offer to take her in hand and help her to straighten her life out, but Erin couldn't bring herself to take on that project.

CHAPTER 21

Sheriff Wilmot seemed unimpressed by Charley's report that the clans were descending on Bald Eagle Falls to have it out. He shook his head slowly.

"No, I don't see it. Bald Eagle Falls has never been the type of place the criminal element were interested in. Sure, we've had our share of moonshiners and pot-smoking high school students, but we're not an epicenter for drug activity. There's no market here. Why would they waste their time and energy on staking out a claim?"

Terry shrugged. "I couldn't tell you. I don't know the inner workings of these organizations. Maybe Charley Campbell could fill you in a little more about that. I just thought you should know."

Wilmot nodded. "Appreciated. But I haven't seen too much to bear the rumor out."

"We have had a few bad characters around the last few days who aren't normally part of the picture here."

"Not unusual after a murder. People want to see where it happened. It will quiet down again."

Terry had expressed the same possibility himself, so he just nodded. Only time would tell.

"Erin," Sheriff Wilmot hadn't acknowledged her up until this point, but having dealt with the possibility of organized crime invading Bald Eagle

Falls, he noticed her waiting for the handsome Officer Piper and took advantage of the opportunity.

"Morning, Sheriff."

"Can you tell me of any reason Charley's fingerprints would be on your rolling pin?"

"Oh… well, I assume she's the one who took it from my kitchen, so she would have gotten her prints on it then."

"She didn't cook with you at any point?"

"No. She'd hardly ever even been in my kitchen. We didn't bake together."

"And when you loaned her the rolling pin—"

"I never loaned it to her," Erin cut him off. "I never would have given it to anyone to use on gluten doughs. It would be contaminated, and I wouldn't be able to use it for my gluten-free doughs. I wouldn't want to take the chance, however slim, of ever poisoning someone."

"I see. She had led me to believe that you had let her use it. But in fact…"

"I told her several times that she couldn't borrow any of my pans or equipment. Again… it wouldn't have been safe for my customers. She seemed to really have difficulty understanding that. She didn't just ask once, and she kept insisting that I would just have to wash them afterward."

"Couldn't you?"

"I couldn't wash them and be one hundred percent sure that there wasn't a single particle of flour in it. And for some people, one particle would be enough to make them sick."

"I see." He nodded slowly. "So, when you went over to The Bake Shoppe to get the rolling pin back, you were prepared for there to be trouble."

"I was ready for an argument," Erin admitted. "But I wasn't planning on beating anyone to death."

"Of course not." But Sheriff Wilmot pursed his lips and seemed to be considering the idea.

Erin hesitated. "Charley said she never took the rolling pin. She said that she wasn't the one who took it. She had never touched it."

"Well, obviously she had touched it. Fingerprints don't lie. If she hadn't ever had the opportunity to use it while it was at your bakery, then she was the one who took it."

Erin didn't know what else to say. The next question was a logical one—had Charley been the one wielding the rolling pin when Don Inglethorpe had met his demise? Erin wasn't sure she wanted to know the answer.

~

In spite of the way the day had started and being short on sleep, Erin ended up having a pretty good day with Terry. She was able to forget about the heavy pall hanging over her and just to enjoy herself and spend time in the moment. It was almost like being on vacation. What little spare time she had was usually filled up with running errands, making lists, cleaning the house, and planning out advertising campaigns. Doing nothing was a rare treat, especially if she could do it with Terry Piper.

Erin was feeling tired, but relaxed and satisfied when Terry dropped her off at home at the end of the day. She let herself into the house and reached over to disarm the burglar alarm, then saw that it was already off. She checked to make sure that the door was shut.

"Jeremy? You home?"

He didn't answer. Erin walked by his bedroom to put her purse in her own, and saw that he was sitting on the bed, phone to his ear. He gave Erin a little wave of greeting. Erin put her things away and went into the kitchen to feed the animals and take a look across the back yard to see if Vic was home.

Reality started to reassert itself. Erin frowned and the knot began to tighten in her stomach again. Was it only a matter of time until organized crime made it to Bald Eagle Falls? Or had it already?

Vic was just arriving home, saying goodbye to Willie before retiring. Erin drew back from the window to give them their privacy. She looked in the fridge for anything good to eat, even though she wasn't actually hungry. In a couple of minutes, she heard Willie's truck engine roar to life and Vic came in the back door, smiling and relaxed.

"You look like you had a good time," Erin observed.

"We did. I think…" Vic hesitated before finishing, "I think we're finally over all of the bumps and can just move steadily forward." She gave Erin a grin. "And you and Officer Piper? I got my fill of gossip at the ladies' tea this morning. It would seem that you have been seen together around town."

"Well, of course. Where else would we be seen?" Erin asked, trying to mask her self-consciousness. "We have been seeing each other for quite some time now. You already knew that."

"But you haven't slept over at his house before." Vic's voice was full of teasing innuendo. Erin had always been very careful not to poke her nose into Vic's business or to tease her about her relationship with Willie, but she was starting to regret that fact. She would feel better if she knew that she had given as good as she was getting.

"We couldn't very well sleep here, could we?" she asked archly.

Vic's eyes got wider. "Why couldn't—oh, because of Jeremy! Where is Jeremy?"

Jeremy joined them in the kitchen a minute later, having pulled himself away from his phone call. "Is that my sister's voice I hear?"

"Jeremy, didn't you know you were supposed to be chaperoning these young people?" Vic demanded, gesturing to Erin.

"Chaperoning them?" Jeremy repeated. He looked quickly at Erin, and then back at Vic. "You're pulling my leg, right?"

"Of course I am. But you could have been a gentleman and spent the night in my apartment so that Erin could have *her* gentleman over."

"I... well, I suppose... but I didn't want to be in your way in case you brought *your* guy back..." He was turning quite red. "I mean, it's one thing to have an older couple that you don't really know around, it's a little different when it's your little sister, who used to be... and I don't really know..." he broke off, scratching the back of his neck and looking incredibly uncomfortable.

Vic was laughing so hard Erin was worried she was going to pop a blood vessel.

Erin raised an eyebrow at Jeremy. "An older couple? Are you serious?"

"Well... you're older than me," Jeremy protested, turning from the hazard of thinking about what his sister might be doing to repair the damage his words had done. "I just meant—older than me," he protested. "You're older than I am. Not by that much, but..."

"I'm not much older than you and neither is Terry," Erin agreed. "Now Willie, he's older than either of us."

They both looked back at Vic, who was standing with her hands on her hips.

"You just go there," she challenged Jeremy.

"Uh, no. I wasn't going to go there. You can do whatever you want with whoever you want." It was going to be a long time before all of the blood suffusing his face faded. He clearly did not want to be imagining his younger sibling with Willie.

"I clearly need to find a place of my own soon," Jeremy said. "I had no idea that it was such a hotbed over here. You guys need your privacy, and *someday* I'm going to need mine."

"Not too soon, I hope," Vic said in a parental tone.

"You're younger than I am," Jeremy repeated. "If you're old enough, then I certainly am."

"You make sure you wait until you're ready and have someone really special that you plan to spend a long time with."

Jeremy chuckled. "You're going to make a good mom, Vic."

She grinned at him, pleased. Then Vic turned her attention back to Erin. "Things went well with Officer Piper? The two of you... enjoyed each other's company?"

"We always do," Erin said evenly. "And that's all I'm going to say on the matter." She looked at Jeremy seriously and then back at Vic. "We need to talk."

"Okay." Vic nodded. She would know that they needed to discuss the living arrangements before too much more time passed, but she didn't know there was more to it than Erin's need for privacy or the difficulty in keeping Jeremy's presence a secret from Terry Piper.

CHAPTER 22

They all withdrew a little reluctantly to the living room and sat down. Erin sighed.

"Jeremy... we're going to need to know what's going on. We can't just keep hiding you here. You really need to fill us in."

He chewed the inside of his cheek. "It's not that easy."

"A lot of things are hard. But you still have to deal with them. You need to tell us what it is you're running away from. What you're hiding from. Don't try to tell me that you just need to find yourself. You could have found yourself a home without hiding from the police."

"I really can't talk about it," Jeremy protested. "I don't want to get anyone else in trouble."

"Well, if you're in trouble, you're already getting us in trouble, because we've been aiding and abetting you. You'd better tell us just what it is that you've gotten us into."

"Erin," Vic protested, "we don't need to know everything. Jeremy is entitled to his privacy..."

"Is the Jackson clan trying to take over Bald Eagle Falls?" Erin asked flatly.

Vic stared at her, mouth open. Then when neither Erin nor Jeremy laughed, she looked at Jeremy, who was no longer red with embarrassment, but as white as a ghost.

"The Jackson clan doesn't want anything to do with Bald Eagle Falls," Vic asserted.

"They didn't," Jeremy agreed. "But because of everything that's been going on lately, they might just have changed their minds."

Vic shook her head. "That doesn't make any kind of sense. What would they want to do with Bald Eagle Falls? There's nothing here. The biggest criminal enterprise is jaywalking, and there's only one street you can even cross against the lights. There's no reason for the clan to bring any of their crap here."

Jeremy was looking at Erin. "How did you know?"

"I have my sources. So explain to me how you're involved here. Were you sent to scout it out? To keep an eye on things? Are you supposed to do something, or just sit back and report on everything that happens?"

"I was supposed to be involved," Jeremy said with difficulty. He gave Vic an apologetic look. "They wanted me to... to do things that I couldn't."

"Who wanted you to?" Vic demanded.

"They said... it was time for me to prove myself. That I've just been living off the clan and getting all of the benefits, and I hadn't paid my dues. So, it was time to join an operation and show that I was really Jackson material."

Erin shook her head.

"So, you were supposed to do what?" Vic demanded. "Kill Don Inglethorpe?"

He cut his eyes toward her and his expression didn't change. He swallowed and kept his eyes down, lips tight.

"Is that it?" Erin asked. She had assumed that he would be involved in some lower-level activity. Reporting back to his organization on numbers. Maybe testing out some drug distribution or trying to spot the soldiers from the opposing clans. She hadn't expected it to be anything big.

"I don't know who killed Inglethorpe," Jeremy said cautiously. "It wasn't me. It wasn't anything to do with me."

"But if you had stayed home, it would have been," Vic suggested.

"I don't know. It might have been clan. They had more than one thing going on. I'm sure there were lots of ways I could have cemented my position with the clan."

"I don't understand," Erin said, shaking her head. "I get that these organizations run along family lines... but... you're saying you don't have a choice whether to be involved or not? If you're a Jackson, you're expected to be a criminal, doing whatever it is they want you to?"

Jeremy chewed on his lip. It was Vic who tried to put it into words.

"You're raised that the Jacksons are on the side of the angels. Anyone who opposes them is obviously on the devil's side. So that makes it right to protect your family's safety and freedom. It's okay to do things that you've been taught were wrong, because that's part of being a Jackson and protecting our way of life."

"Did they expect you to be like that too?" Erin demanded. "I mean, you were just a kid before you left home. A minor. They didn't ask you to break the law for them, did they?"

"It's small things when you're younger," Vic said. "Little things are easier, and then it doesn't bother you as much when they ask you to do the big things."

"Like killing someone?"

Vic looked at Jeremy. "I was never told to kill someone. I was told to get rid of problems, yes, but no one ever told me anything like that."

"Soldiers aren't really told ahead of time what they're going to be asked to do," Jeremy said quietly. "I guess they figure that you'll do what you're told in the heat of the moment. You don't have time to think about it, you just do what the boss tells you to do, and if you feel bad about it after, you have a drink and you laugh about it with the others, and then you're one of them, and you can try to forget about the details."

Was that how it had been for Charley too? Just acting and reacting in the heat of the moment, until she wasn't a living, breathing individual anymore, but a robot, programmed to do what the mob wanted her to do? Was it any wonder that she hadn't shown any emotion after Bobby had died? That she hadn't known what she felt like at the time, not until weeks later when she was faced with another death and the potential loss of her business?

"Then what are you doing here?" Erin challenged Jeremy. "It seems to me that if you wanted to avoid the clan and start life fresh, you wouldn't come to the one place that they're concentrating on at the time."

"I didn't know what to do. I wanted to protect Vic. I thought it would be easier if I was closer." Jeremy looked at Vic and swallowed. "I knew I wouldn't ever be able to talk her into leaving Willie and the bakery and running away somewhere else. So I thought I would stay here... keep an eye on things… make sure that if there was violence, she would be out of the way."

"But you couldn't guarantee that, could you?" Erin pointed out. "You haven't stayed with us. You don't know what might happen while we're out. Who else might get killed. Maybe someone like Inglethorpe, a pillar of the community. Or maybe someone's wife or child. Or someone's sister."

"I didn't want anything to happen to either one of you," Jeremy reiterated. "I came here to protect you."

CHAPTER 23

They had gone to bed without anything being resolved. Jeremy didn't want to leave, but likewise didn't want to talk to Terry to tell him what he knew. Vic didn't want to kick him out and was worried about their security. It had failed before, and they couldn't be sure that it would keep them safe in the future.

Vic ended up calling Willie to come back to the house. She had Jeremy go back to the spare room and didn't tell Willie their specific concerns, she simply told him she needed him there and asked him to stay. Maybe Willie already knew there was clan activity going on around Bald Eagle Falls. He had, after all, been part of the Dyson organization at one point, and still had occasional contact with them to help with computers or one of Willie's other specialties.

"Should we all stay in the house?" Vic asked Erin. "Would you feel better if Willie was there?"

"No, you can stay in your apartment." They couldn't all be in the main house without Willie figuring out pretty quickly that there was someone else there who shouldn't have been. It would look pretty suspicious if Erin wouldn't allow them to sleep in the empty bedroom. "I'll be just fine here with the burglar alarm and Orange Blossom. You know he'll attack anyone who tries to break in during the night." Erin laughed. It was Orange

Blossom who had fended off the previous intruder, until Vic had been able to get there with her gun.

"You should have some protection," Vic encouraged. "I can leave you with this."

She patted her concealed weapon. She had a permit for it and knew how to use it properly, but Erin did not. At some point, she might have to break down and do as they were all telling her to and take a firearms course and practice shooting at the range. Then she might feel confident enough to have a gun and to use it if she needed to.

But it was Erin's opinion that if she weren't armed, there would be less opportunity for anyone to shoot her. They would see that she was just an inexperienced, unarmed civilian, without any ties to organized crime or any kind of crime at all, and they would leave her alone. They would let her go.

"No. No guns. I'll be just fine."

"You should call Terry," Willie said, a twinkle in his eye, "I'm sure he wouldn't mind acting as your bodyguard."

In spite of herself, Erin felt herself blushing again. She glared at Willie, then made a shooing motion with her hands.

"I'm going to sleep now. No need for extra people or guns. Everybody out."

Willie obeyed, chuckling. Vic gave Erin a quick hug and whispered in her ear that Jeremy would look out for her.

Erin was too tired to do anything but go to bed. She'd been up too late the night before and had early bakery hours in the morning.

But sleep eluded her as she thought about Don Inglethorpe and the pool of blood and about Jeremy and Vic's other brothers.

They were all expected to be soldiers for the clan. What if they refused?

What if they accepted?

"Somebody didn't get enough sleep over the weekend," Adele observed, when she caught Erin yawning. Erin tried to cut the yawn short, but it was no use. She smothered it with the back of her hand.

"I had a hard time sleeping last night," Erin explained.

"And maybe you didn't get to bed until late Saturday night."

Erin looked at her. "You live in the woods, isolated from everyone else. How do you know about that?"

"I have my sources."

"Well, that's freaky. Have you got Skye spying on me?"

Skye was Adele's crow. Or a crow that sometimes spent time with Adele; she didn't claim any ownership over him. Adele didn't answer. She just looked mysterious, not filling Erin in on who her source might be.

Adele had come in the afternoon, when the bakery was usually quiet before school let out and people started rushing in to pick up something to go with dinner. She was the only one there.

"I had a run-in with a trespasser a couple of days ago," Adele said, as she waited for Vic to ring up her total.

"Who? A kid?" Erin asked.

"No. A young woman. I'm still not sure what she was out there for. She said she was just out for a walk, but..."

"You didn't know her?" Vic asked. "I think you know pretty much everyone in town now, don't you?"

Adele nodded. "She wasn't from around here. I would say she was native to Tennessee, but not to Bald Eagle Falls."

"What did she look like?"

"Army fatigues. Long, blond hair. Little or no makeup."

Erin thought she recognized the woman who had rear-ended the drug dealer's car in the description. She wished she had taken a picture so she could show it to Adele.

"Long nose and a big mouth?" she asked Adele, a bit embarrassed to be pointing out anyone's flawed features.

Adele nodded. "Sounds like you know her."

"No. Just saw her once. A couple of days ago. She rear-ended a guy on Main Street."

"That was not very bright. It isn't like we have heavy traffic."

"It might have been intentional... I don't know. I couldn't say for sure. But she certainly didn't seem upset about it. And she basically got away with it, because the guy she hit didn't want to open his glove box for Terry."

"You don't know who she was?"

"No. Terry would know her name. You didn't find out anything? Just that she was out for a walk?"

"That's as far as it went. I told her she was on private property and where the boundaries were, and she eventually went on her way. But I don't like people with guns hanging around on the property."

"Back up a minute!" Vic interjected. "This woman had a gun?"

Adele looked surprised at the question. "A hunting rifle. I mentioned that, didn't I?"

"No, you sort of missed that part!"

Erin tried to reconcile the picture with a drug dealer. But army fatigues and a hunting rifle didn't sound like a drug dealer or anyone else from the clans. It sounded like someone who was out hunting or participating in some war games.

"Did you ask her name? Or for some ID?" she asked Adele.

Adele's eyes were surprised. "I've never done that before."

"If we've got trouble coming into Bald Eagle Falls, then maybe we should start. If you don't know who it is, I mean."

"What trouble?"

Erin looked at Vic. "Well, we can't say for sure, but rumor has it… that the Dyson and Jackson clans are battling for possession of Bald Eagle Falls. No verification that it's true, of course, but here have been more strangers in town lately."

Adele considered this seriously. She took her bag of baked goods and her change. "I'll keep my eyes open. But I don't know why they would be interested in Bald Eagle Falls."

She turned and took a step toward the door, then froze.

CHAPTER 24

*E*rin looked to see what had caught Adele's attention.

"Speaking of unsavory strangers," Adele murmured.

There was a man getting out of a shiny red convertible outside the bakery. He was middle-aged, but had an irresponsible playboy look about him. His hair was artfully mussed, and he had laugh lines around his eyes and mouth. Adele turned and looked at Erin.

"Do you think I could sneak out through the kitchen?"

Erin was floored. Adele was always so calm and serene. She never seemed to hesitate over anything. She avoided crowds and preferred to be on her own, but she had never gone so far as to avoid contact so obviously.

Erin didn't want to set the precedent of allowing a customer to walk through off-limits areas, but Adele was different. There was no one around to see the breach, and she was sure that Adele wouldn't take advantage of the situation, assuming that letting her into the kitchen once meant she was allowed to use it any time she liked. Adele had always gone to great lengths not to take advantage of Erin's hospitality.

"Okay," she said quickly, as it became apparent the stranger was headed straight for Auntie Clem's, "go, go!"

Adele scurried around the counter, past Erin and Vic, and into the kitchen. Vic looked at Erin in surprise.

"What was that all about? I was sure you were going to say no."

"I know. I would have, but…" Erin looked toward the door.

The man walked in through the door, making the bells jangle. He was wearing a simple white t-shirt and cargo pants, but somehow made them look as if he'd just stepped off a yacht. He gave Erin and Vic a smug smile.

"Hello, ladies. How are you this fine afternoon?"

Erin had not been expecting the New England accent. She had opened her mouth to greet him and ended up just staring at him, mouth open.

"Good afternoon," Vic greeted cheerfully. "I don't think I've seen you in these parts before."

"No ma'am," he agreed. "First time I ever set foot in town. My name is Rudolph Windsor."

Even Vic was speechless for a beat. Then she smiled.

"Welcome to Bald Eagle Falls, Mr. Windsor. I'm Vic and this is Erin. What can we help you with?" She gestured to the bakery display case.

Windsor barely looked at the baked goods. He clearly wasn't there to buy a turnover.

"I wonder if you fine ladies would be able to help me. I am here looking for my wife." He looked at each of them expectantly. "That would be Adele Windsor."

There was a long pause while they considered what to tell him. Adele clearly did not want to meet up with him. She had never spoken of her husband; they had only recently discovered she was even married.

"Your wife," Vic repeated. "Adele has never mentioned you."

"Well, I'm hurt." His smile suggested that he was not. He didn't give the impression of being a family man. "To tell you the truth, Adele and I have been estranged. But she is still my wife, and I'd appreciate it if you could point me in the right direction?"

"She lives backwoods," Erin finally found her voice. "You'll need someone to show you the way. She doesn't have an address you can put in the GPS."

"I'm sure I could find it if you just point me in the right direction. I am pretty good at finding things."

Something about the way he said it gave Erin the willies. She rubbed her arms, not sure why she would be getting goosebumps in the Tennessee heat.

"Maybe Terry could help," Vic suggested.

Erin nodded, relieved to find a solution. She didn't get a good feeling about Rudolph Windsor and didn't want to give him directions to Adele's cottage. "I'll text him."

She did so, giving him a heads-up that Rudolph Windsor was not someone that Adele wanted to see. He acknowledged the message.

"Should just be a couple of minutes," Erin told Windsor.

He smiled and nodded, pleased with the way the matter was progressing.

"Could we get you a cookie and an iced tea while you're waiting? First cookie is always on the house."

Windsor looked down his nose at the display case, shaking his head. "I eat low carb," he advised. "This stuff is pure poison to the body. Worse than cocaine."

Vic bristled at that and Erin held up a hand to stop her from going off on Windsor. Best if he were still in one piece when Officer Terry Piper got there. "Different strokes for different folks," she murmured.

"But your baking—"

"Shh."

Vic subsided. "I'd better go check on those cookies," she muttered, and retreated to the kitchen.

Windsor gave Erin another sardonic smile. He turned and looked out the front window, waiting for his escort to show up. When he saw the uniformed police officer and his K9 partner approaching, he did not look pleased. Erin saw him take a quick look back and forth, looking for a way to avoid meeting him.

Terry opened the door and walked in. He nodded to Erin, and turned his polite, no-nonsense, public-service smile on Windsor.

"Good afternoon, sir. Something I could help you with?"

Windsor took another look at the door. "I think it's all taken care of, officer." He cast a glance over to Erin for confirmation.

"This is Terry."

Windsor didn't seem to know what to do about that. "I don't think we need to put the police force out. I can find the way on my own."

"What was your name?" Terry asked, flipping his notebook open and holding his pen at the ready.

"Rudolph Windsor."

"And where are you from?"

"I don't see why you would need to know that."

"Are you refusing to answer?"

The superior smile was gone from Rudolph's face. He licked his lips. "No need to be that way… Massachusetts."

"Boston?"

"Thereabouts."

Erin wouldn't have pegged his accent as Bostonian, but she kept her peace.

"Little bit different coming to a small town like Bald Eagle Falls," Terry commented.

"Yes… it certainly is."

"So, Miss Windsor knows you were coming to see her?"

"*Mrs.* Windsor," the man retorted. "I should know. I married her."

"And she knows you're coming?"

"Is there some kind of law out here that I'm not aware of? That a man isn't allowed to visit his own wife without some kind of appointment?"

"If we actually knew you, that would be a different story. But we like to look after our own. I don't know you from Adam, and even if you are who you say, that's no guarantee Miss Windsor didn't come here with the express purpose of leaving you behind. The fact that you're avoiding my question suggests that she doesn't know you're here."

"Look, Officer," Windsor attempted to turn on the charm, smiling in a way that made Erin's flesh crawl. "There's no bad blood between my wife and I. I appreciate your desire to protect your citizenry, but you don't have the right to keep me from visiting her or to detain me. So rather than making a big thing of this… I'm just going to leave."

He held up his hands like he was fending off an attack and retreated from the bakery. Terry swiveled, watching him go.

"Where's Adele?" he asked Erin, without turning back around to look at her.

"I'm right here, Officer Piper."

Erin startled at the voice behind her. She hadn't expected Adele to still be in the kitchen, but well on her way home. Adele appeared in the doorway with Vic.

"I'm sorry to cause all of this trouble. I just lost my head when I saw him. It's okay, really. There's nothing to be concerned about."

Adele wasn't the type to lose her head. Erin studied her for a minute, wondering what the story was. But Adele was a very private person and she wasn't about to tell them about her personal life.

"Have you ever had a restraining order against him?" Terry asked.

Adele walked past the counter into the front area of the bakery. "No. No restraining orders."

"Does he have a criminal record?"

"He might... I don't know."

"You don't know if your husband has a criminal record."

"People often don't know everything about the people they live with. Rudolph has a past that I was not involved in. It's been some time since I left him. Even while we were together... I wasn't with him every minute of the day, and there were nights he didn't come home... Could he have a record? Of course. Does he?" She shook her head. "I have no idea."

Terry scratched his chin, considering this. Erin figured that since Adele hadn't immediately jumped in to say that there was no way her husband could have a record, that she was aware of criminal activities that he might be involved in. The way she answered suggested that it was entirely possible that he'd been caught breaking the law at some point.

"How do you want this to be handled?" Terry asked. "Do you want him to stay away from you and your house? Do you have reason to get a restraining order?"

"No... I shouldn't have run away. I could have just stuck around here and dealt with him face-to-face out in public. I just hate having my dirty laundry spread out for everyone to see."

"Do you feel safe seeing him? If you don't want this guy showing up on your doorstep, we should set up a meeting away from the cottage. Do you know what he wants?"

"What Rudolph always wants. To get back together. But that's not going to happen."

"You're not worried about any violence?"

"No. We had... different lifestyles. But he never hit me."

"Still, you make sure you meet with him in public, a restaurant or somewhere people won't overhear your conversation but are around if he does get angry."

Adele nodded. "Okay. I will. Sorry for the trouble, Officer Piper. I didn't mean to cause any concern."

"No problem. I'd rather be here when I wasn't needed than not be here when I am. He knows I'm around and that people are keeping an eye on things. He'll think twice before doing something stupid."

"Oh, you don't know my husband," Adele said, her mouth curling into a slight smile. "He's never in his life thought twice before doing something stupid."

CHAPTER 25

*A*fter hearing that Adele had made arrangements to have supper with her husband at the family restaurant, Erin and Vic decided they needed a night out as well. They booked a table of their own and were pretending not to watch Adele and Rudolph as they ate their dinner. Erin and Vic were just there in case Adele needed them, like Terry had said. They both had Terry on speed dial, so he could be there in a few minutes if it looked like things were getting heated between the two.

But so far, things seemed perfectly calm. More than that, Adele and Rudolph seemed positively friendly with each other. Adele wasn't smiling, but she wasn't scowling, either. That blanched, worried expression she'd had when she had first spotted Rudolph was nowhere to be seen.

Rudolph himself was in fine form. He was practically gushing over Adele. He beamed at her and frequently slid his fingers through his hair as he flirted with her. He sat across the table and held her hand for several minutes at a time. Erin couldn't hear the conversation between them, but there didn't seem to be any harsh words. No argument.

"Well, this isn't as exciting as I expected," Vic grumbled.

"We don't actually want it to be exciting," Erin countered. "We don't want Adele to be in any danger."

"I don't mean I want her to be in danger, just not to be sitting there smiling at him and pretending she likes him. If she doesn't want to be with him, then why can't she look like it? She can't be that afraid of making a scene. She's just letting him walk all over her."

"Nobody's walking over anybody. She's just having dinner. And I assume he's paying, so she gets something out of it. She said that she's not getting back together with him. She's just humoring him by having dinner and a discussion. She'll let him down easy and he'll go back to Mass, and that will be that. No need for any fuss or bother."

"I know." Vic sighed. "I shouldn't be wanting them to argue. I just feel like it would be healthier if they did. They should get their problems all out in the open."

Erin smothered a smile. "I think that's the whole point of eating here. They want to lay it all out on the table, discuss things civilly, and then come to some kind of settlement. Which would preferably be Adele going home and Romeo leaving town."

They were both quiet for a minute, watching Rudolph talk earnestly with Adele, his cheeks slightly flushed, leaning toward her as he caught her up on his life or asked her for a favor or whatever he was there for.

"Don't look now," Vic murmured, "but I think it's your favorite blond accident victim."

Erin looked around. "Accident victim?" She spotted the woman in army fatigues. "Oh, her. She wasn't the victim, she was the one who caused the accident."

They gazed at her, trying to glean anything they could by looking at her. She stood by the hostess podium, waiting to be seated. She looked just as Adele had described her, with the camouflage shirt and pants. Just no gun. What exactly had she been up to in Erin's woods with a gun? Out hunting? But hunting what? There were still plenty of people around Bald Eagle Falls who hunted for their own food, but they didn't do it right in town. They would go out farther into the wilds and look for deer or other big game.

The woman looked like a hunter, so maybe she had just been in the wrong place, thinking she was on public land and would be able to bag something.

The woman looked over and saw the two of them staring at her. She raised her brows and gave them a questioning smile. Erin didn't know what to do; should they acknowledge that they had been looking at her, or pretend that they had just happened to be looking in that direction? She looked at Vic to see what she thought.

"Oh, sheesh," Vic murmured. "She's coming over here."

"Well, you're the one who wanted some excitement."

"I wanted to watch someone else get into an argument, not me!"

The woman had a slow, rolling gait that brought her efficiently to Erin's and Vic's table without even a whisper of sound.

"Hi. I'm eating alone today; would you mind if I joined you?"

Erin looked at Vic, who looked back at her, and neither of them was sure what the proper protocol for such a situation was. It would be rude to turn the woman away without a good reason, but they were there to spy on Adele, not just to eat and visit.

The woman waited for a few moments, then pulled out a chair and sat down.

"Rohilda Beaven," she introduced herself. "Folks call me Beaver."

"Beaver?" Erin repeated. She looked around to see if someone was secretly filming them. It had to be some kind of joke. People didn't just invite themselves to join you at your meal. And women did not go by nicknames like Beaver. Even if they did have strange Christian names like Rohilda. What kind of a name was that? Danish?

"Beaver," the woman agreed. She crossed one ankle over a knee, spreading out to take up plenty of space. Like a cat puffing out its fur to make itself look bigger. She seemed to be taking up as much real estate as possible. "And you are...?"

"I'm Vic, and this is Erin."

"Vic and Erin. Nice to meet you. I hope you don't mine me horning in on your dinner too much? I'm usually a loner, but the way you were watching me when I came in... I thought maybe you wouldn't mind."

"No, of course not, we wouldn't want you to have to eat alone," Vic assured her. "Erin and I spend so much time together, it's probably a good thing to have someone else join in to spice up the conversation."

Beaver nodded. "Are you two a couple?" she asked, making a gesture to include them both.

Erin was taking a drink of her RC and just about sprayed it across the table. She was used to hearing comments made to Vic about her gender identity, but it had been some time since anyone had accused the two of them of being an item.

"No, no," Vic tried to cover Erin's spit-take. "We work together. And I rent an apartment from Erin. We don't live in the same house and we're both... We're both straight."

"Oh, okay." Beaver shrugged. "Sorry. I just thought maybe you were out on a date. You said you spent a lot of time together, so I figured..."

"No. We both have boyfriends," Vic said firmly.

Erin nodded in agreement. She wondered whether Beaver was gay herself or had just made a wrong assumption. There were stereotypes about a woman in army fatigues or with a brush cut. Not that Beaver had a brush cut. She had a beautiful long ponytail which would have had to be done up in a tight bun if she were actually in the army. And then there was the name Beaver. What kind of a name was that for a woman?

"I don't. No boyfriend or girlfriend. So, no judgments here." Beaver looked around for the waitress. It was a few minutes before she managed to get someone's attention to order a drink and get a menu. Then she flipped through it in a slow, relaxed pace. "What's good here? There anything special?"

"It's all good," Vic said. "All done from scratch, even the mashed potatoes. I don't think there's anything bad on the menu, do you, Erin?"

"No, I haven't ever been disappointed."

"The two of you work together? Where do you work?" Beaver asked.

"I own the bakery," Erin offered. "Auntie Clem's Bakery. That's me."

"You're Auntie Clem?"

"No, I'm Erin. My aunt was the real Auntie Clem. I named it after her, because I inherited from her, so I had enough money that I could take a run at opening a place of my own. It was really a great break for me."

"Sounds like it," Beaver agreed. "I wouldn't mind if someone would die and leave me a business. That seems like a pretty sweet deal."

"You wouldn't want someone you loved to die, though," Vic pointed out.

Beaver considered this seriously before finally nodding agreement. "No, you're probably right there. I wouldn't want someone I loved to die. But someone else could, that would be okay."

Vic shook her head, bemused. Erin decided to try to steer the conversation to something a little less morbid.

"So, what about you? Are you a hunter?"

"I'm a *sort* of a hunter," Beaver said with a mysterious smile. "You could say that."

"I hear you were over on my property earlier and Adele sent you on your way."

Beaver looked around and saw Adele talking with her husband at their table. "That one, you mean? Yeah, she told me it was private land and I couldn't be wandering around on it. You pay her too?"

"Uh, well, she's my groundskeeper. She makes sure that no one is messing around with anything out there, and she gets free rent of the summer house. It works out for both of us."

"You might want to suggest she start carrying a gun. Anything could happen out there, and she wasn't even armed. You don't know what kind of people you're going to run into."

"What's that supposed to mean?" Vic challenged. She looked Beaver over, her brows drawing down in anger. "Is that a threat of some kind?"

Beaver's eyes widened, either surprised or pretending to be. "A threat? Me? Heavens, no. What reason would I have to threaten anyone?"

Vic dialed back her tone. "Okay, then. I just wanted to... We've had some things going on in town. There are some shady people hanging around, and we're a little worried about them causing trouble. So I just... I wanted to make sure you weren't with them and weren't making some kind of threat..."

"I'm not with any one." Beaver slurped an ice cube out of her glass of water and chewed it. "I have seen some characters around town, though... I think I know what you're talking about."

"That man that you rear-ended," Erin said. "He's one of them."

Beaver laughed. "Oh, you heard about that, did you? I guess word does get around, even if you're not from these parts. Yeah, I hit the idiot."

"You know him?"

"I know his kind," Beaver said, her mouth twisting into a sneer of distaste. "And I figured I'd give him a hard time."

"You really shouldn't do things like that! If you'd made him mad enough..."

"Nah. He wouldn't have done anything. What's he going to do, shoot me there on Main Street? He couldn't do anything that might attract the attention of the police. When that cop came afterward..."

"Then he made a break for it," Erin agreed. "But if you provoke someone like that enough..."

"He'd have to get permission from whoever his boss is. And then he'd have to find me. And he'd have to get the drop on me. Because I'm always armed and I'm no shrinking violent about using my weapons."

"His *boss*," Vic repeated. "What do you know about him, then? I just knew he was from out of town…"

"That guy? He had drug dealer written all over him. But not a kingpin. Just the guy at the bottom of the totem pole, finding new clients and doing the street-level sales. Not the kind that climbs to the top. They always die before they get that far."

Erin's stomach turned over at Beaver's casual tone. Bragging that she always carried a gun and then talking about how soldiers like that drug dealer were just going to die… she didn't like the cold, greasy feeling the conversation left her with.

Glancing over at Vic, she saw her own feelings etched on Vic's face.

CHAPTER 26

*T*he waitress brought Erin's and Vic's meals and took Beaver's order. Erin looked down at her food, no longer hungry.

"Don't wait for me," Beaver said. "I'll probably catch up to you. My parents always did say that I eat way too fast. I never slow down and enjoy the meal."

Erin didn't believe it. Everything about Beaver was thought out and deliberate.

"Where did you say you're from?" Erin asked, though she knew very well that Beaver hadn't said anything about where she hailed from.

"Here and there," Beaver said. She creased her napkin and unfolded it again several times. "I've been all over."

"Like Erin," Vic offered. "I think she's been everywhere. Me, I just grew up on a farm here in Tennessee, and I've hardly even been out of the state. Redneck girl if you ever saw one."

"I haven't lived *everywhere*," Erin countered. "Mostly northeast. I spent my first few years around here, but after that… Maine, New York, eastern seaboard… other places. I haven't lived west coast or anywhere past the Midwest."

Beaver nodded. "I've been everywhere."

"Army?" Vic suggested.

"Army brat," Beaver admitted. "Never got the knack for staying in one place after growing up like that. I stick around too long, and my feet start to itch. My mom said she always knew when she got to the bottom of the moving boxes… then it was time to start packing again. Didn't matter whether it took her two weeks or two years to get everything unpacked, as soon as she emptied that last box, Dad would get new orders and they'd be on the road again. So I'm more comfortable living out of a suitcase than confined to one place."

"That's hard for me to believe," Erin said. "I was always being moved from one place to another. There was nothing I wanted more than to just have one family and stay in one place. I love having a house of my own, knowing that I don't have to ever give it up to go somewhere else. It's mine for good."

"Never say never," Beaver warned. "Fate is always listening, and just like my mom unpacking those last boxes… as soon as you say you're safe and secure and no one can take anything away from you… that's for sure when you start to tempt fate."

"I don't believe in fate." But Erin couldn't deny the foreboding Beaver's words stirred up in her. Had she become too complacent? What if something did happen? What if she did lose everything, like she always had before?

"I think Erin's been through enough in life," Vic said. "She's burned through all of her obstacles. Leave some for the rest of us."

Erin chuckled and shook her head.

She was trying to eat her ribs daintily, but it was no use. She couldn't help getting sauce on her fingers and on her face, and eventually, she just had to give up trying to keep them clean. "Just don't look at me," she said. "This is way worse than it should be. You'd think I would have learned how to eat by now."

"You just look like you're enjoying it," Beaver said. "If I was you, I'd make as big a mess as I could. If you're going to get dirty, you might as well get really dirty!"

The waitress eventually brought over Beaver's steak and potatoes, and Beaver proceeded to cut everything up efficiently. She didn't exactly stuff her face, but she was making her way through her meal a lot more quickly than Erin had expected. Beaver looked at Erin.

"I did warn you. I'm going to be done before you are."

"You probably are," Erin admitted, looking at the couple of bones she had cleaned off. She still had a long way to go.

"It's not a race," Vic said primly. But she was eyeing Beaver's plate, looking at her own and calculating how long it was going to take her to finish.

Beaver looked over at Adele and Rudolph. She studied them for a few minutes.

"You said that *she* rents from you. Not her and her husband."

"That's right," Erin admitted. "He doesn't live here. He just showed up today. She's supposed to be turning him down, but it doesn't look as if she is. They are looking pretty friendly."

"She'll turn him down," Beaver said certainly. "She's got a good head on her shoulders."

"What makes you think that?" Vic asked. "You only just met her today for two minutes. How did you even know that they're married? We didn't know until this afternoon."

"I know his kind."

"I hope she's not going to take him in," Erin said.

Beaver continued to watch the interplay between Adele and her husband.

"What is it you do?" Erin asked. "You know that we are bakers and you said you're sort of a hunter, but that just leaves me wondering what it is you actually do?"

Vic cocked an eyebrow at Erin. Erin was normally reluctant to pry into people's personal lives. Too much experience with foster care, where the social workers and foster parents weren't supposed to share information about their kids' backgrounds even with the other kids, and asking was taboo. She usually just sat back and let other people do the asking, or watched and waited until people revealed themselves.

But there were too many people with unknown pasts showing up in town lately. Erin was too anxious not to ask. It was obvious Beaver was holding back, giving only general answers and focusing the conversation on things other than herself. Normally, people loved to talk about themselves.

Beaver didn't answer at first. She was intent on eating her steak and potatoes, and was putting them away at a surprising rate. After a few minutes of silence, she wiped her mouth with her napkin and looked at Erin.

"Okay," she said, "why not? I'm not the kind of hunter you might think I am. I don't hunt animals."

Erin waited, but a more full explanation was not forthcoming. Erin ran through the possibilities. Maybe Beaver was a bounty hunter or a private investigator. Maybe she was like Alton Summers, someone skilled at tracking down heirs or other people who had dropped off the radar.

But if she wasn't hunting animals, what was she doing with a gun?

CHAPTER 27

*B*eaver had remained coy about what exactly it was she hunted, just grinning at Erin's and Vic's questions and giving nothing away. But they had her name, assuming that she hadn't made up Rohilda Beaven, and that at least gave them some leverage to figure out more.

"We should give her name to Terry," Erin said as they discussed Beaver, sitting in the living room making their plans for the next day. "He can run background on her."

"He already has her name from the accident forms," Vic pointed out. "He's the one who isn't sharing information."

"Oh, yeah. Well… he can't, really."

"But we've got her name, so at least let's do an internet search. She's bound to have social media accounts that say something about who she is and what she does."

"You think if she's involved with one of the clans she's going to say that on Facebook?"

"Well, maybe not that," Vic said, "but she said she's a hunter, which would make me think she isn't with the clans."

"That could have been misdirection. Or she might be… hunting people." Erin remembered Beaver chewing her gum, clearly enjoying winding up the drug dealer, and then later grinning away as Erin and Vic

134

tried to figure out what she meant by saying she was a hunter. She shuddered.

"A hit man?" Vic said skeptically, "I wouldn't think so. Those kind of people don't generally go around announcing what they are. Let's just look."

Erin couldn't see any harm in looking the woman up, especially if Terry already knew who she was. "Okay, fine. Let's see who she is."

Vic eagerly pulled out her tablet and tapped in a search. "I'm going to assume that Rohilda is spelled just the way it sounds..."

"I don't have any idea. It should give a suggestion if not." Erin waited for the results.

"There are some news articles," Vic announced. She tapped on one, and her eyes skimmed back and forth as she read the page. She started to laugh.

Erin relaxed. Not a hit man, then. At least they didn't have to worry about that.

"She's a treasure hunter. She's not hunting animals or people. She's hunting for treasure or artifacts."

"The little scamp. Why didn't she just tell us that?"

"Because it was more fun to keep us guessing, obviously."

Erin shook her head. "What a brat!"

Vic was chuckling. "Well, it made our evening more entertaining." She scrolled down the article, her eyes wandering over it. "So... what do you think she's doing in Bald Eagle Falls?"

Erin considered. "Good question... but you get them in this area sometimes, don't you? With all of the mines and the possibility of Confederate gold. I remember talking about that when I first opened up the bakery. Remember the map of Clementine's that we found in the recycling?"

Vic nodded. "Yeah, that's right. That's one of the fun things about spelunking around here, the idea that one day you might run across a treasure that no one else has seen in a hundred years. That there is still a big haul just sitting out there somewhere, untouched. I guess that must be what Beaver is here looking for." Vic grimaced. "I really don't like calling her that. It seems disrespectful."

"It's what she wanted to be called. You've had experience with people who won't call *you* by the name you want to be called."

"I do at that," Vic admitted.

"I think she enjoys making people uncomfortable, don't you? The way she was acting when she rear-ended that drug dealer. Making us try to figure out what kind of a hunter she is. She likes stirring the pot and then sitting back to see how people react."

"Do you think she *did* rear-end him on purpose?" Vic asked.

"I don't know. It certainly makes me wonder."

"That's crazy." Vic grinned. "She's quite the woman."

"I don't think she's as crazy as she would like us to think."

"No. I agree with you there. It seems very calculated."

"With all of these new people around town, I thought she was one of the clans. I really did. It's a relief that she's just a regular person. Or however much of a regular person she can be as a treasure hunter. I think all of those people are a little bit crazy."

"Maybe you have to be in order to believe there's some wonderful treasure buried around here, that if you can just find it, you'll be set for the rest of your life. It's exciting if you believe it. If you don't believe it, then it's just a dream and there's really no point. Unless you really just like crawling around in caves."

Erin's goosebumps returned. She shivered from deep down in her stomach and tried to force her mind away from her cave experiences and pretend that she was only thinking about Beaver.

"Sorry," Vic said.

"I'm fine," Erin brushed off her concern. "That's all in the past. I don't ever have to go into another cave again if I don't want to."

"No. I just wish... you hadn't been through all of that and you were interested in going spelunking with me. I think it's really interesting."

"That's fine. You can go with Willie to any cave you want. I'm just not interested."

"When he took us together, you did okay at that."

Erin had gone with Vic, with Willie as her guide, back when she was trying to prove to herself that she could and wanting to impress Willie. Now that Willie and Vic were together... she didn't have anything to prove to him. He couldn't care less whether she wanted to crawl around in the caves. He could take Vic into his mine or exploring other caves and it didn't bother her one bit. In fact, she enjoyed it.

"I guess we'd better be getting to bed," Erin looked at the time on her phone. "In spite of all of the potential excitement tonight, nothing actually happened, and we need to be up as usual tomorrow morning."

"I'll just go say goodnight to Jeremy, then I'll head out."

Erin nodded. Vic knocked softly on Jeremy's door and then poked her head in.

"Hey, Jeremy. I'm just knocking off."

Erin couldn't make out his murmured reply. She looked over her lists for the next day and carefully layered them into a pile. Whatever was going on in Bald Eagle Falls, she certainly wasn't going to solve all of its problems. She would leave the detecting to Terry and the police department.

~

Melissa was at the bakery at opening the next morning, her curls practically bristling as she waited to gossip with Erin and Vic. She looked like she'd been waiting all night and could barely contain herself.

"You were at the restaurant last night," she said. "What do you think?"

"Um... about what?"

"About Adele and Rudolph, obviously," Melissa said irritably. "They were together at the restaurant. You were there, so dish."

"There's nothing to dish," Erin said, raising her hands in a shrug. "We weren't sitting with her. We couldn't hear anything they discussed."

"They're still married," Melissa pointed out, as if Erin might have missed this point. "If they have been apart since before she moved into town, then why are they not divorced? Why isn't he her ex-husband instead of her husband?"

"Not everybody wants to rush right into divorce," Erin said uncomfortably. "Some people do a trial separation... decide whether it's really what they want, or whether they might want to get back together instead."

"And he does, doesn't he? He wants to get back together, and Adele said she didn't, but she was sitting with him at the restaurant. Just the two of them, holding hands. You don't hold hands with your ex."

"He isn't her ex, you just said that."

"I know that!" Melissa nodded emphatically, her dark curls bouncing all over. "That's what I'm saying! They're still married and they're still holding hands. What have they been doing since they separated? It's like... what if he's been undercover and it was all just a hoax, being apart. What if he's finished whatever he was doing, and now he wants to get back together again, because they didn't *really* break up, it was just because of his job."

Erin tried to follow the convoluted logic. "You think... he's an undercover cop? Is that what Terry said?"

"No, no!" Melissa flushed red. "He didn't tell me anything. I know he looked Rudolph up, but he wouldn't tell me anything about it and didn't leave any reports to be filed. But why didn't he? Is he trying to keep something from me?"

Terry knew he had a couple of leaks in the department, and Erin figured he knew exactly who they were. He probably just didn't want Melissa spreading the results of whatever searches he had done far and wide.

"Well, if he didn't tell you what the results were, you can't assume that Rudolph is undercover. Maybe he's just what he appears to be. Some bored playboy who thought he'd try to get back together with his wife."

"I don't think so. I think he's up to something. He must have been undercover. Otherwise, why would she just accept him back? I sure wouldn't take my husband back if I thought he'd been fooling around on me. I'd want him out of my life for good."

"But we don't know that's what happened."

"Have you seen the guy? Of course that's what happened. He's fooling around, cheating on her, and then he expects her to take him back again. And instead of telling him to hit the road and not bother her, she's holding hands with him!"

"So, which do you think? That he's a playboy or an undercover cop?"

Melissa spread her hands wide, exasperated. "How am I supposed to know? Terry should have told me something."

Not if he wanted it kept quiet.

"How about the other guy?" Erin asked, on a whim. "You know, the one that Rohilda Beaven rear-ended. Did you find anything out about him?"

"Bo Biggles?" Melissa asked, then laughed. "I can't believe that's actually his name. Can you imagine walking around with a moniker like that?"

"Bo Biggles?" Erin repeated. "Yeah, I would think he would have changed it!"

"Well, Rohilda goes by Beaver, so what are you going to do with that?" Vic said.

"Beaver?" Melissa apparently hadn't heard this tidbit. "For a woman? I can't imagine being taken seriously with a name like Beaver. She doesn't use it for real life, right? Just for a silly nickname. I mean, you couldn't rent a house with a name like Beaver. You'd be a laughingstock."

"This Bo Biggles," Erin tried to redirect Melissa, "he's a drug dealer?"

"Terry told you that?" Melissa asked.

Erin evaded the question. "It was pretty obvious."

"Is he with one of the clans?" Vic asked. "Is he with Dysons? It gives me the creeps, thinking that they're in town."

Melissa shook her head. "No, I think he's with your clan. Jacksons."

"Not *my* clan," Vic countered. "I'm not part of that family anymore. Remember, they disowned me. I couldn't be part of it if I wanted to."

"But it's still your clan. They're still your family, whether you stay with them or not."

Vic shook her head. "I got away from all of that when I left home."

Melissa sighed loudly. "Fine then, Bo is with the clan you used to belong to. The Jacksons. But really, you can never leave the clan," Melissa said ominously. "It doesn't matter if you want out, they'll follow you and they'll make sure—"

"Melissa," Erin interrupted. "What did you say you wanted to order? Are you looking for something for the department or for yourself?"

Melissa looked at the display case, her mouth open. She looked at Vic as if she were going to continue the conversation, then apparently caught Erin's warning look and decided she didn't want to be thrown out with no one to gossip with and no baking.

"Maybe a muffin for lunch," Melissa said. "No turnovers today?"

Erin had pulled a couple of batches of turnovers out of the freezer, but she couldn't quite bring herself to make any more since Inglethorpe's death. She remembered him asking her about turnovers, and then the shock of walking into the crime scene and thinking the blood was cherry pie filling. She wasn't sure she'd ever be able to make cherry turnovers again. Hopefully, she'd be able to bring herself to make blueberry or apple.

"Sorry, nothing right now. They're time intensive, so I have to find the time to make them. Not like muffins, where you can just mix up the batter and pour it into the cups."

"They sure were good. I hope you make some more soon."

Vic looked in Erin's direction. "We'll have to see."

They managed to keep Melissa focused on choosing the baking she wanted to buy, and then hustled her toward the door as other customers arrived. Melissa went, knowing that she wouldn't be able to speak freely in front of others. Melissa wouldn't gossip about police files with just *anyone*.

Erin was the one who solved mysteries and had some influence over Terry. Erin was practically family.

Erin sighed as she and Vic dealt with the next few customers, until it was quiet and they were left alone together again for a few moments.

"So," Vic drawled, lengthening her words. "Just what *do* we think about Adele and Rudolph?"

CHAPTER 28

*E*rin dreamed she was back at the bakery. At first, she thought she was in her own kitchen and she looked around, trying to orient herself, but nothing was in the place it was supposed to be. Then she realized she could not be in Auntie Clem's kitchen, but rather was in The Bake Shoppe.

"I don't know where you put anything," Erin muttered, turning around again and trying to decide where to begin.

She went to the fridge and opened it to see what had been prepped. She and Vic always made some batters and doughs ahead so that it would be quick to get started in the morning and the flours would have had a chance to soak and soften. But there was nothing in the fridge.

Except... maybe there was. When Erin looked more closely, she realized that her rolling pin had been left in the fridge. She reached in and grabbed it. The marble was as cold as ice, and when she turned it and examined it more closely, she realized that it was sticky with cherry sauce. But the smell was not the smell of cherries. Erin gagged at the cloying, coppery smell. It wasn't cherry sauce at all.

She turned around and saw the body lying on the floor. It wasn't Mr. Inglethorpe this time, but someone else who was vaguely familiar.

Even though she was starting to realize that it was a dream, she tried to identify the shape on the floor. Who was it? Who had Erin hurt this time?

She stepped closer, her shoes sticking to the floor like they did in a movie theater.

"Mr. Inglethorpe…?"

There was white powder everywhere. Erin tried to avoid getting any of it on her. Had someone opened a bag of flour? Everything was going to be contaminated and she wouldn't be able to serve anything safe.

"It's not flour," Vic laughed. "It was never flour."

"Okay. I think… it's time to go back to Auntie Clem's. I don't want to be here anymore."

Erin tried to leave, but her eyes were drawn again to the figure on the floor. She should have recognized that uniform. It was as familiar to her as the dimple in his cheek. Erin crouched down beside him. "Terry? No! Terry, what happened? Who did this? Who could have done this?"

She couldn't rouse herself from the dream. She tried to pull herself from its grip, but she couldn't escape.

"Help me! I need help! It's Terry!"

"What's wrong? Erin? Erin, are you okay?"

Erin tried to pull away from the grip on her arm. Then she jumped, feeling the sensation of falling. And then her eyes were open, and she was lying on her bed, awake, staring up at Jeremy's face. He looked anxious, his mouth turned down and his eyes squinted at her in concern.

"Are you awake? Erin, are you okay?"

"What happened?"

"Nothing happened. You were just calling out. I thought… I didn't know whether I should wake you or not."

Erin gripped Jeremy's hand. "Yes. Yes, I couldn't get out of it."

She didn't let go of Jeremy's hand. He looked at her for a minute, then sat down on the edge of the bed.

"It must have been pretty nasty."

"Yes…" Erin was breathing as evenly as she could, but couldn't seem to quite catch her breath and calm herself down. Her heart was thumping wildly. "It was Terry…" She gulped. "I guess it's normal to have nightmares after something like that."

"Like that? You mean the murder?"

Erin nodded. "Yeah. It was… kind of a gruesome scene."

"That would be tough," Jeremy admitted. "Sometimes… things stick with you. Even when you think it should just be a minor thing. When it's something bigger like that, it must be worse."

Erin nodded. She could feel Orange Blossom sleeping curled up next to her leg, and she reached out and patted him and scratched his ears. Orange Blossom awoke and started purring loudly.

"But Terry's okay," Jeremy said. "Nothing is going to happen to him. Everybody is safe. You can just take a breath and relax. Go back to sleep."

"Right," Erin agreed. "I'll just close my eyes and go back to sleep."

No problem. She could do that. She did that every night. It was simple as pie.

Cherry pie?

Erin shuddered. She looked at Jeremy. She was still holding on to his hand. Probably harder than was comfortable for him. But it was comforting to her and she wasn't ready to let go.

"It will be okay, Erin," Jeremy said. "Really. Your friend is okay. There's nothing wrong with him. If you just go back to sleep, in the morning everything will be fine, and you'll feel much better. Okay?"

"You're just a kid, what do you know?" Erin laughed.

Jeremy looked at her for a minute, not answering.

"I'm just joking," Erin said uncomfortably.

"Just close your eyes. Go back to sleep."

Erin took in a long breath and blew it out very slowly. She was just starting to relax and to quiet her mind when the phone rang.

Both she and Jeremy jumped.

"Oh, no." Erin looked at the phone, afraid of what she was going to see. Terry calling her to tell her that something was wrong? Vic? Somebody calling to tell her that something had happened to Terry?

Jeremy looked over at it, reading the screen. "Unknown caller."

"I hate those... I don't answer them, but I always wonder. Late at night like this, no one should be calling. It has to be important, right? It's not just a curious client hoping I'll make cupcakes for a birthday party."

"You don't need to answer it. If the person won't let you see their caller ID, that's their problem."

Erin pressed her lips together anxiously. She wanted to do the right thing, and she was too worried to let the call go to voicemail in case it was something important and she was really needed. If it was just a spam call, she could hang up.

She took a breath and picked up the phone. She swiped it to answer the call.

"Hello?"

"Send your friend Jeremy out and no one will get hurt."

Erin stopped breathing. She looked at Jeremy. "What?" she squeaked.

"You heard me. We want to see the traitor. Face-to-face. You shouldn't be protecting him."

"I'm... I'm not doing anything wrong..."

"Tell Jeremy we want to talk to him."

Erin shook her head emphatically. "No."

Jeremy was staring at her, his brows drawn down, unable to hear the voice on the other end.

Erin tried to analyze the voice. Terry was going to ask her to describe it. But she knew by the robotic quality of the voice that it had been altered. It didn't matter whether it sounded like a man or a woman, it could be totally different in real life.

"Who is it?" Jeremy asked urgently.

Erin pulled the phone away from her face and deliberately pressed her finger over the smooth glass of the screen, ending the call. If the caller thought that she was going to listen to them threaten Jeremy, they were wrong. He was her guest and she wasn't turning him over to some psychopath to do whatever they wanted with him.

"Erin. What was all that about?" Jeremy demanded.

"Wrong number," Erin said tersely. She tapped until she found Terry's speed dial, and tapped it.

"Wrong number? You don't talk like that with someone who calls a wrong number."

"No," Erin admitted, "you don't."

"Then who...?"

Terry answered his phone as soon as it rang on his end. "Erin? What's wrong?"

"I just got a threatening phone call. On my cell phone. Could somebody trace it? Could you come here? You'll need backup. At least, I think you will. He said 'we' like there was more than one of them..."

"More than one of who, Erin? What exactly was this call about? Was it something to do with Don Inglethorpe's death?"

"I don't think so. I don't know. Can you come?"

"I'm on my way. I'll get the others dispatched. But you need to tell me what you can about what we're walking into. Do you have some reason to believe that this person is going to hurt you? Did they utter threats? Do you know who it is?"

He gave a quiet command to K9, and Erin heard him start the engine of his car. He called the dispatcher on his police radio. He'd stay on the phone all the way over to her house to make sure she stayed calm and was safe.

"It's... they're threatening someone else. I'll explain better to you when you get here. But they said they wanted me to send out... this other person and to turn him over to them. But I'm not going to do that."

"Of course not. I wouldn't expect you to."

His engine raced in the background. Erin waited to hear the sound of his siren or engine approaching the house. She really wanted to know that he was there and would protect her. He and the others in the police department. She tried to shake loose any fear that they wouldn't be able to handle it. Of course they could handle it. There probably wasn't even more than one person involved. The caller was just saying 'we' to scare her. To make himself sound stronger and more threatening.

"Who is there with you, Erin?" Terry asked quietly.

"It's... Jeremy, Vic's brother."

"Jeremy?" Terry's voice was surprised. "When did he get there?"

Erin didn't bother trying to answer that one. Jeremy was looking at her, shocked that she had revealed his identity to the police. Now what was going to happen to him? She didn't know what kind of trouble he was in, but with murder and drug running and maybe all-out drug war going on, Erin wasn't about to keep quiet. They needed to know everything in order to act. They had to know everything there was about the situation.

Jeremy didn't run away. Maybe he was worried about what was going to happen the minute he walked out the door. Maybe he wanted to stay and make sure that she was okay. Or maybe he just didn't know what to do.

"Sorry," Erin breathed. She shook her head. "I really... don't know what else to do."

"You're doing the right thing," Terry said firmly in her ear. He didn't ask her what Jeremy was doing there. Would he assume that Jeremy had just gotten there? Or as soon as Erin had said it, did he understand that Jeremy had been there for several days and Erin had been lying about it or avoiding telling him what was going on?

"Almost there, Erin," Terry said calmly. "Can you tell me if the burglar alarm is set?"

"Yes… I set it."

"So, no one is going to get into the house?"

"No. I mean… I don't think so, but last time they did. There's no one inside yet." She looked at Jeremy for confirmation. She needed to know that there was no one else there. That the two of them were alone.

"No one," Jeremy confirmed. He walked to the doorway of the bedroom and looked toward the living room. "We would know it if someone had broken in."

"Okay. No one else here," Erin told Terry.

She could hear his car then. No siren, but she could hear the roar of his engine and then he skidded to a stop outside the house. She waited. He said he would call the others as well. She didn't want him to get hurt. He had been dead in her dream. Had she just put him in the crosshairs of someone who was willing to kill for what he wanted?

"I'm here, Erin. I don't see anyone. But I might have spooked them pulling up."

"Wait for backup. Don't get out yet," Erin begged him. "I don't want you to get hurt."

"I won't. It's okay. There's no immediate danger that I can see. As soon as it's clear, I'll come inside, and we'll talk about what happened and how to protect you."

"I'm more worried about you."

Terry chuckled. "No need to worry about me. I'm just fine."

Erin looked at Jeremy. He knew about Erin's dream. Was it a premonition? Precognition? Had she known what was going to happen before it did?

But she tried not to read anything into it. After all, in her dream, the body had been in The Bake Shoppe's kitchen, not in her bedroom or somewhere else in the house. And he'd been beaten with the rolling pin. While she did have a rolling pin in the house, it wasn't a big heavy one like the marble rolling pin she had lost and that had been in the dream. Whoever wielded it as a weapon would need a lot of strength to do the kind of damage that Don Inglethorpe had suffered.

"Here come the others," Terry advised.

It was a moment before Erin could hear the other vehicles, but then she heard them pull up to the house, one of them behind and another one in front. Terry coordinated the approach and they cleared the front and back yards and checked the doors to the garage and Vic's apartment before Terry knocked on the front door. Vic hadn't come out of her apartment, so Erin assumed that she had been told to wait there.

Erin went to the door and opened it. She fell into Terry's arms.

"Thank you so much for coming. I was so scared." She felt his arms go around her and hold her tight. Everything on his utility belt was jabbing into her stomach and body, but Erin didn't care. For the first few minutes, she just wanted to be held and to know that he was safe and so was she.

"I had a dream," she murmured into his chest. "I dreamed that you were hurt…"

"I'm fine, Erin. You didn't call me because of a dream, did you? You said that someone was outside? Someone called you?"

"I don't know who it was. They used a voice changer. You can try to trace the caller, right? It said unknown, though, so it was blocked. I just don't know if you'll be able to find out who it was."

"Well, let's get all of the facts established first. Can I come in?"

Erin gave a little laugh and stepped back. "Yes, of course, come in."

They entered and sat down on the couch. Erin cuddled up to Terry's warm, strong body, looking for comfort. Jeremy reluctantly joined them, ducking his head low at Terry's questioning look. Terry looked at Erin, kissing the top of her head. "I suppose we should also get Vic in here? Does she know what's going on?"

"She doesn't know what happened. I just called you."

"But she knows that Jeremy is here?"

Erin swallowed and nodded.

"Am I the only one who didn't know about this?"

"No," Erin protested. "Vic and I are the only ones who know. Not anyone else."

"How long?"

"Wednesday."

"He's been staying with you since last Wednesday?"

"Yes. Wednesday night."

Erin felt like a child caught with her hand in the cookie jar. And one that she knew very well she wasn't supposed to be sticking her hand into. But she had gone and done it anyway.

She had lied to him and hidden things from him. How would he be able to trust her again?

CHAPTER 29

*T*erry clicked his radio. "Bring Vic into the house."

There was a brief acknowledgment from Tom, and in a few minutes, he was leading Vic into the house in her nightgown and house-coat. Vic's eyes were wide and worried. "What happened? Is everybody okay?" Her eyes went to Jeremy, but she didn't know what to expect.

"Everyone is okay," Terry confirmed. "There was a threatening phone call, and Erin called me. Exactly what I would expect her to do. Unlike lying to me about Jeremy living at the house. How long did you think you were going to be able to keep that charade going?"

"I've been looking for a place of my own," Jeremy said. "I wasn't plan-ning on staying here forever. Just for a few days. The lies are my fault. I asked them to please not let anyone know that I was staying here. I was worried… I wanted to keep it a secret."

"They had their own free will. They didn't have to agree to any terms or conditions they didn't want to."

"I wouldn't turn my own brother out," Vic protested.

"If he dictated terms that you were weren't willing to comply with, you would not have let him stay."

Vic looked for a way around that argument, her face getting red. "It's my fault too," she told him. "Erin wouldn't have agreed to keep it a secret if I hadn't asked her to."

"I think Erin is fully capable of making her own choices," Terry said slowly. "She's a big girl. She has a mind of her own—as we all know."

Erin felt her own face getting hot. The way that he said it, it was hard not to automatically fight back. But he had every right to be bitter and disappointed in her. She had chosen someone else's wishes over telling him the full truth.

"So this is why..." Terry started out. He looked at Erin. She felt tears springing up to her eyes and wanted to tell him that what he was thinking was not true. She hadn't just suggested that they go out to a movie and then to his house because she was trying to distract him and lead him away from Jeremy.

"This is... why I didn't want you staying over," she admitted. "Why I said we should go to your place instead. Because I wanted privacy."

"Jeremy would have given us privacy," Terry said. "It was more than that."

He was obviously hurt. Erin couldn't think of what to say to make it better. Terry's face was frozen like a mask. He looked at Jeremy. "I think you're the one we need to hear from. You're the one who knows what's going on here. Why exactly did you want to stay here and why didn't you want anyone to know about it?"

"I'm trying to find my own way," Jeremy said, sticking to the story he had told Vic and Erin. "I just needed somewhere to crash while I figured out what to do with my life. I need to get my own place... and a job... There's a lot to do before you can really get established independently."

Terry rolled his eyes. "What a load of crap. No one has to hide out because they're looking for a new job. Try again."

Erin had been feeling much the same way. She was pleased that she was finally going to hear the real story. She was proud of Terry for also recognizing that the story Jeremy was telling them didn't make sense. There had to be more to it.

Jeremy sat there, his hands folded, staring down at them.

"I do want to get out. I do want to get out on my own and be my own person."

Terry nodded and waited. The silence grew out uncomfortably long. Vic did her best to coax Jeremy on. "Come on, Jer. We're your friends. Tell us what's going on."

"Things at home..." he darted a glance at Vic. "Things haven't been good."

"Why? What happened?"

"It's just that... now that we're all getting older, we're supposed to be getting more responsible... taking more on... being better contributors."

Erin nodded. "That makes sense."

"Only... that didn't mean just taking on more chores at the farm. The farm hasn't been operating at full potential for a long time."

"What?"

"We still farm some," Jeremy explained. "But the money that we make from the farm... That's mostly just for show. You know: 'This is how we make a living. Nothing suspicious about that, is there?'"

"Who would you say that to? The police?"

Jeremy hesitated, then nodded. "Yeah. It was all for show... for the cops... any authorities who came around to make sure that everything was kosher. And Dad still loves the farm and likes taking care of the horses and other animals, and planting crops, and all of that stuff that..." Jeremy shrugged uncomfortably, "all the other stuff that we all really hate doing, because it's so dang boring."

Vic nodded slowly. "I know it can be boring... but I thought you still did it. Daniel and Joseph... they aren't running the farm? They aren't taking over from Pa?"

"They'll take it over, but the farm isn't ever going to be what it used to be. It's just an excuse now. A front."

"A front for what?" Terry asked.

"I guess you probably got that figured out already. A front for the Jackson clan."

"You're going to have to be more clear about that," Terry said slowly. "Tell me what kind of operations they're running that your farm is covering for?"

"The farm isn't covering everything, It's just a little part of the picture."

"Which is?"

Jeremy swallowed and looked at Vic. "I'm not really ready to start talking about everything the clan is doing. I'm not sure I'll ever be ready for that. Not unless I want to get myself killed."

"What were you expected to do? If you were not running the farm anymore, but were expected to take on more responsibility, then what are we talking about?"

"Uh... whatever they asked... whatever they thought we could handle..." Jeremy gave an uncomfortable shrug. "I used to think that it was all a pretty good deal. We didn't have to do anything much, but we got all of these perks from the clan. Money. Admiration. Whatever we wanted, really. We could go out and party and pretend for the girls that we were gangsters, and the clan would cover the drinks and the venue and whatever else... we could be the big fish. It was all a pretty good deal."

"Until they actually expected you to start paying dues. You were in debt to them and you had to do what they wanted."

"Yeah... pretty much."

"You were expected to do what you were told and not to argue about it."

Jeremy nodded. "Suddenly everything went from not doing anything, and getting whatever we wanted to... 'you owe us big after all we've done for you.' And without the farm to support us, how are we going to take care of Mom... what are they going to do to survive, now that all of that income from the farm has disappeared? If we even wanted to keep the farm, then we had to do some jobs... you need to hurt someone or make something right... take care of any little problems... and I don't..." Jeremy's voice choked up and he had difficulty going on. Erin felt tears in her own eyes. Jeremy was just a kid. Barely older than Vic. Barely an adult. But they had a tight grip on him, and they weren't letting go.

"So I thought... I'd come out here and stay with Vic. Make sure she was okay. She's the only other family I've got... or the only family that I feel like I can trust who isn't under the clan's thumb... and so Vic and Erin said I could stay here in the house or with Vic. There was more space here, so that's what I did. I didn't think anyone would really care. No one would follow me."

"But it sounds like tonight, they did." Terry looked down at Erin. "What did they say to you on the phone? Did they say it was about Jeremy? Did they threaten you or him?"

"They said I should send him outside to talk to them. That he was a traitor and I should just send him out and they would take care of it."

"Did they threaten you?"

"I..." Erin was having trouble recalling exactly what had been said. "I really don't know. They wanted me to send Jeremy out. They knew him by name. They knew he was here."

"And you told them no? Did you ask them who they were? Why they wanted Jeremy?"

"No, I don't think so. I'd just woken up from a nightmare and I was kind of freaked out. I was trying to calm myself down when the phone rang. I just didn't know what to do, except to call you."

"It was the right thing to do," Terry said. "I'm glad you didn't hesitate to bring me into it once you knew there was danger." His mouth was a long, thin line, completely serious with no hint of dimple or good humor. "I wish you had trusted me before this, but…"

"I trusted you. Jeremy asked us to keep you out of it, not to tell anyone that he was here, so… I agreed to do that. I'm sorry. I didn't want to keep anything from you, and I didn't want to mislead you about anything, I just did what Jeremy asked me to. I thought it would just be for a day or two, and then everything would go back to normal again."

"Do you think there *was* someone outside the house, or do you think it was just a threat? Was it to flush him out?"

"I… I didn't doubt that there was someone outside waiting for him."

"Did you hear any vehicles leaving? Did anyone pass by your windows in either direction?"

"I… I didn't hear anything," Erin said uncertainly. She looked at Jeremy. "Did you?"

"No, I didn't hear any engine… if they had a vehicle, it must have been a block away, out of earshot, and they didn't gun it out of here. I suspect that when Erin hung up on them, they knew what was happening and quietly left."

"You hung up on them?" Terry asked, his mouth quirking up slightly.

Erin nodded. "Well… I guess I did. I didn't see any point in letting them threaten me. They had their say and I wanted you to come and… take care of it. And I wanted to make sure that you were okay, and my dream wasn't real."

His look had softened a little. "What exactly was it that you dreamt?"

Erin thought for a moment about whether she could tell him about it, and then shook her head. "Just a dream," she said. "I guess I must have been thinking about Don Inglethorpe when I went to bed, and my brain changed that into thinking it was about you." She swallowed. He could figure it out from there.

"I'm sorry, Erin. You know… you might want to reconsider seeing someone… I know you said you don't want to, but sometimes it's for the best. We all need help sometimes. If you were on the police force, there would be mandatory counseling. It's not weak to need help working through something."

"I'm working through it my own way."

"I think your brain is trying to work through it… but you could maybe speed the process along if you were willing to take it a step further."

"Weren't we talking about Jeremy?"

Terry conceded and turned his attention back to Jeremy. "So what made you decide to come to Bald Eagle Falls?"

"I told you. I wanted to be with Vic. I knew she'd put me up for a few days while I figured out what to do."

"Except that meant that you could be traced. If you had just left town and gone for parts unknown, you would be a lot less traceable than if you stay here with your sister. Anyone could follow your trail here. And with all of the new activity in town… the timing seems just a little suspicious. If you wanted to get away from the clans, then why would you put yourself right into the middle of the playing field?"

"I just… wanted to get away, and to make sure Vic was okay."

"We've got all kinds of out-of-town representatives hanging around, causing trouble." Terry leaned back, looking at Jeremy as if he were one of them. "We've got drug dealers and enforcers and we've got other people who seem totally unconnected, but I sure wouldn't bet the farm that they aren't clan… It's all connected, somehow."

"I wouldn't have come here if I thought it would put Vic in danger. Or Erin. I'm sorry. I didn't think I was important enough for anyone to care about."

Terry let it go. "Who do you think came for you tonight?"

CHAPTER 30

*J*eremy's face was an unreadable mask. In an instant, all of the caring and animation was gone from his face and he was like stone. "I don't know."

"You must have some idea. Who would they send after you?"

"I hardly know anyone that active in the organization. Everybody my age was just like me... taking part in the benefits without really doing anything to earn it. So, I don't know who they'd send."

Vic bit her lip and looked at Jeremy. "Did the others know where you were going?"

"No. I just told you that. No one else knew where I was going."

"I don't mean the bosses in the clan, I mean... the family. Joseph and Daniel. Did they know? Did Pa?"

Jeremy shook his head. "No. I didn't tell them where I was going. I just got on a bus and left. There wasn't anyone to say goodbye to. I just packed my bag."

"But your family knows about Vic living here. So they could probably figure out that if you needed a place to stay, this is where you would come."

Vic and Jeremy looked at each other. Vic nodded slowly. Jeremy still denied it, but Erin could see it was more out of fear than belief. Had he been betrayed by his own brothers? Had they just told someone where

Jeremy might have gone, or had one of them actually been waiting outside the house for Jeremy? Or could it be their pa? Erin hated to even consider the possibility.

"Regardless of why Jeremy came or who else might be in Bald Eagle Falls, what are we going to do now?" Erin asked. "How are we going to keep Jeremy safe? People are after him. It doesn't matter if it's somebody in the family or someone more distant. What do we do next?"

Vic looked at Terry. Terry sat there, saying nothing, considering the question.

"You're not responsible for me," Jeremy said quietly. "I got myself into this mess, I'm the one who is responsible for getting out of it. Not you. There's no need for anyone else to jump in and help me."

"Of course there is. You're here. You're family and you need somewhere safe," Erin told him.

"I'll leave town. I can't stay here and make you or Vic a target."

"I don't want you leaving town," Terry said. "Not before I can establish whether you're involved in anything that's going on. If I have to, I'll take you into custody."

"You can't do that!"

"Not forever, but maybe a couple of days will give me time to sort things out and figure out what to do with you. Do you have any outstanding warrants for the work you've been doing for the clan?"

Jeremy's face tightened. "No."

"You're sure?"

"Go ahead and check."

"I will."

"There has to be somewhere Jeremy could stay that no one would think to find him," Vic said. "What about with Adele?"

Erin grimaced. "I don't think that would be a good place for him. The summer house only has one bed and an open plan, so neither of them would have any privacy. We don't know whether Rudolph is staying with Adele..."

Terry frowned. "Why would her ex be staying with her?"

"He's not an ex," Erin reminded him. "They're still married."

"Doesn't mean he has to stay with her. After all of the dramatics earlier, why would she allow him to stay with her? In a one-room home with no privacy?"

Erin and Vic exchanged glances. "They met at the restaurant. Like you suggested, a public meeting…" Erin started.

Terry nodded, encouraging her to go on.

"We happened to be there for supper too…"

"Happened to be."

"We wanted to make sure everything was okay, that he didn't get abusive with her."

His eyes were narrow. "And how did he behave?"

"They seemed to get along together really well. Holding hands, eye contact, deep conversation… that's why I say, he could be staying there. I know she said she wouldn't take him back, but a lot of women say that, and then they do. Even when it's a really bad relationship. She said he came to get back together with her, and it looked like he was getting on pretty well."

Terry shook his head. "I didn't get a good vibe from the guy."

"Did you run a police check on him? Does he have any police history?"

"Fraud and theft. Nothing violent, no drugs."

"And he doesn't have any connection to the clans?"

"None immediately apparent."

"What about treasure hunting?"

Terry frowned. K9 shifted his position and let out a loud sigh, expressing his displeasure with having to lie in one place for so long. Terry patted his side.

"Why are you asking about treasure hunters?"

"Just because of Beaver… Rohilda…"

"I thought you said you were staying out of trouble."

"I am. I haven't done anything. We just met her at the restaurant. She was evasive about what it was that she did, so we looked her up."

"You need to stay out of it!"

Erin was surprised and hurt at the snap in Terry's voice. She swallowed and turned away from him, looking for Orange Blossom. The cat was watching her from the hallways, ears pricked forward while he watched K9. Erin smacked her lips to call him, but he paid her no attention.

"It's not Erin's fault," Vic said. "Beaver really did just walk up to us and invite herself to our table. And I was the one who said we should look her up. I didn't think it could hurt anything to look her up on the internet to see what it really was that she did. I figured she was just winding us up."

"And you think that people who want to hide who they are put it on the internet?"

"No," Vic's voice took on a belligerence Erin had rarely heard in her. "I figured if she was really someone dangerous, we wouldn't find anything online. How does us looking her up damage your investigation? We haven't interfered with anything!"

"You need to stay away from these strangers and just keep your head down. You shouldn't be doing anything that will attract attention to you. You made yourselves obvious at the restaurant. That will make people ask questions about you. When they find out who you are and your histories…"

Erin did have a reputation for having put more than one person in jail for crimes committed in Bald Eagle Falls. And Vic had, under her previous identity, been part of the Jackson family. Someone who, like Jeremy, might have benefited from clan activities and be expected to prove her loyalty and do something in return. If Beaver or someone else who had seen them at the restaurant had thought they were acting suspiciously and started asking questions, they might decide that Erin and Vic were getting too close to their secrets and had to be eliminated.

"I'm sorry," Erin said. "I didn't realize…"

"You know it's dangerous in Bald Eagle Falls right now. You were the one Charley told about it. If *she's* scared, don't you think you should be too? Don't you think maybe you'd better stay out of the way?"

Erin looked over at Vic. "Why *did* she come over to us? People don't just invite themselves to other people's dinners."

Vic frowned. Her arms were folded across her chest and she had adopted a very aggressive posture. Having her brother threatened and Erin called out by Terry brought out her protective mama-bear streak.

"It wasn't anything we did. She just looked around while she was waiting to be seated and saw us. So she came over and asked if she could join us."

"But why?" Terry asked. "How obvious was it that you were there to watch Adele and Rudolph?"

"Well… it might have been obvious."

Terry looked at his watch. "I'm going to check out the summer house as soon as we're sure everything is secure here."

"Aren't you already sure of that?" Erin asked, the anxiety that had waned since his arrival already building back up in her chest at his words.

"The sheriff was just going to check out the garage and the loft to make sure everything is safe."

"The loft?" Vic demanded. "I didn't give you permission to search my apartment."

"We don't need your permission to search the loft," Terry said evenly. "We have reason to believe that there may be a dangerous person on the property. Criminal threats have been made. We need to assure ourselves that there is no further threat. It's our duty to protect the citizenry."

"But there wasn't anyone in my apartment. I was there, so I know it's clear. You don't need to search it."

"It's procedure. It won't take long. Then you can go back to bed if you like."

"I don't want anyone searching my apartment."

Erin looked at Vic, not understanding the irritation in her voice. "They're not going to mess with anything. They're just making sure it's safe."

"I don't like having my privacy interrupted. And I don't like my civil rights being violated."

Terry's voice was calm and even. "No one is violating your civil rights. Yes, you have a right to privacy, but you give up some portion of that right in a case like this."

"It won't be long," Erin repeated, wishing she could say something else to make Vic feel better. But she couldn't understand why Vic wouldn't want her apartment to be cleared just like the rest of the property.

"You're going to stay here for the rest of the night?" Erin asked Jeremy. "You won't be able to find anywhere else tonight."

"I don't know if that's a good idea," Terry said with a frown. "Whoever called is going to know that he hasn't left. They could come right back, and with no warning this time."

"I'd rather someone else was here with me. And Jeremy shouldn't have to find somewhere else in the middle of the night."

"We can provide Jeremy with somewhere for the rest of the night."

"What, sleeping at the police department?"

"I'm not sleeping in a cell," Jeremy interrupted. "I didn't do anything wrong. I might have done something stupid, but I didn't do anything wrong."

"You can sleep on Sheriff Wilmot's couch with a blanket and pillow," Terry said. "We don't even have a holding cell. So just cool it."

"Okay," Jeremy gave a little shrug. "Sorry, but I'm a little sensitive…"

Erin still didn't want Jeremy to have to leave the house in the middle of the night. And she'd sat on that couch; she remembered how uncomfortable it was. He'd be better off sleeping on the floor.

CHAPTER 31

om stuck his head in the door. He nodded to Terry. "Sheriff said to let you know it's all clear."

"Great. Vic, if you want to go back to your apartment, you can. Or if you'd like to stay here with Erin, I'm sure she wouldn't mind. Jeremy, I think, should come with me. I don't want him drawing unwanted attention to you girls."

"I can handle it," Vic said, patting her side.

Erin frowned, studying her. "You have a holster on under that housecoat?"

"You really should too. Especially when stuff like this keeps happening!"

"It doesn't *keep* happening, this is the only time..." Erin trailed off. It wasn't the first time she'd had to call Terry to the house to take care of an intruder. And it wasn't the first time someone had threatened her or someone in her home. She didn't like Vic sounding like it was something that happened all the time, but she also couldn't deny that it wasn't the first time they'd had to make an emergency call in the middle of the night.

"If it makes you feel better, I'll call Willie," Vic suggested to Terry.

"Well, yes, I'd feel better if I knew he was here."

"You think the poor women can't look after themselves?"

"Let's just call it a southern gentleman looking after the ladies," Terry said, and he gave Erin a little squeeze. "I'm just old-fashioned that way."

161

Vic snorted. "Good way to hide your chauvinism."

"Give him a call. I want to head over to Adele's to make sure everything is good over there."

"Go ahead. You heard what the sheriff said, it's all clear, and he and Tom are still here to defend the helpless ladies. You don't have to wait until Willie gets here."

"And *I'm* still here," Jeremy pointed out, gesturing to himself.

"No offense," Terry said, "but I know Vic, and I suspect she handles a gun just as well, if not better than you do. What I'd like is someone with a bit more muscle and experience, and that's what Willie's got."

"I can shoot—" Jeremy started to protest. Then he met Vic's eyes and faltered. "Okay, she can shoot better than I can. But two guns are still better than one."

"Are you armed?" Terry hadn't done a pat-down of Jeremy or Erin when he had come in. They had been completely focused on the outside threat.

Jeremy's hand dropped and Terry went stiff. He was off the couch and onto his feet before Erin realized what was happening.

"Hands up!" he ordered Jeremy. "Keep them away from any weapon!"

"I'm the one who told you—" Jeremy raised his hands in the air slowly, moving with caution.

"Just be still. What have you got?"

"Handgun in a back holster."

Terry lifted Jeremy's shirt to reveal it and then removed it carefully from the holster.

"What else?"

"That's all."

"What else, Jeremy?"

"I just got out of bed. What makes you think I'm sleeping with my guns on?"

"Hands on the wall."

Jeremy obeyed, grumbling to himself. Terry put his hand on Jeremy's back, holding him still.

"Now, are you going to tell me, or you want to get it automatically confiscated because you're lying to an officer?"

"I'm not."

Terry started to pat Jeremy down, his fingers firm and deliberate.

"Ankle," Jeremy admitted, before Terry got down past his waist.

Terry continued his careful pat-down, until he reached Jeremy's ankles. He lifted Jeremy's pajama pant leg to see the other holster, holding a second small gun. Terry removed that one too.

"And is that it?"

"You know that's all there is. You would have found anything else." Jeremy's voice was sullen, almost a pout.

Terry looked at Vic. "You know he was carrying concealed weapons?"

Vic licked her lips and shook her head, looking at her brother. "No. I didn't know."

"You have a concealed carry permit?" Terry asked Jeremy.

"Not exactly."

"Then you're not supposed to be walking around like this, are you?"

"I'm in my own home. Sort of. Not out in public. You can't arrest me for having a gun in my own house."

"You'd be surprised what I can do. I'm going to go over to Adele's to make sure everything is okay over there, and then I'm going to be back here. I'll take you to the police station for the rest of the night, however long that ends up being, and the girls can go back to sleep." He looked at his watch. "For a couple of hours, anyway. You might want to open the bakery late today. Give your bodies long enough to rest and recover."

Erin nodded her agreement, but she knew she wouldn't. She would still get up at the regular time and open the bakery on time, even if it meant that she only got two hours of sleep all night. She wasn't going to let the bad stuff going on around Bald Eagle Falls be a detriment to her business.

"I'll see you in a while then," Terry told them all. Hearing the finality in his master's voice, K9 got up and stood at the ready. Terry kept both of Jeremy's guns.

"You can't take those," Jeremy protested.

"We'll see about that. I'm not leaving them with you right now, anyway." He walked out the door. Erin could see him hand the guns to Tom and saw him make a motion toward the house, leaving him with instructions.

Erin waited until Terry was in his car and on his way before pulling out her phone and dialing.

It took a few rings for Adele to answer the phone. She didn't sound tired when she answered, but then, she was usually up late and slept later in the morning than Erin.

"Erin? Is something wrong?"

"We had a bit of trouble over here. I wanted to call and give you a heads-up that Terry's on his way over. Just to make sure that everything is okay with you. He got it into his head that somebody might make trouble for you, so he's going to head over there and have a look around."

"Right now?"

"He's on his way." Erin expected Adele to hang up, but Adele stayed on the phone.

"You are all okay?"

"We're fine. There was a threat, but nothing came of it. I think we'll be just fine for the rest of the night. Terry just wants to make sure everything is kosher."

Erin could hear the smile in Adele's voice. "If he's looking for kosher, then he maybe shouldn't be looking for it with a Wiccan."

"Ha. Right. Well, he'll come make sure it's… whatever you would say."

"I think that's him now," Adele said. Erin couldn't hear the noise of the car approaching. She waited. Adele spoke to someone else. "We've got a visit from the police."

"Police?" Rudolph's voice was thick with sleep or maybe with drink. "What are the police doing here?"

"Just doing a check. Don't be a pain. Don't cause trouble."

There was a knock at the door. Adele answered it. "Officer Piper. Come in."

"Mrs. Windsor." Erin kept waiting for Adele to hang up the phone, but she kept the line open and Erin could hear most of what was going on. "And Mr. Windsor."

"What are you doing here?"

"There's been some trouble at your landlord's house. I'm just checking to make sure that no one ended up out here. People will be trying to get out of town, and I wouldn't want them thinking they could hijack your ride or steal your money."

"No one is going to do anything to me," Rudolph growled. "I can take care of myself, thank you."

"Never hurts to have the police around to make sure everything is peaceful. I'm sure you'd rather not have any trouble."

"Well," Rudolph's voice was still belligerent, "you can see that everything is fine here. So you can get on your way."

"Can I talk to you for a moment, Mrs. Windsor?" Terry asked, ignoring her husband's rancor.

There was a pause, Adele considering the request. Then she made a murmur of acknowledgment and Erin could hear them both moving, then heard the bang of the door and the gentle whistle of the night breeze across the phone mic.

"What else can I do for you, Officer Piper?"

"I just wanted to talk to you about your husband. I was surprised to find him out here. Are you... is he here with your permission? No coercion? You don't mind him being here?"

"Yes, Officer. No need for concern."

"Okay. I just wondered because earlier... you were trying to avoid him."

"And I told you I shouldn't have done that. These things are better dealt with face-to-face than trying to avoid contact. It's fine. Don't worry about it."

"You haven't seen anyone out here tonight?"

"No sign of anyone."

"I'm going to take a look around. Just make sure there's no unusual activity."

"I'm not sure how you're going to find anyone in the dark."

"I have a flashlight."

Erin looked out her own window. She didn't know how much difference it was going to make. Anyone would be able to see the beam of the flashlight before it reached them, and move out of its way if they didn't want to be seen.

Erin heard the rustle of footsteps. Adele brought the phone back up to her face. "Everything is fine. Your officer will take a few minutes to look around and then he'll be back to you. Alright?"

"Thanks," Erin said. "I'm glad everything is okay."

Before Adele hung up, Erin heard Rudolph growl at Adele one more time.

∾

Before Terry could get back from Adele's, Erin heard another approaching engine. A big engine, like a truck. It approached at a fairly high speed and screeched to a stop close by. Erin tensed up, unsure what she was going to be facing. Someone who had decided they could take on the last two cops in the police department and didn't have to wait for anyone or anything? The bad guy, come back to take Jeremy this time without any hesitation or negotiation?

But then she heard a voice greet the sheriff and she settled down, recognizing the familiar rumble. Willie was in the door a few minutes later.

"What's going on?" he demanded. "What happened?"

Vic hurried over to him to give him a big hug. "Not much time for talk," she said. "Everybody's okay, but people know Jeremy is here and we need to protect him. Terry wants to take him into custody and make him sleep at the police department."

"That doesn't sound like a whole lot of fun," Willie said. "I can tell you from experience that their facilities are not exactly the Ritz."

Erin wondered when Willie had had the opportunity to enjoy the police department's hospitality.

Willie looked at Jeremy. "Jeremy. How long have you been here?"

"A few days."

"I should have guessed that something was up. So, what do you need?"

"We need to put him somewhere no one is going to find him," Vic said. She looked Willie in the eye. "We can do that, right?"

Willie nodded. "Sure. I know of places."

Vic made a hurrying motion to Jeremy. "Go with him. Before Terry gets back."

Jeremy and Willie looked at each other, then left together. Vic looked at Erin. "You don't know where they went," she said firmly.

"Well... no, I don't."

Vic nodded. She gave a big sigh and rolled her eyes. "What a night." Erin was sitting alone on the couch, so Vic sat down beside her and gave her a sisterly hug. "How about you, are you okay?"

"I am right now... whether I'm going to fall apart in another hour when the adrenaline wears off, I don't know."

"I hear you," Vic agreed.

Erin looked at her young assistant. Despite the fact that Vic claimed to understand, Erin didn't know if she really did. She wasn't the one who had seen Inglethorpe dead and bloody. She wasn't the one getting crazy calls in the middle of the night.

"Are you going to be able to get back to sleep after all of this?"

"I don't know," Vic looked at the wall. "A little too late to be taking sleeping pills. What about you?"

"I don't think so."

"Then after everyone is gone, why don't we just throw a movie on, and we'll veg and watch it. It will be more relaxing than tossing and turning or having nightmares all night. How does that sound to you?"

Erin nodded. "Yeah. That sounds good." It would help her to relax just knowing that she didn't have to try to sleep. And if either or both of them did fall asleep, that would be just fine.

CHAPTER 32

hey both had bloodshot eyes at the bakery the next morning. Erin took a break from the baking to hold an ice pack over her eyes to try to disguise them. It was best if the customers didn't know that they had been up all night.

It soon became obvious that even though the incident had taken place late at night and the police had not used any sirens, everyone knew something had happened at Clementine's house. Again.

Even Charley, when she stopped by in the afternoon, was up on the gossip. She wasn't a fully accepted member of the Bald Eagle Falls community, but she was still attached to the grapevine.

"Are you going to tell me what happened last night?" she demanded from Erin, as if Erin had been trying to keep a big secret from her.

"Not much to tell," Erin said with a shrug. "We just got a phone call, I was a little worried about it, so I called Terry... everything ended up being okay. Nothing happened."

Charley learned in. "Come on, give me the real scoop!" she insisted. "That's just what you tell everyone else. I want to know the sister's inside scoop."

"The only scoops we have are ice cream," Erin pointed to the cold case. "You pick out your flavor, and I'll give you a scoop. Two, even."

"Erin! Come on, don't be a tease. I'm worried about you."

168

Erin had a pretty good idea that Charley wasn't asking because of her deep concern over her half-sister, but due to her own curiosity and wanting to know what was going on with the clans in Bald Eagle Falls.

"We got a threat," Erin said. "Sort of a threat." Because she couldn't remember exactly what the voice had said to her. Had he threatened her at all? "So I called Terry. When he got there, whoever had made the threat was gone. End of story. Terry spent a bunch of time looking around, and Vic and I sat up watching movies because we were too hyped up to go back to sleep after the visit from the police."

"You don't look like you slept."

"Well, that would be why.'" Erin studied Charley critically. "You're actually not looking like you got a whole lot of sleep yourself. Are you okay?"

For a moment, Charley gave her a deer-in-the-headlights look, and then she managed to mask it. "I sleep just fine in this Podunk little town. Why wouldn't I?"

Erin wasn't so sure of that. "You weren't feeling too well the other day."

"I'd just had a bit much to drink. I'm sorry I bothered you. Sometimes… a story needs to be told. That one kind of got away from me. I didn't mean to bother you and your sweetheart with my tales of woe."

"You *can* talk to me about Bobby," Erin said. "It sounds like you're really missing him."

"What's to tell? If he was still alive, we'd be together. But we're not. I don't have what it takes to do a memorial or something for him. I just wish… that I could have the chance to mourn him. But that's not the way things work in this life, is it? We all have to keep on living, even if someone we love dies. Life goes on. There's no point in making a tragedy out of it."

"It was tragic. You loved him and you must really miss him."

"You know what else I miss?" Charley asked.

"What?"

"Being in the know. It used to be, I pretty much knew everything that was going on. Top level stuff. Anything important, I knew about it. I knew where Bobby was and what his plans were, even if they were just to go out on the town and have drinks with his buddies. I knew what the Dysons were doing and what my place was and what I was supposed to be doing."

"Did you know they were interested in Bald Eagle Falls and were planning on coming over here?"

"No. No one had hardly even heard of Bald Eagle Falls. Nothing ever happened here, so why would anyone care about it?"

"But they do now."

"Yeah, my wonderful sister attracted their attention. And I moved here, and I guess they caught up with everything else. Now, it's the place to be. Everyone wants a piece of the pie."

Erin saw cherry pie in her mind's eye. When was she going to stop conjuring it up out of thin air?

"What pie?" she asked. "What exactly is it they're trying to do? Cook and sell drugs? I can't imagine there's that much of a market out here."

"If there's a big enough market to support you on baking, then there's enough for a drug trade."

"But I'm sure... not that many people would buy drugs."

"No. But they'll pay a lot more for dope than they will for sugar. Sugar may be a gateway drug, but it's not going to put a lot of cold hard cash in your hands. Drugs, on the other hand..."

Erin remembered her dream. The part of the dream where she had seen the flour on the floor of the bakery, and Vic had told her it wasn't flour. Or maybe it had been Charley. Had Charley been in that dream as the other baker?

"But you didn't... I mean you don't... You're not looking to get in on the drug trade, right? You wanted to run the bakery, not a front for the drug trade."

"My plan was to have a legitimate business," Charley agreed. "But it looks like that's a dream, now. No one is going to let me open the bakery, which means I'm just going to go further and further in debt until I can get a job that pays more than the grocery store does. And where am I going to get that, other than going back to crime? Man, Erin. You're so lucky. You just fell into this whole thing. I feel like it's all just such a mess. Everything I touch turns to dust. I might as well not even try."

"I wish you wouldn't give up. Isn't there any way to talk the trustees into letting you open it up? Just even on a trial basis?" Even as she encouraged Charley, she felt a stab of anxiety. She wanted her sister to succeed, but not at the expense of Auntie Clem's.

"No. They're not going to do it. They're too afraid of the negative press about people dying there. Pretty soon, everybody will think that just setting foot inside the door could be enough to get someone killed."

"That's ridiculous."

"Yeah, but we're talking about people who still practically believe in fairy tales. These aren't rational human beings. They're superstitious. They believe all of it. They might say that they don't, but they totally do."

"I know they're superstitious, but believe me, they all want The Bake Shoppe to open again." Erin let out a sigh. It was true; she could see it whenever she looked at her church ladies. They told her how much they wanted Erin to succeed and how good her baking was, but they made no secret of the fact that they missed The Bake Shoppe and that if they could, they would just buy regular food at the regular bakery. They didn't want gluten-free baking and other specialty baking. No one except for Erin and the few who need gluten-free or other special diets.

"You and me," Charley sighed. "It seems like one of us has to fail while the other succeeds."

"Yeah."

"I always hoped that we could be like the brothers in that story."

"What?"

Charley grinned. "There's this story about these two brothers, and they ran competing businesses. I forget what they were supposed to be, but their shops were right next to each other, and they had this vicious rivalry going on for their whole lives."

"Okay."

"Well, after they both died, when people went in to take care of all of their personal effects and to sell the stores, they found out that there was a tunnel between the two stores. The two brothers had really been devoted to each other and had spent all of their time together in the evenings. The rivalry had all been for show."

"Why would they do that?"

"I guess people thought they were getting a good deal, because the rivalry kept the prices honest. Or they liked the drama or liked to gossip about them. Whatever it was... it was the magic ingredient in their businesses..."

Erin shook her head. "Funny story. I think I might have heard it before. It *would* be fun if our stores were side by side and connected by a tunnel." But then, Charley drove Erin crazy, too. If Charley had been back and forth to Erin's house and business twenty-four hours a day, Erin might just do something she'd regret.

"There are supposed to be tunnels between some of these buildings," Charley offered.

"What? In Bald Eagle Falls?"

"Yeah, you know, dating back to civil war, or something. People who needed to hide or to escape. They could slip through the underground tunnels and stay safe. Or maybe it was just a way to get around without having to face the Tennessee heat!"

"Which buildings were supposed to have tunnels?"

"I don't know. Most of them, I think. So people had somewhere to go that was safe. It's kind of fun to imagine."

"There isn't any tunnel in my basement."

Charley shook her head. "Mine either. I checked! If there is any tunnel down there, it's been bricked over so no one can access it."

Erin thought of the bricks that lined a couple of the walls of her basement. Not the whole basement, just a couple of walls. Had those walls been made differently because they were built at a different time? Was there something to hide or had they just shored up a crumbling wall?

Like Charley had said, it was fun to imagine. But that's all it was, just make-believe.

Charley looked over the baked goods and picked out a hand-shaped loaf of multigrain bread and a couple of cookies. When she left and Erin looked around to see the rest of her customers, she saw Rohilda Beaven standing nearby, her expression thoughtful.

Mary Lou approached the counter. She seemed like she was in better spirits than she had been lately. Maybe things were going better for her little family. Erin didn't want to inquire too closely, in case it made Mary Lou uncomfortable, but she was glad to see her friend in better spirits.

"I think maybe we'll have a pizza night," Mary Lou pronounced, looking into the display case. "I don't know when the last time was that Josh and I just had a fun, mother-son time together. Things have been so stressful the last couple of years..." A shadow passed over her face. "I don't want to lose him. He's only going to be home a couple more years and I want to make sure we maintain a good relationship."

Erin nodded. She pointed at the pizza shells. "You want the herbed crust? Or the one with cheese baked in?"

"The herbed looks very nice. And I don't think it's too... uh, highbrow for a teenager, is it? I don't want to look like I think we can't let down our guards and enjoy ourselves."

"I don't think it's too high-brow," Erin said. "Pizza is pizza. You're just going to cover it up anyway. He'll like it."

Mary Lou nodded. "It's a deal, then." She looked over at Vic as Erin packaged the pizza shells up for her. "And how are you, Victoria? Enjoying your brother being in town?"

Vic froze, mouth open, hand hovering over the cash register as she moved to enter Mary Lou's purchases.

"Uh... what?" she eventually managed.

"I saw your brother the other day. Tall boy, long blond hair?"

Vic nodded slowly. "I didn't think he'd been out at all. Where did you see him?"

Mary Lou frowned. "Oh, you would ask me that, wouldn't you? It was just casual, I didn't stop to talk to him, so I'm not sure even what day it was... I think I saw him over at the business center? I assumed he was seeing a lawyer, maybe for your folks. But I really don't know who he was visiting over there. There are a lot of different offices he could have been at."

"Yes, that must be it," Vic agreed. If she had continued to question Mary Lou about the meeting, she would draw attention to it, and that was not what she wanted to do. Why would Jeremy tell them that they had to keep his visit under the radar, and then go out during the day where anyone could see and recognize him? "It's been nice to have a little visit with him. I don't see my family often enough."

"No," Mary Lou agreed. "I imagine you'd see them more if you lived the values that you had been raised with."

Erin gave Mary Lou a warning look. If she were going to go any further along that vein, she was going to get herself thrown out of Auntie Clem's. Erin didn't allow any harassment of her employees.

"Anything for dessert?" Erin prompted.

"No, with just the two of us, I have plenty in the freezer still."

Vic rang up the purchase and completed the transaction. Mary Lou smiled politely and wished them both a good day before leaving the store. Vic looked over at Erin, her eyes wide.

"Why would he have been where people could see him?" Erin demanded. "I thought he didn't want anyone to know he was here!"

"I don't know. It's bizarre. Maybe he did have to see a lawyer or do some business over there."

"But if it were me... and I wanted to stay unseen... I'd ask them to come to my house. Or to see them after hours. I wouldn't just go out in the middle of the day when anyone could have seen me."

"Maybe she saw someone else and just thought it was Jeremy."

"No... who else is she going to see that she could mistake for him? How many young men do you know of in Bald Eagle Falls who wear their hair long like Jeremy's?"

"Well... I don't know about at the high school. Some of the teenagers have less conservative styles."

"But who is going to mistake Jeremy for a teenager?"

"I just don't know." Vic shook her head anxiously. "They might. I don't understand what's going on here."

"Where did Willie hide him?"

Vic looked quickly at her. "Don't talk about it. I don't want anyone to overhear and figure it out."

Erin thought of how Beaver had been standing so close, listening to everything that was being said when Charley was there earlier. She had been very stealthy. Erin hadn't even seen her come in. She had just been lurking there, listening in on the gossip. A treasure hunter? Was that all she was? Someone who thought she could line her pockets with a quick job? Read some old blueprints, poke around, and find the secret lost treasure of...

"Erin."

Erin snapped to attention, looking at Vic. "Sorry! Lost in thought."

"I said I don't actually know where Willie hid the you-know-what." It took Erin an extra second to remember that Vic was talking about Jeremy, not some buried Confederate gold. "I figured the fewer people who know, the better. I can hardly slip up and give it away if I don't really even know."

"Yeah, good plan. I'm sure he knows lots of good hiding places."

Willie was a kind of a treasure hunter himself, at least as one of his lives. He was the type who could never have his finger in just one pie. His mining was a kind of treasure-hunting, and he knew a lot of the natural caves and tunnels that went through the mountain.

"Terry was not too pleased that Jeremy took off," Erin commented.

"Uh, no. I don't think pleased is the word I would use." Vic gave an impish grin. "Holy cow. You would have thought that Tom had let the crown jewels walk out the door while he was on watch. Tom did the right thing. He didn't have any reason to stop Jeremy. He wasn't under arrest. He could come and go as he liked."

"Terry would have found some reason to take him in, I think."

"Probably. But luckily, Tom is not Terry."

Erin wiped down the top of the counter and then went around the display case with her cloth to wipe away children's fingerprints and nose prints from the other side of the glass. "You don't think there are really any tunnels between the old buildings, do you? Or lost treasures?"

"I would say no, that it was just a silly fairy tale… except that every few years, something like that turns up. Someone actually does find a treasure or a secret tunnel that was used for smuggling during the war. Just when you think you know what's real and what's not, something like that will come and knock you off your feet, and then for weeks after, you're second-guessing everything you've ever heard."

"Hmm." Erin buffed the surface of the glass lightly to bring out the shine. "So, you think that's really why Beaver is here? She really is looking for old gold? Some Confederate payroll or pirate booty? It just doesn't seem like she's the type of person who would be hunting that kind of thing. She seems to be so… I don't know…"

"I still don't know just what Beaver is and what she's up to. I do know that I don't like her hanging around here eavesdropping on conversations."

CHAPTER 33

*E*rin descended the back stairs to grab another bag of buckwheat flour. There was a noise ahead of her that made her freeze for a moment on the stairs, listening for more and trying to identify what she had heard. Maybe she had just been hearing something from the bakery overhead. Vic had put something down on the floor, and the sound had carried through the joists, echoing to make it sound like it had originated downstairs instead of upstairs. Erin resumed her descent, holding on to the handrail for balance as she strained her ears for another sound. She reached the bottom of the stairs.

"Anyone down here?"

She listened, but there was no response.

Going down to the basement still gave her a twinge of anxiety now and then, since that was where Angela had expired, and Erin had been the one to discover her body. Even though she knew it wasn't her fault and that nothing like that would ever happen again, she couldn't help feeling a pall every time she went downstairs. Not something she would *ever* tell Bella.

The basement consisted of both the tiny public restroom for customers and the storeroom stocked with dry goods. She hadn't ever had any problem with customers going into the "employee only" area, but maybe she should put a locking door on the storeroom just to be sure. Especially with so many undesirables in town.

The door to the commode was slightly open, but the room was dark, the light switch turned off. Erin turned the other direction and looked around the storeroom, watching and listening for movement. There was no one there. It had to have been a noise from upstairs. Erin took one more look for anything that was out of place. She couldn't see anything wrong, but had an unsettling feeling that things had been moved.

She hefted the large bag of buckwheat flour and took one more look around.

"It's fine," she murmured. "Everything looks just the same as always."

As she went by one of the brick-faced walls, she couldn't resist thumping it, listening for a hollow echo or feeling for some give indicating that it was a false wall, maybe on a swivel so it opened like a doorway to let her into some long-forgotten passageway like a scene out of Scooby-Doo. But it felt like a solid wall, just like she had always assumed.

She climbed the stairs back to the kitchen.

"Everything okay up here?" she asked casually before putting down the bag of flour.

Vic didn't answer. Erin let the bag land on the floor with a little thump. She looked up, but Vic wasn't there.

"Vicky?"

Erin walked out to the front of the shop, expecting to see Vic wiping out the display case or clearing the cash register. But there was no one there. Erin looked around, surprised, then returned to the kitchen. Vic had probably just taken the garbage out. She glanced toward the back door. It was not quite shut tight. Vic would return in a moment.

Erin waited. She measured out the flour for the various batters that needed to sit overnight. When Vic got back, Erin could tell her about her paranoia over something happening in the basement and they would laugh about it.

After a few minutes, Erin started to get worried. She went to the back door and called out toward the dumpsters in the alley.

"Vic? Everything okay?"

There was no answer. Erin stood there in the doorway, watching and listening. Vic was sure to come around the dumpster and see her standing there waiting any second. Maybe she had put her earbuds in and was listening to music or was on a call, so she hadn't heard Erin.

But as the seconds ticked away, she knew something was wrong.

"Vic? Vicky, are you there…?"

The night was quiet. She could hear the occasional car making its way down the nearby streets, but nothing unusual. Erin stepped out of the safety of the bakery and walked, her heart in her throat, to the dumpster. There was no one around. Erin looked around. Had someone interrupted Vic while she was emptying the garbage? Someone had called her and she'd gone to talk? But there was no one in sight.

No one at all.

CHAPTER 34

S tay where you are, Erin, I'll be right there," Terry advised. "Did you try calling her on the phone?"

"No." Erin patted her pockets for her phone. That was a good idea. Wherever Vic was, she would have her phone on her. "I'll try that." Her pockets were empty, and frustration boiled over. "I can't find my phone! I don't know where I left it!" She scanned the counter for it. Had she left it in the basement?

"Erin."

"What?"

"You need to just calm down. You're talking to me on your phone, so stop looking for it. I'm going to hang up so you can try her. I'll be there in two minutes."

"Oh." Tears sprang unexpectedly to Erin's eyes. "Right. Okay. See you in a minute."

She ended the call and hit the shortcut for Vic's number.

"Come on, Vic. Answer the phone."

But the phone just kept ringing until it went to voicemail. Erin stared down at the phone in disbelief.

"Come on!"

"Erin?"

Erin looked up and saw Willie standing in the back door. She breathed out a sigh of relief.

"Willie! Vic must be with you!"

He shook his head. "No, I just came to pick her up."

"But..."

"We were supposed to go out tonight. Isn't she here?"

"No. She was... and I went downstairs to get some flour, and when I came up, she was gone."

"What do you mean, she was gone? Where did she say she was going?"

"She didn't say she was going anywhere. She just wasn't here anymore."

"That doesn't make any sense." Willie looked around, his eyes worried, as if she might just appear.

The front door bells jangled, making Erin jump. She whirled around and looked out through the doorway to the front to see Terry walking in with K9. She blinked at him in surprise. "Did you pick the lock? How did you get in?"

"It was unlocked."

"No, it wasn't. I'd already locked it for the night and turned the sign over."

Terry looked back at the door. "The sign is flipped over, but maybe you got interrupted before you locked it. Is that when you realized Vic was gone?"

"No. I locked it before I went downstairs. I haven't been back out to the front since then."

"Let me and K9 have a look around."

Terry walked through the main floor of the bakery and didn't appear to see anything amiss. He went down to the basement, taking the back stairs down and then the front stairs up.

"Everything is quiet. No sign of anyone else here. Just... no Vic."

"I don't understand it." Erin's voice was too high and strident. "I just went downstairs!"

"She can't have gone far. You called me right away, right?"

"Yes. It was just a few minutes... I came up and I thought she was outside for a minute... but she never came back in."

"I want you to think about what you heard while you were downstairs," Terry said calmly. "Were there any voices? Could you hear her moving anything around? Doors opening?"

"I thought I heard something downstairs. But there couldn't be anyone downstairs, so I thought Vic must have put something down or knocked something over in the kitchen, and it just sounded like it was downstairs."

"What did it sound like?"

Erin tried to replay it in her mind. "Like... somebody brushed by something in the storeroom. Like they were wearing or carrying something metal that dinged off of a shelf support. Not loud. Just... it was out of place, because I knew there couldn't be anyone down there."

"But there could have been."

"I'd already locked up, so no one could get in the front. The customers had all gone. It was just me and Vic."

"But you don't track everyone coming in and going out. You wouldn't necessarily know if someone went down to the loo and didn't come back up again."

"That couldn't happen again."

"It could. You can't watch everybody at the same time. You have your own jobs to do, and so does Vic. You trust people to go down to the restroom and come back up again without any direction or supervision."

"But I went down there, and there was no one there."

"Not that you saw," Terry agreed, "but the front door was unlocked."

Erin deflated. "If the front door was unlocked, that means someone unlocked it and went out that way after I had locked up. I was on the back stairway, so they used the other and got out. But I didn't see anyone down there."

"Would you have seen someone going up the stairs when you were going down the others?"

"No... but if the noise I heard was in the storeroom, like I thought, then they didn't have time to get to the other stairs."

"What about the restroom? Did you check inside?"

"Yes. It was empty."

"You checked? You went in?" Terry persisted.

"I... I looked in the door. It was cracked open. The bathroom was dark... so I didn't go in."

"So someone could have hidden there until you got your flour and went back up, then they just went up the stairs at the same time as you did."

"But that doesn't explain what happened to Vic. If someone was downstairs, what happened upstairs? Where did she go?"

~

Everybody was called in. Once again, the Bald Eagle Falls police force was stretched to its limit trying to help Erin. She felt guilty at having called them in yet again, but what else was she supposed to do? She couldn't just ignore Vic's disappearance.

Terry walked around the outside of the building with K9 before anyone else could get there and mess up the scent trails. When he came back, Erin raised her eyebrows hopefully, but he shook his head. "Nothing, sorry. He's not a scent dog, but I was hoping he might be interested in something that would give us a clue... but he just sniffed around a bit in the back parking lot and didn't find anything."

"If somebody was here... Vic might have gotten into a vehicle there, and K9 couldn't follow her scent any farther than that."

"Yeah, it's possible. This whole thing... it's unbelievable. For her to just disappear into thin air like that!"

"She didn't disappear into thin air. Somebody took her. Somebody else was in the bakery, and they took her."

"Whoever was in the basement went out the front door. They wouldn't take Vic out that way. People would see and would know something was wrong."

"Then there were more than one of them. Someone went out the front door, maybe to keep a lookout, and someone else came in the back while I was still downstairs, to take her away. I can't believe that she didn't scream or fight or something."

"They must have caught her off guard. Might have covered her mouth or gagged her. Or hit her over the head or even drugged her. There's no telling. But we know that she wouldn't leave without telling you where she was going or leave Willie in the lurch when they had plans. Vic's just not irresponsible like that."

"No. She'd never do that."

"What if it was Jeremy? If he came here and told her she had to go with him right away, but she had to be quiet and not say anything to anyone, would she do it?"

Erin ran the scenario through her mind. She knew how much Vic loved her family, even if most of them had disowned her. She loved Jeremy even more for being the one member of her family who supported her. If he was in trouble and needed her help and said to be quiet and not talk to anyone… she would have done it in a minute. Erin sighed.

"Yes. If it had been Jeremy… she would have done it."

"So scenario one is that she's with Jeremy. Do you know if she had any contact with him after Willie took off with him yesterday?"

"No, not as far as I know."

"She didn't even talk on the phone with him, text him?"

"No… she was working all day. We took our breaks, but she was just visiting and eating during our breaks. Not on her phone."

"Can you remember what she was wearing?"

Erin did her best to remember Vic's outfit that day, but it was a challenge. They wore aprons and hats and Erin didn't really notice what was on underneath. There had been days when she'd gone home only to find that she'd been wearing mismatched shoes all day.

"Nothing unusual happened today? You didn't… see anything when you went downstairs or out to the dumpster? You didn't smell anything out of place?"

Terry knew Erin's sensitive nose. She closed her eyes and breathed in and tried to remember. Any soap or cologne? Body odor? Some other smell that shouldn't be there?

"No. I can't think of anything downstairs. Just… dust. Concrete. Nothing really out of place."

"Okay. That's fine. There isn't always anything to smell."

"Are we going to call people in to do a search? Like when Roger disappeared?"

"No. When Roger disappeared, we knew he was wandering, and the best bet was to get a lot of people out looking for him. But this… it's different. She probably didn't go under her own power. She isn't just wandering around somewhere. She's locked away somewhere, and we don't know where."

It was an impossible task. Erin didn't even know where to start. She didn't even know what to put at the top of her list.

"Let's talk to Willie," Terry said. "He could have the key."

Erin knew that Terry had already tried to talk to Willie about it once. But Willie was stubborn. He wanted to find Vic, but he wasn't about to break any confidences to do it.

"Vic wouldn't want me to tell anyone where Jeremy is," he told Terry bullishly.

"What if Jeremy came here to get her? She would have gone with him. Where would they have gone?"

"He isn't the one who took her away."

"You don't know that."

"I do. It wasn't Jeremy. It was someone else."

Erin rubbed her forehead. "Who would take her? You've got to help, Willie, you have to have some idea. Didn't she tell you... something that was bothering her? Something she was thinking of doing? An idea she had about things that were going on in Bald Eagle Falls?"

"You girls talk way more than Vickie and I do. You know her every thought. I'm just the guy she hangs out with occasionally when her mean old boss gives her a few minutes off."

Erin gave him a wan smile. "I should give her more time off. She should have more time to spend with her friends and family."

"No" Willie put a warm hand on Erin's arm. "It was a joke. That's not what I'm saying at all. Vic loves her job. She loves working here and earning her own paycheck. It's the best thing for her."

"Who would take her? I don't understand why anyone would take Vic."

Willie shook his head. "I don't know... it could be to get to one of us, or to get to Jeremy. We don't know until they tell us."

"But what if they don't tell us? What if they just did it... to keep Vic quiet about something? Or to punish someone? Or because... I don't know, a random attack? Then what good is sitting around here waiting for someone to tell us going to do? They might have already... done something to her. I can't stand to think of it."

It wasn't like Erin needed much imagination to think about what Vic might be going through. She had been taken before, and so had Bella. It was like Erin had a curse. Everyone around her was attacked or kidnapped. But she hadn't done anything! She hadn't been asking questions and getting people upset. She had just been in the bakery, doing her job. It wasn't fair. Especially not to Vic.

"We're not just sitting around waiting," Willie promised. "I'm not going to sit around, and Terry and the police department are not just sitting around. We're going to figure out what happened. We're going to dig down to the heart of it and we're going to find Vic."

Erin nodded, a tear running out of the corner of her eye and down her nose, to dangle precariously at the end. Erin wiped impatiently at it. Crying wasn't going to do any good. It was time for actions. Or at least for lists.

"All the stuff that's been going on in town... is it all connected? It has to be, right? But I can't make it all fit together."

"All of what things?" Terry asked. "Which things in particular are you trying to connect?"

"Well..." Erin sniffled, "first of all, all the new people hanging around town. Are they all related to each other? To the clan war over Bald Eagle Falls?"

Terry grimaced. "I wish I could answer that one. There have been representatives from both the Jacksons and the Dysons, as well as some hoods that we can only assume are from smaller organizations. Drug dealers and other lowlifes trying to ply their trade..."

"Like Bo Biggles," Erin contributed.

Terry's eyes narrowed at her. "Yes. Like him. He's not the only one hanging around, but he's been one of the most visible. I've done my best to run them out of town, but they're all digging in their heels. It isn't easy. I've been talking to the feds about getting a task force in here to deal with things before they get too bad, but they're not inclined to actually do anything until there have been more deaths, or at least some blood on the ground."

Erin remembered the red pool of blood around Inglethorpe and felt nauseated. Terry must have seen a change in her pallor. He gripped her by the elbow. "Whoa, now. Hang in there."

"I'm okay."

He didn't let go. "You sure?"

Erin swayed slightly. Maybe it was a good thing if he continued to hold on to her, just for a few minutes. "Go on. Inglethorpe's death isn't enough? Why do they have to wait?"

"Because they want proof that we really do have a situation here. Something that needs their intervention. It has to warrant the amount they have to spend on it, which is a pretty penny. So I get where they're coming from... but on the other hand, I think we've given them some pretty convincing evidence of what's going on here and they could just take it at face value and come."

Erin nodded. "So... Don Inglethorpe... you do think he was part of the clan war?"

"I'm convinced he was… I'm not entirely sure how, but it's just too much of a coincidence that he died right at the onset of a gang war over Bald Eagle Falls. I don't think that it was Charley or anyone who was jealous or angry about a court case he had screwed up. He was seen arguing with a man and a woman the day before he died. Outsiders, not Bald Eagle Falls residents. I can only assume that they were clan and he was either arguing that he didn't want to be involved in whatever they were doing… or asking for a bigger cut."

"What do you think they wanted him to do?"

"He's a lawyer, so your guess is as good as mine. Set up some fraudulent corporate structure? Money laundering? Some other kind of fraud? I have no idea."

"He was killed at the bakery."

Terry's eyes stopped moving around and he looked at her for a moment. "Yes. He was killed at the bakery. If he wasn't there to meet Charley, and she wasn't the one who killed him, then why was he there?"

"Were the people who were arguing with Inglethorpe Bo Biggles and Rohilda Beaven?"

"What makes you think that?"

"I don't know. Just the way that they had that accident on Main Street… I'm sure they knew each other. I don't think it was any accident. So if they were both from out of town, and knew each other, I thought maybe they were the man and woman who were arguing with Inglethorpe."

Terry nodded. "I can't really get into that investigation in any detail. But if it were Biggles and Beaver, what would that tell you? How would that help us to find Vic?"

"If we know who it is, then we know better where to look. Right now… I have no idea where to look. I don't know why she was taken or where they would have taken her."

"I've called in the Staties to put up some road blocks, in case they're not out of town yet. There are too many backwoods roads to stop everyone leaving Bald Eagle Falls, but we can at least put roadblocks on the main highways. We could get lucky if someone tries to smuggle her out of town."

At least he was doing something. With every second that ticked by, Erin grew more anxious.

"But they're not the only ones who are new in town. There's also Adele's husband…"

Terry nodded. Willie looked at him. "You think he could be involved somehow?"

"It's hard to nail the guy down, he's a pretty slippery fish. He's been involved in a lot of fraudulent activity in the past… He's mostly a loner, or works a scam with one or two other people. Does that mean that he's not involved with any of the locals? Not necessarily. It's a small world, especially when you're looking at criminals. They all meet each other sooner or later. So, he could be related. He says he's just here to see Adele, and she confirms that, but you know you can't trust the guy."

"So probably a weasel," Willie said, "just not our weasel."

Terry laughed. "Exactly."

"And what about… Jeremy?" Erin was afraid to voice the question. She wouldn't have said it in front of Vic. She wouldn't have ever gossiped about him with Willie or anyone else. But she knew that he was involved in the clans and it seemed highly unlikely that he hadn't known something was going down in Bald Eagle Falls before arriving. He knew what was going on, or he had been sent and had been conducting business the whole time he'd been there.

Willie and Terry both looked at her, then exchanged glances with each other. All of them knew that Jeremy had to be a suspect, but none of them wanted to admit it. Erin had put it into words. Could he be at the center of the trouble? The person who had killed Don Inglethorpe?

"Mary Lou said that she'd seen him around town. But he was supposed to be staying in Clementine's room and keeping his head down. So that's another thing that doesn't add up."

"Do you believe that he just came to see Vic and stay with her?"

Erin shook her head. "Why would he say he didn't want the police around if he was just there to be with us? He was hiding from someone. And that someone tried to get him out of there last night. He eludes them, and then Vic is taken…"

"Jeremy has to be mixed up in this."

Terry looked at Willie, but Willie again shook his head. "Jeremy is right where I left him. And I'm not going to lead the bad guys right to his doorstep. We need to hang back and look around, see who is left."

"The one guy that we know for sure is involved from the Jackson clan is Bo Biggles. So I guess I go haul his butt in and lean on him until he talks."

Erin couldn't restrain a nervous giggle. "I've never heard you talk like that before."

"I don't normally have to get all Kojak in a case, but this one is getting on my nerves. Every time I turn around, there are clan connections, but nothing to arrest them for. That's what they're counting on. That we won't be able to get them on anything until they are thoroughly entrenched. Then it will be like picking burs out of a dog's fur."

"What should I do?" Erin asked. Terry was going to lean on Bo Biggles, but that left her alone. No Vic, no Jeremy, no Terry. She wouldn't have anything to do while she sat around waiting to see if Terry's interrogations produced any fruit.

"Go home and wait there. I don't want you in the way. That means you're not asking questions and not trying to track down Vic, you're just waiting for the police to do their job. Understand?"

"I'm not going to mess it up. I just... don't know what to do with myself while I'm waiting."

He gave her a brief hug. "You'll find something. Bake a cake. Make a list. Call your sister."

"Okay."

~

Willie followed Erin home in his truck to make sure that she got home safely and there was no one lying in wait there. He took a look around the outside of the house before letting her approach, then once she opened the door and disarmed the alarm, walked through the house, just to be sure.

"Last thing we need is you disappearing too. You call if you're worried about anything. If you get a call or you think there's someone around, anything at all, okay?"

Erin nodded.

"You should call someone. Don't sit here by yourself going crazy. You need someone to help hold things together."

Erin considered the advice. He was probably right. She was feeling very vulnerable about not being with Terry and not having Vic's support. With everything else that had happened in Bald Eagle Falls, she'd always had a friend to rely on. But with Vic gone, Erin had no one to fill that void. She wasn't going to pick her sister, in spite of Terry's advice. Charley just wasn't on the same wavelength as Erin, and would wind her up instead of helping to calm her down.

Adele, though… Erin had always found the tall, slim redhead to be a stabilizing influence. Even when everyone else was in a panic, Adele would stay calm and not get hysterical or blame Erin for being afraid.

"Okay. I'll give Adele a call."

"Good. Make sure it's her before you open the door. I don't want you disappearing too."

"Where are you going?"

It was strange that he wasn't helping Terry, but if all Terry was doing was interrogating a suspect, Willie couldn't very well help with that. And staying home waiting for a phone call wasn't going to get him any closer to the answers.

"I'm going to drive around… I've lived in Bald Eagle Falls for a lot of years, and I'm hoping I'll be able to get a feeling for what's out of place or who is not behaving the way they should…"

"You don't think it's Bo Biggles?"

"I know who the guy is. I'm sure he is wrapped up in it all somehow. But is he the one who took Vic?" Willie waited a few beats, and Erin wasn't sure whether he was expecting her to fill something in or was just thinking about it. Finally, he shook his head. "If he took her, then it was under orders. I can't see him doing something like that on his own. If he's involved, then maybe Terry can get something out of him. If we're lucky."

Willie took one more look around the house to make sure that everything was okay, then said goodbye and headed out. Erin wanted to stay at the door and see him off, but he wanted her to be inside with the door locked to be sure she was safe. So she locked it as soon as he was out and watched the truck drive away.

"Good luck, Willie. Please find some sign of her."

After the truck was gone, Erin sat down on the couch, scooping Orange Blossom to nestle in her arms. She juggled out her phone and dialed Adele's number.

It rang a few times, though looking at her watch, Erin wasn't sure why. Adele was usually quite active in the evening, stopping by Erin's shop if she needed something for the next few days, running any other errands, and then up throughout the evening and night for whatever it was she did.

Gathering herbs, praying, communing with nature, and any of the other things she valued.

"Hi, Erin."

"Adele! Are you busy, or could you come over? Something has happened…"

"What? What's happened?"

"It's Vic. She's… missing. I don't know what to do."

"Call the police! Don't wait around. What happened? Were you supposed to meet up? Wasn't she working today?"

"We were both working today. I went downstairs to get some flour, and when I got back upstairs, she was gone. Just like that. No sign of her."

"Willie didn't pick her up?"

"He's out looking right now. I mean, not looking for her, because if she was out there, we'd be able to find her, but looking around to see what's not right, you know?"

"You need to get the police onto it too."

"They are. Terry knows. Everyone has been brought in. They've looked around the bakery, and Terry is going to… question some people who might be involved."

"Where are you?"

"I'm at home."

"I'll be right over."

"Are you sure? I don't want to put you out if you had other plans tonight."

Adele didn't answer immediately. One thing that Adele never did was answer a question quickly. She thought about it, composed her answer, and then thought about it some more. "Do you really think that I wouldn't drop everything for you and Vic?"

Erin felt her face flush. "Well… okay. I just don't want to put you out."

"Don't be silly. I'll be exactly where I need to be."

Erin breathed a big sigh of relief after she hung up the phone. She looked around the room, trying to figure out what to do while waiting for Adele. She could change into her pajamas, but then if Terry found something and suggested they go out somewhere, she wanted to be be prepared. She could make herself a sandwich, but she really wasn't hungry. She could sit down and make a list, but she wasn't sure what to work on. Something for Vic, to help find her? Or one of her regular lists, with her plans for the next day on it? She was going to have to go into work, and what if Vic hadn't been found and couldn't be there? It was inconceivable that she would have to work with her best friend and colleague still missing.

The doorbell rang a few minutes later, and Erin went to get it, surprised that Adele had gotten there so quickly.

She went to the door and opened it, but there was no one there. Erin looked around, frowning. Why ring the doorbell and then run away? Unless it hadn't been Adele, but someone that didn't want her to see them.

Looking down, Erin saw a small cardboard box, and her heart sank. She wasn't sure what she was going to be facing, but she had a pretty good idea she wasn't going to like it.

CHAPTER 35

When Adele did arrive, some time later, Erin just stared at her, her whole body numb, with no idea what to say.

"Erin?" Adele moved closer to her. "Erin, the door was open. Are you okay? You really do need to lock it, especially with all of this stuff going on."

Erin just stared back at her.

"Erin, what's the matter?" Adele looked at Erin's face, then looked down at the package in her lap. "What's that?"

"That's... the end."

"The end of what?"

"The end of everything," Erin said flatly.

She should have known, when she had first come to town, that it would happen. It was too good to be true. Sooner or later, it was all going to come crashing down, she was going to lose what she had, and she would be out on the street again, on her own, with no way to support herself or place to sleep at night.

Because that's how it was for Erin. Anything else was just a pleasant interlude. It had been nice to live in Bald Eagle Falls, to bake at Auntie Clem's Bakery and think that she had a chance to make something of herself. But it had all been superficial. When the time came, it was just all over.

Adele sat down next to Erin and touched the box. "Can I see?"

Erin didn't stop her. She didn't offer the box to Adele. Adele tentatively slid it out of Erin's hands. Erin didn't look down at it. She already knew what it said. She already knew her life at Bald Eagle Falls was over.

Adele opened the box and teased out the piece of paper, holding it by the very corner in case it was evidence.

If you ever want to see James Jackson again, leave Bald Eagle Falls for good. Take nothing with you, just get out of town.

Adele frowned, looking down at it. "James Jackson?"

"Vic."

"Oh. I see. So you think this person has her?"

Erin nodded.

"Have you called Officer Piper to show it to him?"

Erin shook her head.

"You should. He can help you sort it out."

"There's nothing to sort out. I have to leave."

"You can't just leave Bald Eagle Falls."

Erin lifted her shoulders in a hopeless shrug. "How could I do anything else? Vic needs me. They'll kill her."

Adele looked down at the paper. There was no threat to kill Vic, but they did use 'ever again' which suggested that they might do something drastic if Erin didn't follow their instructions.

"What am I going to do with the animals?" Erin asked.

Her chest hurt. She could hardly think, but she knew that she needed to leave, and if she wasn't allowed to take anything with her, then that included the animals. She couldn't take her adored furry friends with her. She couldn't just turn them over to Doc to try to find homes for them. There just weren't enough families in Bald Eagle Falls who would take in a couple of stray animals and keep them safe as indoor pets. If he found anyone, she was sure they would just be turned loose in someone's back yard to come and go, and it wouldn't be long before they disappeared. That was the way it was with outdoor animals in a small rural community.

"Don't worry about the animals," Adele said, putting her hand over Erin's. "If you had to leave, I could take them."

"They'd drive you crazy in that little tiny cottage."

"We'd work it out."

"Then I should go. The longer I think about it, the harder it's going to be."

"Erin. Call Officer Piper."

Erin stared at Adele for a long time before finally nodding. "Alright. I will." She patted her pockets until she found her phone, and looked at it for a minute before she could remember how to turn it on and call Terry.

"Erin?" He answered almost right away. "Any word?"

His question cut Erin to the heart. It told her immediately that he wasn't making any headway. Her only hope was to do as the note said, and to hope that the note-writer did as he said he would and let her see Vic again.

"No... I... I got a note."

"What kind of a note? From Vic?"

"No. From someone else. I guess whoever has her. It says if I want to see her again, I have to leave Bald Eagle Falls. I have to leave forever."

"What? What are you talking about?"

"The note says that I need to leave and not take anything with me."

"And then what?"

"I guess... they'll let Vic live."

"Erin! Who delivered the note? Where did it come from? Are you home?"

"Yes, I'm home. I called Adele to come sit with me, because I didn't want to be alone. I thought it was her when the doorbell rang. But it wasn't. It was... someone else. Someone who left a package, with a note."

"A package? What's in the package?"

Erin looked at the box that Adele was holding. "I don't think there's anything else in it. Just the note that I have to leave town." Erin let out a long breath. Her heart rate was starting to return to normal. "Adele said that I should call you."

"Of course you should call me. You know that. I don't know what to do, Erin. We're still looking for Biggles. I don't have a clue where he's gone to ground. We're not getting anything from our usual sources. I don't know whether to stay here, or..." He made a decision, his voice changing. "I'll come to you. It's evidence. I need to see it with my own eyes and take it into evidence. Maybe the note will sound like someone and I'll know who wrote it."

"You don't think it's Bo Biggles?"

"I don't like to say, but... I don't think he has what it would take to pull off a kidnapping like this. And dropping off the note with you while we were looking for him… I just don't see him doing this."

"How well do you know him?"

"Not well. Not well enough to say no for certain… but I'll come over there. We'll get it sorted out. Once I look at the note… we'll know what it is that we're supposed to do next."

"Okay."

"Hang in there. I'll be right there. Have Adele make you some tea."

"I don't want tea."

But Terry had hung up and was no longer on the line. Erin lowered her phone to her lap.

"Tea?" Adele repeated.

"Terry said to get you to make some tea. But… I don't really want anything. I should get going."

"Not before he gets here. Just wait."

Erin reached over and picked up Orange Blossom, who was snoozing on the couch nearby. He startled and made a sleepy noise, looked to see who had picked him up, and started purring his loud, thrumming purr. Erin scratched his ears and patted him. She'd rescued him when he was just a starving, homeless kitten, and she was going to have to let him go to someone else. Someone else who wouldn't have nearly the same ideas about how to care for a cat as she did.

"Just stay put and let me get you something. Have you had any supper?" Adele asked.

Erin shook her head. "No."

"You need to get something in you. You can't be expected to make any kind of decision without having had something to eat."

Erin remained on the couch, staring forward, unfocused, while Adele looked through the fridge and cupboards to see what was available. By the time Terry got there, Adele was handing Erin a sandwich and a cup of tea.

"It isn't much, but you need to get something inside you. This is better than nothing."

"Terry…" Erin bumped away Adele's hands with the food offering and stood up, falling into Terry's arms just like she had done before. Was she ever going to develop any relationships that would last more than a year or two? She had thought that Bald Eagle Falls was her place. The place she would be able to make her own and live for the rest of her life. "Terry, I don't understand what's going on. Why would they take Vic? What does it have to do with me? What did I do? What do I know or have that they would care about?"

"We don't know that. There's no way for us to know." He looked at the package on the coffee table. "Is that it? Can I see it please?"

Adele nudged it toward him. "I'm sorry, both of us have handled it. I tried to only touch the edges of the note."

Terry took it out carefully, like Adele had. He read it over quickly out loud.

If you ever want to see James Jackson again, leave Bald Eagle Falls for good. Take nothing with you, just get out of town.

"Okay," Terry cracked his knuckles and considered the message. "Okay, it's not a lot to go on, but it gives us a little. First off, it calls Vic by her old name. So it's someone from her past."

"Or someone who doesn't know what she goes by now," Adele suggested.

"No, I don't think so," Erin said. "Anyone who knew she was here would know what she goes by. Much better than her dead name."

Terry looked startled. "Dead name?"

"That's what she calls it. It's a name and identity that's dead to her. That person doesn't exist anymore. Just Victoria. There is no more James."

Adele looked at Terry. "Do you think there's some significance to that?"

"To the fact that he calls her by something she calls her dead name? I certainly hope not. Just an unfortunate coincidence. It doesn't mean that she is dead or that he's threatening to kill her. There's nothing in this note that says what he will do if Erin doesn't do what she's told to. It's just an empty threat. We don't even have any evidence that the person who wrote this note has any idea where Vic is. It could just be someone who wants Erin to leave town."

"But who would want Erin to leave town? From what I've seen, she's got a lot of friends here. Even the people who might not consider her a friend... I don't see a lot of animosity toward her."

Erin thought about Charley. It would be an opportune time for Charley to get Erin out of the way. First try to frame her for murder. Then send a threatening note to try to get her to leave town. Then there would be no more competition in Bald Eagle Falls. How could the trustees turn down the opportunity to have the monopoly on baked goods in Bald Eagle Falls?

"I don't know… Everyone has been pretty good," she said, not voicing her thoughts.

"Let's keep analyzing the note," Terry said. "Probably someone who knew Vic, who shares a past with her."

"Someone who doesn't accept who she is," Erin suggested.

"Right. Could be an old friend, love interest, a family member, someone who feels betrayed by her changes and leaving town. Could that be all that it is? Someone who is jealous of Vic? It could be that it isn't even anything to do with the murder or the drug activities."

"Jealous how?" Erin demanded. "That's she's working with me? That she has a job? Because we're just friends, it's not like we're in a relationship."

"If it was *that* kind of jealousy, then I'd expect them to be targeting Willie."

"Have you talked to him? He said he was going to drive around, see if he could spot anything out of the ordinary."

"I haven't talked to him. I've been trying to track down Biggles. But he seems to have disappeared."

"Then he's got to be the one that has Vic," Erin said. "If he's the one person who we can't track down, then he must be the one who has Vic."

"There are too many people in Bald Eagle Falls for us to track them like that." Terry shook his head, scratching the back of his neck. "He's just the one person I thought might have some insight, and he happens to be out of touch. There could be a lot of other people who we can't reach right now, and a lot of different reasons for not being reachable."

"Is there anything else?" Erin bent her head to look at the words. "I don't recognize any expressions that anyone we know uses. It could be anyone."

"I'll put an APB out on Bo Biggles. If he's still around, we'll track him down. If he's left town… I'll go to the next thug on the list. We'll find Vic."

"And I should get ready to go," Erin said. "I should pack a bag and leave town."

Terry looked at Adele, then looked out the window. Erin could tell that he wanted to argue with her. He wanted to tell her, like Adele did, that everything was going to be fine and she should just stay around there until he managed to figure out where Vic was.

"I don't want you to go anywhere. But if you want to follow the instructions on the note and relocate for a couple of days until we have Vic back safe and sound, you're welcome to do that. I don't know if it will do any good. I don't know what it is these guys want. But I can have Tom watch the house and see if there's any suspicious activity after you leave."

Erin nodded. "I'm not sure where to go… but I have to try. If it can help Vic…"

"It's not going to help Vic," Adele disagreed. "Following the demands this guy or these people make just means you're caving in to the demands of a terrorist. It won't help Vic, and it won't help the next person who ends up in the same situation."

"It's up to you," Terry repeated. "But if you're going to leave… I wouldn't pack a bag. Tuck a few toiletries into your purse, but no suitcase or duffel bag."

"Why not?"

"Because he says to take nothing with you. If you want to appear to be obeying the instructions, you need to leave empty-handed. Or with no more than you would normally take out to the car."

"Right. Of course."

"Don't you think someone is going to snatch Erin as soon as she is out of sight?" Adele demanded.

"I don't know what's going to happen if she does what they tell her to. I suspect they just want her out of the way."

"But you can't know that."

"Of course not. But do you think I could stop her? Really?"

"You could put police protection on her."

"I can't put police protection on her, and watch the house and the bakery, and chase down Biggles and any witnesses or potential informants. We have a very small department. We can do more once we get some help from the feds, but until then, it's just the three of us, and we're stretched thin. Erin… if you go, you'll let me know where you're going to? And you'll let me know when you're safe?"

Erin nodded. She looked out the living room window and felt incredibly vulnerable. Who knew how many of them there were out there, and whether they had evil designs on her? She should have gotten a gun and learned how to use it, like Vic said. At least then, she would have some kind of protection going out on her own. But Vic had a gun, and that hadn't stopped her from being kidnapped and taken away. She hadn't even made a sound. She had just disappeared.

"I think you should go back to the bakery," Adele said suddenly.

Terry and Erin both turned and looked at her in surprise.

"Why?" Erin asked.

"If Vic was taken from there… there must be some kind of clue about who did it and where they took her. If someone wants Erin to leave, then they don't want her to go back to the bakery. There must be something there that she might accidentally unearth. Right?"

Erin shook her head. "We already looked all over for any sign of what happened to Vic. Me and Willie and the police, we all looked for anything… but there were no clues."

"But somebody doesn't want you to go back there."

Erin looked at Terry. "Well, should we go have a look, then? One more time? After that… I'll take off. We'll just check the bakery one more time."

He nodded. "Fine. I'll take you there on my way back to the police department. Are you coming along too, Adele?"

Adele surprised them all by saying yes. "One more set of eyes. Who knows, maybe I'll see something that both of you managed to miss."

Without a word, Erin picked up her purse and headed for the door. She couldn't let herself think about anything she was leaving behind. Only about Vic, out there somewhere, alone and vulnerable to some gangster.

CHAPTER 36

*W*hen she opened the door, she was startled to see a figure move away, trying to disappear into the shadows. But the streetlights were too bright, and the figure was too close to the house, as if she'd been sneaking close to look in the window.

"Wait!" Erin shouted. "Stop right there!"

Terry pushed past her to apprehend the subject. Erin knew who it was by the blond hair that flowed down her back.

"Stop right where you are, ma'am," Terry said warningly, holding K9's collar as he strained eagerly for release. "I'd like to talk to you."

Beaver turned her head, realizing that she'd been caught and there was no point in trying to pretend otherwise. She swung back around, her body loose and casual.

Adele came out of the house and stood beside Erin, watching.

"Officer Piper," Beaver greeted. "Fancy meeting you here. I would have thought that you had enough to investigate without stopping innocent people on the street. Don't you have a murder to investigate? And somebody said something about some kind of drug war?"

"What are you doing here?" Terry demanded. "You don't live around here."

"There's no law against me walking down the street, is there?"

"I'd like to know what you're up to. What are you doing lurking around Erin's house? Do you want to be arrested for trespass or loitering?"

"Nice try. You don't have anything on me. You'd better get on with whatever you were doing. Chasing after me is only going to slow you down."

"It seems to me that you know a little too much, Miss Beaven. Maybe you can explain that to me. What are you doing skulking around Erin's door?"

"I just thought… I was thinking I might ring the bell and chat. Erin was nice to me when we met at the restaurant and I was feeling a little lonely."

Terry got closer to her. "If you have nothing to hide, how about letting me see if you're carrying any weapons?"

"Weapons? Why would I be carrying around any weapons?"

"You want to prove that?"

Beaver eyed Terry and K9 thoughtfully. Eventually, she lifted up the edge of her jacket to reveal a gun holstered at her waist.

She continued to watch Terry with eyes narrowed like a cat's. Erin felt the knot in her stomach tighten. Was this why Beaver had approached her and Vic at the restaurant? Had they given something away when they had talked to her? Something that had gotten Vic kidnapped?

"Take it out and drop it on the ground," Terry instructed. "Do you have anything else?"

"I might have a throw-down in an ankle holster," Beaver admitted. "Would you expect me to have anything less?"

"What exactly does a treasure hunter need all of this weaponry for?"

"You'd be surprised about how emotional people can become while treasure hunting."

Terry let out a bark of laughter. "Oh, you think so, do you? After you drop that gun, I want you to take out the one in the ankle holster. Slowly, letting me see your hands at all times."

They were all quiet while Beaver obeyed Terry's instructions. Both guns were dropped on the pavement.

"Kick them away," Terry instructed.

"Here I thought you were going to forget that part."

"Any other weapons on you?"

Beaver lazily chewed on her gum, mouth wide and loose. "I guess that depends on what you'd call a weapon," she said finally.

"Any more guns?"

"No. No guns."

"What else, then? Knife? Taser? Pepper spray?"

"Yes."

"Which one?"

"All of the above."

They all stared at her. She had a hunter's jacket with all kinds of pockets on the outside, and probably the inside as well.

"Take off your coat and put it down," Terry instructed.

Beaver rolled her eyes and followed his instruction, moving slowly and keeping her hands in view as much as possible. She held the jacket at arm's length, then gave it a little toss to put some distance between it and her when it fell.

The halter-top she wore under the jacket didn't leave much to the imagination. Her body was lithe and tightly-muscled. Her movements were loose and fluid and had given the impression she was soft, but it was obvious just looking at her arms that there was nothing soft about her. Removing the jacket bared a sheath on her arm with the handle protruding. She had a tattoo on her arm, originally black, but old enough that it was starting to blue. Terry approached her, getting close enough to kick the laden jacket farther out of the way.

"Hands up."

Beaver raised her arms obediently. Terry gave K9 a command to sit and guard, and he obeyed, nose and ears pointed intently at Beaver.

Erin was anxious about the fact that Terry hadn't asked Beaver to remove the knife from the sheath. How quickly would she be able to pull it out and attack Terry if the mood struck? He seemed to care more about the tattoo than about the threat.

"You were Airborne?" he demanded.

Beaver gave a little shrug, very casual, as if it were nothing.

"Who are you with now?"

She started to smile, as if she were trying to suppress it but couldn't quite manage.

"You're investigating this? For what department?" Terry persisted.

"I'm afraid I'm not authorized to tell you anything, Officer Piper."

202

"But you are investigating it."

She just raised her eyebrows.

Terry looked at Beaver, considering. "What do you know about what has happened today? You know we had a kidnapping?"

"Unfortunately, I was in the wrong place when that went down... close by, but not close enough to see or hear what was happening. I was checking out... another possibility."

"And do you know about the note Erin was sent tonight?"

"Are you going to keep me standing here with my arms up all day?"

"Uh, no. Go ahead and put them down."

Beaver put her arms back down to her side, and for a moment everybody just stood there, considering the situation.

Despite Beaver not confirming that she was working for some federal department, Erin no longer felt threatened by her. While it was possible that someone ex-army would be involved in a drug war, she didn't get that feeling from Beaver, and obviously Terry didn't either.

"So?" Terry prompted. "Did you know that Erin got a delivery tonight?"

"I knew something was going on. But no, I don't know any details. What was it? What did the note say?"

Terry told her about the note. Beaver nodded, chewing her gum and considering the details thoughtfully.

"Do you know who it is?" Terry asked. "I haven't been able to track down Biggles tonight. It could be something to do with him."

"You've got people working on that? I can have mine look into it."

"Any help we can get at this point would be appreciated. I'm not getting anywhere very fast. We are a small-town police force and we haven't had any response from the federal agencies we've reached out to." Terry gave her a nod. "Except for you, I guess."

"I'll see if I can find anything out. But I haven't seen Biggles for a couple of days. I think he's pulled out."

"Then who has been sent in his place? Because the Jacksons aren't going to give in that easily. If they felt he was compromised and pulled him out, they would send someone else."

"That was my thought," Beaver agreed, giving nothing away with her casual, lazy expression.

"We were going to go back to the bakery. I don't know if we can find any clues there. I don't know how all of us could have missed anything, but we'll check, just in case."

"It's a good idea," she agreed. "Mind if I tag along? Just as an interested civilian. I wouldn't mind having a longer look around."

Terry looked at Beaver for a minute, weighing his answer, then nodded. "We'll all go together. But I expect you to behave like a civilian, and that means you do what you're told."

"Of course." Beaver looked past him to Erin. "Just like Erin always does what she's told."

Erin could feel Beaver laughing at her. Just how much did the woman know? Was she talking about the events that had occurred since Erin had moved back to Bald Eagle Falls, or did Beaver know even more than that, back into Erin's history?

Terry shook his head, obviously sensing that Beaver wasn't going to be quite as cooperative as she suggested.

"May I retrieve my gear?"

Terry hesitated, looking at the discarded guns and equipment jacket. He hadn't had Beaver's identity verified. She could be anyone. She could belong to one of the clans. But Terry had a pretty well-developed instinct.

"Yeah, go ahead," he agreed.

Beaver made quick work of gathering up the tools of her trade and shrugging back into the jacket.

~

At the bakery, Erin looked around, not sure what to expect. Everything looked just as she had left it, nothing out of place. It was just her bakery, feeling a little empty without Vic there to help her, even with Terry and K9, Adele, and Beaver there.

"Vic was up here, cleaning up and getting things ready for tomorrow. I went downstairs to get a bag of flour and I heard something down there."

"Your visitor bumping into something," Beaver said.

Erin looked at her searchingly. Just how much did Beaver know about the visitor?

"I told myself that it wasn't really a noise downstairs, it was just Vic putting something down upstairs. I got the flour... didn't see anyone down there and went back upstairs. Vic was gone. I looked around for her and thought she must have gone outside to the garbage bin. But she didn't come back in, so I called Terry."

Terry nodded. "We conducted a scene survey. There was no sign of her. The front door was unlocked, giving the impression that someone had been downstairs who had gone out the front, but there had to have been someone else here too, because they wouldn't have kidnapped Vic and taken her out the front door. There's too much activity on Main Street. Someone would have seen them. But no one had; they must have gone out the back."

Beaver nodded her agreement. Adele looked around thoughtfully. She wasn't familiar with the kitchen, so maybe she could spot something that Erin and Terry couldn't. Beaver too, with her sharp hunter's eyes, might see something.

Beaver walked around the kitchen area, peering into the tiny office. She looked at the back door, the one they had come in.

"No sign of forced entry."

"It would have been unlocked," Erin said. "We never lock the door during the day. We are always in and out throughout the day."

"Even after your rolling pin was stolen, you didn't start locking the back door?"

Erin started to ask how Beaver knew about that, then stopped. Of course Beaver knew about the rolling pin. That was part of the murder case, and whoever had sent her in wouldn't have done so without having first read all of the information they had about the murder. The point about the rolling pin having been stolen from Erin's bakery had been left out of the newspaper, but Erin assumed that it had been passed on to the various federal agencies that Terry had asked for help.

"I... yeah, I guess so. I just figured that Charley had taken it... She's had a pretty hard time since the murder. I really didn't think she'd be back for anything else."

Beaver's eyes were intense, despite the impression of laziness she exuded. "How is Charley doing?"

"Not good. She's been pretty upset, drinking, thinking a lot about... problems that she had."

"With the Dyson clan?"

"She was missing Bobby... but I think it was more that she was trauma- tized by everything than that she actually missed him personally. I know they were together as a couple, but... I think it was more about being kicked out of the clan than actually missing her old boyfriend."

"Do you think she was the one who killed Don Inglethorpe?"

"No. I know it looks like it, on the surface... but if you look deeper... he was the one who changed his vote to allow her to open the bakery. So he was the one she should have been the most grateful about... I can't see why she would have hurt him."

"Maybe he was threatening to change his vote again. Maybe he was blackmailing her, demanding she pay him or he would change his mind again, on the eve of the opening."

Erin shrugged. She shook her head. "I don't think that's what happened."

"Let's go downstairs," Terry suggested. "I want to have another look at what's down there that our visitor might have been messing around with."

"There isn't anything down there," Erin asserted. "Just storage and the loo."

"Let's check it out anyway. I want everyone to stay together."

They all followed after Terry, in single file down the narrow, steep stairs. There wasn't a lot of room at the bottom to mill around and take everything in. Erin moved into the storeroom where there was a little more space. She looked around. She drew in the smell of the place. Dust and concrete, just like she'd told Terry.

Terry and Beaver looked around with professional eyes. K9 sniffed around curiously, but nothing appeared to grab his attention. Adele's approach was different. Her eyes closed and she just stood in the middle of the room, listening or communing with the spirits or whatever it was she did. Maybe she was praying. Erin wouldn't discount it. Finally, she opened her eyes again.

"There's something down here," she said.

Erin was surprised. "What? We already looked..."

"It's something you can't see." Adele walked a slow circle around the outside of the room. Erin tracked Adele with her eyes.

Something they couldn't see?

"Charley said there were secret tunnels between some of the stores. But I couldn't see anything down here. I kind of... looked earlier."

"Secret tunnels?" Terry asked. "Old wives' tale."

"Maybe," Beaver said, "maybe not."

They all turned and looked at her.

"There is a rumor circulating that a tunnel under the bakery is being used to store drugs."

Erin's stomach dropped. "Storing drugs? But there isn't even a tunnel here, you can see that. If there used to be, it would have to be behind one of the bricked walls," Erin motioned. "But I've already looked at them and they are solid. There's no way to get into a tunnel, if there ever was one."

Everyone went to the brick wall, looking over it and feeling it for some kind of mechanism to open it up. Erin looked at the floor. If someone else were using it to store drugs, then it would have been opened and closed recently, but there was no sign of the concrete beneath the wall having been scuffed or disturbed. She shook her head.

"There's no way."

The others looked at her. Erin shook her head.

"If someone had been using a tunnel down here for storage, I would know about it. You couldn't have people coming in and out of here without me knowing about it. And there would be signs. Marks on the floor, streaks in the dust. If there *is* a tunnel down here, it hasn't been accessed in years."

"People can get in and out of here without you knowing about it," Beaver pointed out. "Your intruder earlier got in and out without you seeing. Charley stole your rolling pin. You leave this room accessible so that people can use the restroom."

"But if shady characters were in and out of here, I would notice."

"I don't know if you would. And you're not here at night when people could come and go and move product without you being any the wiser."

"We're in pretty early in the morning. I've never seen any sign that anyone else has been in here while we've been gone. I don't have a bunch of extra keys floating around. You couldn't use a place this small without leaving some kind of sign of your coming and going."

Just as she said it, there was a noise over their heads. They all looked up automatically at the same time.

Erin had hung back while the others looked at the wall, so she was the closest one to the door. In a split second, she was heading up the stairs, determined to see the intruder this time.

She didn't even think about what she was doing or what she would do when she got up the stairs and confronted the burglar face-to-face. She didn't have a weapon or any kind of training.

The trespasser obviously heard her coming. There was the sound of retreating footsteps as Erin barreled up the stairs, the others calling after her. Erin heard them and put on an extra burst of speed. She needed to see who it was. Who was it that was holding Vic? She needed to find her friend and to see that she was safe. As she got up the stairs, she saw a slim figure with shaggy, long blond hair.

"Jeremy!"

CHAPTER 37

*T*he young man turned to look back at her, and she saw that she was mistaken. It wasn't Jeremy, but an older man who looked quite similar to him. Her mind flashed through scenarios as she tried to find one that fit. It wasn't Jeremy or Vic. It was someone who shared similar features, like she and Charley did. Daniel or Joseph.

"What are you doing here?" Erin demanded. "If you're trying to help, you need to stop!"

But his look back had been fleeting and he wasn't stopping to chat. Erin watched his retreat, unable to keep up with him. She eventually stopped in the parking lot outside the bakery as the figure disappeared into the darkness.

The others caught up with Erin.

"Did you see anyone?" Terry asked, reaching for his police radio.

"I… I think one of the Jackson boys."

"One of the clan? Biggles?"

"No… I mean… one of Vic's brothers."

Terry raised his eyebrows. "Oh, is that so?"

"Not Jeremy. It wasn't Jeremy. One of the others…."

"I'll put out a bulletin. Can you describe him?"

"Just like Jeremy," Erin said. "But a bit older."

Terry called in to his dispatcher and gave them a description, as well as the possible identity of the burglar. They returned to the kitchen of Auntie Clem's.

"Did you know that any of the others were in town?" Terry demanded.

"No. I swear, I didn't. I just knew about Jeremy. I don't know why any of the others would be here."

"Well, he was here for something."

"Maybe he's just looking for Vic," Adele suggested. "Word is bound to have spread about her being missing. There's been enough time for someone to get here from Moose River."

"Then why didn't he stop when I called to him?"

"That part isn't really surprising," Terry said. "They're up to their necks in clan activity. Whether they're here on the clan's instructions or on their own, they really wouldn't want to have to stop and explain themselves."

"I suppose not." Erin sighed and looked around. She still had no clue who had come into the bakery to take Vic or where they had gone. They hadn't left any trace behind.

"I don't see any sign of him—of them here," Adele said, echoing Erin's thoughts.

There was an acrid smell starting to waft into Erin's nostrils. She looked toward the door, wondering if it were coming from outside. "Terry do you smell—wait; the tunnel is under the bakery."

Terry looked at her blankly. Everyone looked at her as if she were speaking another language.

"Not Auntie Clem's Bakery," Erin said. "What about The Bake Shoppe?"

It made perfect sense. The murder hadn't taken place at Auntie Clem's. Erin darted out the front door. If there was a tunnel under The Bake Shoppe, then all of the pieces of the puzzle fit. She could see the whole picture. She ran across the deserted street and down the block so she could access the alley behind The Bake Shoppe. It was getting to be a familiar route. Terry and K9 loped at her side, and Beaver not only kept up despite her load of paraphernalia, but passed Erin with a long, easy stride. Adele lagged somewhere behind.

Erin was focused only on getting to The Bake Shoppe. She was irritated with Beaver for passing her and going first. Wasn't there some kind of professional courtesy that the locals should be allowed in first?

When they reached the back door of The Bake Shoppe, the door was hanging open, the strike plate ripped from the splintered doorframe. Rohilda Beaven had some serious skills. Erin flashed back to entering the bakery once before when the door had been broken. She tried to focus in the present. She wasn't going to find a dead body this time. Just because it had happened before, that didn't mean it was going to happen again. Besides, Beaver was there ahead of her. Erin wouldn't be the one discovering a body this time.

Terry made a motion for Erin to stay back, and murmured to K9. K9 was totally focused, his ears forward and eyes alert, nose pointed like an arrow into the bakery.

Erin entered two steps behind Terry. She was not about to wait outside or to be the last one in the door.

The murder had been there. The drugs were being stored there. It followed logically that the bakery is where they would be holding Vic.

The kitchen was quiet and empty. There was no sign of having been a bloody murder there in the recent past. Charley had scrubbed every last spot away, hoping to be able to reopen.

And now she would be able to reopen, and it would be Erin who was out of business.

Beaver's sidearm was out, but held down at her side. "This floor is clear," she advised in a low voice. "There is only one set of stairs."

"Let me go down first with K9."

Beaver didn't look happy about the suggestion, but she nodded agreement. Terry pulled out his gun.

"Erin, I don't have to tell you to stay put until we've cleared the basement, do I?"

Erin nodded. "I will."

Beaver gave Erin a long look before nodding she was satisfied that Erin would behave herself. Terry spoke to K9 in a low voice, Erin couldn't make out all his words. K9 listened alertly, his body still. Then they started down the stairs. Beaver followed close behind, her gun held ready, close to her chin.

Erin stood by the stairs, listening intently. She heard a confirmation of "clear" from each of the professionals, then a low discussion between them.

"Can I come down?"

"You can come," Terry called back. Erin still hesitated for just a moment before descending the stairs. It wasn't her store, and she didn't exactly have permission to be there. At least she knew, with Terry calling her down, that they hadn't discovered another body or other crime scene.

The storage space was similar to Erin's. Walls lined with shelves of cans or bags of dry goods, as well as a few aisles of freestanding shelves. The walls themselves were of varying building materials. Erin looked down at the floor. It was swept clean, no dust or scuff marks to show where anyone had been.

"Don't touch anything," Terry warned as he looked around.

"I won't." Erin scanned for any sign of a door. A hole or a crack in the wall, a hinge or swivel of some sort. There was nothing obvious. If there was an old tunnel, it was well-hidden. "You're the treasure hunter," she said to Beaver. "So where do you think it is?"

The woman gave her a grin. "You might think that's just a cover story, but it's not. I actually do hunt treasure as a hobby."

"As well as working for the government?"

"No comment. Treasure hunting is fun and relaxing. Going new places and trying to solve hundred-year-old puzzles. Great way to vacation. And if you actually find something, all the better."

"So what do you think? Is there a tunnel down here?"

"I'd like to see some old blueprints, but so far I haven't been able to get them for any of these buildings. They are too old; if anything was ever filed municipally, it's long since been destroyed. Measuring out the room might help. But it's going to take some time. I don't see anything obvious, no more than in yours."

"If there is, they might have hidden Vic there. She could just be a few feet away from us and we wouldn't know it."

"You're right," Terry admitted. They were all silent, straining to hear any sound behind the walls.

"Vic?" Erin was afraid to shout; she didn't want to attract any bad guys. But she called as loudly as she dared. "Vicky? Can you hear me? We're here. Where are you?"

They again waited, but could hear no voice or other noise in response.

K9's nose was quivering as he looked around the room, looking at Terry and obviously wanting to explore, but too obedient to break away from his master's side. His ears swiveled this way and that.

"Let him go," Erin suggested. "Tell him to find Vic."

Terry looked down at K9. The dog was practically vibrating, he wanted to explore the room so badly. "Is Vic here, K9? Find Vic. Go find Vic."

K9 rocketed away from Terry and started to cast for scent along one wall of shelves. He gave a sharp bark, pushed his body partway into the shelf, and scrabbled with one paw at the seam where the wall met the floor as if trying to dig.

Erin looked at Terry. They all hurried toward the wall, surrounding K9 and looking for some sign of a door.

"Help me pull the shelf away from the wall," Terry told Beaver.

Erin didn't see how they could move it. It was piled with heavy cans and fifty-pound sacks of flour. They would have to clear it off before it could be moved. But Terry and Beaver positioned themselves on either end and gave it a heave. It didn't budge an inch. They both pushed and wiggled and shook it, looking up and down for some way to move it. But K9 must have just been chasing a mouse. There was no way that shelf was moving.

"It's bolted to the wall," Beaver pointed out, indicating a couple of anchors near the top.

Terry stepped back, his face sweating, lined with worry. "I don't see how the tunnel could be here."

But the treasure hunter wasn't ready to give up. "Don't be so quick to accept things as they appear." She walked along the shelf, examining it from all angles. "There's a way in. If the shelf is anchored to the wall, that means that the whole wall moves."

"This isn't TV," Terry said impatiently.

"I've seen all kinds of hidden rooms. Even now, there's a huge demand for safe rooms either to store valuables in or to escape to in case of a home invasion or looting. They can be incredibly well-hidden." She inched along the wall, reaching through the shelves to prod anything that displayed some variation from the wall or shelf around it. Knotholes and planks and discolorations. Like Terry, Erin thought it was too hokey to be real. The tunnel had to be a red herring. A rumor someone had started to throw people off the track of whatever it was they were really doing.

Then there was a loud click. Erin's mouth dropped open in surprise. Beaver was a strong woman, that was obvious from what Erin had seen of her body when she had taken the bulky jacket off, but she did not have the strength to move six hundred pounds of dry goods on her own. Yet she was pulling on something, and the shelf and wall were sliding forward as if on wheels. The whole section of shelving and wall swiveled around and doubled back against the wall beside it. K9 was squirming around the corner before Beaver even had it pulled all the way open, Terry calling him to stop and stay. The hole behind the shelves was black as pitch, but when the shelf stopped in its full-open position, there was another click, and fluorescent lights blinked and flickered to life.

There was a body writhing on the floor, K9 attacking and trying to get a purchase. But then Erin realized that it was Vic, and K9 wasn't attacking her, but was nosing her worriedly and licking her face. Erin dashed forward, pushing by Terry before he could process what was going on and call K9 off. Erin dropped to her knees beside Vic and pushed K9 hard out of the way. Vic's mouth was gagged and her eyes were wide with alarm. Erin levered the knotted cloth out of Vic's mouth and pulled out the rag that was stuffed inside it. Vic coughed and retched and lay on her side, breathing heavily, but no longer kicking.

"Praise the Lord," she whispered. "All praise the Lord and the Bald Eagle Falls police department."

Terry was beside Vic and worked on her hands, cuffed together behind her. As soon as he released her, Vic brought her hands around in front of her and wiped her face.

"Dog drool. I do not need a doggie face wash on top of everything else!"

Erin laughed. Tears of relief ran down her face. No matter what else she had lost, she still had Vic.

Terry looked down the narrow tunnel, swearing under his breath. Erin looked. Pallets of packages shrink-wrapped for shipping ran down one side of the tunnel. Hundreds and hundreds of white bricks.

"They really were storing it here. Using this as their shipping center or a way station," Terry marveled.

"How much is all of this worth?"

"Thousands," Terry said. "Maybe millions, I don't know."

"Enough to get the feds to listen to your requests," Beaver said, chewing her gum open-mouthed.

"Oh, dear."

Erin looked at Adele, who had caught up with them and followed them to the tunnel. She stood there, white-faced, looking at the drugs and at Vic. Terry was working on getting Vic's legs free, then she sat up. Her own face went pale.

"Adele! What are you doing here?"

Adele just looked at her, not answering. Erin looked back and forth between them. There was definitely something going on that she hadn't caught on to.

"I called Adele to come sit with me when you disappeared and Terry was trying to track down suspects," Erin explained. "Why… wouldn't she?"

Vic rubbed the insides of her wrists gingerly.

"Because her husband is the one who nabbed me."

CHAPTER 38

$\mathcal{E}$rin felt her own eyes widen. She looked at Adele and knew by her sheet-white face that she had already known or guessed as much.

"I didn't have anything to do with it," Adele said, shaking her head. "I swear to you, Vic, I had no idea what he was up to."

"You didn't know that he was the one who kidnapped me, or you didn't know anything about this caper?"

Adele swallowed. Terry was watching her carefully, but didn't interrupt, letting them talk it out naturally.

"I didn't know why he was in town," Adele said. "I knew something was up, but I didn't know what. I didn't know about the drugs, or that they were going to take you. I didn't know any of it. He put on that he was only here to see me… but I… there was something different about him and I knew he wasn't telling the full truth." She gave a little laugh and shook her head. "There's one way to know for sure when Rudolph Windsor is lying, and that is that his lips are moving."

"You told me that he was just in town to see you," Terry said. "You said that he wasn't involved in anything criminal."

"As far as I knew, he was in town to see me. That was before I'd even talked to him, so how was I supposed to tell you any differently? I told you as far as I knew, he didn't have a criminal record. I left it completely open. It was up to you to find out whether he did or not."

"He does," Erin contributed. "Terry said he has a record for fraud and theft. But nothing related to organized crime. We didn't know he had anything to do with the clans. What... which clan did this?" Erin motioned to their surroundings.

"Jacksons," Vic said bitterly. "Of course. It was Aunt Angela's bakery. I don't know if anyone knew about the tunnel while she was alive. But some time after that, they started moving in..."

"This is a pretty big depot," Beaver observed. "It takes a long time to move that much dope. Engineering that door wouldn't have been an overnight job, either. They've been around here for longer than a few weeks. This operation has been going on for some time."

Vic stared at Beaver. "Beaver?"

"We think she's with DEA or something," Erin filled Vic in. "She won't say, but..."

"With an operation like this, you can bet that they know that we're here now," Terry said in a low, serious tone. "I'm surprised that there weren't guards outside or in the tunnel ready to take us out when we got too close. I didn't see any electronic monitoring, but you can be sure we set off alarms somewhere." He chewed his lip. "It's not safe for us to stay here, and we don't have the manpower to safeguard it."

"Help is on its way," Beaver said serenely, "if they're not here already. You think I would come down here without pulling my own alarm cord first?"

She stopped, cocking her head to listen. Erin tried to hear any footsteps or other sounds indicating that other people were upstairs.

"The good thing about this little storehouse is that its security relies on there being zero traffic. If you suddenly have a bunch of people coming and going into a shop that is supposed to be deserted, people get suspicious and take notice. They couldn't be seen coming in. All movement of product would have to be in the dead of night. They could process during the day, cutting, weighing, and packaging, as long as no one could see inside the store. But they could only move goods when there was absolutely no one around."

"So that's why there were no guards?" Erin asked. "And does that mean... Charley didn't know what was going on here, under her own nose? Could it go all the way back to when Angela was still running The Bake Shoppe, as long as they only operated during the night?"

"Charley might not have known. But she's a Jackson, so it's hard to be sure whether she was in on it or not."

"She was a Dyson more than a Jackson."

Beaver shrugged. "We'll keep an eye on her. I didn't see her spending any time here at night."

"Angela couldn't be here while the bakery was operating because of the contamination. So no one would have thought twice about her being here at night when everyone was gone."

"There will be an in-depth investigation."

"It was Rudolph who brought you here?" Adele asked Vic, tentative.

Vic nodded. "He's the one who grabbed me and brought me here. He talked to other guys, but he's the only one I saw enough to recognize."

Adele shook her head. "Where did he go? Did he tell you what he was doing after he left you here?"

"No. Just said he was taking care of things."

Erin had a sinking feeling in her stomach.

Vic turned to her, as if she had said something audible. "What?"

Erin took a deep breath and let it out. "Auntie Clem's."

"What about it?"

Erin took Vic's hand, more to get strength from her than to give it. "Before we left there, I smelled gasoline."

Terry looked at Erin sharply, his face suddenly gray. "What?"

Erin just nodded. Terry moved quickly, heading out of the tunnel, through the store room, and up the stairs quickly, clicking his radio to talk to the dispatcher. Erin knew she had to follow him and find out how bad it was, but she delayed. She needed a few more minutes of not knowing.

Vic moved slowly, obviously stiff from lying on the floor. Erin helped her to her feet, and the taller girl leaned on her as they walked toward the stairs.

"I'm sorry," Adele said, still ghastly pale. "I didn't know. I'm so sorry."

They walked by Beaver and stopped for a minute, back in the more familiar surroundings. The tunnel filled with drugs had been like another world. The Bake Shoppe storeroom was so like Erin's own, it was like stepping back out of the magical wardrobe.

They gave each other an encouraging squeeze, then made their way up the stairs.

Beaver had said that her people might even be there already, but Erin hadn't taken it literally. The bakery proper and the street outside were a beehive of activity, with yellow warning tape being strung up, bright lights shining on the scene, and black-jacketed figures everywhere. Erin didn't look across the street to Auntie Clem's Bakery, but instead looked for Terry and K9. She could already smell the smoke.

"How bad is it?" she asked when she saw him.

Vic was pulling on her hand, trying to get her to go to the window where they would be able to see the front of Auntie Clem's.

Terry looked grave. He shook his head. "It's bad, Erin. They're trying to control the spread. The other businesses. Some of them have residences over the stores."

"Why would someone do that?" Vic demanded. "What's the point in burning Auntie Clem's?"

Erin tried to speak around the lump in her throat. "Because we wouldn't tell them where Jeremy was. Or they knew we were getting too close to figuring out about The Bake Shoppe and were trying to distract us."

"Jeremy! Is he okay? They kept demanding to know where he was, and I said I didn't know…" Vic's eyes filled with tears. "They kept making threats, and I was so scared of what they were going to do to me. They kept describing how they were going to torture me and saying such foul things…"

Erin pulled Vic down into a hug. "It's okay, Vicky. It's okay. You're safe and so is Jeremy. There is only one person who knows where Jeremy is, and that's Willie."

Vic snuffled into Erin's shoulder. "And Willie? Where is he? What if they got him?"

"Willie's the one who called in the fire first," Terry said. "I'm sure he's probably over there now. Give him a call, but don't be worried if he doesn't answer his phone, he might be occupied with the fire."

"I don't have my phone," Vic patted her pockets. "They took it away. I guess maybe they thought that Jeremy would call. Or that he would be in my contact list. I guess… I'll just wait until Willie is done."

"No." Erin pulled out her own phone. "You'll call him now. He doesn't have to come over here, but he needs to know that you're okay."

Nodding and wiping her nose, Vic took Erin's phone. She unlocked it and called Willie. There was a long half-minute while they waited for him to answer or for it to go to voicemail, and then Willie answered. Vic looked toward the front window as she spoke to him, reassuring him that she was okay and would meet up with him once they were both free of their responsibilities.

"And Jeremy's safe?" Vic asked.

Erin couldn't hear Willie's answer, but she could see the relaxation of Vic's expression and knew he had answered in the affirmative.

"Everybody's okay."

CHAPTER 39

There wasn't a lot for Terry and the little Bald Eagle Falls police department to do once the feds descended on the town and took over the fight against the clans. He sat at the small grouping of chairs in the front section of The Bake Shoppe with the others, waiting to be consulted on any local issues.

"At least we're getting answers to some of our questions. I guess the rest will come out over the next few weeks—or months—while they investigate."

"Like who actually killed Don Inglethorpe?" Erin asked.

He nodded. "They'll have to go through his books to see if he was laundering money... he might have kept files on what was going on here... we know he had some kind of falling out with the Jacksons before he died. They wanted something from him that he wasn't willing to give."

"He'd promised Charley that she could open the bakery," Erin said. "Maybe the clan didn't want her to do that because they couldn't operate without her figuring it out."

Vic nodded. "Rudolph said Inglethorpe didn't know a good deal when he saw it. So I guess they couldn't convince him to do what they wanted him to, and they ended up killing him... I don't know, to get him out of the way?"

"He'd been over at Auntie Clem's asking me about financial stuff.

Turnovers," Erin remembered. "Uh—turnover. He went back over to The Bake Shoppe and…?"

"Maybe he went looking for some bill or insurance policy from their files," Vic suggested, "and he walked in on the drug operation. You said that they could process during the day," she said to Terry, "so maybe he walks in, and they're cutting the powder, or packaging it for sale…"

"Oh." Erin thought back to the scene she had walked into that day. A smear of flour on the counter. The door to the basement standing slightly ajar. "There was white powder on the counter, and an electronic scale. I thought Charley had been making pie."

Terry nodded. "So maybe Bo Biggles or one of the others had been processing powder. Inglethorpe walks in and realizes that the clan *is* operating out of The Bake Shoppe whether he likes it or not."

Vic shuddered. "And goodnight Mr. Inglethorpe."

Since Terry was the one who had suggested that they could find Rudolph Windsor by tracking Vic's phone signal, and the kidnapping was in Terry's jurisdiction, the feds agreed that he could have the first crack at interrogating Rudolph, provided a certain Rohilda Beaven was allowed to sit in on the questioning.

Terry agreed to their terms and he was the one to sweat Rudolph under the cool fluorescent lights of the police department's interview room. While it looked more like a community center multipurpose room with its nondescript carpet and lightweight tubular furniture, Mr. Windsor was looking distinctly uncomfortable waiting for the ax to fall.

He kept darting looks at Beaven, who was sitting in a chair with her arms folded, the chair tipped back on two legs, reclined against the wall. She looked casual and comfortable, a sight that was apparently winding Rudolph up considerably.

"So, Mr. Windsor," Terry said slowly, "we have a considerable number of federal charges piling up against you. Congratulations on finally making it into the big leagues."

Rudolph swallowed. He wiped his sweat-beaded brow. "Look, I'm sure we can work something out. I'm just a small fish in this operation. I was taken advantage of. I really didn't know the whole picture…"

"If you didn't know the whole picture, then how can you tell me anything worthwhile?"

"I know enough to help you. It's just that… I didn't know at the time… what they were planning. It wasn't until the end that it all started coming together and I realized…"

"You are the one who kidnapped Victoria Webster. Kidnapping is a very serious charge with heavy sentences."

"It wasn't just me. There were others involved. I can give you their names. I had to do it, because if I didn't… they would have hurt me. My family. My own life was in peril."

"Maybe you should have gone to the police."

"They were watching me all the time. They didn't trust me. That's a point in my favor, isn't it? That they didn't trust me?"

"No, it just tells me that they knew you for what you were. Somebody unreliable, impulsive, and only looking out for number one."

Rudolph rocked back and forth in his seat. "That's not the way it was… if you'll just let me tell you my story, you'll see…"

CHAPTER 40

*E*rin could tell that Vic was watching out the living room window, even though she was trying to look relaxed and casual, as if everything was perfectly normal and they were just visiting before bed like they usually did.

The truth was, Erin was watching too, and not much was making it to the lists she was working on. All of the things she had to do following the fire at the bakery. Talk to the insurers to find out when the claims adjuster was going to make it out. Decide if there was any way she could stay in Bald Eagle Falls, maybe finding a job at the General Store or one of the other businesses. Find out what she was required to do about her employees following a disaster that shut down the business. She sighed.

Vic opened her mouth to talk to Erin about it, then her head snapped around as Willie's truck pulled in front of the house. She hurried to the door and was standing on the front steps when Jeremy climbed out of the truck and ran up to her. They hugged and held each other, talking over top of one another. Eventually, Willie managed to push them into the house, and they moved apart to bring Erin and Willie into the conversation.

"Where were you?" Vic asked. "I was so worried about you. If the clan had found you…"

"Willie put me down a mineshaft," Jeremy said. He shook his head. "I

SOUR CHERRY TURNOVER

mean *literally* down a mineshaft! He gave me blankets, flashlights, and food, but it was not the best camping experience that I've ever had! Man, is it dark down there! And still! Without the light, I would have gone crazy."

Erin shuddered. There was no way Willie would ever have gotten her down a hole. She'd had enough of caves and underground. She was glad that she hadn't known where Jeremy was. "Isn't that the first place anyone would look if they knew that it was Willie who had hidden you?"

"Nobody knows where all of Willie's mines are," Vic laughed. "I sure don't."

"Aren't they all on public record?"

Vic looked at Willie for his answer.

He just raised his eyebrows and smiled politely. "Where's Terry? I thought he was coming too."

"Not here yet." Erin shrugged. "I assume he'll be here as soon as he can get done at the police department. It might take some time."

"Let's get some food out," Vic suggested, "this is supposed to be a celebration."

Erin went with her into the kitchen and they worked side by side, pulling frozen baked goodies out of the freezer and arranging other finger food on platters. Orange Blossom made an appearance, yowling and begging for food. Vic flicked him a small piece of pepperoni.

"Don't give him that!" Erin protested. "It bothers his stomach and he'll keep me up all night with his... er, gastrointestinal distress."

Vic giggled.

"I'll take him to your apartment," Erin warned. "You can deal with it!"

"I won't give him any more."

Marshmallow made an appearance as well, alerted by Orange Blossom to the fact that there was food on offer. Erin gave him a few pieces of carrot and flicked a couple of kitty treats across the floor for the cat.

She gazed sadly at the cookies that were defrosting. The end of Auntie Clem's Bakery. The insurance wasn't going to cover rebuilding and replacing everything that had been lost and what she was going to owe her laid-off employees. She'd already spent the rest of her inheritance on rebuilding the garage and putting in the loft apartment for Vic. And the burglar alarm and other security equipment to keep them safe. The bank wasn't going to give her a loan when she didn't have collateral, and she wasn't going to mortgage

Clementine's house, especially not when she didn't have a regular income. She kept going in circles and couldn't find a way to get the bakery back in business.

There was a knock at the door, and she heard Terry's voice when Willie answered it. She poked her head out the kitchen door.

"Send K9 in for a cookie! He deserves it after finding Vic in the tunnel for us."

Terry told K9 to 'go get a cookie,' and the dog bounded excitedly into the kitchen. Orange Blossom jumped back and puffed up, hissing his objection to the big dog being allowed in his territory. Erin gave K9 a doggie biscuit from the cookie jar and scratched his ears and praised him, telling him what a good dog he was for finding Vic.

She washed up, and once they had everything ready, they bussed the platters into the living room. Erin was surprised to see Beaver there as well. She gave Erin an easy smile.

"I hope you don't mind me crashing your party. Officer Piper said you wouldn't mind and that there would be good food."

"Uh… no, that's fine." Erin looked at Terry. She couldn't help a little twinge of possessiveness over him. She didn't like this woman getting friendly with him and showing up with him at what was supposed to be a private celebration. "Of course you're welcome. You were a part of the rescue."

The only person who wasn't there was Adele. She had seemed deeply embarrassed by her husband's involvement in the whole thing and had retreated to her solitary cottage.

They helped themselves to the goodies while Erin got out some wine and soft drinks that had been chilling in the fridge. Beaver ended up sitting next to Jeremy and the two of them exchanged stories, laughing with their heads close together. Vic looked at Erin and raised one eyebrow. Erin shrugged back.

"So, how did it go with Mr. Windsor?" Erin asked Terry. "Did you get anywhere with him?"

Terry looked over at Beaver, who nodded at him to go on. Erin appreciated that Beaver was open to Terry talking to them about it, but didn't like their apparent ability to read each other so easily.

"It went better than I would have predicted." Terry sat forward on his seat. "I told you before that Windsor didn't have any apparent connection to the clans. He hadn't had any dealings with organized crime before, so I didn't see how he could have been involved in the drug running. He wouldn't have had enough pull as an independent operator, and he'd need a good 'in' to be involved with either of the gangs."

Erin nodded her agreement. Windsor hadn't seemed like the type to be involved with the clan. He was an outsider, from New England rather than Tennessee, and he wasn't related to anyone. He was the kind of guy who was always running his own brilliant scams but could never get ahead of the big operators.

"The last stint he served was in the Tennessee Penitentiary."

No one else saw the significance to start with. Then Vic's eyes lit up as she made the connection. "That's where Davis is."

Terry nodded. "That's where Davis is."

"Did they know each other?" Erin asked.

"They were in the same block. Apparently, they developed quite a friendship."

"So, when he got out, Davis set him up with the Jacksons?"

"Introductions were made while he was still inside. And it would appear that Davis had ideas about how to make money off of the bakery even while it was shut down."

"It was Davis's idea to use the tunnel?"

"I'm not sure whose idea it was initially. Davis doesn't strike me as an idea man, so it might have been Trenton's. But whoever it was, the boys obviously had knowledge of the tunnels."

"But Davis couldn't make money off of it if Trenton was the one running the bakery," Erin said. "If they both knew about the tunnels, then Davis couldn't use them without Trenton's knowledge, like they could when Charley was in charge. He'd have to give him a cut."

Terry nodded slowly. "Another nail in Davis's coffin. More evidence to suggest that he fully intended to kill Trenton right from the start. Joelle wouldn't have known about the tunnel."

"Good news for Charley. She can get the bakery opened and maybe not even have to split it with Davis. At least Bald Eagle Falls will still have one bakery."

"It will work out, Erin," Vic said. "Somehow we'll work it out."

Erin didn't believe it, but she didn't want to argue about it. She was mentally exhausted.

"So, is it all over?" she asked the room at large. "Is there going to be retaliation? Are we going to be targeted?"

Terry and Beaver looked at each other. "I think we'll be able to get most of the major players behind bars," Beaver said slowly. "There are always dangers with organized crime... bosses still directing operations from inside, or family members retaliating against those who put their loved ones behind bars. So it's impossible to say that it's over for sure. But my best guess... you and Vic should be safe. You didn't actually go looking for trouble. You were defending yourselves and your loved ones."

Erin breathed out. There were no guarantees, but she was glad to hear the opinion expressed by the federal agent. Maybe things would be quiet. For at least as long as it took Erin to figure out what she was doing or where she was going next.

"And what about Jeremy?" Vic asked, looking at her brother.

Beaver grimaced. She looked searchingly at the platters of food and picked out a cookie. She nibbled at it while considering her answer.

"Jeremy had certain commitments to the clan. He bailed out and betrayed the trust his family and the clan had in him. They were pretty intent on finding him before he could talk to the authorities."

"But I didn't snitch," Jeremy said. "They might have thought I was going to, but I didn't. So now that it's all over... they should just leave me alone."

"You have any plans to go back to the farm now?"

"No way!"

"My point exactly."

"What about witness protection?" Vic asked. "You could help him to change his name and get situated where no one could find him."

"For that, he *would* have to testify against them, and it would have to be something big enough for us to hang a case on. Is that what you want?"

Jeremy shook his head. "No." He looked at his sister. "No, Vic. No way. I'll do my own thing. I'm not important enough for them to be spending a lot of time and resources on."

Erin had tried to outrun her troubles before, but it seemed like it didn't matter how many times she changed her name and took up residence in a new town, she couldn't ever leave her past behind.

"You could get some *unofficial* help from an agent," Beaver said. "It would be a good idea to keep in touch with someone who knows the tricks of the trade."

A slow smile spread over Jeremy's face. He nodded. "That sounds like a good plan," he agreed.

EPILOGUE

*B*ella sat down with Erin at the library table. Erin knew she still had to go over termination pay with Bella and to apologize to her for not being able to keep the business going after the fire. The very thought of the conversation tied her in knots.

Bella had been a good employee. She was young and would be able to find work again quickly enough, though there weren't a lot of openings in Bald Eagle Falls and she might end up having to go to the city to find something.

"Vic told me how stressed you've been over the bakery," Bella said. "She said you didn't think you could find a way to start it up again after the fire."

Erin nodded, both grateful to Vic for breaking the ice and ticked off with her for not leaving it to Erin. It was Erin's job to do, no matter how much she dreaded it.

"You had insurance though, right?"

"Yes... but it's not enough to rebuild and buy everything I would need to start over again. There's next to nothing recoverable. I can't get a loan based on the property value and a business plan, not with another bakery opening any day now, one with a wider customer base. I'm not going to mortgage Clementine's house, I won't risk it." Erin was irritated by having to explain it all over again. Everybody thought the insurance company would just hand her a check and she'd be all set.

Bella didn't look dismayed by this news. Maybe she already had a new job lined up.

"What if you didn't have to rebuild? What if there was another possibility?"

Erin stared at Bella.

"What if there was another bakery that was already set up and you could just step in?"

"The Bake Shoppe?" Erin demanded. "I can't exactly walk in and take over Charley's business."

"Now that Davis has pled guilty and Charley's getting the whole of Trenton's estate, she's looking for a partner to invest in The Bake Shoppe so that she'll have the money to get a house."

Erin felt the first real glimmer of hope. "Well... I've got money I could invest, and I could help run it... but The Bake Shoppe is a conventional bakery. I'd have to give up on the idea of having a gluten-free, specialty bakery." Was half a dream better than no dream at all? She hated to think of Peter and her other precious customers having to go back to driving to the city to get second-rate factory-made gluten-free products.

"You'd have to discuss that with Charley." Bella had a mischievous twinkle in her eye, "but she figured that since that was your specialty, and you're the one with experience running a business like this..."

"You think she'd be open to making it gluten-free? Just like Auntie Clem's?"

Bella sat back in her chair, looking like the cat that swallowed the canary. "Well, that's what she *said*."

"You negotiated me partnering with my half-sister to open a gluten-free bakery without even talking to me first?"

"I know your business. I didn't want to get your hopes up with a bunch of pie-in-the-sky ideas..."

"Gluten-free pie-in-the-sky," Erin giggled, feeling giddy. "It won't be Auntie Clem's, but I think I'm okay with that."

"Oh. She did say something about your name having better goodwill than The Bake Shoppe, with all of its associations with the Plaint family and murders and organized crime activities... so she'd like to open it as Auntie Clem's..."

Erin didn't know whether to laugh or cry, so she did both, unable to contain herself, in full view of all of the patrons of the Bald Eagle Falls public library.

APPLE-ACHIAN TREASURE

AUNTIE CLEM'S BAKERY #8

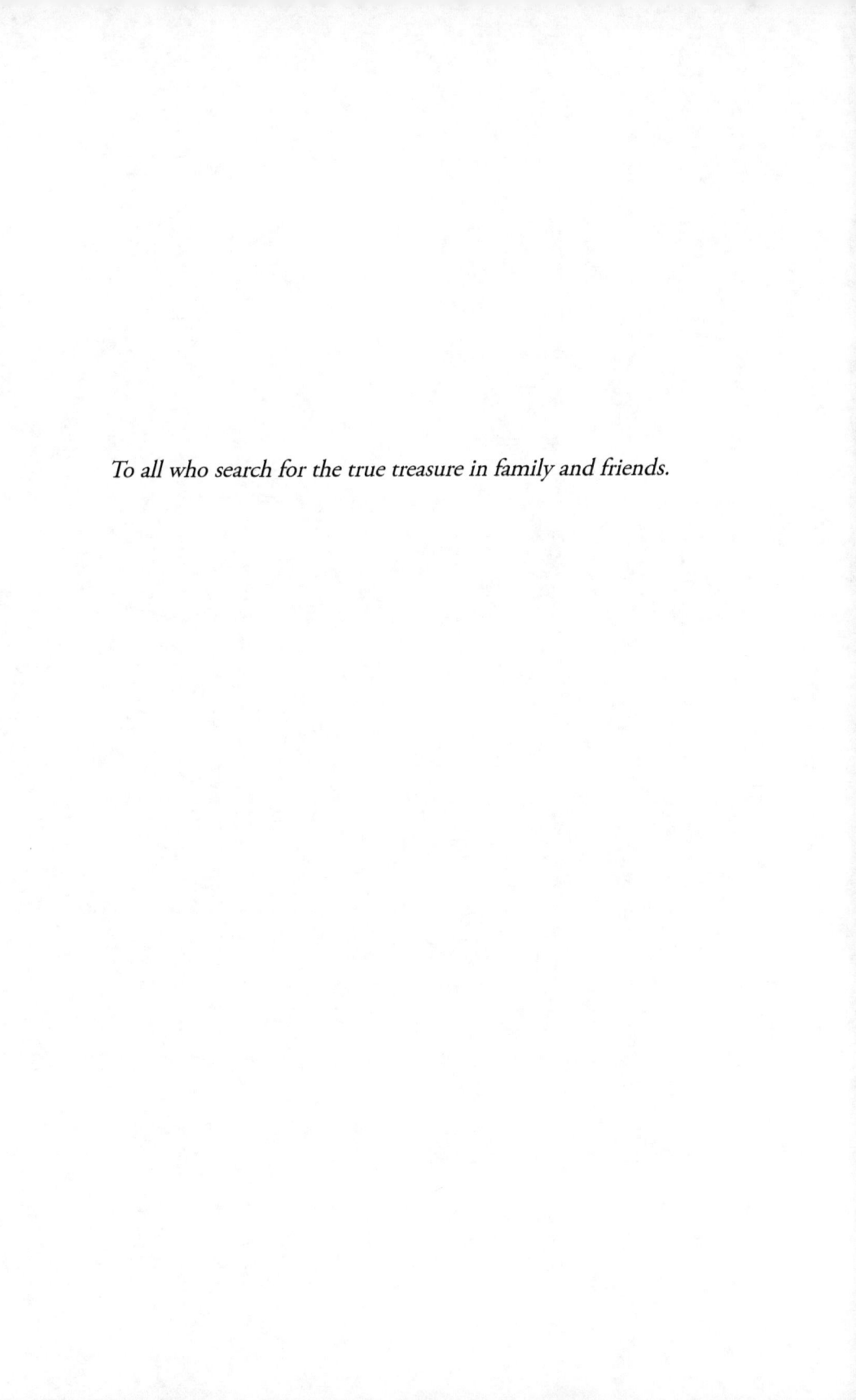

To all who search for the true treasure in family and friends.

CHAPTER 1

*E*rin fit her key in the lock and found herself holding her breath as she turned it. The lock clicked smoothly open and Erin pushed the door open. She turned to look back over her shoulder at Vic as she entered.

"It feels pretty weird," she said.

Vic nodded. "I know. But it's just a different location. It's still Auntie Clem's Bakery."

Erin took a deep breath in and let it out again. "Yeah... just the same."

But it didn't feel the same. She knew she should be ecstatic about being able to open the bakery again. If not for her half-sister, Charley, allowing her to become half-owner in The Bake Shoppe and to reopen it as Auntie Clem's Bakery, that would have been the end of Erin's dream. She would have had to liquidate everything and to figure out how she was going to make a living without the bakery.

Charley's offer had seemed like a godsend at the time, but Erin had become increasingly worried about how it was all going to work out. She barely knew Charley. They hadn't grown up together and their personalities were diametrically opposed. It seemed like everything Charley did rubbed Erin the wrong way, even when she wasn't really doing anything wrong.

And now they were connected not only by blood, but in the business. They had to agree on advertising campaigns, product lines, prices, and

237

promotions. They had to agree on everything that Erin had previously set up, like the ladies' tea after Sunday services, catering for the book club at The Book Nook across the street, and the children's cookie club.

Even just stocking the kitchen had been an ordeal, since Charley wanted to use all of the equipment that had remained from The Bake Shoppe and Erin couldn't use gluten-contaminated bowls and baking sheets to make her gluten-free baking. While Charley had agreed to continue to keep Auntie Clem's Bakery gluten-free, she didn't have the understanding Erin did and thought that they could cut a few corners. Erin wasn't willing to put the health and lives of her allergic or intolerant customers at risk.

Erin turned on the lights and looked around the kitchen. It was her bakery. It was the new normal. She and Vic could continue to work together, just as they had in the shop that had burned down. It would be almost the same.

Almost, but not quite.

Vic strode into the kitchen, where she pulled a clean apron off the hook and tied it around her slim form, then put on a hat, making sure that her long blond hair was all properly tucked away. Normal, routine actions, just like she had followed every day at the old Auntie Clem's. Erin followed suit. She was considerably shorter than Vic and her hair was shorter and dark. She felt a little better once suited up. Her uniform helped to set the mood.

She went to the fridge and started pulling out the batters they had made the night before, working through her mental checklists to get everything started in the right order so that they would have the case filled efficiently by the time the bakery opened in a few hours.

"Do we have chocolate chip muffins today?" Vic questioned.

"Yes. And blueberry. And the rice bran. I'm going to work a high-protein muffin into the lineup once we've had a chance to settle back into the schedule. Not today, but maybe next week. I'm hoping we can tap into the low-carb and paleo markets."

Vic nodded, already aware that Erin had been working on it. "You're finding some low-carb recipes that don't rely on nut flours?"

They worked side by side, finding their rhythm even in the less familiar kitchen.

"I'm focusing on some of the less allergenic seeds like *sacha inchi*. It's one of the new flours out there and becoming more available. We can grind it here so that we know that they haven't been processed on the same equipment as peanuts or tree nuts."

"You're always on top of all of the new developments."

"Well, that's my job."

Vic glanced at the clock on the wall. "I thought Charley said she was going to come in this morning to help out."

Erin didn't look at Vic and tried to keep her expression neutral. "That's what she said."

"But you didn't expect her to get here, did you?"

"Uh… no. She's really not a morning person, and this is early even for morning people. Maybe if Charley came in and helped out now, and then went home and went to bed…"

Vic chuckled. "She's like a teenager. If she wants to be a business owner, she's going to have to make a few changes to her lifestyle."

Erin turned on one of the mixers, then went around to the ovens, setting the preheat temperatures. It was the coolest part of the day, but that was about to end. Once they had the ovens going, even the best air conditioning wasn't going to keep it cool.

"It's supposed to be fall, but I'll be glad when the temperature starts to drop."

"Still got a ways to go before then."

They worked in silence for a few minutes. "When do you think Charley is going to show up?" Vic asked.

Erin straightened and looked at her. "Are you trying to get me to badmouth my new boss?"

"She isn't your boss, she's your partner."

"I'd like to think so," Erin said slowly, "but I don't think that's the way she sees it. If we can't agree on things, who do you think is going to get the final say?"

"You're partners. You'll work it out together."

Erin shrugged. That remained to be seen.

"So…?" Vic pressed.

"I think we'll be lucky to see her before noon."

Vic giggled. "How about a bet? If she gets in before noon, you win. After noon, I win."

"And what do we win?"

"How about… a foot massage."

Erin shook her head. "Okay. You're on."

~

Charley didn't make it in before noon. Vic was chuckling to herself.

"I'm looking forward to that foot rub," she commented.

"I did say we'd be lucky to see her before noon. I hope nothing happened to her…"

"Nothing happened to her. She's just sleeping, like every day."

"I know… I just worry."

"She's fine. She said she was going to be here, but she hasn't got the sense of a cross-eyed goose. She's just like a kid. She's going to have to grow up if she's going to run a business."

Erin raised her eyebrows. Vic herself was barely an adult.

"I'm grown up," Vic shot at her. "It doesn't have anything to do with chronological age."

"No, you're right. She may be a few years older; she may even have been on her own for longer than you have, but she doesn't have the same sense of responsibility."

Vic nodded. There were parallels between Vic and Charley. Both had left home at an early age, rebelling against the way that they had been raised. But Charley had left, apparently, because she wanted a more exciting life on the opposite side of the law, and Vic had come out about her gender identity, transitioning to female. Despite her not aligning herself with the gender she'd been raised as, Vic still had strong moral standards and an attachment to her family. They were the ones who had forced her to leave. Erin was glad that Jeremy, one of Vic's older brothers, had recently moved into town. It was good for Vic to have contact with someone in her family. Jeremy accepted her for who she was and did his best to respect her identity.

"Think she'll show up after lunch?" Erin asked.

"Do you want to go double or nothing?"

"No. Just wondering. It's opening day, you'd think she'd at least make an appearance."

"You would think," Vic agreed.

Mary Lou and Melissa arrived together. Erin was glad to see them together more often again lately. Mary Lou needed the support of her friends more than ever, and Erin suspected that Melissa wasn't having the easiest time since she had started visiting Davis in prison. The ladies of Bald Eagle Falls were not very tolerant of what they perceived as wrong choices.

Mary Lou looked around the bakery and raised her brows. "I was expecting a better turnout for your opening day. Isn't this a little... quiet...?"

Erin shrugged, her face getting warm. "We actually didn't want to do a great big grand reopening. We didn't think it was a good idea, after..."

Mary Lou gazed at her blankly.

"Because of the deaths," Melissa piped up eagerly. "Angela was killed on opening day of Auntie Clem's Bakery and Mr. Inglethorpe was killed the night before the grand reopening for The Bake Shoppe. Were you afraid of jinxing it?"

"No," Erin insisted, though she had to admit to a little superstitious twinge over the thought of another murder around the bakery opening. So far everything had been quiet, and she hoped that it would stay that way. They didn't need any bodies to spice things up. "I just didn't want people to make that association." She looked significantly at the other patrons of the bakery, hoping that Melissa would get the hint and keep her voice down. "Even if it's unconscious... I didn't want them to think... bakery opening... someone might die..."

"That makes perfect sense," Mary Lou acknowledged.

"It's really too bad, though," Melissa said. "I wouldn't mind a free muffin..."

Erin smiled. "You buy a dozen for the Police Department, and I'll throw in a free one for you."

"You'd do that anyway."

Mary Lou and Melissa looked through the case at the baked goods on offer.

"I think... a loaf of the rustic bread," Mary Lou pointed to a hand-shaped loaf. "That would go nicely with supper. And maybe some cookies that I can throw in the freezer. We don't go through them very fast, with it just being Josh and I now, but we are starting to get a little low."

"Anything in particular, or just an assortment?" Erin asked.

"Surprise me."

Erin suspected that Mary Lou wasn't going to be eating any of them anyway. She was very careful to maintain her slim figure. Josh, on the other hand, was a teenager and could probably put away the whole dozen in a sitting without consequences.

"How are the boys?" she asked politely.

"As well as can be expected. Josh is finding high school very challenging. And Campbell… well, I don't know what to think of Campbell. He at least calls me once every week or so, which is more than one can expect from a boy his age. He says he's well, that things are going fine… but he's not going anywhere. I don't even know how he's supporting himself without any marketable skills."

"You don't know what he's doing?"

Mary Lou shook her head. "He's *finding himself.* Whatever that means."

Erin wasn't sure how to respond to that. She finished assembling the cookies for Mary Lou and handed them over to Vic to ring up at the till. She looked at Melissa. "So, a dozen muffins?"

"No, not today. Maybe on Friday. How about…" Melissa studied the display case seriously. "How about a brownie?" She motioned to the chocolate-dipped brownies that Erin had recently added to the product lineup. "Those are addictive. They should be a controlled substance."

Erin nodded. "You'd better not tell Officer Piper that. I don't want him slapping me with any fines. Or jail time."

Melissa gave one of her wide smiles, her eyes dancing. "What you and Officer Piper do behind closed doors really isn't any of my business…"

For the second time, Erin felt a wave of heat go over her face, and was sure that this time she was turning a brilliant red. She shouldn't let Melissa get to her like that. Blushing would only encourage her in the future. But she couldn't keep a dispassionate mask when she thought about Terry Piper and their relationship. They had only recently taken things to the next level with the good-looking officer, and Erin wasn't to the point where she could be casual about it.

"You mind your manners," Vic drawled, her southern accent more pronounced than usual. "Don't be teasing Miss Erin or she'll be adding something to your tea this Sunday."

Melissa responded with a blush of her own. She tittered and gave Vic the money to cover her bill. "I don't know what you're talking about, I'm sure."

It wouldn't have been so bad if Officer Handsome himself hadn't happened to enter the bakery at that very moment.

The bells jingled as Terry walked in the front door, K9 poised at his side in perfect form, as usual. Erin's heart skipped a beat at the sight of her sweetheart in uniform, but she was already embarrassed by Melissa's comments and couldn't help but feel even more awkward at his appearance on the scene. She glanced over at Vic.

"I uh, just have to go check on those cookies. Can you get K9 a biscuit and see what Terry wants? I'll be right back!"

Vic looked surprised. Erin turned tail and dashed into the kitchen, needing to get out of sight to compose herself. She ran cold water into a clean cloth and pressed it to her cheeks, trying to cool them off and remove the color. Terry would be wondering what she was so flushed about.

Not like he wouldn't wonder why she had suddenly fled at his appearance. That wasn't something she normally did.

Erin took an extra few seconds to gulp down a glass of water, then returned to the front before everyone could start to wonder what had happened to her. But that last swallow water went down wrong and she inhaled half of it into her windpipe, resulting in a fit of coughing just as she walked through the door. If she'd been trying for an unobtrusive re-entrance, she had not succeeded.

Erin turned away, coughing into her elbow, and then turned back, her face just as hot as it had been when she'd left.

"Sorry. I'm not contagious. Just some water that went down the wrong way."

"Are you okay?" Terry asked, looking concerned.

"I'm fine, really. Just some water." Erin cleared her throat the best she could, trying to suppress any further coughs. "How are you today?"

"It's a beautiful day out. Things have been pretty quiet. I'm hoping that the crime level in Bald Eagle Falls has gone back to normal."

"You think that the trouble with the clans is done?"

"Considering the fact that we managed to confiscate several millions of dollars' worth of drugs, hopefully they've decided that Bald Eagle Falls isn't the best place for a storage and shipping depot, and we won't be seeing any more of them."

"I sure hope so," Erin said fervently.

Terry nodded. "How has the first day back been?"

Erin breathed out. She blinked to clear her teary eyes and studied the officer. Taller than she was, dark haired, perfect build, and that cute little dimple in his cheek when he smiled at her. "Actually, it's been pretty nice. It felt good to get back into the routine again. When I wasn't working, it just felt... disorderly. I didn't feel like my life was going the way I wanted it to. Like things might just fall apart at any minute."

"But coming back, everything has fallen back into the old patterns?"

Erin nodded. "It feels good."

"It actually does," Vic agreed. "Unlike Erin, I actually enjoyed my time off, but I was ready to come back. The structure and the routine are good, but even more than that... the paycheck... visiting with customers... eating at regular intervals instead of grazing all day." Vic patted her flat belly. "I was starting to put on weight..."

"You were not," Erin disagreed. "You haven't put on an ounce since you moved here."

"Well, that's not exactly true. But considering I wasn't getting enough to eat before I started working for you, those first few ounces were okay. It's the ones since then that are the problem."

Erin just shook her head.

"See you later, Officer Piper," Melissa gave Terry a little wave before leaving. She did some office administration for the Police Department on a part-time basis, and quite enjoyed the prestige of her role, even if she wasn't an officer herself.

Terry nodded to her and Mary Lou as they headed out the door. "Ladies."

They were just coming up on the after-school rush when Charley finally showed her face. She rushed into the bakery through the front door, red-faced and flustered.

"I can't believe how the day has gotten away from me!" she exclaimed. "I was just doing some administrative work from home, you know, making sure that all of the advertising is lined up and that the bank has made all of the appropriate arrangements and all that..." All work that Erin had already attended to herself. "And before I knew it, it's afternoon and I still haven't made it over to the bakery! How did it go? Do you need anything?"

They were, of course, long past the point that Charley could have helped with anything, unless she wanted to take over the register during the rush or help with the cleanup after closing. Erin just looked at her.

"I was working," Charley insisted. "I was just doing it from home instead of here. It's so hot in the kitchen and that little office…"

The office was bigger than the one Erin had used in the original Auntie Clem's Bakery, which had been hardly more than a closet. With a desk fan on the heat was nearly tolerable.

"I didn't say anything," she asserted. "Things went pretty well. We had a good amount of business."

"Good. I was a little worried after we decided not to do a big grand reopening. I mean, I didn't *want* to do a big reopening, I just had some… last minute qualms. What if nobody came? What if not enough people knew that we were open for business again today…?"

"There's nothing that says you have to make all of your money the first day," Erin reassured her. "Even if opening day didn't go well, there's lots of time for word to get around that we're open and to get people in. But, nothing to worry about, it went just fine."

"Good." Charley put a stuffed shoulder bag that doubled as her brief-case down on one of the little wrought iron tables at the front of the bakery. "I'm new to this whole 'business owner' thing. I don't want to screw it up."

"That's why you've got us," Vic offered, putting her arm around Erin's shoulder to remind Charley that she was there too, part of a package deal. "We know how to run a bakery."

Charley didn't quite make a face, but her look at Vic didn't convey that she was thankful to have Vic there helping to look after things. She and Vic had never quite clicked. Erin wasn't sure whether it was a personality thing, or whether there was a certain amount of jealousy between her sister and her best friend, each of them wary of the other intruding on their relationship with Erin.

"I'm glad I've got you," Charley agreed, but her words were aimed at Erin rather than at Vic. "Whenever I start to panic about not knowing everything there is to know about the business, I just remind myself that you've done all of this before. I can't imagine how difficult it must have been for you to start up Auntie Clem's Bakery with no one to tell you how to do everything. How did you manage?"

Erin motioned Charley to move to the side so that she wasn't blocking paying customers.

"I read lots. Talked to my lawyer and accountant. Wrote out my business plan and goals and milestones…"

"You're so organized. You always know exactly what's coming next, don't you?"

Erin only wished that were true.

CHAPTER 2

*W*hen they arrived home after closing the bakery, Erin saw that Rohilda Beaven's big white truck was parked in front of the house.

"Looks like Jeremy has company," she observed, and pulled around to the back to park in the garage.

"It's amazing how well they get on together," Vic said, shaking her head. "You'd think that with Beaver being older than him and a federal agent, they wouldn't have anything in common. But they get along like a house on fire!"

Erin winced at the expression. They had almost lost the house to fire once, and the original Auntie Clem's Bakery burning down was still too recent and a sore spot.

"Or like something on fire," Vic amended quickly, then tried again. "Or... like a pig and mud. They belong together!"

"They really have seemed to hit it off," Erin agreed. She unlocked the back door, pausing and calling out to warn Jeremy and Beaver that they were no longer alone. "We're home, Jeremy!"

They could hear the murmur of voices for a moment, then Jeremy's door opened, and he entered the kitchen.

"Hey Erin, hey Vic. How was the first day back?"

"It was good," Vic offered, giving him a quick hug. "Beaver's here?"

"She'll be out in a minute. We're just getting things packed up and ready to go."

Erin felt a little pang at the thought of Jeremy moving out. It had sometimes been awkward with him there, especially when he had been trying to hide out from the clans and the police. She had told him that he needed to find his own place, but she still felt responsible for him and like she might be turning him out of the nest too quickly.

"Everything is arranged at the new place?" she asked.

"Deposit and first month have been paid," Jeremy agreed. "So, it looks like I'm all grown up after all. My first place all my own."

Erin suspected that most of the money for the basement suite had been put up by Beaver, since Jeremy had just recently landed a job and hadn't likely received an advance on his paycheck. But he hadn't told her what arrangements were being made and it wasn't any of her business how he had managed to rent a place so quickly.

"It will be nice for you," Erin said. "You won't have me and all of the critters underfoot."

Orange Blossom, Erin's cat, was rubbing up against her legs meowing noisily over their conversation. Marshmallow was closer to Jeremy, and he bent down and picked up the brown and white rabbit. Marshmallow kicked his back legs, not liking to be lifted into the air, but Jeremy held the rabbit snug against his body and settled him down.

"Actually, I'm going to miss these guys. The house never seemed lonely with them around. My apartment is going to seem awfully quiet after being used to them running around here."

Erin wasn't about to offer that he could take one of them with him. She wouldn't be able to bear to part with either of them and would never separate the two. The cat and rabbit had grown remarkably close to each other.

Jeremy's bedroom door opened again, and Rohilda joined them in the kitchen. Her tall, lanky body, which always gave the impression of being slow and lazy, was anything but. She was strong quick, and graceful. She just conserved her energy until she had a need for it. She gave them a smile, chewing on a wad of gum. Her nose and lips were too big for her face and her blond hair was more like Jeremy's unruly mane than Vic's sleek, smooth hair. All together, she was not unattractive, but didn't have the type of beauty that society typically worshiped.

Erin had learned to appreciate her open, honest manner. Unlike the women of Bald Eagle Falls, whom Erin found difficult to read, with Beaver what you saw was what you got. She never put on a false front.

"Good evening," she greeted Erin and Vic. "Uneventful day at the bakery?"

Erin nodded vigorously. "Luckily, yes! I don't know what I would have done if... something... had happened. I might have a breakdown and never recover."

"Good thing we didn't have to find out."

"So..." Vic looked at Jeremy and back at Beaver. "I guess you're leaving tonight...?"

"Everything is packed up and ready to go," Beaver agreed. "Jer can sleep in his own bed tonight. I need to go back to the city for a few days, so he'll have some time to settle into his new digs. I'll be back for a day or two on the weekend." She looked at Jeremy with affection.

He grinned back at her. "I told her she could stay, but she doesn't want the commute. So, I guess I just get a few days here and there whenever she can fit me in. I feel used."

"You'd better not complain," Vic warned. "The lady is good with a gun."

Beaver grinned and nodded, chewing on her gum.

"I'm not complaining," Jeremy assured her, and put his arm around Beaver to pull her close for a moment. "I'm perfectly happy with being used."

Beaver laughed and gave him an embarrassingly passionate kiss. Erin looked at Vic and rolled her eyes.

"Did you work today?" Vic asked without waiting for Jeremy and Beaver to finish.

Jeremy pulled back from Beaver. "Yep. I don't work the long hours you two do, but I put in my time."

"What exactly is it that you're doing?" Erin asked. While he'd told her before, she never felt like she'd gotten a full explanation.

"Just keeping an eye on things," Jeremy said. "Making sure that no one bothers the crops."

Erin studied him, trying to make sense of the explanation. She knew that he was working on Crosswood Farm, but he had refused to tell what kind of crop he was guarding. It didn't seem likely that it was any of the crops that were widely farmed in the area. After all, why would fields need to be guarded against intruders? There was no reason for people to come in and steal corn or apples. What was the benefit, unless they were starving? It was harvest time, so the plants would be mature, but she couldn't see why anyone would be interested. Was there a black market for cider?

She was afraid that what he was doing wasn't quite as innocent as he made it sound.

Terry had said that they had eradicated the drug trade in Bald Eagle Falls, so Erin told herself it couldn't be anything to do with the clans. Jeremy had done his best to get away from the Jackson clan that he'd been born into. She couldn't see him giving in and just going right back to a life of crime. And she couldn't see Beaver letting him. Beaver didn't contradict anything Jeremy had said about his job, so either she knew the details, or she was satisfied that as much as he had said was the truth.

It just didn't make any sense to Erin.

"You've got to be on the lookout for poachers," Jeremy told Erin, watching her face carefully. "You'd be surprised at how much illegal trade there is around here."

"Poachers... so does that mean you are guarding animals? Not plants?"

He kept his face carefully blank. "I'm not allowed to talk about it."

"Not allowed to?"

"It's in my employment contract."

"So, your job is watching to make sure nobody steals a bunch of plants?"

He shrugged.

Erin looked at Beaver again, trying to read her expression, but she was even more closeted than Jeremy, giving Erin a cheeky smile that betrayed nothing of what she knew or didn't know about Jeremy's new job.

CHAPTER 3

*J*n the aftermath of the fire at old Auntie Clem's and the opening of the new bakery, Erin hadn't had time for much other than business arrangements. Even when she took some downtime to relax, it was usually to bake and experiment with new recipe possibilities.

Now that the bakery was open once more, she couldn't bring her brain to focus on anything else business-related, so Erin instead pulled out one of Clementine's fat genealogy files and started to leaf through it for old stories about Bald Eagle Falls and its residents. She'd never been much of a fiction reader, but she found history fascinating, and the stories of the old Bald Eagles Falls residents, progenitors of Erin and her friends, were particularly enthralling. They were people who had lived right there, had established the traditions that became ingrained in Bald Eagle Falls life, and had passed on names and physical and personality traits to the people Erin knew.

She carefully unfolded yellowing old newspaper articles, the dust tickling her nose, and dug up the past lives of Bald Eagle Falls. It was almost voyeuristic. She read in fascination about the ways they had lived and died. Where there were pictures, she studied them closely, sometimes with a magnifying glass, searching for familiar features and taking in the old-fashioned clothing and equipment. It must have been an interesting—and difficult—time to live.

She opened up a letter written on thick paper that had been folded twice, the paper almost brown with age. The old-fashioned cursive writing was difficult to read, but she was getting better at it after puzzling through dozens of letters. This one appeared not to be a letter, but a poem.

The treasure it enfolds
Where lies there forest gold
A king's ransom hid amidst
The warrens of the moles
The gift of life to those who toil
Each day to reap the sterile soil
Be wise if thou would life preserve
And no lord be forced to serve

Erin read over it a few times. She felt a thrill of excitement.

She tapped out a quick text to Vic.

Do you want to find a treasure?

It was a few minutes before Vic messaged her back a questioning smiley face. Erin grinned.

Come and see!

She looked out the attic window toward the apartment loft over the garage, where Vic's light was still turned on. In a few moments, she saw Vic's door open and saw the girl silhouetted against the light from inside for a moment before she hurried down the stairs and headed toward the house. Erin picked up the poem and went down the attic stairs to meet Vic in the kitchen. Vic stopped for a moment to make sure the burglar alarm hadn't been armed yet, then turned to look at Erin.

"A treasure? What's all this?"

Erin held the paper out to her, and Vic took it carefully by the edges. She didn't have as much practice as Erin did in reading the old-style script, so it took her a few minutes to puzzle through the short poem, then she looked at Erin, eyes sparkling.

"Gold? Where did you find this? And how do you know it wasn't already found a hundred years ago?"

"We'd have to do some more research before we'd know one way or the other. Go through the rest of the file, the newspaper archives, see if there's anyone around who can remember what it's all about. I just thought…" Erin shrugged. "It sounded like fun. I've never had a real-life treasure to find before."

"And we needed another mystery to solve since no one was killed at the opening," Vic teased. "You might get bored without something to challenge that noggin of yours."

Erin rolled her eyes. "Honestly, what I need is something to take my mind off of Charley and whatever her next idea is going to be. This looked… promising."

"Forest gold," Vic said slowly, meditating on it. "A king's ransom. That's got to be pretty big. I mean, we're not just talking a few coins, here."

"Yeah. It has to be something good. Everyone says there is treasure hidden around here, right? Well… maybe there is. What if we could find it?"

"That would solve a lot of problems. Nothing like a little gold to smooth your way."

"So, you want to find out more?"

"Why don't we look through the file? We can do that tonight without having to go to anyone else or go to the library."

"It's upstairs. I'll go get it."

Vic was waiting on the couch when Erin brought the bulging file down the stairs. She laid it on the coffee table, being careful to keep everything in order and not let the papers spill out in an avalanche.

"It's like an archeological dig," she said. "Everything related to the poem should be in the layers around it, so we don't want to get them out of order."

"Right here in the middle?" Vic indicated the two stacks of paper. "I guess I'll take the top, and you can go through the bottom. You've already looked through the top anyway, haven't you?"

"Yes. You're sure you don't want to go through the bottom together? I don't think there was anything about treasure in that half."

"No, you go ahead and take the bottom. If there's anything about a hidden fortune or a treasure map in the top, I'll find it."

Erin shrugged. "Okay."

She took her half, and they started to go through the piles a page at a time. Orange Blossom had been sleeping on the arm of the easy chair but, hearing the rustling of paper, he woke up, stretched his body out slowly, and wandered over to see what they were looking at, making inquiring noises.

"Nothing interesting to kitties," Erin said, pushing him away with her toe. "Just boring old papers."

He went around her foot and approached Vic's pile. Vic pulled them away. "Nope. Not today, Mr. Blossom. I need to look at these."

Orange Blossom jumped up on the coffee table, sniffing all around the empty file folder. He sneezed three times, shaking his head briskly between each sneeze.

"Oh, gross!" Vic protested. "He sprayed cat snot on my papers!"

"Oops," Erin laughed. "I don't imagine that's good for them."

"If the oils from our skin and the acid in the paper can make it degrade, I hate to think of what cat snot could do."

Vic did the best to dab at the wet spots with a tissue and waved the papers in the air to dry them out.

"Have you found anything about the treasure?" Erin asked.

"No, not yet. Just lots of marriage and death records and what dresses everyone is wearing to what parties." She sighed. "Were people really so shallow? That's all they had to put in the newspaper?"

"Well, it isn't like today when we can gather news from all over the world. They probably didn't even hear much from outside the county. It was all local news. So, the social stuff became really important."

Vic shook her head. "I love a nice party dress as much as the next girl, but this is going a bit too far, if you ask me."

Erin looked at the additional articles she had read through. "There's a bunch of war stuff too. You don't really think about how it affected people out here in the hills. You think they were far away from the fighting, and their lives would just go on as normal. But people from all over sent their sons to fight, and the war disrupted all kinds of infrastructure and people's ability to earn money. It's no wonder someone would write about finding treasure to save your life and not have to serve anyone else. It sounds like things were pretty grim."

"I guess it must have been important to keep up appearances," Vic said, fingering through her social notices, "even if they were dirt-poor and having trouble making ends meet."

"I guess."

"Did you find anything else about the treasure?"

"I don't know." Erin had her fingers marking a couple of places in the file. "This one talks about people trying to solve a riddle. And this one talks about them waiting for gold to come in to pay for shipments of corn that had been sent to the front."

"Maybe related and maybe not," Vic agreed.

She pushed Orange Blossom off the coffee table in order to put her pile of papers back into the file folder. He landed awkwardly on his back, flipped over, and jumped to his feet. He licked down the fur on his back and glared at Vic.

Erin laughed. "Stay out of the way and you won't get pushed off."

Vic looked toward the back of the house and Erin heard the growl of a truck engine a moment later.

"That will be Willie," Vic said. "We'd better head to bed if we're going to be up in time in the morning."

"Okay. Say 'hi' to Willie for me."

"He says 'hi' back," Vic said. She gave Erin a quick hug around the shoulders and headed out. "I'll arm the alarm," she called back to Erin.

"Okay. Thanks."

Erin put her papers back into the folder. "And off to bed for us too," she told Orange Blossom. He immediately took a few steps toward the kitchen doorway and looked back at her expectantly. Erin followed him and, as soon as she was in the kitchen, she heard the patter of Marshmallow's paws behind her. She gave them each their treats and shut off the lights.

~

"We should ask Beaver for her thoughts on the hidden treasure," Vic suggested to Erin while they prepared the baking the next morning. "She's the one experienced at this kind of thing."

Erin thought about it. "I guess that would be okay," she agreed. "I don't think she's the kind of person who would take off on her own to claim it for herself, do you?"

"No." Vic considered the matter herself. "I know treasure hunters are known for having no honor… but I think Beaver does. It isn't like she took all the credit for the drug bust, did she? She could have. She could have said it was all her doing."

Erin had been thinking the same thing. "We could ask Terry what he thinks."

"You're going to tell Terry?"

"Of course!" Erin was surprised Vic would even ask. "Why wouldn't I?"

"I just wondered... he might not like you... you know... detecting."

"It's not detecting. Not like asking about a murder. I'm just... looking into something from the past. Genealogy. He won't care. There's nothing dangerous about it."

Terry didn't welcome the idea quite as much as Erin had hoped he would. His mouth formed a straight line and his forehead creased as he thought about it.

"It's just an old poem," Erin said. "I'm sure it probably won't even lead to anything; it's just something sort of fun to look into. It's not like it's a crime. It's not something dangerous."

"I'd agree, except that I know the way you seem to stir things up... just because you don't think there's anything to it or anything to worry about, that doesn't mean it's true. You seem to have a knack for finding dangerous things, even if it doesn't seem like there would be anything to it. Treasure maps and hidden tunnels... they shouldn't be real... but they are."

Erin tried to shrug it off.

"I really don't think this is anything that's going to attract any attention. We'll keep it quiet. Just me and Vic."

"And Jeremy and Beaver. And whoever else you happen to ask for background information from. Maybe the librarian."

"And you, but you're not going to suddenly turn into a homicidal maniac, are you?"

He didn't crack a smile at her teasing, which told Erin that he really was worried.

"Really, it's just a poem," she said. "It will probably turn out to be something some high school student wrote for an English assignment. You really think there is a chest of gold buried out there in the forest somewhere?"

"No... but people can act strangely when they think there is. You don't know how people might react to the suggestion that there's a treasure to be found. What happened when you told people that there was a locked cabinet in your basement that might hold some kind of key to finding an ancient pirate treasure?"

"Well… someone broke in." Erin hadn't even thought about that. They would have to be careful of security and make sure they didn't tell the wrong person what they were looking for. "I'll be careful, Terry, but I really don't think you have anything to worry about."

Terry sighed and shook his head. "Famous last words."

CHAPTER 4

*I*n spite of Terry's concerns, Erin forged on ahead. She agreed that they would need to make sure that the wrong people didn't find out about the poem and what they were looking for, but she still wanted to find out more about the poem, who wrote it, and what the treasure was that was possibly hidden somewhere in the forest. What were the chances that it was still there after so many years? If it had even existed, the chances that it would still be there were, Erin thought, pretty slim. But it would be fun to try to find out anyway. Like geocaching, it would be fun just to see where the clues led them, even if they didn't find anything that had intrinsic value.

They decided to have supper with Beaver and Jeremy at the Chinese restaurant and, after eating, Erin pulled out the poem, which she had carefully protected in a plastic sleeve and transported in a clipboard to make sure it didn't get folded, crushed, or torn. Erin gave a little preamble about looking through Clementine's genealogy, then handed the poem across the table to Beaver and Jeremy to have a look at.

Beaver's eyes gleamed as she read through the poem. Her smile was wider than ever. She passed it over to Jeremy for him to read. "Got the treasure-hunting bug?" she asked Erin. "This looks like a lot of fun."

"Do you think it's real?"

"If you didn't make it up, it's real. But a real what, we don't know. Is it actually a clue to a treasure? A real treasure? Something that is still valuable

258

today? And if it is, has that treasure been found, or is it still out there? How many people know about it? How many people have looked for it? What are the chances it has been found?"

"Well, I guess the chances are pretty good that it might have been," Erin said, shifting uncomfortably. "I mean, it's been a long time, so someone might have found it just by accident, not even looking for it. And if a lot of people know that it exists or have looked for it…"

"Right," Beaver nodded. "Don't get your hopes up too much. There is no guarantee that this treasure is even around anymore. If there is a treasure. It could just be a poem."

Erin nodded.

"Was there anything else with it? Something that might indicate that it is legitimate?"

"It was in a folder with a lot of other stuff, but none of the other papers I went through mention it at all. So, I don't know… I found some other newspaper clippings that might be related."

Erin withdrew the other clippings from her clipboard, likewise preserved in plastic sleeves to keep them from tearing or being damaged.

Beaver took the other two articles and read them through slowly. She pursed her generous lips, thinking it through.

"You're right," she agreed. "They could be related or could be nothing to do with the poem. You could just be making connections between things that are completely unrelated to each other. It's pretty tenuous." She looked at them again. "Solving a riddle… it could just be some kind of crossword or brain teaser that the paper had published the previous week. There might have been a prize for being able to crack the code. If it was related to your poem, then they might have figured out what it meant a hundred and fifty years ago. Do your newspaper archives go back that far?"

Erin shook her head. "I haven't looked yet, but I doubt it. Though Aunt Clementine got this from somewhere. Someone still had old newspapers around twenty years ago when she was on a genealogy kick."

"This wasn't clipped from any official archives. It's original. If it was in archives, she would have done a microfiche print or photocopy. No archivist is going to let you clip out of the original paper."

"No," Erin agreed. "But Clementine had a lot of stuff that was original papers."

"She must have known someone who hoarded them. Or she had them herself from an ancestor's collection. Sometimes old papers were used as insulation in walls or attics. She might have come across it during some renovations."

"I don't know when it was she built the reading room in the attic. She could have found it then."

Beaver nodded. "You never know what you're going to find in old attics and crawlspaces."

"What's the other one?" Jeremy asked.

Beaver slid them over to him so that he could read them as well. Jeremy read over the description of the payment the town was awaiting for the crops that had been shipped out.

"How much would they have been expecting to get for one shipment of crops? It wouldn't have been a king's ransom. Just part of one year's earnings."

Fresh off the farm himself, Jeremy would have a pretty good idea of how that worked. "One portion of one year's crops wouldn't even be enough for the farmers to get through one year. It certainly wouldn't set anyone up for life."

"No, I guess not," Erin admitted, with a twinge of disappointment.

"A king's ransom might well be an exaggeration," Beaver said. "If it *was* the payment for the crops that was lost or hidden, it might still be worth quite a lot... just not as much as you would hope."

"Or it might be practically worthless," Vic put in. "We don't know how big this crop was that they sent to the troops, how many farms it was from. If it was just one or two farms, then we could be talking about ten bucks each for the laborers."

"Gold is still worth something, though," Erin argued. "Ten dollars of gold a hundred and fifty years ago would be what now?"

Beaver gave a grin. "It would still have some value. Especially since we don't have to pay anybody's wages with it this many years later." She took a sip of her green tea. "I just don't want you getting your hopes up. You might think that because you found a tunnel full of illegal drugs on your first try that treasure hunting is easy, and it's not. I've looked for a lot of treasures over the years, and I've only been successful in a handful of cases. Enough to keep me looking for more, but the actual value of what I have found so far doesn't amount to even a fraction of a king's ransom. If you're looking for this, it should be because of the challenge, not because you think you're actually going to make a fortune."

Erin nodded. "To be honest, I just want something to do that isn't related to the bakery and Charley. I want a diversion. Reading through genealogy stories is fun, but this is even better... I kind of like solving puzzles."

"Kind of," Vic agreed with a wry grin. "What did Officer Piper have to say about it, by the way?"

"It's just a poem," Erin said, not answering the question. "There's no harm in seeing if we can figure it out."

"Well," Beaver positioned the poem in front of herself again, reading it through. "With the mention of moles, I'd say our first clue leads to an underground tunnel. Now you wouldn't know anything about underground tunnels in these parts, would you?"

Erin laughed. "Well, it's not in the tunnel under the bakery, I can tell you that. I think the DEA would have mentioned if they'd found a stash of gold down there with the drugs."

"Or else the Jackson clan made off with it when they first discovered the tunnel," Beaver agreed, "and if they did, they're not very likely to share that news with us."

"But what are the chances that it would have been hidden in that tunnel? Or in any of the old tunnels that were right in town? If it was you, wouldn't you hide it somewhere more remote? I wouldn't want people stumbling over it here in town. If those tunnels were used regularly during the war, then they would have been too well-known to hide anything really valuable. You wouldn't want some other person in town just stumbling across the treasure."

Beaver nodded. "You're probably right. Though we don't know how many people knew about the tunnels, or if they knew about all of them, or if each family only knew about the ones that were connected to their homes or businesses. There were probably some tunnels that were only known to the owner."

"So, you think we should try to find as many of the old tunnels in town as we can?"

"No."

Everybody just looked at Beaver. She took a long sip of her tea and grinned at Jeremy.

"I think that after the big drug bust, everybody is looking for signs of tunnels under their houses and workplaces. It isn't exactly a secret anymore. One thing you need to know about treasure hunting is that if you look in the same places everybody else is looking, you're not going to find anything. It would be a waste of time for us to go around town trying to find all of the old tunnels. Everybody else is already doing that, and they've either found a tunnel and aren't going to tell you about it, or they don't want anyone looking for tunnels on their property. They're not just going to invite you in to look at their basements while you try to catalog all of the old tunnels in Bald Eagle Falls."

"We could make it into a contest," Vic suggested. "We could have everybody who has found a tunnel make a submission to a contest, and then the person we draw or the person who knows the most about the old tunnel system wins a prize..."

"Of what? A gluten-free muffin? Nobody is going to tell you about their secret tunnels for even a full box of muffins."

"The town could enact some kind of law that all of the tunnels have to be registered," Jeremy suggested. "For safety reasons. An inspector has to go check out each one to make sure that it is safe and isn't going to collapse. Then there would be a record of where they all were, and we'd probably be able to find a few new ones that hadn't been discovered yet between dead-end tunnels..."

Beaver was shaking her head. "None of that would be of any help to us. Like I said, you're just looking where other people have already been. There's no point. And even if you did get the town to enact a law like that, most people would decide that their secret tunnels were their own business and they'd refuse to register them. You wouldn't even get enough votes on the town council to pass a law like that."

"Let's assume it's not in the townsite," Vic said. "Like Beaver says, everybody is already looking for those tunnels. There are plenty of places outside the townsite a treasure could have been hidden. It's not necessarily a man-made tunnel. It could be a natural cave or a mine."

Erin gave a shudder.

"You wouldn't happen to know anyone who is an expert on caves around here, would you?" Beaver asked with a grin.

Willie had been invited to dinner, but he'd had other things to do and hadn't been able to join them. Erin hadn't thought about him being a resource in their search for the treasure, or she would have tried to schedule a better time for their dinner so he would be able to join them. It made sense, when she thought about the "warrens of moles" in the poem that they should be looking for tunnels, caves, or mines. And that was Willie's purview.

"Do you think Willie would be able to help us?" Erin asked Vic.

"Sure. But you know... he's not the treasure hunting kind."

It seemed like a strange thing to say. Willie spent much of his time mining or exploring caves or old mine shafts, which sounded exactly like treasure hunting to Erin. Erin frowned at Vic.

"But... that's what he does."

"Mining isn't the same as treasure hunting," Vic disagreed. "It's science based. He knows which mines are more likely to produce because of the surrounding geology and what he's taken out of there before. Treasure hunting is... pretty much chance. If he agrees to help out, it will probably be for a fee. And not a portion of whatever you find, an up-front fee."

"Oh." Erin hadn't thought about that. Of course, she knew that Willie was involved in a wide variety of money-making ventures. He wasn't the kind of guy who was satisfied working one job and making a regular salary. He followed his interests and did a lot of smaller jobs on a short-term basis. If he were going to waste time looking for treasures in caves, then of course it would be for a fee. He wasn't going to take time out of paying jobs for something that was just for a favor. "Yeah, that makes sense. We'll have to talk to him about what his fee would be."

"If you're just doing it for fun, you don't want to be pouring money into the venture," Beaver warned. "If Willie doesn't want to help just for the challenge, you might not want to run up your costs. There are bound to be other people who have some knowledge of caves in the area, old survey maps, things like that."

"Yeah." The wind had been taken out of Erin's sails a little. She had hoped that she would be able to figure out the clues to where the treasure might be with a little ingenuity and the help of her friends. She hadn't considered having to pay for professional advice. She looked down at the poem in front of Beaver. "So, what else? Do you think there are any other clues as to where it is in the poem? If it's supposed to direct us to the treasure, it doesn't seem like there are many things to point to a particular location."

"No, you're right. Talking about those who toil... that lends some credence to it being the lost payment for the corn crop... sterile soil, though... that could be something else. Some of the other words in the poem might be locator clues, too. King and lord are both named, so you might be looking for a location that is named after someone with high-ranking authority. Or for a castle-shaped landmark. Life preserve... I don't suppose they had any animal preserves back then... but I might look into whether there were any endangered species they were trying to protect."

Erin jotted words down on her napkin, listing the clues and then places or ideas that came to her mind. Her excitement started to rise again. "I'm going to need some maps. And to do some more research on the area around here. And there might be something in the clippings Clementine kept about royalty; I wasn't looking for that..."

CHAPTER 5

*R*elaxing after a long day of work at the bakery and butting heads with Charley, Erin decided to let the animals out for a frolic in the back yard. They were pretty good about staying in the yard. Marshmallow sometimes attempted to burrow out under the fence and Orange Blossom sometimes jumped up on top of it, but when Erin told him to cut it out or she wouldn't let him out in the yard again, he would jump down, glaring at her, and go eat the longer grass at the back fence, which he would then throw up in the house. Marshmallow didn't pay any attention to her one way or the other, and it was just a matter of making sure any previous attempts to burrow were filled in and shooing him out whenever he tried to dig his way out again.

They were both happy exploring the smells of the large back yard and pretending they were out in the wild. Erin watched Orange Blossom stalking butterflies and grasshoppers, pretending he was a mighty hunter like his progenitors.

"Just don't bring me anything dead," she warned him, not wanting to be faced with any surprises if he happened to catch a mouse or vole.

His ear twitched at her words but, other than that, he ignored her and continued his hunt. Marshmallow had disappeared around the corner of the garage, so Erin got up to find him and shoo him back into the main part of the back yard where she could watch him.

As she approached the rabbit, she saw Adele coming down the worn path from the woods. Adele waited to make sure that Marshmallow wasn't going to make a break for it before she opened the gate to let herself in. But the rabbit seemed to be enthralled with whatever it was he had found growing beside the garage. Erin remembered that was just about where she had found him the first time, a young rabbit, injured by one of the pieces of equipment that had been clearing away the rubble of the old garage.

Erin waited until Adele was through the gate and had closed it again before giving Marshmallow another nudge.

"Come on, you. Come back to the yard where I can see you."

Marshmallow chewed on a plant, resisting her foot.

"Marshmallow. Come on, bunny. I don't know what you're eating, but it's probably not good for you. Come to the house and I'll give you a nice piece of apple."

He didn't move. Erin bent down and picked him up, wrapping her hands around his soft belly and picking him up to move him a few feet away. Marshmallow hopped back toward the house, acting as if he didn't care. Erin looked down at the plant he'd been grazing on. Yellow leaves and bright red berries.

"Do you know what this is?" she asked Adele. It wasn't one of the plants she recognized by sight. Granted, she only had a limited knowledge, but she knew most of the plants that grew around the house so that she could be sure the boys weren't poisoning themselves on whatever they were eating.

Adele took a few steps closer and crouched down. She didn't give any immediate sign of recognizing it.

"Maybe I should take a picture and look it up," Erin suggested.

Adele took another minute, then looked up. "You don't need to. It's wild ginseng."

"Ginseng?" Erin raised her brows and looked at it. She knew a little bit about ginseng from Clementine's stores of teas that Erin still served at the ladies' tea every Sunday. It was supposed to give energy and alertness, to help boost the immune system, and a whole host of other uses. Like some other herbs, the list of what ginseng might do was probably longer than the list of what it couldn't do.

Adele nodded. "You're very fortunate. Wild ginseng is a rare find these days. It used to be more plentiful, but it was over-harvested for the Asian market and just about disappeared from these mountains. The Chinese call it 'manroot' because of the shape of the roots. In these parts, they called it 'sang' and the people who made a living searching for it were called 'sangers.'"

"So, I shouldn't pull it," Erin suggested.

"Oh, no. I wouldn't do that. In fact, I'd suggest that you take these berries," Adele indicated the red, wrinkled berries, "and plant them in similar spots around the yard, then make sure the rabbit doesn't eat them when they come up."

"Can I use it? Like ginseng you would buy at the store? It's not toxic or anything?"

"No, it has many beneficial properties. If you're going to use it, may I make a suggestion...?"

"Sure, of course."

"A plant like this takes five to ten years to grow. It's just coming into maturity and the age that it can be legally harvested. Since it's in your own yard and you're using it for your own purposes, you don't need a license and you don't have to wait until it's ten years old, but if you were harvesting it for commercial purposes, there is a long list of regulations to adhere to. The part that you want to use is the root..." Adele pushed her finger down into the ground and followed the stem down underground and cleared soil away from the top part of the large, parsnip-like root. "This rhizome. If you were harvesting it commercially, you would dig up the whole thing, because the Asian market only wants intact roots, especially if it's the classic man shape. But if you're just using it for yourself, you don't need to sacrifice the whole plant. Just cut off an inch or two of the root, dry it, and use it as you wish. Leave the rest of it growing, plant all of the seeds it produces and, in a few years, you'll have a good crop of ginseng available."

Erin nodded. "Okay. I don't need to do anything special to treat the roots? Just dry them?"

"You can use fresh roots as well, especially for tea, but it is usually preserved by drying. Just wash and lay out in the sun, make sure it doesn't get moldy."

"And it's not going to hurt Marshmallow? Eating the leaves?"

"The leaves aren't normally used. Deer and rabbits eat them in the wild. It might make him a bit more frisky, but it won't hurt him."

CHAPTER 6

With the animals back where she could see both of them once more, Erin sat down in one of the outdoor chairs with Adele, and they watched the pets while relaxing in the fresh air.

"So... how is everything going?" Erin asked. "Is everything back to normal?"

Adele didn't answer for a while. She watched the animals, considering, and Erin wasn't sure whether she was going to attempt an answer. Adele looked up at the sky. Erin took a quick glance up to see if she could see Adele's pet crow, but she couldn't pick a black speck out in the blue sky and fluffy white clouds.

"I guess I'm waiting to see if everything goes back to normal," Adele said slowly. "In the past... things haven't turned out well when Rudolph has shown up. He has a way of attracting people's attention and making them uncomfortable."

He had done more than make people uncomfortable in the short time he had been in Bald Eagle Falls. But Erin kept that comment to herself. Adele knew as well as anyone what had happened. She didn't need to be reminded.

"He's a handsome guy," she commented. "I would imagine people notice him."

"If he was just handsome, that would be one thing," Adele said, nodding. "People might notice a good-looking guy, but then forget about him ten minutes later. But with his personality, his need to be the center of attention and to make sure everyone sees him and takes notice…"

Erin nodded. She had not been particularly comfortable around Rudolph. He had definitely come across as someone who was self-important, who expected people to do what he said because he was rich or had influence.

"Yeah. He does kind of come across that way."

"He has a lot of flaws. I never found much reason to stay with him… I was attracted to him, and things would go well for a while… but before long, he was looking at other women, hardly taking any notice of me at all, chasing these big deals or unsavory deals… and I would just get so fed up with him and cut him off."

"And then he'd come after you and you'd fall for him all over again?"

Adele made a face. "It makes me sound shallow. I knew we weren't good for each other, but when he would come after me…"

"I don't think it makes you shallow if you loved him. You can't just turn that off because you want to."

"There has to be more to a relationship than attraction. Falling in love is no excuse for staying with someone who is ultimately going to be bad for you. The whole idea of falling in love…"

Erin waited. Adele shook her head and puffed out her breath. "I don't know how to put it. Attraction isn't love, and the whole idea of falling in love just because you're physically attracted to someone… I guess I thought I was above that. I was better than that."

"We can't help how we feel."

"We can help how we act. It isn't enough to be physically attracted. There are people all over the world who don't act just because they are attracted to someone they see. If they're already married, or not social equals in their society, or there are other reasons that the relationship is a bad idea, people choose not to act on mere attraction. And it sounds simple. It sounds easy."

Erin watched Orange Blossom stalk a butterfly. "It sounds easy," she admitted. "It sounds like you should just be able to turn it off and make a better choice. But people all over the world make the wrong choice, too. It isn't that easy."

"No," Adele agreed with a sigh. "It isn't."

They were silent for a while. The breeze blew Clementine's wind chimes, and Erin listened to the soft musical background it produced.

"For what it's worth, I'm sorry," Erin told Adele. "I know this couldn't have been easy for you. You didn't ask him to show up and... do the stuff he did. And now people are acting like you were involved. When it didn't have anything to do with you."

"It doesn't matter where I went... sooner or later, he would get bored with his life or the affair or the sure thing that never panned out, and he would look for me again. I'd end up falling for him again, acting like a silly schoolgirl instead of like a grown woman with a mind of her own, letting him back into my life again, somehow thinking that things would be different this time. This time he would really mean it and he would stay, and things would work out between us. But that's not the way it worked. People don't change." She gave her head a bitter shake. "People never change."

Erin turned her head to look at Adele.

"Sometimes they do. If they really want to."

"The trouble with Rudolph is, whether that is true or not, is that he never wanted to. He never saw any reason to change."

Erin decided to give Charley a shot behind the counter for the ladies' tea on Sunday. Charley had made it to a few of the teas as a customer, so she knew what went on and was usually able to get herself out of bed and to get there in time. That would give both Vic and Bella the day off so they wouldn't have to pay for employee time. Charley wouldn't have to be there early for baking, as they generally prepared an assortment of cookies and treats ahead of time rather than baking on Sunday.

Charley arrived before church services let out to help Erin to arrange the trays and get everything prepared.

"Thanks for doing this today," Erin said, not sure how to say 'thanks for waking up on time' in a diplomatic way. "It's a nice break for Vic and Bella."

Charley nodded. "Sure, of course." She was a little flushed, and looked around as if she were sure she had forgotten something. Erin had been doing the ladies' teas enough times that they were now routine, but she recognized Charley's anxiety over getting everything set up right and presenting herself as a professional. "It's my place too, so I should be the public face at least part of the time."

"Don't worry, everything is fine," Erin assured her. "There isn't a lot to do for the tea. I do one big urn of black tea and make sure there's lots of hot water for anyone who wants a different blend or herbal tea. Everything else is prepared. The ladies just like to come and visit."

"It didn't seem like anything when you were doing it. But now that I'm partially responsible for seeing that everything runs smoothly..."

Erin nodded, chuckling. "Then it's a little bit different, isn't it? It will be just fine. If anybody needs anything, they'll ask."

Charley gulped. "Right. It will be just fine."

They worked on setting the treats out on trays. "I was wondering," Erin said, "what your family was like. Your adoptive family, I mean. You were with them right from the time you were a baby, right?"

It seemed strange to Erin that Charley had ended up being so rebellious when she'd been raised in a normal two-parent home her whole life. Erin understood kids like Reg ending up on the wrong side of the law. Multiple traumas, inconsistent parenting, no support system once they aged out of care; it was only natural for them to fall into street life, to be distrustful of anyone who tried to tell them what to do, and to scrape up what living they could by whatever means they could find. But Charley...

Charley looked at Erin for a moment, then went back to arranging sweets.

"Yeah, I've been with them for as long as I can remember," she agreed. "They picked me up at the hospital when I was just a few days old."

"And what are they like? What do your parents do?"

"They're good people... just your normal, everyday Joes. My dad does bodywork and my mom is a schoolteacher. Elementary school. Good, stable upbringing. Someone to help me if I ever ran into problems with my schoolwork. Good, loving influence." Charley flashed her a look. "So where did they go wrong, huh? Or is it just in the blood?"

"I didn't mean that. I just wondered... I don't know much about where you came from. I'd like to. You know about me."

Charley laughed and shook her head. "I know about you? Not much, Erin. Grew up in foster care. Inherited a bakery from your aunt. Started playing detective. It's not like you've divulged much to me about your life either."

Erin frowned. She checked on the tea, even though she knew it was just fine and didn't need any fiddling. "I've told you more than that."

"Really? Hmm… let's see. You have a foster sister named Reg. I know that because I met her. You had one named Caroline who died because she was celiac and wouldn't follow a gluten-free diet. And…? Have I missed something?"

"I was through a bunch of different homes," Erin said. "There isn't really one home that I consider my family or the one main influence on me. It was all pretty chaotic."

"How old were you when you went into care?"

"Eight." Erin was happy to have one question that was easy to answer. She hadn't expected the conversation to backfire on her. "Or, right before I turned eight. I was in foster care for my eighth birthday."

"So, you must remember something about your parents. About my birthmother."

"A little. It's not really clear. But some."

"So, what was she like? Did you bake with her? Is that where you got your love for cooking?"

"No… not that I remember. I don't think… I don't think baking was something she was ever interested in. I liked playing at the tea shop with Clementine. Maybe we baked cookies once or twice there. I don't remember much about my mother. Just… being around her. In the car. At home. Maybe… watching TV or cleaning…" Erin shook her head. "It's pretty fuzzy. I remember going for walks with my dad. He'd take me out, and we'd skip rocks… collect pinecones…"

"You don't remember doing anything with your mom?"

"Maybe playing with dolls once… She probably worked. I was probably at daycare or school during the day and only saw her for a couple of hours during the day."

Charley raised her eyebrows. "I can remember doing things with my mom at that age, and she was a schoolteacher, so she worked all day and then marked papers or prepared lessons in the evening after I went to bed. But I still remember playing with her and cooking supper together."

"There's a lot of stuff from around that time that I don't remember. With the car accident and losing both of my parents, it was a traumatic time." Erin knew she shouldn't have to feel defensive about not remembering much about her mother or their spending time together, but she couldn't help it. She wanted to be able to remember more about her parents. She had tried. "I just wondered what yours were like," Erin said, trying to bring the conversation back to Charley. "What it was like growing up around here. I mostly grew up in the north, you know."

Charley paused in her cookie-arranging. "I think it was a good place to grow up. I loved my mom and dad. We had a nice family. I always wanted brothers and sisters, but I understood they couldn't have them naturally and that it's just not that easy to adopt. They didn't have any involvement with any of the clans, it was just a normal upbringing."

"So…" Erin trailed off, not sure how to ask the question in her mind.

Charley held her gaze, not looking back down at her tray. "So, what happened to me?" she asked. "Why did I turn out like I did?"

Erin shrugged. "I guess. I just wondered…"

"Plenty of kids raised in good homes end up in trouble," Charley said with a shrug. "It doesn't mean there's anything wrong with their parents or with the way they were raised. It just means they… went off the rails. It can happen to anyone. I didn't really like being the good girl. I didn't enjoy all of those things that I was supposed to… going to school, getting good marks, finding a good job and growing up to be a conservative, responsible person. I wanted something more interesting. Something more exciting. I'm sorry, but being good isn't always a whole lot of fun."

Erin gave a little laugh of disbelief and shook her head. "That just sounds so…"

"Silly? I suppose so. Here I am, great upbringing, middle class home, no problems with abuse or drugs or parents who didn't give me enough time. Maybe some of it is nature. I gather that our folks weren't exactly the salt-of-the-earth types. Maybe the Plaint blood is a little more… adventure-seeking."

"I don't know… the ones that I met turned out to be pretty nasty to each other. There was a lot of dysfunction in that family."

"But maybe you can't just blame it all on how their parents raised them. Maybe some of it is just genetic. I have a genetic predisposition to… be an adventure-seeking free spirit. Not to be tied down by convention. Not everyone does want to settle down and raise a family and be responsible parents."

Erin looked away from Charley, readjusting the arrangement of her tray. "And what about you? You don't ever want to raise a family?"

"I think that what's more important to you is 'do I want to settle down and be a business owner?'" Charley pointed out.

"Yeah, I guess. I thought you'd already decided that."

"I did. But it's not easy. And I'm really more of a take-the-easy-way-out person."

"You've hardly even started. You're not considering giving it up already, are you?"

"No. I'm going to stick it out. You can't just give up after a few days. Not when it's taken months to actually get here."

Erin nodded. "Okay. Good. And if you do want out... you'll give me some warning, right? We'd need to find someone to buy you out, and I can't do that right now. I don't know who in Bald Eagle Falls could, but we'd have to try to work something out."

Charley made a motion to brush the topic aside. "Don't worry about it. I'm not taking off any time in the near future."

"Okay." But the talk about the Plaint family made Erin uneasy. Each of the family members that she had dealt with had been unpredictable and left the rest of the family in the lurch. Not of their own free will, but each of their exits had been abrupt and had left some significant ripples.

"We'd better get these out," Charley said. She picked up her tray and took it out to the front of the store. Erin silently followed with her tray and returned to the kitchen to grab the urn of tea and to fill a couple of teapots with boiling water as the first of the church ladies entered the front door, their entrance marked by the friendly jingling of bells.

CHAPTER 7

*E*rin was surprised to have Rohilda Beavan show up at the ladies' tea. She hadn't talked to Beaver about it, though she supposed she had probably mentioned it in passing. She hadn't thought that Beaver was a churchgoer, and generally those who didn't attend church weekly didn't go to the ladies' tea, though of course, there was no rule to stop them from doing so.

Beaver's presence was definitely noticed by the regulars, who watched her awkwardly and didn't quite know how to respond to her wide smile, lazy drawl, and constant gum chewing. Moreover, Beaver was dressed as she usually was, in camouflage cargo pants, a tank top, and a hunting jacket, while the usual attire for the women at the ladies' tea was a conservative dress, with only the occasional pantsuit. Erin and Charley were wearing slacks, but the church ladies were all in dresses.

Erin could see that Mary Lou was making an effort to include Beaver and make her feel at home, which Erin appreciated. Mary Lou had found herself on the outside of the group for several months and perhaps that ostracism had made her more sensitive to others around her who didn't quite fit in or look or act the way that they were expected to.

"So… Rohilda… have you moved into Bald Eagle Falls?" Mary Lou inquired, taking a sip of her tea. She did not have any of the sweet treats.

She never did. Erin admired her willpower in being able to turn them down.

"No," Beaver responded, leaning her chair back onto two legs, her own legs spread wide, taking up lots of space. "Not full time, anyway, just visiting with Jeremy."

"It's good that he managed to find a place of his own. He seems like a very nice boy." Mary Lou glanced at Erin as if weighing her words and left whatever other comment she had about Jeremy unsaid. Maybe a dig about Jeremy being normal, unlike Vic. Mary Lou had never quite been able to accept Vic's gender identity, though she and Vic had come to an understanding on the matter. Mary Lou would keep her religious opinions about the rightness or wrongness of Vic's identity to herself so that she and Vic and Erin could at least be polite acquaintances, if not friends. In the months since Mary Lou's husband had gone away, Mary Lou had discovered that her good friends from church were not nearly as supportive as she would have expected them to be, and her friendship with Erin and Vic had become more important.

"He's great," Beaver gave Mary Lou a wide smile. "A lot of guys feel threatened by me, but he's very accepting."

"You're quite a bit older than Jeremy, aren't you?" Clara Jones asked, leaning forward and inserting herself into the conversation.

"A bit," Beaver agreed. "Doesn't seem to bother him any." She winked at Clara.

Clara gave a little gasp of shock. Erin tried to suppress a smile, not looking at Charley.

Beaver chewed her gum and looked back at Mary Lou, her eyes dancing.

"And how are your boys?"

Mary Lou gave a restrained smile. "Josh made the basketball team, so he's quite happy about that."

"And how is Cam doing?"

Conversations around them ceased, the other ladies darting curious looks at Mary Lou and Beaver. Erin realized she'd never heard Mary Lou's older son ever called anything but Campbell. Not only that, but he had been living out of town since before Beaver had shown up.

Mary Lou looked at Beaver, her lips pressed together tightly. "Campbell is fine, I suppose. Not that he tells his mother very much."

"Boys." Beaver rolled her eyes in sympathy.

"Do you... know Campbell?"

Beaver shrugged. "We've met."

And Beaver was a federal agent involved in drug enforcement and had done undercover work. Erin could see these facts flash through Mary Lou's mind as she tried to decide whether that meant her son was in trouble.

Beaver's merry eyes went momentarily serious. "He's okay," she told Mary Lou.

Mary Lou touched Beaver's arm. "You're sure?"

Beaver nodded. "Would I lie to a mom?"

Mary Lou's gaze was intense. "Yes, I believe you would."

"Okay, maybe I would," Beaver agreed with a laugh. "But I'm not. He was just fine last I saw."

Mary Lou sipped her tea. Beaver looked away from her, glancing around at the other ladies who had been listening in on the conversation.

"I hear there's some kind of fall fair coming up. What y'all doin' for that?"

They were clearly reluctant to change the subject, wanting to eavesdrop more on what was going on with Mary Lou and her family, but they were too polite to be that obvious about it. So, they turned to describe what crafts, baking, or other items they were preparing for the Fall Fair.

"What about you?" Beaver asked Erin. "You must be planning something special."

Erin nodded. "I don't want to say too much about it yet, I want it to be a surprise. But it is a traditional Tennessean dessert, and Vic is helping me out with all of the details to make sure that all of the usual rules are complied with, even though it will be gluten-free."

Beaver raised her eyebrows and took another cookie off of the platter closest to her. "I gotta say, I haven't ever tasted gluten-free like this before. Are you sure you're not just trying to pull one over on us all?"

"They're gluten-free!" Erin assured her. "Cross my heart!"

"We'd know if they weren't," Clara Jones offered. "Little Peter Foster, for one, wouldn't be able to eat them. He'd be sicker than a dog if Erin was trying to pull something off as gluten-free when it wasn't. And there are a few other people around town who need to eat gluten-free who could tell you they are."

Beaver grinned, nodding. Erin didn't get the feeling that she doubted at all that the treats were gluten-free. She was just being polite and encouraging conversation.

"Well then, I'm looking forward to whatever it is you and Vic are going to pull together for the Fall Fair. It sounds like it's going to be a lot of fun."

"You'll be there, then?" Lottie Sturm asked.

"I expect to be. Of course, work can always throw a wrench into the works. It isn't like I haven't ever had a day off get rescheduled before. But if I can, I'll be there."

"Is Jeremy doing anything for it?"

"I imagine he'll participate in some of the animal handling. He hasn't said yet what he's going to do."

"What about you?" Erin asked. "Are you going to do something?"

"Well, y'all don't want to taste my cooking. So, I won't be submitting any baking or preserves. Maybe I'll go out for the shooting. I'm not bad with a gun."

She patted her waist. Erin swallowed, unnerved by the fact that Beaver carried a gun with her so casually. People didn't attend the ladies' tea wearing guns. It just wasn't done. Something about it being on a Sunday made Erin think that Beaver should have just left her gun at home, even though Erin herself was an atheist. It just didn't seem like it was right for Beaver to bring a gun to the after-church tea.

When Terry dropped by toward the end of the tea, Erin knew that he would be wearing his gun, but somehow that was different. Terry was a police officer in uniform. And a man. Erin apparently had some hitherto unrecognized sexist viewpoints when it came to women wearing guns.

"We've had women win the sharpshooter contests before," Mary Lou commented. "It wouldn't be unheard of if you beat out all the men."

Beaver nodded at this, chewing her gum. "That'd be sweet. I wouldn't mind that at all."

The conversation seemed to have gone back to normal topics. Erin went around with the teapot to refresh anyone's drinks, listening to the casual gossip about what was going on in town.

Nothing to do with her this time. No murders or other mysteries to be solved. As far as everyone was concerned, everything was back to normal. It didn't matter that Auntie Clem's Bakery had moved across the street or that Charley was there helping out now that she was part owner. Everyone seemed completely comfortable with the way things were.

Erin didn't bring up her new mystery. She wasn't about to have the whole town searching for her treasure. Or even worse, spoiling her hunt by telling her that the treasure had been discovered long ago or that it didn't really exist.

She intended to have a good time finding that out for herself.

CHAPTER 8

$\mathcal{A}$t the end of the tea, Terry did show up with K9 at his heel to help tidy up, snitch a couple of leftover cookies, and offer to take Erin out for the afternoon. Erin sighed as she gathered teacups to be washed.

"I'd love to go somewhere... but I think I'm going to need to go into town to run a few errands. We did run into a few things that we need to buy for the bakery that we hadn't thought about before. We made do without, but it's easier when you have everything you need."

"How long is that going to take? Maybe we could go into the city together and catch a movie when you're done?"

"I just don't think I'll have time," Erin said reluctantly. "Once I get things done... it would be too late for a matinee, and that means it would be in the evening, and I'd be late getting back and wouldn't be in on time. I just don't think it's going to work this week."

Terry nodded slowly. He looked down at K9 instead of at Erin. "Seems like you've been pretty busy all the time lately. Should I be taking the hint?"

"No," Erin insisted. "No, it's not that at all. I'm not trying to put you off. I have been extra busy, but that's just because of reopening the bakery. After a couple of weeks, it should settle back down to normal again. Then we'll be able to do something."

"You're sure? It's better if you are open about it and just come out and say so if you don't want to see each other anymore."

"I do. I do. I'm not trying to avoid you or push you away. It's just a lot of work. You don't want to come into the city and hold my bag while I shop, do you?"

Terry made a face. "Not my favorite thing to do."

"Then don't worry about it. Things will settle down again and go back to normal."

"And then it will be the Fall Fair. And then you'll be thinking about Halloween and Thanksgiving…"

"Thinking about Halloween and Thanksgiving didn't stop me from spending time with you last year. We just have to fit each other in where we can. Sometimes you're on shift, and sometimes I'm busy with bakery stuff. It will work out if we both want it to."

"As long as you do."

"I do."

"Okay." Terry picked up another cookie. "But I need sugar to comfort myself."

Erin laughed and motioned to the plate. "Take as many as you like. I'm just going to toss them out."

"That would be a waste of good cookies," Terry said through a mouthful, and grabbed two more off of the platter.

K9 looked up at Terry and whined at him.

"K9 wants his too. Come here, K9, come and get one." Erin called K9 over to the cookie jar.

He looked at Terry, and when Terry signaled to him, he trotted over to Erin eagerly to get his treat too. They both munched on their cookies while Erin and Charley carried dishes back to the kitchen to be washed.

Eventually, Erin brushed off her hands. "Okay. That's it for me. I'll see you tomorrow."

Charley looked at her. "I wasn't planning on coming in tomorrow."

"Didn't you sign up for the early shift?" Erin teased.

Charley shook her head adamantly. "I've come to the conclusion that the only way for me to make the early shift would be to stay up and do it before going to bed. There's no way I can get up that early."

"People do it all over the world."

"They're not me. You ask my mom; I was always impossible to get out of bed in the morning. My body just isn't made for mornings."

~

Erin and Vic hadn't made any plans to see each other in the city, but Erin looked up from her shopping at the kitchen supply store to see a familiar blond head going down the next aisle over. She studied the girl for a moment to make sure she was right, then called out to her.

"Victoriaaaa…"

Vic's head snapped around. She saw Erin and her jaw dropped. She started laughing. "Erin! Aren't you supposed to be taking it easy this afternoon?"

"And I thought you were supposed to be out with Willie."

"I am. Willie?" Vic looked around. "He's around here somewhere. I must have lost him back in appliances. He was looking at something he thought he could use…"

"What are you doing here?"

"We just came out to eat, and I thought that since I was right here, I'd pop in and pick up a few of the things that we needed, and then I'd just text you and let you know that I got them so that we wouldn't both buy the same things. I thought I could save us some time. But you came anyway. I told you to rest this afternoon."

"I couldn't rest, knowing that I still needed to get things for the bakery. I have all of my lists, and today was the only day I was free to run errands. Otherwise, I'd have to wait until next week…"

Vic shook her head. "You're a workaholic. Where's Charley? I bet she's not out taking care of business today. She's out looking after number one, right?"

"She came to the ladies' tea today. But, no, I don't think she's doing anything else today. I think she was taking the rest of the day off."

"And you should have too."

"Said the pot to the kettle."

Willie came around the end of the aisle looking for Vic and put his hands on his hips. "I wasn't told this was an official meeting."

"It's not!" Erin insisted. "It was just chance that we both ended up here. We both thought we could save the other some time. And here we are."

"Using twice as much manpower instead of half," Willie observed. "Well, make quick work of it. Get what it is you need, and then I'll take both of you out to dinner."

"You can take Vic. No need to take me. I'm going to run a few other errands and head back to Bald Eagle Falls."

"Not without supper, you're not. You're here, so you're having supper with us, young lady."

"It's your date night. I'm not going to interfere."

"It's not interfering if you're invited. Now get what you need." He made a hurry-up motion with his hands. "Skedaddle. The faster you get done, the sooner you can have dinner and be on your way. We won't stop anywhere too formal. It will be quick. But you need to eat, so don't argue with me."

Erin shrugged widely and shook her head. She and Vic quickly divvied up the list of supplies they needed to get and went in opposite directions, gathering them up and meeting up again at the till. Willie was standing at the front of the store waiting for them when he was done, with a shopping bag of his own.

"Good. Now there's a pub just down the end there that serves the best wings you ever had. Quick and easy. How about it?"

"I'm yours," Erin said, giving in. He wasn't going to let her back out graciously, so she might as well eat. As he said, she was going to have to anyway.

Once they were settled, Willie tore into his first wing and narrowed his eyes at Erin.

"So, when are you going to tell me about this treasure hunt of yours?"

"Oh..." Erin looked at Vic, surprised. "Well, I didn't really want to bother you. Vic said you were pretty busy with other stuff, so..."

"I want to hear about it. Don't listen to Vic. You know how she is."

Vic laughed. "Does that mean you're offering your services to Erin for free?" she asked. "Because I think we'd better be up front about the arrangements. Do you want to hear, or do you want her to hire you?"

"I want to hear," Willie said. "No charge. If I can think of any way to help, I will. I'm not that miserly."

"I didn't say *miserly*," Vic returned. "I said careful with his money."

Willie made a face at her, then turned his attention back to Erin. "There is a poem? I don't suppose you have it on you?"

"I can remember it," Erin advised. She closed her eyes and envisioned the paper, then recited it to him. Willie thought about it, pursing his lips.

"Interesting. Not a lot of clues in there. At least, not at first. But there may be more than you think. What have you thought of so far?"

"Well… we might be supposed to start at a place that has something to do with a king. Something that has the name of a king or president, or maybe somewhere that looks like a castle or is named after one." Erin looked at Vic. "Right?"

Vic nodded vigorously. "That's where Beaver said to start."

"Good thinking. Well, there are a few places that might fit the bill. We have a rock formation locally known as the turret, because it looks like a castle turret. We have a King's Creek. There is no end of places that could be named after kings like James or Richard. As well as anyplace named after dead presidents. Because they are the kings of the United States."

Erin nodded. "Yeah. I was looking at a map, and there are a lot of places… but I don't really know where to start. I can see them on a map, but I don't know how big an area is covered or how to narrow it down to something searchable. Searching all of King's Creek or James's Forge… I don't know. Is there anywhere that really jumps out at you?"

"We have to look at the rest of the poem for other clues to narrow it down. It has to be somewhere underground, because of the reference to moles."

Erin's stomach gave that familiar nauseated turn at the thought of searching for anything in underground tunnels. "But that doesn't mean that the treasure is in a tunnel. It could just be a clue to something close. Or it could just mean that it's buried, not that it's in a tunnel."

"I'm thinking it means a tunnel," Willie said firmly. "I can't think of any other way that it could be in a mole's burrow. But that doesn't narrow things down a lot, because the number of caves and tunnels in Tennessee outweighs the number of caves in any other state. If you want caves, this is the place to be. But I don't know whether it is a manmade tunnel or a natural cave. I'm thinking manmade, since it talks about toil."

"You don't think that just relates to the crops that the gold was supposed to be payment for?"

"It could be. But you have to look at everything in the poem as having a double meaning. One that is obvious, and one that could mean something else. It has to be understood on more than one level."

"Okay. Maybe a manmade tunnel. And something to do with a king."

"King Solomon's mines?" Vic suggested. "Isn't that a thing? I think there's a movie."

"There is," Willie agreed. "It's from a book. But the book postdates the poem, so I don't think that's what they're referring to."

"But King Solomon goes back to ancient times, doesn't he?" Erin asked. "Isn't he a Bible guy?"

"He is a Bible guy. I don't know if there really is a legend about King Solomon's mines, but if there is… according to the movie, they were in Africa, not Tennessee. I don't think you want to be traveling all the way to the dark continent to try to find this treasure, do you?"

"No," Erin agreed, her face getting warm. "But it could still be a clue. What if there is a Solomon's Creek or Bible Bog?"

Willie nodded his agreement. "Sure. You'll have to see what you can find on the map. But remember that you're looking for something that existed a hundred and fifty years ago, not a new development. You might need to order some old maps to be able to figure it out. It could be some-where that doesn't exist anymore too. It might be a ghost town or a farm that changed its name a hundred years ago. Survey maps are probably the best bet, they'll refer to local landmarks of the time as much as possible. I have a few that I could lend you."

"You don't know of a King Solomon river, do you?"

"No. Nothing that pops to mind."

"How about the rest of it? Any ideas as to what the other clues might be?"

"Did you find anything in the newspapers of the time? Anything that was happening in the area at the time?"

"Mostly war stuff, births, deaths, marriages… there wasn't really a lot of real news. So-and-so's barn burned down. There was a big cucumber crop. I don't know. Nothing that seems like it would have much significance."

"Have you gone to the library archives or just looked through Clemen-tine's files with Vic?"

Erin looked over at Vic, seeing that she had already told Willie all about the evening they had spent looking for clues in the dusty file. "So far, just Clementine's files. I'm not even sure how far back the library will be able to go."

"If they don't have anything, some of the bigger libraries in the capital might have something. I know some of them have archives that go back that far. Don't know how much local color they'd have. Might not be helpful at all."

Erin nodded. "Okay."

"Remember that if Clementine had all of the information in her files, she probably would have figured it out herself. The fact that she never figured out that there really was a treasure or where it might have been suggests that she never had the full story. She just had the poem, and didn't have enough background to make it into anything meaningful."

"I guess that makes sense." Erin had been wondering whether she would need to look through all of Clementine's other files and genealogy books to find more clues, but Willie was probably right. If Clementine had had all of the clues, there wouldn't have been a mystery.

"So, I'll need to go to the library. And you have some maps that I could look at that might be better than Google maps?"

"Google maps has its place, especially if you can spot changes in terrain from digging, but it isn't as likely to give you those historical names. We'll need to work on the assumption that whoever wrote that poem lived around here and would have had limited transportation abilities."

"How limited?"

"Horse and wagon. A king's ransom of gold is too heavy for a man to carry. Limiting it to... say three days' wagon ride?"

"Which is?" Vic prompted.

"Maybe sixty miles."

It was still a pretty fair distance, but not so daunting as having to consider all of Tennessee.

CHAPTER 9

*E*rin had told Terry that she would be able to keep the treasure hunt a secret, shared with only their few close friends, but rumors spread much more quickly than she ever would have predicted. Searching through newspaper archives at the library attracted a certain amount of attention, even when Erin said it was for genealogy. Everyone she saw there wanted to know what genealogical line she was working on and who she was looking for. With all of the shared kinship in Bald Eagle Falls, everyone was related to everyone else, and anyone who was interested probably knew the genealogy of the whole mountain. Going back a hundred and fifty years was nothing; everybody seemed to know their family trees at least that far back. Many of them from memory.

As much as Erin tried to bluff her way through the conversations, it soon became obvious to people that she had something to hide, and the attempts to discover what she was working on became more and more of a problem. Erin neglected to close her clipboard one day, and the eagle-eyed librarian seemed to have read the poem from all the way across the room.

"Is that what you're up to?" Betty Thompson demanded. "You think there's a buried treasure?"

"I don't know," Erin said, trying to brush it off. "It's just a poem. I haven't found anything in the archives that would back it up."

"There have always been rumors of treasures hidden in these parts. If we knew which one the poem is talking about…"

"I'm not sure. I'll need to do some more research."

Betty was staring at Erin's clipboard, even though she had closed it when Betty approached, and Erin knew by the look in her eye that she was reconstructing it and visualizing it in her mind's eye. Betty Thompson's photographic memory was a legend in Bald Eagle Falls and made her a fantastic resource as a librarian. If she saw something once, she would remember it, and when you were looking for it again, she could pinpoint it in seconds. Faster than a Google search on a super computer.

"The paper and the script would suggest wartime," she said slowly, "so they're not talking pirate gold or early colonial days. More likely gold payroll. Preserving life could be referring to armies or soldiers. Not being forced to serve could refer to slavery."

Erin blinked at her. "Wow. You really are good. I don't know how you even saw that."

"All I need is one look, my dear! You know who is really good with civil war history? Edna, come over here!"

Erin tried to protest, holding up her hand to stop Betty, but Betty talked right over her protests, inviting Edna, a white-haired woman a few tables away, to come over to ask for her insights. Edna came over to them, and Erin again tried to politely wave them off.

"No, really, it's okay, I just wanted to work on this by myself—"

"Nonsense," Betty said jovially, "the more people who can help, the better chance you'll have of solving this. Now let's have a look…"

In spite of Erin's attempt to keep the poem out of sight, Betty quickly slid the clipboard out from under Erin's hand and opened it up to show to Edna. Erin was loath to kick up a big fuss in the middle of the library, attracting even more attention to her treasure hunt. She sat there with her mouth open, trying to think of what to say to dissuade them from their course.

The two women read over the poem again and discussed what the various lines of the poem might refer to. Erin couldn't help getting drawn into the conversation and gave in to listening to their insights and asking more detailed questions about the history of the area and the way that payment, and gold in particular, would have been handled a hundred and fifty years before.

Edna was definitely an expert on the matter, sketching out a rough map for Erin and pointing out the different routes that would have been used for transporting crops to market and gold back home, identifying the various landmarks along the way, and suggesting where a delivery might be lost or hijacked along the way.

"Wow, this is more than I ever could have gotten from a newspaper article," Erin said, amazed at the deep knowledge Edna and Betty had, "I didn't even know where to start."

"I would say that you need to look for mines and caves in this general area," Edna said, tapping her finger on the hand-drawn map. "It's close enough that someone in Bald Eagle Falls could have run into the wagon, but far enough away that the other residents would never know that the delivery had come so close. There are a few old mines around there. One person or a small group of people would have to be able to get the gold from the wagon to the hiding place, and gold is heavy, so they wouldn't be able to move it far. It's rough going out there in the wilds. It wasn't a highway like we're used to now. Just a rough track, and moving the treasure out of the wagon into a cave or mine would have been even rougher, cutting through brush and moving over uneven ground."

Erin nodded. "I know someone who might have some maps of the area and could help me out."

The women exchanged glances with each other.

"Willie Andrews," Betty asked.

Erin shouldn't have been shocked. Everybody in Bald Eagle Falls knew everybody else's business, and of course they would know that Erin knew Willie and that he was involved in mining and other ventures and would have all kinds of maps of the area. But she hadn't been expecting them to make that connection quite so quickly.

"Uh…"

They smiled at each other, as if she were some cute two-year-old who didn't understand the ways of adults.

"I really don't want this spread around," Erin hoped to mitigate some of the damage. "Do you think you could keep quiet about it? I don't want other people joining in the search… you know…"

"Of course not," Betty agreed. "This is your little treasure hunt, and good luck to you! We're not going to spread it around to all of our friends."

But Erin had a sinking feeling that each of them would tell at least one other person. And two more people aware of the hunt became four more people, and it wouldn't be long before everyone in Bald Eagle Falls had heard about Erin's possible hidden gold and were on the hunt for it as well.

~

Meanwhile, life went on at Auntie Clem's Bakery. Erin worked long hours and there was always plenty to do, not leaving her a lot of time for treasure hunting. She also had the Fall Fair to prepare for.

Vic sat down beside Erin to show her the recipes that she had gathered.

"So, this is how a Tennessee stack cake is made. It's not like any other layer cake you ever made. It's not all light and fluffy and loads of icing."

Erin skimmed the recipes for the pertinent details, frowning. "No... this is very different..."

"The layers are real thin," Vic explained. "You bake them like cookies, not like cakes, so that they're kind of hard and dry. They're dark and spicy, like gingerbread cookies."

"Okay."

"And you make the apple sauce. It's not applesauce like you buy in a jar at the store. You have to make it out of dried apples, and it's real thick and flavorful."

"And then you layer them."

"Right. A layer of cake, and then a thick layer of the apple filling. You have to have at least six layers for a genuine stack cake, and some of them are as high as fifteen layers. That's a sky-high stack cake."

"And the apple filling is supposed to soak into the layers of cake."

"You have to wrap it up real tight and let it sit for a full day. Better if it's three, but never less than one. The moisture from the apple filling gets into the cake and makes it real moist and rich."

"I've never heard of anything like that before."

"People who lived in these parts had lean times. They had to figure out ways to preserve food and then use it. No one wants to just eat dried apples all day. You make yourself a stack cake, and you've got another way to use that apple harvest. It's so good."

"And it should work well as a gluten-free recipe," Erin mused. "Since it's not something that's light and fluffy and has an open structure like angel food cake, you don't need to rely on gluten to help it to rise and hold its shape. It's okay if it's flat."

"It's supposed to be flat."

"And the lack of gluten will keep it nice and tender. It won't get rubbery like when you over-mix a wheat flour muffin batter. And the apple sauce will keep it from being dry and crumbly."

Vic nodded. She was getting more familiar with how gluten worked in baking and how to adjust for its lack. "That's one of the reasons I thought of stack cake."

"Brilliant. And we'll add our own twist, something just a little different that will combine the old and the new…"

"You're not already doing that by making it gluten-free?"

"No. I don't want them to be able to tell it is gluten-free. But I do want to give it something extra to give it a little update."

They were in the kitchen cleaning up when Vic's phone rang. Since they had already closed up shop, she stopped and took it out of her apron pocket. Her forehead creased in a frown, and she tapped the screen to answer it.

"Hello? Yes?"

Erin saw Vic's face rapidly lose all color. She hurried to Vic's side to catch her by the arm before she could faint.

"Vicky? What is it? What happened?"

Vic lowered the phone from her ear, staring at Erin, her eyes wide. "It's Jeremy."

"What happened?"

"He's been shot."

Erin's hand tightened on Vic's arm. She shook her head slightly, not believing it.

"What? How did he get shot?" Her mind went immediately to Beaver and her gun. Why hadn't she protected him? Or had Beaver been the one who had shot him? Had they had a lover's quarrel? Had they been target shooting and hadn't been careful enough?

Or had it been the Jackson clan?

What could possibly have happened?

"I don't know. They've taken him to the hospital. In the city. I have to go. Can I use your car?"

Erin took a quick look around the kitchen. All of the ovens were turned off and all of the batters and doughs were in the fridge. "We can leave the rest. I'll drive you."

"I can drive myself. You can get Terry to pick you up or you can walk home."

"I'm not letting you drive after having news like that. And I want to be there at the hospital, not at home waiting to find out what happened."

"You don't have to come."

"I know that. I want to. He's my friend."

Vic swallowed and gave a quick nod. "Okay. Thanks. You're sure we can leave everything?"

"It's just dirty, nothing is going to go bad. We'll take care of it later."

Vic headed for the back door. Erin shut off the lights and locked the door behind them.

CHAPTER 10

*I*t seemed like it took forever to get to the hospital. As Erin drove, she remembered Willie driving her when she had been poisoned. He'd grabbed Terry's police vehicle and sped all the way there. Erin wished that she had lights and a siren or a police escort, but she didn't and that meant that she couldn't speed all the way there. It just wasn't safe. She pressed the gas as far as she dared, not wanting to get pulled over and to have to explain to a policeman why they were going so fast.

Vic's hands were in her lap, her long, white fingers twisting together in her anxiety to get there and find out what had happened.

"I'm going as fast as I dare," Erin told her.

"I know. It's okay. We'll get there. I'm sure it's nothing. He probably shot himself in his foot loading his gun." She gave a little laugh that ended up sounding like a squeak or a hiccup.

"Yes. It's probably nothing," Erin agreed. But she didn't think it was nothing. If it was nothing, then Jeremy himself would have called Vic instead of the hospital. He would have laughed and made a big joke out of it, like he did about everything.

Finally, they were into the city, and Erin navigated the streets, keeping an eye out for the 'H' street signs indicating the route to the hospital. She hadn't been there enough times to know the way without them. She pulled up to the emergency doors.

"You go ahead. I'll go find parking and see you in a few minutes."

"Thanks, Erin." Vic jumped out, slammed the door behind her, and dashed in through the doors.

Parking was always an issue at the hospital; space was at a premium and they charged an arm and a leg for it. Erin laughed grimly at the thought of a hospital charging and arm and a leg, but she knew it wasn't really very funny. She was just anxious.

She had to work her way through the maze of hallways from the parking structure, following cryptic signs and ending up in the wrong wing more than once. Finally, she made it back to emergency after going out of the hospital and walking around the outside to the doors she had dropped Vic at.

She looked around the groups of chairs for Vic. She wasn't there, but was standing near the triage desk looking lost.

"What is it?" Erin asked, the pulse in her throat pounding so hard she could hardly hear. "What did you find out?"

"He's in surgery. He got shot in the torso, they won't say how bad it is."

"How did he get shot?"

"I don't know yet. They said someone would come out to talk to me. There are police…" She looked over her shoulder to the area behind the security glass where doctors and nurses were busy with their usual activities. There were several dark-uniformed cops in close conversation with each other. As Erin watched, one of them broke away from the group and swiped his card to open the security door that got him back into the waiting area. He nodded at Vic.

"You're Jeremy's sister?"

Vic nodded. "Yes. What happened? Is he going to be okay?"

"We still need to finish taking statements." He motioned them toward the grouping of chairs close by.

Erin guided Vic over to one of them and sat down beside her, keeping a comforting hand on her shoulder. The policeman remained on his feet.

"As I say, we're still investigating, but the bottom line is that he was shot at work, exchanging gunfire with a poacher."

"At work?" Vic echoed. She shook her head. "How does he get in a gunfight with a poacher in broad daylight?"

"The farm has had issues with poaching, which is why your brother was hired. We'll have to have some discussions about whether everyone was properly licensed and registered. As you say, it was pretty bold, planning a daylight robbery, but that appears to be what happened."

Vic rubbed her hand across her eyes and forehead. "What are they growing that is so valuable? Please tell me it's not drugs. Are they growing marijuana or poppies?"

He gave a sympathetic smile. "Everything appears to be legal."

"Well, thank goodness for that."

Erin noted that the officer still hadn't disclosed what it was that they were growing.

Time passed slowly. Erin sat and rubbed Vic's back and they spoke quietly to each other in fits and starts, mostly sitting silently, but occasionally talking about something unimportant as it came to mind. Erin watched the clock on the wall, as she was sure Vic did, willing the time to pass faster and for Jeremy to be out of surgery, fully restored.

After a couple of hours, Vic looked up, her eyes tired and swollen.

"Your knight in shining armor has arrived," she observed.

Erin followed Vic's gaze and saw Terry approaching with K9 at his side. He spotted the two of them and moved with more certainty.

"Vic. How is he? Do you know anything?"

"No, not yet. He's in surgery. Took a bullet somewhere in his body. That's all we know. Just... waiting for word of how the surgery goes."

Terry shook his head. He pulled a chair over, scraping the floor noisily. "I can't believe it. I figured he'd get in trouble while he was with the Jackson clan, or trying to get out of it, not when he got a legitimate job."

"It is legitimate, right?" Vic asked.

"As far as I can tell. I'm not getting any chatter that there's anything illegal going on. It seems to be all above-board."

"I can't believe it either. He's a good shot, so how did this poacher get the drop on him?"

"It sounds like there was more than one of them. So, he might have been pincered between two of them. I can't imagine that they'd be intentionally approaching him rather than trying to get... whatever it was they were trying to get, but there's no telling. Maybe he snuck up on one and didn't see the lookout."

"Did he get any of them?"

"We think so. They got away, but there is enough blood at the scene that he probably got at least one of them. We don't know how badly or how far they'll be able to travel. It will take time to do all of the blood analysis, of course; we're just going from droplet patterns at this point. They'll do typing and maybe DNA to sort it all out. If they think it's important. It might not really matter."

"Why wouldn't they?" Erin demanded. "They'd want to track down and arrest whoever these poachers are, wouldn't they? Why wouldn't they follow up on every lead?"

"Because testing takes time and money that could be better spent on other things. A couple of poachers don't rank high on the priorities list. Not when you've got drugs, gangs, and murders to deal with. Nothing was actually stolen, so there are no losses. It's just Jeremy's injury. Weapons and assault charges. And more than likely, they'll catch these guys when they show up somewhere for medical care. No need to waste money on unnecessary testing."

"It isn't important that Jeremy got injured?" Erin asked in disbelief.

"Not in the grand scheme of things, no." Terry looked away uncomfortably. "That doesn't mean that I don't care, it just means that's the way they prioritize resources. Of course, I care that Jeremy got hurt. I'm here. I want to support Vic and to make sure he's okay. It's not 'nothing' to me. But to bureaucrats who don't know him... it doesn't mean much to them. Just one non-fatal injury."

Vic choked up. Terry reached out to her and Vic held his hand.

"He's going to be okay, Vic," Terry said. "He'll be laughing about this before you know it."

"You don't know that. He could... he could be badly hurt. He could be..."

"Let's not jump to conclusions. I'm sorry. I didn't mean it to sound like that. He's going to be okay."

"If he is, he'd better not go back to this job again," Vic said forcefully. "He can find another job. This is crazy. Who shoots someone over a cornfield? I can't understand it."

"Corn?" Terry repeated.

"I don't know what they're growing. No one has actually said. But the policeman who was here and talked to us said that it wasn't drugs. It wasn't anything illegal. I can't think of what anyone would be growing that was that valuable."

"Maybe some kind of orchid," Erin suggested. "I know there are some really rare species that are really hard to grow. They need special greenhouses and monitoring equipment... maybe it's something like that."

"Maybe it is. I don't know." Vic ground her teeth. "Orchids!"

They were all quiet for a while. Terry looked at Erin.

"Do you want me to take you home? You can leave your car here for Vic."

"No, I'm not going anywhere. We need to know that Jeremy is out of danger."

"Oh, I know. I meant after that. When everything is sorted out and you're ready to go."

Erin shook her head. "No. I'll stay. Thanks."

"Okay..."

Erin looked at him. "What?"

Terry raised his brows questioningly.

"What's that tone?" Erin asked.

"No tone."

Erin looked at Vic for confirmation. "There was a definite tone," she insisted. "So, what is it? What's the problem with me staying here?"

Vic gave a little nod of confirmation, looking at Terry curiously. "There was something."

"No tone," Terry insisted. "I was just thinking that... you seem to have gotten pretty close to Jeremy. It seems strange that you're so protective of him and concerned about him when really, you hardly know him." He paused. "Because you really do barely know him, don't you...?"

Erin blinked. "You're jealous? I'm here because I'm concerned about my best friend and her brother, and you're jealous over that?"

"I just wonder... if it's more than that."

"Oh, good grief!" Erin blew her breath out in exasperation. "I'm not secretly in love with Jeremy. I'm here to support my friend. I care about Jeremy. I can care about someone without being... in a relationship with him."

"Of course you can," he agreed, his voice carefully neutral.

"And I do care about him. But we're not in a relationship. We're just friends. Like you say, we really don't know each other very well. But I know Vic."

He nodded slowly. "He was living in your house."

"I told you that there was nothing going on between us. He had his room and I had mine. I'm at the bakery all day and I just squeeze in a few hours of sleep each night. I don't have time to be running the bakery and going out with you and carrying on a torrid affair with Jeremy on the side."

Vic snorted and started to laugh. "A torrid affair?" she repeated. "Erin and Jeremy?"

Terry's face flushed red. "I never said that. I just worry that… there was more going on than Erin and Jeremy would like to admit. I don't even mean there was anything going on between them physically, but you don't know what people are thinking about… and they were living together, keeping it a secret."

"Because the Jackson clan was after Jeremy. You know exactly why he was living there. And you know that I told you as soon as I could. Before he wanted me to."

"Yeah."

"You think that he didn't want me to tell you because he had designs on me? He was hoping that if he kept it a secret that he was living there that… somehow, he'd get his chance with me? Even though I was still dating you?" Erin shook her head vehemently. "There's no way, Terry! And you know he's with Beaver now, so why you're still worrying about anything…"

Vic frowned and looked around. "Beaver."

Erin looked over at her, the same thought crystallizing in her mind. "Where *is* Beaver? Why isn't she here already? Didn't anyone let her know what was going on? Wouldn't Jeremy have asked them to call her?"

"If he could have," Vic agreed, "but maybe he couldn't."

"He had them call you."

"They called me… but I was his emergency contact at work. He told me that he put my name down because he wasn't sure where things would go with Beaver or if she'd always be available if something happened. You know, if she's undercover, they wouldn't be able to reach her, and she wouldn't be able to reach any of us. They wouldn't know to call me if they couldn't reach her."

"Do you have her number? Maybe no one has contacted her."

Vic shook her head. Erin looked at Terry. "Do you have her number? Or could you get it from someone?"

"I have it," Terry confirmed. He pulled out his phone and turned it on to check the contact phone numbers. Erin looked at Vic while Terry was looking it up.

"Me and Jeremy," she scoffed. "I mean, Jeremy's a nice guy, but I'm in a relationship already. And so is he, now. I love him like a brother. I never looked at him any other way."

"I know that," Vic said, but there was something in her eyes.

Erin frowned, getting a headache from the tension across her forehead. "Not you too? I didn't have romantic feelings toward Jeremy."

"No."

"Are you saying that he has feelings for me?"

Vic took a little too long to answer the question. Erin's heart beat faster. She looked at Terry, who had looked up from his phone and had his eyes fixed on Vic's face.

"He might have had an interest," Vic said carefully. "He wouldn't horn in on another man's girlfriend, so it's not like he would ever do anything about it, but that didn't mean he didn't have feelings."

"But he's with Beaver now."

Vic nodded quickly. "Yes. And they're getting along famously. I'm just saying that I wouldn't be able to say that he never had any feelings toward you."

"I'm older than he is," Erin dismissed.

"So is Beaver."

"Well... yes."

"So maybe he likes older women."

"That's just..." Words failed Erin. She looked back at Terry. "That doesn't mean anything. It doesn't mean there was ever anything between us. Maybe he liked me, I don't know, he never said or did anything inappropriate. We never did anything."

CHAPTER 11

*E*rin was sitting with her hands over her eyes, elbows resting on her knees. She was done with talking. Done with trying to figure out how Jeremy could have been shot over some plants. Done with trying to explain to Terry that she wasn't attracted to Jeremy and he wasn't attracted to her and there was no need for concern. She was so done with waiting for the doctors to come out and tell them how Jeremy had fared with his surgery that she was at the end of her rope.

She heard the thud of approaching boots, and didn't look up, knowing that it wasn't going to be the doctor. Not in boots.

"So just what did that boy do now?" Beaver's voice was loud over the muted whispers of the emergency room.

Erin dropped her hands from her eyes and looked at Beaver. "You made it."

"Of course I made it. Now somebody tell me what's going on."

Even though Beaver's body language said she was completely relaxed and her voice was good-humored, Erin was sure she detected something around Beaver's eyes that said that she was just as concerned about his welfare as everyone else who was waiting there.

"We don't know exactly what happened," Erin sighed.

"He was shot at work," Vic explained once more. "Poachers. More than one, according to Terry," Vic nodded to him, and Terry nodded. "They exchanged gunfire. Jeremy was hit somewhere in the body. He's in surgery." Vic pressed a button on her phone to wake up the screen. "He's been in there for two and a half hours."

"He was shot at work? I thought I was the one who was supposed to have the dangerous job. Isn't that what we agreed to?"

Erin couldn't bring herself to laugh at Beaver's humor. Beaver looked at the sad little group. She dragged a chair over.

"If he's been in there for two and a half hours, then they are probably almost done," she said. "The doctor will be out before long, telling us that everything is going to be just fine. Then I'm going to kill him."

"The doctor or Jeremy?" Vic asked.

"Jeremy. Definitely Jeremy. How could he do this to me?"

Vic shook her head. "How could he do this to any of us? He was supposed to be safe. He left the farm and left the clan and he was supposed to be safe now. I wasn't supposed to have to worry about him anymore."

"Either he didn't get the memo, or he didn't understand it," Beaver grumbled.

"I don't know what I'm going to do," Vic said. "If I have to tell my parents that he's…" she gulped. "I just can't do it, Beaver. I can't call them and tell them that something happened to him."

"You're not going to have to. He'll tell them himself when he gets out."

Vic sighed and shook her head, unconvinced. Erin grasped her hand and gave it a squeeze. She didn't have the words to make Vic feel better. All she could do was be there.

"Where's Willie?" she asked.

"He was doing a long courier run. He couldn't get back. He'll turn around as soon as he can and meet us here."

Erin nodded. "He probably won't be long, then."

"No." Vic turned and looked at the entrance. "Shouldn't be too long."

Beaver pulled out her phone and started tapping away on it. Erin was relieved not to have to carry on a conversation again. She just covered her eyes and waited some more. Surely, as Beaver said, it wouldn't be too long before Jeremy was out of surgery and they would have something to tell them. They would say that he'd need some time to recover, but then he'd be just fine.

～

It was still another hour before a tired-looking woman in scrubs came out and looked around.

"Family of Jeremy?" she asked.

Vic stood up like a shot. Erin and the others got to their feet more slowly.

"How is he? Is he going to be okay?" Vic demanded.

"He's going to be okay," the doctor said. She put her hand on Vic's arm. "Just calm down there, hon'. Take a deep breath."

Vic did so, swaying slightly on her feet.

"Are you the girlfriend or the sister?" the doctor asked.

"Sister."

"He's in recovery now, and he's awake and asking for you. And you," she turned and looked at Beaver. "You must be the girlfriend."

Beaver nodded. "Yep. But I don't know if you actually want to invite me in there right now, because I might just try to knock some sense into that boy."

The doctor gave a little smile. "I don't normally encourage that sort of thing, but I hope this is the last time I'll see him on my table. I know that boy's insides a lot better than anyone should."

"He's really okay?" Vic asked. "Where did he get shot? Where did the bullet go in?"

"He's okay," the doctor confirmed. "He's stable for now, and he's awake and alert. We'll need to keep an eye on him to make sure that he doesn't get an infection and that we patched up all of the appropriate holes, but I think you can expect a full recovery. He seems like a strong boy, so I imagine he'll bounce back from this pretty quickly and be back out there causing trouble again. I'd just appreciate it if you make sure that he doesn't end up on my table again."

"Yeah," Vic said sourly. "We'll work on that."

"He took two bullets to the torso, but he was lucky and everything seems to be clean. No major organs, intestines are intact, it was mostly just muscle and a lot of blood."

"Two bullets." Beaver shook her head. "Well, he's got me beat. I've only ever had one at a time."

The doctor's jaw dropped as she looked at Beaver. Erin waited for Beaver to laugh and say that she was just kidding, but Beaver didn't. She just gave Erin and the others raised eyebrows and a rueful smile.

"How many times have you been shot?" the doctor demanded. "And what exactly is it that you do?"

"If I told you that, I'd have to kill you," Beaver quipped. "Let's just say that my job has certain hazards. I don't plan on getting shot again, if that makes you feel better. It wasn't a whole lot of fun the first time. Or the second, for that matter."

"You're pulling my leg."

"Nope." Beaver hooked a finger into her collar and tugged back her shirt to show off a scar below her collarbone.

The doctor looked closely at it and shook her head. "You might not be the best person to tell Jeremy to stay out of trouble."

"Maybe I *am* the best person to tell him, since I have the most experience in the area. At least, I assume so…" She looked at Terry, who shook his head, and then at Erin, who shook hers.

"I've never been shot," Erin said. "I *almost* was once, but Vic shot him." She nodded to Vic.

The doctor made a noise of disbelief.

"But you've been *almost* killed the most times of any of us," Vic said. "Unless Terry…"

Terry again shook his head. "I may be a cop, but I've led a pretty charmed life. I've never been in any life-threatening situation. And I plan to keep it that way."

"Good goal to have," the doctor agreed. "Well, I don't want all of you back there, but maybe if sister and girlfriend would like to come and just say hello to him, then we need to let him rest for a while. He'll need a lot of sleep the next few days for his body to recover and start building up strength again. It was quite a shock to his system."

Vic and Beaver followed the doctor out of the waiting room into the area beyond the security glass. Erin sat back down again, letting out her breath in a long stream.

"Okay. I'm beat. That was scary."

Terry nodded. He sat down beside her again and reached over tentatively to massage her shoulders. Erin melted into him, letting the muscles relax under his practiced hands.

"Oh, that feels good. I was so scared."

"We all were," Terry agreed. He didn't sound jealous like he had before. Maybe he had finally gotten it through his head that Erin wasn't scared because she was in love with Jeremy, but just because he was a friend and that he was Vic's brother.

"You won't ever get shot, will you?" Erin demanded. "I've decided I don't like you being a cop. I don't want to ever have to be here waiting to see if you're going to come out okay."

"I can't promise that nothing will ever happen to me, but neither can you. It wasn't that long ago that you were here after being poisoned and we were all sitting around here wondering whether Willie had gotten you here in time."

"Oh…" Erin smiled weakly. "I'd forgotten about that. All of it is sort of a blur, for a few days."

"But you're okay now, and you're not going to get poisoned again, are you?"

"No." Erin was definite about that. "It's not going to happen again. What are the chances that I would get poisoned twice, anyway?"

"I have no idea. But with you… I suspect it's higher than with most of us."

"It's not my fault. I didn't really do anything to attract attention. People just… think that I know things when I don't."

"They'll think it less if you don't ask so many questions."

Erin shrugged. "Well, I'm not asking anything now. We haven't had any murders and I'm not going to upset anyone. That's all over."

"Now you're just hunting treasures."

Erin looked sideways at him. "Well… yeah. But that's not the same. It doesn't belong to anyone. It isn't anyone's secret. It isn't related to anyone dying or poisoning anyone. It's just… something fun to do."

"If you want something fun to do, take up geocaching. Or knitting. Or needlepoint."

"I'm not taking up needlepoint."

"Or knitting," Terry prompted.

"Not knitting, either."

Erin saw Willie looking around at the other people in the waiting room and waved to get his attention. He joined them, looking at Vic's empty chair.

"I gather she's in with him?"

Erin nodded. She relayed the details the doctor had given them. Willie sat down.

"I guess I missed all of the fun stuff. But I can't say I'm disappointed about that. Poor Vic. I'm glad you were here for her."

Erin nodded. "I'm not sure it did any good, but I'm glad too. Hopefully, after this, Jeremy will find something else to do. I don't want anything like this to happen again!"

"I wouldn't have expected it with a job like this," Willie said, shaking his head. "I've heard some pretty interesting things about operations like this, but I don't think violence is high on the list of expectations."

"Operations like this?"

Willie raised his eyebrows and looked back and forth at the two of them. "Well… places that grow valuable plants or raise endangered species. There are always poachers, but you don't usually see violence like this."

"What do you know about this farm that Jeremy's been working on?" Terry asked.

"They're well-known in the business," Willie said slowly. "Good reputation. I haven't heard about them doing anything underhanded. They stick to the rules for harvesting plants, have a good reputation for quality goods. No counterfeit plants."

Erin shook her head. "I've never heard of this kind of thing going on at a farm. What's gotten into people?"

"It isn't common for people to get shot," Willie repeated. "There is theft, yes. There's a reason they hire security, especially during harvest. But believe me, no one could have predicted that this was going to happen to Jeremy."

Erin sighed. "Okay. Got it."

Terry scraped back his chair as he got up. "I don't know about you two, but I'm going to need a coffee if I'm going to stay here much longer. Willie?"

"Love one," Willie agreed.

"Erin?"

Erin shook her head. "Not so close to bedtime, I'll never get to sleep. Something non-caffeinated."

"I'll see what I can find. No Monster energy drinks, then?"

She punched him lightly on the arm. "No Monsters."

Terry and K9 left in search of beverages. Willie gave a deep sigh and leaned back in the chair. Erin knew from experience that there wasn't really any way to get comfortable in the hard plastic chairs. She could see a couple of people who had fallen asleep, but she had no idea how they had managed it. She could only guess that they were very sick. She tried to cover a yawn, but was too tired to repress it. Tears leaked out the corners of her eyes.

"Long day," Willie acknowledged. "You guys are up so early in the morning."

"Yeah. I don't know what I'm going to do tomorrow. I'd call Bella and see if she and Charley could open, but Bella has never prepped by herself, and I'm sure there's no way Charley would be able to get up that early."

"You might just have to open late or be closed for a day."

"I hate to do that."

"Of course. But people will understand. And it isn't like you're providing emergency services. People will survive without their morning muffin."

"I know…"

Willie changed the subject. "How's the treasure hunt coming along?"

Erin was glad to talk about something else, though she wasn't sure she wanted to be talking about treasure hunting when Terry made his way back with their drinks. "Interesting! I learned a lot from Betty and Edna at the library. They really know their stuff."

"They do," Willie agreed. "If you want to know about the history of Bald Eagle Falls, you couldn't ask for much better. But…"

Erin looked at him, frowning. "But what? They're not making it up, are they? They do know what they're talking about."

"They know what they're talking about. It's just that they talk about it an awful lot."

"Meaning…"

"Meaning you may have let the cat out of the bag. Loose lips."

"They said they would keep it quiet. They understood and said they wouldn't talk about it…"

"Uh-huh." Willie's skepticism was clear. "I wouldn't count on it."

All of the effort she had made to keep her treasure hunt quiet, and they were going to spoil it for her. "So I guess I'd better get out ahead of it. Did you find some maps for me?"

Willie looked blank for a moment, as if he'd forgotten all about it. "Yeah, they're in the truck. I can give them to you tonight. You know what you're looking for?"

"I have a better idea." Erin told him about Edna's knowledge about the routes that a payroll wagon probably would have taken. "Do you want to get your maps now? We could look at them together?"

Willie shook his head. "I don't think we need other people seeing us looking at them. Or listening in." He glanced around. "It may look like nobody is listening to us, but I can assure you that's not the case. Half the people here who look like they are sleeping are probably eavesdropping on our conversation. They don't need to see what those routes are that Edna told you about."

Erin looked around at the bored and sleeping people in the waiting room. No one twitched or gave her any sign that they were listening to the conversation between her and Willie. No one smiled to give away the fact that they knew they had been caught. A nurse moved around picking up newspapers, coffee cups, and candy wrappers.

Erin was pretty sure that no one was really listening to them.

CHAPTER 12

*W*hen Vic got back from seeing Jeremy, she looked exhausted, but there was a light in her features that hadn't been there before she went in to see him. Erin was relieved. She was comforted by the fact that Vic looked peaceful and relaxed instead of more wound up about Jeremy's injuries.

"He's going to sleep now," she told Erin. "He needs his rest. But he really is okay."

"He talked to you?"

"Yeah. He wasn't all loopy, but he was a bit… sedated still. Not quite his usual self, but he was trying. He looked a lot better than I expected him to."

Beaver nodded her agreement. "I'm sure I didn't look anywhere near that good after I got shot," she contributed. "They've given him plenty of blood, so that helps. But he seemed… strong. Like there was no doubt he was on the road to recovery."

Vic smiled. "It's such a relief. When we get home, I'll call Mom and let her know what happened. I didn't earlier because I didn't think there was any point in upsetting them when I didn't know how he was."

"Will they come out and see him?"

Vic shrugged. "I don't know how things are between them. I never really asked. I assume they're not real happy about him leaving home and splitting from the clan, but it isn't like they kicked him out like with me. I think they're still on speaking terms."

As much as Vic loved her family, they were not prepared to talk with her for as long as she was living a life that was so different from what they had raised her to.

"I love my family," Vic said, echoing what Erin was thinking. "But they can be pretty hardheaded sometimes. Rednecks." She gave a little laugh.

"Are you ready to go home?"

Vic yawned and nodded.

"Are you going with Erin or with me?" Willie asked.

"Oh..." Vic looked form one to the other uncertainly. "I don't know. How are you doing, Erin? Are you okay to drive? Do you need someone to keep you awake?"

"I'm pretty wound up. I don't think keeping awake is going to be a problem."

"Are you sure? I'll go with you if you need someone. I don't want you having an accident on the way home from the hospital."

"I'll be fine. I'll walk out with you, though, Willie has some maps for me."

Erin was sure that whoever had designed the hospital and the parking around it had to have been on drugs at the time. Or maybe none of it was planned and it had just been added on to haphazardly until it was a complete mess that no one could have sorted out. She suspected that even the people who worked at the hospital didn't know their way around the place. They'd know the places that they needed to go, but not the whole hospital. She had walked with Willie and Vic to Willie's truck to get the maps. Willie had not been able to find any parking near to the emergency entrance, of course, because there wasn't any, but he hadn't picked the same parking structure as Erin. It was on the opposite side of the hospital. Erin didn't try to cut through the hospital, it was much easier to go around the outside, even if it was longer physically.

As she walked around the building, she could hear another set of footsteps. At first, it didn't really enter her consciousness, but as she got farther away from the doors, she became more aware. Someone was headed the same direction as she was. That wasn't surprising. The hospital was teeming with people, and even that late, there were plenty of people who were coming and going to the parking structures.

Choosing to go around the hospital instead of through it might not have been the safest choice. The parking lots were not well-lit and, since most people did travel through the hospital rather than around it, there were not a lot of people outside. The farther she went around the hospital, the darker and quieter it became. Erin swallowed and clutched the maps to her and tried to breathe normally. There was no point in getting worked up over nothing.

She thought of Beaver's gun. Vic had encouraged Erin to get a gun and go target shooting with her for some time, but Erin just didn't feel comfortable about guns. Walking by herself in the dark and lonely parking lots around the hospital, she suddenly wished that she had made a different decision. She wished she had at least something in her purse that could be used as a weapon. Maybe not a gun, but at least pepper spray or a taser. She should have had Terry or Beaver escort her to her car. Everybody had gone their different directions without paying any attention to the possible dangers. The hospital was busy; who was going to get mugged there?

Erin sped up her pace, looking behind her to reassure herself that it was just another visitor like her, going back to his car. It was too dark to get a good look at the person behind her in just a quick glance, and she wasn't going to turn around for long enough to get a good look.

Her heart was pounding and she was breathing heavily, unable to get enough oxygen. She wasn't even close to her car. Where was a security guard? Wasn't there anyone patrolling the area outside the hospital?

Erin spotted a side door and broke into a run to reach it. She wrenched the door open and jumped back into the safety of the hospital. She stopped there for a minute, trying to catch her breath and calm the wild pounding of her heart.

She was fine, safely inside the hospital again. Perfectly safe.

She started walking again, more relaxed, chuckling at herself for being so paranoid just because someone was walking behind her in the dark. Inside where it was bright and she could hear the constant hum of voices and see people hurrying from one hall to another, she felt much better.

Erin went back to navigating the signage to find her way back to the parking structure she had parked in. She asked for directions a couple of times along the way, trying to avoid getting lost.

As she was leaving the hospital once more in the final stretch to the parking structure, Erin spotted a security guard.

"Oh, hey! Would you be able to walk me to my car? I was a little nervous earlier that someone was following me." She gave a little self-depre-cating laugh. "I'm just over here in D-East." She pointed.

The guard looked at her for a moment, not answering.

"I guess maybe you have certain rounds you're supposed to do. I was just hoping maybe you could go this way…"

"Of course." He smiled and nodded. He had a big flashlight on his belt that he pulled out and clicked on. Comforted by his presence, Erin calmed down and walked with him into the parking garage. He stayed with her while she found her level and parking space.

"Thanks so much," Erin told him gratefully. "I really appreciate it."

He nodded and gave her a salute with his flashlight, then turned and walked back out.

Erin fumbled for her keys, having difficulty finding them in her purse in the dimness of the garage. She should have had the security guard shine his flashlight on them before he left. She put her maps on top of the car so that she would have both hands free to look for the keys, and eventually managed to tease them out and juggle them to find the car key.

"There you are," she said softly, and fit it into the lock.

Suddenly she was struck with a blinding pain in the back of her skull and fell forward against the car. She tried to hold herself up, but her knees buckled and she hit the pavement. Erin tried to sort out the sensations.

A shape beside her.

The purse being yanked off of her shoulder.

And then running footsteps.

CHAPTER 13

*E*rin closed her eyes, the world spinning around her. What had just happened?

It was dark and cold on the ground. She had a splitting headache. No matter how hard she tried, she couldn't seem to get to her feet, even holding on to the car. The lighting of the garage, which had previously seemed dim, had grown blindingly bright. She reached up the car door, feeling for her keys. Had whoever had taken her purse taken the keys too? They hadn't taken the car, at least.

Erin's fingers touched the keys. She pulled the key out of the lock and felt the fob for the panic alarm. She had set it off by accident more than once, but now that she needed it, the key fob felt foreign in her fingers. Erin concentrated, running her nail over it, feeling for the cracks of the buttons. One of them had braille over it, but that wasn't the alarm key. She couldn't remember the layout of the buttons. Erin mashed her thumb down, catching all of the buttons at the same time, and held them all down until the car alarm started to shriek.

She sat leaning against the car. It was a long time before anyone came around to check on the alarm. People were too accustomed to hearing car alarms ringing for no reason. They just tuned them out. Erin knew she usually did. When she noticed a car alarm, it wasn't usually with any sort of concern, but with irritation that someone hadn't turned it off.

Then there was a man standing over her, calling to her. "Ma'am? Ma'am, are you okay?"

Erin groaned. "Does it look like it?"

"I'm calling for help. Just hang in there."

What else was she supposed to do?

"Sure," Erin muttered.

He talked on his radio to his dispatcher, relaying their location.

"Did you fall down?" he asked her. "What happened? Does it hurt anywhere?"

"My head. Someone stole my purse. I think they hit me on the head."

He muttered a curse and crouched down beside her, pulling her head back gently from the car to have a look at it. "Oh, yeah. He hit you."

There was a stabbing pain and the spinning sensation increased. Erin moaned. "Don't do that."

He released her head slowly, letting it rest back against the car again, where she was sitting propped up.

"Did you see him? The person who did this?"

"No. I don't have eyes in the back of my head."

"Of course not," he agreed. He checked in on his radio again, asking for an ETA on the paramedics. "They're coming," he reported back. "Hang in there."

She thought he might be the same guard who had walked her into the parking garage.

Time was fuzzy. She didn't know how long she waited there, the man talking to her occasionally, before she finally heard the ambulance siren. Had they actually dispatched it from somewhere else? They were at the hospital, but no one could just come out to help her?

The man waved down the ambulance and reported Erin's condition to them as he walked them over. Erin listened to him describe the injury to her head and her state of responsiveness. The paramedics came over and had a look for themselves.

"Yep, pretty good blow to the head," one of them confirmed. "How are you doing, ma'am? Are you in a lot of pain?"

"Yes."

He worked over her, evaluating her as they talked, checking her pulse and her eyes.

"Can you stand up if we help you?"

Erin avoided shaking her head. "No."

"Okay, we'll get the gurney over here and get you onto it. How long ago did this happen, do you know? Do you know what day it is?"

Erin cleared her throat. Too many questions too fast. "Just give me something for the pain."

"We'll let the hospital do that once we get you stabilized. Can you tell me what day it is?"

"I don't know. Wednesday. Not the weekend."

"Can you tell me your first and last name?"

"Erin. Uh. Erin Price. Price."

"What were you doing here today, Erin?"

"My friend… her brother got shot. I brought her over and was sitting with her."

"Ouch. Don't like to hear that. Was he okay?"

"Yeah. Okay. They said he'd be fine."

"Good. Let's get that gurney over here and get you onto it. How's your neck? Feeling okay?"

"Yeah."

They prepared to move Erin. She looked at her car shining softly in the lighting of the parking garage and wondered what she was doing there.

"I need to get home," she told the paramedic preparing to lift her.

He looked down at her and raised one eyebrow. "You'll get home, but we need to take care of you first. I don't think you're going to be going anywhere tonight."

"But I have to get to the bakery in the morning. I need to go home and get some sleep."

"You'll be able to sleep here. Let's see how you feel when you wake up in the morning, huh?"

That seemed to make some kind of sense. Erin nodded, which made her feel drunk.

"Okay."

"Okay, honey. Now let's get you moving."

The two of them managed to lift her up onto the gurney, and they rolled her inside the ambulance. Erin looked around. She couldn't remember ever being in an ambulance before.

She must have been in one after the accident that took her parents' lives. It had been just the three of them, and they were all taken to the hospital.

But Erin couldn't remember the details. Maybe she had been unconscious. Or maybe it had just been too traumatic or was too long ago.

"Do you think I'll remember this time?" she asked the paramedic who climbed in beside her.

"Remember what, sweetheart?"

"That I rode in an ambulance."

"Hmm. Maybe, maybe not. I think you're pretty shaken up."

"Yeah."

"Just rest for a bit. Even though we're already at the hospital, this is still going to take a while."

"Okay."

But Erin didn't like the way the world spun even faster when she closed her eyes, so she kept them open, watching everything sway around her as the ambulance made its way back around the hospital to the emergency entrance. Around, and around, and around. She couldn't seem to get away from the hospital.

"The Hotel California," Erin murmured.

The paramedic grinned at her but didn't say anything.

They went back around to the ambulance loading bay, and the paramedics took her into the hospital. There, Erin was expected to answer their questions all over again, but they didn't seem inclined to answer any of hers.

"When can I go home?" Erin demanded. "I need to get home."

"You need to just rest and let us help you," a large black nurse told her sternly.

Erin was cowed by her and tried to stay quiet. But she was confused by everything going on around her. "Is Jeremy okay?"

"Jeremy? Who is Jeremy?"

"He was shot. He was here earlier."

"Oh, the GSW that came in on the last shift? I don't know. Sounded like he was doing okay. We don't really hear back after they go to surgery."

"The doctor said he was okay."

"Then you don't need to worry about him, do you? Can you tell me your birth date?"

Erin had a hard time dredging it out of her memory.

"How about your social security number?"

Erin gave her head a tiny shake. "No, I could never remember it. My purse…"

The nurse looked around. "I don't think you were brought in with one."

"Someone stole it."

"Oh, dear. Is that how you got hit on the head? You poor thing."

There was a red light blinking on a camera in the corner of the room, and Erin wondered if they were going to show her a video. She did her best to stay focused on what they were saying around her, but she was getting very tired and the nausea and vertigo were not helping.

"Can I go to sleep?"

"You can," one nurse said, patting her hand, "but someone will probably wake you up again. Just be warned."

"Okay."

Erin closed her eyes and drifted off.

There were doctors and nurses coming and going in a sort of a blur, but when she woke up fully the next time, it was to Terry shaking her arm. Erin startled and looked at him.

"What time is it? I'm going to be late opening the bakery!"

"It's okay," he assured her. "Don't worry about the bakery. What happened? I called you and you didn't answer. I was afraid you fell asleep at the wheel and went off the road."

"I didn't fall asleep," Erin said. "I didn't go to sleep until I was here, and the nurse said it was okay. I asked."

"What happened?"

"Someone stole my purse. They hit me on the head. I was in the garage."

"You were mugged?"

"Yes."

"You really are a magnet for trouble." Terry stroked her chin gently with the backs of his fingers. "My poor girl."

Erin closed her eyes. "That feels good."

"I shouldn't have let you walk to your car alone. I didn't even think about the danger... It's so dark and lonely at night..."

"I didn't walk alone. I had a security guard."

"You did? You had someone escort you to your car?"

"Yeah. Someone was following me. I was worried... I didn't want anything to happen to me too, so I went back in and I asked."

Terry nodded. "That was a smart thing to do. So, what happened? It wasn't the guard who hurt you, was it?"

Erin thought about it. "No. He didn't see anyone there... neither of us saw anybody... so he left. I just had to get into my car."

"But there *was* someone there."

"I never saw him coming. He just hit me."

"You didn't see who did it? Get a look at his face?" Terry asked.

"No. He hit me from behind. I didn't even know there was anyone there until he hit me. I felt like I got hit by a truck."

"Did you see him after? Running away?"

"No..." Erin thought about it. "I heard him. I might have seen a shape. Just a dark shape. But I didn't ever see his face. He made sure of that."

"His footsteps when he ran away, did they sound like he was tall or short?"

"I don't know. Tall. Maybe."

"And the person who scared you earlier, who you thought might be following you? Did you get a good look at him?"

"No, not close enough to even tell if it was a man or a woman. Actually, I'm sure it was a man, but I'm not sure how."

"You might have been able to tell from his gait or his smell. His shape or the clothes he wore. It's easy to be wrong, but if you had an impression, at least that's something."

"I guess."

Erin thought about smell. She was usually good about smells. Was that what had suggested to her it was a man? A musky cologne or male body odor? Pheromones?

Had it been the same person who had followed her both times, or had it just been a coincidence? Had she made herself a target by looking too vulnerable?

"Erin?"

She realized that she had been drifting off. She tried to sit up. Terry readjusted her pillow, but it was flat and didn't give her any lift. Erin wasn't in a permanent bed yet and she didn't know if they could raise the head of the bed. Or if she really wanted them to. She might just want to go back to sleep.

"Will they look for my purse?" she asked Terry. "I mean, after he's got what he wants, he'll just dump it, won't he? I have other things in there I want back."

"I'll make sure they look. Actually, I might be able to track your phone. I can see where he is if he has it or where it is if he dumped it."

"That would be good," Erin agreed. She didn't like the idea of someone else having her stuff. Or of their just dumping it like it was garbage. Having been a foster kid without any possessions of her own to speak of she grew attached to things. It was hard to let go.

"I need a notepad."

Terry frowned. "A notepad? What for?"

"I just... I might want to write things down. And I need a notepad to write them in."

Terry patted his clothes. He pulled a small spiral notepad out of his shirt pocket and tore a few sheets out. He put them on the small table beside her, putting a pencil on top to keep them from flying away when someone walked by and stirred the air. "It isn't much, but it will do in a pinch," he said. "I'll get you something better if I can't find your purse."

Erin let out a sigh. Anyone else probably would have teased her or would have told her it wasn't important and that she didn't need to write anything down. But Terry knew how important it was for her to be able to get her thoughts down on paper to sort them out. He was a good man. "Thank you," she told him, her eyes warm with tears.

"You're welcome. Do you want me to stay here with you, or do you want me to see if I can find your phone and purse?"

"I think I'm just going to close my eyes for a while longer. Would you see if you can find them?"

"Sure." Terry bent down and gave her a kiss on the forehead. "You have a good rest. I'll be back in a little while." He smiled. "Don't you go getting into any other trouble while I'm gone."

"I won't."

~

There was a lot of talking and commotion and people going back and forth holding discussions in loud voices, and Erin didn't know how she was going to be able to shut them out and get any rest but, in a few minutes, she was asleep again, or at least in a half-asleep state, her mind jumping from one thing to another, not constrained by the real world.

A few doctors or nurses spoke to her. Erin wasn't sure if she made any sense when she answered them, because she couldn't remember the conversations afterward. There was another policeman who wasn't Terry. Too many people coming and going.

She didn't know what time it was when she was finally moved out of the emergency room into a ward where it was quieter and she could sleep for real. Or at least, she was moved into the hallway of a ward, which apparently didn't have any free beds for her. But she was just glad to be out of the high-traffic emergency room.

It was much quieter and more peaceful. She closed her eyes and was able to get past the half-sleep state into a more restful sleep.

CHAPTER 14

*W*hen Erin woke up, Terry was asleep in a chair nearby, which he had apparently pulled from some other room in order to be close to her. K9 was lying on the floor at his feet, also asleep. Erin moved around restlessly, trying to find the comfortable position she had just been in, but her whole body ached and was insisting that she needed to move around and stretch her muscles. Any position she tried to settle into, she felt like she was lying on lumps and bruises.

There was something stuffed beside her on the bed, and when Erin craned her neck to see what it was, she saw her purse. She pulled it up onto her stomach and went through it to see what was there and what was missing. Everything seemed to be accounted for other than her cash. Even her phone and credit cards were still there.

Her movements apparently woke K9, and he nudged Terry awake. Terry looked over at Erin and gave her a sleepy, concerned smile. The dimple in his cheek was just visible. "There's my girl. Did you get some sleep?"

"A little."

"Can you tell if anything is missing?" He nodded to her purse.

"Just my cash. Everything else still seems to be there."

He shook his head. "Lazy muggers. If he's going to go to all of the work of knocking someone down, he could at least try to make use of the credit cards and the phone."

Erin chuckled. "I'm glad he didn't. There wasn't even that much cash in it. If he needs it that badly, then he's welcome to it. I wish he'd asked instead of hitting me over the head."

"I put your keys in there too, after checking out your car to make sure everything was undisturbed. It doesn't look like he even opened the door."

"No," Erin agreed. "I was just unlocking it when he hit me, and he ran away without trying it. I guess I was lucky."

"He might still have gone back once the paramedics took you away. Was there anything valuable in the car?"

"No. I don't keep anything in there. I just…" Erin thought about her movements the night before, replaying it in her mind, feeling like she was missing something important. "No, I just…"

Terry studied her, waiting for her to work it out.

"I just put Willie's maps on top of the car so that I could use both hands to get out my keys. Were they still there?"

He shook his head. "No, I didn't see any maps. What were they for?"

"For the you-know-what." Erin looked around to make sure no one was listening in. "Willie said to be careful about talking about it here. You know, the poem, and where it leads."

"Oh." Terry's face cleared and he nodded. "I got it."

Erin looked down at her purse again, frowning. She looked through the loose papers that she tried to keep organized with envelopes and paperclips but couldn't find it.

"That's… it's missing. He *didn't* just take the money."

"What else is missing?"

"The poem."

~

Erin was waiting for word from the doctor that she could be discharged when Vic walked in, pushing Jeremy in a wheelchair. He was dressed in a hospital johnny, but looked remarkably well, as if it were just a Halloween costume.

"Vic! Jeremy! How are you?"

"I am just as good as you, if not better," Jeremy said with a grin.

"I just got bumped on the head. You got two bullets in you."

"Yeah, but the doctor fixed me all up. You didn't get any work done. I'm good as new."

"Are you going home?"

He hesitated. "Well, not quite yet."

"Then I'm in better shape than you are. I'm just waiting to be released."

"That's because you've got someone to take care of you when you get home. You've got Vic and Terry around, so you're not on your own."

"What about Beaver? Can't she look after you?"

"No, she's got to get back to work. She won't be able to stay close by like Terry and Vic."

"They've got to work too," Erin said. "Though if I called them, they could come. But I'm not going to need to do that, because I'll be back at work, not at home."

"You're not ready to go back to work," Vic said sternly.

"I have to! We have to keep the bakery running."

"We'll keep the bakery running. You need to stay home until you're healed. You're not allowed to come back in while you're still concussed."

"Why not? It's not affecting me. Other people would be around."

"For the same reason you're not allowed to drive," Vic said. "You need to do what the doctors say."

"They didn't say I couldn't drive or work."

"Well, I'm saying it."

Erin rolled her eyes. "How are you feeling?" she asked Jeremy, cocking her head to look at him. "You sure are looking a lot better than I would have expected."

"I'm sore all over," Jeremy admitted. "Apparently, getting shot is sort of the equivalent of being trampled by a horse. I'm not just sore where the bullets went in, it's like I have the flu or got beaten up."

"Me too. I only got hit once, on the head, but I feel like he must have punched and kicked me once I went down, because everything is tender. Every time I move, I find a new bruise or sore muscle."

Jeremy nodded. "We make a good pair. Maybe we should both just go back to your place and we can take care of each other and commiserate over our injuries."

Erin looked over at Vic, who shook her head.

"I don't think that's a good idea. Jeremy's not ready to go home yet, even if he thinks he is. If one of you fell down and needed help getting up, you'd both just end up on the floor. Neither of you is supposed to be doing any heavy lifting."

"I'm not going to fall down," Erin said.

"Neither am I," Jeremy agreed.

"You guys are incorrigible. Quit it. Besides," Vic raised an eyebrow at Erin, "I don't think your man would be too happy about Jeremy staying at your house again."

Erin shrugged stiffly. "He might not be, but I don't make all of my decisions based on what he does or doesn't want, either. I'll do what I think is best."

Vic raised her eyebrows. "Well, I don't think I've heard you talk that way about Terry before. Are you sure it's not the concussion talking?"

"No... it's me. I know he doesn't like everything I do. But I'm my own person. I'll do what I need to do."

Vic nodded. "I've always said so. Good for you. If he's expecting you to be some shrinking violet who does everything she is told and just stays in the kitchen all day, he should think again. You might act like a pushover sometimes, but underneath, you're pretty tough."

Jeremy looked at Vic, frowning. He looked back at Erin.

"I don't know if women like being classified as tough any more than as a shrinking violet, do they?"

Vic shrugged. "It depends on the woman. I'd rather be tough than a cupcake. I think Beaver would say the same thing. Erin might like cupcakes, but I don't think she wants to be one."

Erin laughed at that. "No, I don't," she agreed. "I am my own person. I don't know why Terry is acting like he owns me or can control what I do. I'm not a child."

"He just wants to protect you," Jeremy said. "He's a cop. It's in his DNA. He wants to protect people, and especially the ones closest to him. He's not telling you that you can't be the person you want to be, he just wants to keep you from getting hurt and is trying to encourage you down the pathway he thinks is safest."

"He can't keep bad things from happening," Erin pointed out. "No matter what he does, he can't predict the future and he can't keep things from happening to me, or Vic, or even himself. You can go down all the safe garden paths you like, but that doesn't keep you from being run over by a bus."

"Or hit by a mugger," Jeremy agreed.

"Or shot by a poacher," Vic added.

"It's just not feasible to avoid every danger."

"Of course not," Jeremy agreed. "But that doesn't mean Terry won't try. And as far as me staying at the house with you... well, it's perfectly understandable that he doesn't want another guy horning in on his territory. Even if you're not his *territory*. I know he doesn't own you. But he doesn't want another guy looking at you. Trying to have a relationship with you."

"Well, I told him that wasn't the case. You were just a friend staying over for a few days. I told him there wasn't anything between us, but he still gets all... manly about it."

Vic laughed. "Well, you wouldn't want him to stop being manly, would you? I don't think you would have picked a cop in uniform if you didn't like that about him."

Erin's face warmed. She rolled her eyes and looked around the room, looking for some way to change the subject.

"Personal preferences aside... I do want to talk about the schedule at Auntie Clem's. We can't let it just stay closed until I'm feeling better. I don't know how many days it will be before I can put in a full day. I might only be able to come in for a few hours at a time at first, until I'm sure that I've got my mojo back."

"Don't worry about it," Vic said. "We'll take care of everything. Bella was in early this morning and Charley is taking over at noon. Then I'll do late shift and make sure everything is prepped again for the morning. It's not as easy to run the shop with just one person on shift at a time, but it's possible, especially if we're not putting in full-length shifts. You can put up with it being harder if you know you don't have to be there as long. We might work it so that we overlap by an hour over the usual rushes; we'll put our heads together and see what we can come up with. In the meantime, you're not allowed to worry about anything. You just rest and be reassured that we're holding things together until you're healthy again. Really healthy, not forcing yourself to come back because you're afraid everything is going to fall apart."

"Are you sure?" Erin was already worrying about how hard it would be for each of them to run the bakery by themselves. She had done everything by herself for the first little while, before taking Vic on as an employee, and it had been exhausting. There had to be a way to set up the shifts so that two people could cover each shift...

"Leave it to me," Vic insisted, staring at Erin as if she could see right into her mind to what she was thinking. "You don't need to think about it at all. Bella is happy to take the early shift. She doesn't have any classes that interfere and she's a farm girl, so she's used to being up early. Obviously, Charley can't take the early shift, but she's fine once she's out of bed. She doesn't even have to make anything for the middle shift, she can just man the counter. But she likes to cook, so I think she'll still put in a tray of cookies when she has a lull. Then I'm there at the end of the day to make sure that everything is cleaned up to your usual exacting standards and that all of the batters are ready for when Bella gets there in the morning. We all get our preferred time of day, I still have time to check in on Jeremy or you, and nobody is trying to shoulder the full burden."

"I suppose." Erin had to admit, it sounded like they had everything worked out. She wanted to fix it, but if there was nothing to fix, she should just let them do it their way and not try to come up with a better idea.

"Why don't you work on the mystery while you're recovering?" Jeremy suggested. "You can look at the poem and see where the clues lead you. Maybe you'll be able to find something out that you weren't able to see before, when you were so busy and distracted by other things."

Vic bit her lip and gave Jeremy a warning look.

"What?" Jeremy shook his head, eyebrows down. "What did I say?"

"Terry told me. When Erin got mugged, they stole the poem and Willie's maps."

Jeremy looked surprised. He opened his mouth to speak, then did a sort of double-take and looked at Vic again, opening and closing his mouth like a fish on the other side of the aquarium glass.

"Yeah," Vic confirmed. "Someone else is trying to find the treasure. Someone who is willing to hurt people to find it."

CHAPTER 15

*a*s far as Terry was concerned, and probably the rest of the men who were her friends too, Erin should just drop the treasure hunt nonsense and do something that was safer. But as Erin had said, she wasn't about to live her life the way that Terry or anyone else said that she should. She had always found her own path in the world and was her own person, and that wasn't going to stop. She wasn't going to be cowed just because someone had hit her over the head and taken the poem and the maps.

Willie said that he hadn't given her the original maps, just good quality copies, which he could run off again and, while Erin hadn't made any copies of the poem, she had read it enough times that she had it memorized. As soon as she got home and was alone, she wrote it out again, just the same as it had been on the original. Maybe not exactly the same, because she couldn't replicate exactly the swoops and curls of the old-fashioned script that it had been written in, but she did the best she could to keep the spacing the same and to exactly replicate each word and mark that had been on the original paper in case there was any significance in the way they lined up.

She wasn't going to give up on finding the treasure. Maybe someone else was looking for it, but that didn't mean she was just going to go away. She had a head start on whoever was just picking up the hunt. Maybe it was only a few days of research, but she knew more than they did, and that meant she could get to the treasure faster.

She studied the words of the poem. She couldn't do much about the maps until Willie got her new copies. She had looked at them only briefly, and she had only a rough idea of the topography and roads from what Betty and Edna had drawn for her, but it was enough for a start.

She went back to Clementine's files and thumbed through the labels on the folders. Nothing on lost treasure. Nothing on old legends or untold riches. But she might have something in one of her files that would point Erin in the right direction.

She started at the front of the drawer and looked carefully at each folder, rating them as to which was most likely to hold clues to the treasure hunt poem, and then she went through each of the likely folders from front to back, examining every single page and clipping carefully. She had all the time she needed.

She had all day for as many days as she decided to tell her employees that she needed to be home, and they would keep the bakery running in her absence. She wouldn't draw it out any longer than she needed to, of course, but she could take all the time she needed, and why not do something productive with it?

"Here, look at this." Erin knew that Vic was tired and probably just wanted to get into a hot shower and some comfy clothes for the evening. She'd be up at the hospital again in the morning to check on Jeremy and see if he needed anything. Even if she wasn't working her usual long hours, she was still keeping herself busy for most of the day. "It will only take a minute."

Vic sat down to look at the file Erin had pulled out.

"This is a file on Orson Cadaver."

Vic's eyes widened and she opened her mouth to make a crack about the name.

"I know," Erin said, "spooky name, right? Anyway, this is a great, great-something uncle of mine. He was raised dirt poor, never had a single possession, and then suddenly he starts spending a fortune in gold coins."

Vic took the folder from her and read through the first paper or two. "It was modern currency, not like he dug up a pirate treasure."

"I know. It was modern, and he said he earned it legitimately. But get this—he would never say how he earned it. Just that it had been honest work. But with the amounts of money that he had suddenly come into, everybody thought he'd robbed a wagon train or hit it big in the mines. Or that he found a pirate treasure and cashed it in for modern gold. He would have had to pass it through someone else to get it laundered. No one knew for sure how he had gotten the money in the first place."

"That is kind of suspicious," Vic admitted. "Where did he live? Right here in Bald Eagle Falls?"

"No, down in the valley. He'd been trying to farm, but there wasn't enough flatland. The soil was the wrong pH or something and wouldn't grow corn or the other crops he tried. He did something else every year, and just got further and further behind. Then suddenly, he is successful, but he won't tell anyone what it was he planted, and no one knew what it was he took to market. He drove wagonloads of product into the market for sale, but it was covered up and nobody knew who he sold to or what commodity it was he was selling."

"Maybe he was a witch," Vic suggested. "It all sounds pretty dark and mysterious."

"A witch?" Erin repeated.

"You know, selling potions or elixirs or turning coal into gold. Something sinister and unexplainable."

Erin gave Vic a look. They both knew that Adele, an actual witch, didn't do anything of the sort. "I think he might actually have found the gold for the corn crops. Or the soldiers' payroll that disappeared. The timing is right. Of course, he never says so, because neither one was intended for him. But if he had been lying in wait along one of those routes that Edna pointed out..."

"It would take more than one man to take down all of the guards transporting a big payment like that. They wouldn't have sent it on its way without lots of protection."

"Maybe he had help. Maybe he hired someone else to help him. If he did, we don't know what happened to them. Either he paid them off well so that they wouldn't talk about it, or he got rid of them some other way."

Vic gave a shudder. "You really think this is the guy? He's the one who hid the treasure?"

"It makes sense. I haven't come across anyone else in the family who suddenly had more money than they should have. This guy was as poor as dirt before this, then suddenly starts paying for everything with gold coins. They had to come from somewhere, but he would never say where. And he didn't have any heirs. After he died, people went looking for his money. They found a few gold coins, but no fortune. Like they just found his spending money, but the real money was somewhere else."

"Like the bank, maybe? Why didn't these guys ever use banks?"

"Maybe they weren't secure then like they are now. Or they weren't being run by someone trustworthy. Weren't insured. Things weren't regulated like they are now, were they?"

"No, you're right there," Vic admitted. "But if they all looked for it at the time, then what makes you think that we're going to find anything now? They would have looked pretty carefully."

"But they didn't have the poem."

"If the poem is related to Orson, then why wasn't it in that file instead of the one you found it in?"

"I don't know. Maybe Clementine didn't know they were related. Or maybe she didn't want someone else to know."

"Or maybe they're not related."

Erin shrugged. "Maybe not, but looking is fun, isn't it?"

Vic laughed. "It is, kind of. So, what's your next step?"

"As soon as I get the maps from Willie, we go down to see if we can find Orson's old house. I think there's enough detail in this file to identify where it is once we have the map. And then... maybe we find more clues."

CHAPTER 16

*I*t was a few days before Erin was able to get away with Vic to try to find Orson's old homestead. She had to first convince everybody that she was well enough to be working again, and then, once she was well enough to work, she had to be at Auntie Clem's doing her job until she could arrange for a day off for both her and Vic. Since everybody had been putting in extra hours, it didn't seem right for Erin to take the first opportunity to get a shift off again. But when Saturday afternoon rolled around, Bella was happy to take a quiet shift and let Erin and Vic go off treasure hunting. Though they didn't tell her that was what they were going to do. They might have led her to believe they were going into the city to visit Jeremy or to take him out on a day trip. Jeremy *was* getting pretty eager to get out of the hospital, feeling like he could be back to his normal activities again in spite of the gunshot wounds.

"Do you think we'll be able to find it?" Erin asked, as Vic followed her instructions through the overgrown backroads to try to find the old homestead.

"If it's there, we'll find it," Vic said. "The cabin, that is. I'm not guaranteeing anything else."

"We don't even know if there *is* anything else," Erin said agreeably. "Who knows?"

"Right. If it's still standing, we'll find the cabin."

Erin studied the survey map closely. It wasn't easy to compare the roads and trees they were passing with the flat survey map and to match everything up properly. "I think there should be another road to the right, about three hundred yards ahead."

"Okay…" Vic was already going pretty slowly, but she hit the brake and they both watched for a break in the trees where there might be an access road. Some of the roads they had taken to get there had been pretty questionable. They might have been roads at one time, but Erin wasn't sure that they could be called roads anymore.

"There."

Vic turned the car slowly in. "Maybe we should have waited and gotten one of the boys to come with their trucks. I'm a little worried about your car's suspension handling this off-roading."

"We're not off-roading," Erin corrected. "These are roads. They're just very… not very well-maintained anymore. They've been replaced by paved highways, so people don't really use them anymore."

"Not very well-maintained." Vic snorted. "You have a talent for understatement."

Erin grinned. She looked back down at the map, trying to pick out landmarks, topography, and distances. "We'll go in a curve around a hill, and when we get to the opposite side, there should be a fork in the road, and we're to take the left one."

"Left fork," Vic confirmed. They again watched intently out the windshield as the barely-visible track wound around the hill. "Here? Is that a fork?"

"I don't know. It could be." Erin tried to compare it with the map. "Let's give it a try."

"Are you going to get me lost?"

"We can't get lost; we have a map."

"That doesn't mean we know where we are."

"We know where we are. We're… somewhere on this map. Somewhere on one of these maps." Erin shuffled through them. "We're not going to get lost."

"Don't lose track of which one we're supposed to be on," Vic said nervously.

"I'm not going to mix them up. We're on this top one. Or was it this one?" Erin looked slyly sideways at Vic, who shook her head at Erin baiting her.

"Okay, where after this?"

"Looks like about two miles. We just keep following this road. And then eventually, we'll be up to Orson's house."

"I sure hope it's still there," Vic said. "I don't see much other development out here. Doesn't look like anybody is even farming this land anymore. So hopefully…"

Erin looked at the land with new eyes. There were areas that were clear of trees and the land was fairly flat. But she wasn't sure she would have tried to farm it. It would have taken a lot of work to plow the land, breaking the soil and moving the rocks out of the fields, trying to keep the trees from creeping back in on them.

"This really is wild," she said.

"Yeah, it is," Vic said. "A lot more remote than my farm."

Erin remembered Vic's family farm. It had been more like the farms she was accustomed to; much flatter, with a country farmhouse and a big red barn.

They were both watching the odometer to see how far they had gone. Erin looked out the window and started scanning for any buildings or fences or signs of the old farm. The country looked untouched other than the faint track through the trees that Vic was trying to follow without jostling their brains out. Erin was starting to regret having tried to find the house so soon. She was still having headaches following her mugging and the bumps and ruts in the so-called road were not helping.

"What's that?" Vic pointed.

Erin could barely see the outline through the trees. "Is it a house? I think it's a house! I think that's it!"

Vic got as close as she could. The trees were doing their best to take back the clearing that had once been made, and they couldn't drive right up to the house. It was very small, and Erin was worried it was just an outhouse or shed until they got closer. It was larger than it looked from the road, but still very small when compared to Clementine's house or most of the homes that Erin had grown up in.

"It guess this is it," she said, looking around for any other buildings. If there had been barns and other outbuildings, they had been reclaimed by nature; Erin couldn't see any sign of them. The house must have been sturdily built to have resisted the advances of time.

Vic parked the car. They both got out, looking around. There was no sign of other human life around them. The birds were singing and the sun was shining. The leaves were rustling in a slight wind. But it seemed like it had been a hundred years since another human being had set foot on the property.

"Just look at it," Vic breathed.

They walked toward the house. Old and gray from the weather, but the corners still mostly square. The windows were broken and a couple had tattered curtains behind them. As they got closer, Vic called out.

"Hallo the house! Anyone home?"

Erin looked at her.

"There's no one here. That's obvious."

"Well… it's still rude to just walk in."

"Even if there's nobody there?"

Vic shrugged. "What can I tell you? Even if you don't think there's anyone home, you should always call just to be sure. I was always taught that."

"Okay!" Erin laughed and continued to walk toward the house.

There was still no answer, but neither expected there to be. Erin expected Vic to knock on the door when they got to it, further demonstrating her training in southern manners, but Vic did not. She put her hand on the doorknob and waited for a moment.

"Do you want to open it?" she asked. "He's your uncle."

"Go ahead."

"On the count of three?"

Erin again laughed and waited for Vic to count it off and open the door. It wasn't locked and swung open under her hand. They walked in and looked around the interior of the house.

It was empty. Any furniture that had once been in the house was long gone, other than a kitchen table made of a slab of wood, and a broken-down rocking chair across the room by the fireplace. It was mostly a one-room home, with partial partitions built up between the kitchen and the seating area, and a little niche Erin thought must have been for a bed. Very small and cozy. Even smaller than the summerhouse on Erin's property that Adele lived in.

"See any clues?" Vic asked.

Erin searched the room. There was no desk with hidden compartments. There were no cryptic notes scribbled on the walls. Anything that had been left in the house was long gone.

She walked around the little room, looking at the plank wall, where there could obviously be no hidden rooms. In places there were wide cracks between the planks where the sun came in from the outside.

"There's something there," Erin pointed to the floor at a cut-out square.

"A trapdoor," Vic observed. "There must be a root cellar."

They went over to it together. Vic put her finger into a little notch cut-out and gave a tug. The trapdoor no longer fit well in the space. It took a bit of pulling and tugging before Vic was able to lever it up. Erin looked at the narrow stairs that led down into the darkness. It was more like a ladder than a staircase. Erin wasn't sure how anyone would walk down it.

"You want to go down?" Vic asked.

"It's worse than the basement at Bella's house."

"Definitely."

Neither one of them made any move to go down the steps to see what was down there.

"If there are any clues, they're going to be down there," Vic said. "You can see there isn't anything left up here."

Erin looked around. She looked up at the roof of the house. No attic, just the inside of the roof that kept out the rain. Or mostly, anyway. They could go outside and look for a barn and other outbuildings. There might be more clues as to what Orson Cadaver had been doing in the outbuildings. Erin hadn't been able to see any from the car, but that didn't mean they didn't exist. One just had to look harder.

"You want me to go first?" Vic asked.

"Yes."

"If I go down there, you have to too."

"I don't know about that."

"Come on, Erin. You can do that. It's not a cave, it's just a basement. And there won't be any hidden corners. You'll be able to see everything when you get down the stairs."

Erin crouched down at the edge of the hole. "Maybe I could just poke my head down and not go down at all."

"I'll go first, but only if you promise you'll come too."

Erin let out a puff of breath. "Fine. I'll go down. Unless you fall and break your leg. Then I'm going back to the car to get help."

"I'm not going to break my leg."

"You might. Those stairs don't look very safe."

Vic stopped arguing and walked around the trapdoor, trying to figure out the best way to get down the dangerous-looking stairs. She finally decided to approach it like a ladder. She went down it backward, feet first, holding on to the sides of the stairway to stabilize herself.

When she got to the bottom, she put her foot out to feel for another step, then looked down and saw that she had made it. She pushed away from the stairs and looked around.

"Come on down."

"Is there anything to see?"

"Erin you promised you'd come. So, come."

Erin hesitated. But she had promised, so she slowly climbed down the stairs the same way as Vic had. They held their phones up with flashlight apps on to explore the tiny cellar.

"Not much here," Erin muttered.

"Nope."

It was a dirt floor. There were a couple of shelves that might have once held preserves. There was a wooden plank box with a lid torn off. Erin bent over it, shining her light into the box.

There were a few twisted shapes. Old parsnips and potatoes or other roots that Erin wasn't sure about that had dried out and petrified long ago. She poked around at them with one finger, worried about stirring up spiders or something worse. Nothing jumped out at her. There was no journal or note or other clue hidden under the old vegetables.

Erin stood back up. "Well... let's explore a little more upstairs and outside. Maybe there are some other buildings that might give us a clue."

CHAPTER 17

The upstairs was no more enlightening than it had been the first time they looked at it. Erin looked again for any hidden panels, notes folded up and stuffed into the cracks of boards, or anything else that might give them a clue as to the hiding place of old Orson's fabled gold. There was nothing in the house.

Outside, Erin looked out at the forest. If Orson had indeed cleared a field, it was barely detectable a hundred and fifty years later. The trees had reclaimed the area.

There was a scattering of low plants with bright yellow leaves dappling the shadows under the trees. Tennessee autumn came much later than Erin was used to in Maine, but she had noticed some changes and variations in the foliage.

"I'm going to get the map." Erin returned to the car to get the map to see if there were any other buildings or landmarks marked on it that they should look at.

Erin returned to where Vic was standing.

"Do you see anything?" she asked.

Vic motioned to the trees to their right. "I think there's a building over there. Maybe some pieces of an old barn."

Erin squinted, but couldn't see anything through the trees that looked like a building. She looked at the map in her hand, then she and Vic walked over to have a look. Erin had been looking for a building that was still standing, like the house, so she hadn't seen the timbers that were on the ground. They walked around the perimeter of the pile of wood pieces, looking down at the ground and the area around for anything that they might have missed.

"You want to look through this?" Vic asked, motioning to the boards. "It could take a while."

"Let's just have a quick look," Erin said. "We can look more later. If it looks promising or if we can't find anything else."

They moved in. Erin thought belatedly that they should have brought work gloves and shovels and rakes. Any other implements that would let them handle the old boards and detritus without getting dirty or putting nail holes in their hands. As it was, they handled the boards delicately, trying to avoid slivers or dirt. Or spiders or other crawly creatures that might like hiding in the pile.

"Looks like there was a fire," Vic pointed out, as they got down a layer and encountered boards that had been blackened to charcoal.

Erin agreed. "I guess that's why it's not standing anymore. If he did leave any clues here, they would have been destroyed."

"Depending on what kind of clues they were. If he left another note with a poem…" Vic wiped her forehead with the back of her arm.

"There could still be a strong box or coins. They would have survived. But chances are, whoever burned it down would already have looked through the debris for anything like that."

"It might not have been burned down deliberately. Could have been a lantern or a lightning strike. And who knows how long ago. It might have just happened last year." Vic studied the wood, looking for clues. "Longer ago than that, though, I'd say. There's a lot of overgrowth. If it was just last year, there wouldn't be so much growth over top of the site. This looks like it's been here for a long time."

"Yeah." Erin looked at the pile. It had been there before she was born. Before her parents or grandparents were born. A long time. It gave her a strange feeling of being small and insignificant. All of that history, all of that time marching by, and nothing had changed. She hadn't changed anything. She and her ancestors were barely a blip in the long history of the place. Nature was wiping out every trace.

She abandoned her search of the wood. If there was anything hidden in the ashes and fallen timbers of the barn, it was going to take a much more involved excavation to get at them. More people, and proper equipment rather than bare hands. She took the map back out of her pocket.

"What do you think? It looks like there were a few roads through here back in the day. But everything is so overgrown, that even the main road is almost undetectable. There's no way we're going to find any of these other roads."

Vic looked at the map, studying the lines and the contours of the topography. "Actually, I don't think those are roads."

"What are they, then? Rivers?"

Vic shook her head and looked at the title and legend on the map. "This was a mining survey. I think those are mines that were dug and then abandoned."

"I'm not going down any old mines," Erin said immediately.

"No, not today," Vic agreed. "We'll need Willie to look to see what kind of condition they are in. They might need to be shored up. Or they might be completely caved in. But we're not going to go anywhere without him having a look first to make sure it's safe."

"I'm not going into any abandoned mines period. I don't care how much money might be down there. I'm just not doing it."

"Okay. That's fine. Leave it to me and Willie."

Erin shook her head. She didn't even want any of them going into an old mine. Just the thought of it made her stomach clench. She and Jeremy had already been in the hospital; she didn't want anyone else put in danger. And she knew how dangerous it could be underground. It wasn't safe for any of them.

"Let's just see if we can find any entrances," Vic suggested. "We're definitely not going in anywhere. But if we can find the entrances and maybe take some pictures for Willie, it will save time. He'll have a better idea of what kind of shape they're in and what kind of equipment we'll need, and we won't have to waste time looking later. And if I'm wrong, and they are something other than mines, then we won't be wasting time coming back for something that isn't there."

CHAPTER 18

ired and grubby after their afternoon at Orson's old farm, Erin and Vic decided to go back to the hospital before heading home to Bald Eagle Falls. It wasn't long before Jeremy would be released. Erin was looking forward to knowing that he was close to home and they could go see him just a few minutes away instead of having to take a couple of extra hours to go to the city and back. It made it quite an ordeal.

"We should stop for something to eat while we're here too," Vic suggested. "Otherwise, we're going to be too tired when we get home to do anything other than put something in the microwave." Which was their usual practice when getting home from the bakery after a long day of work. Either that or having leftover bread or rolls and jam. Either way, they rarely actually cooked a full meal for anything other than holidays.

"That sounds good. I wouldn't mind something other than frozen pasta or casserole," Erin admitted. She didn't normally go out for burgers, but they sounded awfully good after a steady diet of muffins, sandwiches, and frozen dinners.

"We're doing it then. We can either get something at the hospital cafeteria or hit a fast food restaurant on the way home."

"The hospital cafeteria isn't actually too bad. And that will keep the car from smelling like french fries for a week."

Vic grinned. They reached the door to Jeremy's room and Vic looked in to see whether he was alone. Sometimes when they arrived, the doctor or a nurse was there tending to his bandages or checking out his healing bullet holes. Vic stopped in the doorway, frozen. Erin couldn't see past her to see what was going on inside. Her heart started thumping hard in her chest.

"Vic?" she murmured. "What's up?"

Vic still didn't move or say anything. Then there was another voice that Erin didn't recognize.

"Well, look who's here!"

She could have mistaken it for Jeremy's voice, except that it was a bit huskier, and he didn't quite have the same cheeriness that Jeremy usually exuded.

"It's James," the voice went on. "The brother who ain't a brother."

Erin moved to try to see into the room. Vic finally seemed to break free of the paralysis that held her there.

"Joseph."

Vic moved into the room toward her older brother. Then Erin could see him. A man quite similar to Jeremy in looks, but broader and older, without Jeremy's laughing expression. Vic approached him and held her hand out stiffly, not hugging him as she would have Jeremy.

"Hi, how are you doing?"

Joseph gave her hand a couple pumps. He slapped her shoulder with his other hand, looking away from Vic as though he were uncomfortable with her. "How's it going, little bro?"

Vic looked at Jeremy, her eyes hurt.

"Come on, Joseph," Jeremy said roughly. "How would you like it if she refused to call you by your name? I don't care how awkward you think it is. Just start. It will get easier."

Joseph was a little flushed. He looked at Vic again, not sure what to say to this.

"Vic," Jeremy said. "Just call her Vic."

Joseph cleared his throat. "I don't know," he said. "This is all just... I've never called you that before. It's just not your name."

"I was named James Victor when I was born," Vic reminded him. "So, you can't complain that it isn't really my name, even if you aren't comfortable with my gender identity. I am Vic."

"Okay," Joseph nodded slowly. "Vic. How are you, Vic?"

Vic nodded graciously, as if she hadn't had to prompt Joseph with the proper etiquette. "I'm right as rain. How about you?"

Joseph forced a smile. "I can't complain. You taking care of this old guy?" Joseph indicated Jeremy.

"Who are you calling old?" Jeremy shot back. "I could still beat you."

"Huh. Doubt it," Joseph disagreed. "You're looking pretty poorly."

Jeremy shifted, sitting himself up taller on the bed, drawing himself up to look bigger and stronger. "I'll be out of here in no time. The doctors are just being extra careful."

Vic nodded at the repartee between her brothers. "What've you been doing lately, Joe? Haven't heard anything from you."

"Been busy on the farm," Joseph said curtly. "You know how much work it takes to run the place."

Vic looked at Jeremy, who had informed her that the family was no longer running the farm at full capacity, but was merely keeping it running as a front for the Jackson clan. Jeremy shrugged and didn't challenge Joseph.

"Which one of you was it I saw in Bald Eagle Falls a few weeks ago?" Erin asked. "Back when one of you was at the bakery. Before it burned down. Was that you?"

Joseph looked at her, his expression veiled. He wasn't about to give away whether it had been him or not.

"I didn't burn down anything."

"I didn't say you had. I just asked whether it was you I saw. You didn't exactly stay around to talk."

Joseph clearly wasn't about to be drawn into admitting it was him. Erin and Vic had avoiding discussing the fact that it might have been one of her own brothers who had burned down the bakery. Erin didn't want to make Vic feel any worse than she already did about her family situation and what had happened to Auntie Clem's Bakery, but they both knew in the backs of their minds that since one of the brothers had been seen there before the fire, it was probably one of them who had set it. Terry had questioned both brothers, but they had denied being in Bald Eagle Falls or having anything to do with the fire. Erin hadn't gotten a good enough look say which of them it had been.

"I'm just here visiting my brother," Joseph said, gesturing toward Jeremy. "I didn't come here to get into it again with you two about the bakery."

"Get into it again?" Vic repeated in disbelief. "Neither one of us has ever talked to you about the bakery. Don't make it sound like we've been throwing accusations around."

"Maybe you haven't talked to us about it, but that doesn't mean no one has. The cops have been around enough times, and don't think I don't know that it was you two who set them on us." Joseph nodded toward Erin. "It's your boyfriend who's the town cop, right? You can just tell him you were mistaken and to stay out of my business. He's a cop in Bald Eagle Falls, not in Moose River. He's got no jurisdiction out there."

Erin just looked at him.

"You guys just leave Vic and Erin alone," Jeremy told Joseph. "They're family, and you shouldn't be doing anything against family."

"They're not family," Joseph said slowly. "James—Vic decided that when he—she—decided to leave the family and to become…" he motioned widely to Vic's body and went on, uncomfortable. "And I don't know whether the two of you are an item," he included Vic and Erin both in his gesture this time, "but even if you are, that still doesn't make Erin Price family when James—Vic—isn't anymore." He scowled at Jeremy. "They're not family. So, I don't know why you're trying to protect them. If they don't want bad things to happen," he paused, letting Erin think about the bakery burning down, "then maybe you ought to stay out of the way of the clan."

"Staying out of the way of the clan isn't any guarantee of bad things not happening," Vic said. "Just ask Jeremy. He gets an honest job, and what happens? He gets shot by poachers."

Joseph gave an amused grin, his body language loosening a bit. "Well, that ain't nothin' to do with me. I can't help what other people do."

They all stood around for a minute, saying nothing, stuck in an awkward moment where there didn't seem to be anything appropriate to say.

"Well…" Joseph brushed his hands as if they were sandy. "I just came to see how my little brother was doing. I'll tell Mom that you're still in one piece."

"Say 'hi' for me," Jeremy agreed. "I'll be okay. She doesn't need to worry."

Joseph looked at Vic.

"I won't ask you to say 'hi' for me," Vic said slowly. "Since that would just cause more trouble than it's worth. She knows how to find me if she wants to talk. Until then... I guess she'll just have to be in the dark. I love you guys... but things are pretty screwed up right now."

The three looked at each other. Erin remembered a phrase that she'd heard used to describe the Revolutionary War, about how 'brother fought against brother' and thought it apt. The three wanted so badly to just be family and be friends with each other again, but prejudices and criminal activities were keeping them apart.

They had once been so close, working and playing together. Erin could picture them all gathered together around the kitchen table, breaking bread together, maybe with a word of prayer or their pa reading a scripture to them. They had once been united, all working together. But circumstances had twisted everything apart, leaving them broken and unsure how to pick up the pieces.

"I guess I'll see you around," Joseph finally said to Jeremy. He punched him lightly on the shoulder. "Watch out for flying bullets."

He looked at Vic, then walked out without saying anything else to her.

CHAPTER 19

*W*hen Beaver arrived, Vic was sitting on the edge of Jeremy's bed, still looking stricken after her encounter with Joseph, in spite of Jeremy's and Erin's attempts to cheer her up again. It had been a long day, and Erin figured Vic was just too tired to bounce back. She would feel better in the morning.

Beaver looked at the glum faces and raised her eyebrows.

"You'd think I was walking into a funeral," she observed. "Was there bad news? Did the doctor say Jeremy only has a few more hours to live?"

Jeremy rolled his eyes at her. He squeezed Vic's hand and let it go again. "Joseph stopped by for a visit," he said. "It was just a little rough on Vic."

Beaver dropped into a visitor's chair, chewing on her gum. "Why?"

Erin looked for a way to answer and steer the conversation in another direction. Vic didn't need to keep going over the same ground. Jeremy too seemed to be trying to tell Beaver not to pursue it, shaking his head at her. "Nothing. It's fine. How was your day?"

"Joseph is a bully," Beaver said, not to be dissuaded. She kept her eyes on Vic. "Those boys know that turning you out on the street wasn't right, and that shunning you isn't right. But they're being indoctrinated and that's not something that is easy to break free from."

Vic looked at Beaver, her brows drawn down. "How do you know all of that? From Jeremy?" She turned her head to look at her brother.

He gave a self-conscious shrug, looking down at his hands. His normally ebullient manner was muted. "We talk," he admitted. "And Ro hears things through work."

"About Joseph? They aren't into drugs, are they? I don't want to hear that they're part of this drug trade."

Beaver didn't give any indication.

"I know Joseph was being a jerk," Jeremy said to Vic. "But she's right, they're being told all the time what to do and what to think. That kind of... brainwashing gets under your skin and into your brain. They want to do what's right, but it keeps getting twisted around."

"But *you* didn't turn out that way," Erin pointed out. "You've been really good to Vic. You came last Christmas and you came this summer when you thought she might be in danger. You treated her better than that."

"I wasn't there as long either. And me and James—Vic were closer. We were the two youngest, so we did everything together. The others were older, and they didn't really want their annoying little brothers getting underfoot all the time. So... we were closer to each other than Joseph and Daniel were to us."

"They're responsible for their own choices," Beaver said. "But they're older now, they've had to prove themselves to the clan, which means they've had to do some pretty bad stuff. And once you've got that on your conscience, it's easier to just believe the party line that what you're doing isn't really wrong. You go all in, because it's safer and feels better. You want to either be all in or all out."

Erin looked at Jeremy. "And you decided it was time to get out, before you... had to prove yourself."

Jeremy nodded. "I just... I dunno. I'm kind of a baby, you know. I've always had a soft heart. And that's not so good when you're dealing with a group like the Jackson clan. Those people have to be rooted out."

Beaver nodded. "A soft heart is a liability. If you can't break someone of it, you've got to get them out some other way."

Jeremy shrugged. Vic touched his arm, nodding.

"In the rest of the world, it's not such a bad thing to have a soft heart."

"The world still thinks that a man should be macho and not cry at chick flicks. But it's getting better. I feel... more free now that I'm away from the family. While I was there, I felt like that was the only way to be, and that was the only place I'd ever belong. But it wasn't really true. That's just want they wanted me to think."

There was silence for a few minutes while everyone pondered this.

"Do you know about everyone in Bald Eagle Falls?" Erin asked Beaver, "or everyone who is from Bald Eagle Falls?" She was thinking about Beaver knowing details about Mary Lou's son Campbell.

"How could I?" Beaver laughed.

"It's not that big a place. It just seems like… you know about everyone, even people who aren't connected to your job. To drugs and whatever else you investigate."

"I'm not snooping into everyone's backgrounds, if that's what you're asking. We're not allowed to just investigate anyone without a reason. There has to be a reason to start looking at someone. You can't just look up your boyfriend's boss or sister because you're curious."

That somehow made Erin feel more uneasy instead of less. "So you would need to have reason to think that we were doing something illegal before you could look into our records?"

Beaver studied Erin, one corner of her mouth quirked into a smile. "Do you have something in your past that you would rather keep quiet, Erin Price?"

Erin looked at Beaver, her stomach tight and a little nauseated. She did have a past, and she didn't want anyone who felt like it digging into it to find out where she had come from and what she had done in her life.

"Doesn't everyone?" she asked, forcing bravado.

Beaver chuckled. She looked at Vic, who turned red.

"Okay, so I don't exactly like the idea of anyone investigating me, either," Vic admitted. "Everyone makes mistakes. No one wants people looking into their past and judging them by what they've done in the past." She looked at Jeremy, as if challenging him to ask what she could possibly have to be worried about. Jeremy didn't say anything. "I ran away. I was on my own. And there's not a lot of ways for an eighteen-year-old to make it on the streets alone without breaking a law or two. Erin knows I was down and out. I was squatting in the bakery. I didn't know where else to go. And yeah, I might have helped myself to something to eat or drink, and I know I wasn't supposed to be in the bakery, even if I did have a key. I mean, the key wasn't exactly mine, and Erin had no idea that I had it. She hadn't given me permission."

"I've never blamed you for any of that," Erin reminded her. "I know what it's like. I remember having to take care of myself when I didn't have anything."

"Vic…" Beaver shook her head, losing some of her amused demeanor for once. "I'm not investigating you. I'm just teasing. I told you, I can't just investigate anyone I feel like. If I did want to look into your past, I'd have to have a reason. A good one. I really don't think you need to worry that someone is going to slap you into jail for stealing a loaf of bread when you were out on the street."

Vic shrugged uncomfortably. "I'm not proud of everything I've done. I haven't always made good choices." She looked over at Jeremy. "Nobody makes good choices all of the time."

"No."

"So, when are you getting out of here?" Beaver demanded, changing the subject abruptly at the same time as she crossed one leg over the other and spread out to command as much space as possible. "Aren't those doctors tired of you yet?"

Vic nodded. "They must be. I can't imagine having this guy underfoot for more than a few days."

"They're promising me another day or two," Jeremy said. "If they change their minds, I might just have to check myself out anyway. It's really not much fun just sitting around here all day long. I want to be home. In my own space and able to sleep in my own bed instead of this thing, and not to have to listen to pages over the public address system and people walking up and down the halls at all hours or screaming that they want painkillers. It's bedlam."

"You'll be out before long," Vic assured him. "Just stick it out for a day or two longer until they say it's safe to leave."

"I'm with Jer," Beaver said. "I don't think I've ever stayed as long as the doctors wanted me to. You don't want to end up with some hospital infection and have them talking about wanting to cut off an arm or leg because of it. That's just… annoying."

Erin couldn't help laughing. Vic and Jeremy were smiling too.

"How many times *have* you been shot?" Erin asked.

Beaver shrugged her shoulders. "I wouldn't want to say. You know that most federal agents go through their entire careers without ever having to draw their weapon or be injured? Their whole careers."

"How long are those careers?" Jeremy asked.

"Well, that's a good question. I mean, if you decide it's not for you after a year or two, that's different from an agent who's been in for thirty or forty years."

"Do you know anyone who's been in for thirty or forty years?"

Beaver pursed her lips. "No, can't say I do. I don't know how long our director has been in… maybe he has… but I think they all move on to other things after a decade or two." She shook her head. "How about your new adventure? Any closer to getting that treasure?"

Erin looked at Vic, wondering if she should say anything. Vic shrugged and nodded. Erin started in on the latest details about Orson and his unexplained wealth. Beaver's eyes were alive with interest.

"Were you able to find any mines?"

Erin took out her phone and brought up the pictures they had taken at the farm. Beaver flicked through them.

"Well, well, well. Maybe Orson was getting more out of the ground than potatoes. When are you going to go down?"

"I don't know." Erin received her phone back from Beaver. "*I'm* not going down there. Vic is going to talk to Willie about getting the equipment they'll need and having a look. We won't be able to get back there for a few days, and we don't know what kind of shape the mines are going to be in. They haven't been maintained, so it might be a lot of work before we can find anything. If there's anything to be found."

CHAPTER 20

$\mathcal{E}$rin hadn't actually taken a shift with Charley before, so having Vic leave after lunch and Charley take over was a strange feeling. She wasn't exactly worried about it, but wasn't sure how they would get along together and whether it was going to be awkward the whole time Charley was there.

Erin tried to push aside any doubts and to pretend that Charley was just one of her other employees, someone who needed to be taught and trained but was perfectly competent and able to take it all on. She didn't need to worry about whether Charley was her boss or her partner, she just needed to show her the ropes. Erin was the one with experience, so she was the one who needed to show Charley how it was all done.

After the initial awkwardness, they had fallen into a rhythm. Not like the rhythm that Erin had with Vic, but she couldn't exactly expect that the first day, either.

"Here come some more," Charley advised.

Erin looked up from the display glass she was polishing to see the Fosters coming up to the door of the bakery. She gave them a big smile. "Well, here's my favorite customer. How is everybody?"

Mrs. Foster smiled and murmured a greeting while the children hurried forward to have a look at what was in the display case and negotiate what they were going to get. "Charley, this is the Foster family. Mrs. Foster with her son Peter, and Karen, Jody, and Traci. Peter is very sensitive to gluten and is one of my best missionaries. He is always telling his friends that they should come here."

"Sometimes I think we single-handedly keep this place afloat," Mrs. Foster sighed, giving a tired smile. "Considering the number of times a week I am in here and the amount I walk away with."

"Well, we surely appreciate your business," Charley said, nodding graciously. "We couldn't do it without our customers."

"Erin has been so good to us. It's been amazing for Peter to actually have choices, instead of me having to run into the city to pick up a box of factory-produced cookies. He can have all kinds of wonderful baking that he wasn't able to touch before."

Charley nodded.

"Charley is my partner in the bakery now," Erin explained, though Mrs. Foster probably already knew all of the details. "She's the one who helped me to get the bakery going again after the fire. I couldn't have reopened without her."

Charley actually blushed. Erin laughed at her pink flush.

"And she's my half-sister too, but we never knew each other growing up, so we're still getting to know each other."

"You two look alike," Mrs. Foster agreed, looking from one to the other. "I can see the family resemblance. How nice for you to find each other. You don't have any other siblings, do you?"

"No. I grew up with a lot of different families, so I did grow up with brothers and sisters… but none of them were my own blood, and they came and went. I don't keep in close contact with any of them." She thought about Reg's visit and the odd phone calls that she occasionally got from the woman. She worried sometimes about what was going on with Reg. Erin shook off this stray thought. "Anyway, I'm really grateful for Charley. She came into my life at just the right time and really helped me to get back on my feet again."

Charley got pinker still. Erin laughed and looked down at the children.

"So, have you decided what you want?"

"Could we have one of the chocolate chip cookies?" Peter pointed at them. "And one of the ginger cookies. And…" he looked at Jody, "the banana bread? Is that what you want?"

Jody nodded. "I like banana bread," she told Erin, looking down at the loaf of bread in the display case.

"I do too," Erin confessed. "And I like to think they're better for you than the cookies. Less sugar, and the good vitamins and fiber from the banana."

"Know what I like better?"

"What?"

"Pumpkin bread."

"Oooh," Erin nodded. "I'll have to make sure I make some when pumpkins start showing up at the store for Halloween. I love pumpkin bread too."

Erin started to get out the treats for the children. She looked at Mrs. Foster. "And do you know what you want today?"

Mrs. Foster tried to keep Traci from getting her fingers all over the display case. "I'll need some sandwich bread for school lunches. And maybe some biscuits to go with the soup tonight. Do you need anything else, Peter?"

"Breakfast," Peter contributed. "Could I have bagels or muffins?"

"Why don't you just have cereal?"

Peter gave a martyred sigh. "I like muffins and bagels."

Mrs. Foster rolled her eyes. "Fine, then. One or the other, not both."

Peter looked into the display case. "Could I have... the bagels, then. Six?" he looked at his mother for confirmation.

"You make them last all week No more than one per day."

"Okay."

Erin nodded. "Six bagels for Master Peter."

She packaged up the bagels and handed them over to Charley to ring through the till. Charley didn't take them. Her eyes were on the door. Erin looked to see who was there. It was a woman she didn't recognize. Middle-aged, dark hair, pleasant face. Her eyes were on Charley. Erin looked expectantly at Charley, waiting to be introduced. The woman entered and approached them.

"Hello, Charlotte," she said, prompting Charley to wake up and greet her.

"Uh... hi, Mom."

Erin blinked. Charley's mother? She nudged Charley aside to ring through the transaction and handed the baking to Mrs. Foster. Charley was still standing there like she didn't know what to do or say.

"Hi!" Erin said, holding out her hand to Charley's mother. "I'm Erin Price."

Mrs. Campbell smiled and shook Erin's hand. "Pleased to meet you, Erin."

"I'm Charley's half-sister. Biological."

Surprise registered on the woman's face. "Charley's sister?"

Erin glanced over at Charley. She had apparently not bothered to tell her mother about the discovery of her biological sister. Erin had thought that this would be big news, something that Charley would share with her family.

"Uh... yeah," Charley agreed weakly. "Um... surprise!"

Mrs. Campbell looked at the two of them, making the usual comparison of their features. "There is a resemblance," she admitted. "Have you actually done testing to see if you are?"

"Well, no. But Charley's birth date and information all match up."

"We were told that Charley was an only child. There were no siblings."

Erin shrugged uncomfortably. "There were a lot of things said and done at the time that weren't exactly ethical. I was told that my parents had died instantly in the accident, and they both lived for some months afterward. I was never told about Charley. I didn't find out about her being born until I requested my DHS records."

"That all seems very... unlikely."

"You can look at them if you want to. Charley is my mother's daughter. And she did have a DNA test to prove that she was Adam Plaint's daughter. She..." Erin made a motion to include her surroundings. "She inherited this place. So then we went into business together..."

She was probably saying too much. Wasn't it up to Charley to tell her own family about everything she had discovered? Erin didn't really know much about their relationship. Maybe Charley didn't want her family to know anything at all about Erin's mother and Adam Plaint. Erin looked over at Charley, who was still standing there looking thunderstruck that her mother had shown up in her bakery without any warning.

"Charley... do you want to show you mom around or offer her a free muffin?"

"What are you doing here?" Charley finally managed to ask.

"I came to see you. I don't understand why you didn't come home. If you finally decided not to have anything to do with that awful gang, then why didn't you come back home? And why all of the secrecy about this?" She pointed to Erin.

"I just want to live my own life. You don't control me. I can make my own decisions and go wherever I want."

"Clearly," Charley's mother agreed.

"I didn't want to come home like a boomerang kid. You guys don't need that. There's no reason you should have to support me when I'm an adult. I can take care of myself."

"You don't have to do it all on your own. We'd be happy to help. You know that. We've called. We've left messages. I don't know what else to do to convince you that we just want to be a part of your life. Don't cut us out."

Charley's expression was uncertain. She looked at Erin, then back at her mother.

"I think I should check on those cookies," Erin offered, turning to retreat to the kitchen to give them a chance to sort things out without an outsider listening in on their private conversation.

"No," Charley caught her by the sleeve. "I don't want you to leave. It's okay. I'm trying to figure this out. I don't know what to do."

"Well…" Erin looked at Mrs. Campbell and shrugged. "Don't you want your parents to be a part of your life? Just because you're working here and we've reconnected, that doesn't mean that you can't still be part of your family too. If they want to keep in touch…"

Erin didn't say how much she wished she had a family of her own to connect with. It would be so nice to be able to call up parents whenever she got lonely, to have plans with them for Christmas, to have someone to talk to when she was anxious, who was older and wiser and could give her advice. She had friends, but she would have given anything to have a family like Charley did too.

Maybe Charley sensed some of that. She looked away from her mother, biting her lip. "I should have called you back. I'm sorry. I've been sort of a brat. I know you still want to stay in touch."

"You know that the problem we had wasn't with you, it was with the choices that you were making. The people you were hanging around with. But this is nice. You've really turned things around. That makes me proud."

"You didn't come see me when I was in jail."

Mrs. Campbell didn't have any answer to that immediately. She looked into the display case at the various baked treats.

"I don't know what to say, Charlotte. You're the one who didn't want anything to do with us. And you expect us to swoop in the moment you get arrested? We told you that your lifestyle was going to get you in trouble. You pursued it anyway. You suffered the consequences. We couldn't change those consequences. That was something you had to deal with yourself."

"You could still have visited."

"I'm sorry that hurt your feelings. I hope you'll think about how we felt, hearing that you had murdered someone. That everything we had told you was going to happen did. We didn't know what to do or how we would be received if we did try to visit you. You are the one who broke off contact with us and made it clear that you didn't want us to be a part of your life."

"I know."

Erin stared into the display case, hot and uncomfortable. "How about a free muffin?"

Charley and her mother looked at Erin, brows drawn down, their movements mirrors of each other. Charley spread her hands out.

"Why not a muffin?" She said. "Do you want a muffin, Mom?"

Mrs. Campbell pointed to one of the chocolate chip ones. "I know I should probably go with a bran muffin, but those look so good."

Erin got one out and handed it across to her in a napkin. "They *are* really good."

"So, this is a specialty bakery?" Mrs. Campbell looked around. "You have a section that is gluten-free?"

"Everything is gluten-free," Erin informed Mrs. Campbell as she bit into the muffin, rolling her eyes at the moist muffin studded with chocolate chips.

"This is gluten-free?"

"Yes. Everything."

"How do you do that? Do you have a special kind of flour?"

"Most of them are combinations of flours," Charley jumped in, eager to impart what she had been learning. "There isn't one gluten-free flour that can substitute satisfactorily for wheat or other gluten flours. You need a few different ones to mimic the properties of wheat flour."

"Why did you name it Auntie Clem's? Couldn't you name it after one of your real aunties?"

"Oh, that's me," Erin explained. "I operated the bakery across the street before it burned down. Charley helped me get back on my feet, and I helped her open the bakery. She wanted to keep the name of Auntie Clem's because it had a good reputation. People knew what it was and what we offered already."

"You could have named it something else," Mrs. Campbell asserted, looking at Charley.

"I know I could. But that's what I wanted. There's nothing wrong with it."

"No, of course not," Mrs. Campbell said.

"I wanted Erin on board, and I wanted her goodwill. So I used her name. It's sound business practices."

Erin looked again toward the kitchen and the fictional burning cookies. She really didn't want to stay there and listen to Charley and her mother bickering. Some people enjoyed getting into arguments or watching other people's arguments. Erin was not one of them. She was an avoider, through and through. She did whatever she could to avoid getting in the middle of an argument, especially somebody else's argument.

"Are you going to be in town for a while?" Charley asked her mother, looking at the clock on the wall. "We could get together for dinner before you go home, if you want to talk. If you really want to visit," she added, "and not just criticize."

"Of course I do! I would love to get together for dinner. Why don't you come home and we could have dinner there?"

"Mom... I've got to work. I don't have time to drive out to Moose River, have supper, and then drive back. If you want to stick around for a little while, I'll join you when I'm done here. Otherwise, we can set up another day."

"And you'll answer the phone?"

Charley rolled her eyes. "I'll answer the phone."

"What time are you off?"

"We close at five, and then I need to help with the cleanup and tomor-row's prep—"

"I can do that without you today," Erin said. "It won't take up that much time. Then your mom can still get back to Moose River before it's really late."

Charley shot Erin a look, then gave a grudging nod. "Does that work?"

Mrs. Campbell nodded. She smiled at them both. "How lovely. I'm so looking forward to it. Thank you for being so generous, Erin. And thank you for the muffin. They really are fantastic."

Erin nodded. "You're welcome. Come again."

Mrs. Campbell waved and left the bakery. Erin forced a smile at Charley. Charley put her face in her hands, clearly not happy.

"What have I done now?"

CHAPTER 21

*W*illie rolled up to the house and honked the horn. When Erin and Vic didn't immediately join him at the truck, he locked it up and went up to the house. He knocked on the door and tried the handle. It was unlocked, so he went in.

"You girls ready to go?" he asked, looking through to the kitchen.

"Just about," Vic promised. "We're just finishing up on some sandwiches. We'll be well-supplied."

"You didn't need to make anything," Willie said. "We could have just picked something up on the way."

"I wanted to contribute something," Erin explained. "I don't have any caving equipment or expertise, but I can do sandwiches! This way we won't have to stop for food, and we'll have enough that we don't have to stop if you guys are into something and want to keep working."

Willie walked into the kitchen and helped himself to a slice of bacon before Vic could stop him. She tried to slap his hand, but missed. Willie shoved the bacon into his mouth, grinning.

"Okay, I approve."

"I'm still worried about this," Erin confessed. "What if something happens…? I don't want you to get trapped underground."

"No one is going to get trapped," Willie assured her. "I spend half my life underground. I know what I'm doing."

"But this mine is old. We don't know what kind of condition it is going to be in."

"That's why I'm going to have a look," Willie said patiently. "I'm not going to go in if it's unsafe. If we need to shore up the walls, we can get started on that. If it's collapsed, then we can take a look around and see if there is another way to go in. I'm not going to just rush into a mine without being absolutely sure that it's safe."

"But something could happen."

"No. Nothing is going to happen."

"That time before, you got hurt. You hit your head, and there was a pool of blood, and we were so worried about you."

Willie held her gaze. His face was perfectly calm. "Erin. You know I didn't just happen to bump my head. Somebody helped me along. And I'm not going to be alone today. Vic is going to come. Jeremy is going to come. None of us are going to be alone. You're welcome to come along too, if you like."

"No way," Erin said. "There is no way you're getting me underground."

"You go downstairs. It's really no different. It's perfectly safe. I'm not going to take Vic or you anywhere that I think there is any danger of either of you getting hurt. It wouldn't be anything like when you were underground before. We'll all be working together and helping each other out."

"I'm not going," Erin maintained. "I'll stay outside and then I can call for trouble if anything happens."

"Nothing is going to—"

"I know. But I'm going to be there just in case. Besides, whenever you have someone there in case of an emergency, you end up not needing them, right? So as long as I'm there watching for trouble, there won't be any."

Willie sighed and shook his head at Vic. Vic rolled her eyes and shrugged with one shoulder. "You're not going to convince her," she said. "I've done my best. But Erin has already had a couple of negative experiences. It's not because she just doesn't like tight spaces."

Erin shuddered. She started wrapping the sandwiches they had made, neatly tearing the plastic wrap off of the industrial-size roll, wrapping the sandwiches tightly and stacking them to the side. Willie watched her.

"You're not a coward," he told her.

Erin looked at him, her face getting warm. "I sort of am," she said. "I could try to go into the mine with you. I'd have an expert right there on hand. I know in my head that nothing could happen to me down there with you right there. But I don't even want to try. I just want to wrap a blanket around myself and wait for you to come back out."

"That's okay. Vic is right, you do have good reason for not wanting to go down there. That doesn't make you a coward. You are a brave person."

Erin shrugged. "Eh. Doesn't matter. Results are the same."

As Erin wrapped, Willie started to fill the cooler that was on hand. Erin added some boxes of juice from the fridge, napkins, cookies, cut up fruit and veggies.

Willie shook his head. "All of this for one day? It's a feast."

"I know how much you guys eat. There's not going to be much left over. Especially if we end up covering for two meals. You guys will be like the plague of locusts."

"I don't know. This looks like a lot."

"When you're hungry it won't be. Especially with Jeremy along."

They were finally finished getting everything packed. Willie waited impatiently for a couple more minutes while Erin and Vic gave the animals their treats and said their goodbyes.

"You're going to be back tonight," he pointed out. "It isn't like you're going away for a week."

"We'll be back," Erin agreed. She scratched Marshmallow's ears. "Don't you go getting getting into any trouble." She shook her head. "He's has been crazy lately. He's been getting into the houseplants, chewing on the legs of the couch... I don't know what to think. He's always been so well-behaved before."

"I'm sure he'll be fine without you for a few hours."

"I know." Erin said goodbye to Orange Blossom, and then they were on their way. Willie led them out to the truck. He went around to the driver's side. When he looked at Vic, she hadn't climbed into the car, but was standing outside looking down.

"Vic. What's up?"

"No, it's what's down," Vic said.

Willie walked back around the car and looked down at the tire. It was completely flat.

Willie swore. He replayed the trip over to Erin's house back in his mind and shook his head. It had been a perfectly smooth ride with no issues. Which meant that it had somehow gone from fully inflated to completely flat in the twenty minutes or so he had been in the house trying to get Erin and Vic on their way.

"You must have driven over a nail," Vic said, studying what she could see of the tread for the head of a nail.

"Must have," Willie agreed. He went to the back of the truck and moved things around in order to get out his jack and spare tire and the rest of the tools that he needed. Erin stood by feeling useless while Vic and Willie quickly swapped out the flat tire. While Willie put on the spare, Vic was rolling the flat, looking for some sign of why it had gone flat.

When Willie was finished, he went over to look at the tire. "Find anything?"

Vic turned it around and pointed to the wall of the tire. Willie leaned in. Vic pressed her thumb to the sidewall and Willie saw the small slit open up. He looked at Vic, his brows drawing down. "Somebody slashed my tire?"

Vic nodded.

Erin got closer to have a look, though she was certainly no expert on sabotage to tires. She saw the short, straight slit in the tire. "Couldn't it just have popped or burst? It could just be an accident, right?"

"No," Willie shook his head. "I don't think so. That looks intentional."

"But who would slash your tire?"

Willie walked around the truck, looking at the others. If some unknown party had slashed one of his tires, Willie was lucky he hadn't slashed all four of them. Maybe he had been interrupted. Or maybe the perp had just chickened out and couldn't do more than one. At least where it was only one tire, they could fix it immediately and get back on the road.

"There are plenty of people around Bald Eagle Falls who don't particularly like me," he admitted. "I would think that most of them wouldn't care anymore. It isn't like I'm getting in anyone's way. I would think that anyone who planned to do anything would have done so years ago."

"You haven't started anything recently that someone might be upset with you about?" Vic asked.

Willie shook his head. "No, nothing new."

"Then do you think..." Vic trailed off.

Willie looked at her. "What?"

"I just wondered if you think it's because someone doesn't want us going to Orson's mine. Maybe this is a warning to stay away. Or an attempt to get us to stop so they can get there ahead of us…"

Willie let out his breath in a thin stream. "I don't think anyone really cares that much about this treasure hunt," he said slowly. "Although…"

"Erin got hit over the head for the maps and poem," Vic filled in. "So, we know that *someone* is taking an interest. Someone who maybe followed us all the way from Bald Eagle Falls to the hospital. And then stuck around for hours to see you give Erin the maps."

Willie nodded slowly. Erin didn't like the idea. "Maybe we shouldn't go, then. Maybe it's too dangerous. I don't want anyone to get hurt."

Willie loaded the damaged tire into the back of the truck, then put away his tools. He looked at Erin, his face a mask. "I don't think you need to worry about it. If they really wanted to keep me from the mine, they'd know that they had to do a lot more than just puncture one tire. Anyone who knows me knows that I'm handy and that I've got all the tools I need right here in the truck. There's no point in just flattening one tire."

"So you don't think it was intentional."

"Maybe it was, maybe it wasn't. But they didn't flatten all four, which is what they'd really need to do to slow us down for any length of time. Then I'd need a tow and four new tires before I could get on the road. Just slashing one tire… More likely someone who just has a grudge. Doesn't like something I've been doing lately. I don't know who or why. I'll have to think about it."

"Maybe we shouldn't go to the mine today. Then you have a few days to think about it and investigate properly…"

Willie motioned to the truck. "Hop in. I'm not letting this stop me."

Vic got in as instructed. Willie went around to the driver's door again and got in. Erin was the only one left standing on the sidewalk, dithering about whether it was the right thing to do.

"Get in, Erin," Vic urged. "Come on. We're going. We'll pick up Jeremy and between all of us, we'll be just fine. No one is going to come after all of us."

Erin was still uneasy when they got to Orson's farm. But Vic and Jeremy were talking and laughing as if nothing had happened, and Willie didn't seem to be overly concerned about who might have tried to sabotage his truck. No one acted like it was a big deal.

Willie was a lot faster going over the old roads than Vic had been, and a couple of times they overshot a turn. Erin felt rattled to pieces when they got there and was glad to get out of the truck.

Willie got out and started to circle the truck and tramp back and forth over the area where they had parked, the same place that Vic and Erin had previously stopped to have a look around. He was looking down at the ground. Erin followed him.

"What are you looking for?"

"Just checking for any signs that anyone else has been here."

"And… has there been?"

"Impossible to tell." Willie shrugged. "If someone has been here, they didn't make it obvious. Everything is so overgrown, there's no way to know if they were trying to cover their tracks or if there just hasn't been anyone around. At any rate," Willie took a look around the farm, "it doesn't look like there's anyone here now. So why don't you show me the mine entrances. We'll have a look at their condition. That's what I'm here for, isn't it?"

Erin and Vic took the lead, taking Willie to the place they had taken pictures of the entrances to the mines. They too were overgrown, and Erin was sure that all of the supporting beams and structures had given way. It was way too dangerous for anyone to go into the mines in their current condition.

"Not bad," Willie said, which was not what Erin was hoping to hear. Willie pulled out a strong flashlight and shone it around the inside of the entrances. "It all looks pretty clear. Lots of solid rock, so it's held up pretty well."

He took a couple of steps inside.

"Do you really think you should do that?" Erin asked, her voice squeaking up. He had said that he wouldn't go inside. He'd said that he would just look at it. She wasn't ready for him to go in.

"I'm just right here, Erin," Willie assured, his voice close at hand. "I'm not doing anything dangerous. Just having a look at the condition."

"I don't think we're going to find anything in there. If there was anything to be found, then someone would have found it in the last hundred and fifty years. Even if Orson did hide the source of his treasure, it has long since been raided. People would have looked at the mines before anything else. Well, maybe the house first, but the mines would be the natural place for anyone to search for it."

"Don't freak out now," Vic advised. "Why don't you go sit down? If you don't look at the mines, maybe you'll be able to calm down."

Erin moved a short distance away and sat down, but it didn't make her feel better. Not with Willie already inside the mine, and Jeremy and Vic super close behind him, hanging around the tunnel entrances and talking and pointing and thumping the walls. Erin knew that it wouldn't be long before they all decided to go in.

CHAPTER 22

She was right. Within the hour, Willie had brought over half the equipment in his truck. He was suiting up and showing Vic and Jeremy how to handle their equipment, even though Vic had been caving with him before. Erin bit her fingernails. She knew she didn't have any influence over them. If they wanted to go into the mine, they were going to go into the mine. And Erin couldn't control what would happen to them when they did, and neither could they. They could make the choice, but they couldn't choose the consequences.

"It will be fine, Erin," Vic said as she pulled a backpack on. "Willie says it's perfectly safe. Everything still looks strong. There aren't any loose beams or rocks or anything. Everything was built really well. It's in better shape than the house, and you went into the house."

At least if the house had collapsed on them, there would only have been a few boards coming down on their heads. Not half the mountain. They would have been able to push themselves out from beneath the debris. It wasn't the same with crawling into a mining tunnel. They could easily be hurt or killed if there was a cave-in and they ended up being hit, buried, or trapped by falling rock.

"I just don't have a good feeling about it," Erin said, shaking her head. She wished that she hadn't told anybody about the poem. She should have just read it and left it there in Clementine's papers. Clementine had known what she was doing. Just put the poem in with the genealogy papers and leave it there as a bit of history. What had made Erin think that it was a good idea to go searching for hidden treasure? Why had she told Vic about it? She should have known that Vic would instantly want to pick up the adventure. She was always up for a bit of excitement.

"You don't have a good feeling because you're afraid of enclosed spaces," Vic pointed out. "It isn't anything to do with these particular mines. It's just a bad feeling because you had a couple of bad experiences. You can't let that stop you from enjoying life."

"I really don't think you should go in there," Erin insisted. She could feel tears welling up in her eyes, but she didn't care anymore. Let them see her tears. Maybe it would convince them that what they were doing really was dangerous and unnecessary. What did they think? That they were going to go walking into one of those mining tunnels and just find Orson's treasure, lying in the open? Other people had looked for the treasure. They weren't going to find it.

"Erin." Willie approached Erin. He gave her a hug. "It's going to be okay. You don't need to worry about us. If you want to come in, I'll show you. You can see that it's sturdily-built and there isn't any danger to us."

His arms felt good around her. For a minute, Erin just closed her eyes and reminded herself that she was safe. They were all perfectly safe in Willie's capable hands. She knew he was careful. He didn't rush into things. He knew how to handle himself in an emergency. Even if something did happen, Willie would be able to take care of it. He had always come to her rescue before.

"Don't go in there," she told him anyway.

"Do you want to see? I'll show you."

"No. Just don't go in."

He shook his head and gave her another squeeze before releasing her. "It's going to be okay; you'll see."

Erin couldn't help it. Tears escaped her eyes and she turned away from them, trying to find some mental space to get past the feelings of fear and dread.

She could hear Vic inquiring softly, questioning whether maybe they should just give it up if Erin felt so strongly about it. But Willie murmured that Erin would be okay and that she'd settle down once they were inside, and the little group went ahead.

Erin didn't say goodbye to them. She watched them enter the mine one at a time, just waiting for something to happen. But there wasn't a collapse the minute they walked into the mine. She could hear their voices, cheerful and excited, as they started to explore. She stayed near the entrance for a long time, until their voices had faded away. Nothing had happened. They were okay. Just like Willie had said, the mine tunnel was well-constructed and would probably last several hundred more years. Orson had known what he was doing.

They would explore the empty tunnels, see where Orson had dug looking for gold or whatever he had been mining for, and then they would be back out. Even though they had brought enough food for a couple of meals, they would only spend a couple of hours exploring the tunnels, and then decide that there wasn't anything down there. They would all pile back into the truck and go home.

Thinking about the truck, Erin went back to the vehicle to ensure that everything was still in order with it. She walked around it, checking out each of the tires. It was always possible that whoever had slashed the one tire had intended to do them all. He could easily have followed them there, and then once Willie and the others were in the mine, he could sabotage the rest of the tires and strand them.

But everything looked fine. The tires were all fully inflated and there were no other vehicles around. Birds were singing lustily in the trees. A light wind was blowing through the trees. Everything was calm and peaceful.

There was a muffled thud. Erin felt the ground beneath her feet give a shudder, and the birds stopped singing.

A plume of dust or smoke rose in the air.

CHAPTER 23

*E*rin looked around. She wasn't sure what had just happened, but she knew something was wrong. She looked at the truck once more, worried that if someone had messed with it, they wouldn't be able to get back home. But the truck looked fine. Erin pulled out her phone and looked at it. She had no signal. She hadn't expected to have one, but it still made her anxious not to be able to reach out. How had Orson and the other farmers been able to live that way, totally out of touch with each other? No way to communicate unless they got on a horse—or their own two feet—and physically went to find the nearest neighbor. And maybe he would not be there, having gone into town or to some other destination.

During Erin's time, all of those neighbors had moved away, into the cities and other populated centers, leaving the old farms abandoned and isolated.

Erin walked back to the mine entrance. She walked closer to the entrance and listened for their voices.

"Vic? Willie? Is everything okay"

Her voice bounced back to her. Erin had a sick, tight feeling in her stomach. Something wasn't right. She wasn't sure what it was, but she knew there was a problem. What had happened?

"Vic?"

Willie had given Erin check-in times. If they took more than a few hours in the mine and didn't check in with her, then she was to assume that something had happened and to call for help. She would not go into the mine after them, she would get in touch with someone who could do a proper search.

"Willie?"

There was no answer. Erin looked at her phone for the time. They had not been in there for long. It wasn't time for them to contact her. She went to the radio equipment Willie had left behind. It wouldn't work if they had gone down too deep into the ground, but Willie hadn't thought that the tunnels were very deep. Not like some of the caves that he had been in before.

Erin fiddled with the emergency radio. He had shown her how to use it, but everything he had said had gone straight out of Erin's mind. She turned the volume up and clicked the button on the microphone.

"Willie? Can you hear me?"

There was only crackling in response. Erin listened closely, trying to hear through the crackle for Willie's voice. She could just see him rolling his eyes at Vic and making a comment about how she couldn't go two minutes without assuming that something catastrophic had occurred. She waited for his reassuring voice, but couldn't hear anything.

"Willie? Are you there? Come in, please."

Still no response. Erin looked around. The birds were singing once more. A crow circled way up high in the sky up above her, and Erin was reminded of Skye, Adele's crow. He was so smart. Adele had said that crows were one of the smartest birds, approaching human intelligence.

"At least, we assume by the tests that we have done on them that they are *almost* as smart as humans," Adele remarked. "I happen to think that they may just be smarter. How would you test an animal to see if it was smarter than you? Humans only assume that they are the smartest species on the planet. But that's a little arrogant."

"Hey Skye," Erin said softly, looking up at the bird. Of course it wasn't Skye. It was another crow. But she was still encouraged to have the bird fly over her, feeling like she wasn't quite so alone.

"Willie. Vic. Jeremy. Come in, please."

She thought she might have heard a squawk back, but she couldn't make out any words. Erin clicked the mike button and released it. Where were they and why weren't they answering? They shouldn't already be so deep that Erin couldn't reach them.

Erin looked up at the sky at the crow again. What had he seen up there? Had he been able to feel the vibration that Erin had sensed through her feet? What had caused that?

"Willie?" Erin went back to the entrance of the mine and called him again. "Willie! Are you down there?"

No answer.

No sound from inside.

Erin looked at the equipment they had left behind. She put on a helmet with a light, picked up a bottle of water, and stepped into the entrance of the mine.

CHAPTER 24

The entrance tunnel was broad, easy to walk through. Like a hallway. Erin could still see the light from the outside world. Everything was normal and looked perfectly safe. It wasn't like the caves where she had to crawl on her belly because of cramped quarters. But Erin knew it wouldn't be that wide all the way through. Before long, Orson would have figured out that it was too much work to keep cutting that wide of a tunnel through the rock. He only needed to cut it big enough to get himself and his equipment through.

Erin ignored the nausea and how fast her heart was beating. She couldn't afford to be sick and scared. Not if something had happened to her friends.

They hadn't been in there for long. If Erin moved at a quick pace, she would catch up to them. They would be moving slowly, admiring the tunnel and looking for clues. They would all laugh at how she had gone into the tunnel after all, when everything was perfectly fine.

Erin tried to call out to them, but she couldn't get the words out. Her throat was dry and hot and constricted. But she wasn't going to cry. They were going to be just fine. Willie had said so. Willie had said that the tunnel was perfectly safe.

She continued to press forward, trying not to think about the tunnel closing in around her. She was able to move and breathe freely. There was nothing to worry about. In a few minutes, if she kept moving at a brisk pace, she would be able to hear them and to call out to them to stop and wait for her. They would laugh at her being such a paranoid wimp, but she would at least know that they were safe, and she could return to the outside even if she couldn't convince them to return with her.

But in a couple more minutes, the tunnel ended. Erin looked around, disoriented. She turned a slow circle, letting her light shine in each direction, understanding that she must have missed a branch off into another direction. But the only tunnel she could find was the way she had come in. Erin turned again, studying each wall, looking at the way that it was carved out and the supporting beams were placed. She went suddenly cold, and it wasn't because she was underground and away from the sun.

One of the rock walls that she faced was not the same as the others. Rather than being carved out of the mine, it was filled with smaller pieces of rock. Like a giant had taken a handful of rocks and plugged it up.

Erin grabbed a couple of rocks and pulled them away. She threw them down and attacked the pile of rocks with vigor, calling out her friends' names. "Vic! Willie! Can you hear me? Jeremy? Are you there? I'm right here, can you hear me?"

She paused in her removal of the rocks, straining her ears for some sound. She couldn't hear any answering voices. What if something had happened to them? What if rather than just a cave-in of the tunnel blocking their way back, one of them had been hurt? Buried under the pile of rubble?

She worked more frantically, moving rock as quickly as she could, but she didn't seem to be making a dent in it. There could be a mile of debris to pick through, and she hadn't even made an appreciable dent in the edge she could see.

"Come on!" Erin tried to make herself move faster. But even as she tried to force herself, she couldn't help thinking about the logistics of the job. She couldn't just throw the rocks she cleared to the side. If she was able to move enough of the rock out of the way, she would just end up filling the tunnel behind her with rock They had to be transported out of the tunnel. And that would require equipment, which Erin didn't have. She stopped and looked at the problem, forcing herself to slow down and really think it through. Just attacking the fallen rocks by herself wasn't going to do anything for her friends. It was a hopeless venture. She had to get help.

～

Even though she hated to leave them behind and to stop the work on the fallen rocks, Erin forced herself to turn around and retreat down the tunnel. She tripped over a couple of the rocks that she had discarded along the way, making herself grimace at the mess she had left.

She hurried out to the radio equipment. Her eyes teared in the bright sunshine. She wiped away the moisture and picked up the radio mike again.

"Willie? Are you there? Can you hear me?"

She released the button and waited for a response. Her whole body was tense as she strained for an answer. She wanted so badly to hear some kind of response. Something to indicate that they were still alive and waiting for her. There was nothing. Erin's fingers moved of their own accord. She couldn't remember all of the steps that Willie had shown her, but her fingers changed the frequency to the emergency band and she pressed the button down again.

"Mayday, mayday. Is anybody listening?" Did people really say 'mayday' when they were calling for help? Or was that only boats? Would someone monitoring the frequency just laugh at her or think she was some kid fooling around?

Erin heard a response and tried to fine tune the frequency to make it clearer.

"Is somebody there? This is Erin Price."

The crackle she got back was clearer the second time. Erin could make out the words "emergency dispatcher." It had to be the woman who manned the phones back in Bald Eagle Falls, relaying messages to the police officers or volunteer fire department, or who made the decision when to contact emergency services in the city to have them send help.

"There's been a cave-in," Erin explained, tears filling her eyes and choking her throat. "We're on Orson Cadaver's old farm. There's a mine. There's been a cave-in."

"...everyone safe?"

"No." Erin swallowed hard and tried to go on. "There are three people trapped. I don't know if there are any injuries."

"Coordinates?"

"I don't know." Erin looked around her for some clue. She pulled out her phone and launched the map app. Would the GPS work when she couldn't get a phone signal? It looked like the flashing circle was in the right spot on the map, so Erin tapped it and read the coordinates to the dispatcher.

"Again?"

Erin read the numbers as slowly and clearly as possible.

"Once more?"

Erin read them again, feeling frustrated.

There was a burst of crackles. "...stay on this channel..."

Erin wanted to go back into the tunnel and remove more rocks from the caved-in area, but she knew she needed to do what she was told and relay whatever information the emergency responders might need. It would do more good to get the proper help there than it would to try to shift the pile of rocks by herself. But she wanted to do something more active, not to just sit there by the radio waiting for the next question.

The next voice she heard on the radio was one that sent a warm flush radiating from her heart to the top of her head and the tips of her toes.

"Erin?"

"Terry!"

"...what happened?"

"They went down the mine to look for the treasure or more clues. There was a noise... I went to look... can't get them on the radio... there's rock blocking the tunnel."

"Is Willie there?"

Erin nodded, wiping her nose. She took a minute to try to steady her voice before pressing the button on the mike to answer. "He's in the mine."

Whatever Terry had to say about that, he said offline, not into the radio. Erin didn't imagine it was anything that could be repeated in polite company.

Erin knew that Terry liked to call on Willie to help with rescue work or coordinate in an emergency. While it was good that Vic and Jeremy had an expert to help them, Terry could have done with another Willie on the outside to help with the rescue efforts.

"...on my way..." Terry's voice was coming from the radio again. "...be there soon..."

"Okay." Erin tried to hold the radio mike steady, aware that her hand was shaking. "See you then."

Then he was gone. Erin looked at the time on her phone. It would take an hour for Terry to get out to her. Maybe shorter if he used his lights and siren, but he wouldn't be able to get through the rough trails much faster than Willie had. And Terry wouldn't have a map showing where the roads were. Unless he had paper maps in the car to find his way around the old country roads. Hopefully, somebody had thought of that.

~

Mostly, Erin sat by the radio waiting for any contact from the dispatcher or Terry. Every now and then she went back into the mine to shout at the wall of rock, hoping to get a reply from the other side. How deep was the rock? Was there so much that it blocked out all of the sound, or had her friends been hurt or even killed in the collapse?

She had known it was too dangerous to go into the mine. Why hadn't anyone listened to her?

It seemed like a long time before she heard Terry's voice over the emergency band again.

"I'm at Willie's truck, Erin. Are you okay?"

Erin looked back toward where the truck was parked. She couldn't see either vehicle, but didn't doubt that Terry knew Willie's truck when he saw it.

"I'm okay."

"I'm going to be a couple of minutes while I unload his emergency gear. Hang tough."

"Okay."

She was glad to know that he was there. She could feel her heart rate slow and her muscles relax, knowing that the first help had arrived. They were going to need a lot more than just Terry, but at least he was there. It was a start.

Eventually, she could see Terry heading toward her, laden down with backpacks and bags, K9 at his side. Erin got to her feet to help him.

"What can I take?"

He shuffled his load to hand her a couple of first-aid bags. "Here, grab those."

The bags were probably the lightest thing he was carrying, but they were still heavy. Erin was glad for the muscle burn. Glad that she was finally doing something to help. They carried everything to the mine entrance and put them down.

"Has there been any more noise?" Terry asked. "Any more falling rocks?"

"I haven't heard anything."

"Have you been inside?"

"A few times. It doesn't seem like anything else is unstable."

"I'll take a look. Have you heard anything from them?"

"No. Nothing."

Terry looked grim, but didn't say anything negative. "I'm going to take a look at what we've got, and then we'll try to coordinate the rescue efforts. People in town are getting geared up. Some of them are already on their way."

Erin nodded, her throat hot and her eyes tearing up again. Terry gave her a brief hug. "We'll get them out. Don't cry."

"Why did I ever start this? It's my fault they're in there. If I hadn't started this silly treasure hunt, it never would have happened."

"You can't predict an accident like this. Willie checked it out before going in. If he couldn't tell there was a danger, no one could have. There is always a risk in a place like this, but he obviously didn't think there was anything too hazardous, or he wouldn't have gone in. He certainly never would have taken Vic in with him."

"They could be hurt."

He squeezed her arm. "I'm going in. I can't stop to talk about it."

Erin nodded. Terry turned on his helmet light and walked into the mine.

Even though Erin had been in and out several times since the collapse, she was nervous about him entering. What if there was another rockfall and he ended up getting hurt too?

The radio was squawking when Erin got back to it. She couldn't sort out all of the voices. It sounded like the volunteers were being organized, but it wasn't clear enough on Erin's end to be sure how many people were involved or what they were planning to do when they got there.

How were they going to move all of that rock?

Terry was out a few minutes later. He nodded at Erin.

"We're definitely going to need a hand in there. Do you have maps of the mining tunnels?"

"I do, but they're hard to follow. I don't think they're drawn to scale very well, and the landmarks are hard to see or have changed."

She got out the maps and she and Terry bent over them, following the faint lines.

"So, this is where we are?" Terry pointed.

Erin nodded. "Yeah."

"I want to know if there are any other tunnels that lead through to here," he tapped the map, indicating the area hopefully beyond the rockslide. If Willie, Vic, and Jeremy had been safely on the other side of the affected area, they might be uninjured, but their exit would be blocked until they found a way to get all of the rock out of there. There was so much of it, Erin was afraid they would be looking at weeks rather than hours or even days. How would they survive that long even if they were uninjured?

Erin looked for some sign of another way in. The lines were so faint, it was nearly impossible to tell where a tunnel ended and where the ink was just faded. There were a couple of tunnels that might have fed into the one that her friends were in, but she couldn't be sure.

CHAPTER 25

*T*erry had gone to scout around with K9 to see how the other mine entrances looked before making any kind of decision as to how they were going to effect a rescue. If the other tunnels looked unstable, they would need engineers and heavy equipment before they could start anything. Erin was crossing her fingers and hoping that the other tunnels would look fine and they could try to get closer to Vic, Willie, and Jeremy from another direction. She sat babysitting the radio and answering questions whenever she could. Looking up, she saw Beaver coming through the woods toward her. She had a long, fluid walk that made Erin think of a wolf loping across the prairie. Erin gave her a little wave. Beaver looked surprised to see Erin there.

"Hey, how's it going, Erin?"

Erin looked at her. "Well, not so great."

Beaver's eyebrows went up. "What's up? I saw Officer Piper's truck go by, and it's parked down there. I thought I would find the two of you together, where did he go?"

"To see how the other mine entrances look." Erin motioned to the nearest entrance.

"Is he helping with the treasure hunting, then?"

Erin cleared her throat. She searched Beaver's expression for some sign that she knew what was going on, but Beaver's expression, as usual, was pleasant and amused. The emergency radio crackled to life, and Erin tried to understand what was being said. They were just confirming that they had called for help from the heavy equipment team in the city. Erin looked back at Beaver.

"There was a cave-in," she explained. "I guess you haven't heard."

"A cave-in," Beaver repeated. She blinked at Erin, then looked at the entrance to the mine. "Are you talking about right here? Now? Or back when the treasure was hidden...?"

"Now. Just through there." Erin pointed.

"Was there anyone in there?"

"Vic, Willie, and..." Erin had a hard time getting the painful news out. "Jeremy."

Beaver's face was pale. "Are they okay?"

"We haven't been able to get them. I don't know if it's just because of the rock or whether they were injured and can't answer."

Beaver folded to the ground beside Erin. "They're still in there? And you don't know whether or not they are hurt?"

Erin nodded. "Yeah."

Beaver sat there, staring at the entrance to the mine, her face pale and drawn. The usual smile was gone. She still chewed on her gum, but it was slow and uncertain instead of her usual chomping. Erin wondered whether a doctor had prescribed the chewing gum, worried that she'd chew through her fingernails or something else. Beaver was normally a bundle of nervous energy, but usually she was upbeat. Worrying about what had happened to Jeremy and everybody else, the wind had gone from her sails and she just looked anxious.

"They'll be okay," Erin comforted, reassuring Beaver with what she herself wasn't sure of. "Everything will turn out okay. Terry is seeing if he can find another way in, and the town is sending all kinds of volunteers and equipment. I've seen the way they work together. They'll find Jeremy and the others and get them out."

Beaver rubbed her face with her fingertips and shook her head. "Who else? Who is there with him?"

"Vic and Willie."

Beaver nodded. "Willie is good. He knows a lot about what to do in an emergency."

Erin agreed.

Someone else came through the woods toward them. Erin stared at the figure, trying to think of who it might be. As he got closer, she saw that it was a young man, an older teenager or man in his early twenties, slender, not yet filled in after his final growth spurt. His face looked familiar, but she couldn't think of who he was.

"What's going on?" he asked.

Erin frowned at him and opened her mouth to ask him his name. She figured he must belong to one of the nearby farms and had seen the unexpected vehicles or heard on the radio that something was wrong.

"Erin, do you know Cam?" Beaver asked.

Erin stared at Cam, her mouth open.

"Campbell Cox," the boy said. "You're Erin, right? You know my mom."

Erin nodded. "Mary Lou, yes," she agreed breathlessly. She looked at Beaver. "What's he doing here? You said that you knew him... I wondered..."

"We can't get into that," Beaver said. "But he can be trusted."

Erin looked at Cam for a minute, then nodded slowly. "Okay... but trusted to do what? What are you guys up to?"

Beaver looked at Erin for a minute. She shook her head and looked back at Cam. "There's been... an accident. A cave-in." She gestured at the mine.

Cam's face showed surprise. He looked around, as if expecting to see someone sneaking around, eavesdropping on their conversation. "That's not good. Do you think...?"

Beaver shrugged. "I don't know anything yet. But if this was intentional..."

Erin looked at the two of them, frowning so heavily that her head hurt. "What? What are you talking about? If this was *intentional?* It was a cave-in."

"We'll have to wait for the results of the investigation before we know that," Beaver said, shrugging.

"The results of what investigation?"

"Into the cave-in," Beaver said evenly.

Erin stared at her, shaking her head. "You think that somebody did this to them? Somebody caused this cave-in on purpose?"

"We don't know anything about it at this point," Beaver said. "All we know is what you have told us. That Vic and Willie and Jeremy went into the mine and then the cave-in happened. We don't know any more than that, and we only know that because you told us."

"Then what are you doing here?" Erin asked. "I thought you were here because you had heard over the police radio, so you came to help."

Beaver shook her head. "We've been… investigating other things."

"And that investigation led you here. To Orson Cadaver's farm."

"It's an interesting coincidence that this is where your mystery led you," Beaver contributed. There was a twinkle in her eye despite her worry for Jeremy.

Erin tried to understand what the connection between Beaver's investigation and her treasure-hunting could be, and couldn't come up with anything. Obviously, it had been a surprise to Beaver as well. She hadn't expected to find Erin and her friends there.

"What are we going to do?" Cam asked Beaver, looking toward the mine. "Can we call someone to help? And what about the town?" He gestured to the radio and addressed Erin. "Did you call the police? There's a volunteer fire department, they could help."

"Everyone is on their way," Erin told him. "Terry is already scouting around to see if there is an alternate way to get in."

Cam nodded. "Do you want me to take a look around?" he asked Beaver. "Make sure there isn't anyone else around?"

Beaver shook her head. "No. You'd better stay here with Erin. Make sure she's safe until Officer Piper gets back. I'll look around."

Erin expected him to argue. What young man wouldn't argue with a woman who told him that he needed to stay and take the safer course while she walked into danger? Every boy she had grown up with would have been offended by such a suggestion and would not have agreed without significant coercion. But Cam surprised her by not objecting. He just sat down beside Erin while Beaver got to her feet.

"Who are you looking for?" Erin asked. "I haven't seen anyone else around here."

Beaver chewed her gum and gave a loose shrug. "Just anyone who shouldn't be here."

"But everyone has been called to help, so pretty soon, everyone is going to be here, and you won't be able to tell…"

Beaver nodded with grudging respect. "You're right," she agreed. "So, I need to look around before everyone shows up. If there's anyone else hanging around this farm, I need to find them."

"I didn't see any other cars on the road on the way out here, and we parked by ourselves."

"They would at least think to hide their vehicle, I would think. That was one reason I was so surprised to see Willie's truck there, right out in the open."

Erin couldn't help the smile that started to creep across her face. "Did you think that Willie was involved? Everybody is always thinking that he's involved in criminal operations, but he's not. He got out of that, and he doesn't help the Dysons out any longer."

"Never trust appearances," Beaver said. "I have to assume that people are lying. I have to assume that when they say they're not involved, they really are, and I have to act as if it were true. As that old TV series used to say: 'trust no one.'"

"Willie isn't involved in anything. He's in the mine. He's one of the victims here. He's not involved in anything shady."

"Willie went in there with your friends," Beaver said slowly. "But that doesn't mean he was innocent. He may have been stabbed in the back by one of his cohorts. He might be working both sides. He might have taken Vic and Jeremy in there, fully intending to get them out of the picture."

Erin was shocked at the suggestions. It wasn't like she hadn't suspected Willie of shady dealings in the past. She had suspected him more than once, but he always came out innocent, and she didn't think he would ever get caught, even if he were involved in something. But to suggest that he had gone into the mine to rid himself of his girlfriend and her brother... there was no way. Erin knew that he loved Vic and there was no way he would ever betray her.

Beaver was studying Erin's reaction carefully. She nodded slowly to herself as she prepared to look for whatever conspirator she thought might be lurking nearby. "I hope not too," she said. "But I can't afford to trust anyone."

"Doesn't that include me, then?" Erin asked. Beaver had confided in her. She was leaving Erin there where she could cause more mischief. If anyone was to be suspected of causing the cave-in, Erin had to be the chief suspect. She had brought them there. She had allowed them to go into the mines while claiming that she herself was too scared to go inside. She was the one who could most easily have arranged for an accident to occur, all while she sat coolly outside and waited for help that she knew would arrive too late.

Beaver looked at Erin, then looked at Cam. "Keep an eye on her."

Cam nodded, understanding. Beaver walked away, and Erin turned her attention to the young man.

"I didn't do anything."

"I don't think you did," Cam agreed. "But we have to be careful. Beaver is really good at what she does. She wouldn't still be alive if she wasn't."

"What do you know about her? And what exactly are you doing with her? I don't understand how you're involved in any of this. You're an informant? Is that it? But why would she bring you here? I don't understand what someone as young as you could be doing that the federal agencies would be involved. I don't understand what you could do to help them."

Any answer that Cam might have had for Erin was swallowed up when the rescue teams from Bald Eagle Falls began to arrive. They came in groups that Erin assumed must have carpooled together, half a dozen helpers to a vehicle. Some carried rescue or aid supplies with them, food, or equipment Erin was unsure of. They were a strange combination of laughter and grim determination. Excitement to be part of a big disaster and rescue operation, and anxiety about how it was all going to turn out and if they were going to be able to save their friends from injury or death.

They greeted Erin and coordinated with each other, setting up equipment in the glade, going into the mine to have a look at the problem, and discussing the situation vigorously with each other. Erin wasn't sure who was in charge, but someone needed to coordinate everybody before they all started approaching the problem separately and ended up tripping over one another.

Terry returned from his scouting mission and tried to make himself heard above the babble of all of the volunteers.

"Can I get your attention, please? I need everybody to listen so that we can approach this in a coordinated effort and do everything we can to help Vic, Willie, and Jeremy."

The scattered volunteers quieted, listening to Terry's instructions.

"I want you to get together with your teams. Firefighters in a group, Scouts in another. People in charge of food. Communications. Get together with your group and make sure that you have a spokesperson appointed.

We are going to manage all communication through that spokesperson so that I don't have to yell over all of this chaos."

People nodded and smiled their agreement.

"If you don't have a group, stand over here," Terry pointed. "We'll put you where you can be best used. Okay? It's going to be a while before any of the responders can make it from the city out here. I could use a few flagmen for traffic control, to help direct the city folk to the right route and make sure we're sticking to the established roads rather than just driving across private land."

A few hands went up. Terry looked around at them, nodding. "Don, maybe you could take charge of the flagmen and coordinate them."

The man he spoke to nodded agreement, and Erin watched them gravitate toward each other and start to make arrangements for who would stand where and what jobs they would have.

"I want to break this rescue into two approaches," Terry advised. "Until we have experts in here who can tell us otherwise, I want to go in two ways. First, clearing the rocks and rubble out of this entrance," he pointed to the mine entrance that Erin was already intimately familiar with. "There isn't a lot of room to work, but if we could run a line of people outside, passing rock from one person to the next like a bucket brigade, I think that's the quickest way to get rock out of the tunnel rather than just shifting it from one place to another inside. I don't know how much rock is in there... It's a lot. It might be a hopeless venture. But I need a team to get started."

There were nods of agreement.

"Secondly, I want to go in through another tunnel. K9 and I have been exploring some of the other mines and entrances, and I think we have one that has the potential of getting close to this tunnel here, after the cave-in. Assuming that the whole tunnel has not collapsed and that we still have a chance of getting to any survivors... I want to get together a team that can come up with a plan to dig or drill from one tunnel to the other."

He looked around at the grim faces. Everyone was now listening to him, no one was joking around.

"Get your groups together and appoint a spokesperson. I want to talk to the spokesmen in ten minutes." Terry looked at his watch and nodded, marking the time.

CHAPTER 26

*E*rin watched the townspeople organizing themselves and thought that she should attach herself to one of the teams, but she didn't have the energy to do anything but sit beside the radio listening for the updates on when the actual Search and Rescue team would be arriving from the city.

Erin saw a group of the church ladies setting up a folding table. There would be drinks and sandwiches for the volunteers. Erin would normally be there, coordinating the sandwich-making, setup, and distribution with Vic at her side. She looked at the radio, waiting for confirmation that trained rescuers were on their way.

Erin saw Mary Lou coming toward her, a confused expression on her face. Campbell scrambled to his feet.

"Mom!"

"Campbell. What are you doing here?"

"I... er... I was helping out Beaver."

"Beaver? Helping her with what?"

Campbell gave her a hug. "How are you, Mom? And Josh?"

"Fine. We're good. You don't answer my calls. I never know what you're up to."

"Sorry. Just getting myself settled. I get wrapped up and forget to call back until it's late, and then I don't want to call and wake you up."

Mary Lou brushed Campbell's cheek with a kiss, then held him at arm's length to look at him. Erin evaluated him silently as Mary Lou did. He appeared to be healthy. His color and weight were good. He didn't look like someone who was using drugs or partying every night. Erin would have guessed that he had a good job and a safe place to live. Mary Lou dropped her hands, nodding.

"You call me back anyway," she told him. "Even if it's late at night. I want to hear from you. Go ahead and wake me up."

He shrugged.

"I need to help out here… why don't you come tell me what you've been up to." Mary Lou gestured back toward the table where the ladies were setting up the refreshments.

Campbell's eyes flitted to Erin.

"I'm not going anywhere," she told him. "I want to be close to the radio."

He nodded and walked with his mother over to the table.

~

Beaver sat down close to Erin. She looked around, watching all of the volunteers hard at work. Her eyes lingered on Cam, talking to Mary Lou and helping her out at the refreshment table.

"So… what can you tell me about this Orson Cadaver? He was a distant relative of yours?"

Erin nodded. "Lots of years back. I don't know what I can tell you that you don't already know. He came into a lot of money, but nobody knew where it came from. Or no one told, anyway. It seemed like it could match up with the poem, but I don't know. It was only a guess." She stared at the mine entrance. "A guess I wish I hadn't made."

"It's not your fault. You couldn't have predicted that something was going to happen to Vic and the others. You wouldn't have let them go in if you'd thought that they were going to get hurt."

"I was worried… I did tell them not to go at the last minute… but by that time they were already all excited about going. I couldn't stop them."

"Did you have a premonition something was wrong?" Beaver asked. "Why did you tell them not to?"

"I was just… worried about them being underground, I guess. I'm…

claustrophobic after what happened to me in the caves... I couldn't go down there if someone held a gun to my head." She considered for a moment. "Well, maybe if someone put a gun to my head. I did go in there to see what had happened. But I couldn't ever have gone down there to explore with them."

"So, there wasn't something specific that you thought was going to happen? Or anything that triggered the thought?"

Erin thought about it and shook her head. "No, I don't think so. Why?"

"I just wonder whether your unconscious mind had processed something that you weren't aware of consciously. There might have been something that tipped you off to someone else's presence here. Or that made you feel like they were in danger from someone specific."

"Whoever stole the first copies of those maps hit me over the head. They could have killed me. It obviously wasn't someone who had any qualms about using violence. If they're racing us to find the treasure... then that puts all of us in danger."

"Maybe," Beaver agreed. "So what about the cabin? You and Vic explored it?"

"Yes, but there really wasn't anything there. It's been over a hundred years since he hid the treasure... I guess I shouldn't have been surprised that we didn't find anything else. What kind of clue would have survived that long?"

"You never know. Sometimes the darnedest things survive... things you never would have expected to."

Erin sighed. "Well, not in this case. It seems like all that survived was the poem. And if it hadn't talked about moles, we never would have considered looking in the mines. Or maybe we would have, I don't know. But I wish we hadn't. I wish I'd never found that poem."

"But you did." Beaver's burning eyes betrayed her interest in hearing more about the treasure, maybe in finding it herself. "I know you don't have the poem anymore, but could you tell me again what it said? Do you have it written down anywhere?"

"Beaver..." Erin's voice broke and she cleared her throat to try to speak clearly. "They're trying to figure out how to get our friends out of a collapsed mine. If they're still alive. And you're looking for the treasure?"

"I've done everything I could to help. I'm standing by if there's anything else I can do. But in the meantime... why not look into the treasure? If the treasure is what is motivating someone to commit violence, even risking killing three innocent people in one blow, then we need to catch him. Don't you think?"

"Yes."

"Well, the only way we're going to catch him is if we know as much as or more than he does about the treasure. We need to get out ahead of him. We need to try to find the treasure before he does, if it still exists."

"You and Cam… is this about the treasure hunt, or about illegal drugs? I don't understand what it is you have to do with him?"

"Cam's a good boy. He's got a good heart. But he's going to end up in trouble if someone doesn't get him back on track. I hate to see anyone throwing their life away. I really do."

Erin nodded. "I know… I saw it in foster care… it only takes a few steps to go from being an honest, hardworking citizen to someone operating on the wrong side of the law, as if you had no conscience in the first place. I'd hate to see that happen to Mary Lou's son. I wouldn't want to see her hurt." Erin's eyes were attracted back to the entrance of the mine by a group of people who suddenly started talking louder, but then they quieted again and whispered among themselves, giving nothing away. "But I don't want my friends to get hurt either. He came here with you, right?"

Beaver took her time answering, chewing slowly on her gum while she watched Campbell with his mother.

"We came separately," she said finally. "We didn't want to attract attention by being seen together. We expected it to be deserted, no witnesses. When we saw the vehicles, I had to investigate further."

"So if you came separately, you don't know what he might have done before you got here."

"No. I don't."

"And he doesn't know what you did before he got here."

"No."

"And you both hid your cars, so no one knows how long you were here ahead of time and whether you were here before me and the others. Or whether you had time to rig up some kind of booby trap."

Beaver gazed steadily at Erin. "That's right," she agreed. "You know I'm a federal agent. What are the chances that I would give up my whole career to pursue some treasure that probably doesn't even exist?"

"You do hunt treasure."

"Yes, but I do it on my own time and I don't let it interfere with my job. And I don't mug women and collapse mines. That's an ethical violation." She gave a wide grin to signal that she was joking.

"But I don't know that. You could have been involved. I have no way of knowing."

"No, you don't," Beaver agreed.

"Then... I don't think I'm going to tell you anything else. You don't need to know the poem or anything else that we found out. You're on some other case and you just think it may link up to ours. You thought that maybe the two are linked somehow, but you don't know."

"Absolutely right," Beaver agreed.

Erin had expected at least some kind of argument from her. Why didn't she argue and say that she hadn't done anything? At least then, Erin would be able to examine whether what she said was true or not. She was thrown off kilter by Beaver's agreement that all of her conclusions were correct.

"You don't care?"

"Of course I care. But I also don't want you getting hurt or killed. It's better if you don't go around blabbing about the treasure. It's better if everybody just thinks that you have given up. That in the face of this disaster, it just doesn't matter to you anymore."

"And it doesn't," Erin agreed. "I really don't care how much money the gold is worth. It's not worth as much as my friends' lives."

Beaver nodded. She pulled a pack of gum out of her pocket and popped a couple of new pieces of gum into her mouth. She offered the package to Erin, who declined.

"What would you do if you came into a lot of money?" she asked conversationally.

Erin had determined that she wasn't going to answer any more questions, but this wasn't a question about the poem or the treasure. It was just a philosophical question.

"Uh... Well, I don't know. I'd pay Charley out on the bakery, if she'd let me. How much do you think the treasure would be?"

"It sounds significant from the description. Gold is always good. Hundred-year-old gold is even better. And if there are artifacts... things other than gold coins... then that's worth even more."

"Maybe."

"Of course. It all depends on what you find. Gold isn't always gold. It could be... oh, a family Bible, and Orson considered the word of God to be golden. Or it could be family relationships. Or a good crop. It could be something painted gold, or something considered valuable, or it could even be fool's gold, but he hoped it would lead him to a vein of real gold. There's no way for us to know what it was he really valued. At least, not based on the information you have so far."

Erin nodded. She had wondered a few times whether gold was really gold or not. It could mean anything valuable. Or it might just be a poem. There might not even be a treasure. Orson could have had his own fortune from somewhere else. Or he could have had nothing, and his wealth was just gossip run rampant. It was impossible to tell.

"Do you think there's anything hidden in the mine?"

"I think... if there was... It's probably either buried, or someone got here ahead of you. What are the chances that someone blew up the tunnel without knowing whether there was gold in it or not?"

"You think it was blown up?" A band of muscle tightened around Erin's chest. She had been thinking it, in the back of her mind. But she hadn't wanted to actually put it into words.

"Don't you?" Beaver asked.

"I don't know. I really don't. I don't want to think that anyone could be that... that wicked. Blowing it up intentionally when there are people inside... that's horrible."

"Is it more likely that it was an accident?" Beaver asked. "What are the chances of that?"

"We don't have any evidence that it was intentional. And I didn't see anyone around."

Beaver looked around at the woods. "There are plenty of places to hide. Even just going into another tunnel." She motioned toward the entrance to another mine. "You'd have to be pretty brave to take shelter in one tunnel while you cave in another. You'd have to be pretty confident that it wouldn't collapse the tunnel you were in as well. But I don't think it was an accident. These mines have been untouched for a hundred years. Willie wouldn't have gone inside if he hadn't thought it was safe. He's very experienced in the matter. You think he would make a mistake like that?"

Erin wiped her nose. "No."

"Me neither," Beaver agreed.

"So you think... someone got here ahead of us and set explosives to blow up when we went in?" Erin shook her head, having a hard time picturing it. "You think that they were watching to blow it up?"

"Who knows. Maybe they never intended to hurt anyone, and you guys were just in the wrong place when the charges had already been set. But I don't believe in coincidences."

"That's what Terry always says."

"Officer Piper is right. Sometimes there are coincidences, but more often, there really is a link, and not chance."

Erin covered her face, rubbing her eyes. She couldn't understand why she was so tired. She didn't want to do anything but lie down and go to sleep. Even though she knew her friends were trapped or buried in the mine, she couldn't think about it. Her brain didn't want to accept it. She just wanted to go to sleep and let everyone else deal with it. Maybe when she woke up, she'd be better able to deal with it.

"Let me get you a drink," Beaver offered. "Have you had anything?"

"No. I'm not hungry."

"You need to at least keep up your fluids. You don't realize how much you might be sweating off because you're just sitting around. It doesn't feel like you're doing any work, but your body still is." Beaver got up and went over to the table that Cam and Mary Lou were at. She said a few words to them, picking up water bottles and a couple of snacks from the table. She returned and handed one water bottle to Erin and held out a muffin and a granola bar. "Pick."

Erin picked the granola bar. She could eat it later when she really wanted it.

"How are they?" Erin asked, nodding to the Coxes.

"They seem to be handling it just fine," Beaver said with a shrug. "I don't think you need to worry."

"I do worry about my friends. And Mary Lou... she doesn't have very many friends left in this town. I want her to know that I still support her."

"I'm sure she knows that."

CHAPTER 27

There was a sudden buzz of excitement. Erin looked around.
"What is it? What's going on?"

"Let me find out." Beaver got up and circulated with the volunteers, asking quick questions. She returned to Erin's side. "The Search and Rescue team is here. Lots of heavy equipment. Now we'll get something done."

"What? What are they going to do? They can't move the rock much faster than the volunteers have already been doing. You can only take out so much at one time."

"I'm not sure. But I'm sure we can put them to use."

Erin turned away from the gossiping volunteers who were straining for the first glimpse of the Search and Rescue team, and watched those who were still carrying rock out of the mine. There was a big pile that had already been removed. Some of the volunteers had no gloves and had bloody fingers. They all looked exhausted. They would continue to work until they dropped.

Terry hurried over from where he had been working in another mine and barely nodded at Erin. He jogged past her with K9 beside him, headed across the woods to where the vehicles were parked.

"Do you think they can do something?" Erin asked, following Terry with her eyes.

"He apparently has a plan."

They sat, waiting, their thoughts on those who were still trapped inside the mine.

～

There was a lot of equipment brought in, and Erin waited, wondering how long they would be stuck in the cave. What was the limiting factor? Air? Water? Injuries and shock? How long had it already taken and how much longer would it be before they could reach the tunnel? Was it already too late?

Erin held back tears, trying to keep herself under control as they moved the drilling equipment into the tunnel that Terry had picked out. There were engineers who walked around looking at the tunnel and the way that the walls were braced, how the rocks in the collapsed tunnel had fallen, and everything else that their eyes could see that Erin's couldn't. It seemed like it was going to take another two weeks before they would be able to decide whether the tunnel was stable enough for drilling. Erin didn't want to wait. Terry obviously didn't either, shifting back and forth from foot to foot while he waited for them to finish their inspection.

"If they say not to drill, what are you going to do?" Erin asked.

Terry's mouth formed a straight line. "They'd better not tell us not to drill."

"If they say it's not safe, are you going to chance it anyway?"

He shook his head slowly. Not in an answer of 'no,' but thinking it through and unable to make a decision. "I don't want to lose anyone else. I don't want to take the chance of another cave-in. I guess… we have to find a safe way in, or we look for something else. We can't take the chance of hurting someone else."

Erin had been afraid of that. If she were the one in charge, she would be more likely to tell them where they could stuff their engineering degrees and go ahead anyway. Her friends were in there. The family she had chosen. She needed to get them out.

Finally, the engineers and the Search and Rescue team all huddled together in a little group with Terry and the other officers in the Police Department to discuss their findings and make a decision. Terry turned around and gave Erin a thumbs up. A cheer went up from the volunteers who were waiting for the decision just as intently as Erin was. Erin struggled not to cry. It was such a relief to know that they were doing something. No more sitting around waiting, moving rocks out of the way one at a time.

The drilling started.

Erin had no idea how far they had to drill or how long it would take. She held her breath at first, thinking that it would just be a minute or two and then Vic, Willie, and Jeremy would be free. But it went on and on.

Lights had been set up both inside the tunnels and outside where the volunteers were gathered, and they were needed as darkness fell. Erin nibbled on her granola bar. How could it take so long?

Her body was sore from sitting on the ground for so long. Every joint and muscle hurt. She got up and walked around a little, but that didn't do much to relieve the pain. Erin paced back and forth, willing them to finish the drilling and break into the next tunnel, as if she could make it go faster with the power of her mind.

There was a shout from someone, and the sound of the drill pulling away from the rock and then winding down. Erin and the others held their breaths. Was that it? Were they through?

There was a lot of talk, and eventually Terry came over to fill Erin in. "They're moving to hand tools now. If the maps are accurate, or at least close, then we should only be a few inches away from breaking through. But we don't want to injure anyone on the other side or take the chance of another cave-in if we cause instability in that wall. They'll drill a few small test holes, see if they can get any response from Vic and Willie and Jeremy and evaluate the best way to cut through the last little bit of rock."

"We're so close!" Erin clenched her fists, frustrated. "Can't we just drill the last bit?"

"We don't want to hurt them. We have to effect a safe rescue, not a fast one."

Erin growled and continued her pacing.

CHAPTER 28

"They're alive!"

Erin gasped with the rest of the volunteers. Then a cheer went up. Tears were racing down Erin's cheeks. She had never been so relieved in her life. She looked across the glade to Terry, a broad smile across his dust-smeared face. They were alive. She had been trying not to admit to herself that they might not be. They were experienced in cave exploration. They wouldn't have been caught in the collapsing tunnel. But she knew that there would have been no way for them to predict or avoid it.

Erin pushed her way through the volunteers to reach Terry, her legs quaking. Everyone else was trying to crowd closer as well, asking urgent questions, wanting more details. Terry tried to hold them off, using his strong cop's voice to make them back off and let Erin through. Eventually, she reached him.

"Tell me what you know! They're all alive? They're okay?"

Terry put his arm around her to pull her close, but spoke over her to the rest of the crowd. "They're all alive. They have injuries. We have paramedics standing by for when we get through the last few inches so that they can be treated and transported to the hospital right away. Now that we can communicate with them, we can be sure that they are far enough away from the wall for us to drill the rest of the way through. The engineers believe that we can get through the wall without destabilizing it, but we're still going to go slowly and make the smallest possible access hole to get them out. It will take a few more minutes."

"Who's hurt? How badly?" people asked urgently.

"We won't know the full extent of their injuries until we get them out."

Erin looked at Terry, knowing that he was avoiding the question. If they were able to talk to the explorers, then they would have a pretty good idea of how badly they were hurt. Whether the injuries were serious or just minor. But he wasn't revealing anything to the public about how extensive those injuries might be.

Terry answered a few more questions. He gave Erin a squeeze and let her go. "It will be just a few more minutes," he promised. He returned to the tunnel.

The ambulances that had been waiting back where the rest of the vehicles were parked made their way slowly through the trees so that they would be right outside the entrance to the second tunnel as soon as everyone was brought out. Erin watched them get their equipment ready with a sick feeling in her stomach. Gurneys, IV bags, big cases of medical supplies. They kept their voices low and didn't answer any questions. Tom Banks and the sheriff kept the crowds back so that the paramedics wouldn't have to deal with them.

Then there was movement from the tunnel again. Not Terry returning to give them more news, but one of the Search and Rescue workers supporting Jeremy as he walked out. The young man was holding on to the worker, obviously weak, but he was walking under his own power.

A huge cheer went up from the crowd. Jeremy raised his head slightly to look at them, giving a vague nod. The Search and Rescue worker took him directly to the paramedics, who had him lie down on one of the gurneys and began to talk to him and ask him questions. Erin's attention was split between Jeremy and the entrance to the tunnel, waiting for the next person. Eventually, it was Vic she saw, supported on either side. Upright, but not exactly walking under her own power as Jeremy had. Her face was white in the harsh lights.

They waited. It seemed like a very long time before they saw movement from the mine entrance again. Then two burly Search and Rescue workers struggled out, carrying Willie by the arms and ankles, stretched out between them.

A murmur went through the crowd, then another cheer. Everyone was out. They were all alive.

The crowd was surging forward, everyone wanting a better look at how the three friends were. They wanted to talk with them and get their stories. The Police Department and the Search and Rescue workers held everyone back, trying to keep a perimeter around the paramedics and the victims. Erin stayed where she was, watching every move of the paramedics, trying to figure out from their movements just how badly injured her friends were. They didn't move quickly, in a panic. But they were trained to stay calm and deliberate.

Willie appeared to be the most badly injured of the three, but the way the paramedics kept leaning over him, he was asking them questions and making demands regarding his treatment. The paramedics working over Vic and Jeremy touched them frequently to get their attention and ask them questions. All three had IVs in quick order.

Erin saw Tom letting Beaver past the perimeter to go to see Jeremy. Beaver looked back over the crowd and pointed at Erin, then motioned for her to come forward as well. Erin was encouraged by the volunteers and spectators to move forward.

"Go talk to them. See how they are," Mary Lou murmured to Erin as she helped to make space for Erin to get through. Erin's knees were shaking so badly, she didn't know if she could walk that far, but then in a minute she was there, looking back and forth between Willie and Vic, unsure which one to go to.

"Erin. Here. Come here." Willie had spotted her and was motioning impatiently for her to go see him. Erin obeyed, approaching the gurney and looking him over, a lump in her throat. He looked as he always did, grubby, skin darkened by his mining and processing work, but this time there was rock dust streaked with sweat and tears, his mouth a moist red slash across his face.

"Hey, Willie. How are you?"

"Busted my leg," Willie said tightly, motioning toward his right leg.

Erin ventured a glance toward it, worried that she would see white bone sticking out from a mess of bloody, broken skin, but Willie's pants had been cut away and an inflated air splint was in place. There luckily wasn't any obvious blood or gore.

Erin could only imagine how frustrated Willie would have been to be limited in his mobility when he wanted to be taking care of everyone else. He would not have liked relying on the others to move him around and not to be able to get up and assess the situation and try to get them out of there.

"They'll have you fixed up in no time," she reassured him. "They'll get a cast on that at the hospital and you'll be menacing everyone with your crutches for a few weeks."

Willie gave a grin that was more of a grimace. He caught her hand and pulled her closer. Erin leaned close to him, her face warming a little as the paramedics tried to work around her.

"That wasn't a natural cave-in," Willie told Erin. "You tell Terry. They need to look for signs of explosives."

Erin nodded. "They will. Beaver was already saying that she thought it was intentional."

"I think there was a booby trap. Something caught my foot. It was too late to stop. A tripwire."

Erin felt sick to her stomach. That meant somebody had not just wanted to blow up the tunnel to keep anyone else from discovering what they had found in the mine. They had wanted to kill or injure whoever came into the mine.

"I'm so sorry, Willie. I never thought… I never thought that something like this could happen. I knew somebody else was looking for the treasure, but I never imagined someone could do something like this."

"I know." He squeezed her hand. "This isn't your fault, Erin. It was deliberate."

She shook her head, trying to fathom it.

"How is Vic?" Willie asked.

"I don't know. I'll go over and see. She looked pretty pale."

"She was shocky. They need to treat her for shock, even if she doesn't have any other injuries."

"I'll go see her," Erin promised.

She pulled out of his grasp and moved over to the gurney Vic was being treated on.

"How is she doing?" she asked the paramedics.

They didn't stop their work to look at her. "Broken arm. No other major injuries apparent."

"Willie said to treat her for shock."

One of them looked up from the scrapes that he was cleaning. "Of course we are treating for shock. We're not totally inept."

"Sorry. Willie is worried about her. She's his girlfriend."

"We're taking care of her. Which would be easier if we didn't have any interference. She's ready to move, we're just waiting for word from triage as to how everyone is going to be transported."

Erin had seen a helicopter land close by. It couldn't land too near the mine because it was so heavily wooded, but it had found somewhere to put down a mile or two away. They would be able to get one of the three to the hospital much faster than the other two who followed along on the ground.

Erin looked at Vic's face. She hadn't responded to Erin's proximity, staring off into space as if she were deep in thought. "Are you okay, Vicky? You're going to be taken to the hospital soon."

Vic's eyes moved vaguely to Erin's face. "Erin? I'm gonna sleep for a bit longer."

Erin stroked Vic's silky blond hair. "Okay. You can sleep for a bit. I don't think you're going to be putting in a shift at the bakery in the morning."

In fact, Erin suspected that no one would be opening Auntie Clem's Bakery in the morning. Erin would be at the hospital all night herself, making sure that everyone was going to be okay. She moved out of the way of the paramedics to let them do their jobs. She looked toward Jeremy. Beaver was already there talking to him, and the paramedics probably didn't need yet another person trying to get information.

Beaver saw Erin's questioning look and left her spot at Jeremy's side.

"He's okay," she told Erin. "There are no obvious injuries, but I'm worried about any weak spots from his shooting, where he could be bleeding internally. The blast wave that he would have been exposed to if it was an explosion rather than just a rock slide..."

"Willie says it was explosives. He said he thought he tripped a wire."

Beaver swore and shook her head. "What kind of lowlife..." She stopped speaking to breathe and attempt to get her emotions under control. "I've dealt with plenty of treasure hunters before, and they can get very cutthroat about not allowing anyone else near what they consider to be clues or stopping them if they think they're getting close to finding *their* treasure. But booby trapping the mine with explosives... that's pretty bad, even for treasure hunters."

Erin nodded. She didn't know what Beaver might have run into with other treasures she had hunted for, but the idea of someone not even caring if they killed others was almost unbelievable. She wouldn't have thought it was possible.

"So, Jeremy's okay? He's talking?"

Beaver rolled her eyes. "He's talking, but that doesn't mean he's making sense. I guess he's still back there, trying to solve the clues."

"What's he saying?"

"He just keeps repeating lines from that poem. Forest gold. He says he didn't see it. He should have seen it." Beaver shrugged. "I don't think he's hallucinating. I think he's confused and not getting out what it is he wants to say. I want them to get him to the hospital as soon as possible."

"They're just deciding which one to airlift."

CHAPTER 29

*V*ic was the one they ended up airlifting to the hospital, with Jeremy and Willie following by ground in the ambulances. Erin was able to relax for the first time, knowing that they were out of danger and weren't going to die because she had decided to try to solve a puzzle. It seemed more than bizarre that her friends could be put in mortal peril just because of the words of a poem penned over a hundred years before. They didn't even know for sure that there was any gold. It sounded like the clues to a treasure hunt, but there was no guarantee that it was anything but a weird poem. Orson Cadaver might have written it, or it might have been someone else in his family, or even someone that Erin hadn't run across yet in her review of Clementine's genealogy files.

Most of the volunteers were on their way home. They had quickly broken down the tables, gathered up any trash, and gone on their way. They would have work and school in the morning. Erin's eyes lingered on one woman she couldn't place mingled with the familiar faces. She had seen her somewhere recently, but couldn't think of where.

"Are you okay, Erin?"

Erin looked around and saw Adele.

"I didn't know you were here. How long have you been around?"

"I've been here for a while," Adele said vaguely. "I've just been keeping to the background."

Erin knew that Adele was introverted, not someone who liked to spend a lot of time interacting with others, especially in crowds. It was a bit surprising that she would even be there, with all of the chaos and activity going on. Adele preferred the quiet of her woods and the company of Skye and her own thoughts.

Erin glanced up toward the sky to see if the crow was around, but couldn't see him. "Everything is being cleared up now," she stated the obvious. "You could go home."

But Adele wouldn't be heading to bed early. She would be doing whatever it was she did at nights when she wandered through the woods and lit candles and said her prayers or incantations.

"I know," Adele agreed. She looked around. "I thought, though, that I might say a blessing over this area. The evil that was performed here... you don't want it to taint the place. I thought it might be a good idea to leave it with a blessing."

"Oh." Erin nodded her head. If Adele wanted to perform spells, she would not want to do it while there were still women from Bald Eagle Falls around who might see her and decide that they didn't like having a witch around. "Yes, that sounds nice."

Adele smiled. "I know you don't believe in the efficacy of such things. But your friends were injured here, and we don't want that kind of bad feeling remaining in the place."

Erin shrugged. It didn't matter to her what rites Adele wanted to perform.

"Why are *you* still here?" Adele asked. "I thought you would be in the city at the hospital."

"I'm going to catch a ride with Terry once he's done."

"Oh, I see."

"I didn't bring my own car. I came with the others in Willie's truck. And that's evidence for now."

"Do you want me to take you?"

"No, he'll be finished before long. He wants to see how everyone is doing too. Poor Jeremy was still trying to figure out the poem, even though he was in shock. He just kept repeating the line about forest gold."

Adele looked startled. "Forest gold?"

"There lies there forest gold," Erin quoted. "I don't know where it is, if there is any gold, but maybe whoever got here ahead of us and booby-trapped the mine does."

Adele frowned, looking around. It was late and the woods were dark, other than where lights had been set up to mark the way. Adele turned in a large circle, staring down at the ground. Erin wasn't sure if she were already starting her blessing, or if Adele was doing something else.

"Here," Adele said, pointing down. "Do you remember this?"

Erin followed Adele's finger to a plant with yellow leaves and a small cluster of red berries. She was tired and it took a few minutes to remember.

"Ginseng," she looked at Adele for confirmation.

"Ginseng," Adele agreed. "Also known as forest gold."

Erin blinked. "Forest gold?" she repeated. "*This* is forest gold?"

"Wild ginseng is very valuable. Especially the older roots. Sangers made fortunes hunting wild ginseng and selling it to the Asian markets." Adele studied the plant. "This one looks very old. Probably no one has been harvesting over here for decades. They get grazed down by deer and rabbits, so you can't always tell the age from the number of leaves. If you dig it out, you can count the number of scars in the neck, and that will give you its age."

"But you can't make as much selling ginseng as you could back then, can you?" Erin asked. "You can buy ginseng at the store, it's cheap. They must cultivate it, so there wouldn't be much of a market anymore."

"There is still a market for wild ginseng. About one thousand dollars a pound, last I heard. Ask Jeremy."

"Jeremy? What would he know about wild ginseng roots?"

Adele cocked an eyebrow. "He works for Crosswood Farm, doesn't he?"

"Yes. That's where he was working. As a security guard."

"They grow simulated wild ginseng."

"What is simulated wild ginseng?"

"They do the best they can to simulate the wild environment. They don't plant it in fields or greenhouses, but in its natural environment, and then just keep animals and poachers away while it grows. That may be how these plants started out." Adele pointed to a couple other ginseng plants. "But they've been growing wild for a long time since then."

"So, Orson's fortune came from growing ginseng? That's what you think?"

"I haven't seen this many ginseng plants so close together before. Could the poem be about ginseng?"

Erin hesitated, thinking about it. She recited the poem slowly to Adele.

The treasure it enfolds
Where lies there forest gold
A king's ransom hid amidst
The warrens of the moles
The gift of life to those who toil
Each day to reap the sterile soil
Be wise if thou would life preserve
And no lord be forced to serve

Adele nodded slowly. "*Gift of life* and *life preserve* would fit, since ginseng is supposed to be sort of a cure-all. They grow in the ground, where the moles are. Forest gold. References to monetary value."

One thousand dollars a pound. Erin pictured a ten-pound bag of potatoes. That wasn't so much, and ten pounds of ginseng root would be ten thousand dollars.

"That's for five- or ten-year-old roots," Adele said, her eyes on Erin's face. "Some of these are much older. They've been known to go for huge sums at auction."

Around them, people were still cleaning up and hauling heavy equipment away. Terry was putting up warning signs and police tape around the entrances to the mines. All of them tramping through the unassuming little plants without a thought.

"Doesn't anybody know about this?"

"Not as many people know anymore, unless they work for a farm like Jeremy. Hopefully, anyone who came here today was too distracted to notice it. We should see if the Police Department will post guards overnight. Do you know who the land belongs to?"

"It's public land. We checked before we came to explore. Didn't want to get shot for trespassing. Orson might have held title for a while, but it was eventually abandoned. Too far from town, I guess."

"If you want to come back here to collect it, you're going to need a permit. Or get someone who has a permit. They take a while to be issued, and by the time you get back here, all of this could be gone."

It was hard to imagine walking away and leaving thousands of dollars in the ground. But it was also dark, and Erin was exhausted. No one would have the energy to start digging roots at that point, even if they did have the required permits.

"Would Jeremy have a permit?"

"I doubt it. He's not collecting plants, he's guarding them."

"A permit for what?" Erin was startled at Beaver's words. She hadn't seen or heard the woman approach.

"I didn't know you were still here."

Beaver gave a lazy shrug. "I'm still here. I'll head over to the hospital before long, but I wanted to make sure law enforcement here had everything they needed. Bald Eagle Falls is a pretty small place, and this was a big operation. That's a lot for one small police department to handle."

Erin nodded. "They did a really good job, though."

Beaver looked Adele over and raised an eyebrow. "Everything okay here? I'm surprised to see you here."

"I wanted to do my part," Adele said. "I may not enjoy mixing with large groups of people, but that doesn't mean I can't. I wouldn't want to leave my friends in the lurch. I needed to do something for them, however uncomfortable it might be."

She looked at Erin. She hadn't said anything about blessing the ground or whatever it was she planned to do once she had a bit of privacy. Beaver cocked her head to the side and looked at the two of them. She pressed her lips together and raised her hands slightly in a questioning gesture. "What's up? You look as nervous as a cat."

Erin supposed that was probably true. She was anxious and trying not to show it. She wasn't sure what to do with the sudden revelation from Adele. She looked at Adele, wondering whether she should say anything about the ginseng.

"Go ahead," Adele said. "We need to tell Officer Piper about it anyway."

Erin was still hesitant. Beaver was a treasure hunter. Erin wasn't sure how she would react to knowing that there was a treasure trove right under her feet. Beaver waited. Erin looked down at the ground, grimacing, trying to think of the best way to proceed.

"If you need to tell Terry, then go tell Terry," Beaver encouraged. "It sounds like it's out of my jurisdiction, whatever it is. You don't have to tell me anything."

Erin was again confused by Beaver's lack of ego. If she had been a federal agent on TV, she would have had a fit over Erin not answering her questions the instant they were asked. She would insist that Erin was required by law to answer her questions. She wouldn't cede authority to someone else, but would want to run the case herself, even if it were nothing to do with her department. But that was TV. Erin supposed she shouldn't expect real life to imitate television that closely.

"Yes... I guess I should tell him first. Then he can decide what needs to be shared. I don't want to share anything I shouldn't."

Beaver nodded her agreement. "Last I saw, he was over by the—" she turned and saw that Terry was still working around the entrances to the mines. "Well, you have eyes."

Erin nodded to Adele and walked over to Terry. He gave her a smile and a nod, stepping back to take a look at his handiwork.

"You're looking pretty tired. We'll be out of here before long. Do you want to go to the hospital or straight home to bed?"

"Before that... there's another problem."

Terry's shoulders sagged. He rolled his head as if working kinks out of his neck and took a deep breath. "Okay. What's our next problem?"

"Adele is here," Erin nodded in the witch's direction, "and she knows about plants and herbs and such..."

"Yes, of course she does. That's her thing."

"And it turns out that some of these plants..." Erin swept her hand around to indicate a number of ginseng plants among the underbrush, "are very valuable."

"Well, if she wants to harvest some of them, I don't see a problem. It's public land, and people have the right to gather medicinal plants on—"

"But not ginseng."

Terry blinked at her. "Ginseng."

"It takes a special license and Adele doesn't have one. And I don't just mean it's valuable as a medicine. I mean it's... worth a whole lot of money."

"How much money?" his voice was slightly irritated. He didn't want to be having a conversation about valuable plants when he had so much else to be done.

"A thousand dollars a pound for the roots. Maybe more, because some of these plants are so mature. It could be thousands of dollars for each root."

Terry's mouth dropped open. "Thousands of dollars? Are you serious?"

"Adele thinks that's what the poem was about. Ginseng is apparently called forest gold. People make their living off of collecting it in the wild, and these plants have been left to grow for a hundred years, some of them. If we don't leave someone on guard here, and those guys who blew up the mine figure out that the treasure is really ginseng rather than gold, next time we come out here it's all going to be gone and on the black market."

Terry scratched his rough-whiskered chin. "I see."

"It's illegal to harvest unless you have a license. Whoever is looking for the gold probably doesn't have a license, but that won't stop them."

"I see the problem." He looked around for a minute at the undergrowth, thinking it through. "I'll get Tom to stand guard tonight. Someone will need to take over in the morning. I'll have to find out what department is actually supposed to enforce these licenses, but I'm not sure they're going to be willing to send anyone to guard it indefinitely."

"Adele said that I can get a license. Then I can harvest some of it. I don't care about getting it all, but I don't want to see someone rushing in here and taking the whole crop without replanting it like they're supposed to."

"Alright. Let me get people onto this."

"I don't know if you should just leave Tom to guard it by himself. I wouldn't want him to get shot like Jeremy. He might not be as lucky. And it's so remote out here... no one would know if he was injured."

"Jeremy," Terry repeated, looking at her. "Jeremy was shot because of ginseng?"

"Apparently. I didn't know that's what he was guarding, but Adele is familiar with the farm he's been working on. She says they grow ginseng."

He shook his head. "I can't fathom people shooting each other over plants."

Erin couldn't help but smile. "You'd understand if it was marijuana or poppies, wouldn't you?"

He considered. "Those are more in my realm of experience."

"Or even just plain gold instead of forest gold. Until we found out that gold wasn't really gold, this made perfect sense, didn't it?"

"True." He nodded. "I'll get up to speed on this as fast as I can. In the meantime..." He nodded to Beaver. "Maybe you want to get a ride to the hospital with Beaver. I'm obviously going to be out here a little longer than expected."

"Okay. I'll see. Sorry about this…"

Terry nodded. He gave a smile, making the dimple in his cheek appear. "I'd rather know now than have something happen. At least this time, you're not in the middle of the action."

"Well… I almost was."

"I'll see you later. Or tomorrow."

Erin went back over to Beaver and Adele, who didn't appear to be hitting it off. Erin found both women easy to get along with, so she wasn't sure why they treated each other with such wariness. But Adele was hard to know, and if she didn't want to share her reason for being there with Beaver, then that, together with the fact of who her husband was, would be enough to raise Beaver's suspicions about her motives.

"Beaver, are you going to the hospital soon?"

"That's the plan. Officer Piper doesn't want me to stay around?"

"No. He suggested I ask you for a ride to the hospital."

"Sure, of course. Are you done here?"

Erin nodded. There wasn't any reason for her to stay around. Adele wanted to be left alone to deal with her blessing and Terry needed to make sure that the land was properly guarded before he could leave. Erin wanted to get to the hospital and get an update on how her friends were all doing.

"Let's hit the road, then," Beaver agreed. She motioned for Erin to go with her and pulled out a flashlight. "Follow me."

She struck off across the glade. Erin shook her head. "The road is out this way."

"If you go for parking on roads where anyone can see you," Beaver agreed, and gave a grin. "Some of us don't like to paint targets on ourselves."

"Oh." Erin followed Beaver. They worked their way around the house and the debris where other buildings had been built. Erin stopped, looking toward the house. She couldn't really see it; she could just sense that the darkness was a little blacker and more solid there. "We should probably check out the house before we leave."

Beaver looked toward it. "You looked at it earlier, didn't you? You didn't find anything there. I didn't find anything there. There wasn't anyone hanging around the house, everyone stayed toward the mines, where you would expect."

Erin thought about the little house, and about the root cellar beneath it. "I think… maybe I should go in. There's something I should look at."

Beaver raised the flashlight toward Erin's face and paused, looking at her.

"Okay," she agreed. "We'll go check out the cabin."

She and Erin picked their way toward the house. It seemed like it was a lot farther away than it should be, having to watch every step to get there. Eventually, Beaver shone the light on the building. "There it is. You want to go in?"

"Yeah."

Beaver didn't head for the door. "You want me to go in?" she asked finally, as if reluctant to do so.

"It's not haunted."

"Maybe it is, maybe it isn't. I'm not in the habit of going into abandoned buildings late at night."

"We both looked at it before. There's nothing there." Erin took a couple of steps toward the door, trying to convince herself as much as she was trying to convince Beaver.

"Then why do we need to look at it again?"

Erin kept moving toward the cabin. She put her hand on the door handle and it turned in her hand. "It will just take a minute."

Beaver walked her in and shone the flashlight around at the walls. It was very dark. It was just as bare as it had been when Erin had visited it earlier. Erin pointed toward the trap door.

"There's a cellar."

"You want to go down to the cellar?"

"I don't *want* to."

"Then how about we leave it? It's been empty for a hundred years. We don't need to."

"I need to look at it again."

Beaver shrugged and moved toward it. She raised the trapdoor and shone the flashlight down the black hole. "Nothing there."

"Hold the light on me so I can see."

The other woman didn't object. Erin could hear her chewing on her gum. Erin did *not* want to go down that hole. It didn't matter that she had gone down before and hadn't found anything. It didn't matter that she had seen it already. She just didn't want to go down there. It was a dark hole in the ground and no one would want to go down there.

It was difficult to find her footing and she went down the steep stairs unsteadily, constantly worried that she was going to fall down and break her leg. She had a flashback of the splint around Willie's leg. She did not want one around hers.

There were no more steps. Her feet were flat on the floor.

"Can you see anything?" Beaver asked.

"No. Do you want to pass me the flashlight?"

"Not particularly, no." Erin could see it flickering over her head as Beaver shone it around.

Erin pulled out her phone and turned it on. Her power was getting low, but she had enough for a few minutes. She used the screen rather than the flashlight LED to take a quick look around the room. The box in the corner was still there. She went over and looked at the lumps of dried-out roots in the bottom. Potatoes? No. Ginseng. That was what Orson had been harvesting. That was his treasure. Erin used her shirt as a basket and piled the remains of the hundred-and-fifty-year-old ginseng into it. Then she awkwardly climbed back up the ladder.

Beaver looked at the dirty collection of roots. "This is what you came looking for?"

"This is gold," Erin said.

"This?"

Erin nodded.

CHAPTER 30

*B*eaver got Jeremy's information from the reception desk and headed to his room, while Erin got Vic's and Willie's and tried Vic's room first. She wasn't at all surprised to find Willie sitting in a wheelchair beside Vic's bed instead of in his own room. His leg was in a cast, but other than that he didn't look any the worse for wear for his experience. The staining of his skin meant she wouldn't be able to tell if he was pale or if he had bags under his eyes anyway, but he looked bright-eyed and alert.

"Didn't they give you anything for the pain?" Erin asked. "I thought you'd be knocked out." She motioned to Vic, who was sleeping peacefully, her arm in a cast resting on top of the bed sheet.

"I didn't want anything," Willie admitted. "They insisted they couldn't set it without giving me something, but they kept the dose low, so I'm doing pretty well."

"But you must be in a lot of pain. Wouldn't it be better to sleep?"

He shook his head. "I want to hear what you found out."

Erin opened her mouth to protest that she didn't know anything. Then she stopped. Willie leaned forward.

"You always know something, Erin. I want to know what you figured out."

"It was Adele, not me."

"But you know, so spill. They booby-trapped the mine, didn't they?"

This Erin already knew from what she'd overheard from Terry and the other officers. She nodded. "You were right about there being a tripwire. They're going to have an expert come and look at everything, but Terry said he doesn't think it was an expert. Maybe someone who has used explosives for small jobs like stump removal. They only put the charge in one place, instead of in series along the tunnel."

"That's what saved us. If they'd strung it out ahead and behind us…"

Erin closed her eyes, not wanting to think of the devastation that would have caused. "Maybe it was only meant as a warning. Maybe it was only supposed to scare us off."

Willie nodded. "Yeah, it's possible. They cut off our exit, but assumed we'd be able to get out another way. The map wasn't very clear. I figured when I looked at it that we had multiple ways out. Maybe there used to be, or maybe the map was drawn to illustrate what he wanted to have done, not what had already been done."

Erin looked at Vic. "So how is Vic?"

"She's fine. They just wanted to keep her under observation, because of shock, but I'm sure they'll let her go tomorrow. I haven't heard how Jeremy is doing, but hopefully we can all go home tomorrow."

Erin nodded and blew out a breath. "I was so worried. I didn't know what kind of shape you were going to be in when we got to you. If we could get to you."

"The town really came together. There have been people trickling in and out of here all night."

"Yeah. It's really something to see. Bald Eagle Falls really knows what to do in an emergency."

Willie reached over to the bedside table and sipped a cup of water with a straw. "What else?"

"What?"

"You know something else. What is it?"

"Well… we found it."

"Found what?" Willie's eyes widened. "The gold?"

Erin nodded. She proceeded to tell him about the wild ginseng. Willie sat back, thinking about that.

"My grandmother used to gather sang. I never heard her call it forest gold."

"I guess it's really valuable. It's endangered now. You have to have a license to harvest it."

"Orson Cadaver was selling sang."

"That's what it looks like."

"Who would have guessed."

A nurse poked her head in the door. She looked at them and focused her attention on Willie. "You, sir, are not supposed to be here. Do you know how many people are looking for you?"

Willie grinned. "I'm where I'm supposed to be."

"You are supposed to be in your bed sleeping. Now off you go."

"I can't stay here with my girlfriend?"

"No."

"I'm not going to sleep in my bed. At least here, I can rest if I know she's okay."

The nurse strode into the room. Willie released the brakes on the wheelchair. "Okay. I'm going."

She stood with her hands on her hips, watching him go. She didn't assume he was really going to do what he was told. When he was gone, the nurse turned to Vic and checked her vitals.

"You seem to be spending a lot of time here," she said to Erin.

"What?" Erin studied her. She had seen the woman before but couldn't remember where from. The nurse's name tag said Chantel.

"You were here not so long ago after being mugged."

"Oh, yes I was," Erin admitted. "I'm sorry, I don't remember you."

"A knock on the head will do that to you. You're looking a lot better."

"I'm fine now." Erin put her hand over the bump on the back of her head. It was tender, but she didn't feel like she had after being hit. The pain, nausea, and shakiness had subsided quickly, and though it wasn't fully healed, she hadn't thought much about it.

"You should be more careful, wandering around out there in the dark," the nurse said. "Something could happen to you. This time, it was just a knock on the head, who knows what it might be next time."

"I know," Erin agreed. She'd been through enough dangerous situations to realize that things could always be worse. The head injury she'd sustained after first moving to Bald Eagle Falls had been much worse and she'd been afraid she wasn't going to make it. She shook off the images. "But I wasn't out there wandering in the dark. I was going to my car. I even had a security guard walk me out. I wasn't taking chances."

"Still, you don't want to go around taking unnecessary risks. Maybe you should listen to your boyfriend and take up another hobby."

Erin frowned. That wasn't part of the conversation she'd just had with Willie, but one she'd had with Terry when Jeremy had been in the hospital.

"Do I know you?" she asked. "I'm sorry, but are you from Bald Eagle Falls? Or do I know you from somewhere else?"

"No. Just someone you have had the serendipity of crossing paths with." The nurse fiddled with her watch. "Your friend here is going to be just fine. But if the two of you want to keep it that way, I would think about what people are saying. Just mind your bakery and leave the sleuthing to people who are properly trained."

"Umm... okay." Erin nodded. It wasn't like she hadn't heard that advice before. Obviously, Nurse Chantel had overheard one such conversation. "Thank you for your advice."

The nurse looked at her for a moment, as if expecting something more, then she nodded briskly and left the room.

CHAPTER 31

*T*erry was tired, but he was off duty and Erin was sure he'd go home and crash for a few hours very soon.

"You and Adele were right about the ginseng, of course," he advised. "We've called the Department of Environment and Conservation, and they are trying to coordinate someone to keep an eye on the farm; but they don't have their own security force, so they're having to scramble to figure out what they can do. In the meantime, we don't have a large enough team to take over security there as well as maintain order in Bald Eagle Falls, so they are looking at using some other department's agents to keep an eye on things for a while. Who knows, maybe Beaver will end up being one of the people out there guarding it."

"That would be funny. Although I'd be a little worried about her making off with some of the ginseng…"

"Why would you say that?"

Erin shrugged. "I just get the feeling that… she might not be the most… *honest* agent. That's not the word I want… but I'm always wondering what she's up to. She seems like she always has something else going on. Do you have any idea what it is she's been doing with Campbell?"

"Campbell?"

"Cox. Mary Lou's oldest."

"No, I'm not aware of anything. Why? What do you think she's been doing?"

"I don't know. Using him as a confidential informant, maybe. I can't think of anything she would have to do with a teenager like that."

"I guess CI is a possibility. Kids tend to be able to worm themselves into some unhealthy situations. But I don't think that means Beaver is doing anything she shouldn't be."

"You don't think she's the one who set the explosives in the mine, do you?"

Terry sat down and stared into Erin's eyes. "What?"

"It's just that… she was suddenly there. Not in an official capacity, but she was there before anyone else, other than you. And I think… she might have actually been there before you, and just hadn't made herself known to us. I think she and Campbell were already on Orson's farm for some reason."

"What reason could they have? You don't think she was there as a treasure hunter, do you?"

"Why not? You know that's her hobby. This thing with Campbell, I don't think it's official. I think she just knows him personally. She could have been there ahead of us, and she might have had a chance to search the mines and set the charge, booby-trapping it for when one of us came along to see it."

Terry shook his head and took a sip of his coffee. "You think she tried to blow up her own boyfriend?"

"I don't think she knew he was going to be there. She probably thought he was still too injured from being shot and would be staying at home, not out exploring caves with Vic and Willie. I don't think she meant to blow *him* up."

"But you think she set the explosives that injured them. That she didn't care about blowing up Willie and Vic."

Erin sighed. She ran her fingers through her hair. "I don't know. I don't know what to think. I just know… she was on the farm before anyone else. She implied that her case had led her there. But how would a case have led her to exactly the same place as we were going? The Orson farm had been deserted for a hundred years, untouched by anyone, and suddenly it's the center of a treasure hunt *and* a drug investigation? It doesn't make any sense."

"How would she have found out about the Orson farm? Did you tell her? You don't think she's the one who stole the maps at the hospital, do you?"

Erin considered. Could Beaver have hit her over the head and stolen the maps and her purse? Could she really have done that to someone she pretended was a friend? Erin's impression was that it had been a man, but with Beaver's boxy silhouette when wearing her hunting jacket, and her long, loping stride, she might easily be taken for a man at only a quick glimpse in the dark.

"We told her about the farm. Showed her pictures of it. I never thought... I mean, I knew she was a treasure hunter, but I didn't think she'd ever do anything to hurt anyone. I thought there was... some kind of code, that you wouldn't go after the treasure that your friend was looking for. Or that you would only do it together."

Terry nodded slowly. "I guess I'll have to look into it," he admitted. "I'm not sure who to talk to... I don't want to take any flak for throwing aspersions on a decorated agent."

"I know. I don't want to either. But I thought you would want to know. There was so much going on that day, I didn't know if you knew when she got there."

"You're right. It's the kind of thing I definitely want to know about."

When Erin went by Jeremy's room to see how he was doing, she expected to find Beaver there beside his bed, as she had found Willie sitting by Vic. But Jeremy was sleeping and there was no one else in the room. Erin moved around to the side of the bed and looked down at him, trying to assess his condition.

He had an IV line into his arm, but there were no machines monitoring his vital signs, no catheter bag as far as she could see, and no respirator or casts. He seemed like he could just be sleeping. Maybe the reason Beaver wasn't there was because Jeremy was fine, so she had gone home to sleep.

"You want something, or are you just going to stand there?"

Erin jumped and looked down at Jeremy, his eyes looking up at her, squinting against the brightness of the room.

"Sheesh, you scared the heck out of me. I thought you were asleep."

"Well, I was, but people keep coming in and looking at me."

"I'm sorry. I didn't mean to bother you. Just wanted to see how you are doing."

Jeremy lifted his hand to cover a yawn. His limbs seemed to be working perfectly normally. "How about Vic and Willie? Are they okay?"

Erin sat down in the chair next to the bed. "Yes, they're okay. Willie has been up and around. Well, as much as he can with a cast on his leg. Vic is sleeping, but she's not in any danger. And you're okay?"

"Needed a good nap, that's all. The doctors say there's nothing wrong with me. None the worse for wear for my adventure."

"Beaver said… when you came out, you kept saying that you should have seen it. The forest gold."

Jeremy dropped his eyes. He looked embarrassed. "It was right there in the poem, the whole time. I didn't know why I didn't catch on. I mean, you would think that with what I was doing… I would have seen it immediately."

"The ginseng."

He rolled his eyes. "In my defense, I don't spend all day at work staring at the plants. Mostly, I'm looking at the perimeter, watching for any movement. The plants themselves… they're just background. Something pretty to look at."

"But when you came out of the tunnel, you saw it."

"I figured it out just before that. I'd been in and out, and I guess my unconscious mind decided to unlock the puzzle for something to do. I realized that there was just as much ginseng in these woods as there was at work, maybe more. And it wasn't being guarded or claimed by anyone. Just like… gold in a mine."

"Do you think… that Beaver knew about it before you said anything? Or that Willie knew before he went in with you?"

Jeremy shook his head, frowning. "No. No one else knew."

"Somebody knew. Somebody was there ahead of us."

"We don't know that."

"You know it wasn't just a cave-in, right? It was caused by an explosion. Not just old explosives left behind, and not just something that was on a timer or remote detonated. It was a tripwire. They meant to catch whoever was there in a trap, maybe to kill them."

"Then asking whether Beaver knew is ridiculous. She wouldn't have rigged explosives up to blow me up."

"She didn't know you were going to be there."

"No, we didn't tell anyone ahead of time what we were doing, so she couldn't have known that."

"Then she could have set it up to trap Vic and me whenever we went back to look at the mine."

"Beaver wouldn't do that. She likes you guys."

"You've only known her for a little while."

"You don't think I would know whether she was a good person or not? The kind of person who would kill my sister?"

"She's trained in deception."

"It's not Beaver, Erin."

"Then what about Willie?"

"Why would he trip his own explosives? He could have been killed."

"But he's been mining for a long time. He probably knows how to handle explosives."

"He broke his leg! Rocks fell down all around us. The roof caved in. He broke his leg and could barely move."

"That part could have been an accident." But Erin didn't really believe that either Willie or Beaver had been involved, and Jeremy's reaction confirmed her instinct.

"There's no way Willie knew there was a tripwire down there. There's no way he would have led us in there and set off an explosion. No way."

"Okay. I just wanted to make sure."

A nurse bustled into the room. "I see our patient is awake. How are you feeling, Mr. Jackson?"

"Good," Jeremy approved. "Ready to go home."

"We'll have to talk to the doctor about that."

Erin looked at the time on her phone. She hadn't been in there for very long. Jeremy had been awake only a couple of minutes.

"How did you know he was awake?"

"I have eyes, don't I?"

"But you couldn't see whether or not Jeremy was awake. Not from out there."

She raised her eyebrows, then pointed to a small camera with a red light on it up in the corner of the room.

"Big Brother sees all."

Jeremy and Erin both looked at the camera.

"You have patients under surveillance?" Erin asked.

"We have to know if someone gets up and is wandering around or falls down and needs assistance. And the nursing staff is monitored to make sure they are providing proper patient care." The nurse rolled her eyes. "Washing our hands and not slapping the patients around."

Erin was aware of stories that had made it to the news of nurses being cruel to patients or ignoring their needs, especially at nursing homes. "So you can see what's going on from your nursing station out there... all the time?"

"We sure can."

"What about patients' right to privacy?" Jeremy demanded. "Do you have cameras in the bathrooms too? This is outrageous!"

"I told you, it's for your own safety. Don't go getting all worked up. There aren't any in the bathroom. Just outside, with a timer so we know if someone has been in for too long."

Erin could hardly tear her eyes from the camera to look at the nurse. "Do you have sound too?"

The nurse hesitated before answering. "The sound is turned off unless we need to hear what's going on."

"So you *can* listen in whenever you want."

"Whenever it is *necessary*," the nurse asserted, "for patient safety."

Erin looked at Jeremy. He cocked his head slightly, eyebrows raised. Erin stood by while the nurse performed a brief examination in silence, her eyes darting nervously to Erin several times, then she hurried out of the room after a forced smile and "I'll update the doctor. We'll see if he's ready to discharge you."

Jeremy looked at Erin. "Well?"

"I think I know who made it to the mines ahead of us."

CHAPTER 32

Charley had stopped by to see Erin before taking a trip home to Moose river for the weekend.

"You're getting along okay with your mom?" Erin asked.

Charley wrinkled her nose. "I don't know. She won't stop trying to... mother me. It's like she has no clue that I'm an adult now and can make my own decisions. Every time we talk, she's trying to poke her nose into my life and make sure that I'm not getting into any trouble. Always telling me what I should do. She doesn't trust that I can make good decisions. It's aggravating."

Erin nodded. "But you're going back for a visit."

"Yeah. She is my mom, and I should make sure that I see them now and then. She's right about that, and so were you. I might feel smothered by her, but at least I've got a mom and dad around. I should enjoy that while I can."

"Exactly. I wish I still had my parents... though in all honesty, who knows what kind of a relationship we'd have. They weren't exactly a well-functioning unit. We all just have to take what we get and make the most of it."

Charley gave a shrug. "What is the matter with that rabbit?" she demanded.

Erin looked down at Marshmallow, who kept squirming and digging his way under the couch, and then dashing out and zig-zagging around the room. Orange Blossom, spooked by his wild behavior, was perched up on the back of the couch, watching him with ears back and eyes narrowed.

"I'm not sure. I was wondering if maybe he hit puberty, he's been so wild and crazy lately. But he's neutered, so Doc says it shouldn't be hormones. I think it might be the ginseng in the yard. I can't keep him out of it when I take him outside. He just makes a beeline straight for it."

"Well, if it makes a rabbit that frisky, I can see why the Chinese think it could be a magic elixir for humans."

Erin heard a truck engine outside and looked out the window to see Willy pulling up to the curb. Vic leaned over to kiss him goodbye, and then got out of the truck and headed to the house. She let herself in the front door and nodded to Charley.

"Saw your car was here and thought I'd stop in and say 'hi' before settling in for the night."

Charley looked at her watch. "I need to be getting out of here. I told my mom I'd be there before ten."

"You'd better get a move on, then," Vic agreed. She cocked her head at Erin. "And I wanted to check… no word on that nurse?"

Erin put her lists to the side and wrapped her arms around her knees. "No. I'll let you know once I hear, right now they won't say anything except that they're investigating. But I know she's the one who got to Orson's farm ahead of us. Only the person with the maps could have. And that was somebody at the hospital. She knew way too much about the conversations I'd had with Terry and Willie. She didn't just happen to overhear a few words. She had to be monitoring us."

"But she couldn't be the one who hit you, could she? And why would she set explosives to go off when we went into the mine?"

Erin twisted a lock of hair around her finger, frowning. "She must have had someone helping her, because I'm sure she wasn't the person following me at the hospital when the maps were stolen. And they must have figured that the explosion would look like just a collapse. If one could collapse, then anyone would consider it too dangerous to explore the rest of the mines for treasure, and they could do it at their own convenience."

"But we could have been killed."

"I know," Erin agreed. "And I don't think she cared if we were."

~

Erin had initially hoped that Terry would be able to arrest Nurse Chantel right away. Erin *knew* she had listened in on her conversations and plotted to find the treasure before Erin and to blow up the mine with people still in it.

But of course, the nurse was not in Officer Piper's jurisdiction and the police couldn't just rely on Erin's hunch, no matter how convincing. By the time they were ready to take any action everyone had been released from the hospital and was back in Bald Eagle Falls.

Erin and Vic were hard at work preparing for the Fall Fair when they finally got word that an arrest had been made.

Terry leaned up against the display case to fill them in on the details.

"The same surveillance system that allowed her to listen in on your conversations also proved what she was doing. We figured Nurse Chantel would be the one to break down and admit what she and her boyfriend had done when confronted with the truth. But it ended up being the boyfriend who confessed to the whole thing. It seems that Nurse Chantel wasn't one bit bothered that three people were injured in the explosion. In fact, she went to see each of them to see just how badly they'd fared." He shook his head. "The hospital had surveillance video of her checking in on each of them. You know how she was in checking on Vic while you were there?"

Erin nodded.

"She wasn't even assigned to that unit," Terry said. "She busted in there making it sound like she was in charge, but she wasn't. She just wanted to get a peek at her handiwork."

Erin shook her head. She glanced over at Vic. "Can you believe it? Someone in a profession like that, and she doesn't even care about people getting injured or maybe even killed."

"Maybe that's why she's a nurse," Vic contributed. "She might actually get a kick out of it."

Erin shuddered. "Unbelievable. I'm glad she didn't confess, because that means she won't get a deal, right?" She looked at Terry.

"Nope. The lowlife who knocked you out and set up the explosives might, but she won't."

"Good." Erin got a cookie out of the case for Terry. "Chocolate chip?"

"My favorite. I also hear through the grapevine that your ginseng harvesting permit has been approved. You should get the notice any time now. That means you'll be able to go out to Orson's farm to harvest, when you want. No more being on your feet all day to run Auntie Clem's. Dig a few more roots, and you can retire in style."

Vic looked at Erin, her mouth dropping open. "You're going to close Auntie Clem's Bakery?"

Erin shook her head, laughing. "Not a chance! I might hire a couple of other people so we don't have to put in such long hours, but I'm not quitting! I didn't work this hard just to retire to the easy life the first time I found a root worth thousands of dollars."

"They're not *all* going to bring in that much."

Erin knew they wouldn't all be worth as much as one of the old ginseng roots she had retrieved from Orson's cellar, which she had already put up for private auction, but with the number of plants that had been growing on the farm for decades, they could make a comfortable living, as long as it didn't become known where she was getting her money or where she was harvesting the ginseng.

"I have enough to buy Charley out," she said. "If she wants me to. Enough to hire new employees. And maybe if you want to travel, we could go on a vacation or two."

The morning of the Fall Fair was bright and clear. The air was crisp and the sun was shining brightly. Erin checked to see that everything was properly wrapped and arranged at her stand, but Vic had already taken care of everything, even with her arm in a cast.

"You don't have to do anything but smile and accept the compliments today," Vic said. "You did an amazing job on everything. All of your lists are checked off. Now it's time to enjoy yourself."

"I feel like I need to do something," Erin objected.

"Go look at all of the booths. And at the animals and other contest entries. There's lots to see."

"Okay, but I'll come to spell you in a while, so that you get a chance to look around too."

"And we shut down at three o'clock for the awarding of prizes."

Erin nodded. "I'm excited to see who wins. Did you notice that Mary Lou put a jar of jam in the preserves competition?"

"I did! So maybe Jam Lady Jams isn't dead after all."

Erin left Vic to man the booth and wandered among the other displays of quilts, preserves, and all kinds of arts and useful crafts. The variety was stunning.

"I hear you entered something in the baking competition."

Erin turned to see Adele. "Hey, I didn't expect to see you here. Yes, I do have an entry in the baking competition. But I can't tell you what it is."

"I'm patient. I'll find out when they award the prizes."

Erin felt herself blushing. "Well, maybe, but it's my first competition, so I'm not counting on winning anything."

Adele just smiled.

CHAPTER 33

*E*rin couldn't help but be excited and nervous at the awards ceremony. The sheriff was announcing the winners and had been on the tasting committee.

"As always, the baking competition was a tight race. Everything was delicious. The judges tasted, consulted, loosened their belts, and tasted some more." The sheriff jiggled his heavy belt ruefully, drawing laughter from the crowd. "In first place, with a traditional Tennessee dessert, was the mile-high Apple-achian Stack Cake!" Sheriff Wilmot ripped open the envelope. "By Erin Price, of Auntie Clem's Bakery!"

Vic gave a whoop and did a little victory dance. Erin couldn't suppress the big grin that spread across her face.

"I suppose since this came from Auntie Clem's Bakery, that it is gluten-free?" Wilmot directed the question to Erin over the heads of the crowd.

Erin nodded and called back. "Yes, it is!"

"And the entry said that there was a special ingredient included to honor Tennessee's history," Sheriff Wilmot read from the card. "Are you going to reveal that ingredient?"

"Yes. I added ginseng."

"Ahh. There was a time when ginseng grew wild in these parts," Wilmot observed. "Now you have to go out of the county to find it, but maybe one day we'll have it growing wild again here."

Erin nodded and smiled. "Maybe so."

~

Erin spotted Mary Lou later in the afternoon as they were cleaning up their booth.

"How did you do?" Erin asked her.

"Not too badly," Mary Lou said, allowing herself a small smile and smoothed her well-fitted blazer jacket over her hips. "I got first in two categories."

"Not bad?" Erin repeated. "That's great!"

"The preserves don't get as many entries as the baking," Mary Lou said. "You did much better than I did coming in first in baking. The competition was much fiercer."

Erin shrugged self-consciously.

"And Beaver and Jeremy both placed in the target practice," Mary Lou told her. "Jeremy will have to live down the fact that his girlfriend beat him with a gun."

Erin laughed. "At least he has being shot and blown up recently as an excuse."

Mary Lou chuckled. "You must be excited about the prize. Who are you going to take?"

Erin frowned. "What?"

"On the cruise."

Erin shook her head, confused. "What cruise?"

"The first prize is an Alaskan cruise. Didn't you know that?"

"Oh! No, I didn't realize..." Erin had accepted the envelope from the sheriff, assuming it would be a gift certificate for dinner at the family restaurant or a small honorarium. An Alaskan cruise? "I guess... Vic... or Terry... oh boy." How was she going to decide between taking her best friend and her boyfriend? She would be more comfortable with taking Vic, uncertain whether she and Terry were ready for some big romantic trip, but choosing her closest friend over her boyfriend might have negative consequences on their relationship.

"It's four tickets," Mary Lou pointed out, looking amused.

"Oh... well, that would work. Only I can't really leave Auntie Clem's Bakery to go on a vacation right now." Even as she said it, Erin remembered telling Vic that once they got the new workers trained, they could take a holiday together. She pushed a tendril of hair away from her face, feeling herself flush.

"I'm sure you can find a way to work it out," Mary Lou assured her. "It will be good for you to get away from Bald Eagle Falls and all of the drama that has taken place lately."

"Right." Erin nodded, still feeling a little shocked by the news.

Mary Lou smiled and patted her arm. "At least you won't be stumbling over any bodies on an Alaskan cruise."

VEGAN BAKED ALASKA

AUNTIE CLEM'S BAKERY #9

To those who would live in peace

CHAPTER 1

*I*n Erin's dream, it was dark. Pitch black. She was feeling around, trying to figure out where she was and how she had gotten there. Her stomach roiled and sweat dripped down her face and ran down her back. All she could feel around her was rock. At first, she could stand up and walk along the long passageway, but the roof kept getting lower and lower until she was crouching, and then crawling on her hands and knees, worrying about how she was going to slither along on her belly if it got any lower. How was she going to get out if the tunnel dwindled down to nothing?

How had she gotten in there in the first place? She couldn't remember, but her mind flashed back to the time that she had been hit over the head and left bound and unconscious in the endless mazes of underground caves when she had first moved to Bald Eagle Falls. Had it happened again? Or was she somehow back there? Every thought she tried to focus on slipped away from her, as they did in dreams, slithering away along the tunnel into nothingness.

Then it started to get lighter. At first, there was just a faint grayness that Erin barely even registered. But as she continued on, it got gradually brighter and brighter, until she could finally see the walls around her. Rather than getting lower, the ceiling started to rise and, eventually, she was able to stand again, looking around her in confusion. She was in her kitchen at the new Auntie Clem's Bakery. Was there another underground tunnel leading into the bakery? But how had it led into the bakery kitchen, which was above ground, rather than into the basement? Erin shook her head and looked around the way she had come, but was unable to identify the door she had come in.

When she turned around again, she screamed. There was Vic, her lovely bakery assistant, sprawled out on the floor, unmoving, just where Mr. Oglethorpe had lain. Her silky blond hair was spread out on the floor around her head.

"Erin! Erin, wake up!"

It was a few seconds before Erin could make the transition from the nightmare to the real world, where Terry was shaking her. She stopped screaming. Or stopped the strangled sobbing that had escaped her in the midst of the dream.

"It's okay," Officer Terry Piper soothed. "It's okay, it was just a dream, Erin."

She was shaking. Her whole body was vibrating. She melted into his arms, snuggling in close to his warm body and trying to calm herself down.

"Just a silly dream," Erin acknowledged. "It's fine. It was just a dream."

"That's right." He stroked her short, dark hair soothingly.

She breathed in the smell of his body, familiar and comforting, as she pressed her face into his chest. Terry wouldn't let anything happen to her. He wouldn't let her get hurt or kidnapped or trapped in a tunnel. All of that was in the past. Her future in Bald Eagle Falls was bright. Bright and normal, with no more murders or investigations.

"Do you want to talk about it?" Terry murmured.

"I was in a cave... and then in the kitchen, and Vic was there," Erin didn't want to put it all into words, afraid that if she said them, they would somehow become more real. "She was... on the floor..."

She didn't explain any further. Terry held on to her, his grip tightening a little. He kissed the top of her head.

"Victoria is just fine. She's at home sleeping, just like you."

"She's okay," Erin repeated. The memory of Vic and her other friends being trapped in a collapsed mine was still too fresh. It was still all too familiar, that knowledge that something awful had happened to them and they might not get out alive. Erin had been swallowed up by that dread, waiting for the rescuers to drill through the rock and find out what kind of condition her friends were in. The whole time, she kept trying to block out visions of their dead bodies in her mind. Buried by rock.

Erin let out a long, shuddering breath. She turned her head to look at the clock.

"I don't know if I can go back to sleep."

Terry shifted around to look at it himself. It wasn't even light outside, but Erin was used to keeping baker's hours and, even on a day off, her body still expected to get up before dawn to start doing the day's baking. The nightmares often took place just before rising.

"Stay with me just a little longer," Terry suggested.

Erin couldn't turn him down. She nodded and snuggled back down into his embrace.

"Thank you," she told him.

"You just stay there and relax. It will all be okay. It wasn't real."

"I know. I just… it feels real. I get so freaked out."

"Yeah."

She wondered whether any of it bothered Terry. Just because he was a police officer, that didn't mean that he too wasn't affected by the deaths and accidents that they had experienced since Erin moved to Bald Eagle Falls. Even first responders could end up with PTSD. Not that Erin had PTSD.

Terry kissed the top of her head. "When I'm not here…" he trailed off.

They didn't live together. Even if they had, Terry wouldn't be able to be there all the time, because he frequently had to take night shift or answer calls. Bald Eagle Falls had only a tiny police department, so he was often needed. He and Erin still kept separate residences, and though she did stay occasionally at Terry's, most of the time it was Terry who came over to spend the night with Erin. There was little point in doing it during the week when Erin was baking, since the hours that they would actually both be in bed at the same time were so few. So, they were practical and only slept together on the nights that they could both get off, when they could actually spend time together.

"Do you have dreams when I'm not here?" Terry asked.

"Yeah… of course…" And without him there to wake her up from them, the dreams seemed to go on forever. Sometimes it seemed like she was battling her demons all night. Waking up in the morning was a relief, even if she felt like she hadn't had a good night's sleep. She just wanted the nightmares to end and to get on with life.

He gave her a little squeeze. "Have you thought any more about counseling? You've been through a lot and it could help."

"I know." Erin sighed. The last thing she wanted was more hours in a therapist's office. But she was growing more desperate to end the dreams. She had thought they would just fade away as the memory of the mine collapse and the other traumatic events that had occurred in Bald Eagle Falls grew more distant. But so far, that wasn't happening. She supposed it could take months, even years. People dealt with PTSD or other disorders for a long time. "Maybe. I really... I just don't like doctors. I've done enough of that in the past. My social workers were always insisting on different kinds of therapy or counseling. Any time I had a hard time 'settling into' a new family. It was just a... a farce. Some of them were so stupid... I knew the drill better than the professionals did. I could have given them therapy. 'Tell me about your feelings.'"

Terry chuckled. "I bet you'd make a good therapist. You're good at making people feel better."

"That'd be the carbs," Erin laughed. "Donuts really do soothe the soul."

"Well, they certainly don't hurt," Terry agreed.

Erin could hear the smile in his voice and could picture the little dimple that would appear on her Officer Handsome's face as he was speaking.

She shifted restlessly. While it would be nice to fall back asleep in his arms, she knew that it would just begin another cycle of nightmares. She didn't want to keep dreaming. Her body was more than ready to get up. She would let Terry sleep for a few more hours undisturbed.

"I'll see you later," Erin whispered. She kissed him briefly and slid out of bed, not wanting him to be so wide awake that he wouldn't be able to get back to sleep again. His normal schedule did not have him getting up so early. If he got up with her, he would be shorting himself by several hours.

"Good night," Terry murmured. "Come back and get me if you need anything."

"Shh," she told him, and she slipped quietly out of the room, shutting the door quietly so that he wouldn't be disturbed by the sounds of her moving around the house.

Orange Blossom had jumped down off the bed and was trying to squeeze through the door as Erin shut it, letting out a yowling protest when she caught his tail.

"Oh, Blossom!" Erin held the door ajar for a moment to make sure he was all the way through, and then pulled it shut. "You've got to be quicker if you want to get through the door before I shut it." She bent down and held her hand out for him. It was dark, but not too dark for her to see his shape in the hall as he considered whether to approach her and get his pats and ear scratches or whether to remain aloof and express to her how she had injured his pride by shutting his tail in the door the way she had.

Pats and ear scratches won out and he slid his body under her hand, turned, and returned rubbing his jowls against her fingers. He made little inquiring noises as she patted him and scratched all of his favorite places. Erin whispered to him, careful not to wake Terry any further.

"There, that's nice, isn't it? All is forgiven? I'm sorry I shut your tail in the door, but you really do need to be more careful. Maybe you should sleep in your kitty bed instead of on my bed when Terry's here."

He made a chirruping sound, as if to ask why he would want to sleep on a cat bed when he was obviously a human. Erin laughed and showered him with affection. Then she stood up.

"I need to use the commode and then let's decide what we need to do today. I'll make coffee and we'll start a list."

He allowed her to use the bathroom all by herself without pushing his way in or yowling outside the door. He was affectionate and expressive and, in the early days, had frequently disturbed the neighbors with his demands for attention. But he had mellowed. Like a clingy child, he had eventually been soothed by her routines and gotten used to her comings and goings.

But he was standing right outside the door when she came out of the bathroom, nearly tripping her.

"Come on," Erin ordered. "Coffee. Kitchen."

He stared at her like he had no idea what she was talking about, but Erin knew better. He recognized a lot more words than he liked to let on, and sometimes gave away that he understood a lot more of what she said than a cat had a right to. Erin gave him a little nudge with her foot.

"Go on, don't block the doorway. We're going to the kitchen."

He allowed her to push him out of the way, but still gave no indication he understood her.

"Do I have to promise you a treat before you'll go?"

Orange Blossom took a few steps toward the kitchen and looked back to see if she were coming. Erin laughed.

"Uh-huh. I should have known. It's a good thing you don't have fingers, or I'd never be able to get you to do anything."

She followed him into the kitchen and after turning on the light, grabbed the treat can from the pantry. She picked out a few treats and sent them sliding across the floor, laughing at Orange Blossom skittering after them on the polished floor. She heard K9's almost-ultrasonic whine and, when Orange Blossom was finished eating his treat, she let Terry's furry partner out of his kennel. He waited politely for a doggie biscuit and lay down with it between his front paws as he gnawed on it. Marshmallow lolloped in on almost-silent feet, then kicked the cupboard with a hind foot to make sure she knew he was there and waiting for his treat too. Erin gave him a carrot from the fridge, which he started to gnaw on loudly.

Erin put on the coffee and sat down with a notepad to plan out her day. She was still getting used to the idea of having days off like a normal person. The extra money she had made from wild ginseng meant that she could afford to hire a couple of workers to cover the Saturday shifts and some afternoon shifts during the week so that neither she nor Vic would have to work long hours six days a week. The short Sunday shift for the ladies' tea didn't really count, since all of them, even Charley, took turns at that.

Erin had a hard time turning off her business owner's mind on days off. There were promotions and advertising to plan, experimenting with new gluten-free recipes for the bakery, and working out employee shifts for the coming weeks. She tried to schedule time for herself as well, reading Clementine's old journals and thick family history books and files and spending time with Terry and her friends, rather than letting her time fill up with housework and errands.

By the time the coffee was ready, she had several rough lists going. K9 had finished eating his biscuit and was lying companionably beside her, while Orange Blossom was glaring at his rival from across the room, washing his face and pouting. Marshmallow nibbled delicately on what remained of his carrot, watching Erin with one eye.

CHAPTER 2

That guy from the cruise line called again," Vic told Erin, as they started to arrange their baked goods in the display case at the front of the store. Vic moved slowly, her dominant arm still in a cast from the injury she had received in the collapse of a mining tunnel.

"I don't understand why he keeps calling," Erin said. She shook her head in irritation. "Why can't they just mail me all of the details? Are they expecting to do a big media show?"

"He said he just wants to talk to you to go over the specifics of the cruise and how excited they are to have you along." Vic shrugged. "I guess it's probably media attention he's looking for, yeah. But I didn't say anything about media to him. I just said he can come by the bakery any time during business hours. If you had the time, you could talk to him, but otherwise, he'd just have to be content with dropping the information off."

"Okay, thanks. I don't know why it has to be such a big deal. It was a really cool prize, but I don't want to have to keep making appearances just to get the tickets. They got the promotional package they paid for from the Fall Fair for being a sponsor."

"Yeah." Vic adjusted the cupcakes in the display, making sure they were all evenly spaced and shown off to their best advantage. Then she started putting the price tags in place. She had far more patience in arranging them than Erin, who had hit her head on the display case too many times to count.

"Did you ask Willie whether he'd come on the cruise?"

Vic backed up carefully before standing. "He said he'd do it," she announced with a broad smile.

Erin sighed with relief. She wanted her best friend to go along with her and wasn't sure how she would use the four tickets if Vic's boyfriend hadn't agreed to go. She was taking Terry, and Vic was really eager to go along, but it would be silly to use only three out of the four awarded tickets. Willie wasn't really the type who went on cruises. None of them was, but Willie least of all. He was the down-to-earth type who went on vacations to practical places, where he could learn something or earn some money on the side. He wasn't the type to just sit down and relax.

"Oh, good! Then it will be the four of us!"

"It's going to be so fun. I've never been out of the country before!" Vic enthused.

"I've only been to Canada once. One of my foster families did a vacation there. That was around Niagara, not the West Coast. It will be totally different. But Niagara was beautiful."

"I've heard great things about these tours. We're going to have a blast. I know we're only in Canada for a couple of days, but even Alaska sounds like a different country to me. It's not like anything in Tennessee!"

"Well, no!" Erin agreed. She had been looking at pictures online, and she had to admit that it was nothing like any of the places she had lived before. Even if it *was* part of the States, it was, as Vic said, something totally foreign to them. "Do you have a passport?"

"Uh... no. I'll have to apply for one. You can get them pretty fast if you need to, can't you? You can get expedited service if you already have your travel booked?"

Erin nodded. She needed to check the date on her own passport to make sure that it had not expired, but she was pretty sure that she had written down the expiry date on her calendar. Terry wouldn't have any problem getting a passport, if he didn't already have one. "What about Willie? Does he have a passport? Or will he be able to get one?"

"I don't know." Vic frowned at Erin. "Why wouldn't he be able to get one?"

"Er..." Erin fumbled for an answer. She didn't want to be tactless, but she had her concerns. "It's just that with him having been involved with organized crime in the past... I don't know whether he's ever been convicted of anything or has anything on his record that might prevent him from being able to travel."

Vic's brows pressed together. "I never really thought about it. I'll ask him. But he wouldn't have said yes if he wasn't allowed to leave the country."

"He might not have thought about it. If he's never had a passport before... I just don't know. There's probably nothing to worry about and I'm just being silly..."

"I'll ask him."

Erin nodded. "Good. I don't want to run into any surprises!"

The man was short and skinny. Erin was not a tall woman and carefully watched her weight, but she thought that he probably weighed less than she did. He came into the bakery toward the end of the day as people were stopping in to get their last-minute supper baking and desserts before she closed up. Then she and Vic would need to balance the till, clean up, and prep the next day's doughs and batters so that they could soak overnight, one of the many tricks that Erin had discovered greatly improved the gluten-free baked goods.

The man also wore a hat. Most people didn't wear hats. Sometimes the teenagers wore ball caps, usually backward. Some of the older women had floppy-brimmed sun hats to protect them from the Tennessee sun. But other than that, people didn't go around wearing hats. Especially not fedoras or pork pies or whatever it was the little man was sporting. Erin was quite sure that she had never seen him before.

"Hi, how can I help you?"

The little man looked around. He pushed up the brim of the hat a little to look at her, and higher yet to look at Vic. "Which one of you would be Erin Price?"

"That would be me."

He looked back at her again and smiled. "I am Enzo Dimarco. From the Animal Rights Society."

Erin looked at him nervously. She didn't need any militant animal rights people in her bakery demanding to know what animal products were in all of the baking or spray-painting her window because she normally used milk and eggs. The ARS people were well-known for highly-visible, high-handed methods. They were not the kind of people she wanted sticking their noses into her business. Erin glanced out the front window to see if she could spot Terry. He wasn't in sight. Erin saw Vic's anxious look toward her and knew Vic was thinking the same thing. *Don't make these people angry. But get him out fast.*

"What can I do for you, Mr. Dimarco?"

"It isn't what you can do for me, it's what I can do for you!" He gave her a big smile, waiting expectantly.

Erin shook her head slowly, waiting for the punch line. She had no idea what he was there for and what he thought he was going to do for her. Rewrite all of her recipes? While Erin was sure to always keep a few baked goods that were free of eggs and dairy to satisfy anyone who was vegan or had allergies to eggs and dairy, she wasn't going to make her whole lineup vegan. A lot of the gluten-free recipes she used relied heavily on the protein structure of eggs and dairy to replace that of the missing gluten. Vegans who didn't know anything about gluten-free cooking were always complaining about the amount of eggs or dairy used in gluten-free cooking.

Not that there were a lot of vegans in Bald Eagle Falls. Erin had known one, and she wasn't even really a vegan. But Erin ran into them in online forums frequently, decrying the fact that there were so few really good gluten-free vegan baked treats available.

"I am here to give you your tickets for the all-expense-paid Alaskan cruise that you won at the Fall Fair!" he announced loudly, pulling the tickets out with a flourish. He didn't have a very big audience, but he was making the best of it.

"Oh, thank you." Erin reached out to accept them. "I hadn't realized that they were donated by... your organization."

"Just one of the many methods we are using to try to spread the good word about the importance of an animal-friendly society." Enzo beamed at her, but still didn't hand her the tickets.

"What a great idea." Erin waited.

He didn't hand them over.

Erin realized she was going to have to wait until he was finished his spiel, however long that might be. "I'm really excited about this cruise."

"You are going to be treated to a world-class vegan banquet. People don't realize just how tasty and satisfying animal-free food can be."

"A vegan banquet?" Vic drawled. "Isn't that sort of an oxymoron?"

At Enzo's blank look, she clarified.

"That's one of those phrases that contradicts itself. Like jumbo shrimp?"

He continued to stare at her.

"Vegan banquet?" Vic prompted. "Can you ever really have a real banquet without any animal products? You can't call rabbit food a banquet."

He gave her a scathing look and turned back to Erin. "I do hope that you will be more open-minded than your friend. I assure you that you can indeed eat very well on a plant-based diet."

"I'm sure you can," Erin agreed. She didn't want to draw the event out by arguing with it anymore, but she did have her doubts about what a vegan banquet would entail. It would appear that was why the ARS had sponsored the prize for the Fall Fair. They wanted to spread the word about the delights of vegan cookery. "Now, unless you're here to buy something, there are other people who are waiting for a chance to make their purchases before the bakery closes…"

Enzo turned to look at the women hovering behind him, waiting. He had lost a bit of the wind from his sails and was looking rather deflated.

"I do hope that you will enjoy your cruise," he told Erin, finally reaching over to hand her the tickets. "A great deal of effort has been put into making it a premier cruise."

"We're really looking forward to it," Erin said encouragingly, feeling bad for him.

"Maybe you'll even get some ideas for your baked goods here." Enzo raised his brows, looking at the food in the display case. "A plant-based diet is a very healthy way to eat."

"I'm sure it is."

He nodded, said goodbye, and left the bakery. Vic turned, cocking her head at Erin.

"All I can say is, I'd better not get back from our cruise looking like that. Guy doesn't look like he's eaten in a month."

"He probably just has a fast metabolism." Erin didn't want to spread the idea that all vegans were scrawny little weaklings, even if she was a little worried about the fare they were going to be faced with on the cruise.

"That, and he never lifts anything heavier than cruise tickets," Vic agreed.

Erin smiled and shook her head.

Even if they did have a vegan banquet on the cruise, there would be plenty else on offer. That was just one meal, and from what she understood about cruise ship food, there was always a wide variety of food available at any hour of the day. If they didn't like what was offered at the banquet, they could just visit one of the other restaurants and have whatever they wanted.

But even more important than that, she kept in mind what Mary Lou had told her when she had talked to Erin about winning the cruise.

"At least you won't be stumbling over any bodies on an Alaskan cruise."

CHAPTER 3

There was a lot to be done before their cruise, and not a very long time to do it. Erin wished that she had been able to pick her own cruise date instead of having to go with the one that the ARS had picked out. That would have given her more time to get everything into order before having to leave. But Terry was probably right when he said that given the chance, she would just keep putting it off, waiting for the perfect time, and would never actually go on the cruise. She did tend to overplan, and heading into something new and unfamiliar like an Alaskan cruise, she felt more than the usual amount of anxiety over how she was going to get everything done and make sure that they had the perfect cruise experience.

Starting a bakery had been hard too, and she had done that without anyone else's help. And so was reopening the bakery after it was burned to the ground, but at least she'd had other people to help her by that point.

Charley, Erin's half-sister, told her that everything would be fine while she was gone. Charley was a perfectly capable partner who could keep things running for a couple of weeks. Erin didn't need to worry that she was going to come home to a disaster. Everything was running smoothly and would continue to run while she was gone.

"But what about the animals?" Erin asked Terry, heavyhearted when she realized she was going to have to leave them alone for two weeks. There was no way they could come on the cruise. Terry might be able to get permission to bring along K9, being a trained police dog, but Erin didn't have much hope that they'd let her bring a cat and a rabbit along for the ride. Besides that, even if they had allowed the animals along, Orange Blossom tended to be very loud and would probably not have enjoyed a sea voyage. She would have had to deal with constant complaints from the cat and the neighboring suites. Marshmallow wouldn't make any noise, being a rabbit, but he and Orange Blossom were fast friends and Erin didn't want to think about how depressed they would be if she had to separate them, taking only Marshmallow on the cruise.

But with all of the planning and preparation Erin had to do, she hadn't anticipated the problems that Vic would run into.

Erin was sitting in the living room looking through her lists and trying to decide what to tackle next when she heard Vic open the back door and enter. Vic's loft apartment was over the garage just across the back yard, and Erin was used to her coming and going as she pleased.

"Hey Vicky," she greeted, without looking up.

There was a loud sniffle from Vic. Startled, Erin pulled her eyes away from her plans to actually look at her friend. Vic's eyes were red and swollen. "Vic? What's the matter? What is it, sweetie?" Erin shot to her feet and put an arm around Vic, then helped her to sit in the comfy arm chair.

"What is it? What happened?"

Vic wiped at her eyes with the backs of her arms and hands. She sniffled loudly again, obviously well into her cry. "I just…" Vic sobbed and shook her head. Erin stared at her, searching her expression for some clue as to what had happened to upset her. "I don't think I can go on the cruise," Vic said. She wiped her nose again and hiccupped.

"You can't go on the cruise? Why not? Everything will be okay at the shop. They can do without us for a little while. And Willie said he'd go, right? So, what…?"

"My passport."

"What about it?"

Vic gulped. She tried to hold back the sobs. "I haven't legally changed my name."

"Oh." Which meant, Erin understood immediately, that Vic's passport would have to be issued in the name of James Victor Jackson instead of Victoria Webster. "Well… I get why that would be upsetting to you. We can't get it changed before then?"

"It's too soon. And even if we could get a quick name change through…
There's a whole pile of paperwork and a big long procedure for getting them
to change the gender from male to female."

Of course there was. Erin was grateful that there were any procedures in
place at all to allow a transgender woman to change her documentation, but
society wasn't yet to the point where it was quick and painless. There would
be all kinds of doctor's reports and affidavits and explanations about the
transition that Vic had gone through before they would allow her to change
her gender on her passport. Not something that could be done in the brief
time they had before their departure date.

Erin sighed. "I'm really sorry about that, Vic. I never even thought
about it. Do you think… do you think you could manage to go with your
passport in your old name and everything? Or is that asking too much?"

"That's not who I am!"

"I know. But the paperwork doesn't change who you really are. It's just
words on paper. You wouldn't have to be a different person. You don't have
to answer to James or dress as a man. Do you think…?"

Vic sniffled. Her sobs were slowing now that she had gotten the dreadful
news out. But she was still not happy about the prospect.

"I—I don't know." She sniffled and thought about it. "Does that mean I
have to go by James when I'm on the cruise?"

"No, it just means you have to have it on your passport whenever you
cross a border. They can't force you to go by James on the boat."

"And…" Vic wiped the corners of her eyes. "What about when I get the
picture taken for the photo?" Erin could see where Vic's mind was going.
"Do I need to look like a boy for the photo?"

"We'll talk to Terry and see what he thinks. But I don't think so.
They'll want the photo to look like *you*, won't they? If you look like a boy
on the photo and like a girl when you're trying to cross the border, it's
going to cause all kinds of delays. But if you look like the picture in the
photo, they're not going to care whether you've got long hair and
makeup. They just want to make sure you really are the person you say
you are."

Vic looped her hand around her hair, gathering it together and pulling
it all behind her head so that it didn't look so disheveled. She nodded.
"Yeah. They don't care what I look like, right…?"

"I don't think so. I've never heard of anyone having to look like the gender listed on their passport. There are plenty of people who are transgender, this has to have come up a million times before."

Vic was quiet for a while, just breathing, her sobs slowing down. She cleared her throat a few times before attempting to speak again.

"Okay. I'll ask the passport office some more questions about getting my passport under my legal name. But when we get back... I'm going to start the paperwork to get it changed."

"Yes." Erin touched Vic's face and pushed a damp tendril of hair away from her cheek and over her ear. "I think that would be a really good idea."

Vic nodded again and swallowed. "Thanks."

Vic's fight with the passport office wasn't the last bump in the road, of course, but it was the biggest one. Whenever Erin ran into any other issues, she just measured them against Vic's fight to be the person she really was, and they seemed small by comparison.

In a few short weeks, they were on a plane, headed northwest for Vancouver, Canada. They had all arrived at the airport extra early, prepared for delays to be caused by the apparent discrepancy between Vic's legal information and her appearance. But the officials who had checked their paperwork and questioned them simply looked Vic over and asked the usual questions before allowing her to continue. No one seemed to be the least bit concerned about her gender identity.

Erin had also been a little worried about the cast on Vic's arm and the one on Willie's leg, concerned that they would be considered a security risk, but the Canadians seemed to take it all in stride.

Once they were through all of the security checkpoints and waiting for the plane, Vic was practically giddy with relief, and so was Erin.

Erin looked around at their little group, breathing a sigh of relief. "I can't believe we're doing this! We're actually going on a cruise! In a few hours, we're going to be in a different country, and then we're going to get on a boat and go all the way north where there's ice and snow the whole year 'round." Erin shook her head. "I can't believe it."

"Are you going to relax?" Vic teased. "Or do you have a list of all of the things you have to see while we're on the tour?"

Erin hesitated, not answering. Vic broke into peals of laughter.

"You do, don't you? You have a checklist of what to do while you're on the tour. See whales. Eat vegan feast. Touch snow."

Erin's face got hot. She covered it with her hands, grinning in embarrassment. "Maybe!"

Willie and Terry joined in the laughter. Terry put his arm around Erin's shoulders and squeezed her. He bent down so that he could whisper in her ear. "I have a few things I'd like to add to your checklist."

Erin's face got hotter still. They all laughed, relieved and happy to be together, embarking on a new journey. It was going to be the best vacation ever.

CHAPTER 4

They were picked up from the airport in Vancouver by a shuttle bus for the hotel where they would be staying for the first few days, as the tour included an exploration of Vancouver, Victoria, and some of the surrounding areas for the first few days. Erin had been to a few big cities before, so she was undaunted by Vancouver, though the traffic there was something she was glad she didn't have to face herself. Vic had never been outside of rural Tennessee, never even having been to Nashville or Memphis. She said that she had been to Chattanooga a couple of times, but she stared around at the tall office buildings and congested roads of Vancouver with wide eyes and shook her head in amazement.

"It's like New York!" she exclaimed. "I never thought I'd see a city as big as this!"

Erin laughed and shook her head. "It's the big city," she agreed, "but it's no New York!"

"At least they drive on the right side of the road," Vic observed. "I thought they'd drive on the left, like in England."

Erin had to admit that she hadn't been sure about that fact either, but she wasn't going to voice it.

"And I thought it would be snowy." Vic looked around in rapt attention at the green trees and beds of brightly-colored flowers. "It's cold, but there isn't any snow. The leaves aren't even changing color."

"Vancouver stays pretty warm all year," Willie offered. "It's temperate because it's right on the ocean. They rarely get snow, and when they do, it tends to shut down the city. It will get colder as we move farther north. We'll still see ice and snow, but not this far south."

Vic shook her head, bemused. "It seems crazy to call this south. This is the north! It's Canada!"

Erin laughed and nodded her agreement. "It seems strange. But we are in southern Canada. Some of British Columbia is actually farther south than parts of the contiguous United States."

"That's just weird. I get that Alaska is farther north, but it doesn't seem like any of the other States could go this far north."

Erin nodded her agreement.

Vic leafed through the folder that she had been handed when they had checked in with their tour group. Everyone had been given one, and most of them were looking through it to see the details of their tour. Terry frowned and looked sideways at Erin. She was still looking at her own itinerary and had not yet pulled out her tour folder. Erin caught his look.

"What is it?"

"You said that there was a vegan banquet."

"Yes." Erin put her finger on her itinerary so she wouldn't lose her place, and looked at Terry. "Isn't it on there? Maybe they forgot to include it."

Vic also looked up from her brochures, her mouth open. Erin looked back and forth between them, trying to divine what was wrong.

"What is it? Isn't it in there?"

Terry turned around the folder and showed the face of it to Erin. Erin stared for a moment before starting to take in all of the individual details. *ARS Alaska Tour for the Animals. A Vegan Tour.*

Erin blinked. "Yes... but that doesn't mean that everything is vegan, does it? Just that they have this banquet, and options at the buffet..."

Terry shook his head slowly. "Oh, no. Read the description. It is a full vegan tour. No animal products of any kind in any of the meals. The whole time we're on the ship, it's just plant-based foods."

"Oh." Erin pulled out her folder and looked at the title, and then at the welcome message in the letter inserted inside the front cover. She looked at the glossy folders with bright, colorful pictures of Vancouver and Alaska, and pictures of long buffet tables covered with food. All vegan. The whole tour.

"Oh, boy. I had no idea." She looked around at the others. "I'm sorry, I really didn't. I had no idea. I didn't pick the tour out, they just put us into this one. This was the prize that was awarded for the baking competition. I didn't get to choose, and... I didn't realize."

"Maybe we should have figured it out when that little Enzo came to the bakery," Vic said. "The way he was going on about the vegan banquet, we should have asked a few more questions."

"Would it have stopped you from coming on the tour, though?" Erin asked. "If you had known ahead of time that the cruise was all vegetarian, you would still have wanted to come, wouldn't you?"

Her three friends looked at each other with grim faces and didn't answer.

At least while they were in Vancouver, there was plenty of *normal* food on offer. The hotel had plenty of vegan options for their tour group, and the luncheons that they were provided while on the tours of the various sites in and around Vancouver and Vancouver Island were vegan, but there were lots of other options at the restaurants around them. The other members of their tour group were all staunch vegans, it would seem, or at least one member of each of the couples, so Erin and her group were a little isolated from the rest by their eating habits. It was odd for omnivores to be in the minority and vegetarians in the majority.

Still, the food offered on the tour was good and they didn't separate from the group for every meal. Erin was pleasantly surprised by avocado and tomato sandwiches on chewy baguettes, vegetarian sushi, and a wide variety of fresh fruits and vegetables. The men made complaints about not having their meat, but they too seemed to enjoy the heartier offerings of vegan burgers, chili, and stew.

Erin was surprised at how muscular or heavy some of the other members of the tour group were. She would have expected them all to be skinny like Enzo, but she couldn't pick out of the group which of them were vegetarian and which were "omnis" there to support vegan partners.

"I've never had any problem maintaining my weight as a vegan," Margaret, a vegan from Seattle laughed, looking down at her generous figure. She wasn't fat, exactly, but she was certainly curvy. "I have to fight to keep from putting on weight, especially as I get closer to you-know-what."

Erin shook her head, not understanding.

"My hormones are changing," Margaret explained, smoothing her blue blouse over her stomach and hips. "And you wouldn't believe how easy it is to pile on the pounds."

"Oh. I hadn't even thought of that."

Margaret laughed. "Well, why would you? You're hardly more than a child! You don't have to worry about the big change for a couple of decades yet! But be warned, it comes sooner than you think!"

CHAPTER 5

*V*ancouver Island was even more beautiful than the City of Vancouver had been, quieter and quaint. They had all enjoyed riding in the top deck of a double-decker tour bus as it made its way around Victoria. Erin found it a little windy and cold, but it was a welcome relief from Tennessee temperatures, which she still hadn't become accustomed to after living in New England. Although it was the opposite coast, the sea air and brisk winds were more familiar to her and brought back pleasant memories of home that she hadn't known she had.

"I almost don't want to leave BC," Vic said, echoing Erin's feelings. "I know there is going to be a ton more cool stuff to see in Alaska, but it's so pretty here, and the people are really nice."

"I know," Erin agreed. "I wish we had arranged to spend some more time here. It's really nice to get away from work and there are so many more things that I wanted to see here. I could have spent a whole day just in Butchart Gardens!"

The men seemed more interested in getting on with the tour than Vic and Erin were. They were goal-oriented and wanted to see Alaska. That was what they had come for, after all, not wandering around British Columbia.

The morning of day four of the tour was bright and sunny, with just a little wind blowing off the ocean. They repacked all of their suitcases and headed to the cruise ship. Erin stared up at the huge ship that was waiting for them in the harbor. It was bigger than the ferry that had taken them to Vancouver Island. It towered above them, was blindingly white, and seemed big enough to be a city all itself.

Erin hung on to Terry's arm, staring up at the ship. K9 was leashed at his side and had so far caused no problems at any of the checkpoints they had been through. Terry had papers confirming all of his shots and his status as a police dog, and that seemed to satisfy the border guards, hotel security, and tour officials. Erin missed Orange Blossom and Marshmallow, but was glad that they were home where they were happy and that she didn't have to put them in cages or chance that they would be sick on board the cruise ship.

"It's so big," Erin murmured, still staring up at the ship.

"Huge," Terry agreed. He had read off a number of statistics to Erin the night before about the ship, how many people it carried, its environmental controls, how much of every kind of consumable it went through in a year, and everything else he could find about it. But none of that had given Erin the scope of how big the vessel actually was.

Pleasant crew members checked their passports and checked them off of lists, giving them their room assignments and pointing them in the right direction to find them. Terry and Erin were on board first and turned around and waited for Willie and Vic to catch up.

There seemed to be a delay. Erin wondered at first if they were having problems finding their room assignment on the list. It was possible that they had assigned the room under Vic's assumed name and were having trouble reconciling it with her passport. Erin looked down at the dock, focusing on the male crewman who was talking to Vic. Vic's face was red, and she was shaking her head. Willie was trying to step forward to talk to the guard, but Vic was holding out her arm to keep him back. Willie's body language was aggressive and angry.

Vic negotiated with the crewman, and eventually he let her through. Vic went slowly until Willie's papers could be checked and, when he caught up with her, they moved more quickly, until they reached Erin and Terry.

"What happened?" Erin asked, reaching out to Vic, whose red face and shiny eyes gave away her distress.

"He kept saying that he was looking for James, and that I obviously wasn't James. Said he was going to call the police and get us sent back to the States. Or put in jail. He kept saying that my passport wasn't valid and that I couldn't get on."

"It's perfectly valid, how does he think you got into the country?"

Vic shook her head. A couple of tears sped down her cheeks. "He was just being really belligerent and... hateful. It wasn't just that he wouldn't let me on... it was more than that. It was like he really wanted to humiliate me and make a big show of me in front of everyone else."

"I'm going to report him to the captain," Willie growled. "There's no way he should be behaving like that, and I'm sure if they knew, they'd want to do something about it. That guy shouldn't be working around people if he can't be civil. Don't they get any sensitivity training for working in hospitalities?"

Erin gave Vic's arm a squeeze. "Well, you're on now. He can't do anything else to bother you."

~

Once the ship got under way, all of Erin's worries about the ship's crew and the vegan food disappeared. She had been queasy on the ferry when they had gone to Victoria, but everyone had reassured her that she would be fine on the cruise ship. The bigger the boat, the less chance of seasickness. And the Carolina was one of the biggest ocean liners out there. You could have fit four Titanics inside of her. They all assured Erin that she wouldn't have any trouble on the Carolina.

But they were wrong.

The engines had barely started when she started to feel nauseated. It didn't take a storm or even getting all the way out to the water for her to get sick.

"It's just psychological," Terry said. "No one gets sick on a ship this big. You can't feel the ocean. It doesn't rock like a little boat does."

But Erin could feel the rise and the fall of the ship. She could swear it. And even the lazy rocking was enough to set her middle ear into a panicky jig, giving Erin vertigo and making her race to the nearest toilet.

"Maybe it's food poisoning," Terry offered instead. "It could be something that you ate last night or this morning."

Erin knew the difference between food poisoning and sea sickness, and she was definitely seasick.

"I can't do this. We have to go back."

"We can't go back. The ship is going on, and the cruise is all paid for. Even if it is seasickness, it should wear off in a day or two, and then you'll be able to enjoy the rest of the cruise."

"I can't feel like this for two more days." Erin wiped the sweat from her forehead, but more just sprang up in its place. "You don't know what it's like, Terry, it's awful."

She turned to the toilet once more, and Terry withdrew while she threw up, appearing a few minutes later when the heaves had quieted and Erin was just kneeling there, slumped, wondering if there were any point trying to make it to the bed to lie down.

"I know you're feeling bad," Terry commiserated. "Why don't we find out if the ship's doctor can prescribe something for you?"

"Yes," Erin immediately latched on to the idea. "Drugs. Make them give me something to feel better. I can't last like this for two more days. I can't stand it for two more hours. My throat will be raw and my stomach will be turned permanently inside out!"

"My poor girl." Terry bent down to give her a kiss on the forehead, then wrinkled his nose and changed his mind. He stroked her hair instead. "We'll find something that will make you feel better. I'm sorry that you're feeling sick."

"Go find out. I don't want to have to wait."

She knew it was rude to order him around, but she wanted to feel better as quickly as she could, and she knew she wouldn't start feeling better until she got something from the doctor that would take away the awful vertigo and nausea.

Terry gave her another quick stroke. "I'm going to leave K9 here with you. He'll have to keep you company. I don't know how long I'll be."

"You think he'll be busy?" Erin challenged. "We just left, and you said no one else would be seasick. So he shouldn't have anything else to do."

"Well… just be prepared. I don't know how long things take to happen on a cruise ship."

CHAPTER 6

*A*s Terry had expected, it did take some time before he managed to get in to see the doctor and talk to him about Erin's unexpected seasickness. Erin sat in the bathroom, and eventually lay her head on the side of the bathtub, closing her eyes and wondering if she dared to get up and go to her bed. What if she got sick again as soon as she started out? Or what if she got all the way to the bed and then couldn't make it back to the bathroom? She didn't have a basin or anything to use if she started throwing up again once she lay down. So in spite of how tired she was, she stayed there, resting her face on the cool surface of the bathtub and trying to pretend she was somewhere else.

K9 came sniffing around the doorway, looking concerned about her. He sat outside the bathroom and whined.

"You can come in."

He immediately entered the bathroom and went to her, nosing her worriedly and giving her short, encouraging licks. Erin pushed him back.

"I already feel sick enough. I don't need dog drool too."

He sat back on his haunches and panted. Erin patted him for a minute, then closed her eyes again as another wave of nausea engulfed her. She shuddered, wishing she were anywhere other than on board a boat.

When Terry finally returned, he found Erin still in the bathroom, cuddled up with K9.

"Erin. Erin, wake up. Are you okay?"

She opened her eyes and looked at him for a moment before recognition finally entered her eyes. It was hard to believe that in such a short period of time she could go from the bright and vivacious girl that he knew to a hollow-eyed waif. He felt her cheek and took her pulse, then looked back at the doctor, who had followed him into the suite.

"She's not looking too good. Do you want me to see if I can get her to the bed?"

Dr. Duncan O'Donoghue, a smiley, white-haired gentleman in a white lab coat, peered in at them.

"It would be easier to have a look at her out on the bed."

Terry tried to encourage Erin to get up and walk to the bed with his assistance, but Erin was weak and confused and wasn't going to make it even with help. He ended up bending down and working his hands under her knees and back to pick her up. He took her over to the bed cradled in his arms, and laid her gently down.

"Erin, can you hear me? The doctor is going to take a look at you now. Okay?"

She murmured something Terry wasn't sure of, and he moved out the way for O'Donoghue to do his job.

"Has she been sick for long?"

"No. She wasn't sick at all before we left. But as soon as we got under-way, she started throwing up. I wondered if maybe it was food poisoning. I told her it was way too quick to be seasickness…" Terry trailed off.

Dr. O'Donoghue began his examination of Erin, not appearing to have heard much of what Terry had said.

"She had the flu before this?"

"No. Nothing. She was just fine."

"And then she had food poisoning."

"No. Yes. I thought she might because she got sick so fast. But she said she didn't think it was food poisoning."

"She's very dehydrated. We'll need to get her fluids up and to get her on something to counteract the nausea."

"Can you do that here? Does she need to go to a hospital?"

"We're fully equipped to deal with seasickness here, believe me," the doctor said with a charming smile. "We do deal with it quite regularly."

"I thought nobody got seasick on big boats like this."

"No one except for the people who do." He gave a little shrug. "There are always a few who insist on being sick even when they have no reason to."

"Do you think she'll be okay?"

"Yes, she'll be fine once we get her fluids back up. Good thing you didn't wait until tomorrow to see if she got over it on her own."

"That would have been pretty bad? She could have gotten worse?"

Dr. O'Donoghue raised his eyebrows and indicated Erin's form on the bed. "You noted yourself she's already in pretty bad shape. Without the fluids her body needs to function, she could be dead within hours."

Terry shuddered at the thought. He had known that Erin wasn't faking how sick she was, but it hadn't occurred to him that she could go downhill that quickly.

"I'm going to leave her with you for a few minutes and collect what I need," O'Donoghue said. "There's no need to put her in the infirmary when she can be just as comfortable here. She won't be in any danger once we get her fluids back up. I'll get an IV and you can see if you can tempt her with anything from the mini fridge. But not alcohol. Water, Gatorade, juice, or pop. Not too much juice or pop."

Terry nodded. "Okay. Thanks so much."

After he departed, Terry bent in close to Erin and tried to rouse her enough for her to sit up and take some fluids by mouth. "What would you like to drink, Erin? Would you like some ginger ale? Some apple juice?"

"Mmm," Erin shook her head, refusing. "No, nothing."

"You need to get something in you. You've thrown up too much and you're going to get sicker."

"No."

"The doctor said you need to drink something."

Her eyes opened a slit. "I'll just throw it up again." She groaned. "My throat hurts."

"You need to try. Something that will soothe your throat. Do you want water or apple juice? Just some little sips. Or some ice chips. Do you want some ice?"

She nodded. Terry went over to the mini fridge. K9 sniffed Erin and then followed closely behind Terry.

Terry got ice out of the fridge for Erin and crushed it up the best he could in a cup. He went back over to her and sat on the edge of the bed. He had to rouse her again, and fed a couple of tiny chips of ice between her lips. This seemed to wake her up a bit more. She sucked on them and licked her lips, opening her eyes to look for more.

"Does that feel good? The doctors said you need to get down whatever fluids you can. He's going to put you on an IV, and he's going to give you some medicine to take away the nausea."

Erin gave a tiny nod. "Yeah. That would be good."

"I'm sorry you're feeling so awful. You'll feel a lot better once he helps you out."

"Uh-huh."

She didn't seem to have anything else to say. Terry fed her another ice chip. "Hmm, I wonder if these are vegan ice chips."

Frown lines appeared between Erin's eyebrows. "What?"

"I was just saying—"

"Ice is vegan."

"I know. I was just joking around."

"Oh." She blinked at him. "Okay."

Terry held her hand. Her eyes were drifting back and forth like she was reading very slowly. Her face was pale, and her skin was clammy. He wished that the doctor would hurry up and get back with his equipment. Couldn't he have sent someone else to get it, instead of leaving Erin alone with Terry? What if she took a sudden turn for the worse? If she was so gravely ill with dehydration that she could have died if left unattended for a few more hours, then she was in pretty serious condition, and Terry didn't think Dr. O'Donoghue should have left her alone without medical attention.

"K9 took care of me," Erin whispered.

Terry gave her hand a squeeze and looked over at his partner. "He's a good dog. He's very comforting when someone is sick or hurt."

"Special dog."

"Yes. He is. He's quite worried about you, you know."

"Oh?" Erin's eyes drifted over toward K9 to have a look at him. He wasn't, at the moment, looking all that concerned about Erin's condition. He probably knew that Terry was taking care of her and she would be okay.

"He wants you to have something else to drink."

Erin sighed. She closed her eyes for a moment. Terry shook her arm to keep her from drifting off to sleep. "Hey. Stay awake. What can I get you to drink? You want more ice?"

Erin nodded. He put another chip in her mouth.

"You don't think you could have a little sip of ginger ale? The ginger is supposed to be very good for nausea and motion sickness."

"Maybe… just a tiny, tiny sip."

"Attagirl."

Terry went back to the mini fridge to fix her a cup of ginger ale and put a straw in it. He returned to Erin's side.

"Here you go." He held the straw to her lips, and Erin took a little sip. He had hoped that once she tasted it, she would be more inclined to take a longer drink, but she turned her head away from the straw.

"That's enough."

"You hardly had any."

"I know."

Some time passed in silence. "What are you looking forward to the most?" Terry asked, hoping to keep her engaged and to fill the silence while they were waiting.

"Penguins."

"Penguins?"

"Well, puffins. They're fat little black and white birds. Some of them have a crest on their heads. They look sort of like little penguins. They are really cute."

"And they have them in Alaska?"

"Lots of them. There were pictures in the brochures. Didn't you see them?"

"I might have. I was looking more at the mountains and glaciers, I think. It's so… big out there. We haven't ever seen anything like that before. I'm really looking forward to it."

"Yeah… if I can get better."

"You will. You're not going to be miserable the whole trip, I promise. You'll be up on your feet in no time, and you can see hundreds of puffins. And eagles. And lots of… trees and glaciers and rivers…" He tried to remember what else he had seen pictured in the brochure. "And, uh… icebergs and whales. Lots of whales too," he promised.

"Killer whales?"

"Uh… I don't know. Will we see killer whales?"

"I don't know. It would be nice to see some other kind of killer, for once."

Terry chuckled. Erin had seen far more than her share of killers in the short time she had lived in Bald Eagle Falls. It wasn't her fault, he knew, but she did seem to stir things up and ask all the wrong questions of all the wrong people.

Things hadn't been the same since Mr. Oglethorpe. If he were to tell the truth, she had started showing signs of trouble before that. More than the usual concern when something was wrong. More obsessive list keeping. He wasn't sure when the nightmares had started, since they had only recently begun to sleep together, but he was sure that they hadn't just started with the advent of Mr. Oglethorpe's demise.

"Yes, it will be nice to see something like that," he agreed. "So much nicer than catching a human killer."

CHAPTER 7

*E*rin could hear Vic outside her stateroom, talking quietly to Terry. Erin didn't really want to wake up. The medication that the doctor had given her had finally suppressed the urge to throw up whenever she moved, but she still felt unsteady and sleepy. Terry had promised to stay with her until she fell asleep again, then he would go and see what he could scavenge from the vegan buffets.

"Is she going to be okay?" Vic asked.

"She'll be fine. The doctor said that once her fluids are up again, she'll be feeling a lot better. At least now she's not throwing up anymore. She'll want to sleep a lot, but she'll be okay to rejoin the land of the living within a day or so."

"Poor Erin! Who knew she would have seasickness! I can't even feel the waves, can you?"

"All I can feel is the engines. As far as I'm concerned, we're on our own little island. But Erin always was more sensitive about some things."

"That's true," Vic acknowledged. "Can I come in and say hello to her? Is it okay?"

"Let me check with her."

She heard Terry's soft footsteps over the carpet, and then he was beside her, touching her tentatively. "I know you probably don't want to see

464

anyone because you're sick, but Vic wanted to say goodnight. Do you want her to come in?"

Erin nodded. "It's just Vic, it's okay."

"Okay." Terry raised his voice above the whisper he had been using. "Come on in, Vic."

Vic opened the door the rest of the way and slipped into the room. She moved in beside Erin when Terry moved back. She sat on the edge of the bed and stroked Erin's hair back.

"I'm so sorry you're feeling sick, honey."

"I'll be okay. Better now."

"Good. Maybe when you wake up in the morning, you'll be feeling ready to rejoin the tour. I don't want you to miss the totem poles in Ketchikan."

"I'll try."

"Don't worry about it. I don't want you worrying about anything tonight. Just rest and get your strength back. We love you. Willie sends his love too."

"You too."

"Okay." Vic patted Erin on the shoulder and withdrew. "Sweet dreams."

Erin made a noise of acknowledgment and closed her eyes to try to find sleep again.

Terry had feasted on bean chili with some kind of vegan cheese sprinkled over top that he didn't really want to know the source of. It didn't melt quite right, but had been tasty, and the chili had been hearty and spicy, just the way he liked it. He had his concerns about eating vegan for the whole tour, but suspected that they'd still have more opportunities to order non-vegan food at restaurants or tourist stops. They'd survive it somehow, and if he happened to lose a little weight on the trip, it wouldn't exactly be the end of the world. He wasn't overweight by any measurement, but he wasn't underweight, either. He could lose a few pounds without missing it. And it would give him an excuse to eat just a few more of Erin's cookies when they got back to Bald Eagle Falls. They were only a few days into their trip, and he already found himself missing her mouthwatering breads and desserts.

K9 walked at Terry's side, heeling close as he always did. He attracted a lot of attention on the tour, which wasn't used to having animals along, and all of the women and a lot of the men couldn't resist stopping to talk to him and to pat him and tell him what a good dog he was. K9 was a good dog, but it was funny how many people went out of their way to tell him so.

K9 looked up at Terry and whined.

"What is it?"

K9 edged away from Terry's side, looking back at him in what Terry immediately recognized as 'follow me' body language. They were close partners, and Terry understood many of the dog's movements and expressions instinctively. He raised his brows at the dog.

"We're not on duty, you know."

K9 hadn't moved very far away from him. Just an inch or two farther than he would normally walk. He looked at Terry again, encouraging him to follow.

"Okay," Terry gave in. "What is it?"

He followed K9. The dog moved faster once he knew that Terry was with him, off into a corridor Terry didn't recognize, then out to the observation deck. Terry saw a woman walking along the rail, staring out into the sea. He didn't think anything of it at first. There would be a lot of people coming and going and looking out over the ocean over the next couple of weeks. The woman was short and slight, like Erin, with dark hair, in a similar cut to Erin's, though it was styled in a messy, casual, just-got-out-of bed do.

Terry's heart gave a painful throb when he realized that it actually was Erin. He didn't need K9 to guide him the rest of the way to his girlfriend's side.

"Erin? I didn't expect to see you up. How are you doing?"

She didn't look at him.

"Erin?" Terry put his hand gently on her shoulder, not wanting to startle her. "Erin, are you okay?"

She continued to stare out over the water. Terry tried to see her facial expression better. She didn't smile at him, but had a sort of vague, blank expression.

"Erin, are you okay?"

She still didn't respond to her.

"You're sleepwalking," Terry discerned. The medication or the unfamiliar surroundings must have stirred things up and she had started to wander. He shuddered to think of what could have happened to her as she wandered the decks alone, and stood by the railing looking out into the sea. What if she'd ended up in the water? It could be hours before they figured out that she'd gone overboard and then it would have been too late to do anything about it.

Terry caught Erin by the arm and pulled her gently away from the railing. "No puffins today. Let's go back to bed, and maybe when you get up in the morning you can look at the water."

She allowed herself to be led. Terry took her back to their stateroom, his heart pounding harder whenever he thought of how close she had come to disaster. Wasn't there any kind of security on the ship to prevent people from wandering like that? Surely there were other people who had been sick, sleepwalking, or drunk wandering the decks. There should be some kind of patrol to make sure that no one ended up in the drink.

He was relieved when he got Erin back to the bed. He settled her in. She didn't seem to be aware that she had been anywhere else or that he was there with her. She just murmured something about missing a deadline and closed her eyes to go back to sleep.

Even after Terry tucked Erin in for the night, she was still restless and he stayed just on the edge of sleep, alert to her every movement. He didn't want to sleep soundly while she got up again to wander around unsupervised.

Erin's movements got increasingly erratic and Terry knew she was dreaming.

"Shh, it's okay, Erin." He patted her shoulder, trying to soothe her. "Everything is okay."

"No…"

"You're safe. It's just a dream."

She pushed his hand away. She moved her head back and forth, starting to cry out in her sleep. Terry prodded her.

"Wake up, sweetie. It's just a dream. Wake up, you're dreaming."

It took some firm shaking before Erin finally emerged from the dream. More than he usually had to do. Terry assumed that was because of the medication the doctor had given her.

"Terry?"

"It's okay. It was just a dream. Do you want to tell me about it?"

Though she had been pushing him away, she cuddled close to him.

"Oh. I dreamed…"

He waited, but she just snuggled in closer, not finishing her sentence. In a minute, her breathing started to draw out again, and he thought she was back asleep already. Usually she didn't go back to sleep so quickly after her nightmares. She was obviously being affected by the medication, dehydration, or being in an unfamiliar setting.

Just as he was falling asleep, she started to moan and cry again.

CHAPTER 8

$\mathcal{E}$rin was on her feet the next day, though she was still a bit wobbly. Her face, when she looked at it in the mirror in her bathroom, was as pale as she'd ever seen it. Terry assured her she was looking better, which made her wonder just how bad she had looked the day before.

Even though she still wasn't feeling quite up to snuff, she didn't want to disappoint Vic by not going along on the tour and she didn't want Terry to have to stay behind to look after her. Truth be told, she wanted solid ground under her, if only for a few hours.

She oohed and aahed and took lots of pictures of the totem poles, but secretly, she was still too ill to follow much of what the tour guide was saying, and she found the stylized images and faces of the totem poles ghoulish. Nightmares were something that she really didn't need any more of. She tried to just enjoy her time being with her friends and walking on solid ground again.

"It's so cold!" Vic complained, wrapping her arms around herself. "Don't they know it's still supposed to be fall? Not winter?"

"The weather's a lot colder in the north," Erin observed.

"Sheesh. Why would anyone ever live here? I can't imagine being this cold all the time."

"You'd get used to it," Erin said. "This is probably still pretty mild weather for the locals. You've got thin blood, living your whole life in Tennessee."

"I wouldn't want to get used to it. I'd rather just go somewhere warmer."

"What are you going to do when we go for a tour of the glacier?"

Vic made a worried little moan. Willie pulled her close against himself. "We'll just have to buy her some warmer clothes. Can't have my girlfriend getting cold feet."

Vic and Erin laughed. Vic looked at her watch. "How much longer before we can go back to the boat?"

~

Erin sat at the table with the others for supper, though she wasn't sure she would be able to eat anything. Vic was starting to come around to the concept of only eating plant foods on their cruise, finding versions of most of her favorite foods available, though Willie and Terry didn't seem to have fully bought into the idea yet. Vic was showing the menu to Erin and offering suggestions to the men at the same time.

"See, they've got burgers and everything. You can get all different kinds. I tried one yesterday, and you couldn't really tell it was any different than a regular beef burger. It was just like any burger you'd get at any restaurant."

"I don't think I'm up for burgers," Erin said, queasy.

"If you don't like the ones that are like beef burgers, they've got portabella mushroom caps. They're grilled, and that's sort of a cool idea. A little bit lighter if you don't feel like something that heavy."

"If I wanted to eat a mushroom burger, I'd put mushrooms on top of my beef," Willie said. "That's the way I've always had mushroom burgers. Some nice sautéed mushrooms and onions, that's the way to go. Put it on top of a Quarter Pounder, and you've got a real meal. Just mushroom… You're missing the whole point."

"I was saying for Erin. I know you're not going to pick the mushroom burger. Why don't you have the chili? Terry had it yesterday, and you really liked it, didn't you?"

Terry nodded. "It was good. I'd skip the cheese, though. It's just… too fake."

Willie nodded, considering his menu. "That's a possibility."

"What do you want, Erin?" Vic persisted. "You want something lighter, like soup or salad?"

"I don't know."

One of the other tourists beside them at the long banquet table leaned toward Erin, observing her distaste with the menu. "If you want something else, you can ask if the chef will prepare it for you," he offered. "They have all different vegan diets if you don't like one that is so full of processed foods and substitutes. There are cleaner options, if you're looking for something specific."

"Vegan diets?" Vic asked. "Isn't there just one vegan diet? Eliminating all animal products isn't strict enough?"

The man shook his head. He leaned even closer to Erin, making her uncomfortable. He was a solitary traveler, and she could understand that he might want to interact with the other tourists at dinner instead of just eating by himself, but it made her nervous when he got inside her space. She was already uncomfortable enough physically with her motion sickness, she didn't need another irritant. She shuffled her chair another inch away from him. He was a tall, spare man, with eyes that bulged and hair that was thinning quite a bit on top.

"There are a lot of different kinds of vegan diets. You can have diets that are basically just a version of the SAD diet, with all kinds of processed foods, oils, sugar, all that stuff—"

"SAD?" Vic repeated.

"Standard American Diet. And then you can have diets that don't allow processed foods, or that don't allow extracted oils, or sugar, or any high-fat or calorie-dense foods. Or you have the ones that only allow above-ground plant parts, no roots or tubers. Or fruitarian diets, that only use the ripe seed-bearing ovaries of plants. Or only cast fruits or nuts. There are those who will only eat leaves and not anything with seeds in them, but those tend to be very calorie-restricted, and you can't live on them long-term. If you're into calorie restriction, there are also juice fasts, water fasts, or breatharians…"

"Breatharians?" In spite of the fact that Erin didn't want to encourage his interest in their company, she had to ask about that.

"People who claim to live without any food or drink, just getting their nourishment from the air and the sun."

"You can't do that!" Vic scoffed. "That's a really good way to die!"

The man shrugged. "It isn't a diet I would try. But there are people who claim to live on air, some for a very long time. Calorie restriction is supposed to extend your lifespan."

"Hate to break it to you," Willie interjected, "but eliminating all food and drink from your diet isn't going to make you live longer. It might cut your lifespan short by quite a bit!"

"Like I say, I don't think that's one I would ever try. I think you have to be a yogi before you can do that, and I'm not that devout about anything."

"That's a lot of different diets," Vic said. "I never would have guessed there were so many different ways to be vegan. I thought it was just one diet."

"That's not even all of them," the man went on. Erin tried to remember his name. Blaine? Brent? Something that started with a B. "You've got the people who only eat at certain times of day or certain days of the week. Different forms of intermittent fasting. They hope to get some of the benefits of calorie restriction, but without completely depriving themselves."

"What about you, Brett?" Terry asked. "What kind of vegan are you?"

"I'm just your run-of-the mill vegan right now. To tell the truth, I'm not even one hundred percent vegan all the time. I've done short stints with fruitarianism, and I always feel great when I'm doing it, but I can't stick with it. I'm too tempted by all of the other great stuff to eat. I initially thought maybe I'd do fruitarian for the length of the cruise. They have great juice and smoothie bars, and buffets full of lots of wonderful fruit options, even with dragon fruit and persimmons and other fruits that you don't see in the fruit options at most restaurants."

"But… you changed your mind?" Terry prompted.

"Yeah. There's just so much good food here. They've got world-class chefs, preparing their signature dishes and just about every cuisine you could think of. Why would I restrict myself when I've got all of those options available? It makes more sense to do the fruitarian thing when I'm at home, and to try everything I can when I'm on vacation."

Erin nodded. "Makes sense."

"Anyway…" Brett gave a little shrug, looking at the menu lying on the table in front of Erin. "I was just trying to say… you didn't look too thrilled with the menu, and I thought I'd point out that if there's something else you're in the mood for, or they don't have something in the menu that suits your dietary pattern, the cooks would be happy to oblige. They're very good.

I heard one chef say that he likes it when someone makes a special request on a cruise like this, because otherwise he's just making the same five dishes over and over again hundreds of times. So you'd actually be doing them a favor if you asked for something special, not irritating them."

He sat back in his chair and beamed at her.

Erin shook her head, smiling at him. "It's not that I'm following some super-strict diet, or even that I have allergies. It's just that… I'm suffering from motion sickness and I really don't feel like eating right now. I took some medication, but my appetite is really off. I don't feel so nauseated anymore and I wish I could take advantage of all of the great options here, but I just really don't feel like eating right now."

Brett nodded wisely. "You should ask for a fruit platter. Fruit is very healing when you've been sick. It's light, just sweet enough to tempt you…"

"Yeah, maybe," Erin agreed.

They went back to looking at their menus, and eventually everyone had settled on what they wanted to eat. A few other couples and families were seated while they were waiting for their orders and, as getting to know each other was highly encouraged and the tables and chairs were set in configurations intended to promote visiting, the dining room was soon buzzing with chatter as people tried to get to know each other.

"So, what is it you do?" Brett asked Erin.

"I'm a baker. I bake gluten-free breads and bake for other special diets, like people who are vegan or have allergies. Everything is gluten-free and nut-free. I try to offer foods that are free of any of the major allergens, so I always have one or two things available for purchase that are vegan. I don't know if that had anything to do with me winning the tickets for the cruise…"

"Oh, you won them? How did you win tickets?"

"I entered a stack cake into the baking competition at our fall fair. The ARS guys had sponsored the prize, so that's what I got."

"What is a stack cake? Is it vegan?"

Erin took a few minutes to explain what a traditional Tennessee stack cake was and how to prepare it. "It would certainly be possible to do vegan," she said. "A lot of recipes that were developed to help people use their dry goods storage or rations during wartime were free of milk and eggs, so they end up being vegan. The stack cake that I cooked had eggs in it, but it wouldn't be hard to make vegan."

"You can't just take out the milk and eggs and expect it to turn out the same way," Brett warned. "It changes all of the chemistry when you start swapping them out."

Erin looked over at Vic grinning.

"I think I know that!" she agreed.

"That's what Erin spends all of her spare time doing," Vic declared. "Any time she's not working or planning her work, she's experimenting with new recipes and new ways of making traditional foods. She's really good at figuring it out—"

"I make plenty of mistakes," Erin interrupted. "Some of the stuff that I come up with is barely edible. but I'm getting better. I learn a little more each time about how the different ingredients interact together."

"Do they know you're a baker?" Brett demanded. He waved to one of the wait staff, motioning them forward. "You need to tell them that you're a baker and you know how to do all of that stuff."

Erin raised her hand to try to stop him, but it was pointless. He was the kind of person who injected himself into a situation whether he was wanted or not, and never quite seemed to know the appropriate way to talk or act. He was soon telling all of the servers about Erin's profession and telling them how they should utilize her during the cruise to come up with a new signature dessert.

Erin just looked at Vic, shaking her head.

Erin had slept so much the previous day that she found herself wide awake at two o'clock in the morning. Terry was lying beside her, his breathing sounding congested, like he might be coming down with a cold. Erin knew he hadn't slept well the night before because he'd been looking after her, and he needed his sleep if he wanted to fight off the virus. She was afraid that her tossing and turning trying to get to sleep was going to keep him awake, so she decided to get up and do something else until she started to feel tired again. Her body's clock was all out of whack; normally she would be in the deepest part of her sleep cycle at two in the morning.

She retreated to the couch and tried to relax there, but her brain was still going a mile a minute. A book might help, but she was worried that any reading light she turned on would waken Terry too. Not only that, but her stomach started to growl, deciding at the most inconvenient time that it was finally ready for nourishment.

Erin held out as long as she could. She knew Terry wouldn't approve of her going off on her own without him, but she was a grown woman who could take care of herself. She was on a ship, where the crime rate was practically nil. There were crew members and security guards and closed-circuit cameras. She couldn't be much safer.

She knew that there were a couple of buffets that were open all night to offer repast to those who gambled or pursued other activities late into the night. There were at least two libraries on the deck layouts she had looked at, and she'd found a secret deck on one of the maps as well. Mary Lou had told Erin before she went on the cruise that nearly every ship had a secret deck, some out of the way, hard-to-get-to deck where those who were looking for peace and quiet could get away from the crowds and scheduled activities and just lie down with a book or have a nap.

Erin walked past K9's kennel on the way to the door. He whined softly at her. Erin stood there for a moment, trying to decide whether to take him with her. Eventually she decided against it. K9 was Terry's dog, not Erin's, and he was a working dog, not a pet. It wouldn't be right for her to be walking around the ship with him when other people weren't allowed to bring their pets on board.

She let herself out of the stateroom as quietly as possible.

Keeping track of what amenities were on what decks, and where on the deck they were was akin to memorizing the layout of a small city, and Erin had to stop to look at directories and maps several times to figure out where it was she wanted to go. She picked up a couple of pieces of fruit from one of the all-night buffets. They looked fresh, and there was enough of a chill in the air that Erin wasn't worried about them going bad because they'd been sitting out for too long.

She suspected that food probably wasn't allowed in the library, so she would find the secret deck instead. Someone else would have left a paperback or a newspaper or something else she could read. Or else she could just stare at the stars and wait for her body to decide it was time to go to sleep again.

She had traversed several decks when she realized she had gone too far, and then that she was at the wrong end of the boat to find the secret stairway. There were several sets of stairs going up to each deck, nice and wide and well-lit and signed, but there was only one staircase to the secret deck, and it was hidden in a corner far away from anything else.

Erin reversed direction and looked around, searching for the doorway. She heard voices and tried to decide whether to see if it was a crew member who could help her or another passenger who might know the way, or whether to keep exploring on her own. It was sort of exciting trying to find the secret deck on her own, and Erin thought that if she kept at it long enough, she was sure to be able to sort it out.

She stopped where she was and listened to the voices, waiting for them to pass by. They were on the outside of the deck and she was on the inside, so as long as she stayed still, they weren't likely to see her or know that they were being observed.

"We need to find out," one of the voices said gruffly. "We can't just wait around doing nothing, or we will never get paid. We need to be proactive."

Erin frowned, listening. Who on the ship was paid on commission? As far as she knew, everyone was salaried.

"I don't like this," the other said, in a breathy, sort of whiny voice. "I didn't want to be involved in anything like this. That wasn't what I signed on for."

"You're in too deep to be backing out now," the gruff voice growled. "We need to show you've got what it takes. If you don't, you're going to find yourself... expendable."

"What does that mean? I haven't done anything wrong. There's no reason for anyone to threaten me."

"The boss ain't happy about the way you're waffling over every order. You need to step it up, or you'll find yourself in trouble. They don't want anyone who isn't totally invested in this."

"I'm invested. I just didn't... I never said I'd be involved in this new stuff."

There was silence. Erin couldn't hear them walking or talking anymore. She pictured them in her mind's eye, standing out on the deck, looking at the stars or the waves or the full moon. Even the seasoned crew members must stop and look at the wonders around them every now and then.

"I told them you were on board. Now you're acting all wishy-washy... My reputation is on the line."

"I'm not trying to get you in trouble any more than I want to get myself in trouble. But I think maybe... I need to walk away from this."

"Walk away from it? You think you can just walk away from it?" There was a definite threat in the gruff-voiced man's tone.

"I won't say anything. I won't expose anyone else. I just think that... for myself... this isn't something I can be involved in."

"You were fine when it was someone else taking all of the risks. But now that you're being asked to take an active part yourself, you've decided that your conscience is bothering you?"

"Well... I just... I guess I've been thinking, and I just can't risk it."

"Maybe you should stop thinking and just listen to what you're told."

"I really don't think I can."

Erin pressed against the wall, ears pricked, hand pressed against her mouth. She didn't even know what the stakes were, and she was all wrapped up in the conversation, worrying about what was going to happen to the breathy-voiced one. Terry said she was always getting involved in things that weren't her business, worrying about things that weren't her problem and people who weren't her responsibility. This was a classic example. Two people she didn't even know, and she wanted to protect the one who was being threatened.

CHAPTER 9

*W*ell... I guess that's what I have to report back," the gruff voice sighed.

Erin breathed out in relief. Nothing was going to happen. Nothing that she was going to see or hear. Whatever drama was left to play out would happen somewhere else, not in her presence. They would move on and she wouldn't have any involvement in it.

She wondered briefly what she would tell Terry, and tried to compose a script in her head that would explain why she had been out wandering on the decks and how she had happened to overhear the strange conversation. She inched closer to one of the portholes that looked out to the outside of the deck to see if she could catch a glimpse of the two men talking. She might not be able to tell Terry what it had been about, but he was going to ask her who had been talking, and she wouldn't be able to tell him anything. She hadn't even seen their shadows or whether they wore uniforms.

She couldn't see much through the porthole. It was at the wrong angle to see the speakers, at least from the angle Erin was at. She got close to the window and pressed her face close to try to see them. If they happened to look up at the wrong time, they were going to spot her, but that was a risk Erin was going to have to take. She could just see the two shapes. Men, average height, one of them quite a bit broader than the other. By their voices, that would be the aggressor. A deeper, raspier voice. Neither was looking toward her, so she couldn't see their faces. The bigger of them was in a white suit, obviously a crew member in uniform. The other was in darker clothes. An off-duty crew member or a passenger, or one of the other men she had seen working in maintenance or other unskilled jobs around the ship.

If they were still talking, they were now too quiet for her to make out their words. Maybe the gruff man had dropped to a whisper to sound more threatening or to give instructions that no one could overhear. They both looked away from the ship, out over the water; there was not any danger they would spot Erin unless they turned all the way around.

The bigger man pointed to something out on the horizon. Erin strained her eyes to try to see what it was he was pointing to, but she could see nothing. She was a few feet farther back than they were, and looking through the porthole, which blocked some of the visibility. Erin pressed her forehead against the wall, trying to make out what it was.

The thinner man leaned forward, straining to see. The big man put a hand on his back, encouraging him to look, pressing him forward slightly.

Then as Erin watched, the big man lifted his hand off of the other man's back, and raised it up high.

Erin strangled back a cry of warning. She couldn't bring attention to herself. She couldn't let either one of them know that she was there.

The man's fist fell, crashing into the other man's head.

There was a shout of pain and alarm, fully-voiced instead of a whisper. The smaller man turned on the other, shoving him back, fighting with him.

The bigger man was landing more blows, trying to beat the other into submission.

Erin looked around for some sort of weapon. She could hit the bigger man from behind, stop him from his attack. But there wasn't anything she could use. Especially not without endangering herself. These were obviously bad people. She didn't want to be caught in their crosshairs.

She could see nothing she could use as a weapon.

She had no way to call for help.

She hadn't seen anyone else close by on the deck that she could call out to. She didn't have a phone or radio or any way to reach Terry or anyone else. She shook her head and bit the inside of her cheek, berating herself for not bringing a phone with her.

While she had looked away to assess any weapons or look for a way to get help, the struggle outside had progressed. The two men fought tooth and nail, the smaller one still getting some good blows in.

It looked like he was going to get away.

But then there was a blow that made the smaller man stop struggling. All of a sudden, he was limp in the bigger man's arms.

Erin held her breath, waiting for him to start fighting back again. Was it just a bluff? His way of trying to get in another blow that would stop the big man in his tracks?

"Oh, please," Erin murmured, waiting for the smaller man to start fighting again. But he didn't move.

The big man's body language relaxed. He looked at the other man in his grip. Then he shoved the other man up against the railing.

Erin thought at first that he was just waiting for the smaller man to come around. That it had just been a warning. The smaller man would change his mind and everything would be fine.

But the bigger man was not waiting for the smaller one to come to again. He folded the man over the top of the railing, which made Erin tense up again.

She took a step towards them, forgetting that there was a wall between them and that there was nothing that she could do to prevent whatever was happening from happening. Her foot and her face hit the wall, and she reached out, but her hands hit the wall too.

She held them around the porthole, staring through it, trying to stop what was going to happen with the power of her mind. She couldn't even use her voice, or the big man would be alerted that he had been observed, and he would go after her next.

After folding the smaller man in half over the railing, the bigger man bent down, picked up his feet, and neatly launched him over the railing. It was a long time before Erin heard the splash of the body hitting the water. Or maybe she just imagined she heard it hitting with the water so far below them. The engine noise seemed too loud for her to have made it out.

CHAPTER 10

S he again tried automatically to step forward to see the body going down into the water, to somehow reach through the wall and stop what was happening.

Pressed up against the wall and the porthole, she bit her lip to keep from crying out, tears streaming down her face.

She didn't even know the man who had gone into the water. He might have been a horrible person. The bigger man might have been completely justified in what he had done. But she couldn't help her emotional reaction.

Erin had seen violence before. Since moving to Bald Eagle Falls, she had seen more than one dead body, victims of violence. But seeing a man killed in front of her was something dreadfully new.

The big man stared down at the water for a long time. Erin was sure that the body must have disappeared under the water long before he turned away. A body dropped into the water would sink beneath the waves, wouldn't it? Or would it float on top of the water if it were not weighed down? She couldn't be sure whether the man was watching the body in the water, or was just thinking over what he had done and what he should do next. He would have to figure out how to explain his actions to his boss.

Finally, the big man started to turn back around, looking away from the water. Erin suddenly realized that she was exposed and ducked back from the porthole quickly, hoping that her sudden movement didn't attract his attention.

She remained frozen, leaning with her back against the wall, straining her ears for the sounds of footsteps. She didn't hear anything. Was he there still, standing on the other side of the porthole, peering in, trying to see her and figure out what she had seen and what he would do with her? Did he know that she was there and was just trying to figure out how to deal with her, or had she pulled back in time before he had a chance to see her?

She held her arms over her stomach, aching and nauseated again. How could she get mixed up in the middle of a murder? Was it murder when the two had been fighting and it was not preplanned? Or *had* it been planned, and she had been as taken in by the big man as the smaller man had been?

Erin tried to quiet her breathing. She tried to keep everything about her still and quiet, sure that the big man would be able to hear the wild thumping of her heart and her quick, shallow breaths. She wouldn't even be able to pretend that she hadn't seen anything if he saw her, he'd know by her respiration.

Then she heard the quiet creep of feet. The man was walking down the promenade away from her.

He might just be working his way toward the door to enter the area Erin was in, but for the moment, at least, he was moving away from her. That at least gave her a chance.

Erin went the other way.

She was hoping for a doorway that would lead her to a more populated section of the deck, and instead found a staircase. She climbed the stairs as quietly as she could, hoping that they would lead to something helpful. Maybe to a crew member who could page the captain for her or who would believe what she had just seen.

One step at a time, her knees quivering and shaking violently, Erin finally made it to the top. She looked around quickly to see where she could escape to next. But she had found the secret deck. It didn't run the full length of the ship, and had only one way in and out.

She had trapped herself.

Erin looked around for somewhere to hide.

She couldn't hear any footsteps approaching, but that didn't mean he wasn't still behind her.

There was no place to hide.

Her legs as wobbly as jelly, Erin staggered over to one of the deck chairs and she collapsed onto it. She picked up the newspaper someone had left behind and unfolded it. If the big man came, he wouldn't find anything suspicious. He wouldn't find a woman who had just watched him commit murder. He would just find an insomniac who had retired to the secret deck to read.

She stayed there for a long time, not reading the paper in front of her face, just waiting for the man's feet on the stairs. But they didn't come. It took time to convince herself that he wasn't just below her, waiting for her to come down the stairs and reveal herself. She breathed out slowly, swearing under her breath.

She finally forced herself to crawl off of the deck chair and over to the stairs to look down, her legs too weak to even stand.

There was no one looking back up at her. Erin gasped for breath, feeling like she had just run a race. If she weren't careful, she was going to start hyperventilating. Or hiccupping. She didn't want to do either one.

She stayed there, sure that the man was still there waiting for her, just out of sight.

Finally, Erin managed to pull herself to her feet, holding on to the railing around the stairs. She tried to look perfectly normal as she walked back down to the deck below her, sure that she looked anything but normal. Anyone looking at her would be able to tell there was something wrong.

But maybe she could just pass it off as seasickness. Everyone knew how sick she had been, even people she didn't know.

She looked around, trying to figure out the safest way back to her cabin. She was turned around, trying to remember whether her cabin was at the front or the back of the boat. She knew which way the killer had gone, but he was far away by that point. He didn't know that anyone had observed him, and he had just gone about his normal business.

Erin crept along the wall, past all of the little shops that were closed for the night, making her way to the stairs at the other end of the deck. She could hear music in the distance, maybe the karaoke bar, and she could hear the loud laughter and excited voices in the all-night casino. It was just a regular night for the other passengers on the ship. No one else knew about the terrible thing she had just seen.

She went instinctively toward the voices. It would be safer where there were people. She didn't want to be discovered wandering around the decks alone, especially not by the man. She didn't have any idea as to his identity. He could be anyone.

Erin was startled by a man stepping out of the casino right in front of her. He caught her as they nearly collided.

"Whoa, I'm sorry. Going a little too fast there. Are you okay?"

Erin nodded, forcing a laugh. "Yes, I'm fine. You just startled me."

He let go of her.

"I should have looked before I leaped. Are you going in for a game?"

Erin shook her head. The last thing she needed was somebody deciding that she needed a little help in the casino. She wanted to get back to her room and go back to bed. "No. I just got turned around. I was going to see if I could get some help back to my room."

"Oh! Well, there should be someone in here who could help you!" The man turned around, waving his arm in a big motion to someone inside. A crew member came out, looking inquiring. "Something I could help you with, sir...?"

"My young friend here is turned around. Looking for her stateroom."

"Certainly," the crewman nodded politely. "What number are you in, do you know?"

Erin swallowed; her mouth as dry as a desert. "I... yes..." she told him where she was supposed to be.

"I can walk you there, miss."

"No! No, I don't need you to walk me there, I just need you to point me in the right direction. I can find the way myself; I just got a little turned around."

He looked her over appraisingly, then maybe after deciding she wasn't too drunk to find her own way, he described slowly which stairs she needed to take to get to her own room and which way she needed to turn once she got down them. Erin listened attentively, realizing that she had, in fact, been going the wrong direction.

"That's great. I know where I am now, thanks."

"Are you sure you wouldn't like a hand back to your room? I can take you." He put his hand on her arm, smiling in a friendly fashion. Erin's skin crawled. She pulled back from him slowly, smiling brightly.

"Oh, no, I'll be just fine. Absolutely. I know where I'm going now. My boyfriend will be waiting for me."

At the mention of her boyfriend, he let go of her arm. Erin swallowed and tried not to betray her relief. She just wanted one thing, and that was to get back to her bed and Terry and the safety of his arms. He would take care of her. He always came to her aid when she was in trouble.

The two men looked at her, waiting for her to make the next move. Erin stepped back, pulling away from them, and moved in the direction that the crewman had indicated. "I've got it now," she reassured them. "Thanks for your help. You've been extremely helpful. Thank you."

She was rattled, and they could probably tell. She sounded like a babbling idiot. Erin glanced back over her shoulder to smile at them again and make sure that neither of them was going to follow her. The man who had almost run into her took off down another corridor, and the crewman gave her another smile and nod and then went back into the casino. She was once again alone.

CHAPTER 11

*F*inding her way back to her room proved not to be quite as easy as she had hoped, even once she had directions. The crewman had rattled everything off so quickly that even when she got to the right deck, she immediately turned the wrong direction and got herself mixed up again.

She stepped out through the door to the outer deck. The sea breeze was cold and helped her feel less nauseated and panicked. She could find her room faster if she just went around the outside like she had done earlier in the day, but looking over the railing down at the water, she felt queasy. If the man came across her, he could throw her over the railing much more easily than he had been able to dispose of the man. Erin was smaller and lighter and was so shaken that she probably wouldn't have even been able to kick him or scream.

Had the man who had been thrown overboard even screamed? Erin played it back in her mind. He had been quiet throughout the fight, until it had been too late. Why hadn't he called for help? Had he been too scared? Worried that he would be in trouble?

He should have screamed.

Maybe then someone would have come upon them who could do something to help. Instead, he had stayed quiet, and gone over the edge.

Erin turned to go back to the inner corridor and was blocked by a large crewman. She looked at his face, panicked, wondering whether it was the same man. Had he seen her after all? Had he followed her? He might have seen her on a surveillance camera and been able to track her at a distance. Now she was trapped, alone once more, close to the railing where he could just pick her up and throw her over, and no one would be any the wiser.

She would just be gone, and Terry would never know what had happened to her.

"No!" Erin protested, putting her hands out to protect herself.

He looked down at her, bemused. "Good evening, miss. Can I help you with something?"

She kept her hands up. It could just be a bluff. He might be the killer and fully intend to murder her once she got close enough or she was distracted by something else.

"I'm going to bed" she told him.

"You're in the wrong place if you're going to bed. You can't sleep out on the deck." He smiled at his own joke.

"I'm not sleeping out here, I was just going inside," she motioned behind him, pointing out that he was blocking her way.

"Are you okay, miss? You been drinking?"

"No, I haven't been drinking. I've been sick. I just wanted some fresh air. And now I want to go back to my room."

He looked at her for another minute, then moved out of the way, letting her past.

Erin breathed a sigh of relief and entered the hall that led to the cabins, looking at the signs to point her in the direction of her room. The crewman stood there watching her until she turned the corner. Erin was worried, flashing back to the man who had followed her at the hospital a few weeks earlier. Even though she had walked out to her car with a security guard, he had still been able to follow at a distance and to wait until she was alone again to attack her.

Now she was all alone again, and the crewman could follow her to some quiet corner and do whatever he liked without anyone being any the wiser. She should have taken K9 with her. He would have provided some protection, at least.

Erin walked faster, looking frequently over her shoulder for any sign of him. She almost walked right by her room.

"Erin!"

She nearly jumped out of her skin before she realized it was Terry. He held his arm out for her, and Erin hurried into the cabin, her body sagging with relief. Terry wrapped both arms around her and closed the cabin door.

"Are you okay? I woke up and you were gone. You shouldn't be out there wandering by yourself."

"Just needed some air," Erin murmured.

"You should have woken me up. We could have gone out together. I don't like you wandering out there by yourself."

"Me neither."

He studied her. "Are you okay? You're pretty pale. Do you need another motion sickness pill?"

Erin nodded. "Yes. And a sleeping pill," she said recklessly.

Terry's eyebrows went up. He knew that she never took sleeping pills. Sometimes she would take valerian or chamomile tea, but she always refused anything stronger, worried about how it would affect her in the morning. Even with her nightmares, she had refused to take anything stronger than her herbal remedies.

"Okay," he agreed. "I just don't know if you can take them both together. I'll look it up, okay?"

He walked Erin over to the bed and sat her down before picking up his laptop to do an internet search on the two medications to make sure they could be taken together.

"I suppose I could just call the doctor."

"No. Don't bother anyone else. The web will say whether they can be taken together."

He looked at her for a minute, then nodded.

"Sure, of course."

In a few minutes, he had satisfied himself that it was okay for her to take both of the pills together. He got a glass of water and gave her the two pills, then put the glass of water on the side table in case she needed it later.

He shut off the light and crawled into bed beside her. Erin cuddled up close, molding her body against his and closing her eyes, trying to lose herself behind her lids.

~

"Hey." Terry was shaking her gently.

Erin opened her eyes and looked around, trying to focus in on the walls around her and to figure out where she was. The surroundings were unfamiliar and, at first, she thought she was back in hospital again. Her head was throbbing and thick and she went back in her mind to the attack in the hospital parking garage.

"Terry? What happened?"

"Nothing happened. You just had a restless night. You took a sleeping pill."

"Oh."

She lay there, trying to remember what had happened. She gradually became aware of the thrum of the boat's engines. The stateroom became more familiar to her. She could smell food cooking on the other decks. They made everything from oatmeal to waffles for the tourists. Erin preferred a lighter breakfast of a piece of fruit and maybe a slice of toast. She was used to waking up early and not having a real breakfast until the first muffins were out of the oven at Auntie Clem's.

"Where are we going today?"

"Today is Juneau. Alaska's state capital. We get to see a glacier and a fish hatchery."

Erin rubbed her eyes. "What happened last night?"

"You went out for a walk, I guess. You should have woken me up."

"I shouldn't have been out there by myself," Erin agreed. She tried to sort out the pictures in her brain. "There was... something bad happened..."

Terry was sitting on the edge of the bed next to her, waiting for her to wake up properly.

"Something bad? What?"

"I... there were two men. They were arguing. And one of them..." Erin remembered the stockier man folding the other over the rail and then lifting him overboard. She stopped, feeling the blood draining from her face. She gasped, her eyes wide as she saw it all happening again.

"Erin...?" Terry's face was concerned. He picked up her hand, then felt her wrist, checking her pulse. "Are you okay? Do you need me to get you something? I thought you would be feeling better today."

"It's not... it's not the motion sickness. It's... there were two men, and one of them threw the other one overboard."

He didn't flinch. He just continued to hold her hand and look into her eyes. "You've had a lot of nightmares lately."

"No, this wasn't a nightmare. When I went out, there were two men arguing, and the one wouldn't do what the other one wanted, and he threw him overboard. They had a big fight and one of them killed the other!"

"It was the medication. It's affecting your dreams. Making you confused."

"No. It really happened!"

He nodded. "It seems very realistic. You'll feel better once you've been up for a while."

"It really happened!"

"Do you want breakfast?" Terry looked at his watch. "It's getting pretty late. We want to be ready when it's time to go on the tour."

Erin looked at the little clock on the bedside table. On a normal baking day, she would have been up for five hours already. She rubbed her eyes again, then massaged the back of her head. She was feeling groggy and like she might be getting a migraine.

Was is possible that she really had just dreamed the whole thing? It all seemed so real.

Was it something that her mind had just produced, the same as all of her other nightmares?

"Just... some fruit. I need a shower and something for my head, do you want to go get something and just bring me something back?"

Terry nodded. "Sure. Not a problem." He sighed and patted his stomach. "On a chilly morning like this, I could really use some bacon and eggs!"

"You could try some of that fake bacon and scrambled tofu." They had all laughed at the idea reading menus the day before. Terry wrinkled his nose. "No... I don't think so. Vegan pancakes are one thing. Tofu bacon and eggs are quite another."

"I hear they're really good. You can hardly tell the difference." Erin couldn't help teasing him in spite of how rotten she was feeling. If she weren't so queasy, she would have been up to trying some of the more adventurous vegan foods, but she didn't think she was ready for tofu for breakfast.

"If you don't watch out, that's what I'll bring you for breakfast," Terry warned.

Erin smiled and ducked her head, deciding she'd gone far enough.

"Have your shower then," Terry said, looking down at his watch again. "I'll be back shortly. We don't want to be late for the tour."

He let go of her hand and left to get breakfast. With a sigh, Erin pushed herself up from the bed and trudged to the bathroom.

~

Vic was bundled up in a thickly padded coat. She smiled merrily at Erin. "It might make me look as fat as Santa Claus, but at least it's warm!"

Erin nodded. "It looks like it. You'll enjoy today's tour a lot more."

"And how about you?" Vic cocked her head, looking at Erin. "I thought you'd be feeling better than yesterday too, but you're still looking pretty peaked."

Erin glanced around. She didn't want anyone overhearing their conversation. The crew members were not their tour guides in Juneau, so she didn't need to worry that the killer might be their guide for the day, but she hadn't seen him well enough to recognize him if he tagged along on the tour in plain clothes. And she couldn't be sure who else might be in on whatever scheme was going on aboard the ship. The other tourists should all be trustworthy, but she just didn't know enough about what was going on to be sure.

"Something happened last night," she told Vic in a low voice. "I'll tell you about it later."

"Something happened? Something like what? Between you and Terry?"

"No. It's not safe, I'll tell you later."

Vic raised her eyebrows, interested. "You'll tell me all about it?"

"Yeah. Later. When we're alone."

"But you're okay, right?"

Erin swallowed. She was more scared than she'd ever been in her life, and she'd been through some pretty stressful situations. She shrugged. "Yeah. I guess."

Terry and Willie came walking down the gangplank. Their heads were down, giving the impression that they were discussing something serious. Willie was walking slowly, somewhat hampered by his cast. K9 trotted along at Terry's side. Vic looked at Erin, her brows furrowed.

"You're sure you can't tell me now?"

"No. Not now."

CHAPTER 12

*E*rin's energy was flagging by noon. She didn't know if she was up to going anywhere else. They went their different directions for bathroom breaks. Vic noticed Erin's expression and gave her a hug around the shoulders. "You want to bow out this afternoon? Go back to the ship and you and I can hang out and talk?"

Erin was hesitant, but nodded. "Do you think the guys will mind? I know Willie is pretty interested in the fish hatchery."

"So they can go. We can split up. I'm sure we won't be the only ones who don't go to the hatchery. We can go back to the ship as a group."

One of the other tourists, a twenty-something with brilliant purple hair and a piercing in her nose, turned toward them.

"A lot of the group will be going back and skipping the hatchery," she advised. "Seeing farmed fish can be very upsetting. I don't know why they even included it on a vegan tour. Seems like they should have figured out that any kind of animal husbandry should be off the table." She gave a short bark of laughter at her unintentional pun. "So don't worry that you're going to be the only ones."

Erin smiled at the girl. "Thanks. I appreciate that."

"Great," Vic said briskly. "It's decided, then. We'll skip the rest of the tour today."

They rejoined Terry and Willie in the main gathering area and Vic told them she and Erin were going to return to the ship with some of the others.

"I'll go with you, then," Terry said immediately.

"No, you don't need to," Erin protested. "You and Willie wanted to see the hatchery, so go. Vic will keep me company. We haven't had any time with just the two of us. We have lots of gossip to exchange."

Terry rolled his eyes. "I should have known." He looked at Vic. "You'll stay with her?" It was more of an order than a question. Vic raised her brows.

"Yeah, I'll stay with her."

"I just want to make sure… she's still not feeling very well, and I don't want her… left on her own."

Vic patted Erin on the arm. "She'll be just fine with me, officer."

Terry looked like he would say something more. Erin knew he was concerned about her having nightmares.

"I'm not going to sleep. I just can't do any more walking. We'll catch some sun on one of the decks."

Terry glanced up at the sky, where the sun was trying to break through a cloud. "I don't think you're going to get very much sun out here. Besides, you'd have to take off your coats and Vic would turn into an icicle."

"We'll find something else to do, then."

Vic gave Terry a little shove. "Go on. I'll take care of her."

~

"What do you want to do?" Vic asked. "Go see a movie? Hit the gym? Maybe a game of checkers?"

"Let's just go to my room," Erin told her. "We need to be alone so that we can talk."

"Okay," Vic shrugged. "Whatever you want."

Her eyes were curious, but she didn't demand to know what it was Erin couldn't tell her yet. She waited, knowing that Erin would spill once they were alone.

It still took Erin a few minutes to find her room, but she was getting faster at it, and it was easier when she was not all turned around and freaked out by seeing a murder right in front of her eyes. Vic sat down on the couch and turned to her expectantly.

"So, what's going on?"

"Last night I went out for some fresh air, because I couldn't sleep."

Vic nodded.

"And I saw... I saw a murder."

Vic blinked. She smiled as if waiting for the punchline. Then the smile disappeared. "What do you mean, you saw a murder? Here on the ship? What happened?"

"Two guys were having a fight. An argument. And then a physical fight. And one of them knocked the other one out... and then threw him over the rail."

"Over what rail?"

Erin motioned to the outside of the deck. "Over the rail. Into the ocean."

"He threw him into the water?"

"Yes!"

"Threw him overboard?"

"Yes. He threw him overboard."

Vic was aghast. "What did you do?"

Erin did her best to describe the minutes after witnessing the murder, when she had hidden, run away, and cowered on the secret deck, sure that he was going to catch her and throw her over the rail as well. Vic shook her head, her face pale and eyes wide.

"Land sakes! You must have been dying! I can't believe it. So, then what? What did they say when you told them what had happened?"

Erin looked down at her nails. "I didn't tell anyone anything. I just... I couldn't handle it. I was so freaked out. Terry just took me to bed, and I took a sleeping pill and went back to sleep."

Vic frowned at this. "You took a sleeping pill?"

"Yes."

"And you just went back to sleep without telling anyone about this."

Erin sighed. "I know it doesn't make any sense when you say it out loud like that, but I was scared. I didn't know who might be involved. With my luck, I'd go right to the crewman who had done it to report what I saw. I couldn't. And I just wanted to forget and erase it and not have to think about it anymore."

"And what about this morning?" Vic grabbed Erin's hand and gave it a squeeze. "You told Terry about it?"

"You couldn't tell by the way he was treating me? Yeah. I told him about it."

"What's he going to do?"

"He doesn't believe me. He thinks it was just a dream. I just imagined it."

"Could you have just dreamed it? You've been sick. Sometimes we dream pretty weird stuff when we're sick. And Terry said... You've been having a lot of nightmares at home. He's been worried about you."

"I know he has. He keeps saying I should get therapy. I don't want therapy. Been there, done that. I don't want to tell anyone all of my troubles and I don't want to meditate or take pills or any of the other things they're going to suggest. I'll just deal with it by myself."

"Okay. As long as... you don't think that's what caused this. Maybe suppressing these dreams and these feelings is upsetting you so much that your unconscious mind is..."

"Throwing up murders in front of my face? You think that if I don't go get counseling, I'm going to keep seeing people murdered?"

"I don't know about that... but you might dream it. They say that your repressed thoughts and feelings come out in your dream. I know that's been true for me. When I'm trying to... be something I'm not or live by someone else's rules... I can tell from my dreams. Things get really disturbing. The feelings have to get out somehow."

"I didn't just dream this."

"I didn't say you did. We're just talking about Terry's theory. If it was a dream, then maybe you should consider therapy. Or if you think that the dreams are getting to be too much, then maybe you should think about it."

"I'm not getting therapy. And I didn't *dream* that someone committed murder last night. Somebody *did* commit murder last night."

"Then you should go to the captain and tell him what happened. They'll have to investigate. They'll have to... I don't know, dredge for the body. Call in the police. Figure out who it is that is missing."

"Yeah." Erin nodded. "That's what I should do. I'm just really afraid that..."

"That he won't believe you? Or that he'll be the guy?"

"I don't think it could be the captain. I've seen the captain, when we first got on the ship, and I'm pretty sure it wasn't him. It didn't look like him. I know I only saw him from behind, but the captain is taller, and he stoops a little bit. I just don't think… it didn't look like him. But I'm more afraid that he won't believe me. He'll be like Terry and just think that it was a dream or that I'm being hysterical. I don't want to be that woman. The one who causes everybody all kinds of trouble making things up. I just want… to do the right thing."

"Telling the captain is the right thing. It wouldn't be right to just pretend it didn't happen. Somebody is going to miss the guy that got killed, sooner or later, and wonder what happened to him."

"Yeah," Erin admitted. She knew it was the right thing. She hadn't been able to think of anything else.

But she didn't want him to laugh at her or make fun of her, or just not believe that anything had happened. There had always been a body before. She'd never had to prove that there actually was a death before. Other than with Bella's grandmother, and everyone had already believed that she was dead.

CHAPTER 13

*C*aptain Aro Jacobi was a tall, spare, serious-looking man. He looked very handsome in his suit and captain's hat and had a full beard. He looked a little like a very neat and polite pirate. He looked at Vic and Erin and sat down behind his big desk.

"Ladies, I understand you want to talk to me about something…?"

Erin didn't know how to start. She looked at Vic.

"Maybe I can anticipate," Jacobi said. "I understand that there was a bit of a scene caused by one of my crew members, Mr. Saville, when you first boarded. I'm afraid that there are people on the crew who are not as… tolerant as they should be. There are still a lot of prejudices despite all of the training that we might do to eliminate it. I apologize for any hurt feelings or embarrassment that you may have suffered."

Vic flushed a brilliant shade of red. "It isn't that," she said uncomfortably. "But… thank you. I do appreciate it."

"I think that you will find that most of the staff is more tolerant. We have a lot of… minorities who take the tours, especially the vegan tour. A lot of the passengers will relate to you and your background. And the staff should, for the most part, feel completely comfortable in dealing with you and any requests or problems that you might have."

"No, it's not that. Really. It isn't anything to do with me. It's Erin," Vic looked back over at Erin, trying to take the focus off herself. "I'm enjoying the tour, really. Things have been okay, other than when I first boarded."

"Good, I'm glad to hear it." He turned and looked at Erin. "And you, my dear? Have you been experiencing any prejudice from the staff?"

"Me? No. I'm… There's no reason for them to… everything has been fine."

He nodded. His eyes were clearly questioning, wondering why they had come up to bother him and take his precious time if there was not something seriously wrong. Erin supposed that there would always be women who just wanted to flirt with him or be invited to the captain's table for supper or get some other sign of favor from him. She cleared her throat and looked down at her shoes.

"I was taking a walk last night. Late. Looking around the ship. I thought I might find the secret deck and spend some time there."

Jacobi nodded encouragingly. "Yes, a ship like this can be quite the adventure. You wouldn't be the only one who was intrigued by its secrets."

"While I was looking for the deck, there were a couple of crewmen on the outside, the observation deck. And they were having a big argument."

Jacobi continued to look at her, waiting for her to get to the point.

"They came to blows… and one of them… threw the other over the rail."

His eyebrows climbed his forehead. Erin looked back down at her shoes, letting out her breath.

"I didn't just dream it. I really did see it happen."

"And who were these crewmen? Did you know them?"

"No. I didn't recognize them. I only saw them from behind, so even if it was someone whose face I would recognize… I never saw it."

"They didn't use names to address each other, even nicknames."

"No."

"Could you see any epaulets or rank insignia on their uniforms? Can you describe them in any way?"

"They were both about medium build… dark hair. It was dark outside, so I couldn't make out much more than their shapes, not their actual hair color. One of them was slim, and the other was quite a bit wider."

He considered this for a few moments. "There isn't anything else that could help to identify them? How skinny? How fat?"

"Not… nothing unusual. Just average."

"I see." He nodded.

"I thought… you know, there must be someone missing from your crew. You can find out who it was, and then maybe you know who he was with. His family will need to know, and you'll want to go back and look for a body…"

"No." He shut her down, shaking his head.

Vic and Erin stared at him. "No what?"

"No, we will not be doing any of that. I'm not in the habit of wasting my time on wild goose chases. I'm sorry, I know you're concerned about this, but chances are, you simply misunderstood what happened. They were pranking you, or you'd had a bit much to drink, or you just saw a couple of silhouettes and you didn't really know what was going on. It's fine. I don't judge you. But I'm not going to waste my time on every spurious report that comes through this office. Now, if you don't mind, I'll get back to my work…"

Erin sat there, frozen. She'd never anticipated that he would listen politely and then write it off. She'd been prepared for some emotional reaction. For mockery, even. She was prepared to be harassed and pushed around. But she hadn't expected to be brushed off.

"If that will be all, ladies…" Captain Aro Jacobi waited for them to vacate his office.

Vic stood up, looking at Erin. Erin got to her feet.

"You aren't going to do anything?"

"No, I'm not." He looked up at her from his papers. "You don't have any sort of proof, do you?"

"No. But when someone turns up missing…?"

"There are thousands of people employed on this ship. Most of them are under thirty. We constantly have people turn up missing. It is not something we worry about. They go off on a bender, stay ashore, fall in love. That's what happens on a cruise. Employee turnover is very high."

"You really don't believe me?"

"I believe that you saw something. But I don't think it is anything for me to worry about. Don't go wandering about the ship at night. That would be my recommendation."

～

They left Jacobi's office in stunned silence, neither of them sure how to process what he had just said. They had been expecting push-back, but not disinterest.

Arriving in the outer office, the reception area, they saw a middle-aged woman, dark haired, slim build, with clothes that looked to Erin to be very expensive, arguing with the receptionist. She looked up as Vic and Erin left Jacobi's inner office.

"Now can I go in?" she demanded. "They're out."

"Ma'am, you'll have to wait until I've had a chance to talk to the captain. You can't just go in unannounced. We have protocols…"

It was the same speech that Vic and Erin had heard when they arrived. Erin hadn't fought it; it made perfect sense to her that Jacobi would have a gatekeeper. You couldn't have the captain being interrupted by every passenger with a beef. He would never get any rest or be able to get his work done. The woman who was waiting didn't seem to agree. She thought she should be able to just walk in and see the captain as she pleased. She walked toward his door. The receptionist stood up and positioned herself in front it.

"Ma'am, do you want me to call security? I need you to sit down and wait until the captain is ready for you."

"Security?" The woman's voice rose several notes. "Do you even *have* security on this boat? There isn't any as far as I've been able to tell!"

"There certainly is," the receptionist said evenly. "Please have a seat in the waiting area."

"I want to speak to the captain."

"Then please sit in the waiting area." The receptionist pointed to the small grouping of chairs. "I cannot do my job while standing over here. Sit down and do as you're asked, and I'll do my best to help you out."

"You're not doing anything!" the woman groused.

Erin wondered what it was that the woman was there to confront the captain about. A theft, maybe? Or some slight by the crew? She didn't have to wait long to find out.

"My name is Carisa Shepherd. My daughter's name is Mackay Shepherd, and she is missing!" the woman insisted. "I would think that would be cause for some concern around here!"

"There are a lot of places to go on a ship like this. She's probably just off with some friends exploring the ship or participating in activities," the receptionist soothed. "You're sure she's not ashore for the tour?"

"No, she is not ashore for the tour. She has been missing since last night. I can't find her. She wouldn't just take off in the middle of the night. She never made it back to our suite."

"Kids do like to test the limits. If you'll just wait for a few minutes, I'll make sure the captain is aware of your concerns and you'll be able to see him."

Carisa Shepherd finally sat down in the waiting area chairs, looking angry and devastated at the same time. Erin realized that she was staring, and the woman had noticed her attention.

"I'm sorry," Erin said. "I couldn't help overhearing. I hope… everything is okay. You must be really scared."

"Of course I am. I can't believe that I can't get anyone on this ship to pay attention to my concerns. My daughter wouldn't just take off. She isn't just playing with other kids. She is missing."

"Where have you looked?" Vic asked. "Is there anything we can do?"

"There's nothing two or three women can do to search the whole ship. I've already looked all of the places where she might have gone on her own. But something has happened to her! She was supposed to be at the teen library, but they said she checked herself out of there around midnight last night. What is the point in having a secure place where teens can visit if they can just leave whenever they feel like it, without their parents being notified?"

"I… don't know…" Erin said. She looked over at Vic. Vic had left home as a teenager. Not a runaway, but a throwaway. Erin herself had been pretty independent as a teen, knowing that she was going to have to live on her own and support herself once she hit eighteen. She had not had to contend with a helicopter mother who wanted to know where she was at all times. True, she had generally had a curfew and had been expected to show up and be in her bed every night, but there were not really any consequences if she did not. You couldn't be with a teenager all the time.

"She probably is just off with some friends," Vic repeated what the receptionist had said. "It's pretty tempting in a place like this to just go off and have an adventure. But I'd be worried too. She doesn't have a cell phone?"

"Nothing works in this ship. They said it's because of all of the steel in the ship, but I think they're jamming signals. It's going straight to voicemail, like the battery is dead or it's been turned off."

Or as if someone were rejecting the calls as soon as they came in. Just because Mom was calling, that didn't mean a kid had to actually answer the call. She should, maybe, but there was no way to force someone to pick up a call if she didn't want to answer it.

"Well, I hope she turns up soon," Vic said. "And if there's anything we can do to help, really, just let us know..."

The woman shook her head. "It's sweet of you to ask, but I need the captain to take action here. I need them to perform a search. You're the only people who have shown any concern at all for my daughter. Everyone else just shrugs and says kids are like that and she'll turn up. But not all kids are like that. My daughter isn't like that. I need to find her. Something has happened to her and they can't keep ignoring the fact!"

They both nodded and made their exit. Erin looked at Vic. "You don't think this is related, do you? This isn't part of what I saw last night...?"

"You said that you saw a *man* thrown over the rail. Not a teenage girl. I think you would know the difference."

Erin raised one eyebrow. "Sometimes it's a little more complicated than that."

Vic chuckled. "Okay, sometimes it is," she admitted. "But I think if the daughter was a transgender man, the mother might have thought to mention that to us. I think we can safely assume that this missing girl has absolutely nothing to do with your man thrown over the railing."

"Other than that they both happened the same night on the same ship."

Vic shrugged. "There are thousands of people on board. I'll bet you those aren't the only two interesting things that happened last night."

CHAPTER 14

*T*he men were not yet back from their tour of the fish hatchery, and Erin did not feel like going back to her room to stare at the walls and be left with her thoughts. She was tired, but she wanted to sleep better when night came, so she didn't want to take a nap.

"What do you want to do?" Vic asked. "There are a lot of different activities we could try. Or we could go swimming. Take in a movie."

"If I go to a movie, I'm going to fall asleep, and it's too cold to swim."

"The water is heated. It looks really nice."

"I would still be cold when I got out of the water. And you'd be freezing the whole time, so I don't know why you're suggesting it."

"I don't know." Vic laughed. "Lots of people keep talking about how lovely the pool is, so I just thought I'd try. What do you want to do then? Go look for some food? Shop?" Her eyes lit up. "We both have a little spending money with us, if you'd like to go shopping."

"No," Erin said firmly. "No shopping. I want to know what happened last night... I can't just forget about it."

"What, then? You want to ask people questions? I don't think that's a good idea."

"No... I just want to have a look around. We don't have to ask anyone anything. I'll just... show you where everything happened. I know there won't be any evidence, but... I think we should look anyway."

Vic shrugged. "I don't think Terry would approve."

"That's why we're doing it when he's still ashore."

Vic grinned. "Okay, then. Lead the way."

Erin took a few minutes looking at the deck layouts and descriptions before she was reasonably sure where it was she had stood the night before and watched the drama unfold before her. She walked along the wall, touching it with one hand, and stopped by the porthole.

"Right here. This is where I was standing."

Vic looked around the interior of the room. There was nothing out of place, nothing to indicate that something violent had happened the night before. But Erin had been inside, and the two men had been outside. They walked down to the door that led to the outer deck and walked along the railing. Erin's stomach felt like it was being squeezed by a strong hand.

She knew she was being ridiculous. There would be no one there anymore. What had happened had taken place hours before and the man who had thrown his companion overboard would not be returning to see if anyone else had noticed something was wrong.

He'd be staying as far away from the scene as possible.

Erin scanned the deck, looking for scuff marks or blood. The fight had been violent, and the man had likely been bleeding when it was over. But she didn't see even a drop of blood. She looked back at the portholes, trying to find the place she had been standing and therefore where the two men had talked and fought. She followed the sight lines in her head, and stopped at a place along the rail, looking for some marking on the surface.

"Right here?" Vic asked, looking down at it as well.

Erin nodded. But there was no sign that a man had gone over the rail. No scratches or blood on the railing. The brushed metal surface shone.

Vic looked over the edge, all the way down to the water. She shook her head. "That's a pretty long fall."

Erin didn't want to look, but she held tightly to the railing and looked down. She felt lightheaded. "Oh boy…"

Vic's hand was on her back. "It's okay, honey. Just take deep breaths. There's nothing we can do from here. If someone went over the rail into the water, there's no way for us to tell from here."

"No."

"So, let's get back from the rail."

Erin nodded, swaying uncertainly. She stepped back from the rail, looking away from the water, trying to ground and steady herself once more. "Oh. What's this...?"

Vic looked as Erin bent down and picked up something shiny from the deck. "What is it?"

"A button." Erin held up the shiny gold button. "From a uniform."

~

Vic stared down at it, looking from several different angles. It was, indeed, a gold button. From one of the crew uniforms. Anyone could have lost it at any time. But it was right where the fight had occurred.

"You probably shouldn't have picked it up. You might have obliterated fingerprints," Vic pointed out.

Erin looked at the button pinched between her fingers. Of course Vic was right. She should have left it where she found it, or picked it up with gloves and put it into a plastic evidence bag. She had contaminated evidence, something that with all of her experience with crime scenes she knew better than to do. Her heart sank.

"But no one else is going to be looking for evidence. The captain doesn't even believe that the fight happened. He thinks that I just made it up, or that if it happened, it wasn't important. I don't understand how that could be. They were fighting about something. Something going on in this ship that was important enough that one of them dumped the other overboard to keep anyone from finding out about it."

Vic stared at her. "What?"

"They were talking about some kind of scheme. Something that the victim said he didn't want to do. He had been involved in it up to that point, but they had asked him to do something he didn't want to do."

Erin stood there, staring at the button, trying to remember the details. It had all happened so quickly. She hadn't been able to hear clearly, or to see their faces or who was talking. But there had been... some kind of conspiracy going on... something that the smaller man didn't want to be involved in.

"What kind of thing? Like burglarizing cabins? Stealing from passengers?"

"Yeah, maybe," Erin agreed. "I don't know for sure what it was. They weren't fighting over a girl or a bet or something. They were arguing about business. Money. And the bigger man, he said something about his boss. So it's something with an organized hierarchy, not just something the two of them were in on."

"Did you tell all this to Terry? And why didn't you bring it up to the captain?"

"Because…. I don't know who the boss is. What if it is the captain? He's everyone's boss, isn't he? He could be in charge of this. Whatever it is."

"I suppose," Vic said slowly. "He could be in charge of something criminal. It's not like he wanted to investigate what had happened."

"Maybe because he already knew. Maybe that's why it didn't come as any surprise to him."

Vic nodded and scratched her ear. "So what do you think it was? It could be theft. Or rigging something illegally in the casino. Or… I don't know, something like smuggling. They are crossing international borders, and I don't know how thoroughly a ship like this is searched when it goes from the US to Canada and back to the US again. They could be smuggling drugs or… some endangered species… I don't know."

"Maybe wild ginseng," Erin said, allowing for a moment of lightheartedness. They had learned recently just how expensive and how much in demand wild ginseng was. It would be easy to smuggle through the kitchens, mixed in with other root vegetables or herbs and spices. It didn't look that much different from parsnips or ginger.

Vic smiled briefly and shook her head. "I highly doubt if it's wild ginseng! But it could be drugs."

"Yeah."

"Do you remember exactly what they said? Did it sound like they were talking about drugs?"

"I don't know… I couldn't hear everything clearly, and I was already panicking… It's all muddled. I was sick and then I took a sleeping pill. I just don't know. I can't think of anything they said that might have excluded drugs… or anything else. They both knew what they were talking about, and they didn't take the time to explain it in general terms."

"That makes sense. I wouldn't talk about it openly if I was involved in something. Even if I didn't think there was anyone around to hear."

"So, what do we do with the button?" Erin held it in the palm of her hand, looking at it.

"I don't know. Ask Terry, I guess. He'll be able to tell you whether you can do anything to force an investigation. We must be able to call the police and get them involved. We're in Juneau, that's the state capital, so there's probably state police here."

CHAPTER 15

They were in the main restaurant when the tour group got back from the hatchery. When she saw people from the tour starting to return to the ship, Erin texted Terry to let him know where they were. The text failed several times before it said it was delivered, leaving Erin with doubts about whether he actually got it or not. They watched the door and waved when Terry and Willie arrived. The men were looking flushed and relaxed, ready for a substantial meal. Terry looked Vic and Erin over as he sat down.

"So... are you feeling any better?" he asked Erin.

He didn't say that she wasn't *looking* much better, but it was implied. Erin shrugged her shoulders. She placed the gold button on the table in front of Terry's plate with a soft click. He looked down at it.

"What's this?"

Erin didn't say 'it's a button,' which wouldn't have been at all helpful. She let him look at it for a minute before he looked back at her face, waiting for an answer.

"I found that on the deck. Where the two men had the fight last night."

Terry looked at Erin, then over at Vic. Vic nodded her head, indicating that she'd been read in on the situation and that she'd been there when Erin found the button. Willie was the only one who was left out, not knowing what Erin claimed to have seen the previous night.

"Let's order drinks," Terry suggested.

None of them were heavy drinkers, but it seemed like an appropriate time to have something with their meal. Erin was exhausted from all of the mental conflict, so she didn't object. The kitchen was carrying a variety of vegan wines and beers, so they placed their orders. Willie's eyes were on the button. He waited for them to tell him what was going on.

"Erin had a restless night," Terry said slowly. "She's been having a lot of nightmares and the night before, she was even sleepwalking. So that's really not anything new. What is new, however, is the fact that she says she saw two crewmen fighting last night, and that one of them threw the other into the drink."

Willie looked from one face to the other. "And you're just getting around to telling me this now? What, we were just going to see if it went away?"

Terry pressed his lips together, saying nothing.

Erin spoke up. "He doesn't believe me. That's why. He thinks I imagined it."

"But we found the button," Vic pointed out. "So it obviously wasn't just a dream."

"That button could have been lost there by any crewman at any time. There's no way to tell whose button it is."

"If we can find someone with a button missing from their uniform…" Erin suggested, "then we could be sure. We'd know who it was that was involved in the fight, and that would be a good place to start the investigation."

"What if someone lost it innocently? What if someone did lose it in a fight, but they sewed a new one onto their uniform before wearing it this morning? Or dumped the old uniform and put on a new one? How are we supposed to prove any wrongdoing? A button doesn't prove anything."

"It's not proof," Erin agreed. "But at least it's a little bit of evidence that I did see something. I was there. It wasn't just a dream. This button isn't just a figment of my imagination."

"It could have been left there by anyone at any time since the boat left port. You have no way of knowing where it came from."

"It's just a coincidence that it was right where Erin said there was a fight and a man was thrown overboard?" Vic demanded. "Whatever happened to 'I don't like coincidences'?"

"I still don't like them," Terry agreed.

The waitress delivered their drinks to them and took their meal orders. Erin couldn't even think of food. She shook her head. "I didn't dream it, Terry. I know the difference between a dream and real life."

"But dreaming and hallucinating when you are sick is different altogether. You don't know how it might have affected you. Hallucinations can seem very real."

"I know the difference," Erin insisted.

"Okay." Terry held up his hands and shrugged. "Okay. Assume it was real. Where do we go from here?"

"I don't know." Erin had been building herself up over the past hour while they talked and waited for Terry to get back from the tour, but her good spirits came crashing down. "We went to the captain and told him about it."

Terry nodded. "And? What did he have to say about it? What is he going to do?"

"He isn't going to do anything at all."

"It's pretty hard to prove wrongdoing when there's no body. There are a lot of issues with accusing someone of murder when you don't have a body."

"But it's possible. You can convict someone of murder without ever finding the body."

"Yes, of course. But if the captain isn't convinced…"

"I don't understand how he could be so blasé about it. He acted like… it wasn't anything to be concerned about. How could you have someone come to you and tell you there was a murder and not even care about it?"

"I understand why you're frustrated. I'll do a bit of research, but the law on boats like this can get a little complicated… I'm not sure who has jurisdiction. If the captain doesn't want to do anything about it, the buck may stop there. That may be all we can do."

"What about the FBI? There must be someone who can open an investigation. A man was killed! It doesn't matter whether he is on a boat or on land, does it? There's still a law!"

"I'll look into it."

Willie took a swig of his beer, watching them. "Do you know who it was? How much did you see?"

"Not enough to identify them. Two men. Medium height. One of them was wearing a white uniform and the one who got thrown overboard wasn't.

But it sounded like they both worked here. I couldn't see their faces, only their backs."

"That's not much to go on."

"I know it doesn't narrow it down very much. But I'm not going to make things up. I'm telling it like it is. That's what I saw."

"I believe you."

Erin felt a warm flush. After everyone else's reactions, she was happy that at least someone believed, without any reservations, that she had seen what she said she had seen. And he cared about it.

"I want to find out who it was. I don't want their loved ones to think that he just... ran off somewhere and never came back. I want them to know how he was killed, and why."

Vic patted Erin's hand. "Of course you do. You're a good person. You care about people. We'll figure it out. If we can. It might take a while."

"It might not be possible without the assistance of the crew," Terry said. "If the captain has said that they aren't going to do anything... the crew members are supposed to obey him. It's a militaristic power structure. The captain is over everyone and he isn't to be disobeyed."

"But people must," Erin pointed out. "This isn't the fourteen hundreds anymore. People can think for themselves and there are other opportunities and other places for them to go if he doesn't like it. It's more important to do the right thing than to just obey a power figure."

"That may be true. But you may also find that the people who tend to be employed here are very young or very poor. Both of those demographics are easy to intimidate."

Erin let out a sigh. She sipped at her wine and stared at the button, trying to figure out what to do about it. There had to be something that she could do to figure out who had been thrown overboard, even if she couldn't figure out who had done it.

"They must be able to tell who is missing pretty quickly. Crew members must have to check in and out. And there must be surveillance. It's not the dark ages. We have the technology."

"Good thoughts," agreed Terry. "If we can get them to cooperate."

∽

They talked about other things and listened to the lounge act and eventually got their plates. Erin still wasn't very hungry, and had ordered a salad and sandwich, but neither appealed very much to her as she sat there looking down at them. Vic had ordered a pizza. It had artichokes and other unusual vegetables on it and no cheese. Terry had encouraged her to order the no-cheese version rather than the vegan cheese, which he seemed to be developing a distinct dislike for.

"If it's not real cheese, they should just leave it off," he said. "They should just leave well enough alone. Some things you just can't replicate with vegetables."

He had ordered a Japanese dish with lots of noodles and rice and fewer vegetables than Erin would have expected. Willie had accepted Terry's recommendation of the chili and had a bowl, sans cheese, for his main course.

Erin picked at her sandwich. There wasn't anything wrong with it but, on the other hand, it wasn't anything very exciting, either. If she were making it, she would have used a rustic loaf of hand-shaped bread, and grilled veggies, and some kind of sauce... she wasn't sure what, yet, but not just mayonnaise. Maybe aioli. Maybe hummus. Something that wasn't just mustard or mayo.

"Not very good?" Terry asked.

"It's fine. I'm just not very hungry. My stomach is still a little queasy."

"You're probably about due for another motion sickness pill, don't you think?"

"Yeah... I guess. I'll have one after dinner, when we go back to our room."

"I thought you were going to do something with us tonight," Vic objected. "Dancing or playing a game or something. You're still not feeling up to it?"

"No. I don't think so. And if you suggest a movie, I'm just going to fall asleep in the middle of it, so you may as well just watch it without me."

"Okay... I hope you're feeling better tomorrow."

"Me too."

Willie had been tapping away on his phone, without any indication of what he was doing, but then he looked up, pushing it away from himself. "Wifi in this place sucks. You're right about there being jurisdictional issues, though," he told Terry. "The jurisdiction of the boat when it is in international waters is the country the boat was registered in."

"I wonder where the Carolina is registered. It's a US tour, so that must be where it is registered."

Willie shook his head. "Nope. According to online chatter, it's registered in Liberia."

Erin blinked at him. "Liberia? I don't even know where that is. Why would it be registered in Liberia?"

"Apparently something to do with favorable tax treatment. In other words, the fewer laws they have to obey, the better. But that also means that if you wanted to open a police investigation, you would have to get Liberian officials involved. You would have to get Liberian police on the ship. And since they are halfway around the world… chances are pretty slim that they would send anyone."

"That doesn't make any sense."

"Maritime law is different. Chances are, if we try reporting it to the Juneau police, they're not going to be able to do much."

Erin continued to pick at her sandwich, thinking about it. Terry tried to catch her eye a few times, but Erin deliberately ignored his glances. What was the good of having an officer for a boyfriend if he wouldn't even use the weight of his position to look into a murder? She couldn't believe that he was just going to stand aside and let an injustice go without being addressed. "There's a missing girl, too," she said.

Terry's head turned toward her. He didn't say anything at first, concentrating on his noodle dish, but he couldn't resist asking for more details. There was his cop's curiosity, even if it was a bit late to the party.

"A missing girl?"

"Yes. We were talking to her mother when we got out from reporting the murder to the captain." Erin looked at Vic. "You might want to tell him that I didn't just dream or imagine it. I wouldn't want him to think that I am just making it up."

Vic rolled her eyes. "Erin… give the guy a break. It's understandable that he doesn't want to believe that there might have been a murder on the ship. And that you might have been a witness… again. This was just supposed to be a vacation. A getaway, to relax and put all of that stuff behind us. Behind you, especially."

"It's not my fault that it followed us here."

"No. I just mean… you can see why Terry doesn't want it to be true. I'm not saying that it isn't. I'm saying that he doesn't want to believe it. He doesn't want to believe that you were in danger. That something could have happened to you here, where it was supposed to be safe."

Erin looked over at Terry. He was watching her seriously. No dimple.

"I'm not making it up about the missing girl, either. Her mother was looking for her."

"A little girl or a teenager?"

"Teenager. Her mother was very concerned, though. She had gone all of the places that the girl should have been. She had never gone back to her cabin last night."

"Kids do things like that. I imagine there are a lot of teens who stay out past curfew on a ship. They want to let it all hang out too."

"Something might have happened to her."

"You think she was thrown over the rail too? I think two people being thrown overboard on one night would be quite a coincidence. I don't think that actually happens very often on cruise ships."

"I didn't say she was thrown overboard," Erin said crossly. Terry might think he was being amusing, but he wasn't. She didn't like his poking fun at her.

Terry frowned. "Did you want me to look into this girl's disappearance too? You said the mother went to the captain. Was he going to start any kind of search for her?"

"I don't know. We didn't stay around long enough to find out."

Erin looked around the restaurant, seeing if she could spot Carisa. She had almost forgotten about the incident with the discovery of the button. But she wouldn't forget Carisa Shepherd's face, so distraught over the disappearance of her daughter.

Vic glanced around too. "I don't see her."

"No, me neither."

"That doesn't mean that they didn't find her," Terry said. "They just aren't eating dinner right now. A lot of people won't eat until later. You guys are used to eating early, and we were hungry after our tour, but," Terry looked at his watch, "it's still pretty early for the supper rush."

"I hope they found her."

"Yeah," Vic agreed. "It would be pretty awful to lose your kid in a place like this. I'd be so worried about all of the things that could happen to her.

You don't know what kind of people might be on a ship like this. I mean, there isn't any screening. You think that everyone is just out to have a nice vacation, but there's nothing to say that a predator couldn't come aboard just as easily."

"I think a predator would be found out pretty quickly," Terry said. "You only have a limited population and a limited area to perform any crime in. There are cameras, lots of staff. It would be pretty hard to commit a violent crime and keep it quiet."

"Unless it was dark and late at night and there was no one else around," Erin said. "Then it might be pretty easy."

He looked at her, shaking his head. "Do you want me to look into this, Erin? Into what you saw?"

Erin noticed he didn't refer to it as a murder. She was surprised that he would even have to ask. Why did he think she had told him about it? Why did he think she kept giving him details and had shown him the button and asked about law enforcement on board a cruise ship? "Yes! Of course I want you to."

"Because you know it's not any of my business, right? This isn't my jurisdiction. Especially not if the law of some other country is in force. We're docked right now, so I think that means we're not in international waters and US law prevails, but I'm not a lawyer and this certainly isn't Bald Eagle Falls. What I'm saying is, I don't have any authority here. No more than you do. As far as the officials here are concerned, I'm just a civilian."

"But that doesn't mean you can't ask some questions, take a look around. Ask them if they'll investigate. I know the captain already said no, but saying no to a couple of women who show up with a strange story and saying no to a police officer is different."

"Maybe. Don't count on it. This is the captain's domain and he won't like having his initial judgment questioned. He wants things his way."

"Yeah. I know. But if you ask... there isn't any harm in asking and in taking a look around, is there?"

"Maybe I'll take a quick look around before I ask him to investigate. So that I at least know what I'm talking about."

"I can take you up to that deck. I'll show you. I'll show you exactly where it happened, and I'll explain it all to you."

"Okay. We can do that after dinner. It's already getting dark, so I don't want to put it off and I don't think you do either."

CHAPTER 16

$\mathcal{E}$rin showed Terry to the deck where she had witnessed the two men fighting, just as she had shown Vic, walking him through what had happened, where she had been standing and what she had seen. She indicated the place where she had found the button on the deck and showed Terry where the wider man had pushed the other over the rail.

"The one in uniform was the aggressor," Terry said. "So it wasn't the one whose body was slid over the rail who popped a button."

Erin nodded. "Right. The bigger one was the one who was dressed up. The other one was just in casual wear."

"And you don't know for sure that he was on the crew. He could have been a passenger or other worker."

"Yeah. Could have been. But I got the feeling… I don't know that it was anything they said or did, I just got the feeling that they worked together. That they were both staff."

Terry walked around, looking for any physical evidence of what had happened. He walked through it himself, looking through the porthole to the place where the fight had taken place. Erin took him up to the secret deck, embarrassed by how frightened she had been, but determined to tell him the whole story and convince him that it had been true, not just a dream.

"Had you been up here before last night?"

"No. Last night was the first time. I just looked on the deck maps, because Mary Lou had said there would be a secret deck. I thought I would find it and just sit there looking at the stars or the water until I got tired enough to sleep."

"You hadn't come up here for anything else before."

"You know I didn't. I'd been stuck in our cabin the whole time, seasick."

"Well," Terry scratched his jaw, "other than when you were sleepwalking, yes."

Erin stared at him. "Sleepwalking? I didn't sleepwalk."

"You did. I went for dinner, and when I came back, you were wandering around on your own. And you were asleep. No doubt of that."

"Where was I?"

"Still on our deck, just wandering the halls and out to the observation area. I was scared that you could have gone over the rail yourself. You could easily have had an accident or done something without realizing it was dangerous because you were dreaming."

"I didn't!" Erin couldn't believe it.

Terry nodded. "You did. That's one reason I figured… that this thing about the fight was just a dream."

"But it wasn't. I've shown you everything. You can see that I didn't just make it up. Dreams are different. The setting changes when your mind goes off in another direction. All kinds of things that aren't possible in real life happen."

Terry nodded. "It holds together when you describe it and walk through it," he admitted. "If it was a dream… I'd expect there to be some contraindications. That you wouldn't actually be able to see them through the porthole. Or that the secret deck was actually three decks away instead of just one. But it's all very cogent…" He looked around. K9 sniffed along the walls, but didn't seem to find anything that concerned him. "You've already been through this to describe it to Vic, but you would have figured out when you were showing her if something didn't fit with the narrative of your dream—your memory."

"But everything fits, because I was here. I really did see it."

"I'll talk to the captain, see if he has any thoughts… I don't know about calling the Juneau police or the FBI. I can't promise anything like that."

"Okay. But you'll talk to him. You'll tell him that you believe me and you think I really did see what I said I did."

"Yeah. I'll do my best. If something really did happen here, he's going to want to know about it. Especially if there is some sort of criminal activity that could reflect back on him or the company. He's going to want to know about that."

"You don't think he's involved, do you? What if he was part of all of this? What if he is the boss?"

"Do you think he is?"

"No… I just worry. Some people are really good at hiding who and what they are." Erin let the words hang in the air. He knew who she was thinking of. He knew all of what had happened since she had moved to Bald Eagle Falls, and how people had fooled both of them, keeping their secrets hidden until they were forced to show their hands. Erin had been the target of unexpected violence more than once. People she had trusted and been friends with until suddenly the whole world had flipped upside-down.

"But you don't think he was involved. From what the men said during their argument? From anything the captain said to you? You don't think he had anything to do with it?"

"No. I'm just worried. I don't want to be a suspicious person, but I can't help worrying now whenever I like someone that they might actually be the bad guy. I hate that…"

"It's hard to realize that you can't trust everyone."

"I never thought I was a particularly trusting person to begin with," Erin confided, staring out at the darkening sky. "Growing up the way I did, I learned you can't trust people to take care of you or to do the things they said they would. I knew that people put on a false front and pretended to be one thing to the social workers when they were something else behind closed doors. But not trusting authority figures is different than not being able to trust anyone, not even the ones closest to you." She turned to look at Terry, staring into the bottomless depths of his dark eyes. Was that how he felt when he looked at her? That even though he loved her, he couldn't trust her?

"It will be okay, Erin. We'll sort it out," he said softly.

"I don't know. Like you said, there are thousands of people on board the ship. How do we figure out who it was? How do we know who on the crew can be trusted and who can't?"

"I don't want you to be off on your own," Terry said, not answering her question. "I want to know where you are and that you always have someone with you."

He didn't say the rest of it. That if someone on the crew found out what she had seen, she wouldn't be safe. There was nowhere on the ship that she could go without being followed. She couldn't go home and lock the door and arm the burglar alarm. She was vulnerable to whoever was involved in the plot.

Erin stayed with Vic and Willie in their room while Terry went to talk to the captain about his findings. He hoped to catch the captain before the usual formal dinner time, when the captain might be drinking or consider himself off duty. He wanted to get him to consider the circumstances as early as possible, because the longer it was before an investigation was started, the less they were going to be able to discover.

"You want to play cards? Watch TV?" Vic asked. "We're on vacation. What would you really like to do? We can go out if you want to."

"I don't think Terry wanted me to. He wants me to stay here with you."

"But you'll be fine if the three of us are together. Nothing is going to happen to all three of us. And out there, where there are a lot of people, that's actually safer than being out of sight in our cabin. If something happened to us here, no one would know it. If we're out there where people can see us, no one will dare do anything to us."

Erin was sure Vic was correct, but she didn't want to be out in public where the crew could see her. What if the killer *had* seen her the night before? What if he had caught a glimpse of her and was just biding his time until he could take care of her?

Maybe he had seen her sometime that night but not put it together that she had seen and overheard them. But now she'd talked to the captain and Terry was going to talk to the captain. They were going to do whatever they could to find out who had been killed and who the killer had been. If they did that, the killer would know. He would know he'd been seen, and by whom. If he hadn't already heard rumors of what she had reported to the captain, he would soon.

"What do you want to do?" Vic asked softly. "Do you want a nap? You've been going all day now. I know you're worried about waking up in the middle of the night, but I think you're safe now. Your body needs the rest."

"No, not yet. Thanks. I'll go to sleep later, after Terry gets back." After she had heard from him. After she knew what the captain had said and whether there was going to be any investigation. "I'll just... I want to think things through."

Willie was sitting at the writing desk. He looked up from his computer. "You have some thoughts on what might have happened?"

"No... I know what happened. I just don't know who or why. Except that the victim was supposed to do something, and he didn't want to."

"An attack of conscience. And that made him too dangerous to the killer, or too dangerous to the entire enterprise. So much so that he had to be disposed of immediately. There wasn't any more attempt to convince him. He wasn't going to leave it to later and see if he could convince him. It was now or never."

Erin nodded. "I wish I knew what it was they were involved in." She looked around for something to write on. Vic caught her look and frowned.

"What are you looking for?"

"I thought there might be... a notepad..."

Vic grinned. "Oh, it's time for a list, is it?" she teased. "Willie, is there some paper in that drawer?"

Willie started opening and closing the drawers of the desk. He handed Erin a scratch pad with the Carolina's logo on it, and a stick pen similarly branded. "I don't know what kind of quality those are."

"They'll do." Erin took the writing implements and sat down on the bed, letting her breath out.

"You really should just write your lists on your phone," Vic pointed out, not for the first time. Erin knew it was pretty old-school to do all of her thinking and lists in longhand, but she just didn't think the same way when putting notes on the phone. And she couldn't help thinking that she was going to lose them if she left them in some electronic cloud.

She knew how the technology worked, and that her lists were probably safer stored on some big corporation's server than on a crinkled-up note in her pocket or purse, but she had an irrational fear that she would lose them. She had to be able to put her hands on them physically. That was the only way they brought her comfort. It just wasn't the same writing electronic notes. She couldn't hold them in her hands.

"I'll just jot a few things down here," she told Vic, not arguing the point. Vic already knew all of the arguments. She just liked to tease.

"You want to know what kind of crimes could be going on on the ship?"

Willie asked, staring up at the ceiling as he thought about it. "I don't know a lot about the statistics, but I would say you're going to have similar crimes to what you would have living in a small town like Bald Eagle Falls. You're going to have drug smuggling and using. People come someplace like this, they want to party, and alcohol isn't going to do it for someone used to more. There must be drug suppliers on board, likely in the crew."

"Why in the crew?"

"Because they're the ones who know the ins and outs of getting things on board. And because they're on every cruise."

Erin wrote drugs down at the head of her list.

"You don't think that was it?" Willie asked, trying to read Erin's expression and body language.

"No... but no reason. It just doesn't resonate. The victim was involved in drug smuggling or dealing, and then they asked him to do something that was beyond what he was willing to do... like what? He was already smuggling or dealing drugs. What would they ask him to do that would be worse than that?"

"No idea," Willie admitted. "What else? Theft. I imagine there is a lot of theft that goes on on a ship like this. People have money. They bring cash or traveler's checks. Jewelry. Electronics. They have a false sense of security when they lock something in their cabin or in the room safe."

"Anyone on the crew could get into the cabin," Vic agreed with a nod.

"But wouldn't the captain know something was going on if there were a lot of reports of thefts?" Erin asked.

"I would imagine there are thefts on every ship. And also people losing things and saying they were stolen. And people saying something was stolen in order to claim it on their insurance. They would be used to a certain level of theft. And as long as the criminals didn't do anything too bold and raise people's suspicions, they could stay below the radar."

Erin wrote it down on her list. It made sense, just like drug smuggling and dealing. But it still didn't strike her as the type of thing that would have produced such a violent response when the thin man had decided to back out. They would just be able to hold his past involvement over his head. *If you talk, we'll turn you in. We have proof you stole this or that.* They wouldn't throw him overboard.

CHAPTER 17

There was a soft knock on the door of the cabin. Erin turned and looked at it, her heart squeezed in her chest. Vic and Willie looked at each other, but neither of them was expecting company. Terry would have just entered. Even if he knocked first to be polite, he would then let himself in if it were unlocked so that they wouldn't have to get up to get the door.

Vic eventually got up and went to the door. She opened it a crack and looked out at the caller. Then she opened the door wider and Erin saw it was Carisa Shepherd.

"Did you find anything out?" Vic asked immediately. "Did you find her?"

"We found her…" Carisa looked far more worried than someone who had just found her lost child had any right to. "but… things are not right."

"Not right," Vic repeated.

"She's in the infirmary, under the doctor's supervision. I didn't know where to go. There's no point in talking to the captain or anyone on the crew. Everybody thinks that I'm just overreacting… You're the only one who really took me seriously and offered to help. I don't really know even what to ask for… I just need someone to talk to."

Vic motioned her into the room. "Come in. Tell me about it."

The woman entered the cabin. She looked at Erin and nodded. Her eyes went over to Willie, widening.

Willie always had been a rough-looking character. At least for as long as Erin had known him. His mining and processing of metals meant that his skin was stained dark. Not like a tan, but he looked like he was dirty. Like he hadn't washed in weeks. Erin happened to know that he was very exacting about his hygiene, but a stranger couldn't tell that. He looked filthy and imposing instead of reflecting the kind of man he really was. He was infinitely gentle and loving toward Vic and a good friend to Erin. He was always willing to lend a helping hand. He'd been involved in rescuing Erin more than once when she got herself into a tight situation.

He had a cast on his leg that matched the one on Vic's arm, something that demanded explanation.

"This is Willie," Erin said. "Don't mind the way he looks. He's a pussycat. He's really helpful. He's been involved in search and rescue, so he might have some input on your daughter and... whatever it is you're worried about."

The woman didn't know how to take that. She didn't know whether to believe Erin or her own eyes. She sat down on the end of the bed and looked at the three of them, the worry and anxiety clear on her face.

"My daughter... Mackay. We found her. But there's something wrong with her. They said that maybe she was drinking too much or taking drugs with the other teenagers. But I know she wasn't with them. If she was with them, I would have found her when I was looking for her, because that's who I went to. They didn't know where she was."

"What's wrong with her?" Erin prompted.

"She can't tell me what happened to her last night. She doesn't remember. She doesn't remember anything after I left her with a group of them at the teen library last night."

"Nothing at all?" Erin found it hard to believe.

"No, nothing. I keep telling her things, that it's been almost twenty-four hours since I saw her last and she doesn't even believe me. She just keeps staring at me and repeating things, saying that she's tired and wants to go to bed now."

"Maybe she just needs to sleep it off," Vic said. "If she did have alcohol or some drug, then she'll be fine after it wears off."

Carisa looked at them, shaking her head. "Something is really wrong. I think... I don't think she was doing ecstasy or some recreational drug with those other teens. I think… someone drugged her. Some kind of… date rape drug."

"Was she… assaulted?" Vic asked delicately.

"The doctor won't perform any kind of examination. He said that there are a lot of false reports of sexual assault on ships like this, because people's inhibitions are lowered and then they have regrets afterward. They do things that they wouldn't do if they were at home, so they feel bad and make up stories about how it wasn't consensual."

Erin's heart thumped and her blood boiled. Trust a man to fly that flag. It wasn't really assault; she just changed her mind afterward. How many men had said the same in the past?

"What does your daughter say? Does she say she was assaulted? Does she want them to do a rape kit?"

"She's barely speaking," Carisa said. "She won't answer questions and she certainly doesn't know what it is she wants. She's all muddled and just wants to go to sleep. I want to know what happened to her. I want them to do whatever they have to do to find out who did this to her. What if we hadn't found her? What else might have happened to her?"

"Where did you find her?" Vic asked, frowning in puzzlement.

"Somebody, one of the crew members, he said he found her sleeping in a storage room downstairs. Belowdecks. How would she get down there without anyone seeing her? They wouldn't let a teenager wander around down there. Somebody must have taken her down there."

Erin looked down at the list she had started on the notepad. That was one thing they hadn't discussed, but it had to be a problem on a cruise ship. Not just with teenagers, but with mature adults as well. The doctor had a pretty glib answer; things like that happened all the time. People drank too much, had too much fun, decided to do things that they would later regret. A casual hook-up led to regrets.

Erin wrote "sexual assault" on her list. Not a crime ring, maybe, but there could be a lot of that going on on a ship like that. Something that the crew would want covered up. Something the captain wouldn't want to investigate. They wanted people to be happy. They didn't want the cruise getting a bad reputation. They wanted people to talk about how much fun they'd had on a tour, not about how they were assaulted.

But that hadn't been what the conversation between the two crewmen had sounded like. It wasn't one of them trying to cover up a chance encounter with a passenger. While that might have been something that went on on a big ship, that wasn't a crime ring. That wasn't what the argument had been about.

"She's in the infirmary now?" Vic asked. "Is she sleeping?"

"Yes. I wouldn't have left her otherwise. The doctor wanted to give her a sedative, but I wouldn't let them. If she's been given something, she needs to get it out of her system, not to have something else added to the mix. I don't want her drugged. I want her to be able to wake up clear-headed. I want her to get it out of her system so she can tell me what happened."

"She still might not be able to remember," Erin told Carisa. She wished she hadn't taken a sleeping pill the night of the murder. While she had told Vic and Terry everything she could about what she had seen and heard, parts of it were still hazy or confusing.

"Maybe not… but she's certainly not going to remember it if we keep adding more drugs to the mix. I'm not going to be involved in doping her up until she doesn't know whether she is coming or going."

Erin was grateful for a mother who cared enough about her daughter to make sure that the doctors did the right thing. Too many women would just have accepted what the doctor said, continuing to give Mackay drugs until it was buried so deeply she wouldn't be able to deal with it for many years.

"Have you talked to the captain about it?"

"I couldn't get in to see him. I'm trying… but they said I'll probably have to wait until tomorrow. There's someone in with him right now, and then he's got dinner, and then he goes to bed. If I want to talk to him and not one of the others, I have to wait until tomorrow."

Erin felt guilty, knowing that the person in with the captain was very likely Terry, and he was pressing Erin's case, trying to get the captain to open some kind of investigation into the crewman who had gone overboard. But at least Mackay had been found. She was safe. They couldn't say the same of the dead crewman.

He was gone, his body was gone, and his family would never hear from him again. It would take time before they even knew he was missing, and then they would waste time trying to find him and figure out what had happened to him. But they would never see him again. Maybe his body would wash ashore somewhere, but it would be unrecognizable or chewed on by a shark. By the time an investigation was started by someone in the USA, it would be far too late to find anything out.

CHAPTER 18

$\mathcal{I}$t was late when Terry returned to Vic's and Willie's room. He looked tired and drawn.

"Did you have any luck?" Vic asked.

Erin waited for his answer, not wanting to sound too eager. He was doing the best he could and, from the looks of him, hadn't had much success.

"He agreed to open an investigation," Terry said.

Erin let out a long sigh. Terry had done it. The captain hadn't been willing to listen to a couple of women, but a police officer leaning in and forcing his hand was different. Erin had no idea what he'd had to say to get the captain to agree, but at least he had done it.

"Thank goodness. Thank you so much, Terry. He just wouldn't listen to me! I did try."

"Of course you did," he agreed. "I never doubted that. He wasn't easy to persuade. I'm afraid I might have extended my reach a little more than was strictly ethical…"

Erin stood up and went to him, giving him a big hug. "And I love you for it. Thank you so much."

He gazed down at her. "You're welcome. I hope that it doesn't backfire on us."

Erin shifted uncomfortably. For once, he wasn't lecturing her on sticking her nose in where it didn't belong. He wasn't getting after her for acting like a detective and interfering with one of his investigations.

Instead, he had aligned himself with her. If it ended up causing problems for his career or putting him in danger, she would never forgive herself. They were facing off against a killer. As happy as she was to be believed and for the captain to start an investigation for that poor crewman who had died, she was afraid that she had just put herself and Terry right in the crosshairs of a killer.

~

It was late and Erin was exhausted. She would have been exhausted staying up that late any day, but after being sick and all of the emotional turmoil of the day, it was that much worse. She couldn't imagine being any more tired.

She walked with Terry back to their cabin, K9 heeling at Terry's other side as usual. Erin looked around the cabin when Terry turned the light on. Terry frowned, looking at her.

"What's wrong?"

"Nothing. I didn't say anything."

"You didn't say anything, but your expression… I just thought…"

"No, nothing. There's nothing wrong." Erin's heart pounded hard.

She didn't like lying to him. But if she told him that she just wanted to be alone, it would hurt his feelings. He didn't have anywhere else to go. She could ask him to sleep on the couch instead of the bed and she was sure he would, but that wasn't the right thing to do. He had done all the right things. He had gone to the captain and convinced him to open up an investigation when the captain had previously refused. Terry had spent all of that time and effort and he was tired too. He hadn't slept well while she was sick.

But she really wanted to be alone. She didn't want to share the cabin. She didn't want to share the bed. She just wanted to be by herself.

Terry took a look around the cabin, searching for something that was out of place. "What is it? Do you think someone has been in here?" He paused considering. "Neither of us has anything valuable. I know I don't. You didn't bring anything, did you…?"

"What would I bring?" Erin laughed and shook her head. Her jewelry was purchased at the department store; it wasn't worth anything. She tended to thrift shop for her clothes to make her money stretch further. Any extra money she made at the bakery went back into the bakery to fund promotions and advertising. She still hadn't looked at getting a new car, despite Terry telling her several times that she needed a new one if she were going to keep driving.

Erin had not brought anything valuable with her. Terry hadn't brought anything valuable. There would be no point in anyone entering their cabin for the purpose of theft.

"I don't think anyone has been here," Erin said, making a motion to downplay it. "I just was thinking about how tired I am. You know how it is when you're so tired you can't sleep?"

"Sure." He rubbed her back and shoulders. "I know what that's like. I've trained myself to sleep pretty well to be able to change shifts, but you're used to keeping the same schedule every day, so your body doesn't know what to do when you change it up."

"Yeah."

"Why don't you lie down, and I'll give you a massage. That will help you relax. If you want, you can take another sleeping pill. I know you don't like to, but I think this is a special case. And you're not going to get addicted just having one every now and then."

Erin shuffled toward the bathroom. "I don't want a massage."

"You don't?"

She shut the bathroom door with Terry looking at her, surprised and confused.

Erin washed her face, hoping that would help lift the fatigue headache so she could concentrate. There was no sound from the cabin at first, then she could hear Terry taking care of K9, putting him into his kennel for the night. She could hear drawers opening and closing as Terry changed out of his daytime clothes.

Erin sat on the lid of the toilet, thinking.

The cruise was supposed to be a holiday. A time when they could let down all of their inhibitions and all of the responsibilities that came from their jobs and just spend time together getting to know each other. So far, that had not happened. Terry had learned plenty of new stuff from Erin. How she got seasick on a boat, even one so big. How she was having constant nightmares and wandering in her sleep. How she reacted when she saw a murder right in front of her.

It was no honeymoon, that was for sure.

If she wanted to look back at the trip with some fondness, she was going to have to be open to having a good time. She needed to go on the tours, taste the specially-prepared signature dishes, and spend time with Terry doing something other than talking about people being killed. She needed to take pictures and act like the other tourists. Relaxed and happy to be there. She needed to stop being serious and earnest and to make Terry happy. Then she would be happy herself.

In short, she needed to be someone completely different.

CHAPTER 19

*E*rin went to bed determined to make the best of the next day of the
tour. She was there for a holiday, so it was time to holiday. She
didn't try to get the extra sleep that Terry said she needed to catch back up
and get over the seasickness and trauma that she had been through. She'd
always managed to keep working at Auntie Clem's Bakery through the other
murders, so there was no reason she couldn't get up and start her day early
just like the rest of the time. Not quite as early as her baker's hours, but still
well before the majority of the ship was stirring.

"You up already?" Terry murmured sleepily as she got out of bed and
headed to the bathroom. "You're coming back, right?"

"No. I'm going to have a shower and then go for a walk."

Terry pushed himself up, looking at her blearily. "You can't be walking
around by yourself. Not after the crew has been told about what you saw."

"It's okay. I'll take K9. He won't let anything happen to me."

Terry considered that, still rubbing his eyes, but didn't seem in too great
a hurry to get out of bed. "I don't know… are you sure…? I should come."

"I want to get an early start. I don't think you want to get up yet, do
you?"

He grunted, a noise that Erin took for 'no.' He scratched his bristly
chin. "I don't suppose there will be many people up and around yet."

"No. And K9 will protect me."

"Okay…" Terry flopped back down again with a grunt. "I'll get up before long. I'll call you when I'm up and we can meet, okay?"

Erin nodded, but wasn't sure he could see her in the dark. "Yeah, that sounds fine. No problem."

She went into the bathroom and showered and got herself ready for the day as quietly as possible, not wanting to bother Terry again. When she was finished and crept out of the bathroom, he didn't stir. She let K9 out of his kennel and took him out of the stateroom with her, closing the door quietly behind her.

"There. It's just you and me. How does that sound?" she said to K9.

He looked up at her alertly, ears moving back and forth. Erin felt bad that she hadn't thought to get a cookie for him. She'd have to wait until she was back in the cabin to feed him and he might be hungry before then.

"Well, if we come across anything you would like before then, you can let me know."

He panted happily and started sniffing around, investigating for anything interesting. Erin called him to heel, and he immediately fell in at her side. It always amazed Erin how well he was trained. Not only would he respond to Terry and his commands, but he had quickly learned to listen to Erin as well and, although she got the feeling he considered her the junior partner, he seemed to be content to work with her. Terry didn't want K9 responding to just anyone's commands; it could cause problems if he obeyed a criminal who told him to sit and stay or to break off of a pursuit. But Terry had quickly come to the conclusion that if they were going to be spending that much time together, K9 would need to be comfortable with doing what she told him to as well. It just made things easier.

Erin went up the stairs a couple of decks, and took a walk around the outer hall, enjoying the fresh, brisk air off of the ocean. She had at least thought to dress warmly.

She saw a man in one of the lounge chairs on the deck and was turning around to avoid him when she stopped and looked again. It was Willie. Erin glanced around for Vic, but she wasn't anywhere to be seen.

"Hey, Willie."

Willie looked up from his paper and smiled at Erin. "You're up early. Feeling better?"

"I'm doing great," Erin lied. If she said it enough times, she hoped to convince herself it was true and to actually start feeling better. "Where's Vicky?"

"Oh, she's off with the others," Willie made a waving motion. But when Erin looked in the direction he had pointed, she didn't see Vic or anyone else. She looked back to him.

"With what others? Where did she go?"

Willie looked at Erin for a moment, frowning. He looked over in the direction he had pointed. "There is a group of the vegans that she's made friends with. You know, people who are more like her."

Erin shook her head. "No. Who do you mean? She's not vegan, so I'm not sure that..." Erin couldn't think of what connection Vic would have made with a bunch of vegans on a cruise. "More like her?"

Willie cleared his throat. "Trans and gay and the whole LGBT spectrum. They've been doing some activities together. Mostly just getting together to talk and swap war stories, I think."

"Oh." Erin wasn't sure what to think about that. She was glad that Vic had found other LGBT folks to hang around with, but she had expected Vic would mostly be spending her time with Willie or Erin or their group. She hadn't expected her to take off to associate with people who had been strangers before the cruise. It was nice that she'd made some new friends, but...

Willie chuckled and nodded at Erin. "You look exactly how I feel," he acknowledged. "I'm glad that she's happy, but..."

"But you thought she'd be spending the time with you."

"That was the whole point of the trip, wasn't it? To spend more time together as couples? It seems a little... I don't know... I'm glad she's found people who relate to her, but I just wanted... I wanted it to just be her and me. And some of the time you and Terry. This feels like... she's just turned her back on us." He held up his hand to prevent Erin from speaking. "I know that's silly. I shouldn't feel betrayed just because she's making new friends. But I can't help feeling... kind of left out."

Erin nodded. "Yeah. Me too. I didn't even know..."

"You were sick, and she was looking for other things to do. It makes sense that she would seek out some new girl friends."

"You're right," Erin agreed. "Well... if you see her, tell her I'm up and around. We can hang out later... do the tour together, maybe, if she's not already set something up with these others."

Willie nodded and lifted his paper again. "I'll be sure to pass that on. Skagway is supposed to be a really interesting little place. A gold rush town." With Willie's interest in mining, Erin could see how it would be right up his alley. He would pick up a lot of nuances and background information in Skagway that would mean nothing to her and Vic and Terry.

"Sure. See you later, then."

~

Erin went on, feeling a little off-balance, but in a way she couldn't blame on the roll of the cruise ship. She glanced around to get her bearings and decided to go up a couple more decks to the restaurant. She wasn't usually one for big breakfasts, but she hadn't eaten a lot in the past few days and thought she might be adventurous and try some of the specially-prepared vegan foods. How was she to know if she liked them, if she didn't try them?

"Oh, Miss Price," a young waiter greeted. "Are you feeling better? It's good to see you!"

"Yes, I'm doing a lot better. Figured I'd better start tasting some of this fabulous food that I keep hearing about."

She had heard a lot of positive feedback, even from Willie and Terry who had been prejudiced against it from the start.

The waiter's face wreathed in smiles. "I'm so glad to hear that! What would you like to start with today?"

Erin picked up the menu already in the place in front of her. She skimmed over it. "Well, I'll start with orange juice and coffee, if that's alright. I'll look this over and you can tell me what's good when you get back."

He nodded and disappeared to get her drinks. Erin turned the pages of the menu, letting her eyes wander over the mouthwatering pictures, though she was a little concerned they would not be as mouthwatering as they looked. When the waiter got back with her coffee and juice, Erin wasn't much closer to deciding what she wanted than she had been.

"Tell me what's good," Erin said. "I hear that you've got a really good chef on board."

"More than one!" the waiter agreed. "Right now, Chef Kirschoff is on. He's mostly doing breakfasts and lunches, but he does have a couple of

533

dinners lined up, so that he can prepare a wide variety of dishes. He really is quite good!"

"What should I order?"

"Do you like pancakes? Are you looking for a big breakfast, or do you just want fruit or something light…?"

"I'm actually hungry this morning. So tell me about the pancakes."

The waiter pointed at various different dishes on the menu, describing them and talking about the highlights of each one. Erin ordered some faux buttermilk pancakes with scrambled tofu and vegetables, and some breakfast sausage patties. She was interested in what was in the various dishes, quizzing the waiter on the details. She tripped him up a few times, but he had a pretty good idea what was in most of them. After he finished taking her order and writing it down, he looked back at Erin.

"Are you a cook?" he asked. "Most people don't have that much interest in what the ingredients are. They just want it to taste good. Of course, there are those who are on special diets and can't have certain ingredients, but other than that, most people don't ask a lot of questions."

Erin nodded. "I'm a baker. I own a gluten-free and specialty bakery in Tennessee."

"Really?" he laughed. "That's fantastic. I didn't know that we had a celebrity on board!"

"I wouldn't put it that way!" Erin shook her head.

"I will put this order in for you, and Chef Kirschoff will probably be out to tell you the answers to the questions that I didn't know."

"He doesn't need to. I was just curious. I can eat anything."

"He'll want to talk to you!" the waiter assured her. He gave a little wave and headed for the kitchen.

Erin looked down at K9. "I'm a celebrity. I'll bet you didn't know that."

He looked up at her, made a grumbling noise in his throat, and lay beside her, still and quiet, as she had told him to.

The chef did come out to talk to her, making Erin a little embarrassed at the attention. But it wasn't like the dining room was full. There was only a scattering of people up, and they were pretty quiet, minding their own business and not openly listening to her.

"Miss Price! It's very good to meet you!" he boomed. He took hold of her hand between two of his and nearly lifted her out of her seat. "I am the chef, and I am most happy to discuss food preparation with you. Tell me all of your questions."

Erin shook her head and repeated a few of the questions that the young waiter hadn't been able to answer. In a few minutes, she and the chef were deep in culinary discussions. Erin glanced toward the kitchen a couple of times, but the chef didn't seem too concerned about the kitchen staff not being able to do without him. Erin knew that they could probably function autonomously. They would know all of the recipes and preparation techniques. He was needed, but not every hour of every day.

"I'm very excited to meet a gluten-free baker," Chef Kirschoff said. "As one specialty cook to another, I spend all of my time on vegan considerations and not much on gluten-free. I have a few gluten-free options, of course, serving dishes with rice or potatoes instead of bread, using tofu rather than seitan, things like that, but as far as the baking side of it goes… I'm sadly lacking there. I'm familiar with the most popular ingredients, rice and sorghum flour and cornstarch, but I haven't had much experience in baking with them myself. I usually buy premade pizza shells, rolls, and so on. But they aren't as good as homemade, and I always feel like I'm doing my customers a disservice by not having my own gluten-free baking on offer."

Erin nodded. "The same here, but in reverse. I know what ingredients to avoid for vegan baking. I deal with a few people with egg or dairy allergies. But I don't have a lot of vegan offerings. A lot of gluten-free baking relies on the protein in eggs and dairy, and doesn't do very well if you don't make the right substitutes. I find it is easier to go from a vegan recipe and to adapt it to gluten-free flours than the opposite."

He nodded wisely. "That makes sense. But since I don't have enough familiarity with the gluten-free flours and chemistry, I'm not yet at the point at which I can substitute on the fly. I have to find recipes others have already developed and go from there."

"Well, if there's anything particular you need help on, I can take a look at it and give you some advice."

"That would be wonderful! One of the specialties when we are here is Baked Alaska, and I would love to be able to offer a version with gluten-free cake as well as the usual. Usually I just leave the cake out for anyone who is gluten sensitive. If you will help me out… if I need any ingredients that I don't have on board, I can have supplies dropped ahead of us."

Baked Alaska. It seemed sort of a cliché to have it on an Alaskan cruise, but it wasn't something she'd had often, and it would be a fun treat.

"Yes, of course. I'd love to help you. I'm sure it wouldn't be too hard."

"Fabulous!" The chef threw his hands up in delight. "That would be a huge help. Thank you very much. And I will be certain to credit you with the adaptation of the recipe."

Erin's face warmed. She smiled at his enthusiasm. "Well, let's see how they turn out before you thank me too much!"

"I have no doubt they will be wonderful."

The waiter arrived with Erin's pancake order, and Chef Kirschoff stayed for a few extra minutes to see how she liked everything before returning to his kitchen. Erin was tentative tasting the tofu, but everything was quite nice, and she was able to tell Kirschoff honestly that she liked it all, even the scrambled tofu. "I wouldn't have guessed it," she said. "I've never had scrambled tofu before, but I wouldn't have guessed that it was tofu instead of eggs."

He beamed at her. "You are too kind! You've never had scrambled tofu before? Why did you come on a vegan tour if you are not vegan? Is your partner?"

"No. None of us are. I won four tickets in a contest."

"Ah! Well, I'm grateful to whoever you won them from. It was a pleasure to meet you."

CHAPTER 20

*E*rin couldn't finish her breakfast, but not because there was anything wrong with it. She just wasn't used to big breakfasts. She left her compliments to the chef, and went on to see if she could find Vic. She wasn't sure where to look, but thought she'd take in some air and explore the ship with K9, and maybe they would be able to find Vic on the way.

She had been wandering for some time from deck to deck, looking at the various spas, stores, restaurants, and other venues, and was starting to think she wasn't going to be able to find Vic before the tour. She couldn't get a good phone signal and wasn't getting any replies to her text messages to Vic. Erin approached a crew member, wondering if it were possible to have a passenger paged. She called out to a man who was cleaning up some towels on the pool deck. He turned around to look at her, and Erin's heart sank right down to her stomach.

It wasn't the crew member who had been involved in the fight—he wasn't broad enough to be—it was Saville, the crew member who had given Vic such a hard time boarding the ship. Erin put her hands up as if to hold him at a distance and tried to figure out what to say.

"Uh... hi. I was just looking for my friend and was wondering if I could have her paged, but you look like you're busy."

He studied her, frowning. Erin took a step back. Even if it wasn't the man who had thrown the other overboard, he could still be involved in illegal activities, and the entire crew knew by now of Erin's accusations. She should have listened to Terry about not going off on her own. She had K9 there to guard her, but she felt incredibly vulnerable facing the man. He sneered at her.

"You're talking about the he-she? The supposed *woman* who boarded with a man's passport?"

Erin choked back her ire at his response. She tried to answer in a calm, respectful way. "She is a trans woman, yes. You haven't seen her around, have you?"

"There's a whole group of those people gathered on the next deck," he pointed a finger upward. "At the juice bar. Chattering away like a flock of magpies."

Erin nodded. "Thank you. That's very helpful. You have a nice day."

He continued to stare at her as if she were something bad he had stepped in. Erin took a couple of steps back from him before looking around for the stairs and making her exit with K9. The dog snorted as they walked away from the crewman, and Erin looked down at him.

"I didn't like him either. But we have to educate people one at a time. Maybe in a few years… He'll be able to change his language and his viewpoint. Right now, he's just ignorant. He doesn't know any better."

K9 looked at her intently for a moment, then went back to just looking ahead of them, his nostrils quivering as they approached the juice bar. Erin looked around at the crowd.

There were more of them than she would have thought, though Erin didn't know if everybody in the group was LGBT or an ally or if some of them had just happened to frequent the juice bar at the same time. There was a lot of brightly-dyed hair, piercings, and unusual clothing and hairstyle choices. People trying to show their independence in more than one way. She spotted the familiar slim blond and moved toward her.

"Vic!"

Vic turned and looked around. She smiled. "Erin, hi! You're up bright and early today."

"Not bright and early by our standards. But I didn't want to stay in bed all day today, either."

"Good. You must be feeling a lot better. Do you want a juice? I could order you something. Maybe something like pear ginger? The ginger is good for nausea."

"I actually just ate in the dining room. So I'm good for a while."

"Oh, great! That's good. Let me introduce you around. Everyone, this is Erin. Erin," Vic pointed to each person in turn, naming them and telling Erin something about each of them. There was no way Erin was going to be able to remember everyone, but she tried to remember other details for the next time she saw them again. Everyone smiled and greeted her. One young woman touched Erin on the arm, breaching her personal space.

"I'm so glad that Vic has a friend like you. It's so nice to have people who just accept you for what you are, and I'm super happy that Vic has you."

"Oh... well, thank you. I just... I don't think Vic is any different than anyone else. She's just a person. She's fun and compassionate... and I just like being with her."

"That's awesome. It's hard to find acceptance like that in the cis community. People can be very prejudiced."

"Yes, we've run into that a few times," Erin agreed, trying to back away from the compliments. She was just being a regular person and accepting Vic as a regular person. There was nothing special about that, even if she did know that the other sort existed.

"You see that?" the girl asked, turning back to the rest of the girls, indicating Erin. "She says *we*. We have run into that. Even though she's not trans, just an ally. That's awesome."

Erin cleared her throat and looked at Vic for help, embarrassed.

Vic just gave her a wide smile. "Accept the compliment, Erin. It's true. You're understanding, where other people... are definitely not."

"Okay, but can we talk about something else now?"

Vic and the others laughed, pleased with Erin's embarrassment.

Erin appreciated the compliments that she got from Vic's new group of friends and they included her as if she were a long-time member of their group, but she couldn't help feeling uncomfortable there. They were Vic's friends, close to her because of their gender identity or attraction, but Erin didn't share those things with them. The fact that they included her just made her feel more awkward and obvious.

She also found herself feeling jealous, as Willie had. She knew that it was perfectly natural for Vic to have more than one friend and more than one interest, but seeing her laughing and relaxing with the group of strangers made Erin feel both irritated and protective. *She* was Vic's friend. She was the one who had taken Vic in, taught her and protected her, and provided her with a home. She was the one who spent just about every day working side-by-side with Vic. She was the one who protected Vic from the self-righteous verbal attacks and preaching of the more evangelical church-goers, those who felt like they somehow had the right and the responsibility to call Vic down to repentance for what they considered her evil ways.

And yet, there Vic was, looking just as comfortable with people she hardly knew. She didn't know what kind of people they were or how they would have treated her in any other situation. It just didn't seem right that Vic should be spending time with them instead of with Erin.

Vic looked at the time on her phone. "I guess we should be getting back to the boys if we're going to go on the tour," she said. "What about you, you're going to Skagway with us, right?"

Erin nodded. She had looked through the brochure to read up on what they would be doing that day, and was interested in seeing the little gold rush mining community, carefully preserved or restored to look just as it had a hundred years earlier, with false-front stores and saloons. It would be like walking onto the set for a movie Western. "Yeah, it looks like it's going to be a lot of fun."

"I think so too," Vic agreed. She looked around at the group. "Well, I'll see whoever is going to go on the tour in a little while. We'll catch up later!"

The others in the group nodded or said their goodbyes.

Erin felt relief as Vic separated from the others and it was just her and Erin going down to their cabins.

"Thanks for putting up with that," Vic said. "It's really neat to find such a strong support group on a cruise like this. I know you don't really have anything in common with them, so thanks for being such a good sport about it."

Erin shrugged. "None of my business who you hang around with. It makes sense you would want more friends than just me."

Vic raised an eyebrow. "You're still my best friend. But it is really nice to find people who I could share some experiences with. There isn't really any kind of support in Bald Eagle Falls. In the rest of the community, I mean, aside from you and Terry and Willie."

Erin nodded and didn't say anything further. They walked down to their deck in silence.

Erin was expecting to see Terry along the way, but didn't. Maybe he was already up with Willie, chatting while they waited for the tour group to gather. Vic unlocked the door to her cabin and walked in. She gave a little cry and stepped back, stepping on Erin's toes and pushing her back into the hallway.

"What is it?" Erin asked. "What happened?" She tried to peer around Vic to see. She did not want to see another body, but she couldn't help looking. Or maybe it was some sort of warning for them to stay out of the investigation. Or a threat to Vic and her LGBT friends.

Vic looked around the room from outside. "It's been burglarized," she said. "Everything has been ransacked."

Erin managed to look past Vic and saw that, as she had said, everything appeared to have been turned over and was scattered around on the floor. Drawers were pulled out, all of the bedsheets were on the floor, all of their suitcases had been dumped and were also lying on the floor, wide open.

"Who would do this?" Erin demanded.

"I don't know. Get Terry."

Erin hurried down the hall to her own cabin and opened the door. But it was empty, Terry wasn't there. She had her phone out in an instant, but it wasn't getting any bars and the wifi symbol was grayed out.

"Are you okay here alone for a minute?" she called out to Vic, "I'm going to have to go upstairs to find someone."

"Yes. Just go."

"Do you want me to leave K9 with you?"

"No, you'd better keep him with you."

Erin hesitated. It seemed like Vic was the one who needed the dog more. It was her room that had been ransacked.

Vic made a shooing motion. "Go on. Go find someone."

CHAPTER 21

*E*rin hurried back up the stairs, almost immediately out of breath because of her anxiety and the effort of running. K9 seemed to sense that something was wrong. He was focused, nose and ears pointed sharply forward, bounding up the stairs in sync with her footsteps. They reached the top and Erin looked around. How was she going to find Terry with the whole ship to search, especially when she was in such a hurry? She didn't want to leave Vic downstairs by herself any longer than she had to.

They should have just locked the cabin and left together. The burglar might still be down on the deck in another room. He might return if he hadn't found what he was looking for. What had he been looking for? It didn't make sense that he was looking for jewelry or other valuables; no one in their group wore expensive jewelry or clothing. They hadn't even paid for their own tickets, but had won them in a contest, so no one could assume by their presence there that they were wealthy.

"Find Terry," Erin told K9 sharply. "Where's Terry? Go find him!"

K9 looked at her, his eyes intelligent, his whole body alert and coiled for action.

"Find Terry," Erin repeated. "Go!"

He took off, bounding ahead of her. Erin didn't know whether he had Terry's scent and knew where he was going, or was just going to start randomly looking for him like Erin would have to do. She looked down the hallway and couldn't see any crewmen or anyone who could help her, so she climbed up the stairs to the next deck. She was getting dizzy with the quick climb, not quite recovered from her convalescence. She stopped with her hand on the railing and looked down the next hallway. There was a movement at the end.

"Hello?" Erin called. "Is someone there?"

A woman stepped back into the hallway from the intersection down at the other end. "Yes? Is something wrong?"

"I need security," Erin said. "There's been a break-in. Have you seen any crew?"

"I haven't seen anyone. Do you want me to help you?"

Erin breathed hard. There wasn't much another passenger could do. "If you could go up the stairs at the other end, and we'll both just keep going until we can find someone. If you find a crewman, then send them down to 232. Okay?"

"Sure." The woman stepped out of sight again and, in a moment, Erin could hear her feet on the stairs at the other end of the passage. Erin took as deep a breath as she could and went up another flight. She looked around, stepping into the open area and looking at the restaurant and store fronts she could see. Why was it that there were always waiters and crewmen around asking her if she needed anything until she actually did, and then there was no one to be seen?

She turned to go up the stairs to the next deck and just about ran into a crewman walking from a restricted staff area to the stairs.

"Oh! Thank goodness. I need help!"

He stopped and looked at her, his eyes going over her slowly. He didn't seem to be in any great hurry to help, clearly wanting to know what it was before he committed. Erin tried to push any judgmental thoughts out of her mind. He didn't know what she needed, and he probably had other duties. Of course he wanted to know what it was before he said he would do anything.

"My friend's cabin downstairs was broken into. Everything has been tossed all over the place. We need security down there and I can't find anyone to help. Can you get someone down there?"

He nodded and keyed the radio mounted at his shoulder. "Of course, ma'am. What's the room number?"

"Two-thirty-two. Thank you so much." Erin breathed heavily several times, feeling like she had sprinted a mile. "I didn't know where to go to find help. Thank you."

He spoke into his radio, explaining the situation, and waited for confirmation. "They're on their way. Cell phones are useless on the ship most of the time. That's why we have the radios," he explained. "I'm sorry you were concerned. Do you want me to walk you back down there and make sure security arrives?"

Erin looked around, wondering where K9 had gotten to. Had he found Terry, or was he still casting about, trying to pick up his scent and get him to go back?

"Uh... no, I'll be okay. I'll just go back down so she's not alone."

"Are you sure? I can escort you."

But Erin wasn't sure about him. He obviously hadn't been happy to see her, and she wondered if he knew who she was and that she was the cause of an investigation. She imagined it had probably caused extra work and trouble for the crewmen, not to mention putting them all under suspicion.

And he was the right height and body shape to be the killer. She didn't want to be alone with him. If he were the killer and he knew who she was... She could have kicked herself for saying that Vic was alone too. She should have told him that Terry and Willie were already waiting down by the cabin. Though that would leave her panicked flight to find a security officer all by herself somewhat unexplained.

"I'll... thank you for the offer, but I think I'll be fine. Thank you for calling them."

"If you have any other problems, there are emergency phones on each deck. Just pick up the receiver and you'll be put through to the officer in charge."

"Oh." It hadn't even occurred to Erin to try that. She had seen the phones near the fire extinguisher and fire hose on each deck, but she hadn't thought that she, as a passenger, was allowed to use them. She had just assumed that they were restricted to crew use, and that if she were to mess with them, she would be fined or charged with mischief. But apparently they were there for the use of the passengers. "Thanks. That's a really good idea."

"I know you haven't been feeling well, so you probably missed that at orientation. But you should make yourself aware of the safety features and emergency procedures on the ship. Just in case something else was to happen that was of concern."

It irked Erin that he knew who she was and that she had been sick. Did everybody on the ship know her?

"Okay. I'd better get down there. Thank you so much for your help, again."

He nodded. Erin forced herself to turn her back on him to hurry back down the stairs to where Vic was waiting outside the door of her cabin. She was down two flights when Terry came bursting through one of the doors into the stairwell. K9 was at his side. He grabbed Erin and pulled her to him in a bear hug. "Erin! What happened, what's wrong?"

"Vic and Willie's cabin was broken into."

"Oh." He breathed out, a sigh of relief. "I was worried that someone was hurt. Everyone is okay?"

"Yes. Sorry. I didn't mean to panic you. I didn't know how to find you, so I just told K9 to go get you."

"Well, he did that." Terry paused to scratch K9's ears and praise him. "Good boy. Good job, K9."

K9 panted happily, his tail waving back and forth like a flag. His tongue lolled out as he looked at Erin, obviously expecting something from her too.

"You are a good dog. You knew just what to do, didn't you? I wish I had a cookie to give you for doing such a good job."

"Just give him a pat," Terry suggested. "If he got a cookie every time he followed instructions, he'd be as fat as a whale."

Erin obliged, patting him and scratching around his ears and collar. "You're a good, good dog, K9." She stood back up straight. "We'd better get back down to the room. Vic was down there by herself and I don't think I should have left her alone."

Terry's lips tightened and he nodded. "No, I don't think you should have."

"I didn't know what else to do, I just knew I had to go get help. I should have told her to lock it and come with me, but we both just automatically thought that she should stay there to keep an eye on things. I guess the burglar is probably long gone by now, but we weren't really thinking."

"It's okay. I'm sure she'll be just fine for the few minutes she was alone."

Erin nodded. "Let's go see."

They hurried down the stairs one more flight. Erin could hear a man's voice as they reached the bottom of the stairs and got to the hallway, and looked down the hall in concern, worried that it was someone harassing Vic. But it was one of the crewmen, a security guard apparently. He looked into the room and instructed Vic to stay outside while he went in to have a closer look. Erin and Terry hurried up, and Erin gave Vic a hug.

"Is everything okay? I really shouldn't have left you here. I'm sorry."

"You did what I told you to. I told you to go get help, and you did." Vic nodded at the room. "A security officer and Terry. I couldn't have asked for much more."

Erin gestured to the emergency phone on the wall a few yards away. "Apparently, we could have just called for security from there."

Vic stared at the phone, then looked back at Erin, laughing and rolling her eyes. "It was right there and neither of us thought to use it. Duh."

Terry shook his head at both of them. "You need to be aware of what you can do. On a ship like this, away from cell towers and with all of the iron in the decks, your phones aren't of much use. So you need to use the intra-ship communications. Like the phone or the crew's radios."

"Yeah. Figured that out now," Vic said. "Thanks for the advice."

Terry shrugged. He looked into the cabin and gave a low whistle. "When Erin said that it had been broken into, I thought it had just been left with the door open. But this is a little more than I expected! They did a really thorough job of tossing it, didn't they? Is there anything missing?"

"I don't know. I backed right out again, and Erin went to get help while I kept an eye on it. I don't see anything that's obviously missing, but I'm going to have to go through everything to be sure. It's not like I had a lot of valuables in there. Do you think this was just theft? They just wanted something that we had left in the safe or on a dresser?"

"If that was all they wanted, the whole room would not have been tossed. I think we have to assume that it was more than that. They were sending you a message."

"What message?" Erin asked quietly, afraid she already knew.

Terry looked at her, his lips a thin line. He spoke quietly, his eyes going to the security officer to make sure he couldn't hear. "I think the message is along the lines of 'mind your own business' and 'don't make trouble.' I really don't like this. I didn't want to have to start an investigation into what you saw the other day, and this just confirms it for me. I don't want to put you girls in danger. You need to stay with us. No more going out even if you are with other friends or with K9. It just isn't safe."

"No way," Vic argued. "I want to be able to come and go as I please. Why should I have to be under guard all the time? It isn't fair."

"Because people have seen you and Erin together, and they know that Erin is the one who claims to have seen someone killed."

"The crewman who called security for me creeped me out," Erin confided. "He was the same body shape as the killer. He offered to come down here with me, and…" She suddenly found herself shaking.

Terry put his hand on her arm. "Erin, it's okay. You're okay. You're safe."

"I know." Erin tried to talk in a normal tone and not let the tears enter her voice. "It's just the adrenaline. I'll be fine."

He hugged her to him, murmuring soothing sounds and waiting for the shaking to pass.

News of the burglary of Vic's room had spread quickly through the ship. Erin would not have expected it to circulate so fast without cell phones and social media, but apparently the traditional lines of gossip were working just fine. It wasn't long before Captain Jacobi put in an appearance to get a report from his security staff. He eyed the people gathered in the hallway whispering.

"People need to go back to their own cabins or to meet for the tour," he advised in a clear, quiet, authoritative voice. "Please don't congregate in the hallways, it is a safety hazard. Everything is under control. You don't need to worry."

"Captain Jacobi," Terry acknowledged as the man reached them. They were still standing outside of Vic's room, though Vic and Willie had now entered to talk to the security officer.

"That applies to you folks as well. There's no good to be done just hanging around here. It attracts extra attention, something you don't want at this point."

"I am a police officer—" Terry started.

"As I told you the other night: not on this boat, you're not. The only police on board the Carolina are my staff. You don't have any authority here. If I tell you that you should move on, then that's what you do."

Terry's jaw clenched. Erin waited for him to get angry and to call Jacobi out for his negligent security and all that had happened to them so far, but he didn't. He just kept quiet, his lips pale and his face a tight mask, and said nothing by way of objection.

"Vic is my friend," Erin said. "We want to be here to support her."

"I understand the sentiment, but I would like you to return to your own cabin or gather with the tour group getting ready to go. You are not helping anything by blocking the passages and drawing attention to the situation."

"But this is serious! People should be paying attention. Someone just broke in here and went through all of Vic's stuff. The whole room looks like a bomb went off."

"Maybe it was personal," Jacobi suggested. "If someone was really out for valuables, they would look in the usual places and leave everything undisturbed so that you didn't even know that someone had been in there. The two of you have been throwing around unfounded accusations and asking questions, Miss Webster challenges the gender norms, and you clearly didn't come for the vegan food. Even if you haven't done anything wrong, you have upset people. Maybe someone is telling you to cool it and just let people enjoy their vacations."

Erin opened her mouth to object, but Terry gave her hand a squeeze. She looked at him and held her tongue.

"How is the investigation into the missing crewman going?" Terry asked, changing the subject.

"The investigation is in the very early stages. The crew has plenty else to do without having unnecessary busywork being thrown at them. So far, I have found nothing to be of any concern."

"Someone was killed!" Erin protested, her voice going up several notes, "How can you say that isn't something to be worried about? I'm not just talking about a room not being dusted properly. A man was killed!"

"So you say. But you have been sleepwalking and hallucinating. I have not found anyone on the crew who has concerns about a missing crewman, or about any other criminal forces on board the ship. You are worried about something that didn't happen. You dreamed you saw something untoward, but I have found nothing to indicate that there is any reason for concern."

"You have a missing man, right? You've at least discovered that, haven't you?"

"You could ask me the same thing at any time on any tour. We always lose crew. Most of the staff are young people. They make bad decisions and decide they don't want to stay on board. They go ashore, drink for a few days, and miss the boat. Or they have a falling out with another crew member and decide they just don't want to be here. It happens on every tour. There are always people who have been offended and think they don't owe me any kind of explanation or notice. It's just something that we deal with."

"So you don't believe there was any violence."

"No," Aro Jacobi shook his head. "I think I made that very clear when you came to meet with me. But you tried to do an end run around the rules, having a police officer pressure for an investigation." Jacobi looked at Terry. "I have a lot to do, and investigating tall tales is not something that is productive. It takes time away from the things I really need to concentrate on."

Terry didn't apologize or back down. But he didn't say anything that would make the captain any angrier, either.

Jacobi sniffed and walked into the cabin to talk to his security officer, picking his way over through all of the dumped clothing and personal items on the floor. Vic returned to the doorway where Erin was standing.

"We should get ready for the tour."

Erin was surprised. "You still want to do the tour? Don't you want to stay here and clean up and see what they have to say?"

Vic shook her head. "I can clean up tonight. And I already know what they're going to say. It's already been said."

CHAPTER 22

*a*s they traipsed after the tour guide, lagging back behind most of
the group, Erin talked quietly to Vic about the recent developments.

"Do you think there was anything stolen? I know you haven't had a
chance to look through everything yet, but do you think there's anything?"

Vic shook her head. "Nothing obvious. Like I said, it wasn't like I had
jewelry or anything else that was worth anything. The safe was still locked,
and my passport and everything was still there. I don't know what else they
would have stolen. My panties? I think that Terry and the captain are right.
It was supposed to intimidate us. Make us think twice about pursuing this
investigation."

Erin glanced over to Terry and Willie, who were having their own low
discussion. "I think that Terry still doesn't believe I saw what I did. He went
ahead and talked the captain into investigating it, but I don't think he
believes I saw anything."

Vic bit her lip thinking about it, then shook her head. "I think you're
misjudging him. He might not have believed it to begin with, but I don't
think he would go ahead and talk the captain into opening an investigation
if he didn't really believe it. He'd still be telling you it was just a dream."

"If he believes me, then why isn't he doing more? He's a cop. He could
be investigating it himself. He could be asking people questions, looking for

any clues that might have been left behind. Why were we the ones to find the button? He should have found it."

"Terry can't investigate. It's not his jurisdiction. He has to stand back and let the captain and the crew investigate. He obviously hates it."

Erin stole a glance at Terry. He didn't look happy, that was for sure. Was Vic right? She had assumed that his frozen expression was because of her, that he didn't want to show her that he still didn't believe her. But was Vic right? Maybe the reason he looked so angry was because he couldn't do what he normally would. He had to stand back and let someone else do the work, even if the job was inferior.

"I don't know. Maybe."

"Do you think they'll find anything out in their investigation? Or do you think they're really investigating it at all?"

Erin thought about it. She eventually shook her head. "I don't think they're doing anything. I mean, the first step would be to talk to me, wouldn't it? If they were really investigating a murder or a missing crewman, then wouldn't they have talked to me? And to the rest of you to see if I was stable? I don't see any sign they're doing anything. No questions, no taping off the area and searching for forensic clues. They hadn't done anything as far as I can tell."

"So you think it's just words? You don't think Captain Jacobi is really investigating it at all?"

"No." Erin sighed. "I never would have guessed that the ship would be so isolated. It's like an island all by itself, with a different culture and social structure and police force. It's really... different than anything I expected."

Vic nodded.

The tour guide had finished his spiel and Erin and Vic looked up and down the street, deciding where to go first. The stores and other buildings were just as they had been shown in the brochure, a little ghost town, looking like the movie set from a western.

"We should look through the shops," Vic said, looking at the brochure in her hand. "We've got until dinner for that. Then after we eat, it's the graveyard tour."

Erin gave a shudder. "Why would we want to go on a graveyard tour?"

"It's really interesting. There are a lot of cool old gravestones, and they have all kinds of stories about the men who are buried there. The famous ones, anyway. I was looking at it online last night, and it's a really cool old place. Actually, there are a few graveyards, but we're just going to the biggest one. If we want to visit one of the other ones, we need to do it on our own, they don't have a tour scheduled."

"I don't know. I'm not big on graveyards."

In fact, Erin didn't even know if she'd be able to set her foot inside of one, not after her last experience.

She'd always been a little paranoid about death. Maybe it had to do with her parents dying when she was so young, or maybe it was just part of not believing in an afterlife. The church ladies seemed much more casual about death and funerals. They believed that there was more after death, that the soul had merely gone somewhere else.

But looking beyond the end of her journey, Erin saw nothing.

It felt good to eat in the dining room together. Erin was hungry rather than nauseated, so she could enjoy it. When Chef Kirschoff heard that they were there, he again made his way out of the kitchen to greet Erin and her friends and to tell them how happy he was to have Erin on the tour with them and how she was going to help him to make a superb vegan and gluten-free Baked Alaska.

"Erin is great at coming up with gluten-free recipes," Vic bragged. "She's always thinking about ways to cook new things without gluten. Stuff that you never see in the stores. And everyone is always amazed at how good they taste. She has the only bakery in Bald Eagle Falls, and everybody goes there, whether they need to eat gluten-free or not."

"Well, not everybody," Erin moderated.

Vic rolled her eyes. "Maybe there are two or three who don't. But people are always saying how good it is."

Kirschoff beamed. "And I have her on my boat," he said expansively, as if it were his very own ship and he'd personally arranged for her to attend.

He pointed out several options on the day's menu and helped them each pick the dishes that suited them.

"We always make sure we have something hearty on the menu for the men," he told Willie, after pointing out the seitan stew. "Men who work hard and need a lot of calories aren't going to be satisfied with a salad, are they?"

Willie nodded agreeably. "I haven't gone hungry so far," he assured the chef. Kirschoff smiled and patted him on the shoulder, and after a few more words, headed back to the kitchen.

"You made a good impression on him," Vic commented, raising an eyebrow at Erin.

Erin's cheeks got warm. "Just a couple of cooks exchanging recipes." She turned her head to look at Terry. His face was alert, frown lines between his brows. "What is it?"

She wondered fleetingly if he'd been bothered by her talking to Chef Kirschoff or thought she was flirting with him.

Terry's eyes focused on her, acting as if he'd been unaware of her presence up until then. He considered her question. "They've paged Captain Jacobi three times."

Erin shrugged. "So…?"

"How can they not know where the captain is? Maybe his radio is not working, but then why wouldn't he get in touch with them after the first page?"

Erin considered. She looked at Vic and Willie, gauging their expressions. Terry was definitely the most concerned of them. Vic and Willie were thinking about his response but, like Erin, they weren't sure what to make of it. It didn't seem like such a big thing for the man to have to be paged three times. Maybe he was doing something important that he couldn't drop. Maybe he had gone off ship for something and word hadn't reached whoever wanted him. The ship had to be able to run without his direct control. The man couldn't be on duty twenty-four hours a day.

"Maybe he's busy," Erin ventured.

Terry didn't argue. He sipped his soft drink and looked around. Erin didn't see anything out of place. Everyone was relaxed, eating their dinners or visiting with each other. The crew members that she could see didn't seem concerned over the captain being paged repeatedly. It couldn't be anything too out of the ordinary.

"I think everything is fine," Erin suggested.

"It doesn't feel right. How could they not know where he is?"

"It's a big ship."

"Yes. It is."

They drifted into other conversations. Erin could tell that Terry was still tense, but she ignored it and pretended that they were all enjoying themselves. She was determined to enjoy her holiday, in spite of everything that had happened. She was there to relax. It was up to the crew to sort out anything on the ship that was not kosher.

Even so, she felt a little tug toward her pocket, where she had the notes on crimes that the crew might be involved in. Someone had made it clear that they could get into the cabins anytime they wanted to. Vic's door had not been forced. It had to be a crew member who wasn't happy with the investigation that she and Vic had started. If Terry hadn't been in Erin's room, she knew her own cabin would have received the same treatment.

A crewman moved across the dining room. Not one of the waiters in a serving apron, but somebody else in uniform. Erin watched him make his way across the dining room, not talking to and greeting the guests cheerfully, as they usually went out of their way to do, but moving with deliberation and a fixed, unnatural smile. He stopped at the table of Dr. O'Donoghue, the ship's white-haired doctor, and bent down to talk to him. Dr. O'Donoghue looked at him sharply. He removed the napkin from his lap and dropped it beside his plate, standing up immediately.

Erin felt Terry stir beside her. She looked at him as he too rose to his feet.

"Terry? What is it?"

"I need to find out what's going on."

The doctor and the crewman were moving at a brisk pace. Terry cut across the room to intercept them at the door. O'Donoghue looked irritated and made a motion to him to go away and not to bother him. The crewman looked up the second the doctor slowed, urgency clear on his face.

"What do you think is going on?" Erin asked Vic.

"I don't know. Something is wrong. A medical emergency, I guess. They needed the doctor, but they didn't want to make an announcement that anyone else would hear."

Terry followed the doctor and the crewman out of the dining room. Erin was surprised that he didn't just return to the table when they made it clear that they didn't want to be bothered. Clearly, he wasn't going to be deterred. Erin wished that the phones worked reliably for texting, but sometimes they worked and sometimes they didn't. She decided to attempt a text to Terry anyway to see if he could tell her what was going on.

Willie was considering the situation. "Terry was already concerned about the captain not answering pages."

Erin's mouth went dry. She took a sip of her ice water, but it didn't seem to help much. "You think something happened to him? That's who they need the doctor for?"

"There can't be very many situations in which the captain would decide not to answer or be unable to."

"Oh, dear. I hope nothing happened to him."

She expected Willie to come back with something reassuring, but he didn't. He just shook his head grimly. Erin looked down at her phone, hoping for a response to her text.

CHAPTER 23

They still hadn't heard anything back from Terry when they were finished dinner. Erin looked at Vic and Willie.

"What do you think we should do?"

"I don't think there's anything we can do," Willie said. "We just need to wait until Terry is finished whatever it is he's doing. It's not really any of our business and he hasn't asked for any help. If there is something wrong with the captain and they need Terry's help, they don't need us getting in the way. We're better off letting him handle whatever it is until we hear back."

"What do you want to do?" Vic asked, maybe sensing how lost Erin was feeling without Terry or at least K9 at her side. "I know Terry said he didn't want any of us alone, so I think you're stuck with us. There are some really cool acts scheduled for the Mermaid room. Do you want to see what's on tonight?"

"I don't know." Erin was disgruntled. She didn't really feel like watching some lounge act or magic show. She knew they were supposed to be really good, but she couldn't focus on a show. "I'm not really interested right now... I need to be doing something to keep myself busy, not just sitting around."

"Well..." Vic cast about for something to suggest. "I'm not really sure what it is you want to do. Do you want to work on some planning for the bakery when we get back? I don't think there's any way you can work on your family history, assuming you didn't bring any of those huge books with you. What is it you feel like doing?"

"Baking."

Vic laughed. "I thought we were supposed to be taking a break from baking. What else do you want to do?"

Erin shook her head. "Really. That's all I want to do. My fingers are itching. I want to make something."

Vic laughed again. Willie gave a shrug. "Why don't you send a message to the kitchen, then? Chef Kirschoff was interested in getting your help. Maybe it's not a good time for him now, but you never know unless you ask. Do you want to see?"

Erin nodded. She immediately felt a warm, comfortable feeling. She wanted to be baking, and maybe if Chef Kirschoff was free, she could. It felt right.

Willie gestured to one of the waiters when Erin wasn't able to catch one's eye. The young man came over, looking inquiring. They were finished with their after-dinner coffees, so he was probably confused about why they weren't getting on their way.

"How can I help you folks?" the waiter asked pleasantly. But Erin got just a hint of a sneer behind his manner. This was someone who had been trained to be polite and courteous, but he was just going through the motions and doing what he'd been taught. He didn't really feel respect toward the passengers.

"We'd like to get a message to Chef Kirschoff," Willie said. He too seemed to be assessing the waiter's manner, his lips tightening as he considered. "Do you think you could do that for us? Or should I get someone else?"

"Of course I can pass on a message for you."

"Erin is wondering whether the chef has some time for baking. She wanted to lend him a hand in some gluten-free cooking."

"It is the dinner hour. I think he's probably up to his chef's hat right now. He shouldn't be disturbed."

"Maybe you could ask him," Willie pressed. "He was quite interested in getting some help from Erin. I wouldn't be so quick to discount it."

The waiter barely managed to avoid rolling his eyes. His body language clearly showed that he was barely holding back telling them off. "Of course.

I'll talk to the chef. But you mustn't be upset if he isn't available. It's a very busy time of day and the kitchen will be hectic."

Erin nodded. "I know. I run a bakery. But if he has a few minutes, or if he thinks he might have a few minutes later on this evening... I'd love to spend some time with him on his recipes."

The waiter nodded, gave a brief bow, and walked away. Even so, Erin could hear him muttering under his breath as he turned away from them.

"First vegan, and now gluten-free. Before long, they'll be trying to survive on water."

Erin looked at Willie and shook her head in amazement. "Can you believe this guy? Good grief. If I had acted like that at any of the jobs I had, there's no way I would have lasted. He'll be lucky if they don't boot him off at the next stop."

Vic giggled. "Some people are so full of themselves." She took a deep breath and put on a superior expression. "Vegan and gluten-free? What will they think of next?"

Erin joined in the laughter.

She looked down at her phone, but there was still no response from Terry. She didn't want to be watching it all night. Or waiting to find out what had happened to him. She wanted to know right away. If she couldn't find out, then she needed something to keep her busy. She couldn't stand to sit around with nothing to do. She'd never been interested in crosswords, knitting, or the lounge acts being advertised in the Mermaid room. She needed to get her hands into some dough and figure out something new to make.

"Try to relax, Erin," Vic suggested. "Or you're going to fidget yourself right out of that chair."

Erin tried to calm her nervous hands and legs and just sit still, quietly and patiently. But it didn't work.

Word came back from the chef that he did, indeed, want to see Erin and would make time for her. The waiter was obviously disgusted by this breach in protocol, but he escorted Erin back to the kitchen as instructed. She said goodbye to Willie and Vic, who were going to go check out some of the shows and maybe do a little shopping, and headed to the back with the waiter. She looked at his name badge. Marvin. Well, Marvin was certainly not going to be getting any tips from her, with the way he was acting toward her. And he wasn't going to be getting any tips from her friends, either.

Chef Kirschoff greeted Erin in the kitchen and gave her a whirlwind tour, moving from one preparation area to another, barreling through the people who were busily preparing the dishes to be consumed in the dining room. It was both busier and better organized that Erin had expected. She had expected chaos, but the group worked like a well-oiled machine, prepping the various parts of the dishes, assembling them, plating them for consumption, and lining them up so that they could be taken to the dining room at just the right moment.

"This is really amazing," Erin marveled. "It's just a couple of us in the bakery kitchen, so we're working on a lot of different things at once, and have specific routines to keep us on track, but this is really taking it to the next level."

"We have several thousand people to feed each day," Kirschoff pointed out. "Not everyone eats here, and the staff have their own kitchens, but we still have to be ready to prepare several thousand plates a day. If we weren't well-organized, there's no way we could carry on."

Erin nodded. "It really is amazing the way you have everyone working here."

She saw a couple of kitchen workers who were not in the crew kitchen uniforms carrying in supplies. Bags of potatoes, flour, and other ingredients that were obviously in high demand in the kitchen. They were dressed in what looked like linen pajamas and had Asian or Polynesian features. Filipinos, perhaps?

They smiled at Erin and bowed to the chef, and went quickly about their work, hauling ingredients up from storage areas to the kitchen and distributing them to the proper prep areas. Erin smiled and nodded back. The workers dropped their eyes and continued to work. Looking around, Erin found them not only carrying ingredients in, but also working over the steaming sinks and garbages, cleaning up any spills, and doing all of the chores that didn't require training.

"Wow. So where do you want to work? Is there space for us somewhere? I didn't mean to interrupt you from your work."

"Everybody knows what they need to do. The chef can take some time away from the food preparation for a while. Sometimes it seems like I'm a kindergarten teacher rather than a cook. Keeping the children from their petty squabbles, redirecting them, seeing that spills get cleaned up and everything gets put away in their proper cubbies." Kirschoff laughed. "The amount of cooking that I actually do myself is trivial."

"That's too bad. I wouldn't want to give up my cooking for a supervisory position. I really need to be able to get my hands into things. It's... therapeutic."

"Yes," Kirschoff nodded and pointed at her. "You are absolutely right. And when you don't get enough time with your hands in the ingredients... it's like you go into withdrawal. When you are a runner and start getting irritable, your family tells you it's time to go out for a run. When you're a cook and everyone starts getting on your nerves, you know it's time to get cooking!"

Erin smiled. She loved to work out her anxieties in the kitchen. She loved to create and come up with dishes that were brand new, something that was just her. Something that had never existed before and would not exist if she hadn't spent the time on it. The fact that it also gave her pleasure to eat and to give to someone else was just an added bonus.

"Come over here. We have plenty of space." Kirschoff took her to a quieter area of the kitchen where there was a clear food prep counter. "Have you been thinking about my Baked Alaska?"

"Yes. I don't think it's anything that's too difficult. The ice cream part is already gluten-free, or can be pretty easily. It's the cake part that you need a gluten-free recipe for, and cake isn't that hard to do." She paused, frowning. "How do you do a vegan meringue? Do you use tofu?"

"No," he smiled. "The meringue is a secret. Although if you look it up online, it's not that much of a secret..."

"Hmm..." Erin considered. "I remember when I was trying to make something for Bertie, I was looking at chickpea brine as an egg replacer in some baking. And it seems to me that it can be whipped up into meringues just like eggs."

"Not just like eggs," Kirschoff said, "but pretty close! The miracle of aquafaba!"

"And it really works? I looked at the pictures online, but I just couldn't imagine that it would actually work. Like maybe it was all just some elaborate conspiracy to fool people into making a big mess..."

"It works. Trust me. I'll show you later, when we make the Baked

Alaska. It is the cake that I am wrestling with. I want something that is not too dense or moist when placed next to the ice cream, but that holds up well to slicing."

Erin nodded.

"And some of the Baked Alaskas also have a crust, like a cookie crumb crust. That's a bit of a question as well. Though I was thinking of maybe doing a pecan crumb crust… if that would work…"

"I never use nuts at the bakery, because they are so allergenic. But I would think that would work. Pecans, sugar, some butter—er, coconut oil?"

He nodded. "Yes, that was what I was thinking. How about your cake recipes, do you have some that might work?"

"Sure. What flavor are you looking for? Chocolate? Vanilla? Or something more unusual?"

"Let me show you what I was thinking of."

CHAPTER 24

*E*rin was soon immersed in discussions and experimentation with Chef Kirschoff, able to put her worries aside for the moment to focus on her love of baking for special diets. Chef Kirschoff was ebullient, always enthusiastic about her suggestions and writing copious notes on index cards that she hoped were all going to be collated somewhere after they finished. He gave orders a few times for the kitchen workers to go pull something out of storage or to see if he had something else. He didn't have a lot of specialty gluten-free ingredients on hand, but they worked with what they had and Kirschoff said he would be able to order anything else for delivery in a few days.

It was a long time before Erin looked at the clock on the wall and realized how late it was getting.

"Oh, I was so wrapped up in this, I wasn't watching the time." She thought first about bed, and then about Terry. She still hadn't heard anything back from him as to what had happened after he left the dining room. She wiggled her phone out of her pocket and looked at it. There was a text from Terry, which had been received almost an hour before. He wanted to know where she was. "Look at that. I didn't even feel it vibrate."

Kirschoff laughed. "You are like me, lost in the world of cooking."

"I definitely was." She tapped out a reply to Terry, wondering whether he would receive it or if it would just be sent to dead air like so many of her texts on the ship had been.

In the kitchen. Are you done?

She waited for a few minutes to see whether it would be delivered or return an error. There was a delay, but eventually it was marked as delivered. Erin was putting her phone back in her pocket, figuring it would probably be another half hour before she heard back from Terry again, or else he would come looking for her rather than bothering to text back, when it vibrated in her hand. She pulled it back out and looked at the screen.

I'm done for now. Ready for bed?

I'll meet you at the cabin, Erin texted back.

There was an almost immediate response. *No walking alone. I'll come get you.*

Erin rolled her eyes. She texted him a thumbs-up and looked around. "He's going to come here to get me. I'll help you with clean-up." She hadn't realized how quiet the kitchen had gotten. They weren't alone by any means, but the dinner rush was over and many of the prep areas that had previously been occupied had been cleaned up and were now vacant. The clink of dishes being washed was like a lullaby.

"Oh, you don't need to help with that. I have people."

"I don't like leaving a mess!" Erin started to pick up the mixing bowls and measuring cups she had used.

"No, no, no. Guests do not do clean-up. You leave everything where it is. I will clean up and my staff will help. You do not clean up."

He took a bowl out of her hands. Erin laughed and shrugged. "Alright," she conceded. "Fine, I'll leave it to you."

He put it back down on the counter and leaned back, considering her. "You are very good at what you do. What has been your biggest gluten-free baking challenge?"

Erin frowned, thinking about it. She had been able to overcome many different obstacles in her baking career, short though it had been. Once she decided what she wanted to make, she thought and researched and worked it out, trying numerous different recipes and solutions until she could make it work. So far, it had stood her in good stead.

"It's hard to say. Probably the pickiest is phyllo type pastries. Turnovers and pastry shells and puff pastries. It can be done, but it takes a lot of fiddling and making sure that everything is just right. As far as the hardest… that would probably be developing recipes that Bertie Braceling could eat. He's not around anymore…" She swallowed a hot lump in her throat, trying not to think about it. "He was a friend who had a lot of allergies and intolerances, and finding ingredients that I could use and making them work together was really a challenge. Just when I would think that I had the right solution, he'd shake his head and tell me that he couldn't have this or that. I think half the time he was just making up bizarre excuses to see how creative I could be. It was a lot of fun, and I developed a couple of recipes that he could eat, but nothing fancy."

"He was gluten-free and had other allergies too?"

"Celiac disease can lead to a leaky gut, which can result in all kinds of other intolerances and allergies. If you have a gut that allows molecules that haven't been broken down to their component parts that the body can use being absorbed into the bloodstream, then your body has to fight them off as invaders, and you start reacting to anything that is in your regular diet. I know a number of celiacs or people with other gut problems that have long lists of things that they can't eat. And the list is always growing and changing as they change their diets."

He nodded. "That makes sense. I am always suspicious of the people who claim that they can't have dozens of different foods. I think they are just being picky because they want things made a certain way. But as a chef, you have to assume they are telling the truth anyway, because if you don't believe them and end up poisoning them…" He rolled his eyes and shook his head. "You could end up with a wrongful death suit, if not in jail."

Thinking of her experiences with Angela and Trenton Plaint, Erin gave a shudder. "Believe me, that is not a situation you want to get caught in."

One of the wait staff appeared at their elbows, hovering close. "Miss Price's escort has arrived."

Erin was surprised at first that Terry hadn't come all the way into the kitchen for her, but decided on balance that probably wasn't a very good idea with K9. The cruise might allow his service animal to come on the cruise, but that didn't mean that animals were allowed in the kitchen. She touched Kirschoff on the shoulder.

"Thanks so much for letting me come and play," she said. "I really needed the distraction, and that was a lot of fun."

Kirschoff gathered his index cards into a pile. "And I have a lot of information I didn't have before, so I can start tweaking other recipes as well. It's important to have a foundation to build on. This was very helpful."

Erin went with the waiter back through the kitchen to the dining room, where Terry was waiting with K9. Though he was good at hiding it, Erin thought he looked tired, lines of fatigue showing around his eyes. Usually, she was in bed before he was, but she'd seen him after enough disasters or long shifts to recognize the exhaustion.

"Should have known I'd find you in the kitchen," he said with a smile.

"Yes, you should have. I was going to get in there sooner or later."

"I hope you didn't make a pest of yourself."

She knew by his tone that he wasn't serious. They headed back toward their cabin.

"So…? Are you going to tell me what happened?" she asked.

"I'm really not at liberty to share anything right now."

"You can tell me something. Was it the captain? Did something happen to him?"

Terry didn't answer right away, walking along beside her at a measured pace. "Yes," he said finally. "It was the captain. I imagine that much will be out by now."

"Was he in an accident? What happened?"

"He's dead."

Erin grabbed Terry's arm. "What? What happened to him?"

"Unknown causes right now."

"Does that mean it was a heart attack or stroke? Or…?"

Terry's face was pale. He considered his answer, scratching his head. "That is yet to be determined. Right now… our initial guess is that it could be an allergic reaction."

"Could be?"

"That's not the only option. The doctor happens to know that he had a severe peanut allergy. But it could have been a heart attack. Or… poisoning."

Erin got goosebumps. She looked up at him. "Are you saying he was murdered?"

"There will have to be an investigation, but I still don't have any jurisdiction."

"Then what have you been doing the last few hours?" Erin looked at the time on her phone, calculating how long he had been occupied, apparently, just in finding out that the captain was dead from possible poisoning.

Terry gave a sheepish smile. "Well, I may have pulled rank as the only actual police officer on board. But that's not going to get me very far. They're already contacting their owners, who I assume will tell them to shut up and freeze me out."

Erin stroked his arm, both to comfort herself and to keep him calm about the situation he faced. "So what will they do? Will they get someone onto the ship at the next stop? What are they going to do with the captain's body?" She had a sudden vision of a burial at sea, disposing of the captain's body before an inquiry could be made.

"They've transferred him down to the morgue. I was overseeing procedures, trying to maintain chain of custody for any evidence, but I'm afraid nobody on board is trained in handling of evidence or crime scenes."

"The morgue? Are you telling me there is a morgue on the ship?"

"There is a morgue on every cruise ship."

Erin's jaw dropped. "Really? You're kidding me!"

He nodded vigorously. "People die on cruise ships all the time. They are old and have a heart attack or die in their sleep, or influenza or norovirus goes through the ship and people start dropping like flies. Or other things happen. You can't predict. So every cruise ship has a morgue that can accommodate at least two or three people, and if they end up with more, they start using the refrigerators."

Erin gaped at him. "Gross! Do that many people really die on ships?"

"Apparently so." He gave a sheepish smile. "I didn't know either. I got my education today."

"So what are they going to do? They must have to call in the authorities now." Erin started thinking about the man who had been thrown overboard. If police were being sent to investigate the captain's death, then maybe they would be open to hearing about the man who had gone over the rail. Maybe it was even connected. "Do you think it has anything to do with the other death?"

"One thing at a time. First of all... no, they're not keen to call in any authorities. I talked to them about it and tried to talk them into something, but they were pretty resistant. They'll talk to the cruise line bigwigs tonight, and my guess is that by morning they'll have a new position, and no one will be coming to investigate."

"But why wouldn't they? The captain has been killed!"

"The captain has died. There's no proof at this point that he was intentionally killed. It might have been natural causes."

"But they'll want to find that out, won't they?"

"As I'm learning more and more about these cruises... I'm not convinced that they will. The operating model seems to be that they cover up anything negative, and continue to make a profit. You don't talk about people disappearing or getting thrown overboard. You don't talk about epidemics on ships, or morgues, or the captain kicking the bucket. Rather than investigating, you cover it up. Getting the captain to agree to open an internal investigation was like pulling teeth. And whether or not this was the result of his agreeing... I don't know. But it's an awfully big coincidence if there is no connection between them."

"And cops don't like coincidences."

"No one likes coincidences."

Erin nodded. She didn't like it either. Was it possible that the captain had found something, so he was killed for it? Or maybe he was getting close to finding something out? They hadn't just thrown him over the rail, so it wouldn't look too much like it was connected; but leaving the body on the ship didn't actually prove anything.

"So what are they going to do? They won't look into it at all? They won't call the police or FBI in to investigate it?"

"I'm doing the best I can, but they're not properly equipped for a murder investigation. And I expect to be told at any point to get out and stay out. I'm trying to preserve any evidence, but for all I know, it could be dumped in the middle of the ocean tomorrow."

"So they'll just keep him in the morgue until... when? Until they're back at Seattle?" obviously, they wouldn't bring him out in British Columbia, getting the RCMP or some other Canadian police force involved. If they had to get police involved, they would want it to be US police.

"That's what it looks like. Then they'll turn the body over to someone... from what I can gather, they'll just notify the family and have them send a mortician to pick him up. They aren't a US ship, so they aren't under any obligation to have the US police conduct an investigation."

"That's insane. Is that what they usually do when someone dies on board? There's no investigation, they just turn the body over to the family when they get home?"

Terry nodded. They arrived at their cabin, and Terry unlocked it. He turned on the light and they both looked around cautiously, afraid of finding that the room had been tossed like Vic's.

"And what about those cruises that take months? They just... keep the body on ice until they get home?"

He nodded.

"But then if the family does want an investigation, it's been five months. All of the evidence is gone and everyone has forgotten what happened."

"Exactly."

"But that's outrageous!"

"It keeps their reported crime rate nice and low. If nothing is ever reported to the police, then there aren't any statistics to show that they're lying when they say there is no crime on board the ship. A cruise is the safest kind of vacation you can take, because there are no reports of any kind of crime taking place. Or if there are reports, they are at a much, much lower level than they would be in the continental United States."

Erin sat down on the bed. "Did you know any of this before we came?"

"No. I'd never heard anything about the crime rates on board cruise ships, or the way that criminal activity is dealt with, or not dealt with."

"What if something happens that everyone sees? What if someone stabs someone else with a steak knife or gets in a drunken brawl over poker? Do they just put them in house arrest in their cabin, and then let them go again the next day?"

"Pretty much. All cruise ships have morgues, but they don't generally have brigs. There is no secure detention area. People simply aren't arrested on board. They're warned off, maybe put in their cabin to cool down, and that's it. If someone is really disruptive, they just put him off of the ship at the next port of call and he can find his own way home."

Erin frowned. "Well, that's one thing if you're put ashore in Alaska, but what if you're halfway around the world? How are you supposed to find your way home?"

"I don't know. That's up to you. I'm told that when you sign on for something like this, you pretty much sign away all of your rights to safety and agree not to sue them. You say that you know you're going into a risky situation, and that you won't hold them responsible for anything that happens on the cruise."

"Do you remember signing anything like that?"

"I remember we had to sign a few forms when we sent them our passenger information. But… I didn't really read it. It was all legalese; I figured it was the same kind of thing as you sign when you go on a bungee jump. They're not responsible if you jump and the rope breaks. But I didn't have any clue that it was so wide ranging, or that we were going into something dangerous. I just figured they use the same form for all of their cruises, whether you're going somewhere politically unstable or prone to hurricanes or somewhere quiet and uneventful, like Alaska. I didn't actually think… that anything untoward could happen on a ship touring Alaska. It isn't like we're early explorers, who don't know the way. It's the same route that thousands of people travel every week. It didn't sound dangerous."

Erin nodded. "I guess there was stuff to sign in the package, but I didn't read it either. I thought it was just that I wouldn't bring drugs on board or sue them if someone stole my diamond broach."

"Exactly." Terry nodded and sat down beside her. "I think that's the impression that they intend to give. This is just paperwork that's legally required for your own protection, sign it and send it back. Who would read all of it? And if you did read it… why would you sign it? Why would you agree that the cruise line and crew didn't have any liability for anything that might happen to you on your vacation, including getting killed, lost at sea, or being put ashore in a foreign country without any way to return home? Would you sign something like that? Knowingly?"

Erin considered it. She held Terry's hand, alternating her fingers between his, then lay back on the bed, relaxing. "I don't know. I might still have signed something like that. Because I didn't think that anything dangerous was going to happen. Why worry that someone says you can't sue them if you lose a finger, if you're not planning on putting your fingers near any blades? It's just one of those things… you do it because it just sounds too ridiculous and far-fetched to be true. Like the liability warnings on trampolines or stereos. Don't operate while sleeping. Don't immerse in water. Don't use as a projectile on a catapult. You just laugh because it's so ridiculous that they would think they have to cover their butts for something like that."

"Yeah. I can see that. You think there's no way that could happen to any reasonable person, so you'll just be reasonable, and you'll never have to worry about the consequences of what you signed."

Terry reclined beside her. "I'm going to have to go back out."

"What? I thought you were done!"

"No. I just thought I'd better take a break and make sure everything was okay with you. You need to get to sleep soon if you're going to go on the tour tomorrow. I'm not sure what I'm going to be doing, but I need to get as much of the investigation done as possible before anyone puts on the brakes. Maybe it won't amount to anything, but I feel obligated as an officer of the law to do what I can, however little that might be."

"Are you going to be up all night?"

"I don't know. Probably not. I assume everyone will want to knock off before long. You go ahead and go to sleep. I'll be back as soon as I can."

"Okay." Erin raised their intertwined hands to her lips and kissed his finger. "I'll miss you."

She was amused to see a little color enter his features. He smiled like he hadn't since they'd first gotten onto the ship, the dimple appearing in his cheek.

"Maybe when I get back, if it's not too late, we could spend a little time together."

Erin nodded. "Yes. That would be nice."

He loosed his hand from hers and stood reluctantly. "I'm going to take K9 with me. Is that okay with you?"

"Yes. I'll be fine. I'll lock the door after you."

"Chain it too."

"I will."

Erin wasn't sure if she would, since if it were chained, she would have to get up from bed to let Terry in when he got back from his investigation. But she wanted to be safe, so she knew she should.

"See you later."

CHAPTER 25

*E*rin took some time to get to sleep, tossing and turning restlessly. In spite of the fact that she'd been fantasizing about being able to go to sleep without someone else in her bed to elbow her or wake her up or whom she had to be careful not to awaken, she missed having Terry there. As much as she worried about keeping him awake with her restlessness and nightmares, it was a comfort to have him there beside her, watching her and keeping her safe, and cuddling her in his arms when she got upset. She finally had the bed to herself, and she didn't like it.

She eventually fell into a restless sleep, but was awakened several times by nightmares, or by the sound of footsteps progressing down the hallway outside and loud voices of people who had been drinking and were on their way back to their cabins. She'd never liked sleeping in hotels, and ships were the same sort of thing, living in close quarters with others and having to hear their comings and goings. She should have put in earplugs, but by the time she thought about it, she was too sleepy to consider getting out of bed to put them in. She'd end up waking herself up more and then wouldn't be able to get back to sleep again.

Just count sheep. Or cupcakes.

She tried to listen to her own advice, but it was not working. She turned over, hugged the pillow to her, and closed her eyes again. She'd grown up living in a lot of different places. She could get to sleep wherever she wanted to. She didn't have to be in her own bed.

At least that's what she kept repeating to herself.

It was amazing how much she missed Terry, when they had only been sleeping together sporadically for a short period of time and had never spent every night together until the cruise. But she missed the feeling of his weight on the mattress and his warmth close to her, knowing that he would hold her if she got scared or upset.

Finally, she heard Terry's key and the door opening. He moved slowly, furtively, so as not to wake her up. She supposed she should tell him that he'd already woken her up, but that seemed rude. She rolled over as if she were still asleep and just trying to get more comfortable. In a minute, she felt his weight next to her and he crawled in beside her, quiet as a mouse.

"You were a long time," Erin murmured, moving closer to him and reaching out for him. "Did you find anything out?"

The smell of smoke clung to him. The captain hadn't smelled like cigarette smoke, but Terry must have been somewhere there was smoke. Maybe one of the casinos allowed the players to smoke. Though why would he need to be in the casino to investigate the possible murder of the captain? Did he already have a suspect and was looking for someone to interview?

"You smell," she told him.

She could hear him breathing. He didn't answer her, but put his arms around her and pulled her close.

As soon as Erin's body and lips touched him, she knew it wasn't Terry. She went rigid and tried to scream, but the man held her head in one big hand, pulling her hard against his mouth, effectively gagging her. Erin struggled, trying to free herself from his grip, still trying to cry out.

He had not stripped down. She could feel his clothes under her hands. In a way, it was a relief, but it also meant that he intended to do what he had come for and get away quickly without anyone being the wiser. He couldn't run out into the passageway naked and expect not to be noticed. She clawed at him, trying to get his throat and face. He pinned her with his weight. Erin kept fighting back, but every self-defense class she'd ever taken had taught techniques to use when standing, facing an attacker. It was completely different with him using his weight to press her down and forcing himself over her face and body.

Erin writhed wildly and managed to get her face free for a moment as he took a breath and readjusted. She shrieked as loudly as she could. At first, she just screamed incoherently, making a noise but not saying anything. Then she yelled for Vic and for Willie. They were only a little way away, and she'd been able to hear people coming and going down the hallway all night. They would be able to hear her through the walls.

Her attacker abandoned the fight, letting her go and racing for the door. He was out of the room, slamming the door behind him, leaving Erin gasping and crying and still screaming on the bed.

CHAPTER 26

*E*rin! Erin, you had a nightmare, it's okay." Vic turned the light on as she entered the cabin and was at Erin's side. "It's okay, you're safe. It's alright."

Erin shook her head. "There was someone in here! It's not okay! It wasn't a nightmare! It was real. Someone was in here and tried to... to assault me."

Vic stroked Erin's cheek. Willie stood in the doorway, watching but keeping his distance, obviously wary of making Erin more upset by simply being a man. He didn't speak or do anything that might aggravate her.

"It wasn't a dream!" Erin insisted. She wiped at her mouth, trying to wipe away his sour taste and the stale smell of cigarettes. Her hand came away streaked with blood. "Look! You see? I didn't just imagine it!"

Vic looked at the blood on Erin's hand, then turned her face to look at it. "You are bleeding. I think maybe you just bit yourself."

"Why won't you believe me? Just because I've had nightmares, that doesn't mean I'm dreaming now. I'm telling, you, there was someone in here. You didn't unlock the door, did you?"

"No," Vic admitted, looking back toward Willie. "The door was unlocked."

"Do you think Terry would have left it unlocked? I locked it behind him earlier, when he went back out to continue the investigation into..."

Erin trailed off, unsure how much they knew or whether she would be breaking confidences.

"We heard," Willie said in a low, gravelly voice. "About the captain, I mean. What a crazy boat this is. There's something really wrong here."

"There is!" Erin agreed. "And someone was in here. They attacked me. He. He attacked me. He tried to assault me. He did this!" She dabbed at the blood at the corner of her mouth. "I didn't bite myself."

"Okay." Vic swallowed strenuously and looked back at Willie, her eyes wide. "Did you see anyone in the hallway?"

"I didn't see anyone when I came out of our cabin. But I wasn't looking for anyone else, either. I was just heading toward Erin. She was screaming and I just came straight here. I didn't look behind me, or down the end of the hall, and if he'd already gone around the corner... I didn't hear anyone running. If I had..." He shook his head at Erin. "I'm sorry. If I'd known, I would have chased him."

Vic helped Erin to sit up and cuddled her close. "I'm so sorry! Do you know anything about him? Did he say anything? Do you know who it was?"

"He stank of cigarettes. He must be a smoker."

Vic nodded. "Okay. Anything else? Any other smells? Could you see anything? Hear anything?"

"No." Erin closed her eyes and thought about it. How had she known so quickly that it wasn't Terry? What had been different about him from Terry? She hadn't known immediately, but when he'd pulled her into an embrace and kissed her, she had known without a doubt. "He... he had a uniform, I think. I could feel... buttons, epaulets... the fabric was stiff."

"So it was one of the crew?" Willie asked.

"Yes. It must have been."

"Anything else?" Vic prompted. "Was he... fat? Skinny? Could you tell how tall he was?"

"No. I don't know, I thought he was just Terry until I touched him. Then I knew. I knew it wasn't him."

"Of course you did," Vic agreed. "You see and touch Terry every day. You would know it wasn't him."

"How did he get in?" Willie asked, looking at the door for evidence. "He had a key."

"Yes. He unlocked it. I heard the key in the lock."

"You should put the chain on too."

"I did," Erin remembered. "Terry said to and I did. He should have just opened the door into the chain and not been able to get it open the rest of the way."

"Unless he was expecting the chain to be on and had some experience in unlocking them from the outside," Willie said. "Most of these security locks are pretty easy to open with a tool or a rubber band. If you know what you're doing, you can have it off in a few seconds."

Erin remembered the jingle of the chain. He hadn't opened the door right into the chain. He'd unlocked the handle, then opened it up enough to disengage the chain, and entered at will.

"Why aren't these rooms more secure? Anyone can just walk in here who pleases? Why wouldn't they have any real security?"

"The crew needs to be able to access cabins when the passengers lock themselves out. Or if someone is hurt or sick. If someone doesn't show up for roll call and doesn't answer their door in the morning, what are you going to do? They need to be able to access the cabins. You just would think that the cruise line would be properly vetting the crew so that they weren't letting criminals into passengers' rooms!"

"He just let himself in," Erin repeated. "How could they let him do that?"

Willie looked up and down the hallway once again. "We'll see whether they picked him up on their surveillance cameras. There are a lot of cameras around, one of them must have picked him up at some point."

Erin just shook her head. She knew for a fact that the crew wasn't going to give up one of their own. They would look at the security tapes and shrug their shoulders. *I'm sorry... it looks like he avoided all of the cameras...*

Vic rubbed Erin's back soothingly. "You'd better go get Terry," she told Willie.

CHAPTER 27

*I*t didn't take long for Willie to return with Terry, who, as well as looking tired, now looked panic-stricken.

"Erin! Are you okay?"

Erin nodded, tears suddenly springing to her eyes. "I'm fine. I managed to scream, and it scared him off..."

"But you're hurt. Willie said he attacked you."

Erin nodded. "Just split my lip. Nothing serious. But that wasn't all he wanted."

He swore and sat on the side of the bed. He reached his arms out to her, but let her come to him rather than embracing her. "Erin, I'm so sorry. I had no idea... I thought you were safe. It was locked and chained, and I didn't think that anyone would break in. Why would anyone risk that?"

"I don't know. I just woke up... he came in... I thought it was you, until I got... close to him, and then I knew it wasn't. He didn't say anything, he just grabbed me and..." She swallowed, unable to describe it in more detail.

"I'm so sorry."

"You don't need to keep apologizing. Neither of us knew it was going to happen."

"I could have left K9 with you. He would have protected you."

"But we didn't know. We thought that with the door locked, it would be okay."

"Yes. I wish… I just don't know what to say. How would anyone even know that you were alone here? As far as anyone knew, you were with me. Why would anyone break in?"

"The crew knew you weren't here with her," Willie pointed out.

Erin felt like the walls were closing in around her. They were watching her. They knew when she was by herself and when she was with someone else. She couldn't get away from the crew, she couldn't know which ones were harboring bad feelings against her and which ones were involved in whatever crimes were happening on the ship. She was lucky that it had only been an attempted assault, and not attempted murder. Or successful murder. How much harder would it have been for someone to enter with a knife and to stab her in the dark? She wouldn't even have known what was going on until it was too late. She crawled into Terry's arms and buried her face in his chest.

"It's okay, Erin. You're okay," he told her.

"But it's not okay! And I can't be with you every second! We need to get off of this ship."

He squeezed her tight. "We'll figure something out. We'll keep you safe."

"How can you? You don't have any idea who is safe and who isn't. The captain didn't know who was safe, and they were his crew! If anyone knows them, it should have been him! And how did that turn out for him? He's dead!"

"I know. I know. We'll figure it out."

The tears streamed down Erin's face. She didn't even try to stop them. Terry held her for some time, not saying anything and not trying to talk her out of being upset. After a while, though, he pulled back from her, trying to look at her face.

"You might be in shock, Erin. Are you cold? How are you feeling?"

"I don't know. I feel… I just feel like I'm falling apart. I don't know how I'm supposed to feel.."

"You're supposed to feel however you do." He put his fingers over her pulse and stared into her eyes. "Let's get another blanket on you. And maybe some tea?" he looked over at Vic. "Can you get room service to bring something down? I don't want you to go get it, I want us all to stay together."

Vic nodded. "Yeah, of course."

She went over to the phone and sat down in the desk chair. She called the room service number and ordered not only enough tea for all of them, but also some pastries and some fruit. She hung up the phone. "It shouldn't be too long. They'll bring it right down." She leaned back in the chair, sighing. "What are you going to do, Terry? Are you going to report this to the police? Or to the first mate or whoever is in charge now? You should tell someone what's going on. This is getting ridiculous. We should have... I don't know. A guard on the door. It's obvious someone is targeting Erin personally, so she needs to be protected. It isn't just dangerous for us to be wandering around the ship alone. It's dangerous for Erin to be here at all."

"You're right. I don't know what I'm going to do yet. I might call some people back in Tennessee to get their input on what action to take. At this point, I'm not sure of anything anymore. And who knows, half of this stuff that they're giving me on not being subject to the laws of the USA could be crap. I'm not a lawyer. All I can do is accept what they're telling me. And with the number of criminals who are apparently on this boat, why would I believe anyone?"

Willie nodded. "I think we should all stay here. In your room. I'm not comfortable leaving the two of you alone. Even though you're here to protect Erin... You're not armed. If someone was to come in here in the night with a knife or a gun, or even just a baseball bat... we can at least improve the odds by having more of us in here."

"I don't think you need to do that..." Erin protested.

"I do. And Terry does too, don't you?"

Terry grimaced. He obviously wanted to say that Willie was wrong and that they wanted their privacy and didn't need him there, but he couldn't bring himself to say it. He knew it wasn't true. There was just too much going on for him to think that he could keep Erin safe all by himself.

"Well... for tonight, anyway. I'm not sure that's feasible in the long term, but I would feel better if we were not alone the rest of the night. I'm sure we'll be fine, the attacker has fled and they're not going to come back here while we're being so vigilant, but I have to be sure. I have to sleep tonight, and I don't think I could if I was the only one here to guard against another attack."

Vic nodded, but didn't say anything.

"We really do need to talk to someone," Willie said. "Even if we can't get anyone to come here to help, someone at home needs to know what's going on on the ship. If something were to happen to us, they need to know what we already know. There is obviously a secret here that is too dangerous to keep."

"Yes. That sounds like an idea. We can do that tomorrow when we go on the tour. We'll be able to use a landline and get a good connection."

"What are we doing tomorrow?" Willie asked.

"We are touring the glacier, for one thing," Vic said. "I'm not sure how much of that will be by boat and how much we will be on land for. But there's bound to be a phone somewhere. We'll call the US and at least talk to someone."

None of them was feeling particularly fresh in the morning. They had drunk tea and eaten donuts late into the night, and eventually Erin couldn't keep her eyes open anymore and drifted off to sleep in Terry's arms. She didn't know when the others went to sleep, but when she woke up in the morning, both Vic and Willie were still asleep on the pull-out couch. Erin knew it probably wasn't comfortable, but at least they had gotten some sleep. She ordered breakfast from room service to let everyone else sleep as long as they could. She would have just gone up to the dining room to eat, if that had been feasible. But with a target on her back, she wasn't willing to do that. Vic would kill her even if a crew member didn't.

The others awoke as the food arrived. Terry stuck to coffee, Vic and Erin had a light breakfast, and Willie cleaned up the rest. He grinned at Erin. "I have a fast metabolism."

"You must. Terry walks all day and still doesn't eat like that."

"I've been blessed."

"We're still going on the tour today, right?" Vic asked. "We're not just going to hide in the cabin all day?"

"No," Terry agreed. "We'll go up on deck and act like nothing has happened. I don't think I'm going to tell the first mate about it. I don't trust anyone on the crew. I don't want to use any ship communications that they can eavesdrop on." He scratched the back of his head, then rubbed his eyes.

"A lot of the tour is supposed to be by boat, so we'll just watch from the deck for that part. Then when we go ashore… I'll make a phone call. Either on my cell if I can get a signal, or on someone's land line. I'd call in rein-forcements, but I'm not sure if there's anything I can actually do. But I want someone to know what's going on. Like Willie said, if something happened to us, I would want someone to know what it is we know. These guys have to be stopped."

Willie and Vic nodded their agreement.

Erin didn't nod, just feeling sick inside. *If something happened to them?* They were making contingency plans for what would happen if all of them got killed and were unable to tell their story. All because Erin had poked her nose into yet another mystery that was absolutely none of her business.

What did it matter if someone on board were smuggling drugs or arti-facts? Weren't their lives worth more than that? Wasn't it more important to keep them all safe?

She wanted to go home, back to Auntie Clem's Bakery to make her gluten-free baking, side-by-side with Vic, with Terry stopping in to refill his water and get a biscuit for K9 every day. She wanted everything to go back to normal, the way it had been before leaving Bald Eagle Falls. It was ridicu-lous that they had left Bald Eagle Falls in the first place. What did they think they were going to find? Some kind of frigid utopia off the coast of Alaska?

Terry eyed Erin. "Make sure you put on a sweater. You're shivering."

"It's cold."

"Yes, it is. But the cabins are kept pretty warm. I'm still worried about you."

"You don't need to worry about me. I don't want anyone worrying about me. I just want all of us to get home in one piece."

"Well, we can't all go home safely if you aren't with us."

Erin sighed. "I wish we hadn't come. I wish I hadn't gone wandering in the middle of the night and seen the murder. What was I thinking? That I could just wander all over a boat filled with strangers and nothing bad would happen to me?"

"We all thought that we would be safe," Vic said. "None of us thought anything like this was going to happen. But it did. We have to accept that and deal with it, right? We just have to."

Erin shrugged. "I'm going to get dressed."

She grabbed her clothes, including a sweater, and went into the bathroom to dress. She splashed cold water on her face and returned to them a few minutes later, trying to act like she was calm and collected even if she wasn't feeling that way.

"Okay. If everyone else is ready to go…"

"We need to go get dressed too," Vic pointed out. "We'll be five minutes, okay?"

Terry agreed. "Five minutes. Then be back here. I want us all to stay together, if we can. Maybe you should bring your luggage in here, and we'll plan on you sleeping on the pull-out for the rest of the trip."

Vic made a face. "I don't think I can sleep on that thing every night. If we don't get good quality sleep, none of us are going to be good for anything."

Terry's lips pressed together. He shook his head in frustration. "If we just knew who was behind all of this… we could get them arrested and feel safe for the rest of the trip."

"Depends how many of them are involved in it," Erin pointed out. "I don't think this is just one man. I don't think the man who attacked me last night was the same man who threw that other man overboard."

"You don't?" he stopped and looked at her. "Why not?"

Erin tried to think through the impressions she'd had of him. "I don't think he was the same build… but I didn't see him in the light, so I can't be sure. And the man on the deck didn't smell like cigarettes."

"He was outside, and you were inside. You wouldn't have been able to smell him."

"I probably could have. And he came inside. We were standing just a few feet apart, and I didn't smell any cigarette smoke."

"Okay. So there are at least two involved in whatever scheme they've got going on. Plus the man who went overboard. How many more do you think could be involved without everyone finding out about it? The captain apparently didn't know about what was going on, or he wouldn't have been killed when he started the investigation."

Vic made a motion toward their cabin. "Going to get changed. We can talk about the rest later."

She and Willie went back down the corridor. Erin sighed. She sat on the bed watching Terry get ready.

"Did you find anything else out last night? About the captain and what happened to him?"

Terry frowned as he dressed. "I shouldn't really talk about an open investigation…"

"What open investigation? There isn't really any investigation, is there? It's just you."

"That's true… but I still feel…"

"Someone else should know what you're thinking. Don't you always have someone to report to when you're investigating in Bald Eagle Falls? You don't just act on your own."

"There's no one else to report to here. They have their security staff, but I'm not confident that they're not involved in some way."

"So tell me. Then at least two people will know what's going on."

He finished buttoning up his shirt and let K9 out of his kennel. "There's not very much to tell, unfortunately. I don't have a lab and there's only so much I can to do investigate."

"He died while he was eating his dinner?"

Terry pursed his lips and looked at her for a minute. "Where did you hear that?"

"I didn't hear it. If you think it might have been an allergy or might have been poisoning, then he must have been eating, or just finished eating."

"Oh." His face flushed a little. "I guess that was a bit obvious. Yes, he was in the middle of eating his dinner."

"Do you know what allergies he had? Peanut? Anything else?"

"That's all that the doctor knew about. I assume if there was something else, he would have told the doctor."

"It could have been something unusual that he didn't think he'd be exposed to on the cruise. Or it was something new. Sometimes people develop new allergies quite suddenly."

"So he could have died from an allergy he didn't know he had?"

"Could have," Erin agreed. She scratched K9's ears. "Did it look like allergies? Or poisoning?"

"I couldn't tell the difference. The doctor figured it was an allergy attack, but there really wasn't anything that would tell me one way or another… spittle around the mouth. Scratches on his arms. The doctor said his throat was swollen. None of that proves one theory or the other."

"If they have a morgue on board, does that mean they can do an autopsy? To figure it out?"

"I don't think it's much more than cold storage. And the doctor isn't a specialist. I don't think he's qualified to do a proper autopsy."

Erin snapped her fingers for K9. He went over to nuzzle her hand and get ear scratches.

"It would figure that this would happen on a day when we're not close to a settlement," Terry said. "All there is here is a nature preserve, but no police force, even if we could get the crew to let them board. And tomorrow we are not scheduled to be ashore at all."

"After that, we're in Anchorage."

"Three days after the captain's death." Terry sighed. "All kinds of evidence could be destroyed by then."

"What evidence have you gathered?"

"What I've gathered is safe for the time being. Fingernail clippings, swabs of his mouth. I kept them with me so that no one can lose them. But in the meantime... we put the food into the freezer to preserve it. And there's the captain's body, his clothes, whatever trace evidence might have been left on him. I didn't have any way to prevent contamination of the scene, any of us might have left fibers or hairs or skin cells behind."

"And none of that is going to matter if no one comes to investigate it."

"Exactly."

CHAPTER 28

*T*hey all tried to behave normally and pretend that nothing had happened. They didn't want to reveal to the rest of the passengers that they had concerns about what had happened to the captain or that somebody had previously been killed on board. A full-fledged panic wouldn't help.

Erin stood at the railing, watching the water for any sign of whales or sharks, and the glacier for any other animal life. The brochure had brilliant pictures of seals, bears, birds, and other wildlife that could be found on the glacier but, so far, she hadn't seen much more than screeching gulls and an occasional eagle floating lazily above them.

Terry looked through the binoculars, scanning along the shore. She hadn't thought that he'd be able to relax and forget about the captain and the investigation, but he did seem to be enjoying himself. He handed her the binoculars and pointed to a spot where Erin could see the black smudges of some sea birds.

"Over there."

Erin looked through the binoculars and took a minute to zero in on the location he had pointed to and focus properly. As the stout little birds came into view, Erin laughed.

"Puffins!"

"You said you were hoping to see some."

"I love them! They're just so cute!" Erin watched them. They weren't doing anything, just standing around looking adorable. Before she won tickets for the tour, it had never occurred to her that she'd someday actually be able to see puffins in person. Maybe if she were lucky, she could see them in some marine aquarium or zoo. But she'd never expected to be floating just off the shores of Alaska, watching puffins in their natural habitat.

Erin lowered her binoculars to make sure that Vic had seen the puffins too. Vic lowered her binoculars at the same time, and they laughed at each other.

"I saw!" Vic confirmed. "So cute!"

"Don't you just wish you could take a couple of them home with you?"

Terry shook his head. "You girls. What would you do with puffins? Don't you already have enough animals?"

"I doubt if Orange Blossom would think much of puffins," Vic agreed. "Other than maybe for dinner. We'd have to keep them at my place instead."

"I want them at mine!"

"Neither of you is going to go home with puffins," Willie said sternly. But he was smiling too. They had all been so stressed with the violent happenings on board the ship that they were a little giddy.

Erin put the binoculars back up to her eyes and scanned for any other signs of wildlife. That was what she had gone on the cruise for in the first place. To see Alaska and all of its open spaces and untouched wilds. It was totally different from anything she had ever seen before.

She had come for the wildlife but had not been prepared for what life could really be like on a cruise ship.

She was both relieved and anxious when they reached the dock and were allowed to go ashore. There was, as Terry had said, no settlement, only the small visitor center and other buildings required to operate the nature preserve. There wasn't enough room in the visitor center to manage everyone in the tour at once, so they disembarked in smaller groups, each waiting for the group before them to receive their orientation and nature talk at the center and then go for a walk through the preserve.

Terry didn't pull rank and tell them that he had to go ashore first because he needed to use the phone. He instead waited patiently with the rest of the group, not giving away that he was interested in anything other than seeing the wildlife like everyone else. He used the binoculars, searching the water for whales. Erin looked away, and when she looked back at him she saw that he had switched his view and was focused instead inside the ship, scanning over the faces of the passengers as they stood visiting and the staff as they supervised, coming and going on various errands. She didn't say anything to him, wondering if he were able to pick anything up by looking at their faces. Would the killer or killers give themselves away in an unguarded moment, dropping the masks that they put on for the passengers and showing their true natures?

Erin looked over the faces of the crew members she could see. She didn't have the binoculars to examine them for smaller details. She couldn't see much more than whether people were smiling or frowning. One crew member stood out to her, scowling rather than smiling helpfully.

It was Saville, the man who had harassed Vic when she had first boarded the ship. Following his angry gaze, she saw that he was focused on Vic once again. Vic was visiting with some of the friends she had made, with the brightly colored hair, piercings, tattoos, and other signs of their non-compliance with society's norms. As if they needed to declare that they were individuals.

Erin drifted toward Vic. She wanted to be with her friend, wanted to protect her from the crewman's wrathful stare, but she didn't really want to be with the new friends Vic had made. There wasn't really a place for Erin in the group.

Willie saw her look and joined her. "Hey. Excited to go ashore and see what other animals are out and about?"

"Yeah." Erin watched Vic. "That will be cool, won't it?"

"I hate that I feel so jealous and protective of her," Willie said. "I don't want to be that way. But every time I see her with that crowd, I feel like... I'm losing her."

"You're not losing her. You are her boyfriend. She's just enjoying having people to talk to who understand her perspective. When the cruise is over, everyone will be going their different directions. Maybe she can keep in touch with them by email or social media, but they don't live in Bald Eagle Falls. They don't even live in Tennessee."

"I know that. But cruise ships are notorious for hookups. I don't want to smother her, but I don't want her... wandering, either. We are supposed to be exclusive, but I don't know; in a place like this..."

"Vic's not going to be unfaithful to you," Erin assured him. But she understood his concern. Vic was young, just figuring out who she was, and was suddenly surrounded by people who could relate to the struggles she had been going through. Willie was an older man, comfortable in his life, ready to settle down with a long-term partner. Erin couldn't see Vic being unfaithful to him, but people sometimes did things that they regretted later, especially when under stress and in new environments. Vic could be tempted as easily as anyone by the siren call of exciting new prospects.

Erin looked at Vic again. She was smiling and enjoying talking with her LGBT friends, but that didn't mean she would ever consider being anything more than friends with them.

"I hope not," Willie said quietly.

Erin looked back for the scowling crewman, but he was no longer anywhere to be seen.

Erin was excited when their group was finally invited to go ashore to explore the sanctuary. She could almost forget that one of the reasons they wanted to go ashore was to make contact with the real world back in Tennessee to try to get help or at least guidance on what to do in the situation they were stuck in. She wanted to see the animals on the preserve or, if she couldn't see them in person, to at least look at the pictures and artifacts that they had at the visitor center.

She saw Terry separate from the group and approach one of the staff to see if he could get access to a phone, but tried not to watch him. If she did, then other people would notice what was going on, and they wanted to keep things below the radar. Erin tried to keep her attention on the talks that were being presented. Endangered species, shrinking natural environment, the ivory trade.

Erin perked up. One of the things that they had speculated about was whether the crew might be participating in smuggling something from or to Alaska. Drugs were an obvious possibility, and they had talked about endangered species, plant or animal. Ivory was something that Erin hadn't thought about. She listened carefully to what the docent was telling them about ivory. While hunting elephants for ivory was against the law and elephant ivory could not be legally traded, there were other sources of ivory in Alaska that were legitimate. Walrus tusks and ivory from ancient mammoths that had once roamed the area were both legal for the native peoples to harvest, carve, and sell.

But it was not legal for just anyone, so that meant there was a black market, and that ivory smuggling did go on. Ivory smuggling was something that someone on the crew could be involved in. They could go ashore and bring back ivory without anyone noticing, especially if they were small pieces. Limited supply meant that the price of ivory was high and would continue to rise.

Could that have been what the two men had been arguing about? Could that be what the captain was killed over? Erin's excitement died down as she thought about it. Would the big man really have killed his companion just because he said he didn't want to smuggle ivory? It wasn't like he was being asked to go out and kill walruses himself. If he had agreed to be involved, then what could he have been asked to do that would have violated his moral standards and made him back out?

Ivory didn't fit. Not unless the ivory trade was a lot more bloody than she expected.

CHAPTER 29

*E*rin stayed with Willie and Vic, even though she wanted to stay back and wait for Terry to finish his inquiries. She couldn't hang around the visitor center as people continued to walk through, not knowing what direction danger might come from. Not many of crew had elected to go ashore with the passengers, but there were a few of them, and Erin didn't have any way to tell which of them might be involved in the plot.

"We'll just take the short loop around the preserve," Willie advised. "By the time we get back, Terry should be done, and we can go back to the ship."

"Are we going to go back to the ship?" Vic asked. "Maybe we should just get off here."

"There's nowhere to go from here. You need a boat to get anywhere. We may as well stay with the transportation that we have, rather than trying to find another way out. We're best off waiting for Anchorage."

"Unless Terry says we should get off here."

"Yes. Unless Terry says we get off here."

Erin let out her breath. "Let's walk, then. Maybe we'll see something cool."

They trailed the rest of their tour group, trying to act natural.

~

When they rejoined Terry, he was stone-faced and didn't say anything to them about his calls. Erin gathered that they had not gone well. He merged in with the group but didn't make any effort to join in the happy chatter of the group. Erin walked with him in silence. After a few minutes, she took his hand. He looked at her, but didn't say anything.

"We're going back to the ship?" Erin asked, as they walked by the visitor center back toward the boat. Terry sighed and nodded.

"We'd better stick with it at least until Anchorage. Once we're there, I'll see if I can convince the first mate to call in the authorities. But I don't have high hopes. My friends have pretty much repeated what we've already been told. I have no jurisdiction. Nobody in the US does unless the cruise line authorities or crew involve them."

"It must be frustrating to be told to stay out of it." Erin meant it sincerely, but she saw by his look that he thought she was needling him. All of the times he had told *her* to stay out of an investigation...

"Do you have suspects?" she asked quickly. "You know, in the *last thing*." She didn't want to specifically mention the captain's death in anyone else's hearing.

"I've asked for the surveillance tapes of areas around the cabin and a log of what they know about what he was doing and who saw him the last few hours. I can't really eliminate anyone until I have those things. Though there are obvious suspects. The person who prepared his meal and whoever brought it to him would be at the top of the list."

Erin thought about Chef Kirschoff and felt sick. There were other cooks on the ship. A lot of other cooks and kitchen staff. The food could have been tampered with at any point along the line; that didn't mean it was her new friend.

She wondered fleetingly whether he could just have befriended her because he wanted to keep track of where she was and what she was doing, and maybe to have a window into the investigation. He hadn't asked her anything about the investigation or the waves she had been making, and he hadn't asked if her boyfriend was the one who was looking into the terrible accident that the captain had suffered.

But he had known where Erin was for the evening and knew when Terry had picked her up and returned her to her cabin.

There was no evidence that he'd had anything at all to do with the accident.

And it could still be just an accident. It might not have been anyone in the kitchen who had contaminated his food. The food might have been contaminated at the factory and there hadn't been any recalls done yet. Or the product had been recalled, but no one had checked the ship's stores for goods that needed to be recalled.

Or the captain might have become allergic to something that he hadn't been allergic to before. Nobody would have known that. Not the doctor, the chef, or even the captain himself. Sometimes those things did just happen out of the blue, and if the allergy sufferer didn't have an autoinjector handy or reach medical care quickly enough, that could be the end of it.

"Terry, did he have an Epi-Pen? Or some other kind of autoinjector?"

Terry would know what she was talking about. He had investigated two other deaths by allergy in Bald Eagle Falls since Erin's arrival.

"Not on him, no. From what the doctor and the crew say, he didn't like to carry it with him. He had one in his office and one in his cabin, and the doctor has epinephrine in the infirmary. But he was one of those people who didn't like to carry one with him. He figured he'd have enough time to get to it if he ever needed it. And he was usually in his office or cabin, where it would be immediately on hand."

"But he didn't use it last night?"

"No. It was still there in his desk drawer. He must have reacted too quickly to get to it."

"How horrible."

Other passengers were looking sideways at Erin, and she realized they were eavesdropping, or trying to. She looked away, toward the bay filled with clear blue water.

"It's such a beautiful day. If it just wasn't so darn cold!"

Vic looked over at Erin and laughed. "I feel bad for all of those birds standing out on the ice," she said. "I've never been so cold in my life, and I'm bundled up! The cold just cuts right through everything!"

"Maybe you need to put on some weight," Willie joked. "Fat is a good insulator."

Vic pretended to slap his arm. "If I was going to live here, I might just have to do that, and then wouldn't you be sorry? But lucky for you, I am not going to stay here any longer than we have to for our tour. Then I'm going home and I'm never going anywhere with ice again."

"Nowhere with ice? No ski vacations? That's it?"

"That's it," Vic confirmed. "I am only taking tropical vacations after this."

"Then you have to get shots and worry about tropical diseases. And the spiders and snakes in warmer climates. All kinds of venomous things."

"I'll put up with bugs. I never minded creepy crawlies. But the cold is just too much for me. My body wasn't built for this climate."

"If you lived here for a few years, you'd get used to it eventually."

"Did you not hear the part where I said I was never going to live here? Or anywhere with ice? I'm not going anywhere cold ever again. I'm just going to go home and sit by the fire and warm my bones until I'm old."

"We should go to Mexico," one of Vic's pink-haired friends piped up, moving closer. "I've been there before and it's great. So warm, and the people and the vibe there are just so awesome. I'm enjoying the cruise too, but cruising in the south is totally different than coming up here to the top of the world. I don't know how people could actually live here year-round. Maybe for the summer, but once it got like this, as far as I'm concerned, everybody should migrate south."

Erin forced a smile. She noticed Willie holding Vic's arm protectively, as if afraid she might bolt if given the opportunity. Poor Willie. He was good to Vic and she'd never given him any reason to be concerned, but Willie was suffering from all of the attention she was getting.

Erin was exhausted after they got back from the tour, though it was only mid-afternoon. She hadn't managed to get much sleep the night before. She suspected Terry and the others were feeling the same way. They all made their way toward the cabins without discussion. Erin wanted nothing more than to lie down and go to sleep. Maybe for the rest of the night. She was feeling bruises she hadn't known she had sustained in the attack the night before, and her muscles ached like she had been doing a strenuous workout. She assumed it was fighting off her attacker the night before that had left her feeling so sore and fatigued.

"I am going to be so glad to just sleep normally one night," she told Terry, as he unlocked the door.

K9 burst into a volley of barks. Erin saw that there was someone in the cabin and let out a shriek, sure that it was either her attacker or Vic's burglar, having returned to finish the job. Terry held his hand out to block her from entering the room, his other hand automatically going to his hip. Erin withdrew, not wanting to get caught in any crossfire if the invader was armed. Willie let out a shout and ran over to help Terry out. But they both stopped in the doorway, and didn't go in to arrest the person who had broken in.

Terry started speaking in a soothing voice, holding his hands up and giving K9 the order to be silent. K9 stopped barking, but still appeared threatening, teeth bared.

Willie withdrew, stepping back from the room. "You might have better luck here," he told Erin.

"What? Who is it? What's going on?"

He motioned for her to go in. Erin peered into the room to see what was going on. She saw a tiny woman cowering in the corner of the room, her entire body shaking. She sobbed and held her hands up in front of her face protectively. Erin's fight-or-flight response ebbed. She stepped into the room and moved slowly toward the woman.

"Hey. Who are you? What happened? Did you get confused about which room was yours?"

Getting closer, she could smell the cleaning fluids that clung to the woman's clothes and hair. She took in the light linen uniform, loosely fitted around the woman's slim form, her brown skin, and her Asian features. Clearly, she wasn't a passenger who had somehow found her way into the wrong room, but a maid who had been cleaning the room and been frightened by K9's threats.

"It's okay," Erin soothed again, reading out to touch the woman. "It's fine. We didn't mean to startle you. You're just cleaning, right?" Erin pointed to the little plastic caddy of spray and squirt bottles and assorted rags and brushes. "You're cleaning?"

The woman nodded. Tears still ran down her face, but she seemed to be more confident with Erin than she had been when confronted by the two men.

"I'm sorry. We didn't mean to scare you like that. You didn't do anything wrong. We just didn't expect there to be anyone in our room."

The woman said something in her own language. Erin didn't understand a word. She shook her head.

"English. Do you know English?"

The woman shook her head impatiently and tried again. Erin thought she recognized a few words of Spanish, but she wasn't sure.

"I don't speak that either. Do you know any English?"

The woman began patting her pockets, and eventually tried to push herself up from where she had collapsed in the corner. Erin reached down and helped to pull her up. The woman was older than Erin had thought from her smooth, unlined face. She was tiny and bent over. She immediately grabbed her cleaning caddy and thrust it toward Erin.

"I know, I know. You're just cleaning," Erin said. "I understand. I'm sorry we bothered you."

The woman again patted her pockets as if looking for something. She shook her head at Erin. "Boss say to clean room," she said in thick, broken English. "No food and no money until they all clean."

Erin nodded encouragingly. "You were assigned to clean these rooms. I get it. You can finish. We'll... we'll go into my friend's cabin while you finish this one."

She looked at Terry for his agreement. Terry looked at her, shaking his head. "No... I don't want anything in here touched. There may be evidence that we don't want to lose. The assault last night, we didn't look for any stray hairs or fibers. We should try to collect whatever trace we can..."

"Oh." Erin hadn't thought about that. She looked at the little woman again. "I'm sorry. I guess we don't want the room cleaned at all." She tried to give the woman a few coins from her pocket. "We don't need you to do anything."

The woman's hand closed around the money and quickly transferred it to a pocket, but she shook her head. "Have to clean." She motioned to her surroundings. "No cleaning, no money."

Terry bent down to pick up a piece of paper that had been left on the writing desk. Erin thought it must be one of her lists, and Terry clearly thought so too, but then he looked down at the paper, frowning. He looked back up at Erin.

"Oh, no..."

CHAPTER 30

"What is it?"

He held the paper back from her, but Erin reached farther and took it from his hand. She looked down at it. Her cabin number. Vic and Willie's cabin number. One on a deck that she didn't recognize. Then a few more words scribbled at the bottom that were apparently written in the woman's native language.

"What's wrong?" Erin asked. "I don't understand."

"This is our cabin, Vic and Willie's cabin, and the captain's cabin."

Erin nodded. "So you're saying that we're getting special treatment? Like the captain?"

"I'm saying… someone gave this woman orders to clean the cabins that might contain evidence from the captain's death."

"But you wouldn't have put it in Vic and Willie's—"

"They know we're all friends. You and Vic are together all the time. They know that I could end up over there, talking with them, maybe ask them to do me a favor and put something in their safe or in their fridge. As a misdirection, or just because mine was full."

"But who would do that?"

"Someone trying to cover up a murder."

"Oh. Oh, no."

Terry held the paper out to the woman. "Have you already done these

596

other rooms? Is ours last or first? Did you clean this room up?" he tapped the captain's cabin number with his finger, looking at her sternly.

The woman was obviously terrified of him. She shrank back, breaking into a long stream of foreign words to express her alarm. She ran for the door, and Terry blocked her. "No, you don't. Stay here. Talk to me."

"I get son," the woman said. "I get son to tell you."

"We'll go together. You're not going anywhere by yourself."

The woman needed this fact repeated several times before she finally seemed to understand. She nodded and indicated with a motion that they would all go together. She grabbed Erin's hand and walked with her, but she wouldn't get close to Terry. Willie ducked out of the way, going to his cabin to update Vic on what was happening. Erin squeezed the woman's hand warmly.

"You do a great job around here," she told the maid. "I rarely ever see any of the cleaners or the other staff, but the ship is always spotless. Ship shape. You do good work."

The woman bowed to her and kept moving. Erin walked along with her, and the woman led her unerringly to a younger man who was working on a vending machine, repairing something wrong with the inner workings. At the woman's burst of words, he looked up at her. He saw Erin holding her hand and looked immediately alarmed.

"What is wrong?" he demanded. "What do you think she did? She wouldn't do anything wrong. She wouldn't do anything to make any inconvenience for you."

Terry spoke to the man. "She isn't in trouble. There's just a communication barrier. She said that we could talk through you."

"Why? What is going on?"

"I need to know whether she has already cleaned this other room or not." Terry held up the note with the cabin numbers on it and indicated the captain's.

The man's eyes flicked over the note and then to his mother. He spoke to her rapidly, looking back at Terry and Erin a couple of times to make sure that they didn't understand what he was asking her. They seemed to be arguing about something. The man eventually shrugged at Terry.

"She has finished the other rooms. She is sorry that she was still in your room when you returned. She did not know that she was going to be done so quickly. If you wish to go and sit in the lounge or the restaurant and have a coffee, she will be finished, and it will be fresh for you."

"She's already cleaned the other rooms?"

The man nodded. "Yes. All done. And yours will be done soon, I promise."

Terry groaned. "That cabin was a crime scene. If she's cleaned it, then she's destroyed all kinds of evidence. Who gave her these instructions?"

The man spoke to his mother. Their conversation grew increasingly heated. The woman kept shaking her head.

"I don't know who gave her these instructions," the man said. "I will try to find out. She will freshen your room and then you can rest and relax."

"I don't want my room cleaned. I need to know where those instructions came from. Someone is trying to hide evidence."

"No, nobody do that. It's just an accident. She should have done yours first. Soon it will be taken care of."

"No. She doesn't need to clean my room."

The man bowed to Terry, pressing forward as if he needed to explain something important to him. "You must let her clean the room," he insisted. "If she does not clean the room, she doesn't get any money or any food. She must do it!"

Terry looked at Erin. They had heard this explanation from the old woman as well. "She won't get any money or food? What do you mean by that?"

The man looked at him as if he were crazy. He spread his hands wide. "Food. She needs food to stay alive. They don't give her much because she is so old. She doesn't get much money to buy the things she needs. If she loses her pay, she will die! You want to kill an old woman?"

"What do you mean? They have to pay her for her job. They can't withhold money, and they certainly can't withhold food. Who told her that?"

"That is the way it works here," the man insisted. He looked around as if worried someone might overhear them. "We must work hard for food and money. Many of us support families back home. We just eat what we can and send all of our money home to our villages. It is hard to make very much money."

"They have to pay you a proper wage," Terry said, shaking his head in disbelief. "They can't withhold her pay. If she's working here, they have to pay her."

The man shook his head. "If she doesn't do everything they say, they will not give her anything."

"Who is your boss? Or her boss? Who is it that handles payroll on the ship?"

The man looked frightened. "You must not talk to them. We want to keep our jobs. You will make them take away our jobs, and then we will starve and our families will starve. They need the money that we send to them. My own children are grown, but they have children who are still small. My mother and I both send them money to live. You cannot take that away. She would rather die than stop sending money to her grand-children."

"Nobody is going to die," Erin reassured. She looked at Terry. "Do you think they've really been told that the cruise line will let them die if they don't do everything they are told?" she asked in almost a whisper.

"At this point... I wouldn't put it past them. If they are murdering to cover their tracks..."

Erin smiled reassuringly at the man. "How many people work here like you do? How many people are from your country?"

The man's eyes went wide. "There are many of us. I don't know how many. There is much work to be done in a ship like this."

"There must be," Erin agreed. "I saw a few of them in the kitchen when I was there with Chef Kirschoff. And if they are the ones who clean the cabins and keep everything well-organized..."

The man's eyes widened at the mention of Chef Kirschoff's name. He made a little bow, anxious and trying to withdraw from the conversation.

"I have been watching the crew members, but the other support staff are nearly invisible," Terry said slowly. "But how could they run a ship like this on the small number of crew they employ? There is a lot of work to be done."

"How do we find out? If you talk to the first mate, what would he tell you? He would just obfuscate, wouldn't he?"

Terry nodded. He looked at their interpreter. "You need to show me."

"Show you?"

"Show me where you sleep. Where your rooms are. I want to get an idea of how many others there are. Are you all being paid such low wages? So low that it is hard to survive?"

The man was beginning to see that he had caused more problems than he had solved with his claim. He shook his head. "It's okay. I will look after my mother. She's such a silly woman. I'm sorry that she interrupted your vacation."

"No." Terry put his hand on the man's arm. "I need to see what you're talking about. This isn't right, and I can get things fixed so that you can make better money and not have to worry about your mother starving or not having any money to send to your grandchildren."

"No. I should not have said anything. She should not have said anything. I should have just kept my mouth shut. We are sorry for the inconvenience."

The man was bowing and trying to pull away. "No, no, please. We have work to do. You go back to your cabin. You enjoy your vacation. We will not disturb you again."

He eventually managed to squirm away from Terry and backed a few steps away. Terry had no authority and couldn't detain the man against his will if he decided to leave.

"We need to find out what's going on here," Terry said. "You take K9. Go back and get Willie. I'm going to find out where these immigrants are being housed and see if I can get an idea of what's been going on."

"Okay." Erin did as he asked her to, leaving Terry with the mother and son duo. She hurried to get back to her cabin to explain to Willie what was going on and to see if he could help.

CHAPTER 31

$\mathcal{W}$illie was standing in the doorway of his cabin, waiting for some word from Erin or Terry. He looked relieved to see Erin and K9.

"What's going on?" he asked. "What did she say?"

"It's all pretty confusing," Erin said. "They won't explain anything in any detail, but it seems like… the immigrants who work here in cleaning and the kitchen and whatever other jobs they do around the ship, are not being paid very well and their money and food is held over their heads if they don't do exactly what they are told. The woman was told to clean our cabins and the captain's cabin. Terry figures because they're trying to eliminate any evidence of foul play. But if she doesn't clean our cabins, then she doesn't get paid and doesn't get food." Erin shook her head at Willie, outraged. "How could they withhold food? They can't keep food and money from these people. They're afraid that they're going to starve!"

Willie's expression was grim. His stone-faced countenance, together with his darkly-stained skin, made him look very threatening.

"So where's Terry? What's he doing?"

"He wants to go looking for the housing quarters for the immigrant workers. Find out what's really going on. He asked me to come get you to help him out. I guess he doesn't want to go down there on his own."

"Down there?" Willie repeated.

"Aren't the staff quarters all belowdecks?" Erin asked. "I thought the upper decks were all for passengers."

Willie cocked his head, thinking about it. He looked at Vic. Vic nodded vigorously. "I studied all of the deck charts. Other than the captain and officers, the staff are all below deck. That means you're going to need someone with authority, because they don't just let the passengers wander around down there."

"Mackay was down there," Erin remembered.

Vic and Willie looked baffled at this remark.

"Who?"

"The girl who disappeared. The one whose mother was waiting to talk to the captain. Remember? She came and talked to us after they found her daughter, and she thought Mackay had been drugged and assaulted. She was found belowdecks. So the public must have some access to the area, or the security isn't very good."

"We'll give it a try," Willie said with a shrug. "Maybe Terry will be able to talk himself in with his police credentials."

"I'll take you to them."

Willie looked at Vic. "We can't leave Vicky here by herself. You'd better join us as well."

Vic rolled her eyes. "As if you were ever going to be able to keep me away!"

Willie chuckled and reached out a hand for her. Vic joined hands with him, and they followed Erin and K9 back to where she had separated from Terry. Erin looked around. "He was just here."

They all scanned the deck. It was pretty quiet, but there was no sign of Terry or the old woman and the man. "Well... he must have seen or heard something... he wouldn't have just left when he knew that we were coming back to help him out. Would he?"

"I don't like this," Willie muttered. "He shouldn't have stayed up here alone. He should have come back down with you."

"Uh-huh," Vic drawled. "But he's a man, and men aren't weak and vulnerable like us poor womenfolk. They can fight off hordes of homicidal crew members with their bare hands."

Erin saw at once how silly it had been to leave Terry alone where he was, despite the fact that he was a grown man, well-trained in control and combat. "I didn't even think… he said to run and get you, and to take K9 with me, so I did. I never thought…"

"Of course not," Willie agreed. "He is perfectly safe by himself in Bald Eagle Falls working by himself, for the most part, so it wouldn't occur to you to worry about his safety. He's the protector."

"What are we going to do?"

"We're going to go belowdecks."

"Really?"

Willie nodded. "That's what Terry was going to do, so that's what I'm doing to do. They can't stop all of us." Even so, he looked around anxiously, as if trying to spot anyone who might be watching them. He wasn't nearly as confident as he pretended to be. "Stick close."

They moved in a huddle, practically on top of each other, to the nearest elevator. When Willie pressed the first of the belowdecks floors, there was no responding light indicator. Willie pressed it again, then another of the lower floors. But none of those numbers would light up.

"You need a key," Vic suggested, pointing to the circular keyhole that would take a round security key.

Willie looked at it briefly, then pulled out a pocketknife and fit the tip into the little nick that the round key was supposed to rotate. He wiggled it and manipulated it until he managed to move the notch around the circle from the off position to the on position.

Erin breathed out. "Nice!"

Willie tried the first belowdecks floor again, and this time, it lit up.

"Easy as pie!" Willie proclaimed.

"I never did understand that expression," Erin mused. "Pie is actually one of the more complicated desserts to make. Harder than cake or cookies. So why isn't the expression 'easy as cake' or 'easy as fudge'? It doesn't make any sense to me."

Willie gave her a look that told Erin she was babbling because of her nervousness and needed to pull herself together. They were going into a risky situation, trying to find out whether people on the ship were being treated as slave labor. Two people had already been killed, possibly for knowing too much about what was going on, and she was chattering on about pie.

"Sorry."

The elevator doors opened. Willie stood to the side and took a quick peek out to see who was there that might be able to see them. There were no security guards and no one who looked threatening, so he stepped out of the elevator car, followed closely by Erin and Vic. They all looked around. It looked pretty much like the other decks, other than the fact that the rooms would all go right to the hull of the ship rather than leaving a walkway around the outer edge. There was nothing noticeably different.

"I don't see any sign of Terry. We should probably go down another floor," he said.

At her side, K9 gave no sign that he could smell his master close by.

Vic and Erin looked at each other and nodded. Erin reached back and caught the elevator door before it could finish closing, and they all got back on. Willie selected the next floor and they went down again. They looked out of the elevator doors again. Still no sign of Terry or anything untoward. Just crew quarters.

"I think we're going to have to go all the way to the bottom."

"Won't that just be storage? With all of the supplies that the ship goes through, there must be a ton of space required for supplies."

Willie considered this. Then he shrugged. "I still think our best bet is the lowest deck."

"Okay."

This time he selected the bottom number on the elevator, and they waited longer as the slow elevator descended into depths of the ship.

This time, when the doors opened, it was different. Erin immediately gagged on the scent of sewage. She wasn't sure she could even go out of the elevator. She wanted to go back up to one of the other decks, one of the clean, nice-smelling ones. Hopefully with a breeze through the ship to keep it fresh.

"Ugh. Is there a leak in a sewage tank down here?" Vic demanded.

"Smells that way," Willie agreed. "That, or there is no plumbing down here, because it's not meant to house people, but just for supply storage, like Erin said."

Erin held her hand over her mouth and nose, nauseated and hoping she wasn't going to throw up. Her seasickness was suddenly back full force. Not because of the motion of the ship, but because of the stench and the thought of people living down there, in conditions that were primitive and unsanitary.

"You okay?" Willie asked.

Erin nodded. "I'm trying."

"I don't want us to separate from each other. Are you going to be able to handle it?"

"I'll have to be able to, won't I?"

"I know it's hard. Breathe through your mouth. Try not to think about it. I still don't see any sign of Terry."

"He could be at any of the other decks. We didn't search the whole ship."

"No, we're just going by instinct. If somebody took him somewhere, they'd want him to be out of sight, not where a passenger or non-involved crew member might come across him. And if Terry decided to start the search on his own, we need to think about where he would go first, and I think he would come down here. This is obviously where the immigrant workers are being housed. Maybe he got the maid or her son to talk to him about it and decided to come down here on his own without waiting for me."

Erin knew that wasn't what happened, but she appreciated Willie trying to make it easier on her, so she nodded and played along. "Well, we'd better look for him, then."

"Quietly," Willie advised, and started moving forward.

They moved together in a tight grouping, eyes alert and bodies tense for action. K9 stuck close to Erin's side, sniffing at the foul air.

They got past the first couple of storage bays, and then reached the one that had been converted to a living space for the lower-class workers. Erin looked around, panting through her mouth, trying to see everything without being sick.

There were mats on the floor. No mattresses, just bare, flat sleeping mats. Some workers were asleep. Maybe they had worked all night and morning and were only able to sleep in the afternoon. Maybe they were sick or suffering from some other ailment. There were obviously a lot of workers on duty; there were a lot of empty mats. Rows and rows of them. There was a little pile of clothes or blankets on or beside each one. At the opposite end of the room there were some privacy screens set up like you would see in an old doctor's office. Erin gathered that's where the improvised toilets were.

Erin moaned. Some of the workers were awake and sat up to look at them, wide-eyed and frightened.

"This is horrible," Vic whispered. "I can't believe they're being treated like this."

"Worse," Erin reminded her. "They're also afraid of starving to death if they don't do their jobs to the liking of the boss, whoever that is."

CHAPTER 32

*D*oes anyone know where the policeman is?" Erin asked. She looked around at the faces of the few people who were awake and looking at her. "You know about the policeman who was investigating the captain's death? You heard about him? Do you know where he is?"

The immigrants looked at each other. She didn't know how many of them understood her and were just afraid to answer. Someone must have heard something about Terry. They knew what was going on around the ship; they were everywhere, like flies on the wall, listening to conversations and seeing things that were going on without being observed. Invisible to everyone because they were so omnipresent and unobtrusive.

But would they know anything about where Terry was? Had he gone off on his own or been taken? She couldn't believe that he had just left on his own, after telling her how she needed to be careful. He had stressed that they couldn't be alone and then he had sent her away and left himself vulnerable. She was really angry at him for that. There was a tightness in her chest that was a combination of anxiety and anger. Fury at him for taking chances when he kept telling her not to.

"Has anyone heard?" Erin asked again.

She looked around. No one seemed inclined to talk to her and help her out. A little boy had been sitting on a mat with his mother, who was still asleep, or pretending to be. He crawled to the edge of the mat, then stood up and crept toward Erin. She realized he was looking at K9, his eyes wide and bright with interest.

"Do you like dogs?" she asked him. "He's a very nice dog. Very good." She scratched K9's ears and crooned at him. "You're a good dog, aren't you, K9? You're a good boy."

The little boy continued to approach. He had his finger in his mouth and moved toward Erin with curiosity and suspicion, watching her every move and staying back. He flinched when she moved or looked at him.

"Dog?" he pointed at K9.

"Yes. You like the dog? Have you seen him before?"

He nodded, but Erin didn't know if he understood that she meant *that* dog in particular, or if he meant that he had seen a dog before. How sheltered had he been from the real world? Had he grown up on the ship, isolated from the land and other pets?

"Was there a man with him when you saw him?" Erin asked, watching the little boy's face carefully for signs of understanding.

The little boy nodded again, his finger still in his mouth.

"Would you like to help me out? We don't know where the man is. The policeman who owns this dog. We think he might be in trouble. He might be hurt. The bad men might have him locked up somewhere."

The boy nodded again.

Erin was doubtful. What could the boy do? Whether he understood her or not, how would he know where Terry was or be able to help her to find him? Could he get the grown-ups to help her? They would be too wise, too careful. If the man they had spoken to was of the same mind as the rest of the workers who were being warehoused belowdecks, then they would not want to take the chance of losing their jobs or their food by helping Erin out. Passengers came and went. They had money of their own. The poverty-stricken workers needed the money and food that the cruise line had to offer. They needed that security.

"Maybe I should just let K9 go and tell him to find Terry," Erin said to Willie. "Do you think? I did that before, and he found Terry and brought him back when Vic was in trouble. Should I just do that?"

"I wouldn't," Willie cautioned. "If someone is holding Terry captive, then you may be sending K9 to someone who is armed, and certainly someone who doesn't have much regard for human life. If he doesn't care about people, chances are he's going to care even less about some dog that shows up and makes trouble. If they have Terry locked up somewhere, K9 isn't going to be able to get in and free him."

"Maybe he can track him, though, and lead us to him. Then we can decide what to do when we know where Terry is and what the situation is."

Willie nodded. "Maybe. Let's not rush into anything. We don't really know much about what is going on or who is running this operation, but they know who we are. If we get into the middle of things, they have a lot more reason to get rid of us than to give up. We don't want to get into something that we can't get back out of."

"But what are we going to do? We need to find Terry and make sure he's okay."

"Let's do that, then," Vic said. "Let's find Terry and make sure he's okay." She looked at K9. "He's helped before. He helped when I was kidnapped. You can't expect miracles from him, but he's a pretty smart dog."

K9 panted, looking from one of them to another, looking pleased with himself.

Erin bent down to talk to him. "We need you to find Terry. But quietly. No barking and no letting anyone see you. Do you think you can do that?"

K9 continued to pant and stare into her face.

Erin rolled her eyes and shook her head. "Do I really think he can understand that much of what I say? He's a smart dog, but he doesn't have superpowers."

"He understands more than you give him credit for," Vic said. "Let's get him to search for Terry."

They each nodded in agreement. The little boy finally screwed up his courage to join them. He crouched down and gave K9 a full-body hug. Erin had to smile. The dog was bigger than the boy. He was maybe three years old. He cuddled with K9 and rubbed his face against his fur, cooing and making noises. Erin didn't know if any were actual words, or if he was just doing the usual baby talk thing that most people suddenly devolved to when faced with a cute animal.

They suddenly heard a gruff voice down the hall. The little boy froze. His mother, who had previously been asleep or pretending to be asleep, sat up and called him over urgently. He scampered back over to the sleeping mat, into her arms. She buried her face against his hair, hiding from whoever was coming. Erin looked at the others in a panic. They couldn't go back the way they had come, and there wasn't any obvious way out of the storage bay they were in. Erin whipped her head around, looking for a way out. Vic grabbed her arm.

"Behind the screens."

"No," Erin resisted. There was no way she was going to go back to where it was reeking of human waste. Vic pulled harder. Willie was nodding his agreement. "Come on, we need to get out of sight, quickly. Or they'll throw us overboard just like that man you saw." He grabbed Erin's other arm and, although she resisted, they pulled her toward the back of the room, past all of the sleeping mats and behind the screens where the smell was the worst. Erin protested.

"No, no, let me go. Not in here. I can't handle it! I'm going to be sick!"

They let her go, and Erin was about to make a run for it when she heard the men come into the storage room.

"Where have they got him?"

"Up in the captain's room. He wanted to go there so badly, so why not? We figured it would make him happy."

"And he'll be taken care of?"

"Of course."

"Is this the end of the mess? Every time I turn around, things are unraveling. This is the worst-run operation I've ever seen!"

"It's not our fault. It was just pure bad luck that that woman saw anything. Who could predict that someone would have been watching?"

"Well, you might have taken a look around to make sure before throwing someone overboard. It would seem like the logical thing to do."

"You don't know what you're talking about," the gruff voice growled, and Erin realized it was the same voice as she had heard that night. She peeked through the vertical space between the screens, trying to see him, but she couldn't. Not from that angle. And she wasn't going to go out to meet him.

K9 was moving around restlessly. Erin made the sign for him to stop and stay, and he was instantly still. Vic raised her eyebrow at Erin, impressed. But Erin couldn't take credit, she wasn't the one who had trained K9. She had just learned the proper commands from Terry. It was Erin who had been well-trained, rather than being the trainer. Otherwise, K9 would probably be just as unruly as Orange Blossom. Erin had problems being stern with her animals. She fell prey to their cuteness.

"Where is the old woman?" The other voice demanded.

There was silence for a moment while they both looked around. "I don't know," the gruff voice replied. "This is her pod. She should be in here. Her son said that she had finished the rooms, so she should have come right back here."

"You think she's wandering around the ship somewhere?"

"She's an old woman. She's tired. She wouldn't be wandering around. Maybe she's in the latrine, I'll check."

There were footsteps, and Erin realized that they were headed toward her and the others. The man was going to look behind the screens for the old cleaner to see if she had really finished the job that he'd sent her to do. They all instinctively backed up, looking for some route of escape. The only way out was the way they had gone in. There was no back exit. There was no way underneath or around.

Erin's heel hit one of the buckets. She heard the liquid slosh around in it, and the movement stirred up the worst smell she had ever smelled in her life. She felt wetness hit the back of her leg and knew that it had splashed onto her and that smell was going to stay with her for the rest of her life, which wasn't going to be very long. She clutched at her stomach.

"No, no, no…"

There was no avoiding it. The same Erin as always got sick on the class field trips or who missed out on Christmas dinner because she couldn't stand the smell of cooking onions; she couldn't resist her body's reaction to the stench and the thought that the foul liquid had just soaked through her pant leg. She had to turn quickly to hit the nearest half-full bucket, letting loose a long, hot stream of vomit and coughing and choking afterward. Her stomach clenched, and she knew that wasn't going to be the end of it. Vic and Willie were both pulling back, not wanting to stand too close to her, but unable to leave the latrine area behind the screen where they might be seen.

The footsteps stopped. The man apparently wasn't so keen on approaching someone who was being violently ill, in the corner of a room that already featured the most horrendous smell he'd probably ever smelled.

Erin prayed that the man would not come back there and that she would not have to throw up again. She didn't believe in God; but the words just came to her mind.

Don't let him come back here. Don't let me have to throw up again. Please get me out of here. Please just get me out of here.

The footsteps started again, but they were retreating rather than approaching.

"I'll come back later," the gruff voice declared, as if that had been his plan all along. "We'd better go check on our new guest and see how he is enjoying the captain's quarters."

"Best quarters on the ship," the other voice said. "I know I'd love to make them mine!"

"You can't just get whatever you want on a cruise like this. There's a certain order."

"You don't think I know that by now? You really are an idiot, you know that? What a slipshod operation this has been. You would think that someone with your experience would be able to run things better than this."

"You don't know what it's like to have to deal with these kinds of people," the gruff voice became wheedling, almost whining. Erin was surprised at the triumph that immediately rose in her chest at the fact that he was being reprimanded and hadn't done a good job. It served him right. After all that he'd put her through and all of the horrible things he had done, it served him right to be mocked and criticized by his boss, or his boss's boss, or whoever had been sent to sort the situation out. "It's not just the immigrants. The crew themselves are impossible to deal with. Always asking questions, acting superior, thinking they are 'all that.' And don't get me started on the passengers, especially this Price woman." He swore. "I can't believe we had the bad luck to be saddled with her on this tour. She should have been kicked off the moment she started making waves. Then we wouldn't be in this predicament."

"We didn't know she was going to be trouble. And we didn't know you were going to let her see you taking care of business. That was your fault, you know."

"It wasn't my fault. She was sleepwalking. She'd been sick and she shouldn't have been walking around the ship like that. She should have been in bed. How am I supposed to be able to keep track of the thousands of different people on this floating tub? I know the patterns of traffic and what people are generally doing at different times of the day. No one should have seen anything. And I checked. I looked around to make sure I was alone. She just happened to be wandering past the window at the wrong time."

"You should have been more careful."

The gruff man swore and cussed under his breath. He clearly knew that he'd screwed up. He didn't need to be told over and over again. He wanted to get out of there and to go check on his prisoner.

"Let's go. We'd better check and make sure he's nice and comfy for the night."

They listened to the retreating footsteps. Erin looked at Vic and Willie, wondering what they were going to do. They couldn't get in the way, and they had found out the information they had been looking for, which was that Terry was being held in the captain's room. For the moment, Terry was safe, but that wasn't going to last. For all Erin knew, they were just waiting for the right opportunity to throw Terry overboard just as they had the crewman who had been causing problems. They would be looking for Erin next, planning to dispose of her as well.

Willie held up his hand for silence until after the footsteps had faded away and he was convinced that the men were gone and weren't going to return. Then he spoke in a near-whisper.

"Terry is in the captain's quarters. He will be guarded, but we can't just wait for them to deal with him. We need to go there, and we need to get him out."

Erin nodded. "Yes."

"They don't have any compunctions about killing. It's just what's most convenient. We need to get Terry out of there before it becomes convenient for them to eliminate him."

Erin wanted to get to Terry as soon as she could. She didn't know how they would do it, but she needed to get there and confirm to herself that he was okay.

"Do you know where the captain's quarters are?"

Willie nodded. "Terry and I were talking about it earlier, so I know where everything is."

"Why was he talking about it to you when it was confidential?" Erin demanded. "He wouldn't talk to me about it!"

"He still probably told you more than he ought to," Willie said, his eyes narrowing slightly. "And you're a civilian."

"So are you."

He considered this. "True... but he needed someone who could help him out. I may not be police, but I have training."

It was a far cry from the past when Terry had been suspicious of Willie's motives. Erin shook her head at the hypocrisy. "What were you going to do? What did he expect from you?"

"Tactical advice. Organizational skills. Getting volunteers organized. I don't know. We didn't really get that far with the details. But those are things that I have experience in, and he was all alone on this cruise, as far as having tactical information went. Of course he had you, and even Vic as a friend, but that's not the same as being able to stand up to an attack by terrorists. You don't have experience dealing with criminals." He reconsidered and raised his eyebrows. "Not in a tactical situation, anyway."

"So he told you that the captain was poisoned."

"Possibly poisoned. Yes. And that, combined with your story about someone being thrown overboard, meant that there is some kind of criminal conspiracy on this ship." He motioned to the immigrants on their sleeping mats. "As we can now see. They are using slave labor, and that is illegal in most places in the world, not just in the USA. They don't want to get caught and they are doing whatever they can to protect themselves."

Erin nodded. As a group, they slowly walked to the end of the screens and peeked out, looking for any sign of the men. They saw only the immigrants who were sleeping there, most of whom were studiously ignoring them. The little boy who had been so enamored with K9 was sitting with his mother, cuddled close. She was not going to let him go and talk to Erin and K9 again. If they didn't know before that Erin and her friends were targets of the men who were controlling them, they knew now. They had seen Erin, Vic, and Willie run and hide.

"Well, I'm not sure what we're going to do, but we should at least reconnoiter."

Erin let Willie lead the way, since he knew where the captain's quarters were. She would have had to study the deck maps and ask questions of the crew, and they needed to get there with as few people seeing them as possible. Willie didn't make conversation along the way. Vic and Erin followed his lead. K9 stayed at Erin's side, alert, his eyes forward. Did he know that Terry was in trouble? Or was he merely curious or interested in his surroundings?

They used the stairs rather than risking the elevator, hoping to stay out of sight for longer. Erin tried to fathom how they were going to do anything to help Terry. They didn't have any weapons or anyone to back them up. But they were free, and Terry was not.

Willie stopped and peeked around the corner.

"Okay. I only see one guard. I don't see the men we heard downstairs, so they must be inside with Terry. We don't know how many men might be in that room."

"You want one of us to distract the guard?" Vic asked.

Erin swallowed. That might work on TV, but would it really have any effect in real life? The guard was there to make sure that no one got in. He wasn't going to be talked into a wild goose chase. Some flimsy excuse for a conversation or to lure him away from the door.

"No," Willie said immediately. "I don't want either one of you to do anything risky. I'm wondering about letting K9 either take him down or lure him away."

Erin put her hand on K9 protectively. "I don't want him to get hurt either. He's part of our family."

"He's not part of the family. He's not even a pet. He's a police dog."

"I don't want him doing anything dangerous."

"I don't plan to make him do anything dangerous. But I want to act wisely here. If it's K9 or Terry, who would you choose?"

Erin stared at him. If she had to choose between the two of them? She wanted to reiterate to Willie just how important K9 was to them, but she already knew the answer to his question. If it was a matter of saving Terry or K9, she would have to pick Terry. But that wasn't what she wanted to do, and she wasn't about to tell Willie that.

"I just don't want you putting him into a dangerous situation."

"We're spending too much time talking," Vic interrupted. "Who knows what they're doing in there. We might not have the time to debate it. We're all going to put ourselves at risk. So let's get to it."

Willie motioned to K9. "Tell him to take down the guard."

"I'm not his handler," Erin said, "I don't know if he'll do that for me."

"He listens to other commands from you. If he won't, he won't, but let's try."

Erin stroked K9's head, worried. "What if they hurt him?"

"The man guarding the door doesn't appear to be armed. An unarmed man is not equipped against fangs. Let's get this done quickly."

Erin took a deep breath. She looked at K9 and gave him the 'attend' command. His body language changed from curious but relaxed to alert, his muscles bunched for action. Erin pointed at the intersecting hallway and gave the 'attack' command. She wasn't sure whether K9 hesitated, or whether it just took a second or two for him to process what it was that she wanted. Then he ran around the corner and was only out of sight for a few seconds when they could hear the scuffle with the guard and his yell of alarm or pain.

Willie didn't give Vic or Erin any instructions as to what they should do, but bolted around the corner himself, moving as quickly as he could with the cast on his leg. Erin didn't put any thought into a plan of attack. She and Vic acted as one, following close behind him.

They saw K9 wrestling with the crewman guarding the captain's room, his jaws clamped around the man's forearm. The man was yelling and trying to pull away, but K9 didn't release him. Willie rushed forward. At the same time, two men burst out of the cabin.

For a moment, time froze; Erin wasn't sure whether everybody actually stopped to consider the situation, or whether time only ceased for her, as she considered the tableau. One of the men was the first mate, and the other was clearly the gruff-voiced, broad-shouldered man Erin had seen throw the other man overboard. Erin had probably seen him around the ship, but it wasn't until then that she could identify him as the killer.

Erin had exchanged greetings with the first mate more than once, and he had had always been courteous and pleasant toward her. Nothing like the expression on his face as he looked at them from the doorway of the captain's cabin.

He looked murderous.

CHAPTER 33

*W*illie went after the broad-shouldered killer. K9 was wrestling the guard. That left Vic and Erin to deal with the first mate. They both stood there frozen, blocking the narrow hallway, waiting for him to make a move.

The first mate muttered an oath under his breath. He was transformed from the man Erin had thought she knew.

"Where's Terry?" she demanded.

The mate didn't answer her. They already knew where he was. She wasn't even sure why she had asked; it was just the first thing that had come to her lips.

"It's over," Vic told him. "We know everything. You can't get away with it anymore."

"This is my ship," the man said, "you have no jurisdiction over me here."

"It's not your ship. It belongs to the cruise line, and I don't think they'd be too happy that you were using slave labor to run it."

"You think they don't know?" the mate scoffed. His eyes went back and forth. "All they care about is the bottom line. They don't care how we increase profits as long as we do. One of the easiest ways to lower the costs to run this ship is to find the cheapest labor possible. That's all we've done here."

Erin thought he was just going to stand there and talk. Vic had engaged him, and he was responding. K9 and Willie were doing their best to subdue the other two men. In a few minutes, it would all be over, and peace would be restored.

But then the mate bolted. He ran straight toward them, leaping over K9 and the guard wrestling on the floor. Erin held up her hands to protect herself and to try to stop him from getting by. She couldn't see what Vic was doing, other than to mirror Erin's defensive motion. The mate aimed for the space between them and, after a very brief struggle, he managed to force his way through. The arm that Erin had thought she had a good purchase on slipped out of her hands, the rough buttons and braids on his uniform scraped over her skin, and he was pounding down the hall away from them. Erin turned to go after him, but she knew it was impossible. He was too big and too strong for her to do anything about, even if she managed to catch up with him. Even she and Vic together were not going to be able to control him, especially with one of Vic's arms out of commission. Vic stared after the man, her face as white as a sheet. She looked at Erin.

"Terry," she said.

They both fought their way toward the cabin door. K9 was still wrestling the guard on the floor, but seemed to have him under control, the man crying and flopping like a beached fish, his struggles slowing. It was harder to get by Willie and the gruff-voiced killer, who were both still on their feet and kept bouncing off of the walls as they struggled, yelling at each other but neither able to gain the upper hand.

Erin and Vic managed to push by them, picking up a few more bruises on the way. They squeezed into the captain's cabin, popping free like a cork.

Erin was overwhelmed by the opulence of the quarters. The killer had said he would have liked to live there, and she had no doubt that the captain's quarters were highly coveted. The carpet was thick plush, the furnishings heavy, dark wood. The lighting sparkled through crystal chandeliers and jeweled lamps. There were paintings of past captains or officers displayed on the walls, as well as award plaques, vintage maps, and old astronomical and seafaring equipment.

"Wow," Vic murmured.

That was an understatement. But despite her initial distraction, Erin had eyes only for Terry, who was tied to a chair in the middle of the room. He had a duct tape gag. Not like on TV where the captive would have one small rectangle of tape sealing his mouth shut, but layers of tape wrapped all the way around his head, between his jaws to form a gag and then over the planes of his face to immobilize his mouth. Likewise, multiple layers of tape wound around each arm and leg to secure his limbs to the captain's chair he sat in.

Erin darted forward to release him. If it were TV, then a couple of rips of the tape and yelps from the hostage, and he would be free, but Terry's captors had been very thorough. Erin used her nails to try to get purchase under an edge and to rip it off, but it was the industrial-strength dinosaur-brand tape that Erin had been known to use for car repairs in the past. She could barely get her nails into it. Erin looked around.

"Scissors. Do you see any scissors?"

Vic hurried over to a heavy antique desk. There were only a couple of drawers to check. Vic came up with a pair of scissors and a boxcutter.

"Here you go."

Erin hesitated, then selected the scissors. "I'll start at his face. You use the blade to free his legs."

Vic nodded her agreement, kneeling down to start slicing the tape between Terry's leg and the chair leg. Erin tried to work the pointed scissor blade between the tape and the skin of Terry's face. She knew she was risking cutting him. His eyes were on her face and he was obviously keeping his head as still as possible as she tried to get under the tape to free him. Terry flinched away a couple of times when the sharp blade bit into his skin instead of sliding smoothly in between his skin and the tape, but he held as still as possible.

Vic looked up from her slow progress. "What can I do to help Willie? I could give him the boxcutter? The duct tape?"

Erin shook her head. She looked away from her scissors momentarily to look around the room. There were no obvious weapons Vic could use to help Willie. If Vic gave Willie the boxcutter, Erin was worried that the killer might be able to wrestle it away, and he wouldn't be trying to get Willie under control, but to kill him.

"See if you can tape up the one that K9 took down," Erin suggested. "Then K9 can help Willie with the other one."

Vic's face cleared. She nodded and picked up the big roll of tape, placing the boxcutter by Terry's feet so that Erin could continue the job once she was finished freeing his mouth and head. Erin continued the work of cutting the tape away, pulling Terry's skin around to try to avoid cutting him as she inched the scissors under the tape, a tiny bit at a time. She cut what she could and continued forward. Terry made a noise, and she stopped. He worked his jaw, which had obviously been held in the same uncomfortable position for too long. Erin waited until he was finished and blinked at her, then continued cutting. She could hear Vic yelling at K9's detainee, and then eventually, telling K9 to "break." It took several times before he was apparently willing to do so, not having been trained to take orders from Vic. Then Vic pointed him toward the husky-voiced killer and ordered him to attack. In a few seconds, they could hear the man protesting as K9 and Willie held him down to tie him up.

By the time Willie and Vic came back into the captain's quarters, Erin was removing the layers of tape from Terry's mouth and face, jerking the tape away from the skin an inch or so at a time, leaving an angry red stripe where layers of skin were pulled away.

Willie knelt down to pick up the boxcutter and swiftly sawed through the layers of tape binding Terry's ankles, and then his arms. Terry moved, massaging his limbs and licking his lips.

"Thanks. You didn't... catch them all...?"

Erin shook her head. "The first mate got away. Do you know anyone else who was involved? Was it just those three and the dead man, or are there others?"

"I don't know how many others may know what's going on, either because they were involved or because they guessed." Terry frowned at Erin. "How much did you figure out?"

"Just what the maid and her son said. That the immigrants were being used as slave labor. We went down below and found one of the storage units they were being kept in..." Erin shook her head, her throat getting hot even just thinking about it. "Sleeping on mats on the floor with buckets for toilets and no other facilities. It's no wonder they were so desperate to do what they were told."

"That's not all of it."

Willie retracted the blade on the box cutter and put it down on the captain's desk. "What else?" he asked, studying Terry.

"That girl who disappeared...? It sounds like they are not just trafficking slaves, but girls too. Some they can coax into relationships and then pimp out much like they would in the city. Same type of conversion. And others they have drugged, like with Mackay, and then threatened to turn them in —to their parents or boyfriends or whoever they are close to. Blackmailed them into doing what they say. It's not a new story… but I had no idea that was going on on cruise ships. You would think they would be too obvious, too easy to catch. But girls go on a cruise for their first taste of independence, or they come on vacation with their families and get lured away or outright kidnapped. Disappearances are not investigated. Parents are told that the girls have just run away. And they never know what really happened."

Erin felt sick. "We need to go after him. Even if we don't know all of the crew who are involved… that can be sorted out later. But the first mate—we know he's the ringleader."

Terry grunted and got unsteadily to his feet. K9 was immediately at his side, whining and pushing his snout into Terry's hand. Terry scratched his ears.

"It's okay, K9. I'm just fine. You did a good job out there, didn't you? Good job! Good boy."

K9 panted, lapping up the attention.

"He really did good," Vic agreed, nodding. "I don't think we could have taken down two of the three without him. And I don't think the first mate would have run if it weren't for K9. He would have stayed to fight."

Willie and Erin nodded in agreement.

Terry rubbed his wrists and gingerly felt the red strip on his face. "Let's go, then. He can't be anywhere but on the ship, and it's pretty hard to hide the first mate."

"Everyone stay together," Erin warned. Terry looked at her and opened his mouth to answer, then thought better of it. He led them out of the captain's quarters, pulling the door shut behind him. They stepped over the tape-bound men in the hallway and kept going without comment.

Terry headed for the dining room, the place most likely to be busy as people were getting back from their tours and either heading back to their cabins for naps, or looking for something to eat, or drinking as they relaxed. They immediately spread out, asking both passengers and crew if they had seen the friendly first mate.

One of the crewmen Erin approached smiled obligingly and keyed his radio. "Looking for Little," he said into it, "anyone seen him?"

There were a couple of responses. Erin made a wide motion to the others. "Deck fifteen!" she shouted.

CHAPTER 34

$\mathcal{A}$s they hurried for the elevator and pressed the buttons, Erin jiggled nervously. Deck fifteen included the children's and teens' areas. The last thing they needed was the first mate taking hostages. She could just picture him standing by the railing, smiling, threatening to throw someone overboard. They needed to get to him before he could.

They arrived on deck fifteen and got off the elevator, looking around. Erin tried to slow her breathing and to convince herself that they would find him, and everybody else would be safe and well. Everything was going to be fine.

"Spread out and look for him," Terry said in a whisper. "Try not to alert him. He's on the run. He already knows he's caught; we just need to find him and persuade him that the best outcome for him would be to turn himself in instead of running any farther. Throw himself on the mercy of the court. If you see him, try to signal whoever is closest to you. Try to keep each other in sight."

Of course, there was no way on the huge ship that they were going to be able to keep each other in sight. Erin thought it was even pushing it to think that they could find the man himself on the ship. But with some luck and the help of the other crewmen…

Erin went her own way, looking around for him. There were a lot of teens around, mostly talking and playing on their phones. The older adults should be easy to see. The uniforms should make them easy to spot. But it was like playing a life-size game of *Where's Waldo?* Erin just couldn't find Waldo.

And then she did. He was up another deck, in the balcony that overlooked the teen pool. Erin ducked back against the wall, hoping that he couldn't see her from his angle or wouldn't look in her direction. He had a good vantage point, which was exactly why he had chosen it. He wanted to see them before they could confront him.

Erin waved in Terry's direction, keeping the motion small so that it wouldn't attract Little's attention. Against all odds, Terry saw her. Erin pointed up at the balcony and he saw their quarry. He motioned to Willie, who managed to get Vic's attention. The four of them communicated the best they could with gestures, then each headed up toward the sixteenth deck from four different directions. For a few minutes, they would each be alone, none of them able to see the others. But then they would arrive on the sixteenth deck and could surround the first mate and take him down before he knew what was happening.

Erin made her way up her assigned stairway, moving as quickly as she dared. She didn't want to be completely out of breath by the time she got to the top, but even just walking normally was getting her out of breath because of the adrenaline dumped into her bloodstream. She waited for a few seconds when she got to the top, trying to quiet her breathing so that she wouldn't be approaching him huffing and puffing like a steam engine, alerting Little. She took a deep breath and stepped out into the hallway behind the balcony. Straight into the chest of one of the other crew members.

Erin excused herself and stepped back and made a motion to step around the man, hesitating for a moment to see who it was and if it was someone who would help them.

That was when she realized it was Saville, the sneering crewman who had given Vic such a hard time.

If anyone was part of Little's ring, it had to be him. He was just the type of man who would have not only helped with the human trafficking rings, but would get a real kick out of doing it.

The man reached for her, his hands closing around her upper arms.

"What's going on?" he demanded. "Where are you going in such a hurry?"

Erin pulled away from him. "None of your business," she snapped. She again tried to step around him, but he seemed oblivious to this fact and didn't move away to give her personal space like a normal person would. Erin stepped forward as aggressively as she dared. She needed to get past him to be in place when Willie and Terry we ready to close in on the first mate. They had to be able to work together to get it down.

"What's wrong?" Saville questioned, looking into her face. "Something is obviously wrong. Where's your friend?" He looked around. "Where are all of your friends? You're usually joined at the hip, why would you be walking around alone like this?" He paused, chewing on his lip as he looked down at her. "It's not safe," he said.

Erin sucked in her breath. She looked at him with new eyes. Had her impressions of him been wrong? Had she judged him just as unfairly as he had been prejudiced against Vic? She looked into his face, trying to read him. He looked concerned. He really did look as if he wanted to help her out. But it could all just be an act. She inched to the side again.

"We need to talk to the first mate," she said, motioning to the balcony. "He's just over there. I need to talk to him…"

The crewman shook his head. "First mate is busy. I can help you with whatever it is that you need. Why don't we go back down to the teen deck or another place and discuss what it is you need?"

Erin stared into his face. "Do you know what he's up to?"

"What do you mean?"

They were both so reluctant to put it into words that they were in danger of refusing to talk to each other at all. Erin finally decided to chance it. If she talked to the wrong person and did the wrong thing, then that was all on her. But she needed to do her best and at least try to help the others to stop the first mate.

"He's been involved in human trafficking on this ship. Terry is trying to get to him to put him under arrest. We're coming from different directions so that he can't see us coming and run or take a hostage or do something stupid like that. We just want this to go down smoothly and for everyone to be safe."

The crewman's jaw dropped open. He gaped at Erin. "Human trafficking?"

"Do you have any idea of the condition that the immigrant labor on this boat are living in? Do you know how much money they're making? Or that he threatens not to feed them if they don't do the job to his standards? They are terrified of starving in the middle of a ship full of all kinds of food from all different cuisines. And that girl that disappeared? MacKay? He was the one who had her drugged, if he didn't do it himself, so that he could get her involved in the sex trade."

"No!"

Erin nodded. Though he protested, she thought from his expression that he actually did believe her. He was horrified, not disbelieving. Maybe he had seen things that now made sense when they hadn't before. Maybe knowing about the human trafficking going on aboard the ship, all of the pieces were falling into place.

"Yes. We need to get to him. So please let me past."

"Hold on…" He stopped her again and thought for a moment. "Let me tell him he's needed. Get him off of the balcony. There are too many people around, and that railing… I'm just saying…"

"He had one of the other crewmen throw someone overboard that first night, just like I said they did. It was all part of the human trafficking. The other guy didn't want anything to do with whatever it was that they were asking him to do. They were afraid that he would spill the beans. So they killed him to keep him quiet. They will silence everyone they can. They kidnapped Terry and were going to kill him, but we managed to spring him. So now we need to do this. We need to get him out of the way before he does something else."

"I'll call him," the man repeated. He clicked his radio and spoke into it, calling Little away from his surveillance on the balcony.

⟋

Erin had no way to signal to Terry and Willie and Vic that the plan was changing and Little was on the move. While she believed the shock she had seen in Saville's face, she still wasn't one hundred percent sure that she could believe him about not knowing what the first mate was up to or that there had been human trafficking going on right under his nose on the ship.

The first mate looked irritated as he went through the door from the balcony, heading to whatever part of the ship the crewman had told him he was needed on. When he saw Saville and Erin standing there, his expression darkened even more, and he looked thunderous.

"What is this?" he demanded. "What's your game here? What is this woman doing here?"

There was no reason Erin couldn't be there. It wasn't an area that was restricted to staff only. She was a passenger and it was a public area. He stalked toward her, jabbing toward her with an accusing finger.

"You just couldn't help making waves, could you?" he demanded. "You couldn't just stay quiet and have a nice holiday like everyone else? I made some inquiries about you, and you're always in the middle of things, making a bigger mess, trying to attract attention to yourself. Well, not on my ship; this is the last place that you're going to try this. You have no idea what you've gotten yourself into, little lady. I am going to—"

"Stop right there!" Terry's shout came from the end of the gallery as he entered from the other end, having discovered the first mate to be missing from the balcony where he was expected to be. "Don't move a muscle, Little."

The mate whirled around. He was apparently not worried about Terry being armed, firearms being prohibited on the ship. But he hadn't counted on K9, even after seeing how he had attacked the guard at the captain's quarters.

"Attack!" Terry ordered, pointing at him.

The mate only had time to put his hands out in front of him in protest, as if the gesture could stop K9's approach. He yelled as K9 jumped on him, biting down on his forearm as he had been trained. Saville put his arm out automatically in front of Erin as if to shield her from attack. When Terry approached, looking threatening, Saville stepped between them. But it was Saville who Terry was focused on, not Erin.

"What's going on here? Did he block you, Erin? Keep you from coming in?"

"Well, sort of," Erin said. "But not like that. Not in a bad way. He said it was safer to get the mate out here, away from the balcony and the other people."

Terry looked at him and backed down a little on the aggression. "Yeah? So he helped you?"

Erin nodded. "Yes. He was helping, not hindering."

"You don't think he was part of this?"

"I don't think so."

"Okay." Terry gave a little nod to Saville. "Thank you."

Then he turned his attention to Little, manacling his wrists with large zip-ties he just happened to have in his pocket. Willie and Vic raced in from different directions, ready to fight a dozen crewmen, but there was no one left to fight. Vic hugged Erin, looking at Saville warily. He gave an embarrassed shrug, his eyes sliding away from her.

Willie bent over to help Terry, but there wasn't anything for him to do. They lifted the first mate to his feet. The man spit curses at them. "There's nothing you can do! You don't have any authority here! I am in charge. I am the acting captain of this ship!"

"Not now," Terry responded. "And we'll see what the FBI has to say about what's been going on here. Human trafficking, kidnapping, murder, attempted murder, sexual assault… I think they're going to have more than a passing interest in you, this ship, and the cruise line. You're not getting away with this."

CHAPTER 35

*E*rin stared out into the water, which looked gray and cold, with wisps of fog hanging over it. She shivered and pulled her layers of sweaters and coats more tightly around her.

"This is our last night on board the ship," she told Terry, though of course, he knew that already.

"Maybe tonight you'll actually be able to get a good sleep."

Erin wondered. While they had detained the first mate and the few crewmen who they knew had been involved in the murder of the captain and the crewman, she wasn't convinced that they had everyone who had known about or been involved in the enslavement of the immigrants or the sex trafficking that had been going on under their noses. Could they really work on the ship without knowing about everything that was going on? Or was it just a few people who had known, and the others were blissfully ignorant?

"It's been an… interesting vacation."

Terry chuckled. He scratched K9's ears. "What was your favorite part?"

"I don't know. Seeing the puffins. Or cooking with Chef Kirschoff."

He nodded. "You'll be glad to get back to your own kitchen."

"Will I ever. I wouldn't have guessed when I left Bald Eagle Falls that I would be this eager to get back to work. But now I'm just looking forward to getting back into the old routines and being able to bake my recipes and see my customers. I want to be back in my bakery again."

"And I'll be glad for you to be there. I've been so worried about you here. In spite of everything that has happened in Bald Eagles Falls, I'll feel a lot better when you're off this ship."

There was a movement in the distance, and at first Erin thought she was looking at the disturbance caused by a small boat, then realized that it wasn't.

"Terry, look at that!" He followed her pointing finger. "Is that a whale?"

He squinted at it. Erin regretted that she hadn't brought the binoculars out with her.

"I don't know," Terry said, "It could be; it looks like there is something big in the water, but..."

A column of water shot into the air, fanning out and falling back into the water. Terry grinned, the dimple appearing in his cheek.

"Well, I guess that's your answer. It's a whale!"

Erin watched, enthralled by the dark form and the others that appeared and disappeared around it. She started to shiver. Terry hugged her.

"We'd better get you inside. It's getting cold. And Chef Kirschoff said something about a special treat tonight."

"This is our last dinner on the ship," Chef Kirschoff declared after the general applause that greeted his appearance. "I have enjoyed cooking for you on this tour, as I have for others. But this tour is special."

Another light smattering of applause.

"This tour is special because we have been graced with the presence of an expert in gluten-free baking. Erin Price, would you stand up?"

Her face burning, Erin stood, gave an awkward wave and bow to the diners, and sat back down.

"Miss Price and I have been putting our heads together to create a specialty dish for your enjoyment. For Alaskan tours, I like to end the tour with Baked Alaska, which I'm sure you know is not a dish that is normally vegan! I have tweaked and adjusted recipes for vegan meringue and ice cream. I also have myriad vegan cake recipes. Up until now, I have not had a good vegan *and* gluten-free recipe for cake that would work well with this recipe. But with the assistance of Miss Price, I can now present you with… *Auntie Clem's Baked Alaska*."

With a flourish, he pulled the cover off of a dish to display the fluffy white swirls of the Baked Alaska. Before the audience had the chance to react, the lights dimmed, and Chef Kirschoff poured a beaker of brandy over the Baked Alaska and lit it. Everyone oohed at the blue flame.

Waiters streamed out the doors to the kitchen, pushing Baked Alaskas to each of the tables and setting the desserts alight.

"This is what you were working on?" Vic asked Erin.

After the flames subsided, the waiter cut open the Baked Alaska, showing off the beautiful deep red ice cream concocted of local raspberries, lingonberries, blueberries, and cloudberries over a thick rich layer of chocolate sponge cake.

"Ooh, that looks delicious!" Vic crooned.

"You might not want any," Erin teased. "It is pretty cold."

But Vic wasn't going to be dissuaded. "First bowl over here," she told the waiter firmly, tapping the table in front of her.

Erin smiled and watched as everyone was served and sampled the layers of the dessert.

"With food like this, I could be vegan all day long," Vic declared.

"It's pretty good," Terry agreed, around a mouthful.

Willie gave Erin a thumbs up, not bothering with speech. Erin dug into her own just desserts.

Did you enjoy this book? Reviews and recommendations are vital to making a book successful.

Please leave a review at your favorite book store or review site and share it with your friends.

Don't miss the following bonus material:
Sign up for mailing list to get a free ebook
Read a sneak preview chapter
Other books by P.D. Workman
Learn more about the author

PREVIEW OF MUFFINS MASKS MURDER

CHAPTER 1

*a*h, finally." Vic took a long breath of air as they stepped off of the plane. "I can get warm again!"

Erin laughed and shook her head at her young, blond assistant. Vic had not been able to get properly warm since crossing the border into Canada. Even though she had bundled up on their Alaskan cruise, she just had not been able to get comfortable.

It hadn't been so bad for Erin. Her body was more acclimatized to Maine weather than to Tennessee, so she had fared better. But she had to admit that she still preferred being warm to cold. And while the cruise had been intended to be a nice diversion from her life in Bald Eagle Falls, things had not exactly gone as planned. A relaxed, carefree vacation it had not been.

"There's no place like home," Erin declared.

"There shorely isn't," Vic agreed, drawing out the words in her longest southern drawl.

"We'll need a vacation from our vacation," Officer Terry Piper said, as the men followed the women off the plane and through the corridor to the terminal.

"You're not kidding about that," Vic agreed.

Erin glanced back at Willie, who was characteristically quiet, to see how he felt about it. His skin, darkly stained from the mining and metal processing he did, was disconcerting to someone just meeting him for the first time, but Erin was so used to it that she hardly even noticed it anymore. A far cry from when she had first arrived in Bald Eagle Falls and had taken him for a dirty homeless man and had been afraid to let him help her carry supplies into Erin's new gluten-free and specialty bakery, Auntie Clem's. Now, Erin wouldn't have given it a second thought. Willie was one of the family. He might be nontraditional, picking up whatever odd jobs he felt like between working his mineral claims, but she knew he was a hard worker, not the layabout that many people seemed to think. He had been in Bald Eagle Falls much longer than she had and the townspeople should have known better. There was still prejudice against people who didn't conform, and Willie was about as nonconforming as they came.

Willie smiled and nodded at Erin, acknowledging her look, but didn't have anything to contribute to the conversation. He moved forward to put his arm around Vic, who also faced prejudice for her gender identity. He bumped against the cast on her arm.

"Just about time to get these off, Miss Victoria." He indicated the cast on his leg as well. "It will feel good to be able to get the darn thing out of the way."

"And to scratch," Vic said fervently. "If there's one thing I want more than to be warm right now, it's to be able to scratch this arm like a dog at a flea circus." She scratched around the end of the cast, sliding her fingers under the edge as far as they could reach.

Terry didn't take Erin's arm, but was trying to keep K9 under control. K9 wasn't usually on a leash, but was well-trained to heel and, other than when he had first met the stray orange kitten who had wandered into Auntie Clem's Bakery, Erin had rarely seen him out of Terry's control. But he clearly knew that they were going home. He was sniffing the air and dragging Terry along, eager to get out of the airport terminal and back to familiar settings.

"Heel," Terry commanded in a low, firm tone. "Come on, buddy. Let's show some professionalism here."

It took a few tries before K9 was finally at his side, behaving as was expected from a veteran police dog. But his nose still quivered and his ears pointed forward.

"Do you think he's looking forward to getting back to work?" Erin asked.

"Animals like routines. He's not used to being cooped up on a ship. Even though I walked him plenty, it's not the same as patrolling all day, and I'm sure he felt it worse than I did. I'm going to have to work off a few extra pounds here…" He patted his sleek belly. Erin couldn't tell that he'd put on any weight, but she knew it was bothering him.

"Who knew you could gain weight eating vegan food?" She laughed. "I was sure we'd all be thin as rails by the time we got back. Unfortunately… no such luck." She was so short, every pound she put on looked like two. Her frame was not nearly as forgiving as Vic's tall, slender physique. "But I can't tell you've gained anything, and after you've been hitting the streets of Bald Eagle Falls again, it will just melt away."

"I hope so. I have no intention of turning into one of those cops with a big beer gut hanging over his belt."

"I don't think you need to worry about that."

Erin couldn't help admiring her "Officer Handsome." He had boyish good looks, cut a very dashing figure in his police uniform and, when she made him smile, had the cutest dimple in his cheek. He was intelligent and kind, and it was a wonder he hadn't been scooped up by some other woman long before Erin had shown up on the scene. But he was married to his work, and maybe no other woman had wanted to compete with that devotion and the long hours of days and nights that he was gone. In a little town like Bald Eagle Falls, with its minuscule police force, he was frequently the go-to man, even when he wasn't supposed to be on call.

It was another hour before they finally got all of their baggage off of the carousel and were on their way. They retrieved Willie's truck from long-term parking and piled everything into the back before climbing up into the seats.

"Are you glad to be home?" Vic asked Erin, looking back over the seat of the cab to where Erin and Terry sat in the second row of seating.

"I'll be glad when I am home," Erin agreed. She might be back in Tennessee, but she wasn't in her house yet, and that was what she wanted. Just to be home and away from all of the drama and excitement that had surrounded their cruise, back in her familiar environment with her lists of things to do and her baker's schedule and something to keep her busy. The idea of a cruise had been nice, and Terry had thought that it would help Erin to be away from the stressful day-to-day business of running a bakery, but it had been more difficult not to have something to keep her hands and her mind busy, so she didn't have to think about finding the body of Mr. Inglethorpe, or the other traumatic events that had preceded the cruise. Erin had to admit that she wasn't a "fun" person. She wasn't interested in going out to a restaurant or dancing or watching a lounge act or going on a tour. She was happier following her set routine.

"You'll be happy to get back to your house, the bakery, and your animals," Terry agreed.

Erin reached down and scratched K9's ears. K9, being a specially trained service dog, had been allowed to go with Terry on the cruise without too much hassle. Erin bringing her cat and rabbit would have been another story, besides which, they wouldn't have enjoyed it at all. Like Erin, cats preferred familiar surroundings and routine. She didn't know what rabbits thought about changes. Marshmallow was pretty chill and took everything in stride, but Orange Blossom, who had grown from that straggly little orange stray to a sleek, luxurious adult cat, would have been miserable.

"I'll be thrilled to see them again," she agreed. "I didn't know how much I was going to miss them. Do you think everything is okay with them?"

"Adele would have told you if there were any issues. They don't take a lot of care, and they're not old, so I don't think a short vacation away from them will have been a big deal."

"She would have told me if one of them got hurt, or lost, or wasn't eating." Erin needed to hear the words to reassure herself. Of course Adele would have let her know. Except that they had not had much contact with Bald Eagle Falls while they'd been on the cruise, telecommunications being pretty spotty. And Adele had known the trouble they had run into there, and maybe wouldn't have wanted to put any more stress on Erin if something *had* been wrong with one of the animals. She might have just kept quiet about it, figuring it would keep until Erin got back.

"I'm sure she would have," Terry agreed. He rubbed Erin's back, digging down into the tense muscles and trying to massage the stress away. "You're going to see them in just a little while."

CHAPTER 2

*E*rin watched out the window, looking at the trees that surrounded
Bald Eagle Falls. It was so lush compared to what they had seen in
Alaska. She had gotten accustomed to the rocky cliffs and sparse trees that
faced the ocean in Alaska, the gray water and clouds more reminiscent of
what she had seen during Maine winters, and she had forgotten how full of
life the Tennessee scenery was, even though it was fall and the weather was
starting to get cooler. The trees were a brilliant canopy of oranges and reds,
something tourists would be flocking from miles around to see.

When they pulled into Bald Eagle Falls, it looked just as Erin had
remembered leaving it.

It wasn't like she'd been away for years. It had only been a couple of
weeks. It just seemed like a lifetime ago. She finally felt like she had a home.
A place where she belonged. She was no longer moving from job to job and
from one sad, empty room or apartment to another. Instead, she had her
own house, courtesy of Aunt Clementine who had left it to Erin in her will
along with the bakery. She was the boss instead of someone who had to
listen to everyone else and obey the whims of some old lady or frustrated
high school dropout. It hadn't been easy, especially when she lost her first
location to a fire, but things were running better than ever at Auntie Clem's
Bakery 2.0, and Erin finally felt like she had some security.

Everything looked just right. A little more gold and yellow in the leaves.

The traffic was the same, the people whose faces she saw as they drove in on Main Street were the same familiar faces. It was all exactly as it should be.

And then they pulled onto Erin's street. She let go of a big breath of air she hadn't realized she'd been holding, the muscles in her body finally relaxing. There it was. Nothing had happened to it while she was gone. It hadn't been burned down or burgled or anything else.

She was the first one out of the truck and was at the door while everyone else was still climbing out and then pulling the luggage out of the back of the truck. Erin unlocked the door and disarmed the burglar alarm.

"Hello?" she called. "Where are my furry beasties?"

There was silence. Orange Blossom was a very loud and vocal cat, so Erin was disconcerted that he didn't answer and rush to the door, complaining loudly about her having abandoned him for so long. She looked around.

"Blossom? Marshmallow? Come on, guys…"

Marshmallow hopped around the corner and slowly approached her, then nuzzled her leg and nibbled at her pant cuffs. Erin smiled and bent down to scratch the white and brown rabbit's ears.

"Hello, Marshmallow. Did you miss me? Was I gone for a really long time? You knew I would come back, didn't you? I hope you didn't worry too much."

He didn't seem to be the least bit concerned about her absence, though her shoes clearly smelled very interesting. Erin moved farther into the living room and nudged him out of the way so that the others would be able to get in the door without stepping on a curious rabbit. She stroked his velvety ears and looked around.

"Where's Orange Blossom? Has he shut himself in the bathroom?"

It wouldn't be the first time. Reg suspected that he did it on purpose just to get attention. She walked down the hall to the bathroom to check, but the door was still open. His litter box was in there, looking as spotless as if Adele had just been there and refilled it. Erin checked the spare room and then her bedroom.

Orange Blossom was curled up in the center of Erin's bed, having made a little nest for himself in the blankets. His nose was tucked into his tail and he didn't move when she entered the room.

"Blossom! Oh, Blossom…!"

She poked and prodded, and eventually he deigned to lift his head and look at her. Then he stretched and tucked it back in again, shutting her out.

"Orange Blossom! What are you doing giving me the cold shoulder? Aren't you happy Mommy's home? We can cuddle up to read, and I'll give you nice treats…"

He ignored her, even though she knew he understood the word "treat." Even just the mention of a treat would usually have him trotting to the kitchen, meowing at Erin to follow and get him the promised goody.

She could hear the thumps of the others putting down the luggage and their voices as they talked to each other. There were footsteps in the hall and Erin turned her head to look as Terry looked in the doorway.

"Everything okay then?" he prompted.

"Sure, fine. I guess he's just mad at me for leaving him alone."

"He'll get over it. Then he'll be bossing you around and demanding that you feed him."

"I suppose. I don't like it, though."

"You're not supposed to like it; that's why he's doing it. To train you not to do it again."

Erin chuckled. "I thought I was the one who was supposed to be training him."

"Hate to tell you this, but…"

K9 made a huffing noise and Orange Blossom's head popped up. He glared at K9 and scrambled to his feet, fur puffing out as he hissed and made his opinion of dogs in the house known to them all. Erin shook her head.

"You're going to have to get used to K9 being around. Any other cat would have accepted him by now. I don't know why you have to be so stubborn."

The cat ignored her, staring at K9 and hissing at him to go away. Erin threw up her hands in exasperation. "Okay. We will leave you alone, how about that?"

She left the room, all of them going back to the living room. Vic was bending down to pet Marshmallow.

"Where's Blossom? Is he okay?"

"Oh, he's in fine form. I think I'm going to have to put up with the cold shoulder for a while. He isn't happy with me."

"His loss." Vic stepped into the kitchen, raising her voice slightly to make sure that the cat could hear her clearly. "I'm going to get Marsh-mallow something out of the fridge."

Erin heard Orange Blossom thump to the floor. She looked at the bedroom doorway and waited for him to come out. A little orange head peeked around the doorframe. When Blossom saw Erin watching him, he withdrew and did not leave the bedroom to investigate the possibility of treats. Erin suspected he was washing, pointedly ignoring her and pretending that he didn't want any treat anyway.

Vic gave Marshmallow a carrot. She looked at Erin and raised an eyebrow. "He isn't going to come?"

"Nope. He's pretty mad. I guess he's mad at both of us, not just me."

"Too bad for him. Shall we all have a quick bite to eat before we go our different directions?" Vic looked at her watch. "It's later than I expected, and I'm beat after the plane trip and waiting around. I'm going to either have a nap or go to bed early."

"You could get out some rolls and jam," Erin suggested. "That's really all we need. Well, it's all *I* need." She looked at Willie and Terry. "The menfolk may need something more substantial."

"A bit of bread and jam is good for now," Willie said. "I'm planning on hitting up Fatburger later on. I desperately need to top up my fat and cholesterol levels."

Erin laughed. "How about you?" she asked Terry. "I could see what else is in the freezer. Maybe you'd rather have a chicken sandwich? Something that will stick with you a little better?"

"Jam is fine. I need to start working this belly off."

It only took a few minutes to defrost some rolls from Auntie Clem's Bakery and to put out the various flavors of Jam Lady jams Erin had in stock. She wondered fleetingly whether Roger would ever be back with Mary Lou again to whip up some more batches of jam. If not, their Jam Lady supply was going to run out and they were going to have to go back to store brands or find another artisanal jam that was made locally. Other brands were sure to cost an arm and a leg. Jam Lady had always been very reasonably priced. Especially since Erin bought it wholesale to sell it out of the bakery.

Conversation lagged as they each spread butter and whatever jam they preferred on their rolls. Erin had given K9 a gluten-free doggie biscuit. He munched on it quietly while they ate. Orange Blossom still didn't show his face.

"Are you going to go back in to the bakery in the morning, or take a few days off to recover?" Terry asked Erin.

"I've just had a vacation. I don't need recovery time."

"Except that you didn't actually rest on your vacation. I'm worried you're going to try to do too much and your health will suffer."

"No, I need to get back to work. I need my job more than sleep."

"Okay… if you're sure."

Erin smiled. "You might make me feel guilty about jumping right back in if you weren't going directly onto shift tonight."

He looked sheepish. "Well… I do want to get back to normal police work. I know my town and what goes on here. I didn't like the uncertainty of living on a cruise ship. It will make me feel better to know what's going on in Bald Eagle Falls and to know that nothing has changed."

Erin took another bite of her sandwich. She understood exactly what Terry was talking about.

~

Muffins Masks Murder, Book #10 of the *Auntie Clem's Bakery* by P.D. Workman will be available at pdworkman.com

ABOUT THE AUTHOR

Award-winning and USA Today bestselling author P.D. (Pamela) Workman writes riveting mystery/suspense and young adult books dealing with mental illness, addiction, abuse, and other real-life issues. For as long as she can remember, the blank page has held an incredible allure and from a very young age she was trying to write her own books.

Workman wrote her first complete novel at the age of twelve and continued to write as a hobby for many years. She started publishing in 2013. She has won several literary awards from Library Services for Youth in Custody for her young adult fiction. She currently has over 60 published titles and can be found at pdworkman.com.

Born and raised in Alberta, Workman has been married for over 25 years and has one son.

~

Please visit P.D. Workman at pdworkman.com to see what else she is working on, to join her mailing list, and to link to her social networks.

~

If you enjoyed this book, please take the time to recommend it to other purchasers with a review or star rating and share it with your friends!

facebook.com/pdworkmanauthor

twitter.com/pdworkmanauthor

instagram.com/pdworkmanauthor

amazon.com/author/pdworkman

bookbub.com/authors/p-d-workman

goodreads.com/pdworkman

linkedin.com/in/pdworkman

pinterest.com/pdworkmanauthor

youtube.com/pdworkman